NEW TOEIC
950
黃金 12 回
完整試題＋線上解析

附實戰／訓練音檔｜核心 900 單｜聽力訓練筆記

①

金丙奇、高京希、朴梓亨——著

suncolor
三采文化

國家圖書館出版品預行編目資料

NEW TOEIC 950！黃金 12 回完整試題＋線上
解析 / 金丙奇，高京希，朴梓亨著；三采黃金外
文小組譯 . -- 臺北市：三采文化股份有限公司，
2024.01　面；　公分 . -- (多益瘋狂拿分；1)
譯自：시나공 토익 950 실전 모의고사 (2022-
2023)
ISBN 978-626-358-239-2 (平裝)

1.CST: 多益測驗

805.1895　　　　　　　　　　112018388

本書勘誤及最新資訊

suncolor
三采文化

多益瘋狂拿分 01

NEW TOEIC 950！黃金12回完整試題＋線上解析

附實戰 / 訓練音檔｜核心 900 單｜聽力訓練筆記

作者｜金丙奇、高京希、朴梓亨　　譯者｜三采黃金外文小組
編輯三部 主編｜喬郁珊　　責任編輯｜吳佳錡　　協力編輯｜劉芸孜、王惠民
美術主編｜藍秀婷　　封面設計｜李蕙雲　　內頁編排｜黃雅芬　　版權經理｜孔奕涵

發行人｜張輝明　　總編輯長｜曾雅青
發行所｜三采文化股份有限公司　　地址｜台北市內湖區瑞光路 513 巷 33 號 8 樓
傳訊｜TEL：(02) 8797-1234　　FAX：(02) 8797-1688　　網址｜www.suncolor.com.tw
郵政劃撥｜帳號：14319060　　戶名：三采文化股份有限公司
初版發行｜2024 年 1 月 5 日　　定價｜NT$1100
　2 刷｜2024 年 7 月 20 日

Original Title: 시나공 토익 950 실전 모의고사 (2022-2023)
Crack the Exam! SINAGONG TOEIC 950 Actual Tests (2022-2023)
Copyright © 2022 Kim, Byunggi & Ko, Kyung-hee & Gilbut Publishing Co., Ltd.
All rights reserved.
Original Korean edition published by Gilbut Publishing Co., Ltd., Seoul, Korea
Traditional Chinese Translation Copyright © 2024 SUN COLOR CULTURE CO., LTD.
This Traditional Chinese Language edition published by arranged with Gilbut Publishing Co., Ltd. through MJ Agency

穩拿 950 分
以滿分為目標的完勝試題

從多益考試創立開始，學習者最關心的便是「快速獲得高分」，時至今日仍是考生最大的需求。那麼，到底怎麼做才能在短時間內考取高分呢？

有人說要去上補習班，有人推薦線上課程，還有人買了一大堆學習書。但親自指導過考生後，我們確信，大量解題是最有效的方法。而比起「大量」，「解什麼題」更為重要。練習再多對得高分沒有幫助的考題，也只是浪費時間。為此，本書如實反映多益實戰趨勢，聚焦必考核心重點題。

100% 反映考題趨勢的模擬試題！
多益考試為了維持特定難度，每次只會重新設計一兩個問題，並對其他題目稍做調整。換句話說，多數題目的類型都一樣，只是改變用詞而已。本書分析新制多益歷屆考古題，找出題型變化的基本類型，幫助考生應對實戰中可能出現的問題。

鎖定高分，扎實訓練 12 回、2,400 題！
本書共收錄 12 回、2,400 道題目。這些試題的效果，已經在同系列的其他書籍中得到驗證。考生平均考取 900 分以上高分，還有許多人獲得滿分。書中所有題目並非從無到有、絞盡腦汁發想而來，而是以實際考題為基礎設計，希望幫助考生避開出題者設下的陷阱。

穩固基本功就靠「聽力訓練筆記／閱讀核心單字表」！
本書不僅收錄 12 回模擬試題，還提供多種學習素材。「聽力訓練筆記」有助於增進聽力及題目理解力，「核心單字表」確保考生穩拿基本題分數。這兩項學習資源雖然被歸為附錄，但只要善加運用，就能讓總分提升 200 分。

我們極盡專業與經驗寫下這本書，對於目標考取 900 分以上的讀者是最佳選擇。最後，感謝 Gilbut 編輯部和各位讀者，你們的大力協助，讓本書得以順利出版。

高京希　金丙奇　朴梓亨

1

完整 12 回「聽力＋閱讀」試題，短時間高分速成！

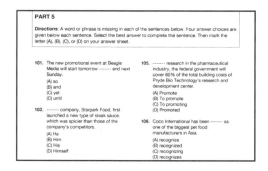

穩拿 950，往 990 滿分邁進

本書適用於目標 900 分以上的考生。題目難度與實際測驗相似或略高，以利達成實戰解題更快、正確率更高的效果。只要認真練習這 2,400 題，就能穩穩拿下 950 分，更有機會挑戰滿分。

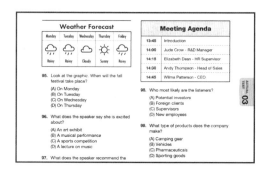

分量 NO.1！12 回、2,400 題扎實練習

三位滿分推手徹底分析多益出題趨勢、精心調整題目難度，設計出 12 回試題。實際考試不考的題目，這本書裡就不會出現。

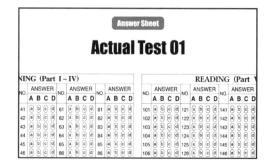

提供空白答案卡，複製實戰情境

在規定時間內，用附錄空白答案卡作答。完全比照實戰情境，上考場就不會心慌。

2 不廢話、只講重點的中譯和解析，迅速掌握考題核心！

---

108. With the purchase of any new cosmetic product from CoCo, a stylish gift bag will be ------- for free.

(A) you
(B) your
(C) yours
(D) yourself

【中譯】購買 CoCo 公司的新化妝品，即可免費獲得精美禮袋。

【重點單字】purchase 購買　cosmetic 化妝品　for free 免費

【考點】所有格代名詞 ★★★

【解說】題目考的是 be 動詞後面的人稱代名詞。be 動詞後面放名詞補語，前提是要與前面的主詞形成相同對象（同格）。禮袋和「你」並不屬於同格，因此將主格／受格代名詞 you 及反身代名詞 yourself 在動詞後充當受詞或修飾整個句子，都是錯誤的。所有格代名詞 your 無法單獨使用，也是錯誤選項。因此，空格處應該填入 yours，以形成「禮袋將免費成為你的」語意。

答案 (C)

題目中譯

通順而正確的中文翻譯，幫助考生理解結構複雜的句子。

核心單字

重點複習出題率及難度最高的單字，不浪費時間記憶已經很熟悉的詞彙。

精準解析

精準解說題目重點和出題方式，幫助考生理解誤答的原因。最後提供三位滿分講師授課的祕密技巧，讀完就跟上完課一樣，分數直升！

3 豐富全面的線上學習資源，分數不再從指縫溜走！

聽力訓練筆記

明星講師授課精華濃縮成 12 回聽力訓練筆記，以最符合大腦吸收方式的「詞塊聆聽法」，打造「聽解同步」的高分捷徑。

Day 01 900 核心單字表

詞彙	字義	聖屆多益考試重點	複習
ability	能力	ability to do 做~的能力；of all abilities 各種程度的	□□□
able	有能力的	be able to do 有能力做 ~	□□□
about to	即將，正要去做~	be about to + 原形動詞	□□□
above all	最重要的是，特別是	新增 / 突顯關係	□□□
abruptly	突然地	abruptly 結束，與會者沒有機會發言	□□□
absence	缺席，缺乏	absence of 缺乏 ~	□□□
accept	接受	accept 提案、現金、職位 ~	□□□
access	接近的機會，存取權限	have access to + 名詞	□□□
accessible	可接近的，可使用的	accessible 文件	□□□

閱讀核心單字表

嚴選多益核心 900 單，呈現字義及考前複習重點，寫完習題後加深印象、考前隨身複習都OK。

[50-52]

50. 主題問題 - 答案在對話前半部 ★
【解說】對話一開始就提到新教多功能工具設計，後續對話延伸這個內容，所以答案是 (C)。(D) 提到對話出現過的 compact，可能會造成混淆。
【重點單字】electric appliance 電器　compact car 轎車

51. 細節問題 - 關鍵詞 agree on ★
【解說】對話中提及多功能工具設計近乎完成，但是「We're still in the process of deciding what to call it ~ we have yet to agree on the best one」，表示他們還沒有決定產品的名稱，所以答案是 (A)。(D) 是陷阱選項，但要先決定產品名稱，才能進入廣告活動階段。
【重點單字】release date 上市日期，發布日期

52. 推論問題 - 答案在對話後半部，專注於男性的聲音 ★★
【解說】第 3 部分中，最典型的考題即是提議諮問題。答案通常出現在對話的最後。本題中，男子提議請大家在員工會議上陳開大家的意見「ask everyone to give some comments at the staff meeting tomorrow」，因此答案是 (C)。(D) 是錯誤的，因為名稱尚未確定，無法投放廣告。
【摘句語詞】ask everyone to give some comments at the staff meeting

實戰、複習 MP3

除了 100% 比照實戰的考試音檔，更提供單題、題組分段音檔，滿足考生練功、模擬應試的需求。

4 線上資源、多種版本 MP3，掃 QR Code 就能取得！

步驟 1

掃描書內 QR Code 進入網頁。

步驟 2

點選要使用的素材或音檔。

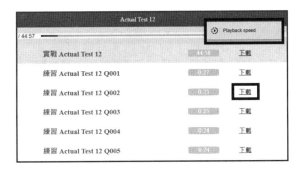

※ 音檔可搭配 7 段速播放器線上聆聽或下載，
　 檔案格式為 MP3。

※ 解析、聽力訓練筆記及單字表可線上閱覽，
　 也可下載使用，檔案格式為 PDF。

多益測驗介紹

什麼是 TOEIC ？

TOEIC 由 Test Of English for International Communication 縮寫而成，中文稱為多益英語測驗，是一種針對非英語母語人士的測試，旨在評估其溝通能力。內容涵蓋商務、日常生活等實用主題，並分為聽力和閱讀兩大部分，各占 495 分，總分 990 分。聽力部分不僅結合美式發音，還融入英式和澳洲發音。

TOEIC 測驗內容

類型	PART	內容	題數	時間	分數
聽力測驗	1	照片描述	6 題	45 分鐘	495 分
	2	應答問題	25 題		
	3	簡短對話	39 題		
	4	簡短獨白	30 題		
閱讀測驗	5	句子填空（文法／單字）	30 題	75 分鐘	495 分
	6	段落填空（文法／單字／句子）	16 題		
	7	單篇閱讀	29 題		
		雙篇閱讀	10 題		
		三篇閱讀	15 題		
總計		7 個部分	200 題	120 分鐘	990 分

TOEIC 出題領域

多益考題主要涉及國際商務與日常生活，不限於特定文化。

國際商務	一般業務	採購、營業／銷售、廣告、服務、合約、研究／開發、收購／合併
	製造	生產流程、品質／工廠管理
	問候	招聘、申請、晉升、退休、工資
	通訊	通知、指導、會議、電話、電子郵件、傳真、公告、協作
	財務／會計	投資、稅務、退款請求、銀行業務
	活動	紀念日、聚會、派對、頒獎典禮
日常生活	文化／休閒	電影、表演、博物館、旅遊、消費、外出用餐、露營、運動
	購物	訂購／預約、變更／取消、換貨／退款、配送
	健康	醫院預約、治療、醫療保險
	生活	故障、維修、日常花費、行程安排

多益測驗報名、應試、成績查詢須知

報名 TOEIC

詳細資訊請至「TOEIC 臺灣官方網站（https://www.toeic.com.tw/ ）」查詢。

① 可透過網路、APP、電話等管道，於規定期間內報名。

② 網路報名時須上傳符合規格之照片電子檔（限 jpg 圖檔），請事先準備好。

應試物品

| 有效身分證件 | 2B 鉛筆及橡皮擦 | 指針式手錶 |

* 有效身分證件包括：「中華民國國民身分證正本」或「有效期限內之中華民國護照正本」；
未滿 16 歲的考生可持「健保卡正本」入場。

TOEIC 測驗流程

① 考試時間約 150 分鐘，測驗中無休息時間。

② 建議至少提前 30 分鐘抵達考場，測驗（含基本資料填寫）開始後即不得入場。

時間	項目
09：30 － 09：50	填寫基本資料及問卷
09：50 － 10：10	確認身分證件及分發試題本
10：10 － 10：55	聽力測驗
10：55 － 12：10	閱讀測驗

* 臺灣考區一般的測驗時間為上午，若遇到場地租借問題或其他原因，可能會更改測驗時間或同時有
上、下午場次，因此確切時間請以考前上網查詢的應考資訊為準。

TOEIC 成績確認

① 網路查詢：報名時有填寫 Email 的考生，可於成績開放查詢期間進入測驗服務專區查詢。

② 成績單：測驗結束後 12 個工作天（不含假日）以平信方式寄出。

PART 1~7 題型解說＆解題策略

Part 1　照片描述（6題）

選出最符合圖片情境的敘述。

題型範例

試題本	音檔
	**1.** Look at the picture marked number 1 in your test book. (A) She is raking some leaves. (B) She is washing her shorts. (C) She is watering some plants. (D) She is selecting vegetables. 答案(C)

題型解說

❶ 第 1 部分中，平均有 3~4 題（約占 60%）描述 1 人／2 人以上的人物行為及狀態，正確答案通常是由現在式或現在進行式構成的句子。

❷ 描述事物／情境的照片及人與事物或情境的複合照片題，平均會出現 2~3 題（約占 40%）。這些題目著重事物位置、擺設型態及情境敘述，正確答案通常是現在式、現在完成被動式、現在被動式及 There 組成的句子。

解題策略

❶ 選擇與照片最相符的敘述

必須熟悉出題者會設計的錯誤選項類型。練習時邊聽音檔、邊看照片，藉由標示 ○ 或 × 確實刪除錯誤選項。

- 出現動詞／名詞指稱照片中無法確認的行動／對象時，該選項錯誤
- 照片中沒有人物登場的情況下出現進行式動詞，該選項極有可能錯誤
- 出現 All、Every、Each、Both 時，極有可能是錯誤選項

❷ 聽音檔之前，預想會出現的單字

在聽音檔之前，先看照片，想像可能出現的動詞或名詞。題目會出現的單字幾乎是固定的，所以看懂照片對掌握內容有很大的幫助。

Part 2　應答問題（25題）

聽完提問或敘述後，在三個選項中選出最適合的回應。

題型範例

試題本	音檔
8. Mark your answer on your answer sheet.	**8.** Where do you usually go for computer repairs? (A) Last Thursday. (B) I think I can fix it. (C) Do you have a problem? 　　　　　　　　　　　　　答案 (C)

題型解說

❶ 從第 2 部分出題占比來看，依序是「疑問句、一般／肯定疑問句、直述句與附加問句、一般／否定疑問句、選擇問句、間接問句」。相較以往，一般問句、直述句與附加問句的比例皆有提升。

❷ 比起直接提供線索的答案，間接透露訊息的答案比例明顯增加。

解題策略

❶ 以經常出現的疑問句句型為基礎，迅速掌握疑問詞、主詞、動詞／形容詞等連續 3~4 個單字的意義（即核心詞、關鍵詞）是解題關鍵。

- 疑問詞＋助動詞〔do / does / did / will / would / can / could / should〕＋主詞＋原形動詞～？
- 疑問詞＋助動詞〔be / has / have〕＋主詞＋形容詞／現在及過去分詞～？

❷ 間接提供線索的答案比例增加，不能預期會有明顯正確的選項。

❸ 熟悉錯誤選項的常見類型，藉此篩選出正確答案。常見的錯誤選項包含：出現題目中的特定單字、與題目中特定單字發音相近的字詞、題目中特定單字會聯想到的字詞。

❹ 絕對不要拖延答題時間。聽完三個選項後，如果選不出答案，便要果斷猜一個答案，馬上進入下一題。第 2 部分每一題只有 4 秒間隔，越是猶豫前一題的答案，就越無法專注於接下來的內容。因此接連失分的考生不在少數。

Part 3 簡短對話（39 題）

聆聽一段 2~3 人的對話，回答相關問題。

題型範例

試題本	音檔
32. Where most likely does the conversation take place? (A) At a restaurant (B) At a hotel (C) At an airport (D) At a food processing company **33.** Why is the man complaining? (A) He did not get a receipt. (B) He was served the dish he didn't order. (C) A bill is higher than he expected. (D) Some food has gone bad. **34.** What does the woman suggest the man do? (A) Speak to a manager (B) Place a new order (C) Check a menu (D) Wait for a replacement 答案 32. (B) 33. (D) 34. (D)	**Questions 32 through 34 refer to the following conversation.** W: Reception. How may I help you? M: This is Wesley White in room 101. I ordered some tuna sandwiches from your restaurant and would like to return them. They smell weird. I think the tuna is not fresh. W: Oh, I'm sorry to hear that. I'll call the chef immediately and ask him to bring you a replacement soon. M: Um... Could you please give me a few minutes to have a look at the menu? I don't want to try the same thing again. **32.** Where most likely does the conversation take place? **33.** Why is the man complaining? **33.** What does the woman suggest the man do?

題型解說

❶ 第 3 部分對話主要談及公司內的各種業務活動和日常生活，如出差旅行、會議、公事等。因此，學習涉及該主題的會話時，熟記各方面的主要詞彙與表達方式非常重要。

❷ 提問比例最高的內容，包括對話主題、對話中提到的問題、談話地點和交談者的工作、對話的細節等。必須了解每一種問題的解答會有哪些線索、通常出現在對話的哪裡，進而習慣高效抓住線索的解題方法。

解題策略

❶ 聆聽對話前，要先了解問題的內容和選項，如此一來，選到正確答案的比例就會大幅提升。如果時間不夠，就先讀問題。

❷ 每種題型的正確答案，線索出現的段落都有其規律，所以在聆聽對話之前，有必要先了解題型及其內容。識別出是哪一種類型的問題後，就該專注聆聽，等待線索出現在對話中。

❸ 不能錯過第一句和最後一句話。這兩個句子通常隱藏著第一個和最後一個問題的線索。

Part 4 簡短獨白（30 題）

聆聽獨白，回答相關問題。

題型範例

試題本	音檔
71. What is the message mainly about? (A) A new library policy (B) An upgraded computer room (C) A special reading program (D) A temporary location **72.** According to the speaker, what can be accessed on a website? (A) A new location (B) A moving schedule (C) Specific directions (D) Discount coupons **73.** What should the listeners do to borrow a laptop computer? (A) Complete a form (B) Show a membership card (C) Pay a security deposit (D) Join a free rental service 答案 71. (D) 72. (C) 73. (B)	**Questions 71 through 73 refer to the following recorded message.** Thank you for calling the Warren Public Library. The Warren Public Library will be closed at the end of August for six months for upgrades and remodeling. For your convenience, we are going to open a temporary library facility located at 911 Harder Street next Monday. Please be advised that we will not provide computer rooms at all for library patrons due to limited space. However, you can borrow library laptop computers as usual if you present your library card to any of our librarians. If you need to get step by step directions for your drive or walk to the temporary library, please visit our website, www.warrenpl.org. Thank you. **71.** What is the message mainly about? **72.** According to the speaker, what can be accessed on a website? **73.** What should the listeners do to borrow a laptop computer?

題型解說

❶ 第 4 部分涵蓋的素材非常多元，主要有說明（公司內部、活動、觀光）、談話／介紹、錄音、廣告、天氣預報、新聞等。

❷ 在第 4 部分中，提問比例相對平衡，包含主題和問題、說話者／聆聽者的地點和身分（職業／工作場所）、具體細節，以及說話者意圖／視覺訊息等。

解題策略

❶ 聆聽音檔前，要先了解問題的內容和選項，如此一來，選到正確答案的比例就會大幅提升。如果時間不夠，就先讀問題。

❷ 每種題型的正確答案，線索出現的段落都有其規律，所以在聆聽對話之前，有必要先了解題型及其內容。識別出是哪一種類型的問題後，就該專注聆聽，等待線索出現在對話中。

❸ 不能錯過前兩句和最後兩句話。這些句子通常隱藏著第一個和最後一個問題的線索，好好掌握的話，相對能確保選出至少兩題的正確答案。

Part 5 句子填空（30 題）

選擇符合語意或文法的適當詞彙，填補句子中的空白。這部分最晚應該在 12~15 分鐘內完成，才能確保第 7 部分有足夠的答題時間。

題型範例

105. Since the copier we ordered arrived -------, it should be replaced with a new one as soon as possible.

(A) damaged
(B) assembled
(C) discounted
(D) unopened

答案 105. (A)

Part 6 段落填空（16 題）

選擇符合語意或文法的適當詞彙，填補段落中的空白。這部分最晚應該在 8~10 分鐘內完成，才能確保第 7 部分有足夠的答題時間。

題型範例

Questions 135-138 refer to the following notice.

If your baggage was damaged while being carried or supported by airport employees or by the airport baggage handling system, please ------- it to the airport baggage office on Level
135.
1. According to regulations, domestic travelers must report damage within 48 hours of their actual time of arrival. International travelers must submit a damage report within seven days of a(n) ------- baggage incident. -------. Office personnel will review reports and evaluate all
136.　　　　　　137.
damage claims. Please be advised that the airport baggage office is only responsible for damaged baggage ------- by the airport staff and the airport baggage handling system.
138.

135. (A) bring
(B) bringing
(C) brought
(D) brings

136. (A) overweight
(B) unattended
(C) forgotten
(D) mishandled

137. (A) Please fill out a baggage damage claim form as directed.
(B) The new baggage handling system is innovative and efficient.
(C) The airport will expand next year to accommodate the increasing demand for air travel.
(D) The airport baggage office will be temporarily closed to travelers while it is renovated.

138. (A) cause
(B) caused
(C) will cause
(D) causing

答案 135. (A) 136. (D) 137. (A) 138. (B)

題型解說

❶ 第 5、6 部分主要考點為文法和詞彙,改版後新增插入句子的題型。即便如此,原先文法和詞彙的部分幾乎沒有變化,只要持續練習、重點加強插入句子的題型,就能穩穩拿分。

❷ 可數/不可數名詞、人稱一致、倒裝句、慣用語、搭配詞、假設語氣、關係代名詞題型有減少趨勢,複雜而須閱讀完全部文章才能回答的題目則比例見長。近年最高頻率的考點包括:

- 混合關係代名詞/連接詞/副詞/介係詞
- 區分不及物動詞/及物動詞
- 第 6 部分:透過前後文選擇代名詞的格
- 第 6 部分:透過前後文選擇特定時態
- 區分副詞連接詞
- 形容詞作為人/物的修飾語/補語
- 複合詞或單數名詞的形容詞或所有格
- 生活英語中的介係詞陷阱
- 強調反身代名詞的問題
- 區分關係代名詞/疑問詞後的 wh- 問句
- 選項中出現多個同義副詞詞彙/連接詞

解題策略

❶ 第 5、6 部分都是先閱讀選項,再預測、推定答案的題型。

❷ 如果選項都是詞形變化,語源相同但詞性不同時,通常都是考單字出現的位置,要先確認空格前後或整句的「主詞/受詞/補語」結構。

❸ 如果選項都是不一樣的詞彙,要盡量確保自己知道每一個字的意思。

❹ 看到連接詞(wh- 問句/關係代名詞、副詞連接詞等),請以「主詞＋動詞」、「一個連接詞連接兩個句子」為基準切分子句,並判斷句子的完整性。

❺ 當看似相同的動詞以不同的形式出現在選項中,按照以下順序篩選答案:(1) 主動/被動、(2) 人稱一致性、(3) 時態。

❻ 出現名詞單字問題時,往前尋找冠詞。如果空格前面沒有冠詞,答案就在於可數/不可數的判斷。

❼ 第 6 部分的句子插入問題,就算選項中的句子語句通順且看似符合文章主題,也須留意要與前後句子有所連結。

閱讀理解（54 題）

閱讀文章，選擇最合適的答案來回答問題。總共由 **29** 組單篇文章、**10** 組雙篇文章、**15** 組三篇文章閱讀題組成。

題型範例 單篇文章

Questions 164-167 refer to the following notice.

Kamon Financial Solutions

Yesterday, management and the owners held a meeting to discuss the future of the company. We have seen a great rise in profits during the last two years and also a large increase in our number of clients. So there are many customers that we are unable to serve from our current office. As such, it has been decided that in order to enable the business to grow, we will move to a much larger new office, which will open on October 2. —[1]—.

To make the relocation to the new office as smooth as possible, we have decided to move the majority of our equipment on September 29. —[2]—. On behalf of management, I would like to request that all staff members come to work that Saturday to help us move to the new location. You will be paid for your time at an overtime rate of $50 per hour. —[3]—. You will be working from 11 A.M. until 3 P.M. In addition, the day before the move, Friday, September 28, management requests that you pack all of your folders and documents into cardboard boxes so that they can be easily loaded into the truck. —[4]—. You will find spare boxes located in the storeroom.

If you have any questions, feel free to contact me directly. My extension is #303. Thank you for your cooperation. Together, we can help Kamon Financial Solutions become a market leader.

164. What is the main purpose of the notice?

(A) To announce a relocation to a new office
(B) To advertise a new product offered by the company
(C) To provide a list of new contact details of clients
(D) To invite employees to attend a conference

165. The word "majority" in paragraph 2, line 2, is closest in meaning to

(A) least
(B) most
(C) absolute
(D) nearly

166. What are employees requested to do on September 29?

(A) Complete some sales reports
(B) Phone some new clients
(C) Come to the office
(D) Park their cars in a different parking lot

167. In which of the positions marked [1], [2], [3], and [4] does the following sentence best belong?

"This day is a Saturday, and our office is usually closed on weekends, so there will be a minimum amount of disruption to our business."

(A) [1]
(B) [2]
(C) [3]
(D) [4]

答案 164. (A) 165. (B) 166. (C) 167. (B)

Questions 181-185 refer to the following announcement and email.

Wallace Zoo Volunteer Program

Requirements:

- 18+ years of age
- High school diploma
- Satisfactory recommendation from previous or current employers
- Ability to commit to one full shift each week
- A clean, professional appearance
- Reliable transportation to the zoo
- The ability to attend employee training

Attendance:

Volunteers will work one full shift each week during the season they are hired. Fall and winter volunteers work shifts from 10 A.M. to 2 P.M. on weekends. Spring and summer volunteers have weekday shifts from 10 A.M. to 4 P.M. However, they might have to work on a weekend shift, which runs from 10 A.M. to 6 P.M. Shifts are assigned by the zoo's assistant manager.

If you are interested in volunteering at the city's best zoo, visit our website at wz.org for an application. If you have any questions, contact Kate Kensington at 703-221-8923 or katek@wz.org. Applications for the spring program must be submitted by the end of the business day on March 18. Training for the spring program begins on March 28.

To: katek@wz.org
From: stevel@pgh.com
Date: March 20
Subject: Volunteer work
Attached: Application; Recommendation Letter

Dear Ms. Kensington;

I'm responding to your advertisement for volunteers at the zoo. I saw the advertisement ten days ago; however, I had an illness that put me in the hospital for the past week. So I was unable to respond until now. I understand that the deadline for the spring program has passed. But I hope that you can understand my situation and let me still apply for it. I have attached a completed application and recommendation letter from my current employer.

Only on weekdays am I available for work. I work at a cinema and must work a full shift on both Saturdays and Sundays. I hope this won't be a problem as I would love to work at the zoo. I am a consummate professional, and I am certain I can do great work at the zoo.

Thank you,
Steve Lionsgate

181. What is NOT a requirement of the volunteer position?

(A) Completion of high school
(B) Attendance at staff training
(C) A recommendation letter
(D) Experience at a zoo

182. On what date were applications due for spring positions?

(A) March 10
(B) March 18
(C) March 20
(D) March 28

183. What does Mr. Lionsgate request in his email?

(A) Consideration for his late application
(B) An extra weekend shift at the aquarium
(C) Information about employee training
(D) More time to submit his high school diploma

184. How many hours will Mr. Lionsgate likely volunteer per day at the time he is available?

(A) 4
(B) 6
(C) 8
(D) 16

185. In the email message, the word "consummate" in paragraph 2, line 3, is closest in meaning to

(A) determined
(B) absolute
(C) independent
(D) meticulous

答案 181. (D) 182. (B) 183. (A) 184. (B) 185. (B)

題型範例 三篇文章

Questions 196-200 refer to the following web page, web search results, and advertisement.

http://www.amityoldtown.com

Old Town in Amity is the perfect place to spend the day with your friends, family, or tour group. You'll love the experience of going on foot through the streets of Amity, which have been preserved to look exactly as they appeared in the 1700s. Go back in time as you tour Old Town.

Discounts are available for groups of 12 or more. In addition, for groups of 15 or more arriving by bus, the driver will get a complimentary ticket. Advance reservations are not required but are recommended for summer weekends. Contact 849-3894 to reserve your tickets today. Group discounts only apply to reservations made at least 24 hours in advance.

Restaurants in Amity

Seascape Features some of the finest dining in the city. Expect to pay high prices, but you'll love the service and the quality of the meals. The specialties are seafood, especially lobster and crab. Located down by the pier.

Hilltop Decorated like an old-style ranch, you'll get some of the finest steaks and ribs in the region. Don't be distracted by the loud music and casual atmosphere. The food here is incredible. About 400 meters from Old Town.

Green Table Enjoy hearty food that takes you back to the 1800s. All the meats and vegetables come from local farmers. Reservations at least a week in advance are a must. Located in the city's center.

Romano's Get a taste of Italian food here. Giuseppe Romano, the owner, has been running this establishment for the past 12 years. It's located just 200 meters from the entrance to Old Town.

Visit Old Town in Amity with the Galway Travel Agency. Enjoy spending a day at Old Town and then dining down by the waterfront. You can do this for the low price of $175.

Your group will depart from the Galway Travel Agency at 9:00 A.M. on August 20. You'll return to the same place sometime around 8:00 P.M. Call 830-1911 for more information. The trip will not be made unless at least 18 people sign up for it.

196. What is indicated about Old Town?

    (A) It requires reservations in summer.
    (B) It has reduced its admission fees.
    (C) It has historical reenactment shows.
    (D) It is designed for people to walk through.

197. How can a group get a discount to Old Town?

    (A) By purchasing tickets a day in advance
    (B) By paying with a credit card
    (C) By having 10 or more people
    (D) By downloading a coupon from a website

198. What is mentioned about Green Table?

    (A) It serves vegetarian meals.
    (B) Its food is locally produced.
    (C) It was established in the 1800s.
    (D) It does not require reservations.

199. Where most likely will the excursion organized by the Galway Travel Agency have dinner?

    (A) At Seascape
    (B) At Hilltop
    (C) At Green Table
    (D) At Romano's

200. What is suggested about the excursion to Old Town?

    (A) It will involve an overnight stay.
    (B) It must be paid for in advance.
    (C) It may receive a complimentary ticket.
    (D) It includes three meals that are paid for.

答案 196. (D) 197. (A) 198. (B) 199. (A) 200. (C)

題型解說

❶ 第 7 部分的新題型，包括 (1) 簡訊／訊息、(2) 線上聊天內容、(3) 三篇文章、(4) 插入句子、(5) 特定片語的內容，所需答題時間較以往多。三篇閱讀題雖然有難度，但整體相較改版前差異不大。請記住，第 7 部分並非全部都很難，而是其中的 3~4 個題組，裡頭的某些問題很難，主要是「有可能／最有可能」這類推理問題。這種題型經常出現爭議，並且很難選擇完全正確的答案，因為有時證據並沒有 100% 清楚地呈現在文章中。此外，大部分問題都很難找到線索，只有在閱讀完所有內容後才能答題。

解題策略

❶ 仔細閱讀文章，尋找題目中的關鍵字。如果想解決所有問題，就得把每一篇文章讀 3~4 遍。每次讀的時候，讀過的內容就會留在腦袋裡，進而提升閱讀速度。練習時，有些人會提前搜索每個問題的關鍵字，在空白處標記出來，這也是很好的解題方法。

❷ 閱讀理解的重點就是在腦袋裡想像情境，所以如果只是讀了單字，卻沒有想到內容，就再讀一遍標題和文章開頭，這樣就能進入整篇文章的氛圍。

❸ 雙篇閱讀題型中，最多只會存在兩個需要在兩篇文章中找線索的連動題。這表示僅閱讀一篇文章，就可以回答 5 個問題中的 3~4 個問題。

❹ 雙篇／三篇閱讀題型中，有一些經常出現的考點：

- 如果一篇文章中出現行程表，另一篇文章就會有相關的變動資訊。
- 如果一篇文章中出現換貨／折扣／退貨的規則，另一篇文章中出現特定人物，則題目可能會與該人要求換貨／折扣／退貨以及是否可行有關。
- 對於特殊文本，例如草稿、發票和確認預約的電子郵件，題目通常會問的是文章的格式或性質，而非裡面的內容。
- 當題目涉及特定人物的事實或推論時，先閱讀由該人物撰寫的文章會更快找到答案。
- 如果題目涉及多家企業，必須先釐清電子郵件頂端收件人／寄件人的公司名稱。

❺ 練習時，解答、批改、參考解析後，一定要從頭到尾再多讀幾遍。這時候，就會發現很多答題時看不到的線索。

❻ 第 7 部分無須做出誤答筆記，但最好寫下每個段落的一兩行摘要，以便在日後復習時有個概述。

目錄

引言   003

本書特色＆使用方法   004

多益測驗介紹   008

多益測驗報名、應試、成績查詢須知   009

PART 1~7 題型解說＆解題策略   010

Actual Test 01   023

Actual Test 02   067

Actual Test 03   111

Actual Test 04   155

Actual Test 05   199

Actual Test 06   243

答案表   286

Actual Test 01 中譯與解答   290

Actual Test 02 中譯與解答   314

Actual Test 03 中譯與解答   339

Actual Test 04 中譯與解答   363

Actual Test 05 中譯與解答   388

Actual Test 06 中譯與解答   412

答案卡   438

分數換算表   449

線上學習資源   450

Actual Test 01

MP3 音檔   解析

最佳解答時間 120 分鐘

開始時間：＿＿＿點 ＿＿＿分

結束時間：＿＿＿點 ＿＿＿分

▲盡量不要在作答中途停下來。
▲請於答案卡上畫記作答。

目標正確題數：＿＿＿／ **200 題**　實際正確題數：＿＿＿／ **200 題**

題數與分數對照，請參考 P449 分數換算表。

LISTENING TEST

In the Listening test, you will be asked to demonstrate how well you understand spoken English. The entire Listening test will last approximately 45 minutes. There are four parts, and directions are given for each part. You must mark your answers on the separate answer sheet. Do not write your answers in the test book.

PART 1

Directions: For each question in this part, you will hear four statements about a picture in your test book. When you hear the statements, you must select the one statement that best describes what you see in the picture. Then find the number of the question on your answer sheet and mark your answer. The statements will not be printed in your test book and will be spoken only one time.

Statement (B), "They are sitting at a table." is the best description of the picture. So you should select answer (B) and mark it on your answer sheet.

1.

2.

▶ ▶ ▶GO ON TO THE NEXT PAGE

3.

4.

5.

6.

▶ ▶ ▶GO ON TO THE NEXT PAGE

Directions: You will hear a question or statement and three responses spoken in English. They will not be printed in your test book and will be spoken only one time. Select the best response to the question or statement and mark the letter (A), (B), or (C) on your answer sheet.

7. Mark your answer on your answer sheet.

8. Mark your answer on your answer sheet.

9. Mark your answer on your answer sheet.

10. Mark your answer on your answer sheet.

11. Mark your answer on your answer sheet.

12. Mark your answer on your answer sheet.

13. Mark your answer on your answer sheet.

14. Mark your answer on your answer sheet.

15. Mark your answer on your answer sheet.

16. Mark your answer on your answer sheet.

17. Mark your answer on your answer sheet.

18. Mark your answer on your answer sheet.

19. Mark your answer on your answer sheet.

20. Mark your answer on your answer sheet.

21. Mark your answer on your answer sheet.

22. Mark your answer on your answer sheet.

23. Mark your answer on your answer sheet.

24. Mark your answer on your answer sheet.

25. Mark your answer on your answer sheet.

26. Mark your answer on your answer sheet.

27. Mark your answer on your answer sheet.

28. Mark your answer on your answer sheet.

29. Mark your answer on your answer sheet.

30. Mark your answer on your answer sheet.

31. Mark your answer on your answer sheet.

PART 3

Directions: You will hear some conversations between two or three people. You will be asked to answer three questions about what the speakers say in each conversation. Select the best response to each question and mark the letter (A), (B), (C), or (D) on your answer sheet. The conversations will not be printed in your test book and will be spoken only one time.

32. Where does the woman work?

(A) At an art supply store
(B) At an art gallery
(C) At a publishing company
(D) At a bookstore

33. Why is the woman calling?

(A) To ask about using a picture
(B) To find out about a new display
(C) To inquire about an establishment's hours
(D) To arrange a special tour

34. What does the man ask the woman to provide?

(A) A registration fee
(B) A digital image
(C) A deadline
(D) An identification number

35. What event are the speakers preparing?

(A) A celebratory party
(B) A company retreat
(C) A fundraiser
(D) An anniversary celebration

36. What does the man offer to do?

(A) Send out invitations
(B) Decorate a room
(C) Bake a cake
(D) Ask Mary for assistance

37. What does the woman say she will do?

(A) Ask for a revised budget
(B) Purchase some supplies
(C) Reserve a room
(D) Drop by a bakery

38. What does the man sell at his store?

(A) Electronics
(B) Books
(C) Furniture
(D) Clothing

39. What do the speakers indicate about the convention center?

(A) It is near public transportation.
(B) The tradeshow was held there last year.
(C) Their hotels are located near it.
(D) They had to take a taxi to get there.

40. How are tablet computers used at the man's store?

(A) To sign up new members
(B) To process payments
(C) To collect customer comments
(D) To check inventory

41. What did the man recently learn?

(A) An executive's schedule has changed.
(B) A seminar has just been canceled.
(C) A shipment should be delivered today.
(D) A meeting room has been reserved.

42. What do the speakers need to do?

(A) Review some materials
(B) Schedule a training session
(C) Practice a presentation
(D) Dispose of some documents

43. What does the woman suggest doing?

(A) Ordering in some food
(B) Making a reservation at a restaurant
(C) Arriving early for rehearsal tomorrow
(D) Having lunch after they are done

▶ ▶ ▶GO ON TO THE NEXT PAGE

44. What is Alice's occupation?

(A) Researcher
(B) Lab technician
(C) Office assistant
(D) Office supervisor

45. What will Alice most likely do next?

(A) Take a tour of an office
(B) Complete some paperwork
(C) Conduct a job interview
(D) Speak with the CEO

46. What does Alice suggest about a software?

(A) She hopes it will be replaced.
(B) It is not working properly.
(C) It costs a lot of money.
(D) She knows how to use it.

47. Where are the speakers?

(A) At a supermarket
(B) At a health food store
(C) At a restaurant
(D) At a warehouse

48. What does the woman mention about the business?

(A) A sale will start there soon.
(B) It was just renovated.
(C) It opened a second location.
(D) Fewer customers shop there now.

49. What does the woman suggest when she says, "We no longer carry a few brands anymore"?

(A) She no longer works in that section.
(B) She is expecting a new shipment of the frozen pizza soon.
(C) Some merchandise may not be available.
(D) She thinks the man should buy something else.

50. What type of item are the speakers discussing?

(A) A food product
(B) An electric appliance
(C) A tool
(D) A compact car

51. What still needs to be agreed on?

(A) The name
(B) The price
(C) The release date
(D) The advertising campaign

52. What does the man suggest doing?

(A) Conducting a customer survey
(B) Redesigning the product
(C) Consulting colleagues
(D) Placing an advertisement online

53. What will happen in ten days?

(A) A new manager will start working.
(B) The athletic facility will be renovated.
(C) New fitness classes will begin.
(D) Another location will be open.

54. What will be offered to members?

(A) A discount
(B) A T-shirt
(C) A new class
(D) A gift certificate

55. What does the man say he will do?

(A) Interview an applicant
(B) Call all the members
(C) Change a schedule
(D) Send an e-mail

56. What are the speakers mainly discussing?

(A) Changing hotel rooms
(B) Relocating an office
(C) Arranging a presentation for clients
(D) Organizing a company retreat

57. What information is Mary missing?

(A) The price estimate for an event
(B) The confirmed venue
(C) The complete list of attendees
(D) A list of potential buyers

58. What does the man recommend doing soon?

(A) Booking a place for an event
(B) Reserving airline tickets in advance
(C) Contacting a local catering service
(D) Rescheduling a company event

59. Where do the speakers most likely work?

(A) At a television station
(B) At a movie studio
(C) At a radio station
(D) At a restaurant

60. Why does the man say, "He has won the award three times"?

(A) To compliment a coworker
(B) To make a correction
(C) To express satisfaction
(D) To reject a suggestion

61. What do the speakers agree to do?

(A) Ask for employee input
(B) Extend a deadline
(C) Postpone an awards ceremony
(D) Hire a new TV show host

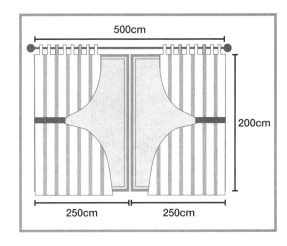

62. Where does the man work?

(A) At an interior design firm
(B) At a bookstore
(C) At a travel agency
(D) At an architectural firm

63. Look at the graphic. Which measurement will change?

(A) 200 centimeters
(B) 250 centimeters
(C) 300 centimeters
(D) 500 centimeters

64. What will the woman most likely do next?

(A) Determine a new price
(B) Order some extra materials
(C) Redesign a sketch
(D) Call another vendor

▶ ▶ ▶ GO ON TO THE NEXT PAGE

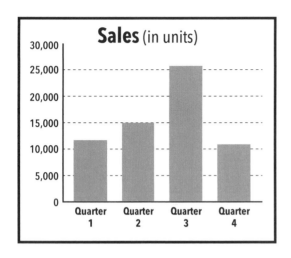

Sales (in units)

65. Where do the speakers most likely work?

    (A) At a mobile phone manufacturer
    (B) At a kitchen appliance store
    (C) At a computer manufacturer
    (D) At a toy maker

66. Look at the graphic. Which sales figure is the man surprised about?

    (A) 12,000
    (B) 15,000
    (C) 26,000
    (D) 11,000

67. Who is Jacob Green?

    (A) A company president
    (B) A marketing expert
    (C) A designer
    (D) An accountant

Madison Fall Music Festival

October 4

Performance Schedule

YELLOW STAGE		BLUE STAGE	
12:00 P.M.	Country	10:00 A.M.	Jazz
4:00 P.M.	Rock	3:00 P.M.	Pop
		5:00 P.M.	Classical

68. What does the woman offer to do for the man?

    (A) Purchase a ticket for him
    (B) Look over his report
    (C) Give him a ride
    (D) Save a seat for him

69. Look at the graphic. What is the man's favorite type of music?

    (A) Country
    (B) Pop
    (C) Jazz
    (D) Rock

70. What does the woman remind the man to do?

    (A) Purchase a ticket in advance
    (B) Wear a jacket
    (C) Bring lots of water
    (D) Arrive in time for the festival

PART 4

Directions: You will hear some short talks given by a single speaker. You will be asked to answer three questions about what the speaker says in each short talk. Select the best response to each question and mark the letter (A), (B), (C), or (D) on your answer sheet. The talks will not be printed in your test book and will be spoken only one time.

71. What is the topic of the conference?

(A) Vehicle manufacturing
(B) Software development
(C) Engineering
(D) Book publishing

72. According to the speaker, what did Brandon Morris do last month?

(A) He installed solar panels.
(B) He won an award.
(C) He participated in a conference.
(D) He gave a speech.

73. What does the speaker remind the listeners about?

(A) A product demonstration
(B) A reception
(C) A speech
(D) An exhibition

74. Where does the speaker most likely work?

(A) At a government office
(B) At a local weather service
(C) At a construction firm
(D) At a power company

75. What is the cause of the problem?

(A) There was some bad weather.
(B) Some machinery is outdated.
(C) There are not enough work crews.
(D) Electricity rates have risen.

76. What should the listeners do if the problem continues?

(A) Visit a website
(B) Call back later
(C) Visit an office in person
(D) Cancel an electric service

77. What is the museum celebrating?

(A) An anniversary
(B) An executive retirement
(C) A new exhibit
(D) A library opening

78. What will the listeners do first?

(A) Introduce themselves
(B) Go on a tour
(C) Listen to a speech
(D) See a film

79. What will the listeners receive?

(A) Free admission
(B) A gift shop discount
(C) A voucher for a free meal
(D) A complimentary souvenir

80. What is the speaker planning?

(A) A business meeting
(B) A client visit
(C) A corporate fundraiser
(D) A vacation

81. Who most likely is the listener?

(A) A travel agent
(B) A train conductor
(C) A seminar organizer
(D) A hotel clerk

82. What does the speaker mean when she says, "I heard that the scenery in Switzerland is stunning that time of the year"?

(A) She is not happy that her trip was canceled.
(B) She agrees with the listener's recommendation.
(C) She encourages the listener to accompany her.
(D) She thinks a purchase will be worth the money.

▶▶▶GO ON TO THE NEXT PAGE

83. What is the speaker's company planning to do next month?

(A) Update its website
(B) Introduce a new product line
(C) Hire more staff for IT team
(D) Attend a trade fair

84. What does the speaker mean when he says, "I must admit that they're quite unique"?

(A) He needs a more detailed explanation.
(B) He just started working at a consulting agency.
(C) He is impressed with some designs.
(D) He is unwilling to follow a recommendation.

85. What does the speaker request?

(A) An estimate
(B) A meeting
(C) A guest list
(D) A shipping address

---

86. What type of business does the speaker work at?

(A) A department store
(B) A supermarket
(C) An advertisement agency
(D) A marketing firm

87. What will the business start doing?

(A) Offering sale prices to regular customers
(B) Reorganizing the displays of its stores
(C) Adjusting prices throughout the day
(D) Renewing some contracts with its suppliers

88. What does the speaker say that David Lowell will do?

(A) Transfer to headquarters
(B) Ask for volunteers
(C) Hire more employees
(D) Explain a new strategy

89. What will the mobile application allow users to do?

(A) Download maps of banks
(B) Edit photographs and movies
(C) Bank online
(D) Make suggestions

90. What does the speaker suggest when she says, "However, there have already been 15,000 users"?

(A) Another location will be open.
(B) A service is popular.
(C) A system is overwhelmed.
(D) A project needs more employees.

91. What can some users participate in?

(A) A contest
(B) A reception
(C) A training program
(D) A focus group discussion

---

92. What is the message mainly about?

(A) A temporary location
(B) Library relocation
(C) New programs
(D) A book club

93. According to the speaker, what can be accessed online?

(A) A list of available services
(B) A promotional code
(C) Membership applications
(D) Directions

94. How can listeners borrow a computer?

(A) By sending an e-mail
(B) By calling before they arrive
(C) By filling out a form
(D) By presenting a library card

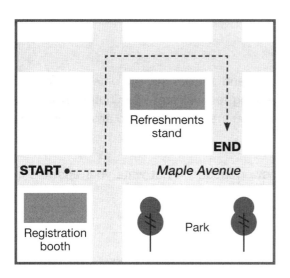

95. What event are the listeners most likely participating in?

(A) An athletic competition
(B) A community cleanup
(C) A charity auction
(D) A city parade

96. According to the speaker, what should the listeners pick up?

(A) A water bottle
(B) A T-shirt
(C) A pair of shoes
(D) A nametag

97. Look at the graphic. Where can the listeners get their pictures taken?

(A) At the park
(B) At the registration booth
(C) At the starting line
(D) At the refreshments stand

98. Who is the announcement intended for?

(A) Airplane passengers
(B) Conference attendees
(C) Hotel guests
(D) Shopping center employees

99. What does the speaker offer to do?

(A) Take drink orders
(B) Provide blankets
(C) Lock up valuable personal belongings
(D) Bring complimentary meals

100. Look at the graphic. Which item is unavailable?

(A) The purse
(B) The necktie
(C) The perfume
(D) The belt

This is the end of the Listening test. Turn to Part 5 in your test book.

▶ ▶ ▶GO ON TO THE NEXT PAGE

READING TEST

In the Reading test, you will read a variety of texts and answer several different types of reading comprehension questions. The entire Reading test will last 75 minutes. There are three parts, and directions are given for each part. You are encouraged to answer as many questions as possible within the time allowed.

You must mark your answer on the separate answer sheet. Do not write your answers in your test book.

PART 5

Directions: A word or phrase is missing in each of the sentences below. Four answer choices are given below each sentence. Select the best answer to complete the sentence. Then mark the letter (A), (B), (C), or (D) on your answer sheet.

101. If you have a question about your bill, your payment options, or applying for or receiving financial assistance, please contact us -------.

(A) recently
(B) really
(C) usually
(D) now

102. Before you leave the office, please turn off the overhead -------, and turn on a soothing, soft nightlight.

(A) lights
(B) lightens
(C) lighted
(D) lightly

103. Our vice president usually attends a marketing conference by -------, but has decided to take Mr. Watson to the one in Los Angeles.

(A) he
(B) him
(C) himself
(D) his

104. It is not fair to judge the candidates on the ability to run a company based on ------- ethnicity.

(A) they
(B) their
(C) them
(D) theirs

105. According to the data, the use of fossil fuels such as coal, natural gas, and oil ------- steadily over the past 150 years.

(A) increase
(B) increases
(C) has increased
(D) will increase

106. Since Joshua Pharmaceuticals moved its manufacturing plant to Spokane, the demand for housing in the city has increased ------- in recent years.

(A) tightly
(B) significantly
(C) distinctly
(D) often

107. ------- of the paintings in our art gallery contains a piece of history that creates a strong impression.

(A) They
(B) All
(C) Each one
(D) Other

108. Teleconferencing technology allows our employees to meet with their clients in other countries without ------- the office.

(A) leave
(B) left
(C) leaving
(D) to leave

109. Bella Corporation currently awards long-serving employees with up to 21 days of vacation ------- three years.

(A) all
(B) much
(C) every
(D) some

110. ------- are the results of the latest residents' survey on the proposed shopping mall construction project.

(A) Enclose
(B) Enclosed
(C) Enclosure
(D) Enclosing

111. After ------- three months of renovations, the manufacturing factory of Ace Technology in Detroit resumed operation yesterday.

(A) mostly
(B) while
(C) approximately
(D) immediately

112. Many companies are currently facing lack of personnel support. -------, there is a shortage of employees who have specialized skills.

(A) Therefore
(B) Otherwise
(C) Moreover
(D) Nevertheless

113. Applicants who passed the final interview for the floor manager position ------- by the human resources director later next week.

(A) have been contacted
(B) was contacted
(C) will be contacted
(D) will contact

114. Some of the directors were very ------- of the new business plan, but the chief executive officer convinced them of its potential.

(A) unanimous
(B) capable
(C) unaware
(D) skeptical

115. ------- new convention centers and hotels being built, London has all the qualifications necessary to become the number one destination for business travelers in Europe.

(A) With
(B) On
(C) To
(D) About

116. Business branding is ------- more important now than ever for local companies because consumer perception and trust are necessary for your business to thrive today.

(A) very
(B) far
(C) extremely
(D) enough

117. Please be ------- that all the flights are currently delayed due to the poor weather conditions and zero visibility.

(A) advise
(B) advising
(C) advised
(D) advisable

118. Construction workers who knowingly fail to comply with safety regulations are ------- to dismissal.

(A) informed
(B) subject
(C) eligible
(D) responsible

▶ ▶ ▶GO ON TO THE NEXT PAGE

119. Dinner will be served at the hotel restaurant ------- after the conclusion of the Annual Conference on New Telecommunication Technology.

(A) shortly
(B) already
(C) frequently
(D) carefully

120. ------- our new car models were released last quarter, they have been astonishingly popular.

(A) During
(B) Since
(C) When
(D) As though

121. In order to ensure the objectivity and the transparency, applicants for business loans must submit several financial documents that have been ------- audited.

(A) primarily
(B) especially
(C) particularly
(D) independently

122. Some customers were ------- with the overall quality of the new products manufactured by the GB Corporation.

(A) disappointing
(B) disappointed
(C) disappoint
(D) disappointment

123. In an effort ------- prices, our company streamlined the production process and minimized package volume and weight.

(A) reduced
(B) reduction
(C) will reduce
(D) to reduce

124. Our warranty does not cover any defects or damage to a product ------- customer's misuse of the product.

(A) in general
(B) alongside
(C) whereabouts
(D) resulting from

125. When you look at stock research websites, they will normally provide you with ratios based on past and ------- earnings.

(A) projecting
(B) projected
(C) projection
(D) projector

126. We usually provide a ------- course schedule for the following academic year so there might be some changes in the future.

(A) pending
(B) sudden
(C) tentative
(D) considerable

127. Unless ------- by one or more parents, minors under the age of 15 are banned from entering movie theaters and amusement parks.

(A) accompany
(B) accompanies
(C) accompanied
(D) accompanying

128. This online presentation will ------- a wide range of marketing techniques and strategies that are effective for your business.

(A) participate
(B) activate
(C) conduct
(D) examine

129. Unfortunately, there are some remote areas in the country ------- our wireless cellular broadband service is unavailable.

(A) which
(B) what
(C) how
(D) where

130. ------- we have suffered more losses this quarter, I see no other way out of this mess than to start making drastic cuts across the board.

(A) If so
(B) Given that
(C) Owing to
(D) Rather than

PART 6

Directions: Read the texts that follow. A word or phrase, or sentence is missing in parts of each text. Four answer choices for each question are given below the text. Select the best answer to complete the text. Then mark the letter (A), (B), (C), or (D) on your answer sheet.

Questions 131-134 refer to the following e-mail.

From: Harry Houston, Plant Manager
To: Plant Employees
Date: March 25
Subject: External Review

I'm writing to inform you that three ------- from Komi Motors will be visiting our plant in
                                    131.

two weeks. Their task is to monitor the ongoing production process and to verify our

automotive parts are being manufactured according to their requirements and standards.

In addition, they will ------- the cleanliness of our manufacturing process.
                        132.

Their review will be released sometime between April 15 and April 17. -------. It is very
                                                                        133.

important that we follow our normal procedures during their visit. If you are planning to

take leave on any day between April 8 and April 10, please inform your supervisor in

advance ------- your replacement can cover your responsibilities.
         134.

Harry Houston
Plant Manager
Houston Precision Machinery

---

131. (A) investors
(B) inspectors
(C) dealers
(D) trainees

132. (A) assess
(B) mark
(C) award
(D) establish

133. (A) Their arrival date has not been confirmed yet.
(B) Even so, our products are highly commercialized in the industry.
(C) Applications must be submitted by the end of next month.
(D) It will be sent to us and posted on our official website.

134. (A) when
(B) because
(C) so that
(D) admitting that

▶ ▶ ▶GO ON TO THE NEXT PAGE

Century Home Interior Design

Change Your Home With Perfection!

Do you want to remodel or build an addition to your home and have no idea what to do?

-------. Here at Century Home Interior Design, we know exactly what it takes to create a
135.

home that is perfect for you. We ------- a full spectrum of renovation solutions for families
136.

who want to turn their house into a true home.

From picking out new wallpaper to building a new deck for your backyard, our design

consultants can perform ------- any task you require.
137.

We have hired experts in nearly every aspect of home design, whether it is interior design,

home plumbing, structural reconfiguration, and more. This guarantees that each staff

member appointed to ------- your family has the experience to give you exactly what you
138.

need.

You can visit our website at www.chid.com for more details, or stop by our office at 1123

King Street to speak with us personally.

135. (A) We have the solutions for your technical problems.
(B) Your interior works have already commenced.
(C) You don't have to look any further.
(D) Our aim is to help you find the best house in the region.

136. (A) provide
(B) were providing
(C) had provided
(D) will be provided

137. (A) recently
(B) almost
(C) enough
(D) carefully

138. (A) assist
(B) treat
(C) affect
(D) introduce

Galaxy Technologies
5174 Richmond Avenue
Houston, TX 77056

Dear Mr. Baker,

Thank you for your inquiry of our X63 laptop computer series.

We are very ------- to enclose our latest catalog. Please note the items in red highlights.
         139.
They are special products that we are offering in set with Wave Printers and Velocity video

cards. Our promotion event ------- only for a month. So do not miss this chance, and
         140.
please take the advantage of the occasion.

We can assure you that our X63 laptop computer series are the most reliable personal

computer you can buy in the market today. Our ------- in it is supported by our two-year
         141.
guarantee and round-the-clock online back-up system that answers any questions of

users 24 hours a day.

-------.
142.

Sincerely,

Donald Harrison
Sales Director
Galaxy Technologies

---

139. (A) please
(B) pleased
(C) pleasure
(D) pleasing

140. (A) continue
(B) continued
(C) has continued
(D) will continue

141. (A) confide
(B) confident
(C) confidence
(D) confidentiality

142. (A) We look forward to receiving your
further inquiry or valued order.
(B) They also need to continually strive to
improve their job performance.
(C) Allow three business days for card
order processing and delivery.
(D) Our company is proud of the quality
products that we manufacture.

▶ ▶ ▶ GO ON TO THE NEXT PAGE

Dear Ms. Davis,

We are terribly sorry to hear about the problems you encountered during your stay at Bella Resort from June 24 to June 29. Please be assured that the used towels and the unchanged bedding you found in your room are not ------- of the high standards of
143.
service on which our resort has built its reputation. All of our rooms are usually equipped with fresh towels and bedding before guests are allowed to check in. We apologize for the

-------.
  144.

We would be happy to ------- you with a complimentary one-night stay at our resort,
  145.
including a meal at our Italian restaurant, Luigi's Lasagne. The next time you reserve a room at our resort, simply print out the voucher attached to this e-mail and present it to the front desk staff upon checking in.

-------.
  146.

Truly yours,

James Williams
General Manager
Bella Resort

---

143. (A) represents
(B) represented
(C) representative
(D) representatively

144. (A) factor
(B) attempt
(C) violation
(D) oversight

145. (A) providing
(B) provide
(C) be provided
(D) have provided

146. (A) As always, you will be completely satisfied with our new product.
(B) Please check our website if you need more information about this promotion.
(C) Thank you for your kind words regarding our hotel and its amenities.
(D) Once again, I apologize for the poor standard of service you received.

PART 7

Directions: In this part you will read a selection of texts, such as magazine and newspaper articles, e-mails, and instant messages. Each text or set of texts is followed by several questions. Select the best answer for each question and mark the letter (A), (B), (C), or (D) on your answer sheet.

Questions 147-148 refer to the following advertisement.

BUYNSELL.COM

Rachel Cagle (rcagle@easymail.com)
posted 1 hr ago

Product: *All about Herb Therapy* by Jaquelin Koch

The book is in mint condition and was purchased about 6 months ago for $25.

For those who are interested in herbs or other medicinal plants, you can buy this book from me for $15. The book must be collected by no later than next Wednesday in the Brookside area. The Brookside Community Center would be ideal. I will only accept cash. Please leave me a text message at (647) 555-3921 for further details.

147. What is NOT mentioned about the book?

(A) It is intended for those who want to use plants for medicinal purposes.
(B) It was originally $25.
(C) It is signed by the author.
(D) It has not been damaged.

148. What does the buyer have to do?

(A) Visit the Brookside Community Center
(B) Bring a personal check for $15
(C) Leave a phone number
(D) Pick up the book by next Wednesday

▶ ▶ ▶GO ON TO THE NEXT PAGE

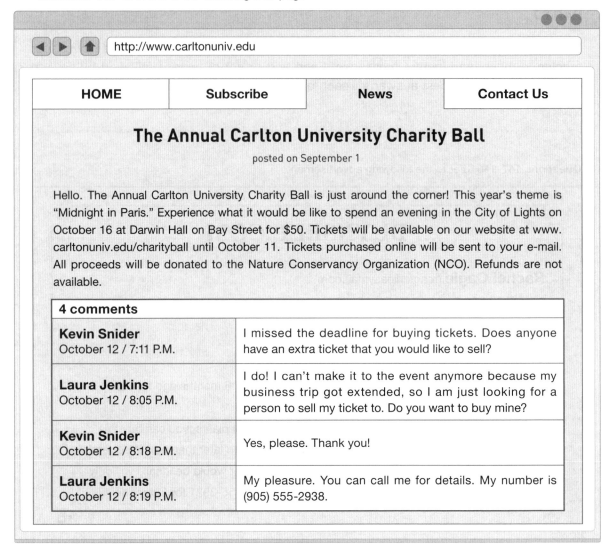

149. What is true about the Carlton University Charity Ball?

(A) It will refund tickets for a limited period of time.
(B) It is taking place in Paris.
(C) Tickets for it will go on sale on October 11.
(D) It is supporting an environmental group.

150. At 8:19 P.M., what does Laura Jenkins mean when she writes, "My pleasure"?

(A) She is excited to go on a business trip.
(B) She is happy to help Kevin Snider.
(C) She is interested in attending the next charity ball.
(D) She enjoys talking on the phone.

Blue Sky Tours

Tasmania Village Tour

August 14, 9:00 A.M. – 6:30 P.M.

*Please arrive at the Hamilton Center 30 minutes prior to the departure time in the morning.

9:00 A.M.	Bus leaves Hamilton Center (please have breakfast before arriving)
10:00 A.M.	Arrival at Tasmania Aboriginal Village
10:15 A.M.	Great Hawk Mountain hiking Hawk Falls sighting
11:00 A.M.	Tour of the Tasmania Aboriginal Museum featuring a special display of Kabu Warseau's pottery
12:30 P.M.	Lunch and free time at Haystack Cafeteria - Free food will be provided.
2:00 P.M.	Tasmania Village onsite tour
4:00 P.M.	Free time in Tasmania Tourists are encouraged to visit the Tasmania Long House, which has traditional sweets and various souvenirs available for purchase.
5:30 P.M.	Departing Tasmania Aboriginal Village
6:30 P.M.	Arrival at Hamilton Center

151. Where most likely can the tourists go shopping?

(A) At the Hamilton Center
(B) At the Tasmania Aboriginal Museum
(C) In the Haystack Cafeteria
(D) At the Tasmania Long House

152. Who most likely is Kabu Warseau?

(A) A tour guide
(B) A curator
(C) An artist
(D) The chief of a tribe

▶ ▶ ▶GO ON TO THE NEXT PAGE

Questions 153-154 refer to the following e-mail.

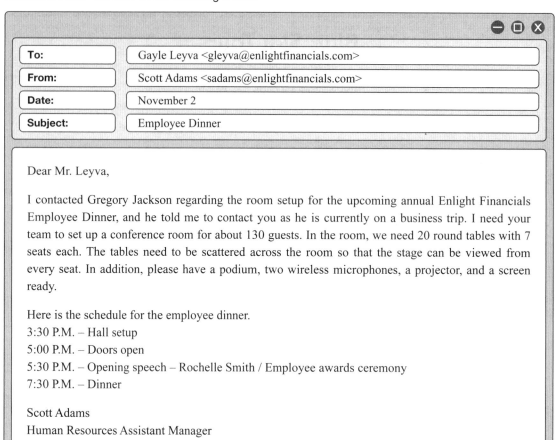

To: Gayle Leyva <gleyva@enlightfinancials.com>

From: Scott Adams <sadams@enlightfinancials.com>

Date: November 2

Subject: Employee Dinner

Dear Mr. Leyva,

I contacted Gregory Jackson regarding the room setup for the upcoming annual Enlight Financials Employee Dinner, and he told me to contact you as he is currently on a business trip. I need your team to set up a conference room for about 130 guests. In the room, we need 20 round tables with 7 seats each. The tables need to be scattered across the room so that the stage can be viewed from every seat. In addition, please have a podium, two wireless microphones, a projector, and a screen ready.

Here is the schedule for the employee dinner.
3:30 P.M. – Hall setup
5:00 P.M. – Doors open
5:30 P.M. – Opening speech – Rochelle Smith / Employee awards ceremony
7:30 P.M. – Dinner

Scott Adams
Human Resources Assistant Manager

153. By what time should the guests arrive at the Enlight Financials Employee Dinner?

(A) 5:00 P.M.
(B) 5:30 P.M.
(C) 7:00 P.M.
(D) 7:30 P.M.

154. What does Mr. Adams request in the e-mail?

(A) A list of available conference rooms
(B) Information about previous dinner guests
(C) A specific furniture arrangement
(D) A list of presentation equipment

Lakeview Inn Somerset
Wireless Internet Connection

Please read the following to use the wireless Internet at our hotel.

1. Purchase an Internet connection card at the front desk.

2. Open the network sharing center on your device. Select the network named "Lakeview Inn Somerset" from the list of available networks.

3. Enter the access code, which is printed on the connection card.

4. Read and accept the terms of use of the Internet.

5. Click on "Access the web."

Please note that you can use the Internet for free on desktop computers at the business center. A wireless connection is not available in the parking area and at the outdoor swimming pool. Call the front desk at extension #555 for assistance and inquiries.

155. What is the purpose of the information?

(A) To inform customers of the steps involved in accessing a service
(B) To announce the launching of a new feature
(C) To explain the details of a hotel policy
(D) To outline the advantages of using a program

156. In the information, what is NOT mentioned as something customers should do?

(A) Enable a function on their computers
(B) Enter their personal information
(C) Acquire a code from the reception desk
(D) Agree to comply with some conditions

157. Where is access to wireless Internet limited?

(A) In the hotel rooms
(B) Around the front desk
(C) In the business center
(D) Around the outdoor pool

▶ ▶ ▶GO ON TO THE NEXT PAGE

Questions 158-160 refer to the following e-mail.

To:	All employees
From:	Jose Scott <jscott@beauchamparts.edu>
Date:	February 17
Subject:	Underground parking space

To all employees,

Yesterday, a technician has found a leakage problem in the underground parking area for staff members. Please be advised that the underground parking space will not be available during February due to the pipe reinforcement construction. It is suggested that all employees use local parking spaces around the school. The school will provide reimbursement for parking fees. A list of available parking areas will be posted on www.beauchampartsschool.com/staff. The construction will neither directly affect our upcoming spring concert, nor will it cause problems for the new student orientation program next week. Thank you for your cooperation.

Jose Scott
Secretary, Beauchamp School for the Arts

158. What is the purpose of the e-mail?

(A) To explain about a new program
(B) To announce the construction of a new parking area
(C) To inform the employees of a possible inconvenience
(D) To describe how to get to the parking lot

159. What will happen next week?

(A) A concert will be postponed until the week after.
(B) The underground parking area will be available.
(C) Parking fees will increase.
(D) An instructional session will take place.

160. What are the employees advised to do?

(A) Avoid driving their vehicles to school
(B) Visit a website
(C) Receive reimbursement for damage to their cars
(D) Participate in the construction

Attention, Rose Cosmetics Customers!

In response to our customers' repeated requests, we at Rose Cosmetics have decided to extend our hours of operation to welcome more guests. Please refer to the following new schedule:

Location		Opening Hours
Richmond	Mon – Fri	8:00 A.M. – 6:00 P.M.
	Sun	9:30 A.M. – 4:00 P.M.
Suffolk	Mon – Fri	8:00 A.M. – 6:00 P.M.
	Sat	9:00 A.M. – 5:00 P.M
Portsmouth	Mon – Fri	9:00 A.M. – 7:00 P.M.
	Sat	9:00 A.M. – 6:00 P.M.

To thank our customers for supporting us, we would like to offer all of our customers who visit one of our stores between May 5 and June 4 discounts on selected items and a special gift with every purchase. For a complete list of the discounted items, please visit our website at www.rosecosmetics.com. We at Rose Cosmetics look forward to seeing you soon!

161. Why is Rose Cosmetics changing its hours of operation?

(A) To regain competitiveness in the area
(B) To attract people from other areas
(C) To accommodate increasing clientele
(D) To address customers' complaints

162. How is the Richmond location different from the other locations?

(A) It opens earlier each day.
(B) It operates on Sundays.
(C) It is currently offering a discount.
(D) It will undergo renovations soon.

163. How can customers receive a free item at Rose Cosmetics?

(A) By visiting its website
(B) By purchasing a product
(C) By talking to a representative
(D) By going to a specific store at a designated time

July 8

Matty Romano
3718 Sunrise Road
Las Vegas, NV 89109

Dear Mr. Romano,

Congratulations! Your application for doing volunteer work at the Evergreen Children's Hospital was received, and you are being given a position in our daycare program. However, before you can begin, you have to provide some additional documents for security issues.

You are required to provide a medical record for the last 5 years (this can be retrieved from your personal doctor) and a letter from your school verifying that you are currently attending classes there. This volunteer opportunity is only available to college students, so it is crucial that you send us this document. —[1]—. The required documents are to be mailed directly to the Evergreen social work office. —[2]—. The documents need to be original and hard copies. Please submit them by no later than July 15.

Per your request, I have enclosed this year's volunteer program schedule. —[3]—. Once we have finished reviewing your documents, we will send you a text message with a link to a web page where you should make an account so that you can check your daily volunteering schedule online. —[4]—.

If you have any inquiries regarding these, please do not hesitate to contact me.

Sincerely,

Judy Cruz
Evergreen Children's Hospital Volunteer Program Coordinator

Enclosure

164. Who most likely is Mr. Romano?

(A) A college student
(B) A hospital employee
(C) A recruiting specialist
(D) A representative of a volunteer group

165. What is Mr. Romano required to do within a week?

(A) Apply for volunteer work
(B) Send an e-mail to Ms. Cruz
(C) Visit Ms. Cruz's office at the Evergreen Children's Hospital
(D) Receive a document from a doctor

166. What was sent with the letter?

(A) A certificate for volunteer work
(B) A letter of attendance
(C) The address of a web page
(D) A timetable

167. In which of the positions marked [1], [2], [3], and [4] does the following sentence best belong?

"The address is posted on our website."

(A) [1]
(B) [2]
(C) [3]
(D) [4]

▶ ▶ ▶GO ON TO THE NEXT PAGE

Questions 168-171 refer to the following online chat discussion.

Jennifer Moss   9:03 P.M.

I would like to remind everyone that all employees in the Advertising Department will be moving to the new office location tomorrow, June 10.

Jennifer Moss   9:05 P.M.

Please finish clearing your desk tonight. If you have not yet been assigned a desk in the new office, please let me know immediately.

Owen Webb   9:08 P.M.

I haven't been assigned a desk yet. I remember speaking with you about it, but you never got back to me after.

Jennifer Moss   9:10 P.M.

Oh, of course! I am so sorry. I was so caught up with other things that I completely forgot to tell you. Your desk has been arranged. I will personally contact you to give you your desk number.

Owen Webb   9:12 P.M.

Thank you.

Simon Halom   9:14 P.M.

Finally, a new office! So, is tomorrow a normal workday, or do we just come in to move our belongings?

Jennifer Moss   9:15 P.M.

Tomorrow is just a moving day. Our new office will open its doors from 9:00 A.M. to 6:00 P.M. Make sure you move all your belongings during these hours.

Tim Belvins   9:18 P.M.

I believe I wasn't assigned a desk, either.

Jennifer Moss   9:19 P.M.

Tim, your desk was not assigned as early as the others because you just transferred to our department a few days ago. However, I have a desk for you. I will contact you personally as well.

Tim Belvins   9:21 P.M.

All right. Thank you.

SEND

168. What is mentioned about Ms. Moss?

(A) She does not have an assigned desk.
(B) She has been very busy for a while.
(C) She works for a relocation service company.
(D) She is the new advertising manager.

169. Why did Mr. Webb contact Ms. Moss previously?

(A) To get permission to transfer to another department
(B) To mention his promotion
(C) To ask for a designated workstation
(D) To consult about his working hours

170. At 9:14 P.M., what does Mr. Halom most likely mean when he writes, "Finally, a new office!"?

(A) He is indicating that he does not want to work tomorrow.
(B) He plans to visit the new office for the last time.
(C) He is concerned about his new position.
(D) He is excited about working in a new environment.

171. What are the employees instructed to do between 9:00 A.M. and 6:00 P.M. on June 10?

(A) Open a new account online
(B) Move some office furniture
(C) Visit the new office
(D) Contact Ms. Moss

▶ ▶ ▶GO ON TO THE NEXT PAGE

Around Nashville – Business Spotlight

July 19

This week's business spotlight is on Bell Laundro and its owner, Ms. Monica Bell. For those who don't know, Bell Laundro is a one-stop place that is a combination of a launderette, a café, and a bookstore and is based on Jackson Street. This new type of self-service laundry is one of the most successful independent businesses in Nashville today. —[1]—.

At first, Bell Laundro was not as successful as it currently is. —[2]—. However, Ms. Bell was not willing to give up on her business. —[3]—. After months of planning, she renovated a part of her laundry into a café-like lounge. —[4]—. In this waiting area, customers can enjoy a cup of coffee and read books while their clothes are being washed and dried.

The customers at Bell Laundro highly value the convenience and high-quality service Bell Laundro provides. Many residents in the area are students at Welch College, who need to do the laundry and buy books for their classes; they know Bell Laundro is perfect to take care of both tasks at the same time.

Ms. Bell was asked by many local colleges to provide tips and advice for students who plan on opening a new business. As a young entrepreneur herself, she seems very excited to lead her class, entitled "Difficulty into Opportunity."

172. What is indicated about Bell Laundro?

(A) It is located on a college campus.
(B) It has been featured in local magazines.
(C) It sells books via its website.
(D) It is a business with an unusual concept.

173. The word "value" in paragraph 3, line 1, is closest in meaning to

(A) evaluate
(B) appreciate
(C) estimate
(D) support

174. What does Ms. Bell plan to do in the future?

(A) Teach college students
(B) Join an organization
(C) Open another branch
(D) Start a new business

175. In which of the positions marked [1], [2], [3], and [4] does the following sentence best fit?

"Surrounded by large launderettes, it was not able to raise substantial revenue."

(A) [1]
(B) [2]
(C) [3]
(D) [4]

▶ ▶ ▶GO ON TO THE NEXT PAGE

Bach's Music Center

Bach's Music Center has expanded to Oakville! We will be having a free open house for our patrons to explore the brand-new center in Oakville, which is equipped with new and improved systems and instruments. Be the first to experience true music at our music center!

Date: July 8
Time: 10:00 A.M. – 5:00 P.M.
What to expect: Taking a tour around the facilities, trying samples of our café items, and meeting our talented instructors.

At Oakville's Bach's Music Center:

- Lyrical Coffee serves delicious and freshly baked goods with a variety of beverage choices to choose from.
- St. Thomas Auditorium, an indoor performance hall with 150 seats.
- Project Eisenach, a junior music class for children under 11 years old.
- Bach Studio – Learn how to sing with a professional vocalist. The first vocal training class ever to be provided at Bach's Music Center.

Oakville's Bach's Music Center will first open our doors to the general public on July 11. We will provide visitors with a free music book and a Bach's Music Center T-shirt. More baked goodies and beverage samples will be waiting for you as well!

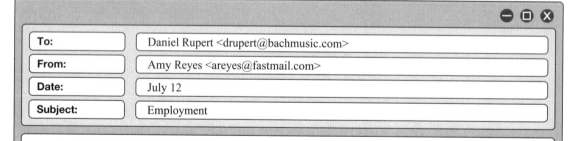

To:	Daniel Rupert <drupert@bachmusic.com>
From:	Amy Reyes <areyes@fastmail.com>
Date:	July 12
Subject:	Employment

Dear Mr. Rupert,

Thanks again for your time yesterday. I was very pleased to see the facility with all the newest systems and equipment. Oakville's Bach's Music Center certainly displays an exciting vibe, and that is why I would love to be one of the music instructors at your music center.

I have worked at several music academies as a piano instructor in the past. I have mostly taught young students because I like to work with children to see them grow as musicians as they take their first step in music education by learning the piano. Seeing children develop a passion for music is my main motive and inspiration.

Please e-mail me back or call me at (510) 555-3937 for further inquiries regarding possible positions at your music center. Thank you for your consideration.

Sincerely,
Amy Reyes

176. For whom is the notice most likely intended?

(A) Music instructor applicants
(B) Current students at a music school
(C) Visitors to Oakville
(D) Music contest participants

177. What will be given to visitors for free on July 8?

(A) A T-shirt
(B) A music book
(C) A trial class coupon
(D) Food and beverages

178. What is available exclusively at Oakville's Bach's Music Center?

(A) Instrument rentals
(B) A concert hall
(C) Vocal training
(D) Discounted music lessons

179. When did Mr. Rupert most likely talk to Ms. Reyes?

(A) During the music center's grand opening
(B) During a concert intermission
(C) During his music class
(D) During an open house event

180. Where would Ms. Reyes most likely prefer to work in the music center?

(A) At the St. Thomas Auditorium
(B) At the Project Eisenach
(C) At the Bach Studio
(D) At the Lyrical Coffee

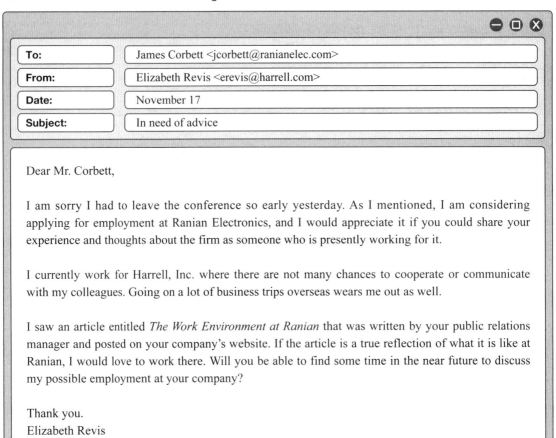

To: James Corbett <jcorbett@ranianelec.com>

From: Elizabeth Revis <erevis@harrell.com>

Date: November 17

Subject: In need of advice

Dear Mr. Corbett,

I am sorry I had to leave the conference so early yesterday. As I mentioned, I am considering applying for employment at Ranian Electronics, and I would appreciate it if you could share your experience and thoughts about the firm as someone who is presently working for it.

I currently work for Harrell, Inc. where there are not many chances to cooperate or communicate with my colleagues. Going on a lot of business trips overseas wears me out as well.

I saw an article entitled *The Work Environment at Ranian* that was written by your public relations manager and posted on your company's website. If the article is a true reflection of what it is like at Ranian, I would love to work there. Will you be able to find some time in the near future to discuss my possible employment at your company?

Thank you.
Elizabeth Revis

To: Elizabeth Revis <erevis@harrell.com>

From: James Corbett <jcorbett@ranianelec.com>

Date: November 18

Subject: re: In need of advice

Dear Ms. Revis,

I am glad you are interested in working for Ranian Electronics. This is to briefly answer your questions before we meet up to discuss Ranian and your employment here in detail.

The article you mentioned, the one written by Ms. Mary Witt, correctly describes the workplace at Ranian. We have many group assignments that require all members to share their ideas and thoughts with one another. In daily meetings, anyone can suggest a new strategy or insight regardless of rank or title. We rarely go on business trips, which should be a positive factor for you. We are more in-house work oriented.

I am free next Thursday afternoon. How does lunch together that day sound? I look forward to seeing you soon.

Regards,

James Corbett

181. What is the purpose of the first e-mail?

(A) To arrange an appointment
(B) To recommend employment
(C) To accept a job offer
(D) To request compensation

182. What does Ms. Revis mention about Harrell, Inc.?

(A) It does not cover employees' travel expenses.
(B) It has vacant positions to fill.
(C) It posts articles on its website.
(D) It conducts business in more than one country.

183. In the first e-mail, the word "true" in paragraph 3, line 2, is closest in meaning to

(A) certain
(B) natural
(C) direct
(D) accurate

184. What is suggested about Mr. Corbett?

(A) He often works at his home.
(B) He used to be Ms. Revis's coworker.
(C) He has known Ms. Revis for a long time.
(D) He attends meetings frequently.

185. Who is Mary Witt?

(A) A personnel manager
(B) A public relations manager
(C) A journalist
(D) A technician

Welcome to the Bernardo Mall

To ensure a pleasant and safe experience for all visitors, the Bernardo Mall's parking policy must be strictly abided by and will be enforced at all times. Please read the following rules and instructions carefully:

- All parking is on a first-come, first-served basis. Park in designated spaces only. The Wells Zone, the parking space for large vehicles, such as trucks, buses, or vans, is located next to Carpe Diem, a toy store. All other types of vehicles should be parked in the Pedro Zone, located near the west wing of the mall.

- Parking is complimentary for the first half an hour for all visitors. Afterward, a rate of $2 per hour will apply. Visitors who spend more than $20 at the Bernardo Mall will have their parking fee waived. The receipts must be shown at each gate when leaving. Although we share parking spaces with several restaurants near the Bernardo Mall, restaurant receipts are not accepted.

- Parking is available during the Bernardo Mall's operating hours, 10:00 A.M. to 10:00 P.M., throughout the year.

- Contact the Bernardo Mall at **customerservice@bernardomall.com** for any inquiries, requests, or complaints.

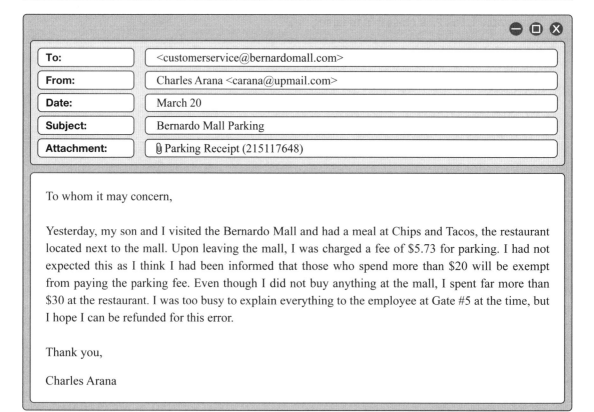

To:	<customerservice@bernardomall.com>
From:	Charles Arana <carana@upmail.com>
Date:	March 20
Subject:	Bernardo Mall Parking
Attachment:	Parking Receipt (215117648)

To whom it may concern,

Yesterday, my son and I visited the Bernardo Mall and had a meal at Chips and Tacos, the restaurant located next to the mall. Upon leaving the mall, I was charged a fee of $5.73 for parking. I had not expected this as I think I had been informed that those who spend more than $20 will be exempt from paying the parking fee. Even though I did not buy anything at the mall, I spent far more than $30 at the restaurant. I was too busy to explain everything to the employee at Gate #5 at the time, but I hope I can be refunded for this error.

Thank you,

Charles Arana

RECEIPT

Bernardo Mall Parking Lot
Receipt Number: 215117648

Parking Location	Wells Zone	Slot Number	B07
Date/Time of Arrival	March 19, 3:19 P.M.	Date/Time of Departure	March 19, 6:41 P.M.

Receipt?	NO	Discount?	NO
Amount Due	$5.73	Hours of Use	3 hrs and 22 min
Amount Paid	$5.73	Payment Type	Cash

Thank you and drive safely!

186. What is implied about the Bernardo Mall?

(A) It has recently amended its parking policy.
(B) It is open every day of the week.
(C) It is currently recruiting customer service representatives.
(D) It may not be available during certain seasons.

187. What is indicated about the parking lot Mr. Arana used on March 19?

(A) It was closed throughout the morning.
(B) It was recently renovated.
(C) It is an underground facility.
(D) It has multiple gates.

188. Why will Mr. Arana be unable to receive a refund?

(A) He did not park his vehicle properly.
(B) He did not spend the required amount of money at the Bernardo Mall.
(C) He did not read the instructions.
(D) He did not contact a customer service representative in time.

189. In the e-mail, the word "far" in paragraph 1, line 4, is closest in meaning to

(A) really
(B) well
(C) beyond
(D) distantly

190. What is NOT true about Mr. Arana?

(A) He drove a large vehicle to the Bernardo Mall.
(B) He dined at Chips and Tacos with his son.
(C) He paid his parking fee in cash on March 19.
(D) He will not visit the Bernardo Mall again.

▶ ▶ ▶ GO ON TO THE NEXT PAGE

Sherman Tours

Sherman Tours proudly presents our special one-day trip to the Grand Canyon. You can enjoy a memorable and comfortable trip to the South Rim of the Grand Canyon in a small group of 6. Our expert guide will drive you to the Grand Canyon and other major local tourist attractions in a spacious van and tell you about the history of, as well as tales about, each place. Note that only members of Sherman Tours can take advantage of this very reasonably priced tour. To register and for further information about our trip to the Grand Canyon, please refer to our website at www.shermantours.com.

http://www.shermantours.com/tourinfo

Sherman Tours

HOME	ABOUT US	TOUR INFO	TESTIMONIALS	BOOK A TOUR

Special One-Day Trip to the Grand Canyon

When:	10:00 A.M. – 8:00 P.M. Available Sunday – Friday (Not available on Saturday)
Where:	From the Flagstaff Airport to the South Rim of the Grand Canyon (pickup and drop-off services included). Lunch at Olivares' Italian and dinner at Mitchell's Diner or All about French on Thursdays.
How much:	$145 per adult $80 per child under the age of 16
Other:	A helicopter ride at the Grand Canyon for sightseeing is available for an additional $200. Dietary preference must be reported in advance. **Click Here** to view pictures of the Grand Canyon and other tourist attractions.

http://www.shermantours.com/testimonials

Sherman Tours

| HOME | ABOUT US | TOUR INFO | TESTIMONIALS | BOOK A TOUR |

"Great Trip to the Grand Canyon"

Reviewed by Samantha Watts
Reviewed on October 10

This was such a wonderful and well-organized tour provided by Sherman Tours. I especially liked the fact that I was never rushed, which enabled me to take in the view and appreciate the nature of the beautiful Grand Canyon. Our guide Joshua O'Neil was very informative, knowledgeable, and entertaining. I greatly enjoyed the delicious dinner I had at All about French as well. I would recommend this trip package to all those who want to have an unforgettable experience at the Grand Canyon in a relatively short time.

191. What is true about Sherman Tours?

(A) It is offering its members an exclusive deal.
(B) It consists of six employees.
(C) It issues a newsletter monthly.
(D) It has a long history.

192. What is mentioned about the helicopter ride?

(A) It must be requested in advance.
(B) It will be given to returning guests.
(C) It is offered for an extra fee.
(D) It is currently available for a reduced price.

193. What is included in the one-day trip to the Grand Canyon?

(A) An airline ticket
(B) Meals
(C) A souvenir
(D) Picture-taking service

194. When did Ms. Watts most likely go on a tour to the Grand Canyon?

(A) On a Thursday
(B) On a Friday
(C) On a Saturday
(D) On a Sunday

195. What can be inferred about Mr. O'Neil?

(A) He is a professional entertainer.
(B) He paid $145 for his tour of the Grand Canyon.
(C) He is a new employee at Sherman Tours.
(D) He gave Ms. Watts a ride to the Grand Canyon.

▶ ▶ ▶ GO ON TO THE NEXT PAGE

http://www.booksworld.com/category

Books World

HOME	RECENT	CATEGORY	ORDER

Bestselling books by category: culinary arts

1. *Behind the Kitchen* by Anthony Barry
   Dreaming of opening a restaurant? Learn to make good money in the food industry with Mr. Barry's insights and advice.

2. *Happy Table* by Karen Wilson
   The food on your table determines you and your family's health and happiness. Directions on choosing the right ingredients and using the right cooking methods.

3. *Understanding the Food Industry* by Rodney Sanford
   You have to understand the industry in order to become successful in it. See how to avoid mistakes that people new to the food industry often make. If you are interested in owning a restaurant, this is a must-read for you.

4. *Food, Language, and Culture* by Rodney Sanford
   What determines the food, language, and culture of a nation? And how do they, in turn, affect the nation and its people? Find out in Mr. Sanford's book that has been translated into more than 10 languages.

Bloomfield Public Library

Events in the Fourth Week of June

June 20, Monday – Successful author and restaurant owner Rodney Sanford visits our library to discuss methods regarding operating a restaurant that are demonstrated in his latest book. Mr. Sanford will sign his book for participants after the event.

June 22, Wednesday – A fun, interactive event full of music for preschoolers and toddlers with their guardians. Songs about the different seasons and weather will be played along with various instruments. No registration required to join this exciting musical class.

To: `<customerservice@bloomfieldpl.org>`

From: Melvin Charles `<mcharles@opmail.com>`

Date: June 27

Subject: Bloomfield Public Library

To whom it may concern,

I recently attended an event held at the Bloomfield Public Library. I was greatly impressed by Mr. Sanford's knowledge and ideas. What he taught me during the discussion session will be a great asset when it comes to executing my own business plan.

In addition, I would like to be notified by text message when the book *Behind the Kitchen* becomes available. It was already checked out when I tried to borrow it. My mobile number is (210) 555-3918. Thank you.

Melvin Charles

---

196. In the web page, the word "good" in paragraph 1, line 2, is closest in meaning to

(A) pleasant
(B) substantial
(C) generous
(D) real

197. What is indicated about the Bloomfield Public Library?

(A) It hosts events for children.
(B) It requires a membership card for event registration.
(C) It is currently hiring new employees.
(D) Its operating hours vary seasonally.

198. What book was signed at the Bloomfield Public Library by its author recently?

(A) *Behind the Kitchen*
(B) *Happy Table*
(C) *Understanding the Food Industry*
(D) *Food, Language, and Culture*

199. What is probably true about Mr. Charles?

(A) He frequently visits the Bloomfield Public Library.
(B) He works at the Bloomfield Public Library.
(C) He would like to buy one of Mr. Sanford's books.
(D) He is interested in opening a restaurant.

200. What does Mr. Charles request the Bloomfield Public Library do?

(A) Inform him of the release date of a book
(B) Notify him of when there will be another event with Mr. Sanford
(C) Let him know when a book is returned to the library
(D) Send a new book to his address

STOP! This is the end of the test. If you finish before time is called,
you may go back to Parts 5, 6, and 7 and check your work.

Actual Test 02

MP3 音檔　　　解析

最佳解答時間 120 分鐘

120 min

開始時間：＿＿＿點 ＿＿＿分

結束時間：＿＿＿點 ＿＿＿分

▲盡量不要在作答中途停下來。
▲請於答案卡上畫記作答。

目標正確題數：＿＿＿／**200 題**　實際正確題數：＿＿＿／**200 題**

題數與分數對照，請參考 P449 分數換算表。

LISTENING TEST

In the Listening test, you will be asked to demonstrate how well you understand spoken English. The entire Listening test will last approximately 45 minutes. There are four parts, and directions are given for each part. You must mark your answers on the separate answer sheet. Do not write your answers in the test book.

PART 1

Directions: For each question in this part, you will hear four statements about a picture in your test book. When you hear the statements, you must select the one statement that best describes what you see in the picture. Then find the number of the question on your answer sheet and mark your answer. The statements will not be printed in your test book and will be spoken only one time.

Statement (B), "They are sitting at a table." is the best description of the picture. So you should select answer (B) and mark it on your answer sheet.

1.

2.

▶ ▶ ▶GO ON TO THE NEXT PAGE

3.

4.

5.

6.

▶ ▶ ▶ GO ON TO THE NEXT PAGE

PART 2

Directions: You will hear a question or statement and three responses spoken in English. They will not be printed in your test book and will be spoken only one time. Select the best response to the question or statement and mark the letter (A), (B), or (C) on your answer sheet.

7. Mark your answer on your answer sheet.

8. Mark your answer on your answer sheet.

9. Mark your answer on your answer sheet.

10. Mark your answer on your answer sheet.

11. Mark your answer on your answer sheet.

12. Mark your answer on your answer sheet.

13. Mark your answer on your answer sheet.

14. Mark your answer on your answer sheet.

15. Mark your answer on your answer sheet.

16. Mark your answer on your answer sheet.

17. Mark your answer on your answer sheet.

18. Mark your answer on your answer sheet.

19. Mark your answer on your answer sheet.

20. Mark your answer on your answer sheet.

21. Mark your answer on your answer sheet.

22. Mark your answer on your answer sheet.

23. Mark your answer on your answer sheet.

24. Mark your answer on your answer sheet.

25. Mark your answer on your answer sheet.

26. Mark your answer on your answer sheet.

27. Mark your answer on your answer sheet.

28. Mark your answer on your answer sheet.

29. Mark your answer on your answer sheet.

30. Mark your answer on your answer sheet.

31. Mark your answer on your answer sheet.

PART 3

Directions: You will hear some conversations between two or three people. You will be asked to answer three questions about what the speakers say in each conversation. Select the best response to each question and mark the letter (A), (B), (C), or (D) on your answer sheet. The conversations will not be printed in your test book and will be spoken only one time.

32. What product are the speakers discussing?

(A) A motor vehicle
(B) A laptop computer
(C) A cellular phone
(D) A television set

33. What caused a delay?

(A) Unavailable materials
(B) Not enough money in the budget
(C) A problem with an engine
(D) A lack of skilled workers

34. What will happen in two months?

(A) Production will start.
(B) A design will be approved.
(C) Customer surveys will be collected.
(D) A new factory will open.

---

35. Where do the speakers most likely work?

(A) At a grocery store
(B) At an electronics store
(C) At a bookstore
(D) At a library

36. What did the woman decide to do?

(A) Improve the website
(B) Guarantee a service
(C) Charge customers for membership
(D) Order more products

37. What does the man expect will happen?

(A) Hours will be extended.
(B) Free delivery will be offered.
(C) More staff will be hired.
(D) Sales will improve.

38. Where does the man work?

(A) At a landscaping service
(B) At a real estate agency
(C) At a public library
(D) At a telephone company

39. What is the woman concerned about?

(A) A material
(B) A deadline
(C) A price
(D) A location

40. What do the speakers agree to do in the afternoon?

(A) Check out a manual
(B) Sign a rental contract
(C) Meet with an owner
(D) Visit a property

---

41. What event are the speakers talking about?

(A) A retirement party
(B) A training seminar
(C) A new cleaning service
(D) An employee appreciation party

42. Why does the man say, "All the recyclables get picked up tomorrow morning"?

(A) To provide a warning
(B) To make a request
(C) To express surprise
(D) To turn down a suggestion

43. What does the man say he will do?

(A) Contact a cleaning service
(B) Go home early
(C) Pick up some trash
(D) Get some cleaning supplies

▶ ▶ ▶ GO ON TO THE NEXT PAGE

44. Where does the man work?

(A) At a train station
(B) At an airport
(C) At a convention center
(D) At a hotel

45. According to the man, what event will take place this week?

(A) A marketing seminar
(B) A trade fair
(C) A music concert
(D) A book release

46. What does the man recommend doing?

(A) Using a shuttle bus
(B) Hiring a local guide
(C) Eating at a restaurant
(D) Taking a taxi

---

47. What does the business want the woman to do?

(A) Design a new recreation area
(B) Take care of online advertising
(C) Create a new web page
(D) Manage customer account

48. Why is the woman the top job candidate?

(A) She has experience working abroad.
(B) She has good recommendations.
(C) Her work is impressive.
(D) Her schedule is flexible.

49. What do the men point out about their resort?

(A) It was recently renovated.
(B) It has beautiful views.
(C) It is popular with guests.
(D) It is reasonably priced.

50. What does the woman say will happen on the weekend?

(A) Some products will be discounted.
(B) New items will be arriving.
(C) Some lighting fixtures will be installed.
(D) The store's hours will be extended.

51. What does the man mean when he says, "I think we'll be seeing each other a lot"?

(A) He accepted a job at the store.
(B) He is happy about a new business.
(C) He has known a business owner long.
(D) He is a member of a shopping club.

52. Why does the woman apologize?

(A) She misunderstood the man's request.
(B) The store is not currently hiring.
(C) A payment method cannot be used.
(D) An advertised item is out of stock.

---

53. What type of product are the speakers talking about?

(A) A kitchen appliance
(B) A musical instrument
(C) A light fixture
(D) A smartphone accessory

54. What is the woman's complaint about the item?

(A) It is missing some parts.
(B) It is making strange noises.
(C) It comes with wrong cables.
(D) It is damaged.

55. What does Stuart recommend doing?

(A) Using a manufacturer's warranty
(B) Visiting another repair store
(C) Ordering some replacement parts
(D) Returning later in the day

56. Where do the speakers work?

(A) At a recycling plant
(B) At a technical school
(C) At a manufacturing facility
(D) At a bicycle shop

57. What are the speakers talking about?

(A) An electric motor
(B) Some safety equipment
(C) A bicycle rack
(D) A steering wheel

58. What does the man ask the woman to do?

(A) Call a supplier
(B) Put up a notice
(C) Sign a document
(D) Send an e-mail

59. Where does the woman work?

(A) At a radio station
(B) At a furniture store
(C) At a computer store
(D) At a department store

60. What is mentioned about recent orders?

(A) They are for smaller quantities.
(B) They are mostly from businesses.
(C) They are always placed online.
(D) They must come preassembled.

61. According to the woman, how does her business stay competitive?

(A) By offering a discount on custom-made furniture
(B) By improving customer service
(C) By increasing online marketing
(D) By providing many items for individual customers

Inspection Report

Item	Action Taken
Laptop Computer	Upgraded Operation System
Photocopier	Replaced Toner
Projector	Broken – Repair or Remove
Printer	Connected to New Computer

62. What type of business do the speakers work at?

(A) At a library
(B) At an electronics store
(C) At a university
(D) At a law firm

63. Look at the graphic. Which piece of equipment are the speakers talking about?

(A) The laptop computer
(B) The photocopier
(C) The projector
(D) The printer

64. What does the man say he will do now?

(A) Order some replacement parts
(B) Speak with a coworker
(C) Clean the conference room
(D) Purchase some new equipment

▶ ▶ ▶ GO ON TO THE NEXT PAGE

Sam's Schedule

To Do	Time
Meeting with Dean	11:00 A.M.
Conference Call	11:45 A.M.
Client Lunch	12:00 P.M.
Factory Tour	1:30 P.M.
Orientation Speech	4:00 P.M.

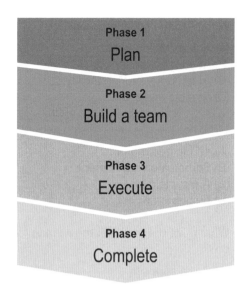

65. Where is the conversation taking place?

(A) In Dean's office
(B) At a restaurant
(C) At a factory
(D) In a conference room

66. What are the speakers going to discuss?

(A) The price of a product
(B) The design of a product
(C) The sales of a product
(D) The advertising of a product

67. Look at the graphic. Why does Sam need to leave early?

(A) He has a meeting with Dean.
(B) He has a conference call.
(C) He has a factory tour.
(D) He has an orientation speech.

68. Where does the conversation take place?

(A) At a job fair
(B) At a meeting for managers
(C) At a marketing company
(D) At a trade show

69. Look at the graphic. Which phase does the man think is important to the success of a project?

(A) Plan
(B) Build a team
(C) Execute
(D) Complete

70. What does the woman say she will do when she returns home?

(A) Register for a course
(B) Apply for a position
(C) Talk to the man on the phone
(D) Submit her résumé

PART 4

Directions: You will hear some short talks given by a single speaker. You will be asked to answer three questions about what the speaker says in each short talk. Select the best response to each question and mark the letter (A), (B), (C), or (D) on your answer sheet. The talks will not be printed in your test book and will be spoken only one time.

71. Where does the speaker most likely work?

(A) At a sporting goods store
(B) At a hardware store
(C) At a department store
(D) At a jewelry store

72. According to the speaker, what should the listeners focus on?

(A) Cleaning the store
(B) Handing out promotional flyers
(C) Providing customer service
(D) Rearranging the shelves

73. How can shoppers win a prize?

(A) By sending a text message
(B) By turning in a receipt
(C) By visiting a website
(D) By completing a form

74. What business is being advertised?

(A) An amusement park
(B) A travel agency
(C) A restaurant
(D) A hotel

75. According to the speaker, what is the business recognized for?

(A) Holding swimming competitions
(B) Using environmentally friendly materials
(C) Drawing foreign tourists
(D) Donating to the local charities

76. What job benefit is given to the employees?

(A) Employee discounts
(B) Chances for full-time employment
(C) Flexible work schedules
(D) Training opportunities

77. Why is the speaker calling?

(A) To make a cancelation
(B) To track an order
(C) To talk about an order
(D) To ask for driving directions

78. What does the speaker imply when she says, "We have orders that we need to fill at the end of the month"?

(A) More workers must be hired.
(B) Her request is urgent.
(C) She can pay a higher price.
(D) Items should be sent by special delivery.

79. What is the listener warned about?

(A) The speaker might not be in her office.
(B) There could be a change in working hours.
(C) A reservation cannot be made.
(D) A schedule has been changed.

80. What type of event is being prepared?

(A) A trade show
(B) A local festival
(C) A charity auction
(D) A fundraiser

81. What news does the speaker announce?

(A) An advertisement was successful.
(B) Posters have been put up.
(C) A venue can be rented.
(D) A dinner reservation has been confirmed.

82. According to the speaker, what is the next phase in the planning process?

(A) Placing advertisements
(B) Signing contracts
(C) Creating a web page
(D) Acquiring supplies

▶ ▶ ▶GO ON TO THE NEXT PAGE

83. What is the topic of the podcast?

  (A) Understanding market trends
  (B) Expanding a business
  (C) Increasing profits
  (D) Helping with starting a new business

84. What type of business does Tina Mellon own?

  (A) A clothing store
  (B) A restaurant
  (C) A financial service company
  (D) A cosmetics manufacturer

85. What does the speaker say can be found on a website?

  (A) An interview
  (B) A business tutorial
  (C) A list of investors
  (D) A job opportunity

---

86. What does the speaker apologize for?

  (A) An unexpected fee
  (B) A long line
  (C) A delayed start
  (D) A crowded bus

87. Why does the speaker say, "And that's our next stop"?

  (A) To suggest purchasing items later
  (B) To complain about a tour schedule
  (C) To advise the listeners to hurry up
  (D) To answer a listener's question

88. What does the speaker say the listeners will enjoy at the Rudolph Bistro?

  (A) The view of the city
  (B) The artwork
  (C) A musical performance
  (D) The fresh food

89. What has the business had difficulty with?

  (A) Hiring qualified employees
  (B) Promoting its newest products
  (C) Expanding into foreign markets
  (D) Retaining staff members

90. What did the speaker do last month?

  (A) She conducted a survey.
  (B) She interviewed some applicants.
  (C) She signed a new contract.
  (D) She went on a business trip.

91. What does the speaker say the company will do?

  (A) Start a mentoring program
  (B) Offer an on-the-job training
  (C) Create more advertisements
  (D) Purchase a new property

---

92. What is Summerville planning to do?

  (A) Widen some of the roads in the city
  (B) Improve bus services
  (C) Encourage residents to use public transportation
  (D) Attract more tourists

93. Why does the speaker say, "It has been successful in other cities"?

  (A) To hire more bus drivers
  (B) To mention a new training program
  (C) To develop another mobile app
  (D) To praise a job well done

94. What are the listeners asked to do?

  (A) E-mail some feedback
  (B) Start taking the bus
  (C) Visit the mayor's office
  (D) Go to other cities

Repairs Plan

Step 1	Inspect a property
Step 2	Make a cost estimate
Step 3	Create a timeline
Step 4	Obtain permits
Step 5	Begin Working

Fayetteville Spring Festival

Saturday, May 2 – Sunday, May 3
Painting and drawing
Local food and performers

◇◇◇◇◇◇◇◇◇◇◇◇◇◇◇◇◇◇◇◇◇◇◇◇◇◇◇◇◇◇◇◇◇◇◇◇◇◇

Saturday Performances
- Marshall Peters Band
- Fayetteville Orchestra

Sunday Performances
- Dave Sanders Comedy Routine
- Redwood Band

95. Who most likely is the speaker?

(A) A construction manager
(B) An architect
(C) A hardware store owner
(D) An interior decorator

96. Look at the graphic. Which step is the speaker currently working on?

(A) Step 1
(B) Step 2
(C) Step 3
(D) Step 4

97. What will the speaker send the listener?

(A) A contract to sign
(B) Revised blueprints
(C) Some samples of material
(D) A cost estimate

98. Why has an event been postponed?

(A) Some fees have not been paid.
(B) Inclement weather is predicted.
(C) Some performers are not available.
(D) Repair work needs to be done.

99. Look at the graphic. Which performance will the speaker most likely go to?

(A) Redwood Band
(B) Fayetteville Orchestra
(C) Dave Sanders Comedy Routine
(D) Marshall Peters Band

100. What does the speaker offer to do?

(A) Volunteer at the festival
(B) Organize an event
(C) Buy some tickets
(D) Drive to a performance

This is the end of the Listening test. Turn to Part 5 in your test book.

▶ ▶ ▶ **GO ON TO THE NEXT PAGE**

READING TEST

In the Reading test, you will read a variety of texts and answer several different types of reading comprehension questions. The entire Reading test will last 75 minutes. There are three parts, and directions are given for each part. You are encouraged to answer as many questions as possible within the time allowed.

You must mark your answer on the separate answer sheet. Do not write your answers in your test book.

PART 5

Directions: A word or phrase is missing in each of the sentences below. Four answer choices are given below each sentence. Select the best answer to complete the sentence. Then mark the letter (A), (B), (C), or (D) on your answer sheet.

101. Due to ------- optimistic and cheerful personality, he later became a radio host in New York.

(A) he
(B) him
(C) his
(D) himself

102. Last week, ------- the euro and Swiss franc weakened 3.1 percent against the U.S. dollar.

(A) both
(B) either
(C) never
(D) whether

103. Our company decided to hire Mr. Kwon ------- our Head of Marketing because his marketing presentation was impressive.

(A) as
(B) by
(C) so
(D) for

104. Due to the heat wave, BK Construction requested an ------- on the new bridge construction project.

(A) extend
(B) extension
(C) extensive
(D) extended

105. Mandoo Electronics shares rose by about 25 percent almost immediately ------- the release of new memory chips.

(A) when
(B) either
(C) aside from
(D) following

106. With improved search technologies, it is not difficult today to locate ------- to purchase old jazz albums from the 50's and 60's online.

(A) such
(B) and
(C) but
(D) if

107. The landscaper hired by Mr. Jenkins used evergreen bushes to create additional privacy in his garden and to mark a natural ------- for his property.

(A) inventory
(B) building
(C) boundary
(D) source

108. Once the new manufacturing plant in Vietnam has been -------, our productivity is expected to increase by about 30%.

(A) constructed
(B) repaired
(C) incurred
(D) indicated

109. Both the exteriors and interiors of our new car models have been ------- redesigned to appeal to domestic and foreign customers.

(A) complete
(B) completing
(C) completely
(D) completion

110. People usually read newspapers and magazines in order to obtain ------- information about a variety of social phenomena.

(A) accurate
(B) obscure
(C) confidential
(D) sensitive

111. Job applicants should be reminded that false information ------- in the interview may result in automatic dismissal.

(A) give
(B) given
(C) giving
(D) was given

112. The newly-developed battery charger is ------- with almost all types of laptop computers in the domestic market.

(A) popular
(B) innovative
(C) compatible
(D) unavailable

113. Ms. Parker is arguing that the idea for the new inventory system was her own and not ------- of Mr. Evans.

(A) one
(B) this
(C) none
(D) that

114. Drivers must ------- with the rules governing driving time and off-duty time if they drive vehicles transporting dangerous substances.

(A) compete
(B) comply
(C) associate
(D) provide

115. ------- on the recent study, some scientists have concluded that North Pole ice cap is being lost seven times faster than it was in the 1990s.

(A) Based
(B) Basing
(C) Base
(D) Basement

116. ------- who is interested in participating in the technology seminar should contact Mr. McGowan by next Wednesday.

(A) Those
(B) Them
(C) Each other
(D) Anyone

117. The recent survey shows that three out of ten adolescents appeared heavily ------- on their mobile phones.

(A) depend
(B) dependent
(C) dependable
(D) dependence

118. The market analysis report contains some errors that Mr. Hopkins ------- before the board meeting scheduled to take place tomorrow.

(A) to correct
(B) correct
(C) has been corrected
(D) will correct

119. James Watt, ------- latest album has

been the top selling album in the country, has received many prestigious music awards.

(A) whatever
(B) whom
(C) what
(D) whose

120. Please write your recent experience with Global Telecom ------- we can improve our customer services.

(A) now that
(B) while
(C) although
(D) so that

121. The guest speaker should stand ------- the audience to foster their positive engagement and participation.

(A) anywhere
(B) somewhere
(C) in place of
(D) in front of

122. The human resources department will ------- plan many activities that the company offers for newly hired employees.

(A) compatibly
(B) meticulously
(C) considerably
(D) enormously

123. It is recommended that all people ------- a copy of their tax returns and receipts in case they are audited in the future.

(A) retain
(B) imitate
(C) complete
(D) arrange

124. ------- selling fewer trucks and sedans, Autotrade Services reported record profits last year.

(A) Through
(B) Despite
(C) Unless
(D) Upon

125. Ace Computer's manufacturing plant has

noticed a sharp increase in productivity ------- the assembly line workers began operating the new machinery.

(A) since
(B) how
(C) even if
(D) as a result of

126. Some of the company's transaction files became damaged ------- being moved to the new data storage system.

(A) in contrast to
(B) in exchange for
(C) in the process of
(D) for the reason that

127. The new office computer course holds thirty employees, all of ------- will learn computer skills, including advanced knowledge of word processing and database management.

(A) who
(B) whom
(C) which
(D) them

128. Although manufacturing jobs have fallen in recent decades, improved productivity has kept manufacturing ------- rising.

(A) amount
(B) quantity
(C) output
(D) consequence

129. Many popular restaurants and hotels are opening their own official websites ------- making reservations and paying with a credit card.

(A) facilitates
(B) facilitation
(C) is facilitating
(D) to facilitate

130. A product that was delivered in packaging will be refunded ------- its original case has not been removed.

(A) therefore
(B) now that
(C) regardless of
(D) provided that

PART 6

Directions: Read the texts that follow. A word or phrase, or sentence is missing in parts of each text. Four answer choices for each question are given below the text. Select the best answer to complete the text. Then mark the letter (A), (B), (C), or (D) on your answer sheet.

Questions 131-134 refer to the following information.

Course Announcement

The Sunhill Community Center is pleased to announce that starting next Wednesday, April 10, Ms. Patricia Hernandez ------- Basic Spanish at the community center. The -------
                                131.   **132.**

meets every Monday from 10:00 A.M. to 11:30 A.M., in room 401.

You can register through our website at www.scc.org, or visit us in person at one of

------- help desks. Tuition is $80 for all four weeks. If you register by this Wednesday, you
133.

will automatically receive a 20 percent discount off of the tuition.

The Sunhill Community Center offers comprehensive foreign language courses starting

next month. -------. More information can be found on the website.
       134.

131. (A) to teach
    (B) is taught
    (C) will teach
    (D) has taught

132. (A) faculty
    (B) board
    (C) class
    (D) committee

133. (A) my
    (B) her
    (C) our
    (D) those

134. (A) You need a college degree to satisfy licensure requirements for teaching.
    (B) No other prior experience may be necessary for our translation jobs.
    (C) All residents of Sunhill age 60 and older can attend our courses for free.
    (D) The community center will be temporarily closed for extensive renovations.

▶ ▶ ▶ GO ON TO THE NEXT PAGE

Hill Valley Widens The Roads

By Alfred Brantley on December 12, 10:15 A.M.

The city council of Hill Valley is about to commence the road expansion construction on

Lombard Street ------- to Hill Valley Convention Center. This construction project consists
        135.

of widening the four lanes of Lombard Street so that it can become an eight-lane roadway.

-------.
 136.

To enable the construction to be ------- safely, Lombard Street will be closed to vehicular
                         137.

traffic between Hill Valley Convention Center and the Art Gallery of Hill Valley. The

footbridge next to Hill Valley Convention Center that leads onto Lombard Street will also

be shut to pedestrians.

The pedestrian footway along Lombard Street that provides access to Hill Valley

Convention Center will not be affected by the work. -------, during this period, public
                                  138.

buses that normally use Lombard Street will be diverted via Valencia Lane.

---

135. (A) committed
(B) pertaining
(C) related
(D) adjacent

136. (A) We are concerned about traffic congestion on roads and air pollution.
(B) It will create many new jobs for local workers and drive our economic growth.
(C) Workplace safety is all about ensuring people are doing their jobs the right way with zero or very little chance of getting hurt.
(D) This work is scheduled to begin around March 1, and is expected to take around three months to complete.

137. (A) completed
(B) intensified
(C) occurred
(D) undertaken

138. (A) Similarly
(B) However
(C) Additionally
(D) For example

Dear Mr. Michael Western;

We received your letter of June 1. We regret ------- you any inconvenience.
139.

According to our shipping company, -------, all one hundred cases were delivered in good
140.

frozen condition and no one on the ship observed any cases defrosting before their arrival

in San Diego. Therefore, we assume that the defrosting process started after the cargo

------- to the warehouse in the harbor.
141.

In order to keep pork frozen, the freezer room must be maintained at temperature of

minus 15 degrees centigrade. We believe that the cases began to defrost due to the

insufficient freezing facilities in your warehouse.

Although we are not prepared to offer you a full refund, we would be happy to give you a

30% discount on your next deal. -------.
142.

We look forward to serving you again in the future.

Sincerely yours,

Nina Lee
Product Quality Control Manager
Andrew Farms, Inc.

139. (A) to cause
(B) cause
(C) causing
(D) caused

140. (A) because
(B) however
(C) thereby
(D) at the time

141. (A) move
(B) is moved
(C) will be moving
(D) had been moved

142. (A) We are not responsible for any lost, stolen, or damaged baggage or personal items.
(B) Freezing foods removes any bacteria and allows the foods to be stored for many years.
(C) With speedy delivery and proper packaging, you can send perishable items to your customers.
(D) We hope this arrangement should cover part of the financial losses you have suffered.

▶ ▶ ▶GO ON TO THE NEXT PAGE

Walnut Creek Hotel

1411 Tremont Street,
Boston, MA 02120
Tel: (857) 770-7000~3
Fax: (857) 770-7004~5
www.walnutcreekhotel.com

-------. The Walnut Creek Hotel is fully furnished and always prepared with lots of love to
143.
receive you; therefore we would like to ask you to take care of it ------- it were your own
144.
home.

All of the hotel rooms have recently been tastefully redecorated and re-equipped,
combining delicate fabrics and rich marble with the latest technology to ensure the most
------- stay by each and every guest at the hotel.
145.

You can get the necessary information on transportation tips and a variety of services for
your convenience at the front desk located on the ground floor. If you need -------
146.
information, please feel free to call us at ext. 101.

We hope your stay in the Walnut Creek Hotel becomes part of the great memories of your
trip to Boston. Thank you again for choosing the Walnut Creek Hotel for your stay and
enjoy your time with us.

143. (A) On behalf of all the staff, a big thank you for your kind gifts and your support this year.
(B) When booking a reservation for a hotel room, guest may be asked to make an advance deposit.
(C) No matter what time of year, this town offers scenic backdrops and views right on your doorstep.
(D) It is a real pleasure to have you as our guests and we thank you for choosing us for your stay.

144. (A) unless
(B) as if
(C) now that
(D) even though

145. (A) satisfy
(B) satisfying
(C) satisfied
(D) satisfaction

146. (A) further
(B) adequate
(C) essential
(D) confidential

PART 7

Directions: In this part you will read a selection of texts, such as magazine and newspaper articles, e-mails, and instant messages. Each text or set of texts is followed by several questions. Select the best answer for each question and mark the letter (A), (B), (C), or (D) on your answer sheet.

Questions 147-148 refer to the following advertisement.

RELAX HERE AT
SERENE SPA

As the premier spa in Southern California, Serene Spa offers services that go far beyond any traditional spa. On July 1, we are opening an additional spa location in San Diego.

Please note that services with asterisk* are available from July 10.

Swedish Massage*	Remedial Massage*	Laser Skincare*
Facials	Waxing	Stone Therapy
Nails	Peels	Aromatherapy

Please print out this page and bring the coupon below.

15% OFF Any Spa Service	**Schedule Your Appointment Today!** - Offer is valid through July 31. - Only one coupon may be used per visit.

---

147. Which service is NOT available on July 9?

(A) Facials
(B) Stone therapy
(C) Peels
(D) Laser skincare

148. What is indicated about the coupon in the advertisement?

(A) It is available for use in August.
(B) It offers a discount only in the San Diego branch.
(C) It has to be printed out in order to get a discount.
(D) It can be used together with other offers.

Questions 149-150 refer to the following text message chain.

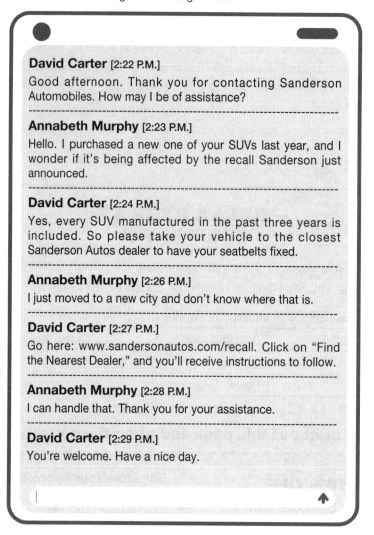

David Carter [2:22 P.M.]

Good afternoon. Thank you for contacting Sanderson Automobiles. How may I be of assistance?

Annabeth Murphy [2:23 P.M.]

Hello. I purchased a new one of your SUVs last year, and I wonder if it's being affected by the recall Sanderson just announced.

David Carter [2:24 P.M.]

Yes, every SUV manufactured in the past three years is included. So please take your vehicle to the closest Sanderson Autos dealer to have your seatbelts fixed.

Annabeth Murphy [2:26 P.M.]

I just moved to a new city and don't know where that is.

David Carter [2:27 P.M.]

Go here: www.sandersonautos.com/recall. Click on "Find the Nearest Dealer," and you'll receive instructions to follow.

Annabeth Murphy [2:28 P.M.]

I can handle that. Thank you for your assistance.

David Carter [2:29 P.M.]

You're welcome. Have a nice day.

149. Why did Ms. Murphy contact Mr. Carter?

(A) To find out how to buy an SUV
(B) To inquire about an engine problem
(C) To ask about a company recall
(D) To request a rebate on a purchase

150. At 2:28 P.M., what does Ms. Murphy most likely mean when she writes, "I can handle that"?

(A) She just followed Mr. Carter's instructions.
(B) She will fix the problem by herself.
(C) She can return to the place she made her purchase.
(D) She understands what she needs to do.

Questions 151-153 refer to the following letter.

October 14

Alice Watts
Patterson Carpets
557 Longman Street
Portsmouth, OH 45662

Dear Ms. Watts,

It was a pleasure to meet with you at the home furnishings expo in Lexington, Kentucky, last week. —[1]—. You spent a lot of time speaking with me about the carpets your firm manufactures. I enjoyed learning about how your products are different from those of your competitors. I shared the samples you gave me with several employees here, and everyone was impressed with their quality. —[2]—. My colleagues particularly liked the selection of colors available.

We have been searching for a new supplier for our interior design company. —[3]—. We feel that your firm should definitely be able to fulfill all of our needs. I wonder if you are available to meet in person soon so that we can discuss a large order. —[4]—. When do you have time to meet?

Sincerely,

Reginald Wellman
Portsmouth Interior Design

---

151. What is NOT mentioned about Mr. Wellman?

(A) He is the owner of a company.
(B) He spoke with Ms. Watts in person.
(C) He works at a place that sells carpets.
(D) He traveled to Kentucky a week ago.

152. What does Mr. Wellman indicate about Portsmouth Interior Design?

(A) It recently opened.
(B) It has multiple workers.
(C) It provides free installation.
(D) It is having a sale soon.

153. In which of the positions marked [1], [2], [3], and [4] does the following sentence best belong?

"I'd also like to talk about a possible bulk discount."

(A) [1]
(B) [2]
(C) [3]
(D) [4]

Attention All Customers of
Ala Moana

Thanks to all our customers for visiting Ala Moana. We strive to provide you with the finest Hawaiian-style shirts, hats, accessories and a wide variety of fashion items through our website.

Today, we would like to announce a change in our shipping policy. Ala Moana previously offered free shipping on all purchases, but due to the increasing fuel costs, we are no longer able to provide this service. Therefore, we must impose a shipping charge on each purchase less than $50. This was an inevitable decision in order to maintain the area's lowest cost of the products.

We ask for your understanding and Ala Moana promises to remain the most competitive Hawaiian fashion provider.

154. What is the purpose of the information?

(A) To advertise an online business
(B) To post a price list of new products
(C) To confirm a recent order
(D) To announce a change in service

155. What kind of business most likely is Ala Moana?

(A) A resort
(B) A clothing store
(C) A tour operator
(D) A shipping service

156. What is NOT indicated about Ala Moana?

(A) Its items can be purchased online.
(B) It has offered free shipping until recently.
(C) Its products cost less than its competitors'.
(D) It will hold a sale for the first time soon.

PUBLIC ANNOUNCEMENT
FOR RESIDENTS OF IRVIING

An area in the City of Irving will be temporarily closed due to the 4th Texas Spring Parade, which will be held near Fritz Park from 3 P.M. to 8 P.M. on May 4.

The road closure will affect:
- The portion of St. Louis Street between Hampton Boulevard and Keys Road

Alternative Routes include:
- Marconi Street
- Bell Boulevard

For additional information, please contact the Traffic Advisory at the City of Irving at 214-885-0830.

157. What is the main purpose of the notice?

(A) To announce the opening of a sports competition
(B) To inform about upcoming traffic interruption
(C) To notify a scheduled road construction
(D) To alert residents to possible dangers on roads

158. Which part of the city will be closed during the event?

(A) The Fritz Park
(B) St. Louis Street
(C) Hampton Boulevard
(D) Marconi Street

▶ ▶ ▶GO ON TO THE NEXT PAGE

Jalalios' Tacos Opens in the Heart of the City of Kearny

by Chritiano Luxemberg

Kearny, August 11 – The residents of Kearny will now be able to enjoy delicious Mexican cuisine in the heart of Kearny. On August 9, the grand opening of Jalalios' Tacos saw local inhabitants flooding into the restaurant.

The owners, Abrahim and Brena Jalalio, are certified chefs who have successfully managed three restaurants in their hometown, Mexico City. Since they moved to the United States last year, they have been planning to open a restaurant in Kearny. When a vacant property, which was once a shoe store, was put on the market on May 22, they did not hesitate to purchase it and then renovate it into a restaurant.

Jalalios' Tacos provides homemade, traditional Mexican fare with a touch of the Jalalios' modern creativity at reasonable prices. Using only the freshest ingredients, Jalalios' Tacos provides not only delicious but healthy food.

Located on the most crowded street of the business district in Kearny, Jalalio's Tacos will now be the favorite restaurant to many businessmen. "I have always been a big fan of Mexican food. I had to eat at the restaurant after trying a free sample at the front door on the opening day. And I was really satisfied with the quality of its food," said Juan Suarez, a customer. On the day before the opening of the restaurant, I interviewed Mr. Jalalio on the outlook of his restaurant. He noted, "I am very pleased to open a new restaurant here on Castanteen Street. I plan to attract university students as well as businessmen. There can be people who have never visited our establishment, but there are none who have just come once."

For detailed information, pricing of the menu and reservation, please call 201-331-9243.

159. What is the purpose of the article?

(A) To advertise a vacant property
(B) To provide information about traditional food
(C) To introduce a new business to the region
(D) To inform residents of an upcoming construction

160. What is indicated about Mr. and Ms. Jalalio?

(A) They have relatives in Kearny.
(B) They previously owned a shoe store.
(C) They use ingredients imported from Mexico.
(D) They have run other restaurants.

161. According to Mr. Suarez, what is true about Jalalio's Tacos?

(A) It is conveniently located near a university.
(B) It gave visitors some food to try.
(C) Its customer service quality is satisfying.
(D) It has been Mr. Suarez's favorite place for a long time.

Questions 162-164 refer to the following review.

A Magical Autumn Night by Blue Souls

Last night, Blue Souls gave a rousing performance to 500 people gathered in the Oklahoma City Plaza. Composed of four musicians from different national backgrounds, Blue Souls is one of the most popular jazz bands in the United States and has been covered in articles numerous times.

Blue Souls was formed four years ago by the world-renowned pianist, David Yakal. Two years after its formation, an old friend of Mr. Yakal joined the Blue Souls. Taylor Clayton, who previously played trumpet in the London City Orchestra, enriched the sound of their performances as a new member of the group. Soon after he joined, Blue Souls was honored with the Best Musician of the Year Award by Oklahoma City for its exceptional quality of brass sound and performance.

The live performance at the outdoor stage of the Oklahoma City Plaza last night showed the audience the unique color of the music Blue Souls play. In addition to their most popular song, *On My Own*, they also performed songs from their upcoming third album, which will be released next month. Their new album contains different styles of music including swing, bossa nova, and modern jazz.

Blue Souls' performance was perfect as usual, but there was a tiny flaw. The concert venue was a little chilly and it would have been better if the organizers had furnished some portable heaters near the seats.

by Lauren Segulla

162. What type of event is being reviewed?

(A) An orchestra concert
(B) A jazz concert
(C) A magic act
(D) A dance performance

163. The word "covered" in paragraph 1, line 4, is closest in meaning to

(A) interviewed
(B) featured
(C) paid for
(D) blocked

164. What is stated about Mr. Clayton?

(A) He plays the piano.
(B) He joined Blue Souls two years ago.
(C) He has been presented an award by the London City Orchestra.
(D) He recently became the leader of Blue Souls.

▶ ▶ ▶GO ON TO THE NEXT PAGE

Mickey Anderson
31 Mountain Road
Cornwall-on-Hudson, NY 12520

April 19

Chelsea Hair Salon
98 Cosmic Drive
Cornwall, NY 12592

To whom it may concern,

I am writing to apply for the advertised position of a fulltime hair stylist at the Chelsea Hair Salon branch in New Hampshire. Although I have enclosed my full résumé with this letter, I would like to briefly summarize my career background.

After receiving the hair stylist certification from the Clark College, I began working at the Berkshire Hair Shop located in Brookline. During the 6 years of employment there, I received professional recognition, including the National Best Hair Perm Styling Award last year. Along with my résumé, I have also added some photos of my awarded hair styles.

Beyond my professional skills, I am an enthusiastic, artistic, and faithful person who is ready to contribute to the national reputation of the Chelsea Hair Salon. I am sure my hair styling will fit the trend-oriented taste of the Chelsea Hair Salon.

Thank you and I look forward to having the opportunity of a personal interview.

Sincerely,

Mickey Anderson
Enclosure

165. Why did Ms. Anderson write the letter?

(A) To confirm participating in an interview
(B) To apply to a hair styling competition
(C) To introduce herself to a potential employer
(D) To offer a job at a hair salon

166. What is included with the letter?

(A) Hair stylist certification
(B) Award prizes
(C) Sample images
(D) Reference from another person

167. According to the letter, what is indicated about the Chelsea Hair Salon?

(A) It is well-known nationally.
(B) It has been in business for at least 6 years.
(C) It has many award-winning hair designers in its staff.
(D) It has a branch located in Brookline.

▶ ▶ ▶ GO ON TO THE NEXT PAGE

Questions 168-171 refer to the following online chat discussion.

Russell Thompson   9:55 A.M.

Hi, Steve and Mark. How's work at the Murray residence going?

Steve Gilmore   9:57 A.M.

We are almost finished. The work took a bit longer than expected because Mr. Murray asked us to cut a tree down after we trimmed the hedges. Don't worry. I put it on his bill.

Russell Thompson   9:58 A.M.

Sounds great. We just got an online inquiry from someone new. Anna Granite requested an estimate for her place. She lives at 88 Butler Drive. Do you think you can go there before heading to the Stanton Place?

Mark Stuart   10:00 A.M.

It's only a couple of blocks away.

Steve Gilmore   10:01 A.M.

Our next appointment isn't until 1:00 P.M., so we'll drop by after we finish here. What does she want?

Russell Thompson   10:02 A.M.

Thanks, guys.

Russell Thompson   10:02 A.M.

Ah, she wants the basic service, but she said her yard is larger than most people's. That's why I want you to check it out.

Mark Stuart   10:04 A.M.

I know the place. It covers around three acres.

Russell Thompson   10:05 A.M.

I guess it will be a big job. Give her an estimate based upon how much work you think it will require.

Steve Gilmore   10:06 A.M.

You've got it. I'll call you when we finish to discuss the matter.

SEND

---

168. Where most likely do the writers work?

    (A) At a pool installation company
    (B) At a real estate agency
    (C) At a construction firm
    (D) At a landscaping company

169. What does Mr. Gilmore expect to do in the afternoon?

    (A) Provide an estimate
    (B) Return to the office
    (C) Visit a client
    (D) Take part in a conference call

170. What will Mr. Gilmore do after meeting with Ms. Granite?

    (A) Contact Mr. Thompson
    (B) Submit a bill
    (C) Purchase supplies
    (D) Send an e-mail

171. At 10:00 A.M., what does Mr. Stuart suggest when he writes, "It's only a couple of blocks away"?

    (A) He can comply with Mr. Thompson's request.
    (B) He does not have time to make a personal visit.
    (C) He does not know an exact location.
    (D) He has visited a house in person before.

To:	All Employees of Pizza Stop
From:	Jason Bonanza
Date:	April 5
Subject:	News

Everyone,

Thanks for all of the hard work you have done to make our pizza shop the top one in the city. Unfortunately, our success has led to several imitators, each of whom is attempting to take business from us. —[1]—. As a result, I've decided to implement a few new strategies to attract more customers. Let me fill you in on them.

First, as of tomorrow, April 6, we're going to provide free Wi-Fi to customers in the shop. The password will change daily, so the servers must inform our diners at their tables. We'll also be increasing the number of electrical outlets near tables. —[2]—. That will enable diners to recharge their electric devices. We'll be closed on April 8 in order for electricians to make those changes here.

Next, the recent survey we took indicated that diners would like more options for pizza toppings. So I'll be changing the menu on April 9. —[3]—. We'll have a total of 25 possible pizza toppings, which will be the most in the city.

Finally, we're introducing Pizza Stop membership cards to our customers. —[4]—. Please see the document I've attached to this e-mail for more information.

Regards,

Jason Bonanza
Owner, Pizza Stop

172. Why will Pizza Stop make changes in its policies?

(A) To respond to customer requests
(B) To reduce spending
(C) To make itself more competitive
(D) To improve its advertising

173. What will happen on April 8?

(A) A shop will not open.
(B) A menu will change.
(C) Internet will be installed.
(D) A sale will begin.

174. What is indicated about Pizza Stop?

(A) It currently has a membership program.
(B) It offers discounts to frequent diners.
(C) It will be adding more tables soon.
(D) It is one of the city's leading pizza places.

175. In which of the positions marked [1], [2], [3], and [4] does the following sentence best fit?

"Holders can receive discounts and various free items."

(A) [1]
(B) [2]
(C) [3]
(D) [4]

Questions 176-180 refer to the following website and e-mail.

 www.hudsoncollege.edu/notice

HUDSON COLLEGE

About	Notice	Academics	Community

Hudson College Lecture Series on Child Education

Department of Child Education and Development proudly presents a series of lectures on early childhood. Lectures will take place at the department every Friday from June 14 through July 5. Renowned professors of Hudson College and professionals from national organizations will provide in-depth presentations about new ideas on analyzing childhood development and appropriate teaching skills.

Seminar Schedule:

Seminar Title and Speaker	Date/Time	Fees
Development of Language in Early Childhood by Mila Trundel, Professor at Hudson College	June 14 2 P.M. – 4 P.M.	$60
Appropriate Curriculum in Childhood Classrooms by Daniel Quinn, Professor at Hudson College	June 21 3 P.M. – 5 P.M.	$70
Managing Childhood and Elementary Classrooms by David Denton, Child education professional at National Institute of Early Childhood Education	June 28 2 P.M. – 4 P.M.	$90
Children's Social Development: Birth through Childhood by Lilith Mills, Child psychiatrist at Cornwall Hospital	July 5 1 P.M. – 3 P.M.	$80

*100 people maximum are permitted to attend each seminar.

If you would like to register for one of the lectures, CLICK HERE. Please note that all classes are on a first-come, first-served basis and the registration deadline is June 1. Contact Carolina Felton at cfelton@hudsoncollege.edu for any inquiries.

Participants who work in the field of child education and development will receive a $10 discount on the seminar entry fee. An evidentiary document must be presented in the process of registration.

To:	Carolina Felton <cfelton@hudsoncollege.edu>
From:	Olivia Kang <okang@hudsonelementary.com>
Date:	June 3
Subject:	Inquiry

As I frequently heard that the lectures Hudson College offers on these topics are very beneficial, I registered for a lecture, which is to be held on June 21. However, this e-mail is actually to inquire if I may make a change to my reservation.

I am a teacher at a local elementary school. Unfortunately, one of my colleagues has taken an abrupt leave for three weeks due to some family issues. I will have to cover one of his classes on Friday afternoon, June 21. I am still interested in taking one of your lecture series and want to know if I can take the lecture led by David Denton instead. I would also like to know, if the change is possible, when I have to remit the additional fee amount and if I am still eligible for the discount.

Thank you. I look forward to hearing from you soon.

Olivia Kang

176. In the website, what is NOT indicated about the lectures?

(A) They are scheduled in the afternoon.
(B) Their registration deadline is June 1.
(C) Only a limited number of participants can take each lecture.
(D) All lecturers are university professors.

177. How can participants register for the series of lectures?

(A) By sending an e-mail
(B) By visiting a website
(C) By calling a school employee
(D) By coming to the event venue

178. How much did Ms. Kang originally pay?

(A) $60
(B) $70
(C) $80
(D) $90

179. On what date does Ms. Kang wish to take the seminar?

(A) June 14
(B) June 21
(C) June 28
(D) July 5

180. What is suggested about Ms. Kang?

(A) She will be on sick leave for three weeks.
(B) She already paid for the additional charge.
(C) She probably submitted a required document to Hudson college.
(D) She participated in the similar lecture series last quarter.

7TH ANNUAL ISEE GLOBAL FORUM ON PSYCHOLOGY
CALLS FOR STUDENT VOLUNTEERS!

ISEE Global Forum on Psychology is a renowned conference for psychologists from all over the world to exchange new ideas. Organizing committee of 7th Annual ISEE Global Forum on Psychology (IGFP) is now recruiting student volunteers for various supporting roles during the upcoming conference scheduled from July 5 to July 10 at the Milano Hotel, Chicago, IL.

Volunteer Responsibilities
• **Event Assistant** – The primary role is to set up and clean the area during and after conferences. Also, an event assistant helps with making photocopies, distributing handouts to participants, or preparing water for speakers. This role may involve light furniture moving.

• **AV Operator Assistant** – This job is to check audiovisual equipment in the conference hall. Setting up a projector and microphones, if necessary, will also be one of the roles of an AV operator assistant.

Applicant Requirements
- Official letter from your school indicating your current student status
- Official proof of proficiency for at least one of the following languages: Spanish, Chinese, or German
- Experience in volunteering at a conference
- Knowledge about presentation equipment is strongly preferred

Application Submission
You need to send a copy of your résumé, a cover letter, and official documents by June 1 to the office of IGFP organizing committee stated below:

Claire Stanley, Personnel Manager
IGFP Organizing Committee, 30 Franklin Dr., Chicago, IL 60007

May 10

Ivan Harfield
22 Roosebelt St.
Bridgeport, IL 60608

Claire Stanley
IGFP Organizing Committee
30 Franklin Dr.
Chicago, IL 60007

Dear Ms. Stanley,

I would like to apply for the student volunteer program at ISEE Global Forum on Psychology. I am a junior at the University of Illinois and am highly interested in the field of psychology. I have participated in numerous conferences on psychology in the past including IWO Psychology and University of Illinois Conference.

Also, I have been involved in many different activities including working at American Student Marketing Association where I interacted with many people from diverse backgrounds. I work very hard to complete tasks given to me. Despite the fact that I do not speak any other language except English, I am sure I can contribute a lot to IGFP.

Please find enclosed the documents you requested. I hope to be contacted for an interview. Thank you for your consideration in advance.

Sincerely,

Ivan Harfield
Enclosure

181. What is suggested about IGFP?

(A) It has been held seven times successfully.
(B) It is sponsored by Milano Hotel.
(C) It will have attendants from different countries.
(D) It provides a certificate to volunteers.

182. What is NOT one of the roles of event assistant?

(A) Handing out documents to participants
(B) Lighting the conference venue
(C) Doing some errands for presenters
(D) Cleaning up when the conference is over

183. When will the organizing committee stop receiving applications?

(A) May 10
(B) June 1
(C) July 5
(D) July 10

184. Why might Mr. Harfield NOT be successful in assuming the volunteer position?

(A) He doesn't speak any languages required.
(B) He didn't submit the documents from his university.
(C) He lacks experience in the field of Psychology.
(D) He doesn't have an academic degree in Psychology.

185. What is indicated about Mr. Harfield?

(A) He may not be available on a certain day during the conference.
(B) He graduated from the University of Illinois.
(C) He is good at handling presentation equipment.
(D) He has attended conferences on psychology before.

▶ ▶ ▶GO ON TO THE NEXT PAGE

http://www.officeshed.com/policies/shippinganddelivery

Office Shed is at your service!

| About Us | Products | Policies | Customer Reviews |

Shipping & Delivery

Office Shed charges a flat rate of $4.50 for domestic standard shipping (5-7 business days) and $6.50 for domestic express shipping (2-3 business days). We currently deliver to the U.S., the U.K., and New Zealand. For detailed rates, refer below:

Destination	Standard Shipping	Express Shipping
United States	$11.00	$15.00
United Kingdom	$13.00	$17.00
New Zealand	$6.00	$8.00

*All prices are in Australian dollars (AUD) unless otherwise indicated.

For registered members of Office Shed, we are now delivering your orders for free for a limited time. This offer only applies to domestic orders.

You will receive a notification e-mail once your order has shipped. After that, you can check the delivery status of your package at no cost by using our program at www.officeshed.com/ordertracker. Please note that you may not be able to track some orders, such as international shipping.

To view our policies on refunds and returns, click **here**, and on membership, click **here**.

OFFICE SHED
Order Confirmation & Receipt

Order Reference: #4865436
Order Placed On: December 12

Shipping Address:
Brooke Binder, 43 Sheldon Rd., Glenhaven, Vic. 4157, Australia

Product Information	Quantity	Price(s)
4-Tier Metal Desk Tray (Color: Black)	1	$10.99
28mm Paper Clips (100/Pack)	3	$6.75
Premium White Envelopes (25/Pack)	1	$8.81
	Subtotal:	$26.55
	Tax:	$2.65
	Shipping Charge:	$0.00
	Total Price:	$29.20
Payment Method: Credit Card (xxxx-xxxx-xxxx-0555)	Amount:	$29.20

In case you need assistance regarding the ordering process, please call the customer service center during our working hours from Monday to Friday between 9:00 A.M. and 5:00 P.M. at 130-111.

To:	<cs@officeshed.com>
From:	<brookebinder@goldcoastmail.com>
Date:	December 17
Subject:	Request

To whom it may concern,

I've been very pleased with the service I've received from Office Shed. However, imagine my surprise when I opened the box and couldn't find the envelopes I had ordered. I suppose someone forgot to insert them while packing my items.

I would appreciate having the price of the missing items added to my account as I will be ordering again in the near future. I hope that you can rectify this situation soon.

Regards,

Brooke Binder

---

186. In the website, the word "flat" in paragraph 1, line 1, is closest in meaning to

(A) insufficient
(B) fixed
(C) reduced
(D) vertical

187. Where is Office Shed probably based?

(A) The United States
(B) New Zealand
(C) Australia
(D) The United Kingdom

188. In the receipt, what is mentioned about Office Shed?

(A) It shipped Ms. Binder's order on December 12.
(B) It sells products made by local manufacturers.
(C) It distributes office furniture.
(D) Its customer service center operates only on weekdays.

189. What is suggested about Ms. Binder?

(A) She purchases frequently from Office Shed.
(B) She paid for her order with cash.
(C) She will receive an e-mail from Office Shed.
(D) She is the owner of a small company.

190. How much money does Ms. Binder request she be refunded?

(A) $2.65
(B) $6.75
(C) $8.81
(D) $10.99

Dove Cottage Inspection Notice

Attention, all tenants. Please note that the annual inspection on the building's heating systems will be performed next week. This process is being done in preparation for winter and will help keep the heating system running properly. As always, Four Seasons Maintenance, a local company, will visit and perform the inspections. The checkup will take about 20 minutes for each unit. If any problems are detected, we will schedule further inspections and repair work for the units.

Detailed schedule of the inspection is stated below:
– Units on Building A: November 3, 12:00 P.M. – 6:00 P.M.
– Units on Building B: November 4, 12:00 P.M. – 6:00 P.M.
– Units on Building C: November 5, 10:00 A.M. – 4:00 P.M.

If you are not available on the scheduled date for any reason, please contact Rosa Velasquez, the property manager, at rvelasquez@dovecottage.com immediately to reschedule your inspection.

Check out the website of Four Seasons Maintenance for additional information about the inspections. Thank you in advance for your cooperation.

To: Andrew Rudolph
Telephone Number: 594-9584-1128

Andrew, this is David. I'm supposed to have my apartment inspected this morning, so I wonder if we can reschedule our meeting until the afternoon. Once the inspectors arrive, the process shouldn't take long. How about if we get together in your office at around 3:00? Let me know if that works for you. David.

To:	Rosa Velasquez <rvelasquez@dovecottage.com>
From:	David Yakal <dyakal@smail.com>
Date:	November 6
Subject:	Inquiries

I recently had my apartment inspected and was happy to learn there weren't any problems with my heating system. However, earlier today, I noticed that the inspection crew cracked my balcony window. This same problem also occurred when the crew visited my place last year. I think the large equipment they use caused the damage.

I would like to be compensated for the cost of replacing the window. I will purchase a new window and install it myself. Then, I'll send you the receipt so that I can be repaid. Please be advised that I will be leaving on a business trip this weekend and won't be back for two weeks, so I'd like to receive the payment before I depart.

I look forward to hearing from you soon.

Thanks,

David Yakal

191. Why did Dove Cottage undergo inspections?

(A) To prepare the building for the cold season
(B) To fix problems with the central heating system
(C) To follow local regulations for residential buildings
(D) To reduce excessive energy use

192. In the notice, what is stated about the inspection?

(A) It requires registration.
(B) It is performed on a regular basis.
(C) It is done by the property manager.
(D) It takes about a day.

193. When most likely did Mr. Yakal's inspection take place?

(A) On November 3
(B) On November 4
(C) On November 5
(D) On November 6

194. Why did Mr. Yakal send the e-mail?

(A) To reschedule an inspection
(B) To request a problem be addressed
(C) To note where he is going on a trip
(D) To inquire about inspection fees

195. What is indicated about Mr. Yakal?

(A) He went on a business trip on November 3.
(B) He recommended an inspection company to his neighbor.
(C) He intends to complete some repairs by himself.
(D) He has contacted Ms. Velasquez before.

▶ ▶ ▶GO ON TO THE NEXT PAGE

Questions 196-200 refer to the following e-mail, announcement, and review.

To: David Linderman <dlinderman@kitavipi.com>
From: Sam Bankole <sbankole@kitavipi.com>
Date: July 9
Subject: Workshop sessions

Dear Mr. Linderman,

I am writing with regard to the schedule for next month's workshop in Istanbul. I reviewed the first draft of the schedule you sent me this morning, and I think I must ask for a change in it. In the morning on the day when the workshop sessions will be held, I have to attend a meeting with an important client in Ankara. The client is coming from Brussels for only two days, and the meeting cannot be rescheduled. My flight back to Istanbul will depart at 11:30 A.M.

I already asked Sayuri Fujita in our department to switch our workshop times, and she agreed to do so. Please reflect these changes in the schedule before it is printed and posted throughout the company to prevent any confusion.

Thank you,

Sam Bankole
Assistant Editor, Editing Department

Kitavi Publishing, Inc.
Istanbul • Ankara • Izmir • Bursa

15th Annual Employee Training Workshop
August 14, Headquarters Building in Istanbul

Time	Workshop Name	Moderator
8:30 A.M. – 10:00 A.M.	Communicating with Both Clients and Colleagues	Sayuri Fujita
10:20 A.M. – 11:30 A.M.	Developing an Idea into a Great Story	Lorenzo Mondi
11:30 A.M. – 1:00 P.M.	Lunch	
1:00 P.M. – 2:30 P.M.	Designing Attractive Book Covers	Katherine Confalonieri
2:50 P.M. – 4:00 P.M.	Editing Your Columns on Your Own	Tyler Butcher
4:20 P.M. – 6:00 P.M.	Time Management – Make It Count	Sam Bankole

*Every attendee will be invited to a luncheon during the lunch break.

All employees are requested to complete this short review of the workshop. You may remain anonymous if you wish. Your feedback will help us improve future sessions.

How was the overall quality of the...

	Excellent	Good	Average	Poor
trainers	X			
presentations		X		
materials	X			

Comments: I really loved the talk by Mr. Mondi. I learned a lot from him. The other instructors were good, too. The microphone kept breaking down during Mr. Butcher's talk, so it was hard to hear him speak.

Name: *Emily Harper*

196. What is not indicated about Mr. Bankole?

(A) He contacted Mr. Linderman recently.
(B) He has a business meeting to attend.
(C) He will visit Brussels next month.
(D) He plans to lead a workshop session.

197. Where most likely will Mr. Bankole be at 11:30 A.M. on August 14?

(A) In Brussels
(B) In Istanbul
(C) In Bursa
(D) In Ankara

198. What time was Ms. Fujita originally scheduled to lead a workshop?

(A) At 8:30 A.M.
(B) At 10:20 A.M.
(C) At 1:00 P.M.
(D) At 4:20 P.M.

199. What is indicated in the schedule?

(A) Kitavi Publishing, Inc. has been in business for 15 years.
(B) Mr. Mondi will lead a workshop on article editing.
(C) Mr. Bankole will be present at Ms. Fujita's workshop session.
(D) A meal will be given to the attendees at the workshop.

200. Which presentation did Ms. Harper like the most?

(A) Communicating with Both Clients and Colleagues
(B) Developing an Idea into a Great Story
(C) Designing Attractive Book Covers
(D) Editing Your Columns on Your Own

STOP! This is the end of the test. If you finish before time is called,
you may go back to Parts 5, 6, and 7 and check your work.

Actual Test 03

MP3 音檔   解析

最佳解答時間 120 分鐘

120 min

開始時間：＿＿＿點 ＿＿＿分

結束時間：＿＿＿點 ＿＿＿分

▲盡量不要在作答中途停下來。
▲請於答案卡上畫記作答。

目標正確題數：＿＿＿／ **200 題**　實際正確題數：＿＿＿／ **200 題**

題數與分數對照，請參考 P449 分數換算表。

LISTENING TEST

In the Listening test, you will be asked to demonstrate how well you understand spoken English. The entire Listening test will last approximately 45 minutes. There are four parts, and directions are given for each part. You must mark your answers on the separate answer sheet. Do not write your answers in the test book.

PART 1

Directions: For each question in this part, you will hear four statements about a picture in your test book. When you hear the statements, you must select the one statement that best describes what you see in the picture. Then find the number of the question on your answer sheet and mark your answer. The statements will not be printed in your test book and will be spoken only one time.

Statement (B), "They are sitting at a table." is the best description of the picture. So you should select answer (B) and mark it on your answer sheet.

1.

2.

▶ ▶ ▶GO ON TO THE NEXT PAGE

3.

4.

5.

6.

▶ ▶ ▶GO ON TO THE NEXT PAGE

PART 2

Directions: You will hear a question or statement and three responses spoken in English. They will not be printed in your test book and will be spoken only one time. Select the best response to the question or statement and mark the letter (A), (B), or (C) on your answer sheet.

7. Mark your answer on your answer sheet.

8. Mark your answer on your answer sheet.

9. Mark your answer on your answer sheet.

10. Mark your answer on your answer sheet.

11. Mark your answer on your answer sheet.

12. Mark your answer on your answer sheet.

13. Mark your answer on your answer sheet.

14. Mark your answer on your answer sheet.

15. Mark your answer on your answer sheet.

16. Mark your answer on your answer sheet.

17. Mark your answer on your answer sheet.

18. Mark your answer on your answer sheet.

19. Mark your answer on your answer sheet.

20. Mark your answer on your answer sheet.

21. Mark your answer on your answer sheet.

22. Mark your answer on your answer sheet.

23. Mark your answer on your answer sheet.

24. Mark your answer on your answer sheet.

25. Mark your answer on your answer sheet.

26. Mark your answer on your answer sheet.

27. Mark your answer on your answer sheet.

28. Mark your answer on your answer sheet.

29. Mark your answer on your answer sheet.

30. Mark your answer on your answer sheet.

31. Mark your answer on your answer sheet.

PART 3

Directions: You will hear some conversations between two or three people. You will be asked to answer three questions about what the speakers say in each conversation. Select the best response to each question and mark the letter (A), (B), (C), or (D) on your answer sheet. The conversations will not be printed in your test book and will be spoken only one time.

32. Where is the conversation most likely taking place?

    (A) At a hotel
    (B) In an office
    (C) On an airplane
    (D) At a conference center

33. What did the man bring with him?

    (A) Some pictures
    (B) Some materials
    (C) A hotel confirmation
    (D) Directions to a hotel

34. Why will the woman call a conference center?

    (A) To reserve a conference room
    (B) To change an arrival time
    (C) To ask to see a room
    (D) To get a schedule of events

35. Where do the women most likely work?

    (A) At a radio station
    (B) At an electronics store
    (C) At an auto repair shop
    (D) At a car dealership

36. What did the man recently do?

    (A) He read a car magazine.
    (B) He found a new job.
    (C) He opened a business.
    (D) He completed an automotive repair course.

37. What will the man do next?

    (A) Publish a book
    (B) Call in a radio station
    (C) Buy a vehicle
    (D) Provide some advice

38. What do the speakers say about Jason?

    (A) He is retiring from work.
    (B) He is getting transferred abroad.
    (C) He is being promoted.
    (D) He is moving to another company.

39. What does the man ask about?

    (A) Preparations for a party
    (B) An upcoming meeting
    (C) A business trip
    (D) An urgent call from a client

40. According to the man, what is he planning to do?

    (A) Go to a golf course
    (B) Purchase a present
    (C) Find another caterer
    (D) Donate some money

41. What is the man surprised about?

    (A) The extended hours of operation
    (B) The location of an event
    (C) The number of attendees
    (D) The price of a catering service

42. What does the woman want permission to do?

    (A) Hire a caterer
    (B) Purchase some presents
    (C) Change venues
    (D) Invite more people

43. What is the woman asked to do next?

    (A) Get a price estimate
    (B) Go over a guest list
    (C) Send out some invitations
    (D) Speak with a board member

▶ ▶ ▶ GO ON TO THE NEXT PAGE

44. Who most likely is the man?

(A) A sales representative
(B) A human resources employee
(C) A customer service representative
(D) A product designer

45. What does the woman imply when she says, "I only purchased it two weeks ago"?

(A) An item should still function.
(B) An item is damaged in transit.
(C) An order has not been delivered yet.
(D) She wants to purchase another audio device.

46. What will the woman most likely do next?

(A) Get some software updated
(B) Get a refund on an item
(C) Refer to a user's guide
(D) Plug a device in

47. Where does the conversation take place?

(A) At a supermarket
(B) At a bakery
(C) At a restaurant
(D) At a cooking school

48. What opportunity does the man offer the woman?

(A) Renewing her contract
(B) Transferring to another location
(C) Managing a bakery
(D) Working extra hours

49. What information does the woman ask about?

(A) Working hours
(B) Company benefits
(C) Hourly wages
(D) Payment options

50. What is the main topic of the conversation?

(A) A relocation
(B) A popular product
(C) A hiring opportunity
(D) A new facility

51. What did the women do today?

(A) They worked on a new design.
(B) They visited a warehouse in person.
(C) They went over a project proposal.
(D) They interviewed job applicants.

52. According to Alice, what information is not correct?

(A) The cost of some items
(B) The address of a building
(C) The size of a warehouse
(D) The number of loading spots

53. What does the woman want to discuss?

(A) Improving the safety rules
(B) Hiring other suppliers
(C) Changing a production process
(D) Offering competitive prices

54. What problem does the woman mention about the extra tiles?

(A) They are unable to be sold.
(B) There is no room to put them in storage.
(C) Some of them were damaged in production.
(D) They are not the correct size.

55. Why does the man say the customers were not happy?

(A) Prices were raised recently.
(B) A website had some problems.
(C) Orders were not received on time.
(D) The quality of some work was poor.

56. What did the company recently do?

(A) Rearranged office supplies
(B) Expanded to a foreign country
(C) Offered employees more benefits
(D) Moved to another location

57. What does the woman say she used to do?

(A) Work out every day
(B) Go to work on foot
(C) Bring her lunch to work
(D) Stay at work late

58. What does the man suggest that the woman do?

(A) Move to a different place
(B) Transfer to another department
(C) Become a member at a gym
(D) Drive to work

59. What is the main topic of the conversation?

(A) The design of a product
(B) A change in an advertisement
(C) A product demonstration
(D) The release date of a new car

60. What does the woman imply when she says, "We have until August to finish the project"?

(A) They do not have enough time.
(B) They need to hire more workers.
(C) They have to work faster.
(D) They can still meet their deadline.

61. What does the woman suggest doing?

(A) Hiring a consultant
(B) Speaking with a coworker
(C) Increasing a budget
(D) Reviewing some calculations

Survey

	Satisfactory	Unsatisfactory
1. Performance	☐	☐
2. Story	☐	☐
3. Graphics	☐	☐

4. If you found something unsatisfactory, what is the reason?

_____

_____

_____

62. Who is the survey for?

(A) Designers
(B) Authors
(C) Game players
(D) Computer programmers

63. How did the man choose the items listed in the survey?

(A) He referred to some online reviews.
(B) He read some articles in the online magazines.
(C) He had a meeting with his colleagues.
(D) He looked at a product manual.

64. Look at the graphic. Which item will be taken out from the survey?

(A) Item 1
(B) Item 2
(C) Item 3
(D) Item 4

▶ ▶ ▶ GO ON TO THE NEXT PAGE

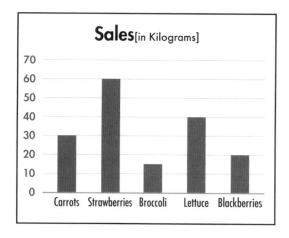

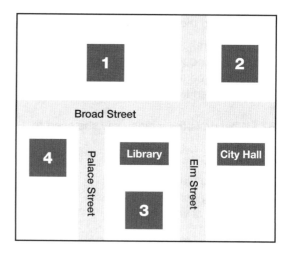

65. What did the speakers do last year?

(A) They bought some fertilizers.
(B) They purchased a new farm vehicle.
(C) They acquired more farmland.
(D) They hired more farmhands.

66. Look at the graphic. Which item will be sold for a lower price this weekend?

(A) Strawberries
(B) Broccoli
(C) Lettuce
(D) Blackberries

67. Why does the woman think more customers will go to the market?

(A) A report aired on a news program.
(B) A newspaper printed an article.
(C) More vendors will be there later.
(D) All prices will be discounted.

68. What kind of business do the speakers most likely work at?

(A) At an advertisement agency
(B) At an accounting firm
(C) At an electronics manufacturer
(D) At an electric company

69. Look at the graphic. Which building will the speakers visit on Friday?

(A) Building 1
(B) Building 2
(C) Building 3
(D) Building 4

70. What does the woman offer to do?

(A) Speak with her supervisor
(B) Change the time of a meeting
(C) Rewrite some presentation material
(D) Change a meeting place

PART 4

Directions: You will hear some short talks given by a single speaker. You will be asked to answer three questions about what the speaker says in each short talk. Select the best response to each question and mark the letter (A), (B), (C), or (D) on your answer sheet. The talks will not be printed in your test book and will be spoken only one time.

71. What product is being promoted?

(A) A blender
(B) A coffeemaker
(C) A toaster
(D) A scale

72. What does the speaker praise about the product?

(A) It is environmentally friendly.
(B) It is inexpensive.
(C) It is portable.
(D) It is accurate.

73. What special deal does the speaker offer?

(A) A discount on cookbooks
(B) Free installation
(C) An extended warranty
(D) Free shipping

74. What will the speaker give a presentation on?

(A) Retaining more workers
(B) Providing cost-cutting ideas
(C) Improving office efficiency
(D) Getting more cost estimates

75. According to the speaker, what has changed?

(A) The deadline for a proposal
(B) A date when the CEO arrives
(C) A visit by a client
(D) A meeting location

76. Why does the speaker say, "You do know Peter from Finance, don't you?"

(A) To express concern about the cost
(B) To confirm a meeting date
(C) To suggest a staffing change
(D) To ask the listener to contact a coworker

77. Who is being introduced?

(A) A CEO
(B) A client
(C) A company director
(D) A government official

78. What is mentioned about an engine?

(A) It is currently in use.
(B) It breaks down at times.
(C) It needs to be improved.
(D) It is in the process of being developed.

79. What is suggested about Susan Darcey?

(A) She was just promoted.
(B) She frequently travels abroad.
(C) She intends to retire soon.
(D) She enjoys assisting others.

80. What is the speaker calling about?

(A) An advertisement about furniture
(B) A sofa delivery
(C) A status on her special order
(D) Some furniture repairs

81. What problem does the speaker mention?

(A) Some material is not available.
(B) An item cannot be repaired.
(C) A price is higher than the estimate.
(D) A deadline hasn't been met.

82. What is the listener asked to do?

(A) Look for another supplier
(B) Change a release date
(C) Visit the establishment
(D) Pick up his equipment

▶ ▶ ▶ GO ON TO THE NEXT PAGE

83. According to the speaker, why is the Impressionist Art Collection popular?

(A) Its admission is free.
(B) It was featured in a TV documentary.
(C) It is the museum's largest collection.
(D) It is updated frequently.

84. What does the speaker imply when he says, "I'm an intern here"?

(A) He is not getting paid for leading the tour.
(B) He needs some help from his colleague.
(C) He might not answer some questions.
(D) He is eager to impress the visitors.

85. What does the speaker remind the listeners about?

(A) A gallery policy
(B) A ticket price
(C) A closing time
(D) A new exhibit

---

86. What is the broadcast mainly about?

(A) Economic conditions
(B) A business acquisition
(C) The results of an election
(D) A completed construction project

87. According to the speaker, what field does Peter Shaw have experience in?

(A) Education
(B) Business
(C) Entertainment
(D) Travel

88. What are the listeners invited to do?

(A) Request some music
(B) Sign up for a membership
(C) Share their thoughts
(D) Enter a raffle

89. What service does the company provide?

(A) Financial consulting
(B) Web security
(C) Online marketing
(D) Property management

90. Why is the speaker unavailable this week?

(A) He is out of the country.
(B) He is at a conference.
(C) He is in a staff meeting.
(D) He is at a training course.

91. What should the listeners do if they need some urgent advice?

(A) Send an e-mail
(B) Visit an office
(C) Call another employee
(D) Call the manager on the cell phone

---

92. Where do the listeners work?

(A) At a university
(B) At a medical equipment company
(C) At a healthcare facility
(D) At a pharmaceutical company

93. What does the speaker imply when she says, "Lots of people know about Leslie"?

(A) She plans to order more office supplies.
(B) The listeners need to sign up quickly.
(C) A venue for a meeting is too small.
(D) She needs to contact Leslie right away.

94. What does the speaker remind the listeners to do?

(A) Make some proposals
(B) Contact some clients
(C) Improve their efficiency
(D) Prepare some documents

Weather Forecast

Monday	Tuesday	Wednesday	Thursday	Friday
Rainy	Rainy	Cloudy	Sunny	Rainy

95. Look at the graphic. When will the fall festival take place?

(A) On Monday
(B) On Tuesday
(C) On Wednesday
(D) On Thursday

96. What does the speaker say she is excited about?

(A) An art exhibit
(B) A musical performance
(C) A sports competition
(D) A lecture on music

97. What does the speaker recommend the listeners do?

(A) Bring their friends
(B) Buy tickets in advance
(C) Call the station
(D) Enter a contest

Meeting Agenda

13:45	Introduction
14:00	Jude Crow - R&D Manager
14:15	Elizabeth Dean - HR Supervisor
14:30	Andy Thompson - Head of Sales
14:45	Wilma Patterson - CEO

98. Who most likely are the listeners?

(A) Potential investors
(B) Foreign clients
(C) Supervisors
(D) New employees

99. What type of products does the company make?

(A) Camping gear
(B) Vehicles
(C) Pharmaceuticals
(D) Sporting goods

100. Look at the graphic. Who will speak next?

(A) Jude Crow
(B) Elizabeth Dean
(C) Andy Thompson
(D) Wilma Patterson

This is the end of the Listening test. Turn to Part 5 in your test book.

▶ ▶ ▶ GO ON TO THE NEXT PAGE

READING TEST

In the Reading test, you will read a variety of texts and answer several different types of reading comprehension questions. The entire Reading test will last 75 minutes. There are three parts, and directions are given for each part. You are encouraged to answer as many questions as possible within the time allowed.

You must mark your answer on the separate answer sheet. Do not write your answers in your test book.

PART 5

Directions: A word or phrase is missing in each of the sentences below. Four answer choices are given below each sentence. Select the best answer to complete the sentence. Then mark the letter (A), (B), (C), or (D) on your answer sheet.

101. James Watson, one of the popular singers in the country, has agreed to allow Coco Jewelry to use ------- name in an upcoming advertising campaign.

(A) he
(B) his
(C) him
(D) himself

102. Bella Communications provides ------- Internet and mobile phone services to local residents.

(A) only if
(B) either
(C) both
(D) but also

103. The firm has been a leading company in educating people to design advertising campaigns more ------- for years.

(A) efficiency
(B) efficiencies
(C) efficient
(D) efficiently

104. Some of the office desks in the personnel department are too heavy for Brian and Harry to carry by -------.

(A) them
(B) their
(C) theirs
(D) themselves

105. Our firm decided to push ahead our original plan for the ------- of the two banks in China.

(A) merge
(B) merger
(C) merged
(D) merging

106. The new desktop computer is equipped ------- the latest word processor softwares and high-resolution screen.

(A) for
(B) by
(C) with
(D) through

107. With two weeks of added musical shows, *Romance With Cats* will ------- run through November 14 at our theater.

(A) now
(B) mostly
(C) nearly
(D) immediately

108. Many companies have been ------- awaiting the new free trade agreement with European countries in the hope of raising their market shares there.

(A) eagerness
(B) eager
(C) more eager
(D) eagerly

109. Mr. Jenkins said yesterday that the exported frozen food products ------- with the food safety regulations of 20 countries.

(A) comply
(B) complying
(C) compliance
(D) compliant

110. According to the data, the number of earthquakes caused by volcanic activity ------- significantly over the last ten years.

(A) increase
(B) has increased
(C) had increased
(D) will increase

111. A work environment that is clean and visually appealing can have a great ------- on your workforce's performance and mood.

(A) impact
(B) comfort
(C) enthusiasm
(D) responsibility

112. Some passengers on the flight were ill ------- arrival at the international airport and were immediately hospitalized.

(A) with
(B) along
(C) upon
(D) towards

113. Please be aware that our data must be ------- transmitted to the central data repository for analysis and feedback.

(A) securely
(B) systematically
(C) precisely
(D) potentially

114. If you are ------- to keep your scheduled medical appointment, please notify us at least two days in advance.

(A) impossible
(B) absent
(C) unable
(D) ready

115. Please fill out the form to see if your office building is ------- from requirements for fire drills and safety inspections.

(A) reliant
(B) exempt
(C) intact
(D) absolute

116. When ------- one of our customer service representatives to ask questions, it would be better to have a list of questions ready.

(A) call
(B) calling
(C) called
(D) to call

117. The investment by One International is the ------- largest foreign direct investment in the nation's financial industry.

(A) every
(B) quite
(C) much
(D) single

118. With ------- facts and evidence, the presentation was conducted in a logical and analytical manner.

(A) attentive
(B) verifiable
(C) incredible
(D) renewable

119. Mr. McDonald was hired only two months ago, but has ------- devised some effective sales strategies for the company.

(A) namely
(B) simultaneously
(C) nevertheless
(D) notwithstanding

▶ ▶ ▶ GO ON TO THE NEXT PAGE

120. According to our office policy, ------- leaves last is responsible for turning off all the lights and locking the door in the office.

(A) several
(B) this
(C) which
(D) whoever

121. It appears that many office workers overuse energy drinks ------- they get tired or stressed from work and their daily routines.

(A) even if
(B) whenever
(C) whichever
(D) so that

122. The magazine was ------- successful, selling many more issues than anyone had thought likely, but its circulation dropped rapidly in several years.

(A) tightly
(B) phenomenally
(C) abundantly
(D) profitably

123. Orders placed to commercial websites in Asia are usually ------- with merchandise from their warehouses in Vietnam.

(A) filled
(B) positioned
(C) occurred
(D) committed

124. Our employees will receive a significant bonus at the end of this year ------- the company's net profits exceed the expectations of the board.

(A) provided that
(B) while
(C) in that
(D) unless

125. Starpark Sports is committed to designing and producing different running shoes that ------- wants to wear.

(A) everyone
(B) anywhere
(C) whoever
(D) one another

126. ------- for our brand to remain popular as it is today, high quality contents need to be provided in convenient forms on the Internet.

(A) Not only
(B) As a result
(C) In case
(D) In order

127. ------- the high waves and bad weather, all the passengers onboard the flight were successfully rescued.

(A) In spite of
(B) On account of
(C) As a result of
(D) With regard to

128. City residents rarely think about growing their own gardens ------- building a small garden is not that difficult.

(A) for one thing
(B) therefore
(C) similarly
(D) even though

129. -------, most of our employees are permitted to leave the office earlier than usual before a national holiday.

(A) At that time
(B) By the time
(C) Once in a while
(D) In a moment

130. In recent years, consumption of electronic products has increased so much ------- today this represents one of the most environmentally problematic product groups.

(A) because
(B) that
(C) when
(D) although

PART 6

Directions: Read the texts that follow. A word or phrase, or sentence is missing in parts of each text. Four answer choices for each question are given below the text. Select the best answer to complete the text. Then mark the letter (A), (B), (C), or (D) on your answer sheet.

Questions 131-134 refer to the following information.

Bella Airlines Frequently Asked Questions

What if I did not receive an e-mail confirmation of my Bella Airlines flight?

-------. Bella Airlines ------- takes up to three hours to send the e-mail confirmation to a
131.   **132.**

passenger after booking. In case you don't receive your e-mail confirmation even after

booking, make sure that your payment was successful. If the payment doesn't show up

on your credit card, it is ------- that your flight reservation did not go through.
                        133.

-------, please call us at 692-9815 so that we can look into the matter. Calls to this number
134.

are paid for by Bella Airlines, making them free for our customers.

---

131. (A) Mobile phones cannot be used during flight at any time.
(B) We will correct your account if the transaction was posted in error.
(C) Your flight details will be sent to the e-mail address you provided.
(D) Please keep hard copies of your purchase order and confirmation number.

132. (A) potentially
(B) normally
(C) accordingly
(D) temporarily

133. (A) right
(B) likely
(C) proper
(D) correct

134. (A) Finally
(B) Moreover
(C) In contrast
(D) In this case

Lucky 7 Mart

"Only the fresh!"

5801 Sundale Ave.

Bakersfield, CA 93307

The Lucky 7 Mart is full of the ------- fruits and vegetables available during all seasons!
135.

From California, Arizona, Florida, and beyond, our ------- is SUPER FRESH! When
136.

available, the Lucky 7 Mart offers fresh local food, which is grown by nearby farmers, to

your family.

The Lucky 7 Mart has products at prices you'll love! We have a fabulous selection of lunch

meats and cheeses freshly sliced to your order! We ------- only the finest beef, grade-A
137.

poultry, grade-A fresh pork, homemade smoked hams, and ground meats. -------.
138.

If you need help while shopping, ask a store clerk. He or she will gladly take you to the

items.

---

135. (A) fresh
(B) fresher
(C) freshest
(D) freshly

136. (A) produce
(B) producer
(C) production
(D) productivity

137. (A) carry
(B) access
(C) transport
(D) promote

138. (A) Learn about our upcoming special
promotions.
(B) Customer reviews have been
consistently positive.
(C) Business competition can be very
fierce, especially in fast-moving
markets.
(D) You'll love our everyday low prices,
on-sale items, and new items.

Questions 139-142 refer to the following e-mail.

To: Charlotte Parker <cp@hdmail.com>
From: Lisa Preston <lpreston@nybc.com>
Subject: Your application
Date: February 14

Dear Ms. Parker,

Thank you for your application for the administrative assistant position. We very much

appreciate your interest in ------- our firm. -------. However, our human resources team
        139.   **140.**

read your résumé with great interest. Your professional experience and educational

background are very -------, which will make you an excellent addition to the firm.
          141.

If you have no -------, we will keep your résumé on file and get in touch with you as soon
       142.

as a suitable position becomes available.

In the meantime, we wish you all the best with your job hunt.

Kind regards,

Lisa Preston
Head of Personnel
New York Business Consulting

---

139. (A) purchasing
(B) visiting
(C) joining
(D) contracting

140. (A) We are concerned about the result of
your job interview.
(B) The position you applied for is no
longer available.
(C) You are highly qualified to be an
administrative assistant.
(D) Our recruiters must go through many
applications to fill a position.

141. (A) impress
(B) impressed
(C) impressing
(D) impressive

142. (A) option
(B) objection
(C) intention
(D) confidentiality

▶ ▶ ▶GO ON TO THE NEXT PAGE

June 20

Miramax Home Improvement

Classic Shades, Inc.

265 Peachtree Street

401 Scott Street

Atlanta, GA 30303

Atlanta, GA 30303

Dear whom it may concern,

We received 40 one-gallon cans of Floral White house paint yesterday, but they are not what we ordered from your company. -------.
143.

Please refer to our purchase order BK365020 of June 12, in which we asked ------- 50
144.
one-pint cans of Snowflake house paint, your product catalog No. SF-909. Please confirm the receipt of this letter and ------- of the request with a fax to 1-800-521-6313 as soon as
145.
possible.

-------, please rush this order so that we may meet our customers' demands promptly.
146.

Sincerely yours,

Aurora Lane

Head of Purchasing

Miramax Home Improvement

143. (A) We are happy to supply you with the estimate you requested.
(B) Unfortunately, the client expressed disappointment at the deadline being missed.
(C) We, therefore, are returning them to your Rocksville plant in Maryland.
(D) Your paint products are most commonly used to protect or provide texture to objects.

144. (A) after
(B) for
(C) into
(D) around

145. (A) routine
(B) execution
(C) termination
(D) collection

146. (A) In summary
(B) In fact
(C) Conversely
(D) Furthermore

PART 7

Directions: In this part you will read a selection of texts, such as magazine and newspaper articles, e-mails, and instant messages. Each text or set of texts is followed by several questions. Select the best answer for each question and mark the letter (A), (B), (C), or (D) on your answer sheet.

Questions 147-148 refer to the following form.

East Village, Inc.

109 Pitts Street
Dover, Delaware 19028

Date of Order: June 5

Order Number: 0194570
Customer Name: Angela Rose
Delivery Address: 42 Charity Dr., Highland Acres, Delaware, 19010
Delivery Date & Time: June 9, 12:00 P.M.
Return Date & Time: June 10, 10:00 A.M.

Items	Qty	Price
Color Reception Tableware Set (Rental)	2	$ 24.00
Flower Decorations – White and Yellow (Rental)	5	$ 20.00
Folding Banquet Table & Chair Set (Rental)	2	$ 40.00
Party Tent (Rental)	2	$ 50.00
	Shipping & Setting	**$ 50.00**
	Total	**$ 184.00**

* We provide corporate customers with a 10% discount.

* Pick-up charge is included in the shipping & set-up fee.

* All items must be ready for pick-up by the return time stated above.

---

147. What is suggested about Ms. Rose?

(A) She resides on Pitts Street.
(B) She is a corporate customer.
(C) She is preparing an event.
(D) She will use the delivered items in the morning.

148. What is NOT indicated about East Village, Inc.?

(A) It charges additional 10% of the service fee for late returns.
(B) It provides a discount to certain customers.
(C) It charges customers a shipping cost.
(D) It will pick up the rental items on June 10.

▶ ▶ ▶ GO ON TO THE NEXT PAGE

Questions 149-150 refer to the following text message chain.

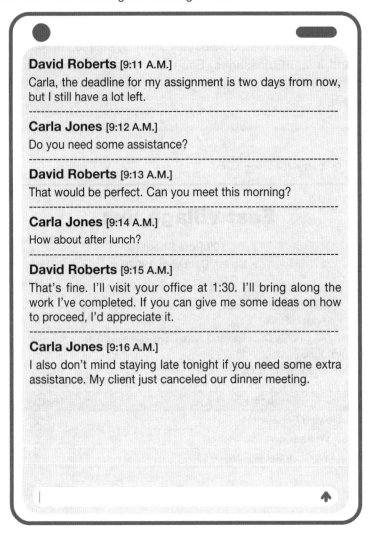

David Roberts [9:11 A.M.]
Carla, the deadline for my assignment is two days from now, but I still have a lot left.

Carla Jones [9:12 A.M.]
Do you need some assistance?

David Roberts [9:13 A.M.]
That would be perfect. Can you meet this morning?

Carla Jones [9:14 A.M.]
How about after lunch?

David Roberts [9:15 A.M.]
That's fine. I'll visit your office at 1:30. I'll bring along the work I've completed. If you can give me some ideas on how to proceed, I'd appreciate it.

Carla Jones [9:16 A.M.]
I also don't mind staying late tonight if you need some extra assistance. My client just canceled our dinner meeting.

149. What is Mr. Roberts' problem?

(A) He needs more ideas for a new project.
(B) He has to complete a project by this evening.
(C) His client just canceled a meeting.
(D) He has not finished some work yet.

150. At 9:14 A.M., why does Ms. Jones write, "How about after lunch?"

(A) To change a reservation
(B) To reject a suggestion
(C) To make an apology
(D) To propose a location

The 2nd Brown Design Competition

Brown, Inc., the leading manufacturer of household goods, is excited to present the 2nd Brown Design Competition. This year's design entry will be of a food storage container, which we intend to develop for the first time in our history.

Various forms of entries including drafts and sketches using different art materials are welcome. Please refer to the previous product designs of Brown, Inc. at www.browninc.com. The portable teapot designed by Walter Cho is an excellent example, as it was the winning design of the Brown Design Competition last year that broke all previous sales records of Brown, Inc.

This year's winning entry will be selected and launched as an official product of Brown, Inc. in the next market year. Also, the first-prize winner will be offered a fulltime employment position with the company. All winners will be invited to the awards ceremony scheduled on August 20 at the headquarters in Dover. The awards will be presented by design executives of Brown, Inc.

In addition, the winners will be given monetary awards worth a total of $6,000.

1st Prize: $3,000
2nd Prize: $2,000
3rd Prize: $1,000

If you are interested in participating, please visit our website at www.browninc.com/ application to download detailed guidelines for submission and e-mail us your entry. The entries begin on July 1, and the deadline for submission is July 31.

151. What is suggested about Brown, Inc.?

(A) It only sells food containers.
(B) It has been in business for two years.
(C) Its portable teapot has been popular with customers.
(D) It will hold the awards ceremony of the competition next year.

152. What will NOT be offered to the first place prize winner?

(A) $3,000 in cash
(B) Invitation to a formal event
(C) An airfare to Dover
(D) A full-time position at Brown, Inc.

153. What is indicated about the application?

(A) It requires a processing fee.
(B) It is due on July 31.
(C) It will be judged by a group of executives.
(D) It has to be submitted by mail.

To: John Baker <jbaker@easymail.com>

From: Amber Lee <alee@hotelconcord.com>

Date: September 20

Subject: RE: About my last visit

Dear Mr. Baker,

First of all, I would like to thank you for your recent visit to Hotel Concord New Orleans. It was truly an honor for us to serve you.

We have received your inquiry. Please kindly accept my sincere apologies on behalf of Hotel Concord for your unpleasant stay at our hotel last week. An unknown error occurred in our reservation system and we apologize for not being able to provide you with the room that you had originally reserved.

To compensate for this inconvenience, we would like to provide you a $200 certificate, which you may use at any branch of Hotel Concord in the United States. You can download the certificate through our official website at www.hotelconcord.com.

Thank you, and I hope to see you again.

Sincerely,

Amber Lee
Manager, Hotel Concord New Orleans

154. What is the main purpose of the e-mail?

(A) To thank a customer for visiting the hotel
(B) To give an excuse about overbooking
(C) To confirm the reservation
(D) To make up for a recent mistake

155. What is implied about Mr. Baker?

(A) He visited Hotel Concord with his family.
(B) He recently wrote an e-mail to Hotel Concord.
(C) He lives in New Orleans.
(D) He paid $200 for his room.

156. According to the e-mail, what is indicated about Hotel Concord?

(A) It will open its website.
(B) Its rooms are currently fully booked.
(C) It has more than one location.
(D) It gives coupons to all first-time visitors.

SAM'S PIZZA

Celebrating the 5th anniversary of Sam's Pizza, we are offering our customers special weekday deals throughout July. Please bring a coupon from below to enjoy delicious pizzas at special prices.

Coupons

$3.00 OFF
On
Any Specialty Pizza

<FREE>
2 Pepperoni Rolls
Or
2 Toppings of Your Choice
With Purchase of a Large Pizza

Wednesday & Thursday
BIG DEAL
Large Cheese Pizza
$7.99
2 For $15.00

BUY 1 GET 1 FREE
Any Large Pizza

- All coupons are for "Take Out" only.
- Only one coupon may be used per order.

157. What can be inferred about Sam's Pizza?

(A) It has been in business for five years.
(B) It closes on weekends.
(C) Its customers don't have topping choices.
(D) It doesn't offer a delivery service.

158. What should a customer do to buy two large cheese pizzas for $15.00?

(A) Pay in cash
(B) Dine in the restaurant on a Thursday in July
(C) Use a coupon on a specific date
(D) Buy another regularly-priced pizza

Tree House Solutions

Are you bothered by household pests such as termites and bedbugs? Tree House Solutions can solve your insect problems with our individualized three-step extermination solution for your home.

1. Detection

Our highly qualified inspectors, who undergo 10 hours of annual training, will start by carefully examining your house after a consultation with you. Then, we will prescribe an optimal treatment for maximum protection based on your unique situation.

2. Treatment

After detection, we effectively and quickly eradicate pests by applying our pest control treatments three times. We have two types of treatments, both of which are non-toxic and environmentally safe: liquid and foam. Liquid treatment is applied to the foundation of house whereas foam treatment is applied to surfaces such as exterior walls and pipes.

3. Monitoring

Our monitoring service ensures the ongoing effectiveness of the protection. We visit your house quarterly for two years and apply additional treatment as needed.

---

159. What most likely is being advertised?

(A) A house cleaning service
(B) A bug extermination service
(C) Environment-friendly interior design
(D) A gardening service

160. How often do staff of Tree House Solutions visit for monitoring?

(A) Once a year
(B) Twice a year
(C) Three times a year
(D) Four times a year

161. What is NOT indicated about the staff of Tree House Solutions?

(A) They must take annual training.
(B) They discuss symptoms with clients before the detection of the cause.
(C) They give a treatment kit to customers who renew the contract.
(D) They use treatments, which do little harm on the environment.

Questions 162-164 refer to the following e-mail.

To:	Jessica Cisneros <jcisneros@sevelia.com>
From:	Mark Demont <mdemont@sku.edu>
Date:	April 15
Subject:	Last Night

Dear Ms. Cisneros,

Since my first visit to Sevelia on its opening night, I have been a big fan. I couldn't believe that a small local restaurant could provide such delicious Thai food with excellent service. —[1]—. Since then, I have frequently visited Sevelia, and I have been delighted every single time until last night.

—[2]—.We ordered two main dishes, but we were served only one. Though we were quite upset about this mistake, we did not have time to wait, so we decided to share the dish and leave. After finishing the meal, I paid with my credit card but did not check the bill or the receipt. —[3]—. However, when I checked the receipt later, I discovered that you charged me for two main dishes instead of one.

It was the most disappointing service I have received in the two years that I have dined at your establishment. —[4]—. Because of this experience, I have to consider whether or not to visit your restaurant again in the future. I demand your prompt attention to this matter.

Thank you,

Mark Demont

---

162. What is the purpose of the e-mail?

(A) To recommend a local restaurant
(B) To ask for monetary compensation
(C) To complain about increased meal prices
(D) To report some poor service

163. What is indicated about Sevelia?

(A) It is a big chain store.
(B) It does not have many customers.
(C) It has been in business for about 2 years.
(D) It recently hired a new employee.

164. In which of the positions marked [1], [2], [3], and [4] does the following sentence best fit?

"Last night, my wife and I went to your restaurant for dinner."

(A) [1]
(B) [2]
(C) [3]
(D) [4]

▶ ▶ ▶GO ON TO THE NEXT PAGE

Old Dusty City Hall Reborn

June 17

The old City Hall located on Vie Street has been subject to much curiosity and anticipation over the past 8 months. Finally, the building will be presented to the public on the night of July 1 under a new name, Indianapolis City Museum for Art.

Ian Kensington, the architect who created the city's icon, Spiral Tower, assumed the responsibility of designing the museum. He worked closely with Dorian Webster, the engineer of the city electricity system, to make the space eco-friendly. Two wings have been added, connecting the museum to a sculpture garden. Windmills and solar panels disguised as sculptures will generate enough power to run the entire museum.

The renovation project was actually initiated by the architect himself. After he submitted the proposal to the city council, he also donated a significant sum of funds to the project. "It is not an exaggeration when I say that Mr. Kensington made the project possible," commented Caitlin Tristan, the mayor of Indianapolis. "He raised the majority of the renovation costs required by hosting fund-raising dinners. All I did was merely approve his proposal."

The museum will open with an exhibition of the renowned photographer, Amy Nijinsky. She will deliver an appreciation speech to Mr. Kensington that night on behalf of the city council.

The museum will be open Monday through Friday from 9 A.M. to 7 P.M. For more information about the city museum, visit its website at www.icma.org.

165. How has Mr. Kensington contributed to the museum?

(A) By allowing his private properties to be used as the construction site
(B) By planning out how the budget should be used
(C) By coming up with the idea of renovating the City Hall building
(D) By organizing the opening ceremony

166. Who most likely is Ms. Tristan?

(A) A famous photographer
(B) A museum curator
(C) A city official
(D) A professional engineer

167. What is stated about the opening ceremony?

(A) It will be followed by a fund-raising dinner.
(B) It will be held on a Monday.
(C) It is an invitation-only event.
(D) It will include a formal talk.

▶ ▶ ▶ GO ON TO THE NEXT PAGE

Teresa Harper   10:48 A.M.

Don't forget about the brainstorming session scheduled for today. The location has changed to room 453, but it's still going to take place at 3:00.

Kate Martin   10:50 A.M.

I'm not going to make it there on time. My meeting at Duncan, Inc. isn't supposed to finish until 2:30. Shall I bring some refreshments for everyone?

Teresa Harper   10:51 A.M.

Why not? Oh, everyone, please remember to print the information I e-mailed you this morning and bring it with you.

Darryl Waltrip   10:52 A.M.

I'm looking at my inbox, and I don't see anything from you.

Eric Reed   10:53 A.M.

Me, neither.

Teresa Harper   10:55 A.M.

Really? I must have forgotten to send it. I'll e-mail it to everyone right now.

Eric Reed   10:56 A.M.

Got it. Thanks.

Darryl Waltrip   10:57 A.M.

I'll read it during lunch so that I'm fully prepared for the meeting.

Teresa Harper   10:59 A.M.

Thanks, everyone. We really need to land this contract, so I hope you have some creative ideas for our proposal. It's due at the end of the week.

SEND

168. Why does Ms. Harper invite the writers to the meeting?

(A) To go over the results of a survey
(B) To consider a recent proposal
(C) To examine the terms of a contract
(D) To come up with some new ideas

169. Why will Ms. Martin be late for the meeting?

(A) She has not prepared for it yet.
(B) She needs to complete a work proposal.
(C) She has to attend a business meeting.
(D) She will be meeting with her supervisor.

170. What does Mr. Waltrip indicate he will do?

(A) Read some information
(B) Print a document for everyone
(C) Set up the meeting room
(D) Let his colleagues know about a meeting

171. At 10:51 A.M. why does Ms. Harper write, "Why not?"

(A) To question the suggestion made by Ms. Martin
(B) To refuse to allow anyone to attend the meeting late
(C) To agree to have food and drinks at the meeting
(D) To approve a request to change the time of the meeting

▶ ▶ ▶ GO ON TO THE NEXT PAGE

Tokyo Daily

"I still cannot believe this is really happening to me," said Sakutaro Kimoto. Mr. Kimoto moved to the United States with his parents from Tokyo, Japan, when he was only 16. "When I first came to New York, I was very lonely. Everything was new and confusing, so I spent most of my time by myself after school. The only way to ease my boredom was to spend time cooking at home." —[1]—.

When he turned 20, Mr. Kimoto started working as a kitchen staff member at a Boston-based Italian restaurant, Charley's, instead of going to college. Recognized for his outstanding ability and effort, he was promoted to head chef in just 2 years. There, he learned to manage a kitchen staff and to cook various Italian dishes. As he built a reputation as a chef, Mr. Kimoto began to consider opening his own restaurant. —[2]—. After working there for 3 more years as the head chef, he left Charley's, moved back to his hometown, and opened a small restaurant, named Iratshai Italy, that specializes in Japanese-Italian fusion cuisine. The restaurant soon acquired considerable local interest and became one of the most popular dining places in the region only a year after its opening.

—[3]—. The establishment has undergone renovations and been enlarged two times already, but it still needs more space to meet the needs of its customers. In fact, the second Iratshai Italy will be opening in Yokohama, Japan, next weekend. "I am so excited to open another restaurant. I am grateful for the opportunities given to me, and I will continue to put all my efforts into serving quality Japanese-Italian foods to local residents," Mr. Kimoto said. —[4]—.

172. What is mainly being discussed in the article?

(A) The achievements of an individual
(B) The requirements for the success of a local business
(C) Dining trends in a local area
(D) Successful ways to open a restaurant

173. What did Mr. Kimoto do for a living right before opening his own restaurant?

(A) A kitchen staff at a restaurant
(B) The owner of Charley's
(C) A student at a college
(D) A manager of a local business

174. According to the article, what will Mr. Kimoto do soon?

(A) Hire more employees
(B) Relocate his original restaurant
(C) Launch another restaurant
(D) Invest in another field of business

175. In which of the positions marked [1], [2], [3], and [4] does the following sentence best fit?

"Mr. Kimoto's restaurant has been expanding in size."

(A) [1]
(B) [2]
(C) [3]
(D) [4]

Magical Intelligence

There is nothing we are unable to fix, so count on us!

Branch Location:

■ Manchester ☐ London ☐ Bradford

Date of Visit and Pick Up: July 6
Work Completion Date: July 22   **Service Number:** CR7902

Customer Information	Service Information
Name: Steve Jackson	**Item:** Washing machine
Address: 134 Ridge Ave., Manchester	**Brand:** Shalatt
Telephone: 161-555-2267	**Model:** S3

Service Description	Rate
• Leaking Washing Machine: Door Seal and Pump Replacement	£65.00
• Visit and Pick Up Service	£15.00
• Delivery and Installation Fee	£12.00
Subtotal	£92.00
Tax	£9.20
Total	£101.20

Payment Received on:	July 22
Form of Payment:	Cash

We especially regard the speed of our service highly, thus, we will refund 30% of all services that take longer than the originally estimated time to be repaired and returned to your home. Indicate the total duration of the process in the survey form that the technician gave you when picking up your appliance.

Magical Intelligence

Thank you for choosing Magical Intelligence! Please take some time to complete the survey below so that we may improve our service and serve you better next time.

Customer Name	Steve Jackson
Date of Receipt	July 22
Service Number	CR 7902
Technician	William Luke

Please indicate the level of satisfaction with...

	Excellent	Good	Fair	Poor
Promptness				V
Quality	V			
Cost		V		

Was the technician...?

	Excellent	Good	Fair	Poor
Professional	V			
Polite	V			
Informative	V			

Please note any comments you might have:

I must say that I am quite disappointed by the service I received this time. The quality of service was fair and satisfying as always, but how long it took was really frustrating. When I called Magical Intelligence on July 2, I was informed that the repair would be completed by July 10. However, I have been forced to go to a local laundry for over 2 weeks now, and my washing machine arrived just yesterday. I think I will have to reconsider coming back for your service in the future.

176. What kind of business most likely is Magical Intelligence?

(A) A local laundry
(B) A shipping company
(C) A repair service provider
(D) An electronics store

177. What is implied about Magical Intelligence?

(A) It requires customers to pick up their appliances.
(B) It offers discounts to all customers.
(C) It has more than one location.
(D) It provides free shipping and handling.

178. What most likely is true about Mr. Luke?

(A) He filled out a survey.
(B) He owns a washing machine made by Shalatt.
(C) He visited Mr. Jackson on July 6.
(D) He is a new employee at Magical Intelligence.

179. What will probably happen in the future?

(A) Mr. Jackson will receive a certain amount of money back.
(B) The fixed washing machine will arrive.
(C) Magical Intelligence will send a technician to Mr. Jackson again.
(D) A discount coupon will expire.

180. What is indicated in the survey?

(A) Mr. Jackson is upset with the quality of the new washing machine.
(B) The cost of Magical Intelligence is the least expensive in the region.
(C) Mr. Jackson has done business with Magical Intelligence before.
(D) Magical Intelligence has been featured in a publication.

▶ ▶ ▶GO ON TO THE NEXT PAGE

To:	Nicholas Kadinsky <nkadinsky@relectronics.com>
From:	Erin Jackson <ejackson@relectronics.com>
Date:	October 10
Subject:	Schedule for October 23 and 24

Dear Mr. Kadinsky,

I am sure you are well aware of your upcoming business trip to Tokyo from October 23 to October 24, but I just wanted to remind you about it.

Your flight will depart from Los Angeles Airport at 7:15 A.M. on October 23 and arrive at Tokyo Airport at 12:50 P.M. (local time). A representative from our Tokyo branch, Takuya Akira, will greet you at the airport to pick you up. Then, you will arrive at Sakura Hotel to have lunch with Tsubasa Honda, the branch manager.

The Futures Conference, where you will deliver your keynote speech, will commence at 4:00 P.M. at the Grande Conference Hall of Sakura Hotel. Afterwards, you are scheduled to attend the banquet to which all chief executives and presidents of companies, who participate in the conference, are invited.

On the following day, you will be attending the board of directors meeting at our Tokyo branch conference hall in the morning to discuss the company's direction in the next financial year. Your return flight departs at 4:25 P.M., and I will pick you up from the airport upon your arrival.

Regards,

Erin Jackson
Chief Secretary
Rami Electronics

To:	Tsubasa Honda <thonda@relectronics.com>
From:	Erin Jackson <ejackson@relectronics.com>
Date:	October 23
Subject:	Lunch Appointment Cancellation

Dear Ms. Honda,

I regret to inform you that Mr. Kadinsky's flight has been delayed due to mechanical problems and therefore, he is unable to have lunch with you today. I have scheduled an alternate flight that departs 2 hours later than originally planned. Please rearrange the schedule accordingly so that Mr. Kadinsky can be picked up from the airport promptly.

Mr. Kadinsky apologizes for not being able to meet with you personally and hopes for another opportunity in the future. Despite the delay, he will be able to deliver his keynote speech at the conference, and the rest of the schedule is to remain unchanged.

Regards,

Erin Jackson
Chief Secretary
Rami Electronics

181. Why did Ms. Jackson e-mail Mr. Kadinsky?

(A) To provide details about an event
(B) To ask for a conference agenda
(C) To outline the plans for a trip
(D) To remind of a department meeting

182. Who most likely is Mr. Kadinsky?

(A) A corporate executive
(B) A branch manager
(C) A regional representative
(D) A chief secretary

183. What will Mr. Akira probably do on October 23?

(A) Deliver a keynote speech at 4:00 P.M.
(B) Have lunch with Ms. Honda
(C) Pick up Mr. Kadinsky from Sakura Hotel
(D) Be present at an airport by 2:50 P.M.

184. What is suggested about the Futures Conference?

(A) It is exclusively for employees of Rami Electronics.
(B) It will be followed by a formal dinner.
(C) It will be held in Los Angeles.
(D) It is organized by Ms. Jackson.

185. In the second e-mail, the word "rest" in paragraph 2, line 3 is closest in meaning to

(A) break
(B) detail
(C) remainder
(D) addition

▶ ▶ ▶GO ON TO THE NEXT PAGE

Make Your Own Magazine

Nielsen Publishing is pleased to announce another addition to our variety of magazines. Over the past ten years, we have expanded our focus from women's interests to other fields. This year's addition will be launched in May.

Make Your Own is the very first magazine of its kind. With *Make Your Own*, you can select topics you are interested in and have them compiled into a personalized monthly magazine. Nielsen Publishing provides twelve different categories from which you may choose. The subscription rate varies depending on the number of categories you want.

Membership	Number of Topics	Subscription Rate
Platinum	6	$200/yr
Gold	4	$170/yr
Silver	2	$145/yr

Platinum members will receive an extra three months of the magazine as well as a free bestselling novel. When you subscribe to *Make Your Own*, enter the book code of the novel you want. The list of books and codes can be found on Nielsen Publishing's website. Gold members will receive an extra month of the magazine.

Check out our exclusive promotion for those who already subscribe to any of Nielsen Publishing's magazines. They will receive a 50% discount for the first year's subscription to *Make Your Own*. This offer will last from May to August.

Subscribe to *Make Your Own* today and have it delivered to you within 30 days!

---

www.nielsenpublishing.com/subscribe/payment/confirmation

Nielsen Publishing Co.
120 Chambers St., New York, NY 10007

HOME	SUBSCRIBE	DONATION	CONTACT US

Subscription confirmed.
Thank you for your subscription to *Make Your Own*!

Date	June 19
Name	Kelsey Perry
Telephone	917-659-7834
Address	98 Mountain Rd., Cornwall-on-Hudson, NY 12520

Payment Received: $200
Subscription Details:

	Business & Economics		Science & Nature		Sports & Recreation		Fashion & Style
	Parenting		Health & Fitness	V	Literature	V	Music
V	Lifestyle	V	Medicine		News & Politics		Children

Your Complimentary Book Code: _____

* For Platinum-level members who leave the book code column blank, a book will be selected randomly.

To:	<customerservice@nielsonpublishing.com>
From:	<kperry@personalmail.com>
Date:	June 20
Subject:	My Subscription

To whom it may concern,

I just realized that I omitted the special code that I was supposed to send you along with my subscription. The code that I want is 5954-93A. Please make sure that it is added to my subscription record. Thank you very much.

I am looking forward to receiving the first issue of my magazine soon.

Sincerely,

Kelsey Perry

186. What is mentioned about *Make Your Own*?

(A) It is popular with its readers.
(B) It will be published monthly.
(C) It will be available in bookstores in May.
(D) It has been published for ten years.

187. What is indicated about Nielsen Publishing?

(A) It specializes in magazines for women only.
(B) It publishes magazines in multiple countries.
(C) Its headquarters is located on Chambers Street.
(D) It has published many bestselling novels.

188. When will Ms. Perry receive her first issue of *Make Your Own*?

(A) In May
(B) In June
(C) In July
(D) In August

189. In which topic is Ms. Perry NOT interested?

(A) Literature
(B) Medicine
(C) Fashion & Style
(D) Health & Fitness

190. Why did Ms. Perry send the e-mail?

(A) To select a free novel
(B) To name the bonus magazine she wants
(C) To praise the quality of the magazine
(D) To ask for an extension on her subscription

▶ ▶ ▶GO ON TO THE NEXT PAGE

International Paliburg Award to Be Given

by Frank Jameson

North Arlington (September 19) – On September 28, the ceremony for the International Paliburg Award (IPA), an award given to authors for exceptional achievements in literature, will take place at the Paliburg Center as it always has for the last 8 decades. The winner will receive $8,000 in cash and a medal. This year, 4 nominees have been selected: Rosa Perry, Justin Otter, Genevieve Swift, and Bruce Moore.

Ms. Perry and Mr. Moore are both award-winning authors. Ms. Perry's nominated work, *Fireworks*, is of the biography genre, like many of her other novels. Mr. Moore's *The Way* is a tragic love story of a young boy named Luke West.

Among the nominations is Justin Otter's *Never Say Never*. During his interview with us at the Paris Book Festival last month, Mr. Otter said that his adventure-themed work is somewhat based on his own experiences as a young student in his hometown of Melbourne.

What is most notable about one of the selected books, *Belonging*, is that it is Genevieve Swift's first novel. "Last year, I finally quit my teaching job to concentrate on writing. When I saw a copy of my novel at a bookstore, I thought that I had finally realized my dream," noted Ms. Swift.

For more information and a list of past award winners, please visit IPA's website, www.ipalibergaward.org.

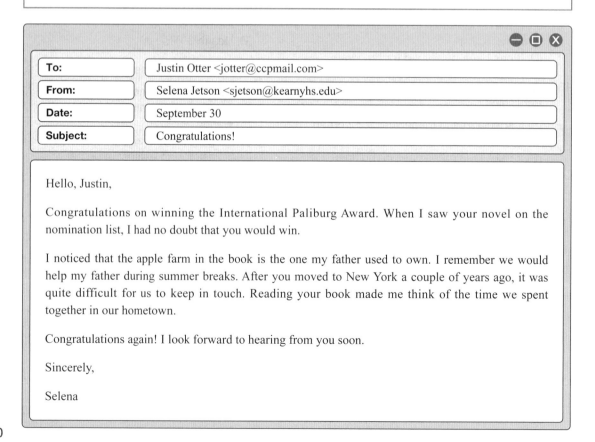

To:	Justin Otter <jotter@ccpmail.com>
From:	Selena Jetson <sjetson@kearnyhs.edu>
Date:	September 30
Subject:	Congratulations!

Hello, Justin,

Congratulations on winning the International Paliburg Award. When I saw your novel on the nomination list, I had no doubt that you would win.

I noticed that the apple farm in the book is the one my father used to own. I remember we would help my father during summer breaks. After you moved to New York a couple of years ago, it was quite difficult for us to keep in touch. Reading your book made me think of the time we spent together in our hometown.

Congratulations again! I look forward to hearing from you soon.

Sincerely,

Selena

For Immediate Release

Primrose Publishing has just signed Genevieve Swift to an exclusive writing contract. Ms. Swift will produce 5 books in the next 6 years. The first book, tentatively entitled *Swan Lake*, is a sequel to *Belonging*, which Ms. Swift published several months ago. More information regarding this new deal can be found at www.primrosepublishing.com.

191. What is suggested about the International Paliburg Award?

(A) It was established about 80 years ago.
(B) It has been given only two fiction writers.
(C) It is sponsored by a local business.
(D) It accepts personal submissions from authors.

192. Who is a former educator?

(A) Frank Jameson
(B) Rosa Perry
(C) Genevieve Swift
(D) Luke West

193. In the article, the word "realized" in paragraph 4, line 3, is closest in meaning to

(A) possessed
(B) fulfilled
(C) recognized
(D) understood

194. What is true about Mr. Otter?

(A) He was hired by the Paliburg Center.
(B) He received a monetary prize.
(C) He won other awards for his work in the past.
(D) He majored in literature.

195. What is suggested about Ms. Swift?

(A) The title of her second novel will be *Swan Lake*.
(B) It was not possible for her to attend the awards ceremony.
(C) She will collaborate with Mr. Otter on a new work.
(D) She works during the day and writes at night.

To: All Employees
From: Erin Lindsey, HR Director
Subject: Employee Training
Date: September 21

We will be installing new machinery this weekend. We are acquiring computers from Synth, Inc., printers from CompuBest, copy machines from Powderhouse, and scanners from Tyndale. Because we are replacing so much equipment, it is imperative that all employees be trained on how to use everything properly as soon as possible. The following is the schedule for the training courses that will be given on Monday, September 28, and Tuesday, September 29:

Dates/Times	Departments
September 28, 9:00 A.M – 12:00 P.M.	Sales
September 28, 1:00 P.M. – 4:00 P.M.	Accounting, HR
September 29, 10:00 A.M. – 1:00 P.M.	R&D
September 29, 2:00 P.M. – 5:00 P.M.	Marketing

Please be sure to attend the proper training session with your colleagues. Speak with me at extension 89 if you are unable to attend your assigned session. I will do my best to assign you to another one.

To:	Harold Martin <harold_martin@powderhouse.com>
From:	Erin Lindsey <elindsey@watsontech.com>
Date:	September 23
Subject:	Thank You

Mr. Martin,

Thank you for informing me about the recent sale that Powderhouse is offering its long-term customers. In light of that information, I would like to purchase six units of the XJ45 instead of only five. I hope you can accommodate this request. I would still like all of the machines to be delivered and installed at the company this coming weekend. Please let me know if there are any problems with my request.

Regards,

Erin Lindsey
HR Director, Watson Tech

Employee Training Comment Form

Training Date/Time: September 29, 2:00 P.M.

Employee Name: Regina Stewart

Comments:

I found the training session to be quite beneficial overall. The trainers were knowledgeable about the equipment they were teaching us to use. They were also willing to answer all of our questions. However, I wish that the representative from Tyndale had provided us with handouts. I had to write down everything she told us instead, and I'm afraid that I was unable to record all of the necessary information.

196. What is one purpose of the memo?

(A) To request work schedules from employees
(B) To confirm an upcoming office move
(C) To assign training slots to workers
(D) To request volunteers to work on the weekend

197. What is suggested about Watson Tech?

(A) It is moving its office to a new location on the weekend.
(B) It is providing its own trainers for the upcoming sessions.
(C) It has purchased equipment from Powderhouse in the past.
(D) It needs new equipment because it recently hired more employees.

198. What equipment was Ms. Lindsey able to purchase for a discount?

(A) Computers
(B) Printers
(C) Copy machines
(D) Scanners

199. What department does Ms. Stewart most likely work in?

(A) Sales
(B) Accounting
(C) R&D
(D) Marketing

200. What problem does Ms. Stewart mention?

(A) The questions that she asked were not answered.
(B) Her training session did not start on time.
(C) She was not provided with written instructions.
(D) Some equipment she trained on did not work properly.

STOP! This is the end of the test. If you finish before time is called, you may go back to Parts 5, 6, and 7 and check your work.

Actual Test 04

MP3 音檔　　　　　解析

最佳解答時間 120 分鐘

120 min

開始時間：＿＿＿點 ＿＿＿分

結束時間：＿＿＿點 ＿＿＿分

▲ 盡量不要在作答中途停下來。

▲ 請於答案卡上畫記作答。

目標正確題數：＿＿＿／ **200 題**　實際正確題數：＿＿＿／ **200 題**

題數與分數對照，請參考 P449 分數換算表。

LISTENING TEST

In the Listening test, you will be asked to demonstrate how well you understand spoken English. The entire Listening test will last approximately 45 minutes. There are four parts, and directions are given for each part. You must mark your answers on the separate answer sheet. Do not write your answers in the test book.

PART 1

Directions: For each question in this part, you will hear four statements about a picture in your test book. When you hear the statements, you must select the one statement that best describes what you see in the picture. Then find the number of the question on your answer sheet and mark your answer. The statements will not be printed in your test book and will be spoken only one time.

Statement (B), "They are sitting at a table." is the best description of the picture. So you should select answer (B) and mark it on your answer sheet.

1.

2.

▶ ▶ ▶GO ON TO THE NEXT PAGE

3.

4.

5.

6.

▶ ▶ ▶GO ON TO THE NEXT PAGE

PART 2

Directions: You will hear a question or statement and three responses spoken in English. They will not be printed in your test book and will be spoken only one time. Select the best response to the question or statement and mark the letter (A), (B), or (C) on your answer sheet.

7. Mark your answer on your answer sheet.

8. Mark your answer on your answer sheet.

9. Mark your answer on your answer sheet.

10. Mark your answer on your answer sheet.

11. Mark your answer on your answer sheet.

12. Mark your answer on your answer sheet.

13. Mark your answer on your answer sheet.

14. Mark your answer on your answer sheet.

15. Mark your answer on your answer sheet.

16. Mark your answer on your answer sheet.

17. Mark your answer on your answer sheet.

18. Mark your answer on your answer sheet.

19. Mark your answer on your answer sheet.

20. Mark your answer on your answer sheet.

21. Mark your answer on your answer sheet.

22. Mark your answer on your answer sheet.

23. Mark your answer on your answer sheet.

24. Mark your answer on your answer sheet.

25. Mark your answer on your answer sheet.

26. Mark your answer on your answer sheet.

27. Mark your answer on your answer sheet.

28. Mark your answer on your answer sheet.

29. Mark your answer on your answer sheet.

30. Mark your answer on your answer sheet.

31. Mark your answer on your answer sheet.

PART 3

Directions: You will hear some conversations between two or three people. You will be asked to answer three questions about what the speakers say in each conversation. Select the best response to each question and mark the letter (A), (B), (C), or (D) on your answer sheet. The conversations will not be printed in your test book and will be spoken only one time.

32. Who most likely is the woman?

(A) A yoga coach
(B) A culinary teacher
(C) A lab technician
(D) A computer programmer

33. What does the woman say she recently did?

(A) Joined a fitness center
(B) Changed departments
(C) Bought some supplies
(D) Reviewed a budget

34. What does the man suggest?

(A) Reusing some items
(B) Buying some more equipment
(C) Meeting with their supervisor
(D) Holding a fundraiser

35. What event are the speakers discussing?

(A) A training program
(B) An orientation session
(C) A charity luncheon
(D) A product demonstration

36. What does the woman imply when she says, "I requested 25 laptops"?

(A) She plans to conduct an online meeting.
(B) A request was not fulfilled properly.
(C) Not everyone will attend an event.
(D) Some machines are not working.

37. What does the man ask the woman to do?

(A) Make a payment
(B) Pick up some food coupons
(C) Reserve an event venue
(D) Clean up a room

38. What problem does the woman mention?

(A) A truck's engine will not start.
(B) An oven is broken.
(C) A bathroom window is jammed.
(D) A sink is leaking.

39. What does the man ask about?

(A) Where some tools are
(B) How much he needs to pay
(C) When a repair can be done
(D) How to complete a form

40. What does the woman say she will do next?

(A) Check her toolbox
(B) Inspect the rest of the house
(C) Look for some parts
(D) Call her supervisor

41. What is the purpose of the man's business trip?

(A) To present some results
(B) To meet with a new supplier
(C) To sign a contract
(D) To demonstrate a product

42. What does the woman suggest the man visit?

(A) A museum
(B) A theater district
(C) A restaurant
(D) A monument

43. What does the man say he will do during his break?

(A) Conduct some research
(B) Reserve a plane ticket
(C) Look for some tickets
(D) Contact his client

▶ ▶ ▶GO ON TO THE NEXT PAGE

44. Who most likely is the woman?

(A) A newspaper reporter
(B) A company owner
(C) A talk show host
(D) An advertising executive

45. According to the woman, why was the man busy recently?

(A) He took part in convention.
(B) He was training some new workers.
(C) He wrote some news reports.
(D) He conducted some interviews.

46. Why does the man say, "My employees are incredibly dedicated and reliable"?

(A) To recommend his workers for new jobs
(B) To help secure a new contract with a client
(C) To address a complaint by a customer
(D) To recognize the contribution of some others

47. What has the man been doing?

(A) Interviewing job applicants
(B) Writing an article on international travel
(C) Going over some survey results
(D) Updating some rules

48. What problem does the woman mention?

(A) Some costs have gone up.
(B) A company's branches are closing down.
(C) Some equipment is malfunctioning.
(D) Writers are reluctant to go abroad.

49. What does the man suggest doing?

(A) Transferring some workers to a new branch
(B) Allowing electronic payment
(C) Producing an online version of the magazine
(D) Hiring more staff members

50. What are the speakers mainly discussing?

(A) An available position
(B) A proposed budget
(C) An advertisement campaign
(D) A business trip

51. What did the man say he received?

(A) A job offer
(B) A meal voucher
(C) Some new information
(D) Sales numbers

52. What will the woman most likely do next?

(A) Meet with a client
(B) Make a presentation
(C) Reschedule a meeting
(D) Attend a luncheon

53. Where does the conversation most likely take place?

(A) At a construction site
(B) At a duty-free store
(C) At a hardware store
(D) At a rental car agency

54. What does the woman say she is looking for in a product?

(A) An extended warranty
(B) Durable material
(C) Ease of transport
(D) Something that is waterproof

55. What will Todd probably do next?

(A) Show a user's guide
(B) Arrange a delivery
(C) Provide a demonstration
(D) Offer a discount

56. Where does the conversation take place?

(A) At an airport
(B) At an office building
(C) At a hotel
(D) At a supermarket

57. Why has the man visited the business?

(A) To install a lighting fixture
(B) To repair some lights
(C) To redecorate a room
(D) To paint some walls

58. What does the woman say happened last week?

(A) Some equipment was purchased.
(B) A new tenant arrived.
(C) Renovations were made.
(D) Operating hours were extended.

---

59. Why does Sarah Doyle want a loan?

(A) To purchase some equipment
(B) To pay her monthly rent
(C) To run some advertisements
(D) To hire additional staffers

60. Why does the man ask for assistance?

(A) He does not do a certain task.
(B) He is helping another customer.
(C) He is currently on his break.
(D) He does not understand a question.

61. What requirement for a loan is mentioned?

(A) A letter of recommendation
(B) Legal documentation for property
(C) Some financial records
(D) A bank account

Restaurant Reviews

Susan's Corner	★ ★ ☆ ☆ ☆
Westside Café	★ ★ ★ ☆ ☆
Steak 45	★ ★ ★ ★ ☆
Thompson Place	★ ★ ★ ★ ★

62. What did the man look over for the woman?

(A) A product review
(B) A meeting schedule
(C) A presentation
(D) A company catalog

63. What is the woman worried about?

(A) An upcoming training course
(B) Her presentation at a seminar
(C) Her performance review
(D) A meeting with a client

64. Look at the graphic. Which restaurant does the man recommend?

(A) Susan's Corner
(B) Westside Café
(C) Steak 45
(D) Thompson Place

▶ ▶ ▶GO ON TO THE NEXT PAGE

	Ground (price per package)	Air (price per package)
1-20 packages	$3.00	$6.00
21-50 packages	$2.50	$5.00
51-100 packages	$2.00	$4.00

Project-Related Agenda Items

1. Timeline
2. Project Managing
3. Budget
4. Vendors for supplies

65. What recently happened to Harrison Manufacturing?

(A) It hired more workers.
(B) It obtained some new customers.
(C) It opened a factory in Europe.
(D) It signed a contract with a supplier.

66. Look at the graphic. How much will it most likely cost to send each package?

(A) $2.00
(B) $2.50
(C) $4.00
(D) $5.00

67. What will the man most likely do next?

(A) Send packaging boxes
(B) Provide his contact information
(C) Sign a contract
(D) Ship some packages

68. Where do the speakers most likely work?

(A) At a library
(B) At a museum
(C) At an art supply store
(D) At an architect office

69. Look at the graphic. Which agenda item are the speakers discussing?

(A) Item 1
(B) Item 2
(C) Item 3
(D) Item 4

70. What does the woman say she will do later?

(A) Contact a colleague
(B) Review a proposal
(C) Post an advertisement
(D) Call in a meeting

PART 4

Directions: You will hear some short talks given by a single speaker. You will be asked to answer three questions about what the speaker says in each short talk. Select the best response to each question and mark the letter (A), (B), (C), or (D) on your answer sheet. The talks will not be printed in your test book and will be spoken only one time.

71. Who most likely is the listener?

(A) An editor-in-chief
(B) A writer
(C) A photographer
(D) A teacher

72. According to the speaker, what is he impressed with?

(A) A budget proposal
(B) A job description
(C) Some photographs
(D) Some samples of work

73. What does the speaker say he wants to do?

(A) Confirm an e-mail address
(B) Arrange an interview
(C) Provide a price estimate
(D) Schedule a release date

74. What will take place on Sunday?

(A) A product demonstration
(B) An information session
(C) A sales conference
(D) A job interview

75. What does the Jospin Institute offer?

(A) Business audits
(B) Computer classes
(C) Online market research
(D) Security consulting

76. Why should the listeners text a number?

(A) To respond to a survey
(B) To receive a newsletter
(C) To request an application
(D) To provide comments

77. What is the speaker mainly discussing?

(A) A departmental budget
(B) A speech at a conference
(C) A new phone system
(D) A new conference room

78. According to the speaker, what should the listeners do if they have any further issues?

(A) Notify an expert
(B) Write an online review
(C) Use some different equipment
(D) Restart their computer

79. Why does the speaker ask the listeners to call him?

(A) To reserve a meeting room
(B) To request new machinery
(C) To ask for a transfer
(D) To order some supplies

80. Who most likely is the speaker?

(A) A restaurant owner
(B) A government inspector
(C) A kitchen staff member
(D) A financial advisor

81. Why does the speaker say, "Our kitchen is always busy"?

(A) To tell the listeners that a wait time could be longer
(B) To explain a reason for a change
(C) To show that a business is successful
(D) To prove that the work will be difficult

82. What does the speaker ask the listeners to do?

(A) Confirm their work schedules
(B) Work overtime
(C) Wear hard hats at all times
(D) Have their name tags on

▶ ▶ ▶GO ON TO THE NEXT PAGE

83. What kind of product is the speaker discussing?

(A) An exercise machine
(B) A software program
(C) A skincare item
(D) A running shoe

84. What will the listeners start working on?

(A) Working with a focus group
(B) Creating some marketing materials
(C) Making a TV commercial
(D) Training some new workers

85. What does the speaker say she will do this week?

(A) Meet with each employee
(B) Arrange a conference call with staff
(C) Travel abroad on business
(D) Visit the company's factory

---

86. What type of business is the news report mainly about?

(A) An airplane manufacturer
(B) A car rental service
(C) An automobile maker
(D) A photography studio

87. According to the speaker, what is the goal of the company's action?

(A) To expand into overseas markets
(B) To help protect the environment
(C) To cut its production costs
(D) To use fewer raw materials

88. What does the speaker imply when he says, "I've already ordered a new one"?

(A) He thinks the vehicles are high in demand.
(B) Some models will not be available soon.
(C) The vehicles' prices are not too high.
(D) He likes the looks of the new models.

89. What problem does the speaker mention?

(A) A shipper is sending items late.
(B) A building needs renovations.
(C) Some products are getting damaged.
(D) Wrong items have been shipped out.

90. What does the company intend to do?

(A) Change its packaging options
(B) Hire another shipping service
(C) Provide more employee benefits
(D) Introduce new policy guidelines

91. What has been prepared for some employees?

(A) Food and drinks
(B) A tutorial for packaging
(C) An employee handbook
(D) Some samples of packaging

---

92. Where does the speaker work?

(A) At a government office
(B) At an elementary school
(C) At an art supply store
(D) At a community center

93. According to the speaker, what is different about this summer's program?

(A) It will include additional activities.
(B) It will be at a different venue.
(C) It will cost money to participate.
(D) It will start later in the summer.

94. Why does the speaker say, "We hope you feel the same way"?

(A) To apologize to the listeners for changing a date
(B) To encourage the listeners to make a donation
(C) To thank the listeners for volunteering
(D) To ask for feedback from the listeners

Catalog

Ivory #R4852	Light Blue #R4853
Green #R4854	Cream #R4855

95. Look at the graphic. Which color is the speaker interested in?

(A) Ivory
(B) Light blue
(C) Green
(D) Cream

96. What does the speaker want to know?

(A) If refunds are allowed
(B) If a special price is available
(C) If an item is out of stock
(D) If delivery can be made for free

97. When does the speaker want to be contacted?

(A) In the morning
(B) At lunchtime
(C) At night
(D) On the weekend

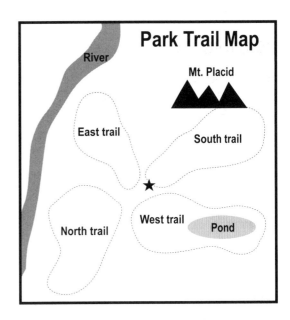

98. Look at the graphic. Which trail does the speaker say is the easiest?

(A) North trail
(B) South trail
(C) East trail
(D) West trail

99. According to the speaker, what should the listeners take with them?

(A) Sunblock lotion
(B) Raingear
(C) Plenty of water
(D) A tent

100. What are the listeners asked to do next?

(A) Complete a survey for hikers
(B) Watch a short video
(C) Look at some photos
(D) Get a permit for hiking

This is the end of the Listening test. Turn to Part 5 in your test book.

▶ ▶ ▶GO ON TO THE NEXT PAGE

READING TEST

In the Reading test, you will read a variety of texts and answer several different types of reading comprehension questions. The entire Reading test will last 75 minutes. There are three parts, and directions are given for each part. You are encouraged to answer as many questions as possible within the time allowed.

You must mark your answer on the separate answer sheet. Do not write your answers in your test book.

PART 5

Directions: A word or phrase is missing in each of the sentences below. Four answer choices are given below each sentence. Select the best answer to complete the sentence. Then mark the letter (A), (B), (C), or (D) on your answer sheet.

101. Regular customers of Coffee House have been surprised at the sharp price increases which were ------- imposed last week.

(A) unexpected
(B) more unexpected
(C) unexpectedly
(D) unexpectedness

102. The weather satellite project began ten years ago, but suffered from several -------.

(A) delay
(B) delayed
(C) delaying
(D) delays

103. The speech of the chief executive officer focused on our Mr. Jenkins and ------- successes in India.

(A) he
(B) his
(C) him
(D) himself

104. Economic uncertainty is one of the biggest challenges we face while doing business in this city, ------- comparatively little effort is devoted to fixing it.

(A) so
(B) yet
(C) nor
(D) although

105. Our town is a ------- community made up of different nationalities, cultural backgrounds, and religious groups.

(A) successful
(B) profitable
(C) diverse
(D) external

106. The president of Speed Freight Services has been considering ------- another warehouse in Toronto in two years.

(A) build
(B) building
(C) to build
(D) built

107. Most employees are ------- to vacation time and vacation pay after being employed for one year.

(A) entitled
(B) eliminated
(C) limited
(D) trained

108. Customers who wish to be ------- should return defective products within three days of purchase and bring an original receipt as well.

(A) fulfilled
(B) reimbursed
(C) exchanged
(D) collaborated

109. ------- the high volume of applications that we receive, only qualified applicants will be contacted next week.

(A) Due to
(B) Aside from
(C) Regardless of
(D) On behalf of

110. It is quite ------- that Bella Motors has become the leader in the hybrid car industry in just six years.

(A) amaze
(B) amazing
(C) amazed
(D) amazes

111. All of the researchers at BK Pharmaceutical's Lab are required to wear safety equipment on the -------.

(A) phases
(B) premises
(C) technologies
(D) remarks

112. The government ------- announced that it would grant generous tax breaks for foreign companies doing business in the country.

(A) immediately
(B) soon
(C) recently
(D) exclusively

113. The environmental project was designed to raise ------- of the serious garbage problem in the oceans.

(A) approach
(B) maintenance
(C) awareness
(D) influence

114. It is ------- necessary to turn off the computer data servers to upgrade their operating system.

(A) lately
(B) occasionally
(C) helpfully
(D) carefully

115. Some employees ------- usually work late are likely to think that the best way to refresh themselves is to get some energy drinks.

(A) who
(B) which
(C) where
(D) what

116. Don't put off making necessary repairs or performing ------- maintenance to make your car last as long as possible in top condition.

(A) routine
(B) beneficial
(C) upcoming
(D) cautious

117. Sign up for the BK Cable Television membership to get hundreds of channels ------- your choice of three sports channels for absolutely no charge.

(A) whichever
(B) plus
(C) additionally
(D) that

118. According to our personnel records, Mr. Jones works the ------- of all of the employees working at Cheese Bread Factory.

(A) hardly
(B) harder
(C) hardest
(D) hard

▶ ▶ ▶ GO ON TO THE NEXT PAGE

119. The health care system is basically a service-based industry and is at ------- just as in other service-oriented sectors.

(A) utmost
(B) farthest
(C) relative
(D) apparent

120. Most people rarely think about sharing their cars ------- crude oil prices are currently rising sharply.

(A) if so
(B) therefore
(C) even though
(D) since

121. Mr. Parker ------- a managerial position last year, but declined since he was looking for a high-paying job.

(A) offers
(B) offered
(C) was offered
(D) will be offered

122. Tourism International will award 'Agency of the Year' to ------- travel agency gets the most votes from the board members.

(A) whoever
(B) whichever
(C) wherever
(D) however

123. The human resources department will come up with several ways to ------- the sales staff to improve their competitiveness in the overseas market.

(A) consolidate
(B) contact
(C) raise
(D) motivate

124. The company cafeteria opens from 8 A.M. to 8 P.M. during the weekdays, so you can plan your lunch and dinner hour -------.

(A) subsequently
(B) seasonally
(C) primarily
(D) accordingly

125. ------- Mr. Brown, actual profit and loss should be precisely reflected in the next accounting report.

(A) With respect to
(B) In addition to
(C) The fact that
(D) As stated by

126. According to our policy, ------- who violates the "no mobile phone" rule can be asked to leave the theater.

(A) those
(B) both
(C) several
(D) anyone

127. The individual ------- responsibility is to trace all business transactions that result in changes in the property and finance of our company is Mr. Brian Walker, the head accountant.

(A) whose
(B) what
(C) whether
(D) this

128. Even though most customers find the new product easy to use, ------- less familiar with it should refer to the user's guide before use.

(A) those
(B) who
(C) these
(D) none

129. Ms. Rodriguez will participate in a training course for her new position, in ------- she will be in charge of statistical analysis.

(A) whom
(B) which
(C) that
(D) where

130. The launch of the new mobile device ------- at least a week after a problem was detected.

(A) were postponed
(B) will postpone
(C) has been postponed
(D) had been postponed

PART 6

Directions: Read the texts that follow. A word or phrase, or sentence is missing in parts of each text. Four answer choices for each question are given below the text. Select the best answer to complete the text. Then mark the letter (A), (B), (C), or (D) on your answer sheet.

Questions 131-134 refer to the following letter.

Dear Ms. Schickler;

In connection with our annual symposium on the electronics industry, we invite an expert in the field to address us. ------- our emphasis this year is on the future of the electronics,
131.
we would be honored if you could speak to us on your experience of business.

Future Electronics Symposium will be ------- at Los Angeles Metropolitan Hotel on
132.
October 1, from 10:00 A.M. to 3:00 P.M. We ------- your speech from 1:00 P.M. to 2:00
133.
P.M., and would like you to speak for an hour including questions and answer period.

-------.
134.
Very truly yours,

Siobhan Kelly
Vice President
Andromeda Electronics

131. (A) Since
(B) Although
(C) Even if
(D) While

132. (A) hold
(B) holding
(C) held
(D) to hold

133. (A) is scheduling
(B) have scheduled
(C) had been scheduled
(D) will be scheduled

134. (A) We very much appreciated your attendance at our presentation on October 1.
(B) As agreed, your payment for our transaction will be made in Canadian dollars.
(C) It is our pleasure to host a number of seminars and presentations related to the international community.
(D) We are pleased to be able to pay your traveling costs and to offer you a modest honorarium.

Dear all staff,

I'm writing to inform you that we have recently revised our business travel reimbursement policy. This policy defines the conditions, rules, and procedures that apply to staff members who undertake business travel ------- the company and where the company
135.
may reimburse the expenses associated with business travel.

From now on, after approval for your business travel, flight tickets and hotels must be booked through the personnel department. -------. If there is any reason you need to book
136.
your business travel, you must ------- the reason in your business travel expense report
137.
and submit all receipts to the personnel department. Additionally, employees ------- up to
138.
$100 per day to pay for your incidentals, including food and ground transportation.

Please be aware that reimbursement will not be made if you do not follow this new policy when booking your business travel.

Do not hesitate to contact me with any questions or concerns.

Truly yours,

Jennifer Grant
Head of Accounting

.

135. (A) in charge of
(B) in compliance with
(C) with regard to
(D) on behalf of

136. (A) You will be satisfied with the quality of our service here.
(B) We should discuss the amount permitted for incidentals next week.
(C) It will help to remove the confusion we had in the past.
(D) To take advantage of this opportunity, you must respond by May 15.

137. (A) document
(B) consider
(C) perform
(D) persuade

138. (A) allows
(B) allowed
(C) will allow
(D) will be allowed

Uptown Furniture

Event Notice

Many thanks for purchasing our couch set. Seats should be comfortable for all members

of family. We greatly appreciate your -------, and we trust that you are getting lots of
139.

enjoyment from your new furniture.

-------. We would therefore be grateful if you could take a moment to complete the
140.

enclosed customer satisfaction survey. Your answers will help us ensure that we always

------- our future customers' needs.
141.

Furthermore, your completed survey will be entered into a special prize draw. The winning

customer will get a $500 gift certificate to use in-store. Please return your survey by July

15 to be included in the draw. The winner ------- on August 1.
142.

ACTUAL TEST ... 04

139. (A) requirement
(B) supervision
(C) custom
(D) prediction

140. (A) Prior experience is preferred for this position.
(B) We always strive to improve our customer care.
(C) All of your complaints are to be treated equally.
(D) It's often used for heavy items like dressers and dining tables.

141. (A) satisfy
(B) desire
(C) research
(D) replace

142. (A) announces
(B) should announce
(C) was announced
(D) will be announced

▶ ▶ ▶ GO ON TO THE NEXT PAGE

Syracuse Chronicle
Culture Section

A New Photo Exhibit Is Coming to Town
Brandon Lee

November 1) Starting next Wednesday, the National Art Gallery will be holding an exhibit on the works of photographer Ms. Cecil Beaton. Ms. Beaton's photos ------- many awards

143.

internationally. The rising artist is renowned for her black and white photos that feature the socially oppressed. She was the sole apprentice of the late Peter Jackson, a prominent photographer who focused on capturing the lives of indigenous peoples. Based on -------

144.

she learned from Mr. Jackson, Ms. Beaton went on to take photos of homeless people, beggars, child workers, and other socially ignored citizens. "Like the indigenous people that are not being fully recognized globally, there are people within our own cities that are being ignored," stated Ms. Beaton. "I wanted to capture their lives through photography

------- my audience can see and reconnect to their forgotten neighbors." The

145.

photographer hopes to contribute to society through her works. -------. The exhibit will

146.

last for four months.

143. (A) receives
(B) were received
(C) have received
(D) will receive

144. (A) that
(B) which
(C) what
(D) how

145. (A) however
(B) although
(C) so
(D) therefore

146. (A) The exhibition will be based on Mr. Jackson's photos on indigenous people.
(B) Several magazine companies will contact her to use her pictures soon.
(C) She plans to donate all of the exhibition's profits to charity organizations.
(D) The photographer mentioned future plans of taking photos of homeless people.

PART 7

Directions: In this part you will read a selection of texts, such as magazine and newspaper articles, e-mails, and instant messages. Each text or set of texts is followed by several questions. Select the best answer for each question and mark the letter (A), (B), (C), or (D) on your answer sheet.

Questions 147-148 refer to the following e-mail.

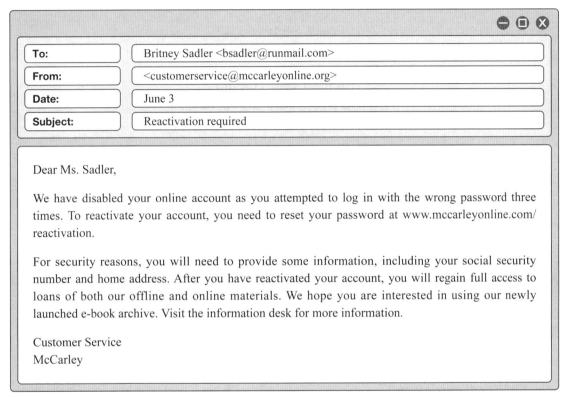

To:	Britney Sadler <bsadler@runmail.com>
From:	<customerservice@mccarleyonline.org>
Date:	June 3
Subject:	Reactivation required

Dear Ms. Sadler,

We have disabled your online account as you attempted to log in with the wrong password three times. To reactivate your account, you need to reset your password at www.mccarleyonline.com/reactivation.

For security reasons, you will need to provide some information, including your social security number and home address. After you have reactivated your account, you will regain full access to loans of both our offline and online materials. We hope you are interested in using our newly launched e-book archive. Visit the information desk for more information.

Customer Service
McCarley

---

147. Why was the e-mail probably sent to Ms. Sadler?

(A) She was unable to purchase a book online.
(B) She canceled a transaction with McCarley.
(C) She needs to renew her account.
(D) She forgot her password.

148. What most likely is McCarley?

(A) A bank
(B) A online bookstore
(C) A library
(D) A security agency

5th Annual Hot Potato Market

A Rock & Roll Night

presented by Iratshai – a local Japanese restaurant

Come and enjoy a night full of energy!
Guest Performer: Green Tomatoes Band

Friday, September 4
5:30 P.M. – 11:00 P.M.

Benson Arts Theater

958 Kyle Street, Bertrand, NE 68927
Second floor

Tickets - $20 (Sales start on August 30)
All proceeds to benefit the Jacksonville Music Academy.
Visit www.hotpotatomarket.org for more information or to reserve a ticket.
You'd better hurry! Tickets are expected to sell out quickly.

* Iratshai 10% discount coupons will be provided to all attendees.

149. What type of event is being advertised?

(A) The anniversary party of a restaurant
(B) A theater opening
(C) Musical entertainment
(D) A local food festival

150. What is NOT mentioned about the advertised event?

(A) Its tickets are available online.
(B) It will help an educational institution.
(C) It will conclude at 11:00 P.M.
(D) Its tickets will be available on September 4.

Questions 151-152 refer to the following text message chain.

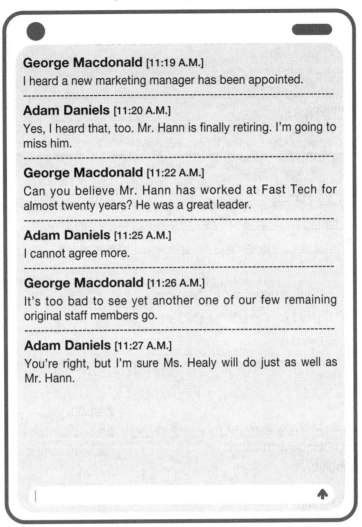

George Macdonald [11:19 A.M.]

I heard a new marketing manager has been appointed.

Adam Daniels [11:20 A.M.]

Yes, I heard that, too. Mr. Hann is finally retiring. I'm going to miss him.

George Macdonald [11:22 A.M.]

Can you believe Mr. Hann has worked at Fast Tech for almost twenty years? He was a great leader.

Adam Daniels [11:25 A.M.]

I cannot agree more.

George Macdonald [11:26 A.M.]

It's too bad to see yet another one of our few remaining original staff members go.

Adam Daniels [11:27 A.M.]

You're right, but I'm sure Ms. Healy will do just as well as Mr. Hann.

ACTUAL TEST 04

151. What is indicated about Fast Tech?

   (A) It has been in business for fewer than two decades.

   (B) It has recently hired a new employee.

   (C) It will post a job advertisement soon.

   (D) It is expanding its Marketing Department.

152. At 11:25 A.M., what does Mr. Daniels mean when he writes, "I cannot agree more"?

   (A) He is indicating that Mr. Macdonald is giving incorrect information.

   (B) He thinks greatly of Mr. Hann as well.

   (C) He does not have any close colleagues now.

   (D) He refuses to work with Ms. Healy.

▶ ▶ ▶ GO ON TO THE NEXT PAGE

Quality Frames

1086 College Avenue
Dayton, OH 45434

Customer Information	
Name:	Victor Clark
Phone Number:	(513)555-2903

Special Memo:

I would like to frame a painting. This painting was painted by my grandfather, and it has a very high sentimental value. As you will see, the painting is timeworn, so please take special care of it.

Frame Type: Michelangelo

Color: Classic Gold & Silver

Pickup Date: July 10

Cost Summary:

- Service: $35.00
- Material Cost: Michelangelo frame (2 5/8 inches): $95.00
- Membership Discount (10%): -$9.50
- Prepaid Deposit: -$30.00

Balance Due at Pickup: $90.50

153. What can be inferred about the painting?

(A) It was created by a famous artist.
(B) Its original frame broke.
(C) It is fragile.
(D) It is expensive.

154. How much money does Mr. Clark need to pay on July 10?

(A) $30.00
(B) $35.00
(C) $90.50
(D) $95.00

Jazzy Numbers

Jazzy Numbers is a 3-year-old jazz instrumental band that has members who play the piano, saxophone, clarinet, double bass, and drums. We have turned out many famous musicians, including Aaron Mills, who is one of our original members. He recently joined the prestigious Ersel Orchestra as the lead clarinetist.

Do you have a passion for jazz music?

Then do not hesitate to apply to be a member! As a freelance jazz band, we play anytime, anywhere for various events such as parties, weddings, and other ceremonies. We are currently looking for new members. All we need is a recording of you playing as well as a brief personal statement by November 3. Once we have evaluated your submission, we will call you for an audition. E-mail Jeffry Henderson at jhenderson@boostmail.com for audition file submissions or questions.

155. What is the purpose of the advertisement?

(A) To announce a retirement
(B) To recruit additional artists
(C) To publicize an upcoming performance
(D) To ask for donations

156. What is NOT true about Aaron Mills?

(A) He will be judging the audition.
(B) He played in Jazzy Numbers about 3 years ago.
(C) He is a well-known clarinetist.
(D) He is currently a member of the Ersel Orchestra.

157. What is suggested about the musicians in Jazzy Numbers?

(A) They record their performances on electronic files.
(B) They are amateurs.
(C) They travel to different places.
(D) They work for Mr. Henderson.

▶ ▶ ▶GO ON TO THE NEXT PAGE

Barney's Hill
Barney's Signature Cereal Bars

Barney's Hill Cereal Bars are made from the traditional homemade family recipe created by Canadian farmer Barney Pierres. For 50 years, Mr. Pierres had run the business, but now his son, Romeo Pierres, has taken over the business. Using no artificial flavors, each bar is filled with toasted oats, cashews, and almonds and dipped in real maple syrup to produce a sweet, great-tasting, wholesome snack that you can take anywhere. Our cereal bars are full of classic crunch and whole grain goodness making them a nutritious snack that will keep you full without guilty pleasures.

- High in fiber and low in sugar
- Zero trans-fats and gluten-free
- Quick and easy to consume
- Provides a boost of energy
- Approved by the Organic Farm Association (OFA)

Visit our website at www.barneyshill.com/naturebars to download a printable coupon. When purchasing a package of Barney's Hill Cereal Bars containing a dozen bars, present the coupon to the cashier and receive a second pack for free!

158. What is the purpose of the information?

(A) To describe the history of a business
(B) To introduce a traditional food
(C) To advertise a product made with natural ingredients.
(D) To show how to cook a homemade dish

159. What is indicated about Barney's Hill?

(A) It prints Mr. Pierres' signature on its products.
(B) Its products are manufactured on a farm.
(C) It is a family-owned business.
(D) It will merge with the OFA.

160. What is available on the website?

(A) Ordering a pack of cereal bars
(B) Downloading an application
(C) Requesting some free product samples
(D) Receiving a buy-one-get-one-free voucher

Questions 161-163 refer to the following e-mail.

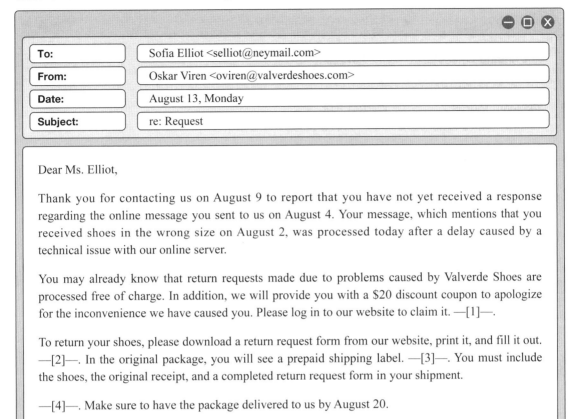

To: Sofia Elliot <selliot@neymail.com>

From: Oskar Viren <oviren@valverdeshoes.com>

Date: August 13, Monday

Subject: re: Request

Dear Ms. Elliot,

Thank you for contacting us on August 9 to report that you have not yet received a response regarding the online message you sent to us on August 4. Your message, which mentions that you received shoes in the wrong size on August 2, was processed today after a delay caused by a technical issue with our online server.

You may already know that return requests made due to problems caused by Valverde Shoes are processed free of charge. In addition, we will provide you with a $20 discount coupon to apologize for the inconvenience we have caused you. Please log in to our website to claim it. —[1]—.

To return your shoes, please download a return request form from our website, print it, and fill it out. —[2]—. In the original package, you will see a prepaid shipping label. —[3]—. You must include the shoes, the original receipt, and a completed return request form in your shipment.

—[4]—. Make sure to have the package delivered to us by August 20.

Truly yours,

Oskar Viren
Customer Service, Valverde Shoes

161. What is implied about Valverde Shoes?

(A) It normally charges a fee for return requests.
(B) It will include a discount coupon in a shipment.
(C) It is currently experiencing technical problems.
(D) It offers discount coupons to return customers.

162. When did Ms. Elliot first report a problem with her order to Valverde Shoes?

(A) On August 2
(B) On August 4
(C) On August 9
(D) On August 13

163. In which of the positions marked [1], [2], [3], and [4] does the following sentence best belong?

"It should be glued on top of your shipment when being sent as our office address is printed on it."

(A) [1]
(B) [2]
(C) [3]
(D) [4]

▶ ▶ ▶ GO ON TO THE NEXT PAGE

Questions 164-167 refer to the following online chat discussion.

Amanda Meester   7:37 P.M.
I just bought a ticket to the Rocking Socks concert! Who else is going?

Liam Morris   7:41 P.M.
I've wanted to go to one of their concerts for such a long time. Their new album is amazing.

Pedro Luther   7:42 P.M.
I know, right? I tried to purchase it at several offline stores, but it sold out very quickly.

Liam Morris   7:43 P.M.
How much was the ticket?

Amanda Meester   7:44 P.M.
I purchased a general admission ticket for $90.

Pedro Luther   7:44 P.M.
Wow. I got mine for $120. Which website did you use?

Amanda Meester   7:47 P.M.
I have a membership at Ticket Legend, so I was able to get a discount.

Liam Morris   7:48 P.M.
Get out! Normally, concerts at Torzia Hall cost well over $100. Will I be able to get a discount if I sign up for a membership?

Amanda Meester   7:49 P.M.
Absolutely. The company also provides additional discounts for first-time users. You should definitely check it out.

Pedro Luther   7:50 P.M.
I think I'll buy all my concert tickets from that website from now on.

Liam Morris   7:53 P.M.
Thanks for the information, Amanda!

Amanda Meester   7:54 P.M.
No problem. I'll see you guys at the concert then!

SEND

164. Why is Mr. Luther's ticket more expensive than Ms. Meester's?

(A) His ticket is exclusive to fan club members.
(B) He did not purchase his ticket at a discounted price.
(C) He purchased a front-row seat.
(D) He paid more than he should have by mistake.

165. What is indicated about Rocking Socks?

(A) Tickets to their upcoming concert are sold out.
(B) They recently debuted.
(C) They are currently on tour.
(D) Their new album is a big hit.

166. At 7:48 P.M., what does Mr. Morris mean when he writes, "Get out"?

(A) He thinks the website is offering a great deal.
(B) He is suggesting that Ms. Meester leave early on the day of the concert.
(C) He will receive the ticket from Ms. Meester once she buys it for him.
(D) He is surprised to learn how easy it is to purchase a ticket online.

167. What can be inferred from the online chat discussion?

(A) Mr. Morris will get a refund for his ticket.
(B) There will be a long line at the Rocking Socks concert.
(C) Ms. Meester will go to Mr. Luther's concert with Mr. Morris.
(D) The upcoming Rocking Socks concert will be held at Torzia Hall.

December 18

Lillie Martinez
Associate Editor
Dysart Publishing
551 Eagles Road
San Diego, CA 92155

Dear Ms. Martinez,

I am a professor of journalism at Cupouse University. I was very impressed with your innovative ideas on creating and using e-publications that you explained in your online column on your company's website. Your knowledge and expertise in the field of editing and publishing are admirable.

In an effort to provide my students with current information on the professional writing field, I have been organizing a program with special guest lecturers. Would you be interested in coming to one of my classes to meet with my students and to deliver a lecture on the same topic as your online column? Last semester, the manager of your department, Mr. Phillips, came to deliver a lecture to the students, and they benefited from it very much.

If you are interested, please contact Brenda Smith at bsmith@cupouse.edu to discuss the date and time of your visit. I look forward to seeing you.

Sincerely,

Joseph Cleveland
Professor of Journalism, Cupouse University

168. What is the purpose of the letter?

(A) To give information about an upcoming event
(B) To compliment a student
(C) To request a web design
(D) To recruit a lecturer

169. How did Mr. Cleveland find out about Ms. Martinez's ideas?

(A) He read an online article that she wrote.
(B) He attended a seminar that she led.
(C) He delivered a speech at her company.
(D) He interviewed her for a report.

170. According to the letter, who previously visited Cupouse University?

(A) A group of web designers
(B) An employee at a publishing company
(C) The head of a company
(D) The organizer of a seminar series

171. Why should Ms. Martinez contact Ms. Smith?

(A) To reserve a seat for a seminar
(B) To submit some documents
(C) To discuss compensation
(D) To arrange an appointment

▶ ▶ ▶ GO ON TO THE NEXT PAGE

August 9 – The Moon Circus is making its first appearance in New York to present *Zora*, a show based on an astounding story of the nature. This latest extravaganza is finally ready for the stage after 2 years of production.

At a press conference held in Philadelphia last week, Mr. Gregory Karminski, the director of *Zora*, described in detail how the show came to be. —[1]—. The show is inspired by Julia Simms' famous work of fiction, *Jungle Tales*, taking on the majestic and wild characteristics of the jungle and its inhabitants.

—[2]—. Mr. Karminski emphasized portraying the colors of nature on the stage that *Jungle Tales* illustrates in words. He paid close attention to the details of the stage designs, costumes, and props to make them look as realistic as possible. He collaborated with Aria Fernandez, a choreographer who created routines for *the Seattle Horizon*, in creating of the choreography that makes the audience feel as if they are in the actual jungle. —[3]—. These efforts contributed to the creation of a masterpiece, a circus that is beyond imaginable.

—[4]—.

Zora's premiere at Loren's Theater will be shown on September 3. The *Zora* National Tour will be visiting Boston and Las Vegas in the future. Do not miss the chance to see the most stunning show of all time, *Zora*, by the Moon Circus.

172. What is the main purpose of the article?

(A) To advertise a movie based on a novel
(B) To introduce a debuting director
(C) To share information about a show
(D) To describe an event featuring animals from the jungle

173. What is NOT indicated about Mr. Karminski?

(A) He talked to a group of reporters last week.
(B) He visited the jungle to prepare for his show.
(C) He worked with Aria Fernandez.
(D) He worked on *Zora* for two years.

174. Where is Loren's Theater located?

(A) In New York
(B) In Philadelphia
(C) In Las Vegas
(D) In Boston

175. In which of the positions marked [1], [2], [3], and [4] does the following sentence best fit?

"The director also worked closely with an award-winning scriptwriter Louis Bell in the making of *Zora*'s script."

(A) [1]
(B) [2]
(C) [3]
(D) [4]

Valley Fitness Center
~ Celebrating our first anniversary ~

"We needed just a year to become
the top personal training provider in the region."

Personal Training Room 201 Availability for December 12 – 16

	MONDAY	TUESDAY	WEDNESDAY	THURSDAY	FRIDAY
9 A.M. – 12 P.M.	Daniel Andrews	Robert Stone	Robert Stone	Alexander Nielson	Allan Grayson
1 P.M. – 4 P.M.	Sylvia Pereira	Allan Grayson	Robert Stone	Alexander Nielson	Sylvia Pereira
4 P.M. – 6 P.M.	Daniel Andrews	Allan Grayson	Daniel Andrews	Victoria Burke	Victoria Burke

This week, Mr. Robert Stone will fill in for Ms. Ashley Snider, who is recovering from a minor injury, and provide personal training for her clients. On Saturdays, all the personal training rooms are reserved for clients to make up for their missed sessions.

To:	Linda Cronin <lcronin@cuzmail.com>
From:	Carl Johnson <cjohnson@valleyfitness.com>
Date:	December 10
Subject:	Your personal training

Dear Ms. Cronin,

We are sorry to inform you that Valley Fitness Center will be closed on Monday and Tuesday of this week due to the unexpected heavy snowfall Sacramento experienced. As a result, your Monday morning personal training originally scheduled to be held in Room 201 had to be canceled. Please call the center at your earliest convenience to discuss a convenient day for you to come to our center for training.

Our records also indicate that your annual membership will expire on December 20. Renew your membership before December 15 to receive a 15% discount on the membership and a special gift. Go to our website to see more than 20 gifts that you can choose from.

Carl Johnson
Valley Fitness Center

176. What is indicated about Valley Fitness Center?

(A) It is a fast-growing business.
(B) It invites makeup artists on Saturdays.
(C) It hired Mr. Stone recently.
(D) It plans to open another location.

177. What is a purpose of the e-mail?

(A) To warn about the harsh weather
(B) To respond to a request
(C) To confirm the shutdown of a business
(D) To announce a schedule change

178. Who did Ms. Cronin intend to receive personal training from?

(A) Alexander Neilson
(B) Allan Grayson
(C) Daniel Andrews
(D) Sylvia Pereira

179. What is indicated about Ms. Cronin?

(A) She lives in Sacramento.
(B) She will renew her membership on Saturday.
(C) She has been a member of Valley Fitness Center for about a year.
(D) She is a personal trainer at Valley Fitness Center.

180. Why should Ms. Cronin visit the website?

(A) To reschedule an appointment
(B) To check out a list
(C) To renew a membership
(D) To receive a discount

▶ ▶ ▶GO ON TO THE NEXT PAGE

Auckara

Auckara is a Pottsville-based convention center that provides venues for both businesses in and residents of Pottsville and Kirington. Our venue experts will not stop until you are completely satisfied.

Featured Venues

Barbara Hall	Catalina Garden
This main hall in the Burton Building is the perfect venue for both business and personal events. Snack bar included. Can accommodate up to 200 people.	A beautiful garden for outside events such as weddings and receptions. Venue availability dependent on weather conditions. Catering service available at an extra charge.
Disquito Hall	**Professionals Room**
This conference hall is equipped with a projector, round tables for groups of 6, and comfortable chairs. Suitable for presentations and seminars with about 40 people.	A classroom-type room ideal for seminars, presentations, and lectures. A whiteboard, a microphone, a laser pointer, a projector, and other necessary items are included. Accommodates about 50 people.

All venues featured on this page are equipped with free wireless Internet. For specific details, the price of each venue, and more information about Auckara, please visit our website at www.auckara.com. Please send an e-mail to our venue manager, Katherine Washington, at k.washington@auckara.com to make a reservation.

To:	Katherine Washington <k.washington@auckara.com>
From:	Rose Guarin <rguarin@voepublishing.com>
Date:	June 10
Subject:	Venue

Dear Ms. Washington,

I am planning to hold a seminar on public relations in July. A colleague of mine, Michael Greenmier, from the Event Planning Department referred me to Auckara after holding a banquet in the Barbara Hall in April. He said the place was very well prepared and its price is reasonable. I am looking for a venue for about 35 people. As the seminar will include discussion sessions, a place where participants can break into smaller groups is needed.

If there is a suitable venue for my needs, please reply to this e-mail with your recommendation. I would like to talk to you over the phone to discuss further details and prices. In addition, as our department will be holding the seminar biannually, I want to know whether I can receive a discount. Thank you in advance for your assistance.

Sincerely,

Rose Guarin

181. What is mentioned about Auckara?

(A) It requires a deposit when reserving a venue.

(B) It may be closed depending on the weather conditions.

(C) It sells equipment for business meetings.

(D) It has venues for various events.

182. According to the advertisement, what is available at all featured venues?

(A) Refreshments

(B) A projector

(C) Tables and chairs

(D) Internet access

183. What is mentioned about Mr. Greenmier?

(A) He works for Auckara.

(B) He will send an e-mail to Ms. Guarin.

(C) He visited the Burton Building in April.

(D) He is knowledgeable about public relations.

184. Which venue would Ms. Washington most likely recommend to Ms. Guarin?

(A) Barbara Hall

(B) Disquito Hall

(C) Catalina Garden

(D) Professionals Room

185. What does Ms. Guarin ask about in the e-mail?

(A) Her eligibility for a discount

(B) The catering service fee

(C) The dates of a seminar series

(D) The size of a venue

▶ ▶ ▶ GO ON TO THE NEXT PAGE

3rd Homemade Cuisine Contest

Food Empire Magazine is inviting amateur cooks to participate in our 3rd annual Homemade Cuisine Contest. We are looking for dishes in the following four categories:

Categories	Judges
Chinese	Donald Liu, owner of the restaurant Red Dragon and author of *Finest Ingredients, Finest Dishes*
French	Corinne Desilets, head chef at the Grand Palace Hotel and author of *The Most Important Factor in Life: Food*
Italian	Mario Panicucci, TV show *Gourmet Spot*'s food critic and author of *The Secret Recipes*
Mexican	Alicia Rodriguez, award-winning food stylist and author of *How to Take the Best Snapshot of Dishes*

The first round of selections will be based on photographs and recipes submitted by the participants. Submit your entries on our website by July 5. On July 20, 15 candidates in each category will be announced. They will be invited to Food Empire's convention center to show off their cooking skills and cuisines in front of the judges on July 30. Two winners in each category will be announced on August 10. All winners will be featured in our September issue with pictures of their kitchens and dishes taken by our professional photographers. First-place winners will be given $2,500 as a prize, and second-place winners will receive a free subscription to our magazine for a whole year.

---

http://www.foodempire.com/contest_submission

Homemade Cuisine Contest
Online Submission Form

Name: Helen McDaniels
E-mail Address: hmcdaniels@riomail.com
Phone Number: 843-555-5265
Address: 35 Khale Street, Roswell, SC 29455

Brief Description of Your Dish:

Classic cream pasta with mushrooms and bacon and home-baked cheese pizza. Affogato with vanilla ice cream as a dessert included as well.

 If I am chosen as a winner of the contest, I approve of *Food Empire Magazine* publishing photographs of my dishes and kitchen.

Please Attach Photos and Recipe of Your Dishes:

📄 Pasta_McDaniels.jpg	📄 Affogato_McDaniels.jpg
📄 Pizza_McDaniels.jpg	📄 Recipes_McDaniels.doc

Homemade Cuisine Contest
Winners Announcement

It is finally time for us to announce the winners of the 3rd Homemade Cuisine Contest!

Chinese	1st Place: Justin Harnois	2nd Place: Robert Wilson
Italian	1st Place: Kimberly Smith	2nd Place: Helen McDaniels
French	1st Place: Brian Lopez	2nd Place: Tyson Sullivan
Mexican	1st Place: Michelle Mason	2nd Place: Joseph Tang

Congratulations to the winners! To see the pictures and recipes of the dishes of the winners,
Click Here.

186. What do the judges have in common?

(A) They have all won awards for cooking.
(B) They went to the same cooking school.
(C) They have each judged the contest three times.
(D) They each wrote a book about food.

187. When is the due date for the first round of selections?

(A) July 5
(B) July 20
(C) July 30
(D) August 10

188. Who most likely evaluated Ms. McDaniels' entry?

(A) Mr. Liu
(B) Ms. Desilets
(C) Mr. Panicucci
(D) Ms. Rodriguez

189. What does Ms. McDaniels agree to do?

(A) Appear on a TV show
(B) Allow Food Empire to check if she is an amateur cook
(C) Photograph the kitchens of the contest winners
(D) Let Food Empire's employees visit her kitchen

190. What is indicated about Ms. Mason?

(A) She will receive a free magazine subscription.
(B) She will be given a monetary award.
(C) She works for *Food Empire Magazine*.
(D) She is a professional Mexican food chef.

▶ ▶ ▶GO ON TO THE NEXT PAGE

Questions 191-195 refer to the following e-mails.

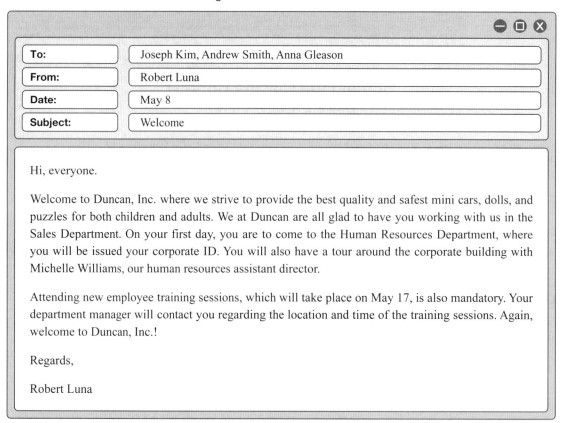

To: Joseph Kim, Andrew Smith, Anna Gleason
From: Robert Luna
Date: May 8
Subject: Welcome

Hi, everyone.

Welcome to Duncan, Inc. where we strive to provide the best quality and safest mini cars, dolls, and puzzles for both children and adults. We at Duncan are all glad to have you working with us in the Sales Department. On your first day, you are to come to the Human Resources Department, where you will be issued your corporate ID. You will also have a tour around the corporate building with Michelle Williams, our human resources assistant director.

Attending new employee training sessions, which will take place on May 17, is also mandatory. Your department manager will contact you regarding the location and time of the training sessions. Again, welcome to Duncan, Inc.!

Regards,

Robert Luna

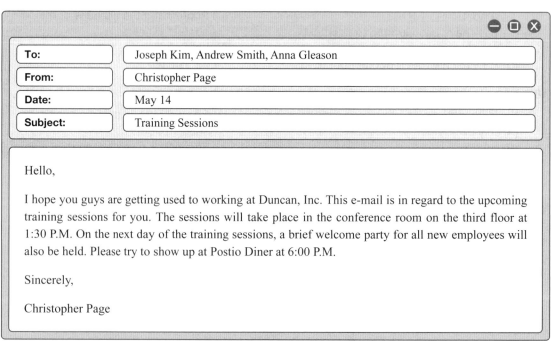

To: Joseph Kim, Andrew Smith, Anna Gleason
From: Christopher Page
Date: May 14
Subject: Training Sessions

Hello,

I hope you guys are getting used to working at Duncan, Inc. This e-mail is in regard to the upcoming training sessions for you. The sessions will take place in the conference room on the third floor at 1:30 P.M. On the next day of the training sessions, a brief welcome party for all new employees will also be held. Please try to show up at Postio Diner at 6:00 P.M.

Sincerely,

Christopher Page

To:	Christopher Page
From:	Laura Morgan
Date:	May 21
Subject:	Your business proposal

Dear Mr. Page,

Thank you for choosing Postio Diner for your company's recent party for your new employees. I hope everyone had a good time at my establishment. As we discussed at the party, we at Postio will be happy to provide food at your annual celebration to take place in June at your company's conference room. Please pay a visit again to talk about the terms and conditions of the contract.

Thank you,

Laura Morgan

191. What is NOT suggested about Duncan, Inc.?

(A) It provides educational courses for its employees.
(B) It recently hired a group of employees.
(C) It sells playthings for children.
(D) It covers employees' tour expenses.

192. In the first e-mail, the word "issued" in paragraph 1, line 4, is closest in meaning to

(A) printed
(B) charged
(C) given
(D) published

193. Who most likely is Mr. Page?

(A) A Sales Department manager
(B) An instructor at a training session
(C) A business owner
(D) A human resources director

194. When did Ms. Morgan and Mr. Page probably meet?

(A) On May 14
(B) On May 17
(C) On May 18
(D) On May 21

195. What does Ms. Morgan ask Mr. Page to do?

(A) Provide catering service
(B) Send an e-mail
(C) Pay for a recent event
(D) Come to her business

Booktree.com is an online bookstore where you can find both new and second-hand books at the most reasonable prices. In business for more than 20 years, Booktree.com is becoming increasingly popular with booklovers and was selected as the Bookstore of the Year by *Trend Today Magazine* last year.

As a summer special promotional event, we are currently giving back 20% of what you spent on your book purchase in Booktree points. This is 15% more than the 5% you usually get. Booktree points are our rewards points that you can use in the future for more books. This offer applies only to your first purchase and is valid until August 30.

Request expedited shipping for only $3.00 and receive your shipment within just 2 days of order. This service is available for domestic customers only.

Booktree.com
Always the best books at the best prices

Order Number:	FS094810	Order Date:	August 28
Booktree Account:	jbrown09	Shipping Date:	September 2
Customer Name:	Joseph Brown		
Address:	425 Cambridge Drive Phoenix, AZ 85040		

Order Details

Book Title	Author	Item Number	Price
The Art of Designing Software	Leonard Castro	D148501	$27.50
Computer Programming Patterns	Frank Mosley	R720958	$16.75
Programming Fundamentals	Howard Jackson	R012290	$31.10
Productive Computing	Lucy Rodriguez	C890271	$28.80
		Subtotal:	**$104.15**
		Shipping and Handling:	-
		Tax (8%):	**$8.33**
		Total:	**$112.48**

Booktree Points Provided on this Transaction:
22.50 Points (Promotional – 20%)

*Return or refund request must be made within 10 days of purchase. Submit an online request or send an e-mail to returnrequest@booktree.com. Refer to our website for detailed return and refund policy.

To:	Joseph Brown <jbrown@bkmail.com>
From:	Customer Service <customerservice@booktree.com>
Date:	September 5
Subject:	re: My Recent Order

Dear Mr. Brown,

We are sorry to hear that you received a wrong book, *Elements of Computer Programming*, written by Dr. Mosley, this morning. I believe there happened to be a mistake in packing your shipment as the author and the price of the book are the same as the one you actually ordered. We will expedite the correct book to your address. Please send the title you received to 55 Ilford Avenue, Houston, TX 73550 at your earliest convenience. In addition, to apologize for our mistake, we have provided you with a $10 discount coupon; log into your account on our website to claim it.

Sincerely,

Booktree.com Customer Service

196. What is suggested about Booktree.com?

(A) It sells used books online.
(B) It has received several awards.
(C) It ships books to domestic customers only.
(D) It launched a magazine last year.

197. What is probably true about Mr. Brown?

(A) He manufactures computers.
(B) He subscribes to *Trend Today Magazine*.
(C) He requested expedited shipping.
(D) He placed an order at Booktree.com for the first time.

198. When was the order sent to Mr. Brown?

(A) On August 28
(B) On August 30
(C) On September 2
(D) On September 5

199. In the e-mail, the word "claim" in paragraph 1, line 7, is closest in meaning to

(A) insist
(B) complain
(C) spend
(D) take

200. How much is *Elements of Computer Programming*?

(A) $16.75
(B) $27.50
(C) $28.80
(D) $31.10

STOP! This is the end of the test. If you finish before time is called,
you may go back to Parts 5, 6, and 7 and check your work.

▶ ▶ ▶GO ON TO THE NEXT PAGE

Actual Test

MP3 音檔

解析

最佳解答時間 120 分鐘

120 min

開始時間：＿＿＿點 ＿＿＿分

結束時間：＿＿＿點 ＿＿＿分

▲盡量不要在作答中途停下來。

▲請於答案卡上畫記作答。

目標正確題數：＿＿＿／**200 題**　實際正確題數：＿＿＿／**200 題**

題數與分數對照，請參考 P449 分數換算表。

LISTENING TEST

In the Listening test, you will be asked to demonstrate how well you understand spoken English. The entire Listening test will last approximately 45 minutes. There are four parts, and directions are given for each part. You must mark your answers on the separate answer sheet. Do not write your answers in the test book.

PART 1

Directions: For each question in this part, you will hear four statements about a picture in your test book. When you hear the statements, you must select the one statement that best describes what you see in the picture. Then find the number of the question on your answer sheet and mark your answer. The statements will not be printed in your test book and will be spoken only one time.

Statement (B), "They are sitting at a table." is the best description of the picture. So you should select answer (B) and mark it on your answer sheet.

1.

2.

▶ ▶ ▶ GO ON TO THE NEXT PAGE

3.

4.

5.

6.

▶ ▶ ▶ GO ON TO THE NEXT PAGE

Directions: You will hear a question or statement and three responses spoken in English. They will not be printed in your test book and will be spoken only one time. Select the best response to the question or statement and mark the letter (A), (B), or (C) on your answer sheet.

7. Mark your answer on your answer sheet.

8. Mark your answer on your answer sheet.

9. Mark your answer on your answer sheet.

10. Mark your answer on your answer sheet.

11. Mark your answer on your answer sheet.

12. Mark your answer on your answer sheet.

13. Mark your answer on your answer sheet.

14. Mark your answer on your answer sheet.

15. Mark your answer on your answer sheet.

16. Mark your answer on your answer sheet.

17. Mark your answer on your answer sheet.

18. Mark your answer on your answer sheet.

19. Mark your answer on your answer sheet.

20. Mark your answer on your answer sheet.

21. Mark your answer on your answer sheet.

22. Mark your answer on your answer sheet.

23. Mark your answer on your answer sheet.

24. Mark your answer on your answer sheet.

25. Mark your answer on your answer sheet.

26. Mark your answer on your answer sheet.

27. Mark your answer on your answer sheet.

28. Mark your answer on your answer sheet.

29. Mark your answer on your answer sheet.

30. Mark your answer on your answer sheet.

31. Mark your answer on your answer sheet.

PART 3

Directions: You will hear some conversations between two or three people. You will be asked to answer three questions about what the speakers say in each conversation. Select the best response to each question and mark the letter (A), (B), (C), or (D) on your answer sheet. The conversations will not be printed in your test book and will be spoken only one time.

32. Where do the speakers work?

    (A) At a retail shop
    (B) At a textile manufacturer
    (C) At a drugstore
    (D) At a supermarket

33. What will happen this weekend?

    (A) A sale will be held.
    (B) Employees will work overtime.
    (C) New equipment will be installed.
    (D) A training program will take place.

34. What does the woman say she has been preparing?

    (A) A work schedule
    (B) A store directory
    (C) An inventory
    (D) An advertisement

35. Who most likely is the man?

    (A) A customer service representative
    (B) An electric engineer
    (C) A sales consultant
    (D) A marketing expert

36. Why is the woman frustrated?

    (A) She does not have her receipt.
    (B) She didn't get the computer fixed.
    (C) She cannot get her money back.
    (D) She had to wait a long time.

37. What is the woman asked to provide?

    (A) An account number
    (B) An item number
    (C) A coupon code
    (D) A street address

38. Who most likely is the woman?

    (A) A bus driver
    (B) A railroad engineer
    (C) A rental car agent
    (D) A bus station employee

39. What problem does the woman mention?

    (A) A phone number is incorrect.
    (B) A meeting was canceled.
    (C) A bus is delayed.
    (D) An Internet connection is not available.

40. What will Steve do next?

    (A) Contact a customer
    (B) Cancel a meeting
    (C) Pay for some tickets
    (D) Ask for a refund on tickets

41. What does the woman ask the man about?

    (A) An auto repair shop
    (B) An upcoming seminar
    (C) Bike parking
    (D) A rental car reservation

42. What problem does the woman have?

    (A) She misplaced her car keys.
    (B) Her car is in the shop.
    (C) Her computer is not working.
    (D) She is late for work again.

43. What does the man suggest the woman do?

    (A) Take some time off work
    (B) Move closer to work
    (C) Speak with a coworker
    (D) Print some files

▶ ▶ ▶GO ON TO THE NEXT PAGE

44. What does the woman congratulate the man for?

   (A) Being promoted
   (B) Getting a transfer
   (C) Receiving a bonus
   (D) Winning an award

45. What is the man looking forward to doing?

   (A) Moving to his hometown
   (B) Signing a new contract
   (C) Working as a manager
   (D) Greeting employees from abroad

46. Why does the man say, "I heard about a new Indian restaurant downtown"?

   (A) To accept an invitation
   (B) To indicate that there is heavy traffic downtown
   (C) To request a change of menu
   (D) To express concern about the cost

---

47. Why are the speakers meeting?

   (A) To have a job interview
   (B) To view a demonstration
   (C) To conduct an experiment
   (D) To discuss a new software program

48. What most likely is the man's profession?

   (A) Chemical engineer
   (B) Software developer
   (C) Automobile designer
   (D) Sales representative

49. What does the man say he likes about the company?

   (A) It pays high salaries to its workers.
   (B) It offers opportunities for personal growth.
   (C) It has offices in many foreign countries.
   (D) It provides gym memberships to its employees.

50. Where does the woman most likely work?

   (A) At a university
   (B) At a medical clinic
   (C) At a shopping center
   (D) At a drugstore

51. What new policy does the woman tell the man about?

   (A) He needs to have a referral.
   (B) He must pay for a cancelation.
   (C) He needs to register in advance.
   (D) He does not need an appointment.

52. What does the man say he will do?

   (A) Fill out a medical form
   (B) Reschedule an appointment for tomorrow
   (C) Arrive after work
   (D) Visit in the morning

---

53. What are the speakers mainly discussing?

   (A) A rescheduled event
   (B) A proposal for expansion
   (C) The impact of a construction project
   (D) Employment opportunities

54. What does the woman mean when she says, "We just got four new interns"?

   (A) There is not enough space.
   (B) She needs additional office equipment.
   (C) They need an orientation session.
   (D) Her department is over its budget.

55. What does the woman offer to do?

   (A) Call Facilities
   (B) Look at the budget report
   (C) Speak with a client
   (D) Address a customer complaint

56. What does the man want to do?

(A) Install an updated version of software
(B) Hire some more employees
(C) Arrange a training session
(D) Schedule a departmental meeting

57. What does the woman suggest doing?

(A) Taking a look at online reviews
(B) Upgrading computers
(C) Taking a client out to lunch
(D) Providing food

58. What will the man most likely do next?

(A) Find some missing supplies
(B) Hire a catering service
(C) Look at a budget
(D) Make a telephone call

---

59. What are the speakers mainly discussing?

(A) A hiring process
(B) A durable device
(C) A timesheet system
(D) A digital door lock

60. What will be provided to employees this afternoon?

(A) A revised work schedule
(B) A new security code
(C) An electronic badge
(D) A laptop computer

61. What does the woman indicate about the XLS 500?

(A) It is easy for employees to use.
(B) It is costly to be installed companywide.
(C) It comes with a two-year warranty.
(D) Its installation work takes long.

Team Safety Helmet Color	
Welders	Yellow
Plumbers	Blue
Bricklayers	Orange
Roofers	White

62. What type of building are the speakers discussing?

(A) A sports stadium
(B) A factory
(C) A parking garage
(D) A shopping center

63. Look at the graphic. Which team of workers will begin in one week?

(A) Welders
(B) Plumbers
(C) Roofers
(D) Bricklayers

64. What will the woman do next?

(A) Put an advertisement online
(B) Visit a project site
(C) Check a construction timeline
(D) Put in an order

▶ ▶ ▶GO ON TO THE NEXT PAGE

Jackson's Ice Cream Shop

Today's Special Prices

Scoop	$2.00
Pint	$3.50
Quart	$5.00
Gallon	$9.00

65. Who is the woman?

(A) A restaurant owner
(B) A delivery person
(C) A school teacher
(D) A company manager

66. Look at the graphic. How much will the woman pay for her order?

(A) $2.00
(B) $3.50
(C) $5.00
(D) $9.00

67. What will the woman do next?

(A) Pay a bill for ice cream
(B) Sample some of strawberry ice cream
(C) Retrieve her purse from her car
(D) Get her car to the mechanic

Credit Card Statement

Date	Description	Amount
February 5	Sylvan Clothes	$73.45
February 9	Bus Terminal	$15.00
February 11	Jerry's Grill	$42.00
February 12	Westside Groceries	$89.98

68. What information is the woman asked to provide?

(A) Her name
(B) Her e-mail address
(C) Her phone number
(D) Her home address

69. Look at the graphic. Which amount does the woman say is not incorrect?

(A) $73.45
(B) $15.00
(C) $42.00
(D) $89.98

70. What does the man tell the woman to do?

(A) Visit the office in person
(B) Provide her account number
(C) Complete paperwork
(D) Speak with his manager

PART 4

Directions: You will hear some short talks given by a single speaker. You will be asked to answer three questions about what the speaker says in each short talk. Select the best response to each question and mark the letter (A), (B), (C), or (D) on your answer sheet. The talks will not be printed in your test book and will be spoken only one time.

71. Where does the announcement take place?

(A) At a movie theater
(B) At a museum
(C) At a television station
(D) At a library

72. What new service does the speaker say is provided?

(A) Online customer support
(B) Complimentary online tutorials
(C) E-book downloading service
(D) Movie streaming

73. How can the listeners get further information?

(A) By reading a brochure
(B) By subscribing to a newsletter
(C) By consulting a librarian
(D) By visiting a web page

74. What is the topic of the workshop?

(A) Hiring new employees
(B) Writing résumés
(C) Marketing goods
(D) Managing workers

75. How will the workshop help the listeners?

(A) It will attract more customers.
(B) It will let them retain clients.
(C) It will let them save money.
(D) It will improve performance.

76. What does the speaker ask the listeners to do?

(A) Sign a form
(B) Watch an informational video
(C) Set up a slide projector
(D) Introduce themselves

77. Where do the listeners work?

(A) At a hotel
(B) At a supermarket
(C) At a restaurant
(D) At a department store

78. What does the speaker imply when she says, "The tourists are flocking to this area"?

(A) More employees will be hired.
(B) Parking will be hard to find.
(C) A deadline is not likely to be met.
(D) A business will become busier.

79. What does the speaker remind the listeners to do?

(A) Pick up their new uniforms
(B) Arrive at work on time
(C) Update a calendar
(D) Wear their nametags

80. What is the speaker calling about?

(A) An equipment order
(B) A mobile application
(C) A job opening
(D) A release of a new mobile phone

81. Why is the listener suitable for a new project?

(A) He is familiar with a city.
(B) He has good leadership skills.
(C) He is a computer programmer.
(D) He is well organized.

82. What does the speaker want to do?

(A) Place an advertisement
(B) Talk about employment opportunities
(C) Consult with an expert
(D) Arrange a meeting

▶ ▶ ▶GO ON TO THE NEXT PAGE

83. What did the speaker recently do?

(A) She started a company.
(B) She requested a job interview.
(C) She wrote a book.
(D) She gave a presentation.

84. What does the speaker imply when she says, "I've worked as a recruiting manager at a few large companies for more than two decades"?

(A) People can trust her advice.
(B) She has an excellent job.
(C) She withdrew her résumé.
(D) She does not work with small companies.

85. What can the listeners receive by checking out a website?

(A) A discount on some course material
(B) A trial version of software
(C) An autographed book
(D) A free consultation

---

86. Who is the speaker?

(A) A singer
(B) An actress
(C) A radio host
(D) A sports reporter

87. What does the speaker say inspired her to choose her career?

(A) Talking with a famous singer
(B) Winning a prize
(C) Listening to an interview
(D) Traveling around the country

88. What will the speaker do next?

(A) Announce some news
(B) Interview some famous people
(C) Answer a question
(D) Play a song

89. What event is being planned?

(A) A charity auction
(B) A sporting event
(C) A fundraiser
(D) A musical concert

90. According to the speaker, what will volunteers be doing for the event?

(A) Serving food to the guests
(B) Putting flower arrangements on each table
(C) Greeting guests at the entrance
(D) Setting up a room

91. What does the speaker ask the listeners for?

(A) A signed contract
(B) A suggestion for a band
(C) A credit card number
(D) A recommendation for a caterer

---

92. Where does the talk take place?

(A) At a conference
(B) At a training session
(C) At an orientation event
(D) At a job fair

93. Why does the speaker say, "Your employees could turn out to be effective product testers"?

(A) To advise selling more products
(B) To suggest an alternative approach
(C) To praise some employees
(D) To recommend hiring more workers

94. What does the speaker give the listeners?

(A) A business card
(B) A website address
(C) A brochure
(D) A picture

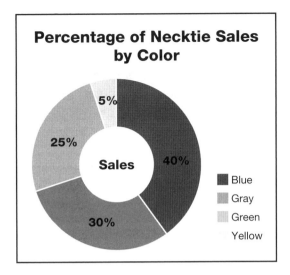

Percentage of Necktie Sales by Color

Sales

- 5%
- 25%
- 40%
- 30%

Legend:
- Blue
- Gray
- Green
- Yellow

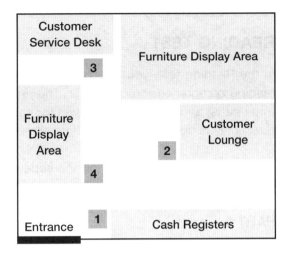

Customer Service Desk — 3

Furniture Display Area

Furniture Display Area — 4

Customer Lounge — 2

Entrance — 1 — Cash Registers

95. Who most likely are the listeners?

(A) Marketers
(B) Designers
(C) Salespeople
(D) Programmers

96. Which aspect of a new product will the team discuss in small groups?

(A) Its size
(B) Its color
(C) Its style
(D) Its price

97. Look at the graphic. What will the color of the new product be?

(A) Gray
(B) Green
(C) Yellow
(D) Blue

98. What is the speaker mainly discussing?

(A) A training session
(B) A yearly clearance sale
(C) A sales conference
(D) A customer appreciation day

99. What are the listeners advised to do when people arrive?

(A) Give them shopping carts
(B) Assist them in finding items
(C) Distribute promotional flyers
(D) Inform them about refreshments

100. Look at the graphic. Where will the additional signs be located?

(A) Location 1
(B) Location 2
(C) Location 3
(D) Location 4

This is the end of the Listening test. Turn to Part 5 in your test book.

▶ ▶ ▶ GO ON TO THE NEXT PAGE

READING TEST

In the Reading test, you will read a variety of texts and answer several different types of reading comprehension questions. The entire Reading test will last 75 minutes. There are three parts, and directions are given for each part. You are encouraged to answer as many questions as possible within the time allowed.

You must mark your answer on the separate answer sheet. Do not write your answers in your test book.

PART 5

Directions: A word or phrase is missing in each of the sentences below. Four answer choices are given below each sentence. Select the best answer to complete the sentence. Then mark the letter (A), (B), (C), or (D) on your answer sheet.

101. The catering service company offers various Italian dishes ------- desserts for special occasions such as anniversary celebrations and business banquets.

(A) and
(B) so
(C) for
(D) nor

102. Consumers need to check whether a product ------- purchase through foreign direct shopping has been recalled.

(A) they
(B) them
(C) their
(D) themselves

103. If you have difficulty ------- a particular book, please come to the circulation desk and ask one of our librarians for assistance.

(A) location
(B) to locate
(C) locating
(D) located

104. Our restaurant ------- the right to refuse service to any patrons if they disturb the enjoyment of other patrons.

(A) guarantees
(B) violates
(C) reserves
(D) grants

105. The personnel manager mentioned to me that the board was ------- somebody to take charge of the new manufacturing plant.

(A) looking
(B) seeking
(C) searching
(D) consulting

106. ------- the lack of research and development for new products, Coco Sports couldn't remain the leading company in the sports equipment market.

(A) Neither
(B) Despite
(C) Due to
(D) Along with

107. Any errors in the articles should be reported to the editing department ------- so corrections can be made before the newspaper is published.

(A) prompt
(B) promptly
(C) prompted
(D) prompting

108. Some local businesspeople were ------- in getting a law passed that promoted fair competition for the protection of consumers.

(A) instruct
(B) instructor
(C) instrument
(D) instrumental

109. The city will provide a variety of complimentary drinks to ------- who participates in the film festival from May 14-19.

(A) anyone
(B) some
(C) those
(D) many

110. Applicants who passed the final interview for the floor manager position ------- by the human resources director later next week.

(A) have been contacted
(B) was contacted
(C) will contact
(D) will be contacted

111. BK Electronics announced its new plan yesterday to ------- their semiconductor manufacturing facilities in Alabama.

(A) extend
(B) accomplish
(C) enlarge
(D) anticipate

112. It is essential that we try harder to improve customer satisfaction levels and keep our company more -------.

(A) competitive
(B) competitively
(C) compete
(D) competition

113. Several investment companies saw the ------- for return at a time of slowing economic growth, and so they launched financial products tailored to the emerging markets.

(A) mark
(B) potential
(C) proposal
(D) allowance

114. Please note that payment for this shipment is due within 21 days of ------- of this invoice.

(A) receiving
(B) receive
(C) receipt
(D) receiver

115. ------- arrival at the airport, every passenger should go through customs, and it'll take about twenty five minutes or so.

(A) For
(B) Upon
(C) Owing to
(D) Despite

116. All the participants in the upcoming forum may stay at the Bella Hotel or the Grand Hotel, ------- they find more pleasant and convenient.

(A) that
(B) whoever
(C) whichever
(D) everyone

117. In order to ------- expenses incurred, it is necessary that original receipts or invoices be submitted with expense claims.

(A) schedule
(B) verify
(C) discount
(D) complicate

118. Hit by the surging costs of raw materials, food -------, steel, and textile industries are pinpointed to have a pretty gloomy economic outlook.

(A) proceed
(B) process
(C) processing
(D) procedure

▶ ▶ ▶GO ON TO THE NEXT PAGE

119. Mr. Stanford ------- the reins of his father's company by stepping down as CEO two years ago.

(A) reported
(B) inaugurated
(C) assumed
(D) relinquished

120. Prices are ------- to change based upon your choice of travel dates, number of travelers, departure city, and your choice of flight, hotels or other items.

(A) public
(B) subject
(C) imperative
(D) willing

121. Anything done to change some major rivers will only destroy the environment and ecosystem ------- repair.

(A) in
(B) toward
(C) beyond
(D) since

122. The assessment report states ------- that improvement to our distribution system has resulted in savings of more than millions of dollars for the past two years.

(A) explicitly
(B) randomly
(C) intangibly
(D) cooperatively

123. Success in this consumer-electronics industry depends on technological capability to introduce new products to the market in a ------- manner.

(A) time
(B) timer
(C) timely
(D) timing

124. ------- the current state of the economy, most customers cannot afford to buy our expensive new products.

(A) Provided
(B) Given
(C) Regarding
(D) Now that

125. Ace Medical has developed several low-cost imaging devices, two of ------- are considered for this year's Brandon Prize for Technology.

(A) them
(B) that
(C) whose
(D) which

126. If Jet Red Airlines ------- outsourcing some reservations jobs overseas, about 1,000 new jobs will be created in California this year.

(A) had started
(B) starting
(C) will start
(D) starts

127. ------- one of us must assume personal responsibility, not only for ourselves and our families, but for our neighbors and our society.

(A) Entire
(B) Every
(C) Total
(D) Complete

128. The company's personnel director will stop accepting applications ------- the administrative position has been filled.

(A) while
(B) once
(C) despite
(D) whereas

129. The new governor ------- to widen the four main highways to accommodate increasing freight shipments and reduce travel delays.

(A) insisted
(B) suggested
(C) supported
(D) proposed

130. ------- you need any help with the presentation or further assistance, please do not hesitate to contact us.

(A) In order
(B) Although
(C) Should
(D) So that

PART 6

Directions: Read the texts that follow. A word or phrase, or sentence is missing in parts of each text. Four answer choices for each question are given below the text. Select the best answer to complete the text. Then mark the letter (A), (B), (C), or (D) on your answer sheet.

Questions 131-134 refer to the following article.

SAN FRANCISCO DAILY

Ace Supermarket Is Expanding Into South America

Peter Smith

San Francisco - March 3) Ace Supermarket, the world's largest supermarket chain based

in the U.S., is planning to get a ------- in the markets in South America. The headquarters
                                    131.

of Ace Supermarket announced yesterday that five branch locations will come to Chile

and Brazil, with the first two supermarkets scheduled to open on March 30 in Chile. -------.
                                                                                      132.

Basically, Ace Supermarket implements a unique ------- of management to open small
                                              133.

supermarkets and provide its house brand products and local agriculture produces with

affordable prices. "We are ------- to open our supermarkets in South America and
                          134.

introduce customers to our high quality products at lower costs," said the spokesperson

of Ace Supermarket Benjamin Wilson.

131. (A) share
(B) foothold
(C) permission
(D) settlement

132. (A) The other three ones will open in Brazil by the end of next month.
(B) About one-fifth of our supermarkets will have energy efficient lighting this year.
(C) They have competed against traditional grocery chains throughout South America.
(D) Many of the stores are being built in overcrowded cities where land is scarce.

133. (A) event
(B) strategy
(C) regulation
(D) control

134. (A) eligible
(B) necessary
(C) capable
(D) eager

▶ ▶ ▶ GO ON TO THE NEXT PAGE

May 30
Mr. Lewis Burton
184 Cheetham Hill Road
Manchester, UK
M4 1PW

Edinburgh College of Art & Design
74 Lauriston Place
Edinburgh, EH3 9DF
eca@ed.ac.uk
+44 (0)131 651 5800

Dear Mr. Burton,

Thank you for your inquiry regarding evening classes at the Edinburgh College of Art &

Design. I am contacting you with details of our classes, ------- the classes that we run
                                                              135.

every week on Tuesdays or Thursdays, as you requested.

First, there is our Beginner Oil Painting class, which provides instruction on basic

techniques and emphasizes the importance of color. Second, there is our Technical

Drawing class, which is designed for those interested in engineering and architecture.

Unfortunately, these are the only ------- classes that we currently run in the evenings.
                                    136.

-------, we do also offer various online classes for individuals who have particularly
137.

busy schedules. Those who enroll in such courses are supplied with a list of necessary

materials that they should purchase in advance. -------.
                                                138.

Best regards,

Annabel Taylor
Manager of Student Services
Edinburgh College of Art & Design

135. (A) specify
     (B) specific
     (C) specified
     (D) specifically

136. (A) midweek
     (B) weekend
     (C) monthly
     (D) annual

137. (A) Indeed
     (B) Nevertheless
     (C) In spite of
     (D) For example

138. (A) We appreciate your interest in
         employment opportunities at our
         institution.
     (B) Further details for all the above listed
         options are available on our website.
     (C) Your application for enrollment in the
         class is currently being processed.
     (D) Please contact me should you wish to
         withdraw from any of these classes.

To: Scarlett Welsh <sw@cocomail.com>
From: Eleanor Fletcher <ef@sjfc.com>
Subject: Record Store Shows
Date: April 21

Dear Ms. Welsh,

It is my distinct pleasure to inform you about the upcoming shows that Stanley Jordan's management is organizing for ------- fan club members.
139.

Mr. Jordan will play twenty-five concerts in Sound Factory Hall, and these shows will provide an amazing opportunity for fans to joyfully ------- a Stanley Jordan performance in
140.
a small, intimate setting. -------, they will be able to meet with their favorite pop singer
141.
during an autograph session, which will immediately follow his performance. Copies of Stanley Jordan's new record will be available for purchase, and fans can also have these signed during the autograph session.

Tickets will be affordably priced and may be purchased online. The record store concerts will take place between May 10 and May 15, and the exact tour schedule will be posted on www.sjfc.com within the next few days. -------.
142.

Best wishes,

Eleanor Fletcher
Manager of Stanley Jordan Fan Club

139. (A) value
(B) valuing
(C) valuation
(D) valued

140. (A) interest
(B) present
(C) benefit
(D) experience

141. (A) Even though
(B) Afterward
(C) Instead
(D) In advance

142. (A) Thank you for your recent inquiry about Stanley Jordan.
(B) You will receive your free tickets within seven days.
(C) Don't miss this chance to see your beloved artist up close.
(D) The first show will be held at the end of the month.

▶ ▶ ▶ GO ON TO THE NEXT PAGE

Cork is essentially a piece of bark from a cork oak known as Quercus suber. The cork tree grows naturally in a region ------- the western Mediterranean Sea. -------. But, so far, the
143. **144.**
results have not been encouraging. Although there is some historical evidence suggesting that cork was used as a stopper about 2,000 years ago, its use became more ------- with
145.
the introduction of glass bottles in the 17th century. In recent years, other alternatives such as plastic stoppers ------- as closures for wine bottles. However, cork still remains
146.
the principal closure of choice for premium wines.

143. (A) locating
(B) exploring
(C) bordering
(D) corresponding

144. (A) Several efforts have been made to grow this species in other parts of the world.
(B) That means there are some trees that are adapted to the Mediterranean climate.
(C) The corking machine should be cleaned and maintained according to the manufacturer's directions.
(D) The region is producing some of the most remarkable grapes and wines in the world.

145. (A) competitive
(B) authentic
(C) prevalent
(D) familiar

146. (A) introduce
(B) are introducing
(C) will be introduced
(D) have been introduced

PART 7

Directions: In this part you will read a selection of texts, such as magazine and newspaper articles, e-mails, and instant messages. Each text or set of texts is followed by several questions. Select the best answer for each question and mark the letter (A), (B), (C), or (D) on your answer sheet.

Questions 147-148 refer to the following information.

East Seattle Laundry
Nicest, Cleanest Launderette in Town!
Open 24 Hours

1. Place your laundry into one of the washing machines.

2. Put laundry detergent into the washing machine. Detergent is available from the vending machine by the front door.

3. Set the washing machine's controls. Generally, hot water is suitable for whites, and cold water for colors.

4. Insert the exact amount of coins required for each machine into the coin slot. Do not open the machine until the washing process is finished.

Call (206) 408-3180 with any problems.

147. What is the purpose of the information?

(A) To inform ways to purchase a washing machine
(B) To explain the procedure of using a facility
(C) To instruct how to request a repair service for equipment
(D) To advertise a laundry service

148. What would a customer have to do if hot water does not come out?

(A) Go to the front desk
(B) Add laundry to the washing machine
(C) Report to an employee on the phone
(D) Insert additional coins

Questions 149-150 refer to the following text message chain.

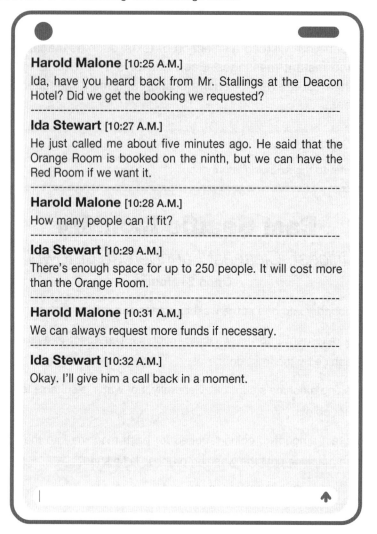

Harold Malone [10:25 A.M.]

Ida, have you heard back from Mr. Stallings at the Deacon Hotel? Did we get the booking we requested?

Ida Stewart [10:27 A.M.]

He just called me about five minutes ago. He said that the Orange Room is booked on the ninth, but we can have the Red Room if we want it.

Harold Malone [10:28 A.M.]

How many people can it fit?

Ida Stewart [10:29 A.M.]

There's enough space for up to 250 people. It will cost more than the Orange Room.

Harold Malone [10:31 A.M.]

We can always request more funds if necessary.

Ida Stewart [10:32 A.M.]

Okay. I'll give him a call back in a moment.

149. What is the text message chain mainly about?

(A) Preparations for an upcoming event
(B) The price to rent a room
(C) The need to book a hotel room
(D) Some changes in the date of an event

150. At 10:31 A.M., what does Mr. Malone most likely mean when he writes, "We can always request more funds if necessary"?

(A) He needs to submit a budget report.
(B) He should talk to his supervisor soon.
(C) He just requested more money for the budget.
(D) He is willing to reserve the Red Room.

THEATRICAL PIZZA

Business hours: 10:00 A.M. – 11:00 P.M.
Open 7 days a week

Small	Medium	Large	Giant
$12.95	$14.95	$18.95	$20.95

All prices are subject to change without notice.
Free delivery on orders of $20 or more.

Pizzas of the Month (Buy One & Get One Free!)	
Vegetarian	Tomatoes, Mushrooms, Red Onions, Green Bell Peppers, Cilantro, Olives
Supreme	Pepperoni, Tomatoes, Mushrooms, Red Onions, Red & Green Bell Peppers, Olives
BBQ Chicken	Special BBQ Sauce, Chicken, Tomatoes, Mushrooms, Onions, Bell Peppers

Visit our website at www.theatricalpizza.com for a complete list of items on the menu.

ADDITIONAL TOPPINGS

Small	Medium	Large	Giant
$1.65	$2.25	$2.85	$3.55

Mushroom, Tomato, Bell Peppers, Cheddar Cheese, Shrimp, Ham, Pepperoni,
Chicken, Roasted Garlic, Onions, Olives, and Many More!

We offer catering services for all types of occasions.
Please call 555-329-0504 for pricing.

ACTUAL TEST 05

151. What ingredient is included in all pizzas of the month?

(A) Cilantro
(B) Tomatoes
(C) Chicken
(D) Olives

152. What information is provided in the advertisement?

(A) The prices of beverages
(B) Rates for catering services
(C) Topping choices
(D) The address of the shop

153. What is NOT indicated about Theatrical Pizza?

(A) It is open on Sundays.
(B) It delivers orders free of charge to some customers.
(C) It has a website.
(D) It recently opened a new branch.

▶ ▶ ▶ GO ON TO THE NEXT PAGE

Nathaniel Cooper Bed

Thank you for purchasing a Nathaniel Cooper bed from Nathaniel Furniture Ltd., the city's best furniture provider. We believe that this bed, which has won awards for its durability, will perfectly satisfy you. Please read the instructions below carefully before you start assembling the bed. —[1]—.

Assembly Instructions

Step 1.   Install the headboard at its desired location.

Step 2.   Attach a side rail to the headboard by matching the red dot on the side rail with the dot on the headboard. —[2]—.

Step 3.   Attach the footboard to the side rails.

Step 4.   Tighten the roll bolts securely to the headboard and the footboard. —[3]—.

Step 5.   Drop in the slats and screw them in by using a screwdriver.

Step 6.   Place the mattress on the frame. —[4]—.

Visit our website to see photographs depicting these steps. If you have any questions regarding our product, please call us at 1-555-932-3333, or send an e-mail to staff@ nathanielbed.com.

154. For whom is this information intended?

(A) Employees at a furniture delivery company
(B) Customer service representatives
(C) Furniture manufacturers
(D) Customers

155. What is indicated about the product?

(A) The bedrails can be used as handles.
(B) Extra items can be used to assemble the bed.
(C) It is designed for young children.
(D) The bed is recognized for its sturdy construction.

156. In which of the positions marked [1], [2], [3], and [4] does the following sentence best fit?

"Repeat the above procedure with the other side rail."

(A) [1]
(B) [2]
(C) [3]
(D) [4]

Questions 157-158 refer to the following receipt.

Caring Hands

24 Franklin Drive
Seaside, OR 97160
(503) 762-0847

April 10, 9:35 A.M.

Item	Qty.	Price	Amount
Pocketbook, *All About First Aid*	1	$2.80	$2.80
Bandage (2ea)	1	$2.00	$2.00
Antiseptic Ointment (25mg)	1	$4.70	$4.70
Painkiller Pills (10 tablets)	1	$4.00	$4.00
Total Item(s)	**4**		
Subtotal			**$13.50**
Frequent-Buyer Discount			**- $2.00**
Balance Due			**$11.50**
Credit Card			**$11.50**
********5621			
Change			**$0.00**

Thank You!

157. What type of business most likely is Caring Hands?

(A) A hospital
(B) A pharmacy
(C) A bookstore
(D) A beauty salon

158. What is indicated about the customer?

(A) The customer works at a clinic.
(B) The customer purchased the items in the afternoon.
(C) The customer paid in cash.
(D) The customer often shops at Caring Hands.

▶ ▶ ▶ GO ON TO THE NEXT PAGE

To: Jake Herald <jherald@chelsea.com>

From: Lilian Mulvey <lmulvey@chelsea.com>

Date: January 23

Subject: Inquiry

Dear Mr. Herald,

On January 2, the copy machine in the Marketing Department broke down. So I submitted a request for a new copy machine to the Purchasing Department on January 8. You told me that it would be handled within a week, but it has now been two weeks since I submitted the proposal, and nothing has been done yet.

Our department is currently using the copy machine in the Human Resources Department. This has caused a serious delay in the preparations for a conference we are holding on January 30.

I hope this problem can be solved shortly. Please let me know if there is anything I can do.

Thanks,

Lilian Mulvey

---

159. What is the problem?

(A) An item has not been replaced.
(B) A conference has been delayed.
(C) Funds have not been provided.
(D) A replacement has not been hired.

160. Where does Mr. Herald work?

(A) In the Marketing Department
(B) In the Human Resources Department
(C) In the Purchasing Department
(D) In the Maintenance Department

161. When was the proposal for a new copy machine submitted?

(A) On January 2
(B) On January 8
(C) On January 23
(D) On January 30

Questions 162-164 refer to the following e-mail.

To:	<jhbuskers@chmail.com>
From:	<tmyers@ggmail.com>
Date:	December 15
Subject:	Congratulations!

Dear members of the Buskers,

I would like to congratulate you on your recent success with the concert at the Cruz Arena. I read on *St. Cruz City Herald* that you are the first musicians to hold a concert there within just three years of your first debut. I was especially impressed when I learned that you have donated a part of the proceeds to the children's hospital.

Both as an owner of a bar and a big fan of yours, I would like to invite you to perform at my bar. The majority of our customers are university students and in their mid-twenties, so I think you will be a good fit for my customers. My bar, Sailboat, is located at 46 Reindeer Dr., St. Cruz City and is open from 8 P.M. to 4 A.M. every day. The time of your performance and your payment are negotiable. Please get back to me if you are interested.

Thanks,

Tessa Myers

162. What is the main purpose of the e-mail?

(A) To address the achievements of a band
(B) To offer a job at a bar
(C) To inform about details of a concert
(D) To confirm a performance schedule

163. Who is Tessa Myers?

(A) A customer at a bar
(B) A band member
(C) A patient
(D) A music fan

164. What is indicated about the Buskers?

(A) It was formed 4 years ago.
(B) It recently recruited a new member.
(C) It was featured in a local publication.
(D) It held a concert at a hospital.

▶ ▶ ▶ GO ON TO THE NEXT PAGE

AMC Steps Forward

By Samantha Provoost, Staff Writer

August 7 — The Brussels-based carmaker, Aqua Motors Corp. (AMC), will begin producing vehicles in China this week as the construction of its manufacturing factory in Beijing is finally completed.

"This is the first step of AMC's strategy to dominate the automotive industry and hold an edge over other competitors in China," explained CEO of AMC, Jean Bergmann. "We had decided to build the new facility to maintain stable sales of our vehicles in the Chinese market and promote future models."

AMC has been gaining popularity in China since the critically acclaimed compact car model, the Jaws, was put out on the market last year. "Demand for AMC cars, especially for the Jaws series, has risen sharply. I believe local customers are interested in the Jaws model because they are affordable, fuel efficient, and creatively designed," commented a local car dealer in Shanghai, Joe Wang.

The company is planning to release an upgraded version of the Jaws, the Jaws-2, in October. The new line of Jaws will feature a built-in navigation system, improved safety technology, and even better fuel efficiency. The newly built plant will be focusing mainly on manufacturing this model to meet the demand in China's major cities such as Chongqing and Tianjin. AMC is currently preparing to aggressively promote the model in China through TV commercials, starring popular Belgian celebrity, Mr. Filip Gilliams. The commercials will be broadcast once the Jaws-2 is released.

165. The word "edge" in paragraph 2, line 1, is closest in meaning to

(A) blade
(B) revenue
(C) advantage
(D) trend

166. According to Mr. Wang, what is NOT suggested about the Jaws model?

(A) It is reasonably priced.
(B) It consumes relatively less energy.
(C) Its sales are quite robust in China.
(D) It is currently being manufactured in China.

167. Where will the Jaws-2 be primarily produced?

(A) In Brussels
(B) In Shanghai
(C) In Tianjin
(D) In Beijing

▶ ▶ ▶GO ON TO THE NEXT PAGE

Questions 168-171 refer to the following online chat discussion.

Rosemary Waters   2:42 P.M.

Hello, Sylvia. How is your training program going?

Sylvia Smith   2:43 P.M.

It's really educational. I'm learning a lot here, and the information should be a big help when I start my official duties next week.

Rosemary Waters   2:44 P.M.

I'm glad to hear that. I'm sure that you'll fit in really well here.

Sylvia Smith   2:45 P.M.

I'm pleased that you're confident in me.

Trent Sutter   2:47 P.M.

Sylvia, when you get here next Monday, please drop by my office at 10:00 in the morning. I have an assignment for you.

Sylvia Smith   2:48 P.M.

I'd love to, but I'm supposed to meet Patsy Roth in HR from 9:00 to noon. Can we meet after lunch?

Trent Sutter   2:49 P.M.

I'm going to be out of the office starting at noon, and I won't be back until Friday. How do you feel about me e-mailing you an assignment?

Sylvia Smith   2:51 P.M.

That works for me. But I don't have a work e-mail account yet.

Rosemary Waters   2:53 P.M.

I'll get someone in IT to set that up for you right now. I'll text you the login and the password within an hour.

Sylvia Smith   2:54 P.M.

Thank you so much. I'll let you know my new e-mail address as soon as I get it, Trent. And then we can get to work.

SEND

168. Who most likely is Ms. Smith?

    (A) A manager
    (B) A trainee
    (C) A customer
    (D) An executive

169. What problem does Ms. Smith have?

    (A) She cannot meet at a proposed time.
    (B) She does not have enough experience.
    (C) She is unable to go on a business trip.
    (D) She has not completed some forms.

170. What does Ms. Waters offer to do for Ms. Smith?

    (A) Arrange for a new computer
    (B) Order her a new desk
    (C) Set up an online account
    (D) Assist her with a project

171. At 2:51 P.M., why does Ms. Smith write, "That works for me"?

    (A) To complain about a new assignment
    (B) To offer to work overtime
    (C) To indicate how busy she is
    (D) To agree with Mr. Sutter's idea

▶ ▶ ▶ GO ON TO THE NEXT PAGE

Come Feel the African Soul!

Brookline, April 22— The sound of Africa comes to Brookline, where many music festivals have been held in previous years. A marvelous outdoor African music festival, the African Soul Festival, will be held at Brookline Square on May 30 and 31. —[1]—. Hundreds of African music fans as well as local residents are expected to attend it.

Hosted by the Recreation Department of Brookline, the African Soul Festival has many notable features. One is the diversity of the music. —[2]—. There will be many different kinds of African music performed, including tunes from Eastern, Central, and Southern Africa.

Many renowned African musicians will fly to Brookline to perform in the African Soul Festival. Papa Kelle, the winner of the 4th African Musicians Contest, will perform on the opening day. —[3]—. Popular in their countries but not yet world renowned artists, such as Alan GaM'olla, Daddy Solomon, and Simba Omonga, will also perform in the festival.

On the first day of the event, samples of traditional African foods and drinks will be served for free near the entrance in the evening.

Tickets can be purchased at the box office near the entrance to Brookline Square on the days of the festival. —[4]—. Tickets are also available at reduced prices until May 20 at www.brooklinetickets.com.

172. What is the topic of the article?

(A) Free performances for residents
(B) A trip to Africa
(C) The history of African music
(D) An outdoor event

173. What is mentioned about tickets?

(A) They will be discounted for a limited time.
(B) They are not available onsite.
(C) They will be given to local residents for free.
(D) They can be reserved by calling the Recreation Department.

174. When will free food be served?

(A) On April 22
(B) On May 20
(C) On May 30
(D) On May 31

175. In which of the positions marked [1], [2], [3], and [4] does the following sentence best fit?

"On the second day, Moulin Noir, a Ska music band now famous after appearing on TV, will participate."

(A) [1]
(B) [2]
(C) [3]
(D) [4]

▶ ▶ ▶GO ON TO THE NEXT PAGE

CALL THE CUE

Seymour Park, London
October 1-5

The International Theatre Society (ITS) once again returns with its 5th Call the Cue! Join our annual week-long festival filled with vibrant performances from both major and independent productions, including the Claymore College of Performing Arts (CCPA).

Main Stage Showcases include:

Day 1   James Garza & Roxanne Swanson performing *Man with the Tiger*

Day 2   Anne-Sophie Wynter performing a series of monologues; Royal Theatre Company performing *Merchant's City*

Day 3   Curtain Call Company performing *Fountain of Color*; Elaine Edina's one-man show

Day 4   Prize-winning scripts from this year's ITS Short Play Competition including Russell Chan's *Yellow Umbrella*

Day 5   JMS Production & the Rhodes Actors Association performing *Dragonia*; Roderick Doherty performing *The Solitary Tree*

And many more! For the complete list of performances on each day, visit our website at www.its.org/callthecue.

A special discount offer is extended to those attending the CCPA. Enter the promotion code CCASTD upon checkout. Proof of enrollment will be requested upon entry.

International Theatre Society
1 Pattison Street, London
0844 555 0787

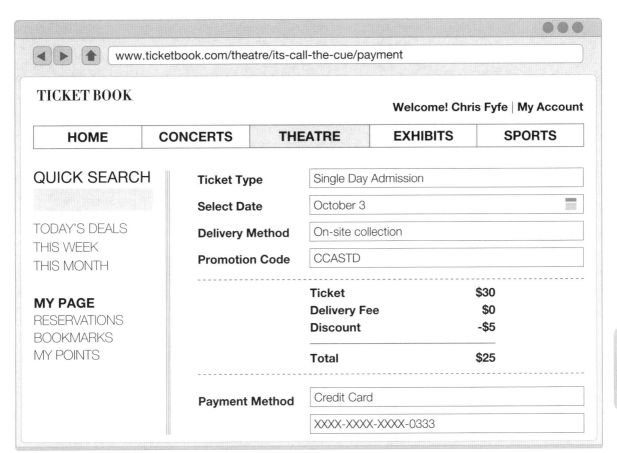

176. What type of event most likely is Call the Cue?

(A) Art exhibitions
(B) A sequence of animal shows
(C) A series of plays
(D) School festivals

177. Who will perform *The Solitary Tree*?

(A) Ms. Swanson
(B) Mr. Garza
(C) Ms. Wynter
(D) Mr. Doherty

178. In the flyer, the word "extended" in paragraph 4, line 1 is closest in meaning to

(A) postponed
(B) created
(C) offered
(D) enlarged

179. What is NOT indicated about the International Theatre Society?

(A) It has arranged festivals before.
(B) It is based in London.
(C) It was established about 5 years ago.
(D) It hosts a short play competition.

180. What is suggested about Mr. Fyfe?

(A) He purchased a ticket for someone else.
(B) He has a membership at ITS.
(C) He is a student at an art school.
(D) He will perform a short play.

▶ ▶ ▶GO ON TO THE NEXT PAGE

Valpoa Cave Tours

Welcome to Valpoa Cave, the amazing masterpiece created by nature. Located in a national park in the province of Laguna, the Philippines, this cave, thousands of years old, is one of the largest tourist attractions in the nation. Choose one of the following tours and witness the magnificence of nature that will take your breath away! In each tour, you can learn about the history, geography, and culture of the region with the help of our guides, who are certified by the National Tourist Association (NTA).

Regular Tour

Includes comfortable rides to the cave in an SUV. 450 pesos per adult and 300 pesos per child (ages 4-11), and children under the age of 4 are admitted for free.

Prime Time Tour

Departs at the time of the day when the most sunlight enters the cave. Adults 550 pesos and children (ages 4-11) 380 pesos, and children under the age of 4 are admitted for free.

Photography Tour

Take your own pictures of beautiful Valpoa Cave. For both amateur and professional photographers alike. Experts are there to help you with camera settings and angles. You can bring a tripod with you. Adults 650 pesos and children (ages 4-11) 470 pesos, and children under the age of 4 are admitted for free.

Open 365 days a year. For reservations and detailed information, visit www.valpoacave.com. For any questions, please send an e-mail to customerservice@valpoa.com or call 632-555-9270.

To:	Valpoa Cave Tours <customerservice@valpoa.com>
From:	Kurt Toka <ktoka@polemail.com>
Date:	July 5
Subject:	About my last tour

To whom it may concern,

Last month, I visited Valpoa Cave with my wife. We enjoyed the beauty of the cave very much. However, the place was too crowded, and I had difficulty taking pictures of the cave, as there was not enough space to set up my tripod. I told David Neeson, our tour guide, about this inconvenience, and he acknowledged the problem. He promised to arrange a partial refund and a set of Valpoa Cave postcards to be delivered to my house within a week as compensation. I have received the partial payment, 200 pesos, which is reasonable because I did enjoy the cave. However, it has been more than 2 weeks, and I have not received the postcards yet.

If you have not yet mailed the postcards to me, could you please include a brochure in the parcel? I noticed a discount coupon on your advertisement and would like to visit Valpoa Cave again in the near future.

Thank you,

Kurt Toka

181. What is indicated about the tours at Valpoa Cave?

(A) They require visitors to drive their own SUVs.
(B) They depart every hour.
(C) They are available year round.
(D) They charge the same fee regardless of age.

182. How can a customer book a tour?

(A) By talking to a guide
(B) By writing an e-mail
(C) By visiting a website
(D) By calling a phone number

183. What is the purpose of the e-mail?

(A) To complain about a tour guide
(B) To inform a person of an item that has not been delivered
(C) To request a complete schedule of tours
(D) To ask about the location of a cave

184. How much did Mr. Toka originally pay for his visit in June?

(A) 200 pesos
(B) 450 pesos
(C) 470 pesos
(D) 650 pesos

185. What is suggested about Mr. Neeson?

(A) He will lead another tour for Mr. Toka.
(B) He will send postcards to Mr. Toka.
(C) He is licensed by an organization.
(D) He brought his own tripod to Valpoa Cave.

▶ ▶ ▶ GO ON TO THE NEXT PAGE

Rudolf Toys

Rudolf Toys is pleased to announce that the annual employee training courses will take place next week. These are held to improve the efficiency and knowledge of the staff. The following is the course schedule:

Project Planning

Setsuko Asada, Marketing Department Director		
Tuesday, June 10	9:00 A.M. – 10:30 A.M.	Room 501

Engineering   *All Engineering Department members must attend.

Orlando Ibrahimovic, Senior Engineering Manager		
Tuesday, June 10	1:00 P.M. – 3:00 P.M.	Room 502

Communication Skills

Anna Dvorkin, Accounting Department Assistant Manager		
Thursday, June 12	1:00 P.M. – 2:30 P.M.	Room 401

Safety Regulations and Equipment Use

Kimberley Jade, Plant Manager		
Thursday, June 12	3:00 P.M. – 6:00 P.M.	Room 603

Following the latter session on June 12, dinner will be served to the attendees. Please arrive 5 minutes prior to the beginning of each session to be seated. No food or drinks are allowed. Any comments, suggestions, or questions should be submitted to the Human Resources Department.

To:	Remy Yves <ryves@rudolftoys.com>
From:	Setsuko Asada <sasada@rudolftoys.com>
Date:	June 3
Subject:	Training Courses

Dear Mr. Yves,

I am writing with regard to the upcoming training courses. I was supposed to lead a session, but I will be unable to do so due to an urgent business trip I must go on. Fortunately, the assistant director in my department, Linda Sommers, is available on the day of my session. She will handle the training course in my place.

Please correct the posts with the schedule at your earliest convenience to prevent any confusion. I am sorry for the inconvenience this may cause. While on my trip, I will be available by e-mail or phone at (135)-555-6432.

Sincerely,

Setsuko Asada
Director, Marketing Department

To:	Remy Yves <ryves@rudolftoys.com>
From:	Anna Dvorkin <annad@rudolftoys.com>
Date:	June 13
Subject:	Thank You

Mr. Yves,

Thank you so much for allowing me to switch course times with Kimberley. I regret only giving you one day's notice, so I am truly appreciative that you were able to make the change.

In addition, this was my first time to lead a training course here. I thoroughly enjoyed the process and hope to have the opportunity to do it again in the future. If you need more assistance from me at a later time, please feel free to ask.

Thank you.

Anna Dvorkin

ACTUAL TEST 05

186. What is indicated about Rudolf Toys in the schedule?

(A) It requires training course attendees to sign up in advance.
(B) It is currently recruiting new employees.
(C) It plans to hold a regular event soon.
(D) It evaluates the performances of its employees annually.

187. What is mentioned about the training course led by Mr. Ibrahimovic?

(A) It requires certain people to participate.
(B) It will last for 3 hours.
(C) It will have refreshments for attendees.
(D) It is intended for new staff members.

188. After which session will a complimentary meal be given?

(A) Project Planning
(B) Engineering
(C) Communication Skills
(D) Safety Regulations and Equipment Use

189. What can be inferred about Mr. Yves?

(A) He will lead a training session.
(B) He is planning to go on a business trip.
(C) He will contact Ms. Asada soon.
(D) He works in the Human Resources Department.

190. When did Ms. Dvorkin lead a training course?

(A) On Tuesday at 9:00 A.M.
(B) On Tuesday at 1:00 P.M.
(C) On Thursday at 1:00 P.M.
(D) On Thursday at 3:00 P.M.

▶ ▶ ▶ GO ON TO THE NEXT PAGE

Scarlatium
Make Your Special Day Extraordinary

Choose the city's favorite place, Scarlatium, to hold special occasions. We have been nominated as the finest service provider in Washington, D.C. in the event management field for the past five consecutive years.

•Banquet Hall

This option includes a ballroom lit by chandeliers, which creates an elegant look. It seats 200 guests comfortably at tables of 10 and includes a stage for speeches.

•Rose Garden

Hold your event under the sun in the elegant gazebo. The bench setting with meals accommodates 300 guests and the banquet arrangement 150 guests. Please note that events may be relocated to vacant ballrooms depending on weather conditions.

•Chapel

High arches and large stained-glass windows provide a divine space for your day. This room is only available for ceremonies as food is not served there. Guests can be served meals in another hall upon request.

•Photography

Hamilton's, a local photography studio, will capture the days' special moments. This service is provided free of charge except during the peak season from March to May.

---

www.scarlatium.com/testimonials

Scarlatium *Make Your Special Day Extraordinary*

HOME	CONSULTING	RESERVATION	TESTIMONIALS

Perfection

- by Nathalie White, posted June 13

Holding my wedding at Scarlatium was a decision I do not regret. The day was flawless, and I have my event coordinator, Evelyn George, to thank for it. Evelyn was invaluable in organizing every detail of the event. I was very stressed out in the morning because I was informed that the audio system was malfunctioning in the room I had booked. I became even more nervous upon hearing that every other ballroom was booked. Then, Evelyn arranged for the event to be held in the garden. She also refunded the money I paid for photographs as an apology. The food served by Scarlatium was beyond my expectations, too. I could not have asked for more.

To:	Jacob Thomas <jthomas@hamiltons.com>
From:	Evelyn George <egeorge@scarlatium.com>
Date:	June 14
Subject:	Re: Payment

Mr. Thomas,

I just read the e-mail you sent me. Please do not be worried as you will receive the payment for the services you rendered for Ms. White at her wedding. While we refunded her money, we still intend to pay you. Once we receive an invoice from you, the payment will be deposited into your account within three business days. Please let me know if you have any other concerns.

Regards,

Evelyn George
Scarlatium

191. In the advertisement, the word "occasions" in paragraph 1, line 1, is closest in meaning to

(A) cases
(B) events
(C) breaks
(D) dates

192. What is mentioned about Scarlatium?

(A) It was founded five years ago.
(B) It only accommodates wedding ceremonies.
(C) It has a space with ornate windows.
(D) It can host a maximum of 300 guests at a time.

193. Why did Ms. White make a post on the web page?

(A) To request a refund
(B) To make a suggestion
(C) To file a complaint
(D) To praise a service

194. What can be inferred about Ms. White?

(A) She requested a refund from Scarlatium.
(B) She initially planned to hold her event outside.
(C) She held her event during Scarlatium's peak season.
(D) She used an external catering service.

195. Who most likely is Mr. Thomas?

(A) A photographer
(B) An employee at Scarlatium
(C) A wedding guest
(D) A Scarlatium customer

ORIENTAL STAR HOTEL

Located in the heart of Bangkok, the Oriental Star Hotel has been hosting guests for the last sixty years. The hotel was recently renovated. Free wireless Internet is now available in the entire hotel. Here are the features of the newly refurbished rooms:

Standard	twin bed, hair dryer, and air conditioning
Deluxe	2 twin beds, hair dryer, refrigerator, and air conditioning
Suite	2 twin beds, living room, 2 bathrooms with bathtubs, hair dryer, refrigerator, state-of-the-art audio system, high-definition television, and air conditioning
Executive Suite	2 bedrooms, living room, 2 bathrooms with bathtubs, hair dryer, 2 refrigerators, audio system, 2 high-definition televisions, air conditioning, and complimentary breakfast

The Oriental Star Hotel's restaurant, Blue Plates, serves food prepared by internationally renowned award-winning master chef Isra Ta. Ms. Ta has 15 years of experience in cooking the traditional foods of Thailand, Korea, Japan, and Italy.

To learn more about the Oriental Star Hotel, please visit us at www.orientalstarhotel.com. Given the large number of visitors during the peak season, we recommend booking a room two months in advance.

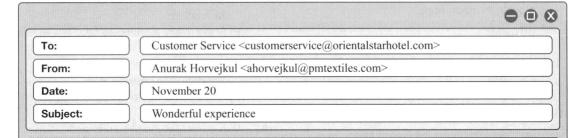

To:	Customer Service <customerservice@orientalstarhotel.com>
From:	Anurak Horvejkul <ahorvejkul@pmtextiles.com>
Date:	November 20
Subject:	Wonderful experience

To whom it may concern,

I am writing to thank you for a wonderful experience at your establishment. I arranged for my client, Tahan Santisakul, to stay at your hotel last week when he visited Bangkok for business. Mr. Santisakul said he was satisfied with the overall service you provided for him. He especially appreciated the free breakfast he enjoyed each morning.

In addition, both Mr. Santisakul and I enjoyed the cuisine at Blue Plates. On November 16, we both ordered the grilled salmon. The head chef herself served us. It was a pleasant experience to speak with someone whom I had seen on TV before. I look forward to doing business with you again in the future.

Sincerely,

Anurak Horvejkul
Account Manager
PM Textiles, Inc.

To:	<reservations@orientalstarhotel.com>
From:	<tahans@promenadecarpets.com>
Date:	December 1
Subject:	Booking

Dear Sir/Madam,

My name is Tahan Santisakul, and I would like to make a reservation at your hotel. I stayed there last month and thoroughly enjoyed it. I will be in Bangkok from December 6 to 12. I hope to have the same type of room that I stayed in the last time.

I realize that I should have made this reservation a couple of months ago, but I still hope that you can accommodate my request. Please let me know if you have any available rooms.

Regards,

Tahan Santisakul

196. What is indicated about the Oriental Star Hotel in the advertisement?

(A) It was closed for a certain period of time.
(B) It is the biggest hotel in Bangkok.
(C) It is located near several tourist attractions.
(D) It has been in business for decades.

197. What is available in a deluxe room?

(A) A high-quality TV
(B) A refrigerator
(C) A living room
(D) A bathtub

198. What is NOT suggested about Ms. Ta?

(A) She has worked at the Oriental Star Hotel for 15 years.
(B) She has won awards for her cooking.
(C) She cooks various styles of dishes.
(D) She is known to people in other countries.

199. What can be inferred about Mr. Santisakul?

(A) He is Mr. Horvejkul's coworker.
(B) He has visited Bangkok many times.
(C) He stayed in an executive suite.
(D) He recently read a magazine about culinary arts.

200. What is indicated about Mr. Santisakul?

(A) He will stay in Bangkok the entire month of December.
(B) He will meet with Mr. Horvejkul daily.
(C) He wants to stay in a different room on his next trip.
(D) He plans to visit Bangkok during the peak season.

STOP! This is the end of the test. If you finish before time is called, you may go back to Parts 5, 6, and 7 and check your work.

Actual Test 06

MP3 音檔

解析

最佳解答時間 120 分鐘

120 min

開始時間：＿＿＿點 ＿＿＿分

結束時間：＿＿＿點 ＿＿＿分

▲ 盡量不要在作答中途停下來。

▲ 請於答案卡上畫記作答。

目標正確題數：＿＿＿／200 題　實際正確題數：＿＿＿／200 題

題數與分數對照，請參考 P449 分數換算表。

LISTENING TEST

In the Listening test, you will be asked to demonstrate how well you understand spoken English. The entire Listening test will last approximately 45 minutes. There are four parts, and directions are given for each part. You must mark your answers on the separate answer sheet. Do not write your answers in the test book.

PART 1

Directions: For each question in this part, you will hear four statements about a picture in your test book. When you hear the statements, you must select the one statement that best describes what you see in the picture. Then find the number of the question on your answer sheet and mark your answer. The statements will not be printed in your test book and will be spoken only one time.

Statement (B), "They are sitting at a table." is the best description of the picture. So you should select answer (B) and mark it on your answer sheet.

1.

2.

▶ ▶ ▶GO ON TO THE NEXT PAGE

3.

4.

5.

6.

▶ ▶ ▶GO ON TO THE NEXT PAGE

PART 2

Directions: You will hear a question or statement and three responses spoken in English. They will not be printed in your test book and will be spoken only one time. Select the best response to the question or statement and mark the letter (A), (B), or (C) on your answer sheet.

7. Mark your answer on your answer sheet.

8. Mark your answer on your answer sheet.

9. Mark your answer on your answer sheet.

10. Mark your answer on your answer sheet.

11. Mark your answer on your answer sheet.

12. Mark your answer on your answer sheet.

13. Mark your answer on your answer sheet.

14. Mark your answer on your answer sheet.

15. Mark your answer on your answer sheet.

16. Mark your answer on your answer sheet.

17. Mark your answer on your answer sheet.

18. Mark your answer on your answer sheet.

19. Mark your answer on your answer sheet.

20. Mark your answer on your answer sheet.

21. Mark your answer on your answer sheet.

22. Mark your answer on your answer sheet.

23. Mark your answer on your answer sheet.

24. Mark your answer on your answer sheet.

25. Mark your answer on your answer sheet.

26. Mark your answer on your answer sheet.

27. Mark your answer on your answer sheet.

28. Mark your answer on your answer sheet.

29. Mark your answer on your answer sheet.

30. Mark your answer on your answer sheet.

31. Mark your answer on your answer sheet.

PART 3

Directions: You will hear some conversations between two or three people. You will be asked to answer three questions about what the speakers say in each conversation. Select the best response to each question and mark the letter (A), (B), (C), or (D) on your answer sheet. The conversations will not be printed in your test book and will be spoken only one time.

32. What did the woman do yesterday?

(A) She conducted an interview.
(B) She gave a presentation.
(C) She recruited a new employee.
(D) She updated a website.

33. What industry do the speakers work in?

(A) Clothing
(B) Electronics
(C) Engineering
(D) Catering service

34. What will the company do next Monday?

(A) Have a meeting with clients
(B) Replace some devices
(C) Negotiate a takeover
(D) Test a new product

35. What does the man ask the woman to do at an event?

(A) Introduce some speakers
(B) Make a list of attendees
(C) Arrange a venue
(D) Sell tickets

36. What kind of event is being planned?

(A) A charity auction
(B) A training session
(C) A fundraiser
(D) A product demonstration

37. What does the man say he needs to do?

(A) Create some invitations
(B) Contact the guest speakers
(C) Hire a caterer
(D) Pay a deposit

38. Where do the speakers work?

(A) At an amusement park
(B) At a bank
(C) At a zoo
(D) At a museum

39. According to the man, what will happen on Tuesday?

(A) A person will start working.
(B) A group will visit a building.
(C) A new program will begin.
(D) An exhibit will be launched.

40. What does the man say the woman should do?

(A) Provide some badges
(B) Collect some tickets
(C) Restock some more brochures
(D) Print some tour schedules

41. What product are the speakers talking about?

(A) A running shoe
(B) A sports beverage
(C) A skateboard
(D) A bicycle

42. Why is the man concerned?

(A) A flight has been canceled.
(B) A factory is located far away.
(C) A workload is too great.
(D) A project is not on schedule.

43. What does the woman suggest doing?

(A) Purchasing a fuel-efficient vehicle
(B) Relocating a factory
(C) Changing a production timeline
(D) Finding a local inspector

▶ ▶ ▶ GO ON TO THE NEXT PAGE

44. Who is the man?

(A) A recruiter
(B) A trainer
(C) An interviewer
(D) A car dealer

45. Why did the woman take a new job?

(A) To be closer to her family
(B) To make a bigger salary
(C) To take a course at a local university
(D) To acquire some new skills

46. What will the woman most likely do next?

(A) Get hands-on experience
(B) Review a manual
(C) Fill out the paperwork
(D) Give a demonstration

47. What is the problem with the elevator?

(A) It is down for maintenance.
(B) It is being cleaned up.
(C) It is not big enough.
(D) It is being repaired.

48. What does Emily offer to do?

(A) Carry some bags
(B) Park a vehicle
(C) Drive the man to the airport
(D) Provide a discount to the man

49. What does the man hope to do tomorrow?

(A) Rent a vehicle
(B) Sell some books
(C) Shop at a bookstore
(D) Reserve a booth for a book fair

50. Who most likely is the woman?

(A) A government inspector
(B) A bus driver
(C) A tour guide
(D) A travel agent

51. What does the man want the woman to do?

(A) Look over some documents
(B) Take a park tour
(C) Give out some surveys
(D) Send him an e-mail

52. What does the woman say she has?

(A) A map of the park
(B) Some nametags
(C) Some visitor passes
(D) An e-mail list

53. What is the conversation mainly about?

(A) A leaking pipe
(B) A broken lock
(C) A missing item
(D) An electrical problem

54. What does the woman mean when she says, "The maintenance team is working on some pipes this morning"?

(A) The man needs to call somebody else.
(B) Some repair work will be expensive.
(C) Some work cannot be done immediately.
(D) The team members are busy all day long.

55. What does the man say he will do in the afternoon?

(A) Visit a warehouse
(B) Meet with a client
(C) Attend a company outing
(D) Prepare some documents

56. What does the woman suggest the company do?

(A) Change the hours of operation
(B) Provide gym memberships
(C) Offer better benefits
(D) Open an in-house health center

57. What does the man imply when he says, "We have lots of employees here"?

(A) The company will add more offices soon.
(B) A suggestion will be too costly.
(C) Some employees will be transferred.
(D) Many of the employees should work from home.

58. What does the man say he will do?

(A) Put off a staff meeting
(B) Review a budget report
(C) Do some research on his own
(D) Add a topic to an agenda

---

59. What does the woman want to purchase?

(A) Postcards
(B) Photo frames
(C) Hanging flowers
(D) Key rings

60. What does Peter say about the engraving service?

(A) It would require additional time.
(B) It isn't currently in stock.
(C) It was featured in a magazine this year.
(D) It is an award-winning service.

61. What does Jason say is available for free?

(A) Engraving service
(B) Delivery
(C) Maintenance
(D) An extended warranty

Jeff's Schedule
Thursday, Nov. 5

9:00 A.M. – 10:00 A.M.	Conference Call with Tudor Pharmaceuticals
10:30 A.M. – 12:00 P.M.	Product Demonstration with Edward Wright
1:00 P.M. – 2:30 P.M.	Contract Negotiation with Stuart Duncan
5:00 P.M. – 6:00 P.M.	Presentation at the Harper Convention Center

62. What is the woman organizing?

(A) A product demonstration
(B) A conference
(C) A charity auction
(D) An orientation event

63. What does the woman ask the man to do?

(A) Fill in for a colleague
(B) Organize a reception
(C) Go on a business trip
(D) Meet with a customer

64. Look at the graphic. Which activity will the man reschedule?

(A) The conference call
(B) The product demonstration
(C) The contract negotiation
(D) The presentation

Last Week's Sales by Team Three

- 30% Eric
- 25% Tom
- 20% Steve
- 15% Peter
- 10% Robert

File name	Size
Kingswood.mov	15MB
Bernstein.mov	30MB
Perez.mov	40MB
LIttlebrook.mov	25MB

65. According to the woman, what will happen next month?

(A) A work schedule will change.
(B) A new worker will be transferred.
(C) A sales promotion will take place.
(D) An employee will stop working.

66. Where do the speakers most likely work?

(A) At an appliance store
(B) At a clothing shop
(C) At an outdoor market
(D) At a tool manufacturer

67. Look at the graphic. What is the man's name?

(A) Eric
(B) Tom
(C) Steve
(D) Peter

68. What kind of business do the speakers work in?

(A) Marketing
(B) Advertising
(C) Manufacturing
(D) Software

69. Look at the graphic. Which file did the man try to e-mail?

(A) Kingswood.mov
(B) Bernstein.mov
(C) Perez.mov
(D) LIttlebrook.mov

70. What does the woman suggest the man do?

(A) Attempt to e-mail a file again
(B) Wait for a manager to come back
(C) Speak with an IT specialist
(D) Have his computer repaired

PART 4

Directions: You will hear some short talks given by a single speaker. You will be asked to answer three questions about what the speaker says in each short talk. Select the best response to each question and mark the letter (A), (B), (C), or (D) on your answer sheet. The talks will not be printed in your test book and will be spoken only one time.

71. Who most likely is the listener?

(A) A government official
(B) A shopkeeper
(C) An apartment supervisor
(D) A delivery person

72. What information does the speaker inquire about?

(A) An apartment address
(B) A place for recycling items
(C) A pickup day
(D) A service fee amount

73. What does the speaker ask the listener to do?

(A) E-mail some information
(B) Return a telephone call
(C) Check some policies for tenants
(D) Call Maintenance

---

74. What does the speaker discuss?

(A) Changing rules
(B) Ordering supplies
(C) Cleaning the office
(D) Getting another supplier

75. What does the speaker request that the listeners do?

(A) Submit their timesheets
(B) Stay late at work this evening
(C) Complete a form accurately
(D) Share ideas for workplace efficiency

76. What does the speaker say is in Sharon's office?

(A) An employee directory
(B) A product catalog
(C) A user's manual
(D) A visitor's pass

77. What product is being discussed?

(A) Pizza
(B) Bread
(C) Coffee
(D) Cake

78. What did Justin Groceries recently do?

(A) It canceled an order.
(B) It changed its operating hours.
(C) It released a new line of pizza.
(D) It increased an order.

79. What does the speaker mean when she says, "I need to hear your thoughts"?

(A) More funding will be needed to meet the demand.
(B) Meetings will be held biweekly.
(C) Some production lines are not working properly.
(D) Some information is needed to make a decision.

---

80. Where does the speaker work?

(A) At a restaurant
(B) At a hospital
(C) At an airport
(D) At a theater

81. What does the speaker imply when he says, "We have a good team working on it now"?

(A) A replacement part will arrive shortly.
(B) A problem will be solved soon.
(C) All of the workers are too busy.
(D) More training is not necessary.

82. What does the speaker say he will do next?

(A) Offer everyone a refund
(B) Change the gate number
(C) Answer anyone's questions
(D) Provide an update soon

▶ ▶ ▶GO ON TO THE NEXT PAGE

83. What are the listeners most likely experts in?

(A) Design
(B) Tourism
(C) Marketing
(D) Computers

84. What does the speaker suggest doing?

(A) Focusing on specific individuals
(B) Releasing a new line of running shoes
(C) Improving the quality of an item
(D) Hiring more marketing consultants

85. What will happen on Friday?

(A) An advertisement will be recorded.
(B) A specific group will be surveyed.
(C) A career fair will be held.
(D) A strategy will be discussed.

___

86. According to the broadcast, what is the sponsor looking for?

(A) Cooking contestants
(B) Celebrity chefs
(C) Product testers
(D) TV announcers

87. What kind of products does the sponsor manufacture?

(A) Computer games
(B) Kitchen appliances
(C) Gardening supplies
(D) Sporting goods

88. What should the listeners interested in participating do?

(A) Visit a store
(B) Mail in a survey
(C) Send a recipe
(D) Make a phone call

89. Who most likely are the listeners?

(A) College students
(B) Writers
(C) Publishers
(D) Business owners

90. Why does the speaker say, "He owns a chain of stores all across the country"?

(A) To put an emphasis on a speaker's qualification
(B) To thank a colleague for his dedication
(C) To encourage the listeners to do their best
(D) To suggest a topic for an agenda

91. What will the listeners get at the end of the day?

(A) A book of coupons
(B) An autographed poster
(C) A signed book
(D) A free subscription

___

92. What will happen next week?

(A) A grand opening
(B) A going-away party
(C) A sale
(D) A road closure

93. What does the speaker want the listeners to do?

(A) Arrive at work on time
(B) Park in a pay lot
(C) Use public transportation
(D) Check a store directory

94. What does the speaker tell the listeners to do by the end of the week?

(A) Put up sale posters
(B) Complete a training course
(C) Confirm their working hours
(D) Read a document

Weather Forecast

Sunday	Monday	Tuesday	Wednesday	Thursday
Rain	Cloudy	Rain	Sunny	Sunny

95. What event is the speaker calling about?

(A) A concert
(B) A sporting event
(C) An interview
(D) A conference

96. Look at the graphic. When will the event take place?

(A) On Monday
(B) On Tuesday
(C) On Wednesday
(D) On Thursday

97. What is the listener asked to do?

(A) Send an announcement
(B) Post an advertisement
(C) Sell some tickets
(D) Change a venue for concert

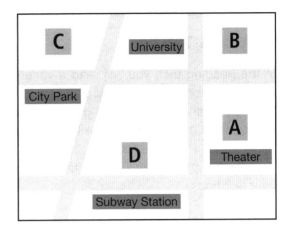

98. What type of business is the speaker discussing?

(A) A retail store
(B) A restaurant
(C) A hardware store
(D) A theater

99. Look at the graphic. Which location does the speaker recommend?

(A) Location A
(B) Location B
(C) Location C
(D) Location D

100. What does the speaker say he will do next?

(A) Show some pictures
(B) Hand out some brochures
(C) Talk about finances
(D) Answer questions

This is the end of the Listening test. Turn to Part 5 in your test book.

▶ ▶ ▶ GO ON TO THE NEXT PAGE

ACTUAL TEST 06

READING TEST

In the Reading test, you will read a variety of texts and answer several different types of reading comprehension questions. The entire Reading test will last 75 minutes. There are three parts, and directions are given for each part. You are encouraged to answer as many questions as possible within the time allowed.

You must mark your answer on the separate answer sheet. Do not write your answers in your test book.

PART 5

Directions: A word or phrase is missing in each of the sentences below. Four answer choices are given below each sentence. Select the best answer to complete the sentence. Then mark the letter (A), (B), (C), or (D) on your answer sheet.

101. Sociologists can help ------- to become aware of the barriers that prevent a social problem from being solved.

(A) we
(B) us
(C) our
(D) ourselves

102. During musical shows, there is ------- basic lighting, but also laser beam projectors or fog machines to maximize visual effects.

(A) even
(B) such
(C) just
(D) not only

103. Mr. Harrison pursued the dream ------- owning a business and learned about everything from business insurance to corporate accounting.

(A) on
(B) of
(C) to
(D) with

104. Boutique Coco is one of the popular clothing brands in Europe which creates the ------- trends in women's fashion.

(A) late
(B) latest
(C) lately
(D) lateness

105. The city council has recently made a law ------- all multinational companies to renew their business license every year.

(A) require
(B) requiring
(C) required
(D) requires

106. ------- to the city from all countries remains strictly controlled to help prevent the spread of the harmful virus in the initial stages.

(A) Enter
(B) Entrance
(C) Entry
(D) Entered

107. Some newspapers say that our new chief executive officer is ------- a leader who changes his management style and his business policies.

(A) much
(B) seldom
(C) almost
(D) enough

108. A variety of methods were ------- to get the word out to potential audiences and to increase ticket sales.

(A) use
(B) using
(C) used
(D) usage

109. It is important to distribute a meeting agenda ------- in advance to allow time for the attendees to do necessary thinking of planning.

(A) well
(B) good
(C) best
(D) soon

110. Delta Securities has outlined its management improvement plan to seek a big synergy effect by ------- Sydney Investment with its own banking subsidiary.

(A) consolidation
(B) consolidate
(C) consolidating
(D) console

111. With his extensive hands-on experience, the personnel manager thinks Mr. Collins is a welcome ------- to the sales team.

(A) nominee
(B) article
(C) realty
(D) addition

112. Due to the ------- cost of renting office space in the business district, an increasing number of companies want to move into the outskirts of the city.

(A) rise
(B) rising
(C) rose
(D) risen

113. The installments of new traffic signals on Devonshire Street has been only ------- successful in lowering traffic congestion.

(A) evenly
(B) permanently
(C) specifically
(D) moderately

114. Thanks to careful ------- and consistent advertising on television, Bella & Andrew has finally become the leader in the global toy market.

(A) planner
(B) plan
(C) planning
(D) planned

115. Social media can be described as new kinds of online media with ------- such as participation, openness, and connectedness.

(A) actions
(B) appearance
(C) symptoms
(D) characteristics

116. Candidates ------- have limited experience in sales will be required to attend training session once hired.

(A) who
(B) whom
(C) what
(D) which

117. There are some strict customs formalities to be gone through before the flight passengers are ------- into the country.

(A) needed
(B) appeared
(C) socialized
(D) admitted

▶ ▶ ▶GO ON TO THE NEXT PAGE

118. In the recent survey of seaport use, many travelers stated that they found the long waiting time at customs -------.

(A) exhausting
(B) exhausted
(C) exhaustingly
(D) exhaustion

119. Customers are invited to tour the manufacturing plant of Winchester Furniture to see ------- their office furniture is made.

(A) whom
(B) during
(C) about
(D) how

120. Our ------- appraisals of the employees are necessary to understand each employee's competency and relative merit and worth for the company.

(A) perform
(B) performer
(C) performance
(D) performing

121. Some advertisers prefer to hand out refrigerator magnets rather than ------- promotional items like pens, towels, or key holders.

(A) other
(B) another
(C) every
(D) others

122. ------- the latest snow storm, our region is currently experiencing a warmer and drier winter.

(A) Since
(B) Despite
(C) Before
(D) During

123. Due to the recent oil price increases, the company ------- its contract to purchase a piece of new heavy machinery until late November or even mid-December.

(A) postponing
(B) has been postponed
(C) are postponing
(D) will postpone

124. Our members can accumulate bonus points ------- they make purchases from any of our affiliated stores across the country.

(A) whoever
(B) whichever
(C) whatever
(D) whenever

125. According to medical experts, ------- who goes outside must wear a mask for protection against viral infections.

(A) anyone
(B) something
(C) everything
(D) themselves

126. Money and trees would be saved if public transportation were free ------- no one would have to print out tickets anymore.

(A) when
(B) because
(C) unless
(D) provided that

127. Many public festivals and events take place throughout the year, but ------- usually do in summer and fall.

(A) most
(B) each
(C) that
(D) another

128. Mr. McGowan will make a presentation about our new mobile phones and there will be a ten-minute question and answer session -------.

(A) before
(B) so as
(C) afterward
(D) subsequent to

129. According to our company policy, ------- is the last to leave the office is responsible for turning on the security alarm system.

(A) that
(B) which
(C) whoever
(D) most

130. In recent years, consumption of electronic products has increased so much ------- this represents one of the most environmentally problematic product groups today.

(A) since
(B) that
(C) which
(D) in addition to

▶ ▶ ▶GO ON TO THE NEXT PAGE

PART 6

Directions: Read the texts that follow. A word or phrase, or sentence is missing in parts of each text. Four answer choices for each question are given below the text. Select the best answer to complete the text. Then mark the letter (A), (B), (C), or (D) on your answer sheet.

Questions 131-134 refer to the following press release.

New Toll on Highway 585

July 17 - Auckland> Mayor Kenwood has approved a new toll for Highway 585, being built

on the outskirts of the city, ------- completion of construction.
                                131.

The mayor's new toll fee will take effect ------- after the new highway has been completed
                                          132.
and the toll booth will be constructed at the first mile marker of the highway. The

electronic toll collection system -------, and it will allow motorists the ease of not having to
                                  133.
stop and pay the tolls.

-------. He said he understood that the fee will be unpopular, but ultimately it will help to
134.
decrease traffic while giving the city the ability to pay for the new local roads without

having to raise taxes.

131. (A) for
(B) upon
(C) because of
(D) before

132. (A) promptly
(B) accurately
(C) consequently
(D) accordingly

133. (A) were installed
(B) will be installed
(C) have been installed
(D) had installed

134. (A) From August to November, roadway toll fees may be paid in cash.
(B) He joined Tourism Department to promote tourist attractions and arouse tourist visit intention.
(C) The mayor addressed the concern of the new highway and the toll that will be applied.
(D) A highly developed highway system will attract tourists into our city for recreational purposes.

Questions 135-138 refer to the following information.

The Energy Battery you have just purchased was designed to last for over four years or about 40,000 miles. Nevertheless, when your battery finally dies, you should dispose of it
------- . Please do not just throw it in a trash can. Most municipalities currently recommend
135.
users simply not ------- their dead batteries away with trash.
136.

Most experts say discarded batteries can cause fires and explosions if they ------- loose in
137.
boxes or bags with metal items. That's why our company offers a quick and easy disposal method to our customers. ------- . If you turn them over to us, our recycling specialists take
138.
care of them in the proper fashion at no additional charge.

135. (A) immediately
(B) properly
(C) confidentially
(D) respectively

136. (A) throw
(B) to throw
(C) throwing
(D) thrown

137. (A) stores
(B) are stored
(C) stored
(D) will be stored

138. (A) Please do not combine old and new batteries or different types or makes of batteries.
(B) Some batteries left in your garage can be the cause for several safety concerns.
(C) All you have to do is return your dead batteries to one of our recycling centers in your area.
(D) New small-size batteries are used in mobile phones and motor-driven electric tools.

▶ ▶ ▶ GO ON TO THE NEXT PAGE

Questions 139-142 refer to the following advertisement.

VIP Membership For Speed Shopping

Tired of waiting for your package to arrive? Desperate for a little bit of shopping therapy?

Hate paying for expedited shipping each time? Become a VIP member today and ------- **139.** those problems. Our VIP members ------- free same-day shipping for an unlimited amount **140.** of deliveries every year. -------, they receive a $30 electronic gift certificate once a quarter **141.** which can be used both in-store and online. -------. For an annual fee of just $18, become **142.** our VIP member today. Take an advantage of this golden opportunity! You will never

regret it!

139. (A) embrace
(B) delay
(C) avoid
(D) accept

140. (A) enjoy
(B) enjoyment
(C) will enjoy
(D) have enjoyed

141. (A) Thus
(B) In addition
(C) In other words
(D) Simultaneously

142. (A) We also provide VIP members with special discounts on purchases.
(B) For spending over $100, you will qualify for free same-day shipping.
(C) Thank you for your hard work and commitment that has made the best sales record this year.
(D) We are surprised that you did not receive your shipment and apologize for the delay.

Dear all,

I would like to officially let you know that Mr. Harry McBain will be leaving us on June 30 to start up his own company. Since joining us five years ago, Mr. McBain ------- a key role
143.
in improving the competitiveness of our company. -------.
144.

Under Mr. McBain's leadership, we realigned our planning procedures, introduced rigorous quality standards, and developed a company-wide competitive strategy. While the process of change was not always easy, we can all appreciate the positive results.

-------, last quarter we estimate that we overtook all of our rival companies in both
145.
revenue and unit sales, for the first time ever. Mr. McBain deserves a great deal of the

------- for this achievement.
146.

Please join me in wishing Mr. McBain all the best and continued success in his future endeavors.

Best regards,

Sally Murphy
Head of Personnel

143. (A) plays
(B) has played
(C) had been playing
(D) will have played

144. (A) The dedication we have shown to our customers has helped us to expand.
(B) He will continue his role as CEO and will be involved in major decisions.
(C) The prices for our services and products vary widely, which often results in confusion.
(D) As a result, we have dramatically grown sales and become a significantly more profitable company.

145. (A) Even so
(B) In the mean time
(C) For instance
(D) On the other hand

146. (A) aspect
(B) credit
(C) reflection
(D) motivation

PART 7

Directions: In this part you will read a selection of texts, such as magazine and newspaper articles, e-mails, and instant messages. Each text or set of texts is followed by several questions. Select the best answer for each question and mark the letter (A), (B), (C), or (D) on your answer sheet.

Questions 147-148 refer to the following advertisement.

HOME SWEET HOME

Presented by *The Houston Daily*

Looking for brand-new recipes for your family?
Supported by the community's favorite restaurant, Deli Neko, *the Houston Daily* will provide cooking lessons to local residents starting next week. They will take place at Deli Neko, and the owner of the restaurant, Minoru Toba, will teach the classes.

The lessons offered are:
• Create Your Own Sushi – Monday 2 P.M.
• Japanese Noodles   – Monday 3 P.M.

You can register online at www.thehoustondaily.com. For detailed information including costs, please contact Vanessa Connelly at 917-803-7552.

147. What is being advertised?

(A) A restaurant
(B) A local publication
(C) Culinary classes
(D) Home improvement service

148. What should interested readers do?

(A) Go to a website
(B) Call a restaurant owner
(C) Visit Ms. Connelly
(D) Buy a magazine

Questions 149-150 refer to the following text message chain.

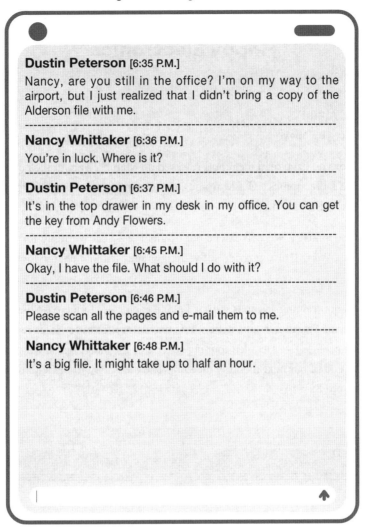

Dustin Peterson [6:35 P.M.]

Nancy, are you still in the office? I'm on my way to the airport, but I just realized that I didn't bring a copy of the Alderson file with me.

Nancy Whittaker [6:36 P.M.]

You're in luck. Where is it?

Dustin Peterson [6:37 P.M.]

It's in the top drawer in my desk in my office. You can get the key from Andy Flowers.

Nancy Whittaker [6:45 P.M.]

Okay, I have the file. What should I do with it?

Dustin Peterson [6:46 P.M.]

Please scan all the pages and e-mail them to me.

Nancy Whittaker [6:48 P.M.]

It's a big file. It might take up to half an hour.

149. What is suggested about Ms. Whittaker?

(A) She shares an office with Mr. Peterson.
(B) She went into Mr. Peterson's office.
(C) She normally stays late at the office.
(D) She could not find Mr. Flowers.

150. At 6:36 P.M., what does Ms. Whittaker most likely mean when she writes, "You're in luck"?

(A) She is working on the Alderson file.
(B) She found the file that Mr. Peterson needs.
(C) She has time to go to the airport.
(D) She has not yet left the office.

▶ ▶ ▶GO ON TO THE NEXT PAGE

Happy Electronics

To: All employees

From: Marie Davis

Date: Monday, April 1

Subject: New Service Policy

I assume that all of you have read the report released on March 27 about the new customer service policy at ST Electronics. ST Electronics, one of our biggest competitors, announced that it will conduct onsite repairs. —[1]—.

To get ahead in the industry, we will extend our original one-year warranty for all our products by two more years. We will also provide software upgrades without charge for those who visit our centers. —[2]—.

In addition, two-hour training sessions will be held in each store to increase the quality of service and to enhance customer satisfaction. It is mandatory for every sales representative to receive this training. —[3]—. Detailed training schedules for individual stores will be announced at the end of our next monthly meeting. The meeting will be held in Conference Room 302A on April 8. —[4]—.

Marie Davis

Marketing Manager

151. What is the purpose of the e-mail?

(A) To provide the history of a company
(B) To solicit feedback from customers
(C) To ask for the agenda of a meeting
(D) To inform employees of some changes

152. What is NOT indicated about Happy Electronics?

(A) It holds meetings on a regular basis.
(B) It possesses more than one store.
(C) It will soon provide a three-year warranty.
(D) It will start doing onsite repairs.

153. In which of the positions marked [1], [2], [3], and [4] does the following sentence best fit?

"The new policy will go into effect on Tuesday, April 5."

(A) [1]
(B) [2]
(C) [3]
(D) [4]

Come to Charlotte, Enjoy the Performances!

Charlotte City Council presents the following series of marvelous performances!
Visit our city and enjoy our different tourist attractions.

• In case of rain, performances may be canceled •

May 4 / Cyche
Charlotte Adventure World / 7 P.M.

Norway's Musician of the Year, Cyche will perform the songs in his 2nd album. Renowned as one of the most enthusiastic singers in the world, he was selected as Musician of the Year by the *Muse* magazine.

May 18 / Kuwaiti Troupe
Charlotte Theater Hall / 7 P.M.

Kuwaiti Troupe will perform traditional Kuwait dance using Kuwaiti musical instruments, rubabah and tanbarah.

May 11 / James McLean
Charlotte Amusement Park / 8 P.M.

Using the traditional Scottish instrument, bagpipes, McLean will sing you amazing songs he himself wrote.

May 25 / Zebras
Light Factory in Charlotte / 7 P.M.

Burundian band, the Zebras, will perform traditional African music with unique instruments and beats.

154. Why will the events be held?

(A) To advertise tour packages
(B) To commemorate a newly constructed amusement park
(C) To promote tourism to Charlotte
(D) To encourage citizens to perform different kinds of music

155. According to the flyer, when will the Zebras perform?

(A) On May 4
(B) On May 11
(C) On May 18
(D) On May 25

156. Where will the dance performance be held?

(A) Charlotte Adventure World
(B) Charlotte Amusement Park
(C) Charlotte City Council
(D) Charlotte Theater Hall

▶ ▶ ▶ GO ON TO THE NEXT PAGE

Peter's Gardening

Dear Customer,

Thank you for using our service. We ask you to complete the form below to help us make our service better with your valuable opinions.

Your Name: Scott Hunt

Phone Number: 214-860-2209

Address: 80 Bearpaw Dr., Irving, TX

1. Which service have you received from Peter's Gardening?

☐ Pruning   ☐ Mowing   ☐ Cleanup   ☑ Total Solution

2. How satisfied were you with the costs?

☐ Very Satisfied   ☐ Satisfied   ☑ Dissatisfied   ☐ Very Dissatisfied

3. How satisfied were you with the time the service took?

☑ Very Satisfied   ☐ Satisfied   ☐ Dissatisfied   ☐ Very Dissatisfied

4. How satisfied were you with the outcome?

☐ Very Satisfied   ☑ Satisfied   ☐ Dissatisfied   ☐ Very Dissatisfied

5. Additional comments :

The total solution from Peter's Gardening succeeded in transforming my garden. I liked the fast renovation progress and the results as well. However, the cost of the service seems a bit high compared to your competitors. I recommend adding a discount for frequent customers like myself.

157. Why was the form sent to Mr. Hunt?

   (A) To collect the opinions of employees
   (B) To get feedback about a finished job
   (C) To ask the customer some questions about an upcoming service
   (D) To confirm a service order from a customer

158. According to the form, what is indicated about Mr. Hunt?

   (A) He recommended Peter's Gardening to his colleagues.
   (B) He thinks the prices of the services is reasonable.
   (C) He received a discount on his service.
   (D) He has received service from Peter's Gardening before.

Questions 159-161 refer to the following information on a website.

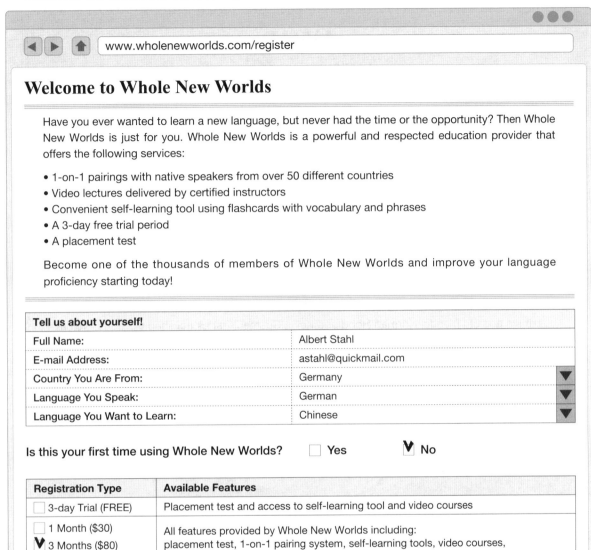

Welcome to Whole New Worlds

Have you ever wanted to learn a new language, but never had the time or the opportunity? Then Whole New Worlds is just for you. Whole New Worlds is a powerful and respected education provider that offers the following services:

- 1-on-1 pairings with native speakers from over 50 different countries
- Video lectures delivered by certified instructors
- Convenient self-learning tool using flashcards with vocabulary and phrases
- A 3-day free trial period
- A placement test

Become one of the thousands of members of Whole New Worlds and improve your language proficiency starting today!

Tell us about yourself!	
Full Name:	Albert Stahl
E-mail Address:	astahl@quickmail.com
Country You Are From:	Germany ▼
Language You Speak:	German ▼
Language You Want to Learn:	Chinese ▼

Is this your first time using Whole New Worlds? ☐ Yes   ☑ No

Registration Type	Available Features
☐ 3-day Trial (FREE)	Placement test and access to self-learning tool and video courses
☐ 1 Month ($30) ☑ 3 Months ($80) ☐ 6 Months ($150)	All features provided by Whole New Worlds including: placement test, 1-on-1 pairing system, self-learning tools, video courses, skill evaluation test and many others

159. What is the purpose of the information?

(A) To recruit new language teachers
(B) To offer a discount for an online publication
(C) To advertise translation services
(D) To promote educational programs

160. What is mentioned about Whole New Worlds?

(A) It offers all of its services for free.
(B) It was recently established.
(C) It has a large number of users.
(D) It is based in Germany.

161. What is suggested about Mr. Stahl?

(A) He plans to register for the 3-day trial.
(B) He speaks Chinese.
(C) He has visited the website before.
(D) He recently took a placement test.

▶ ▶ ▶ GO ON TO THE NEXT PAGE

MEMO

To: All Employees of Hotel Mystic Falls
From: Damon Salvatore
Date: February 2
Subject: The result of the nomination

Dear all employees,

I am glad to announce that Elena Gilbert has been selected as the Employee of the Month. The hotel owner, Robert Hood, will present a recognition plaque to her at the next biannual Mystic Falls Night held in June. Additionally, she will receive a two-day paid holiday and a $300 cash prize.

Since she started working at the Hotel Mystic Falls 3 years ago as a housekeeper, Ms. Gilbert has been an exceptional employee who has displayed continuous effort and devotion. Her excellence in service has been recognized several times by customers.

I would like all employees to congratulate her for this remarkable achievement. Since business partners and old friends, Norman Hood and Kevin Costner, first established the hotel, we have continued the tradition of rewarding employees who demonstrate dedication and passion, and I believe any of you could be the next winner of the Best Employee of the Month.

Thanks,

Damon Salvatore
General Manager
Hotel Mystic Falls

---

162. What is the main topic of the memo?

(A) An award recipient
(B) An upcoming festival
(C) Customer satisfaction survey results
(D) Review of the employees' performance

163. What will most likely happen in June?

(A) Mr. Salvatore will be given a reward.
(B) Submission for a nomination will commence.
(C) A hotel employee will be promoted.
(D) Ms. Gilbert will attend an event.

164. Who is Mr. Costner?

(A) A hotel owner
(B) A friend of Ms. Gilbert's
(C) A co-founder of a business
(D) A housekeeping staff

VEHICLE SALES CONTRACT

J&G Automobile, Ltd.

Contract Number: 121590

This Sales Agreement is made between J&G Automobile, Ltd. (the "Seller") and Michael Bell (the "Buyer").

A. Seller shall transfer the following vehicle to Buyer on February 28.

Maker:	Jensen	Type:	Pickup truck
Model:	J3000i	Color:	Royal Blue
Odometer:	76,291		

B. Buyer agrees to purchase the vehicle from Seller at the price of $19,500 (including tax).

C. Buyer will make a partial installment in the amount of $14,500 on this day and pay the outstanding balance upon the receipt of the vehicle.

D. Seller has presented all inspection records of the vehicle to Buyer and Buyer agrees to purchase the vehicle without warranties.

Signed on February 20 at the J&G Automobile, Ltd. branch in the city of Johnsville.

John Kales	*February 20*
Seller(Dealership Representative)	Date
Michael Bell	*February 20*
Buyer	Date
Kyle Wilson	*February 20*
Witness	Date

ACTUAL TEST 06

---

165. What will Mr. Bell most likely do on February 28?

(A) Sell a vehicle to J&G Automobile, Ltd.
(B) Submit the balance of five thousand dollars
(C) Purchase a one-year limited warranty
(D) Send Mr. Kales a copy of inspection record

166. According to the contract, what can be inferred about J&G Automobile?

(A) It has more than one location.
(B) It is headquartered in Johnsville.
(C) It has many sales representatives.
(D) It sold a royal blue sedan to Mr. Bell.

167. What is NOT indicated in the contract?

(A) The car was manufactured by Jensen.
(B) Mr. Bell will not receive any warranty.
(C) Kyle Wilson is the previous owner of the vehicle.
(D) John Kales works for J&G Automobiles, Ltd.

Questions 168-171 refer to the following online chat discussion.

Glenn Carter   2:29 P.M.

Janet Rudolph from the Amber Café e-mailed me. She wants to double her weekly order. Can we handle that?

Marcus Stetson   2:30 P.M.

I don't see why not. It's not terribly big, so we can do it. What do you think, Greg?

Greg Watkins   2:31 P.M.

The only problem I can foresee is delivery. She receives six boxes every Monday, and if we double that to twelve, her delivery might be too big to fit in my truck with everything else.

Marcus Stetson   2:33 P.M.

Oh, I hadn't considered that.

Glenn Carter   2:34 P.M.

Is it possible to rearrange the delivery schedule? After all, her establishment is only a couple of blocks away. How about delivering her items earlier in the day?

Amy Jones   2:35 P.M.

Let me do it. I drive by her place every morning, so I can drop everything off as I'm going to Harold's Fish and Chips. I can be there by 8:30 A.M.

Glenn Carter   2:37 P.M.

Sounds good. I'll call Janet and fill her in. Are there any problems I need to know about?

Marcus Stetson   2:38 P.M.

We're going to be understaffed this weekend. Brad Howard resigned, and we haven't found a replacement yet.

Amy Jones   2:40 P.M.

I don't have any plans for the weekend.

Glenn Carter   2:41 P.M.

Thanks, Amy. I'll see you on Saturday then.

SEND

168. What is suggested about Mr. Watkins?

(A) He drives a delivery truck.
(B) He works at a café.
(C) He has met Ms. Rudolph in person.
(D) He works late at night.

169. What does Ms. Jones offer to do?

(A) Have a talk with Ms. Rudolph
(B) Find a potential new employee
(C) Deliver some items to a store
(D) Start working earlier each day

170. What will Mr. Carter most likely do next?

(A) Make a telephone call
(B) Redo the schedule
(C) Speak with Mr. Howard
(D) Visit a customer

171. At 2:40 P.M., what does Ms. Jones suggest when she writes, "I don't have any plans for the weekend"?

(A) She needs to earn some extra money.
(B) She has not worked many hours this week.
(C) She expects to be paid overtime.
(D) She is willing to work Mr. Howard's shift.

▶ ▶ ▶ GO ON TO THE NEXT PAGE

Pasadena, April 19 — Today, Brilliance Dairy, Inc., a Los Angeles-based international distributor and supplier of dairy products, announced that Jackson Hofstadter, its chief executive officer for the past 10 years, will retire as of April 30. His position will be filled by the company's current vice president, Penelope Garcia. —[1]—.

Spending his whole career at Brilliance Dairy, Mr. Hofstadter has been loyal to the company since its foundation 35 years ago. —[2]—. "It was wonderful to see the company I have put all my passion into rise to become the number-one company in the industry," said Mr. Hofstadter while reminiscing about the past.

Mr. Hofstadter's successor has a history of service to the firm as long as his. Right after earning a degree in business administration from the University of Boston, Ms. Garcia joined the company's subsidiary in New York, CBS Milk, 25 years ago. —[3]—. She worked as the director of marketing at CBS Milk for 11 years before she transferred to Brilliance Dairy.

"Ms. Garcia was a natural choice for the board of directors. I knew Ms. Garcia was going to be selected when I worked as an assistant marketing director with her at CBS Milk. She is the most effective and dedicated leader I have ever seen," said Sean Cooper, the current managing director at CBS Milk.

Brilliance Dairy has arranged an event to say farewell to its old CEO and to welcome its new one at its headquarters. —[4]—. This event will also celebrate the release of Mr. Hofstadter's book, *Everyone Starts at the Bottom*. "I am indebted to numerous people in the industry in many ways. Now it is time for me to help others by passing on my experience and knowledge through books," noted Mr. Hofstadter.

172. What is indicated about Brilliance Dairy Inc.?

(A) It exports its goods abroad.
(B) It is a competitor of CBS Milk.
(C) It has a large dairy farm in Pasadena.
(D) It is currently recruiting new employees.

173. Who is Mr. Cooper?

(A) The new CEO of Brilliance Dairy, Inc.
(B) The former assistant marketing director of CBS Milk
(C) The current vice president of Brilliance Dairy Inc.
(D) The author of *Everyone Starts at the Bottom*

174. What does Mr. Hofstadter plan to do?

(A) Open a new business
(B) Study business management
(C) Train Ms. Garcia
(D) Share his expertise through writing

175. In which of the positions marked [1], [2], [3], and [4] does the following sentence best fit?

"It will be held on April 30."

(A) [1]
(B) [2]
(C) [3]
(D) [4]

▶ ▶ ▶ GO ON TO THE NEXT PAGE

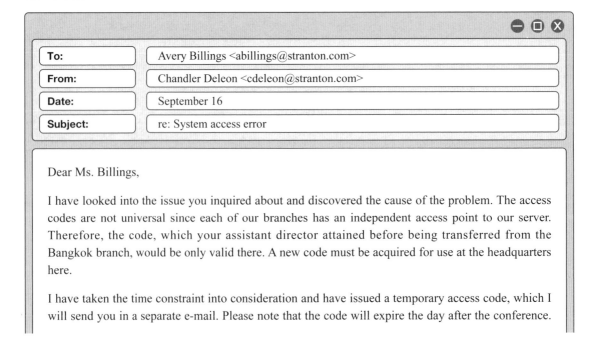

To: Chandler Deleon <cdeleon@stranton.com>

From: Avery Billings <abillings@stranton.com>

Date: September 15

Subject: System access error

Dear Mr. Deleon,

As you know, our department is currently preparing a joint video conference with our Thailand branch and a local business, Diem Home & Living Bangkok. Jessica Diem will join us in the talk to discuss the possible cooperation between the two companies. This conference will be a crucial stepping-stone for our company's expansion into the Asian market.

However, we have encountered a problem while preparing for the conference, which will be held on September 19. Evelyn Forster, our assistant director, reported that she is currently unable to access the company's intranet. She mentioned that she didn't have any problems when she logged in to the system a week ago.

She is a key member in this potential business relationship, and thus, we definitely need Ms. Forster to be able to access all the materials online. Please attend to the issue as soon as possible. Thank you in advance for your assistance.

Regards,

Avery Billings
Marketing Director, Stranton Kitchen Appliances

To: Avery Billings <abillings@stranton.com>

From: Chandler Deleon <cdeleon@stranton.com>

Date: September 16

Subject: re: System access error

Dear Ms. Billings,

I have looked into the issue you inquired about and discovered the cause of the problem. The access codes are not universal since each of our branches has an independent access point to our server. Therefore, the code, which your assistant director attained before being transferred from the Bangkok branch, would be only valid there. A new code must be acquired for use at the headquarters here.

I have taken the time constraint into consideration and have issued a temporary access code, which I will send you in a separate e-mail. Please note that the code will expire the day after the conference.

To gain a permanent code, the individual will need to submit a request online. As indicated in the employee manual, fill out the form found at http://intranet.stranton.com/form/100254 and upload the listed materials.

I will be away on a business trip from September 22 and be out of contact. Should there be any issues while I am away, please get in touch with my assistant, Dan Hadley.

Regards,

Chandler Deleon
Technical Support Director, Stranton Kitchen Appliances

---

176. What is the main purpose of the first e-mail?

(A) To ask for conference attendance
(B) To solicit technological assistance
(C) To inform about business plans
(D) To commend an employee's efforts

177. What is indicated about Stranton Kitchen Appliances?

(A) It is experiencing financial difficulties.
(B) It recruited new employees recently.
(C) It intends to enlarge its business.
(D) It plans to adopt a new system soon.

178. Who has recently joined Ms. Billings' department?

(A) Mr. Deleon
(B) Ms. Diem
(C) Ms. Forster
(D) Mr. Hadley

179. When will the temporary code expire?

(A) On September 16
(B) On September 19
(C) On September 20
(D) On September 22

180. What will Ms. Forster most likely do next?

(A) Submit a report to her manager
(B) Read an instruction manual
(C) Request a new authorization code
(D) Schedule a conference

|||||||||||||||||||||||||||||||||||||||||||||||||||||||||||||||||||||||||||||||||||||||||||

4th Sand & Music Festival
July 13-14, Salisbury Beach

Visit Salisbury, the hometown of many world-famous musicians, to enjoy your summer days and nights with the 4th Sand & Music Festival. The weekend-long festival at the Salisbury Beach will provide all visitors with great food, excitement, and unforgettable memories! Below is the list of activities you can participate in:

Sand Sculpture Exhibition
Walk along the magnificent sand sculptures displayed on the wonderful shore of Salisbury Beach. The theme of this year's exhibition is 'Under the Ocean.'

Beach Volleyball Competition (July 14 Only)
Join us at the coed beach volleyball competition. Quick and easy registration is available online until July 8.

Summer Night Concerts
Enjoy the sound of music calling in the sunsets. A stage will be set up on the shore of Salisbury Beach. The concerts will be held in a local bar if it rains.

Fireworks Display
Experience amazingly beautiful fireworks each night at 9 P.M.

- For further inquiries about the 4th Sand & Music Festival, please give us a call at 555-0095.
- Press must receive official permission to cover the festival. Prior registration by July 10 with Jake Seiz at jseiz@salisbury.com is required.

|||||||||||||||||||||||||||||||||||||||||||||||||||||||||||||||||||||||||||||||||||||||||||

Salisbury Times

By Helena Maliosa

July 15, Salisbury — Last weekend, over ten thousand people attended the 4th Sand & Music Festival at Salisbury Beach to enjoy some exciting activities.

My sons and I personally enjoyed this year's sand sculpture exhibition the most. When I visited the festival with my sons last year, the sand sculpture exhibition only had about 10 sculptures. This year's village of giant sea creatures definitely provided a splendid view. Ten world-class sand sculptors from across the nation built 30 pieces of art.

The first day's jazz concert was a huge success. The large stage set up on the shore actually seemed small among the large crowd. Unlike the jazz concert, the pop concert on the second day was disappointing. It was held in a local pub, and because of the size of the pub, a lot of people could not even enter. Also, the sound equipment in the pub was so dated that the crowd could not hear the music clearly. It seems like the organizers of the festival next year should come up with another indoor venue for concerts.

Without a doubt, the highlight of the festival was the fireworks rounding off each day of the event. The best local pyrotechnic company designed the fireworks this year, and all visitors were invited to watch the fabulous show free of charge.

181. In the announcement, what is mentioned about Salisbury?

(A) It is famous for its weekly fireworks.
(B) It is open to public only in summer.
(C) It is overly crowded with visitors.
(D) It produced some well-known musicians.

182. By when does the registration for beach volleyball competition have to be completed?

(A) July 8
(B) July 10
(C) July 14
(D) July 15

183. What had Ms. Maliosa probably done before the festival?

(A) Registered for a membership
(B) Contacted Mr. Seiz
(C) Paid for admission
(D) Called the organizers

184. What is NOT suggested about the festival this year?

(A) It was held near a body of water.
(B) It hosted the sand sculpture exhibition for the first time.
(C) It was open to children.
(D) It rained on the second day.

185. What does Ms. Maliosa indicate about the festival in the review?

(A) The festival lacks events for children.
(B) The firework display needs more safety staff.
(C) The alternative location for a concert was inadequate.
(D) There were not enough places for visitors to eat.

▶ ▶ ▶ **GO ON TO THE NEXT PAGE**

INCREDIBLE LODGE

Alice Springs, Northern Territory, Australia
+61 230777199

In search of a unique getaway? Then come to the Incredible Lodge for an extraordinary encounter in the heart of the Australian continent. Get in touch with an ancient land and dig up stories buried in the sand.

- Tour Uluru with a guide from an Aboriginal tribe, one of the indigenous people of Australia
- Take part in a festival of the Anangu people, a local tribe
- Take a sunrise camel tour exploring central Australia
- Dine under the beautiful starry sky in the desert

As the biggest hotel in the area, we cater to your every need, including providing an airport shuttle, laundry service, and cleaning at no cost. In celebration of our tenth anniversary, all guests can enjoy a complimentary buffet breakfast.

Visit www.incrediblelodge.com to discover more. Visit before the end of January and receive a 10% discount at our souvenir shop.

INCREDIBLE LODGE

Customer Feedback

Please complete this short survey so that we can better serve our guests.

Name: Kieran Achino   **E-mail:** kachino@mail.com

Date of Stay: January 20-25

Please indicate your level of satisfaction (1 = highest / 4 = lowest)

	1	2	3	4
Politeness of staff	○	●	○	○
Responsiveness of staff	●	○	○	○
Cleanliness of the facilities	○	●	○	○
Quality of your room	○	●	○	○

Most Memorable Experience: The Uluru tour. When I visited Uluru, I was guided by Bakana, who was a wonderful storyteller. She told a traditional dreamtime story of her tribe, adding depth to my experience. It was nice to see her again at her people's festival that night, where she told more stories.

Issues You Had: On the second day of my stay, the air conditioner stopped working. However, the problem was fixed within half an hour of my reporting it. I was impressed with the level of service.

To: All Staff, Maintenance Department
From: Jason Wheelock
Subject: Room Problem
Date: January 30

The air conditioner in room 34 on the third floor has broken down for the second time in the past week. I looked into the matter and discovered that we purchased it more than ten years ago. As such, I've ordered a new unit. It's scheduled to arrive in two days. Once it arrives, please install it immediately. That room will remain empty until the new unit is running properly.

186. For whom is the advertisement intended?

(A) Historians
(B) Business owners
(C) Tourists
(D) Traditional artists

187. What is NOT suggested about the Incredible Lodge?

(A) It only accepts online bookings.
(B) It does its guests' laundry for free.
(C) It can hold more guests than all other nearby hotels.
(D) It opened a decade ago.

188. According to the advertisement, what is being offered for a limited period of time?

(A) Room upgrades
(B) A free camel hire
(C) Complimentary dinners
(D) A discount at a gift store

189. What is indicated about Bakana?

(A) She is a famous author.
(B) She is from the Anangu tribe.
(C) She was recently hired by the Incredible Lodge.
(D) She was satisfied with her recent tour.

190. What is suggested about Mr. Achino?

(A) He felt that the Incredible Lodge was too expensive.
(B) He was somewhat displeased with his tour.
(C) He stayed on the third floor of the Incredible Lodge.
(D) He intends to return to Uluru later in the year.

July 25

Barbados Grill
97A Plate Avenue
Toronto M4C 5B5

Dear Store Manager,

This is to inquire about the billing process during my last visit to your establishment. At 6:30 P.M. on July 20, my wife and I visited your restaurant for dinner before attending a concert. My wife ordered the lamb chops with Italian herbs while I ordered the stuffed pork belly. Each dish was priced at $60. However, I was served the chef's special, which was pork chops with artichokes.

When I spoke to you, you asked me whether I would like to wait for the correct dish or have the served dish. You also said that since it was your mistake, you would offer the $90 dish at the same price as my original order. Since we were pressed for time, I ate the pork chops.

When we were leaving, we were in a hurry so we didn't examine the bill carefully. However, when I received my monthly credit card statement, I noticed that I had been charged $150 for the meal. I hereby request a refund of $30.

We have been customers at your restaurant for almost two years, and this incident has been disappointing. I hope something similar does not happen again.

Regards,

Bruce McGee

July 31

Bruce McGee
555 Victoria Street
Toronto, M3M 5G9

Dear Mr. McGee,

Please accept my sincere apology for the mistake. I spoke with Mark Harrington about your visit, and he confirmed that you were accidentally served the wrong meal and that he offered it to you at a reduced price. $30 has therefore been refunded to your credit card.

I feel bad that something like this has happened to valued customers such as you and your wife. Please accept this coupon that you can use on your next visit. If there is anything else I can do for you, please let me know.

Yours respectfully,

Lorraine Bracco
Owner, Barbados Grill

COUPON
Barbados Grill

This coupon is good for one free chef's special meal.
Please show this coupon to your server when placing your order.
Limit one coupon per customer.

Expiration Date: December 31

---

191. Why was the first letter written?

(A) To describe a pleasant experience
(B) To report a payment error
(C) To make a reservation for a meal
(D) To inquire about the menu

192. What is indicated about Mr. McGee?

(A) He was late for a concert.
(B) He dined with his spouse on July 20.
(C) He likes to try new menu items.
(D) He will not return to the restaurant again.

193. What is suggested about Mr. Harrington?

(A) He was working at Barbados Grill on July 31.
(B) His credit card was wrongly charged.
(C) He is the manager of Barbados Grill.
(D) He usually recommends lamb chops to customers.

194. What can be inferred about Barbados Grill?

(A) It closes at 7:30 P.M.
(B) It offers gift cards to all customers.
(C) It has been in business for about two years.
(D) Its owner cares about its customers.

195. What is the value of the coupon?

(A) $30
(B) $60
(C) $90
(D) $150

Victoria (October 10) – The Flourishing Trees Organization (FTO) will host a fundraising event, the One Earth Festival, at Gilmour Park on Friday, October 13, from 8:30 A.M. to 6:00 P.M. FTO is a nonprofit organization focusing on reminding people of the importance of the environment and nature. This festival is intended to promote the environment to residents of Victoria.

The festival will feature speeches by invited speakers, including Willow Lawrence. "I'm pleased this event will be finally held in my hometown. It's a good cause and will definitely help increase environmental awareness in the region," remarked Ms. Lawrence.

"I want everybody from Victoria to enjoy the festival like people did at previous festivals in other cities. There will be food vendors, short performances, and music concerts by locals," said FTO spokesman Dexter Voorhees. "What is special about this year's festival is that it will be held outdoors for the first time."

Everyone is welcome at the festival. All donations are appreciated. Businesses donating more than $3,000 will be given an advertisement slot on the front page of the organization's website and in its brochure. For more information, please call the planning director, Declan Jackman, at 852-555-0958 or send an e-mail to djackman@ftomail.com.

To: Declan Jackman, Felicia Stewart, Rodney West
From: Jason Greene, CEO
Date: October 11
Subject: Slight Changes

We have had to make a few changes regarding the festival in Victoria. Please note the new duties of the following individuals:

Aaron Hampton: entertainment coordinator
Patricia Ermine: catering coordinator
Rodney West: public speaking facilitator
Nancy Marsh: public relations advisor

If you have any questions, get in touch with me at once. Let's make this year's festival the best one ever.

To:	Declan Jackman <djackman@ftomail.com>
From:	Arnold Xavier <axavier@lesfeuilles.com>
Date:	October 17
Subject:	Thank you!

Dear Mr. Jackman,

Thank you for putting my restaurant's logo on your website and in the brochure. I'm pleased the festival went so well. The entire event seemed to run smoothly. My restaurant has seen an increasing number of diners lately as well as increased sales thanks to the ads.

I was happy to be involved with the event and hope to do so in the future. Please keep me advised of any opportunities that may arise later.

Thank you,

Arnold Xavier
Owner
Les Feuilles

196. In the article, the word "cause" in paragraph 2, line 4, is closest in meaning to

(A) promotion
(B) goal
(C) fund
(D) result

197. What is indicated about Ms. Lawrence?

(A) She will lead a team of volunteers.
(B) She founded the FTO.
(C) She is from Victoria.
(D) She is world famous.

198. According to Mr. Voorhees, what is true about the One Earth Festival?

(A) It is expecting the most attendees in its history.
(B) It has been held in Victoria several times.
(C) It will only admit residents of Victoria.
(D) It took place indoors last year.

199. Who most likely worked with Ms. Lawrence?

(A) Mr. Hampton
(B) Ms. Ermine
(C) Mr. West
(D) Ms. Marsh

200. What can be inferred about Mr. Xavier?

(A) He contributed over $3,000 to the festival.
(B) He sold food from his restaurant at the festival.
(C) He founded Les Feuilles a few years ago.
(D) His restaurant's logo was redesigned recently.

STOP! This is the end of the test. If you finish before time is called, you may go back to Parts 5, 6, and 7 and check your work.

Actual Test 答案表

Listening Comprehension

Reading Comprehension

01

1. (D)	2. (D)	3. (C)	4. (A)	5. (A)
6. (D)	7. (A)	8. (B)	9. (B)	10. (A)
11. (B)	12. (A)	13. (A)	14. (B)	15. (A)
16. (C)	17. (C)	18. (C)	19. (B)	20. (C)
21. (C)	22. (A)	23. (A)	24. (B)	25. (A)
26. (B)	27. (C)	28. (A)	29. (B)	30. (B)
31. (A)	32. (C)	33. (C)	34. (D)	35. (A)
36. (C)	37. (B)	38. (B)	39. (C)	40. (D)
41. (A)	42. (C)	43. (A)	44. (C)	45. (B)
46. (D)	47. (A)	48. (B)	49. (C)	50. (C)
51. (A)	52. (C)	53. (B)	54. (A)	55. (D)
56. (D)	57. (C)	58. (A)	59. (A)	60. (D)
61. (A)	62. (C)	63. (A)	64. (A)	65. (C)
66. (D)	67. (B)	68. (C)	69. (B)	70. (B)
71. (C)	72. (B)	73. (B)	74. (D)	75. (A)
76. (B)	77. (C)	78. (D)	79. (B)	80. (D)
81. (A)	82. (D)	83. (D)	84. (C)	85. (B)
86. (A)	87. (C)	88. (D)	89. (C)	90. (B)
91. (A)	92. (A)	93. (D)	94. (D)	95. (A)
96. (B)	97. (A)	98. (A)	99. (B)	100. (D)

101. (D)	102. (A)	103. (C)	104. (B)	105. (C)
106. (B)	107. (C)	108. (C)	109. (C)	110. (B)
111. (C)	112. (C)	113. (C)	114. (D)	115. (A)
116. (B)	117. (C)	118. (B)	119. (A)	120. (B)
121. (D)	122. (B)	123. (D)	124. (B)	125. (B)
126. (B)	127. (C)	128. (D)	129. (D)	130. (B)
131. (B)	132. (A)	133. (D)	134. (C)	135. (C)
136. (A)	137. (B)	138. (A)	139. (B)	140. (D)
141. (C)	142. (A)	143. (C)	144. (D)	145. (B)
146. (D)	147. (C)	148. (D)	149. (D)	150. (B)
151. (D)	152. (C)	153. (B)	154. (C)	155. (A)
156. (B)	157. (D)	158. (C)	159. (B)	160. (B)
161. (C)	162. (B)	163. (B)	164. (A)	165. (D)
166. (D)	167. (B)	168. (B)	169. (C)	170. (D)
171. (C)	172. (D)	173. (B)	174. (A)	175. (B)
176. (B)	177. (D)	178. (C)	179. (A)	180. (B)
181. (A)	182. (D)	183. (D)	184. (D)	185. (B)
186. (B)	187. (D)	188. (B)	189. (B)	190. (D)
191. (A)	192. (C)	193. (B)	194. (A)	195. (D)
196. (B)	197. (A)	198. (C)	199. (D)	200. (C)

02

1. (C)	2. (C)	3. (C)	4. (A)	5. (C)
6. (B)	7. (B)	8. (C)	9. (C)	10. (B)
11. (A)	12. (B)	13. (B)	14. (B)	15. (A)
16. (A)	17. (C)	18. (B)	19. (B)	20. (C)
21. (B)	22. (B)	23. (C)	24. (A)	25. (C)
26. (C)	27. (B)	28. (B)	29. (A)	30. (A)
31. (B)	32. (A)	33. (C)	34. (A)	35. (C)
36. (B)	37. (D)	38. (B)	39. (C)	40. (D)
41. (A)	42. (D)	43. (D)	44. (D)	45. (B)
46. (A)	47. (B)	48. (C)	49. (B)	50. (A)
51. (B)	52. (C)	53. (B)	54. (D)	55. (A)
56. (D)	57. (A)	58. (B)	59. (B)	60. (A)
61. (D)	62. (D)	63. (C)	64. (B)	65. (B)
66. (B)	67. (C)	68. (D)	69. (B)	70. (A)
71. (A)	72. (C)	73. (D)	74. (D)	75. (C)
76. (C)	77. (C)	78. (B)	79. (A)	80. (D)
81. (C)	82. (C)	83. (B)	84. (D)	85. (A)
86. (C)	87. (A)	88. (C)	89. (D)	90. (A)
91. (A)	92. (B)	93. (D)	94. (A)	95. (A)
96. (B)	97. (C)	98. (B)	99. (D)	100. (C)

101. (C)	102. (A)	103. (A)	104. (B)	105. (D)
106. (B)	107. (C)	108. (A)	109. (C)	110. (A)
111. (B)	112. (C)	113. (D)	114. (B)	115. (A)
116. (D)	117. (B)	118. (D)	119. (D)	120. (D)
121. (D)	122. (B)	123. (A)	124. (B)	125. (A)
126. (C)	127. (B)	128. (C)	129. (D)	130. (D)
131. (C)	132. (C)	133. (C)	134. (C)	135. (D)
136. (D)	137. (D)	138. (B)	139. (C)	140. (B)
141. (D)	142. (D)	143. (D)	144. (B)	145. (B)
146. (A)	147. (D)	148. (C)	149. (C)	150. (D)
151. (A)	152. (B)	153. (D)	154. (D)	155. (B)
156. (D)	157. (B)	158. (B)	159. (C)	160. (D)
161. (B)	162. (B)	163. (B)	164. (B)	165. (C)
166. (C)	167. (A)	168. (D)	169. (C)	170. (A)
171. (A)	172. (C)	173. (A)	174. (D)	175. (D)
176. (D)	177. (B)	178. (A)	179. (C)	180. (C)
181. (C)	182. (B)	183. (B)	184. (A)	185. (D)
186. (B)	187. (C)	188. (D)	189. (A)	190. (C)
191. (A)	192. (B)	193. (C)	194. (B)	195. (C)
196. (C)	197. (D)	198. (D)	199. (D)	200. (B)

Actual Test 答案表

Listening Comprehension   **Reading Comprehension**

03

1. (C)	2. (C)	3. (A)	4. (C)	5. (C)	101. (B)	102. (C)	103. (D)	104. (D)	105. (B)
6. (C)	7. (C)	8. (A)	9. (C)	10. (A)	106. (C)	107. (A)	108. (D)	109. (A)	110. (B)
11. (A)	12. (A)	13. (C)	14. (C)	15. (A)	111. (A)	112. (C)	113. (A)	114. (C)	115. (B)
16. (A)	17. (B)	18. (B)	19. (B)	20. (A)	116. (B)	117. (D)	118. (B)	119. (C)	120. (D)
21. (C)	22. (C)	23. (A)	24. (B)	25. (B)	121. (B)	122. (B)	123. (A)	124. (A)	125. (A)
26. (C)	27. (C)	28. (B)	29. (B)	30. (B)	126. (D)	127. (A)	128. (D)	129. (D)	130. (B)
31. (A)	32. (C)	33. (B)	34. (C)	35. (A)	131. (C)	132. (B)	133. (B)	134. (D)	135. (C)
36. (C)	37. (D)	38. (D)	39. (A)	40. (B)	136. (A)	137. (A)	138. (D)	139. (D)	140. (B)
41. (D)	42. (B)	43. (B)	44. (C)	45. (A)	141. (D)	142. (B)	143. (C)	144. (B)	145. (B)
46. (A)	47. (B)	48. (D)	49. (C)	50. (D)	146. (D)	147. (C)	148. (A)	149. (D)	150. (B)
51. (C)	52. (D)	53. (C)	54. (A)	55. (C)	151. (C)	152. (D)	153. (B)	154. (C)	155. (C)
56. (D)	57. (B)	58. (C)	59. (A)	60. (D)	156. (C)	157. (A)	158. (C)	159. (B)	160. (D)
61. (B)	62. (C)	63. (A)	64. (D)	65. (A)	161. (C)	162. (D)	163. (C)	164. (B)	165. (C)
66. (B)	67. (A)	68. (A)	69. (B)	70. (B)	166. (C)	167. (D)	168. (D)	169. (D)	170. (A)
71. (D)	72. (D)	73. (C)	74. (B)	75. (A)	171. (C)	172. (A)	173. (A)	174. (C)	175. (C)
76. (D)	77. (C)	78. (A)	79. (D)	80. (D)	176. (C)	177. (C)	178. (C)	179. (A)	180. (C)
81. (A)	82. (C)	83. (D)	84. (C)	85. (A)	181. (C)	182. (A)	183. (D)	184. (B)	185. (B)
86. (C)	87. (B)	88. (C)	89. (A)	90. (D)	186. (B)	187. (B)	188. (C)	189. (D)	190. (A)
91. (C)	92. (C)	93. (B)	94. (D)	95. (C)	191. (A)	192. (C)	193. (B)	194. (B)	195. (A)
96. (B)	97. (D)	98. (D)	99. (A)	100. (C)	196. (C)	197. (C)	198. (C)	199. (B)	200. (C)

04

1. (B)	2. (C)	3. (B)	4. (C)	5. (A)	101. (C)	102. (D)	103. (B)	104. (B)	105. (C)
6. (D)	7. (C)	8. (C)	9. (B)	10. (C)	106. (B)	107. (A)	108. (B)	109. (A)	110. (B)
11. (B)	12. (A)	13. (A)	14. (B)	15. (B)	111. (B)	112. (C)	113. (C)	114. (B)	115. (A)
16. (B)	17. (B)	18. (B)	19. (B)	20. (C)	116. (A)	117. (B)	118. (C)	119. (A)	120. (C)
21. (A)	22. (A)	23. (A)	24. (A)	25. (B)	121. (C)	122. (B)	123. (D)	124. (D)	125. (D)
26. (B)	27. (C)	28. (C)	29. (A)	30. (B)	126. (D)	127. (A)	128. (A)	129. (B)	130. (C)
31. (C)	32. (A)	33. (C)	34. (D)	35. (A)	131. (A)	132. (C)	133. (B)	134. (D)	135. (D)
36. (B)	37. (B)	38. (D)	39. (C)	40. (C)	136. (C)	137. (A)	138. (D)	139. (C)	140. (B)
41. (A)	42. (C)	43. (A)	44. (C)	45. (A)	141. (A)	142. (D)	143. (C)	144. (C)	145. (C)
46. (D)	47. (C)	48. (A)	49. (D)	50. (B)	146. (C)	147. (D)	148. (C)	149. (C)	150. (D)
51. (C)	52. (A)	53. (C)	54. (C)	55. (C)	151. (A)	152. (B)	153. (C)	154. (C)	155. (B)
56. (C)	57. (B)	58. (C)	59. (C)	60. (A)	156. (A)	157. (C)	158. (C)	159. (C)	160. (D)
61. (D)	62. (C)	63. (D)	64. (C)	65. (B)	161. (B)	162. (B)	163. (C)	164. (B)	165. (D)
66. (C)	67. (B)	68. (B)	69. (B)	70. (A)	166. (A)	167. (D)	168. (D)	169. (A)	170. (B)
71. (B)	72. (D)	73. (B)	74. (B)	75. (B)	171. (D)	172. (C)	173. (B)	174. (A)	175. (C)
76. (B)	77. (C)	78. (A)	79. (A)	80. (A)	176. (A)	177. (D)	178. (C)	179. (C)	180. (B)
81. (C)	82. (D)	83. (D)	84. (B)	85. (A)	181. (D)	182. (D)	183. (C)	184. (B)	185. (A)
86. (C)	87. (B)	88. (D)	89. (C)	90. (A)	186. (D)	187. (A)	188. (C)	189. (D)	190. (B)
91. (D)	92. (C)	93. (A)	94. (B)	95. (C)	191. (D)	192. (C)	193. (A)	194. (C)	195. (D)
96. (B)	97. (C)	98. (D)	99. (B)	100. (C)	196. (A)	197. (D)	198. (C)	199. (D)	200. (A)

Actual Test 答案表

Listening Comprehension **Reading Comprehension**

05

1. (C)	2. (B)	3. (D)	4. (C)	5. (C)	101. (A)	102. (A)	103. (C)	104. (C)	105. (B)
6. (D)	7. (B)	8. (A)	9. (A)	10. (C)	106. (C)	107. (B)	108. (D)	109. (A)	110. (D)
11. (B)	12. (B)	13. (A)	14. (B)	15. (A)	111. (C)	112. (A)	113. (B)	114. (C)	115. (B)
16. (C)	17. (A)	18. (C)	19. (C)	20. (C)	116. (C)	117. (B)	118. (C)	119. (D)	120. (D)
21. (C)	22. (A)	23. (B)	24. (B)	25. (A)	121. (C)	122. (A)	123. (C)	124. (B)	125. (D)
26. (A)	27. (A)	28. (C)	29. (B)	30. (C)	126. (D)	127. (B)	128. (B)	129. (D)	130. (C)
31. (B)	32. (A)	33. (C)	34. (A)	35. (A)	131. (B)	132. (A)	133. (B)	134. (D)	135. (D)
36. (D)	37. (B)	38. (D)	39. (C)	40. (A)	136. (A)	137. (B)	138. (B)	139. (D)	140. (D)
41. (C)	42. (B)	43. (C)	44. (B)	45. (C)	141. (B)	142. (C)	143. (C)	144. (A)	145. (C)
46. (A)	47. (A)	48. (B)	49. (B)	50. (B)	146. (D)	147. (A)	148. (C)	149. (A)	150. (D)
51. (D)	52. (D)	53. (C)	54. (A)	55. (A)	151. (B)	152. (C)	153. (D)	154. (C)	155. (D)
56. (C)	57. (D)	58. (C)	59. (C)	60. (C)	156. (B)	157. (B)	158. (D)	159. (A)	160. (C)
61. (A)	62. (C)	63. (B)	64. (D)	65. (C)	161. (B)	162. (B)	163. (D)	164. (C)	165. (C)
66. (D)	67. (C)	68. (A)	69. (C)	70. (C)	166. (D)	167. (D)	168. (B)	169. (A)	170. (C)
71. (D)	72. (D)	73. (D)	74. (C)	75. (C)	171. (D)	172. (D)	173. (A)	174. (C)	175. (C)
76. (D)	77. (C)	78. (D)	79. (C)	80. (B)	176. (C)	177. (C)	178. (C)	179. (C)	180. (C)
81. (A)	82. (D)	83. (B)	84. (A)	85. (D)	181. (C)	182. (C)	183. (B)	184. (D)	185. (C)
86. (C)	87. (C)	88. (D)	89. (C)	90. (D)	186. (C)	187. (A)	188. (D)	189. (D)	190. (D)
91. (D)	92. (A)	93. (B)	94. (C)	95. (B)	191. (B)	192. (C)	193. (D)	194. (C)	195. (A)
96. (C)	97. (D)	98. (B)	99. (D)	100. (C)	196. (D)	197. (B)	198. (A)	199. (C)	200. (D)

06

1. (C)	2. (B)	3. (A)	4. (D)	5. (C)	101. (B)	102. (D)	103. (B)	104. (B)	105. (B)
6. (A)	7. (B)	8. (B)	9. (B)	10. (C)	106. (C)	107. (B)	108. (C)	109. (A)	110. (C)
11. (A)	12. (C)	13. (C)	14. (C)	15. (A)	111. (D)	112. (B)	113. (D)	114. (C)	115. (D)
16. (C)	17. (B)	18. (C)	19. (A)	20. (C)	116. (A)	117. (D)	118. (A)	119. (D)	120. (C)
21. (B)	22. (C)	23. (B)	24. (A)	25. (B)	121. (A)	122. (B)	123. (D)	124. (D)	125. (A)
26. (B)	27. (B)	28. (A)	29. (C)	30. (B)	126. (B)	127. (A)	128. (C)	129. (C)	130. (B)
31. (C)	32. (B)	33. (B)	34. (D)	35. (A)	131. (B)	132. (A)	133. (B)	134. (C)	135. (B)
36. (C)	37. (A)	38. (D)	39. (B)	40. (A)	136. (B)	137. (B)	138. (C)	139. (C)	140. (A)
41. (C)	42. (B)	43. (D)	44. (B)	45. (A)	141. (B)	142. (A)	143. (B)	144. (D)	145. (C)
46. (B)	47. (D)	48. (A)	49. (B)	50. (C)	146. (B)	147. (C)	148. (A)	149. (B)	150. (D)
51. (C)	52. (B)	53. (D)	54. (C)	55. (A)	151. (D)	152. (D)	153. (B)	154. (C)	155. (D)
56. (B)	57. (B)	58. (D)	59. (B)	60. (D)	156. (B)	157. (B)	158. (D)	159. (D)	160. (C)
61. (B)	62. (B)	63. (A)	64. (C)	65. (D)	161. (C)	162. (A)	163. (D)	164. (C)	165. (B)
66. (A)	67. (C)	68. (A)	69. (C)	70. (B)	166. (A)	167. (C)	168. (A)	169. (C)	170. (A)
71. (C)	72. (C)	73. (B)	74. (B)	75. (C)	171. (D)	172. (A)	173. (B)	174. (D)	175. (D)
76. (B)	77. (A)	78. (D)	79. (D)	80. (C)	176. (B)	177. (C)	178. (C)	179. (C)	180. (C)
81. (B)	82. (D)	83. (C)	84. (A)	85. (D)	181. (D)	182. (A)	183. (B)	184. (B)	185. (C)
86. (C)	87. (B)	88. (C)	89. (D)	90. (A)	186. (C)	187. (A)	188. (D)	189. (B)	190. (C)
91. (C)	92. (C)	93. (B)	94. (D)	95. (A)	191. (B)	192. (B)	193. (C)	194. (D)	195. (C)
96. (C)	97. (A)	98. (B)	99. (D)	100. (A)	196. (B)	197. (C)	198. (D)	199. (C)	200. (A)

Actual Test

01
02
03
04
05
06

中譯與解答

Actual Test 01

Part 1

1. 美國 W
   (A) She is paying for purchases.
   (B) She is weighing some vegetables.
   (C) She is exiting a store.
   (D) She is placing food in a basket.

   (A) 她正在為購買的物品付錢。
   (B) 她正在秤蔬菜的重量。
   (C) 她正從商店走出來。
   (D) 她正把食物放進籃子裡。　　　　答案 (D)

2. 英國 M
   (A) The man has his hands on the steering wheel.
   (B) A vehicle is being repaired.
   (C) A package is being delivered to a man.
   (D) The man is writing on a clipboard.

   (A) 那名男子把手放在方向盤上。
   (B) 車輛正在修理中。
   (C) 包裹正遞送給一名男子。
   (D) 那名男子正在板夾上寫字。　　　　答案 (D)

3. 澳洲 W
   (A) She is pouring coffee into a cup.
   (B) She is holding onto a handrail.
   (C) She is descending a staircase.
   (D) She is taking a wallet from her backpack.

   (A) 她正把咖啡倒進杯子裡。
   (B) 她正緊抓著扶手。
   (C) 她正在下樓梯。
   (D) 她正從背包裡掏出錢包。　　　　答案 (C)

4. 美國 M
   (A) Some tables have been arranged in the middle of a room.
   (B) Some objects are scattered around on the table.
   (C) Some potted plants have been arranged in rows.
   (D) Folded chairs are leaning against the wall.

   (A) 幾張桌子整齊地擺放在房間的正中央。
   (B) 幾件物品散落在桌子上。
   (C) 幾個盆栽排列整齊。
   (D) 摺疊的椅子靠在牆上。　　　　答案 (A)

5. 美國 W
   (A) Some people are assembled on the patio.
   (B) Some people are adjusting an umbrella.
   (C) A chair has been set on the lawn.
   (D) They are arranging chairs on the patio.

   (A) 幾個人正聚集在戶外露臺上。
   (B) 幾個人正在調整遮陽傘。
   (C) 椅子放在草坪上。
   (D) 他們正在整理戶外露臺上的椅子。　　　　答案 (A)

6. 英國 M
   (A) One of the women is reaching into an oven.
   (B) Some containers are being emptied.
   (C) One of the women is leaning against the counter.
   (D) Some candy is being displayed in a glass case.

   (A) 其中一名女子正把手伸進烤箱裡。
   (B) 幾個容器正被清空。
   (C) 其中一名女子靠在櫃檯上。
   (D) 糖果陳列在玻璃盒子裡。　　　　答案 (D)

Part 2

7. 美國 M 美國 W

   Who is supposed to work at the loading dock this morning?
   (A) Karl and Jeff.
   (B) I know the name of that road.
   (C) More than 10 crates of bananas.

   今天早上誰應該在裝卸場工作？
   (A) 卡爾和傑夫。
   (B) 我知道那條路名。
   (C) 十箱以上的香蕉。　　　　答案 (A)

8. 美國 W 澳洲 W

   When is Margo coming to the product demonstration?
   (A) There's more in the supply cabinet.
   (B) She said she'd be five minutes late.
   (C) Yes, she arrived last Monday.

   瑪歌什麼時候會來產品展示會？
   (A) 儲藏櫃裡還有更多。
   (B) 她說會遲到五分鐘。
   (C) 是的，她在上星期一抵達。　　　　答案 (B)

9. 澳洲 W 美國 M

   Do you work out every day?
   (A) A nearby fitness facility.
   (B) I jog each morning.
   (C) That's not the right size.

   你每天健身嗎？
   (A) 附近的健身房。
   (B) 我每天早上都會慢跑。
   (C) 那個尺寸不對。　　　　答案 (B)

10. 美國 W 美國 M

Where is our team taking the clients out to dinner?
(A) Somewhere in the commercial district.
(B) No, put it here on the dinner table.
(C) They have great vegetarian dishes.

我們團隊要帶客戶去哪裡用餐？
(A) 商業區的某處。
(B) 不，把它放在餐桌上。
(C) 他們有很棒的素食料理。　　　　答案 (A)

11. 美國 W 英國 M

Could you call the Royal Restaurant to make dinner reservations?
(A) Today's chef's specialty.
(B) They don't accept reservations.
(C) Yes, the security code has changed.

你可以打電話到皇家餐廳預約晚餐嗎？
(A) 今天的主廚特餐。
(B) 他們不開放預約。
(C) 是的，安全代碼已更改。　　　　答案 (B)

12. 美國 M 美國 W

How did your presentation go yesterday?
(A) It went very well, thanks.
(B) Sorry, I can't go by bus.
(C) It was a present from my colleagues.

你昨天的報告如何？
(A) 很順利，謝謝。
(B) 抱歉，我無法搭公車前往。
(C) 那是我同事給的禮物。　　　　答案 (A)

13. 美國 W 美國 M

This laptop model here is new, isn't it?
(A) Yes, but it isn't selling well.
(B) We need new cables.
(C) Thanks for leaving it turned on.

這臺筆記型電腦型號是新的，不是嗎？
(A) 是的，但是它沒有賣得很好。
(B) 我們需要新的電線。
(C) 謝謝你讓它保持開機狀態。　　　　答案 (A)

14. 美國 W 澳洲 W

Would you like to see the promotional flyer I designed?
(A) He got a promotion last week.
(B) I'll go to a meeting in just ten minutes.
(C) I resigned last year.

你要看看我設計的促銷傳單嗎？
(A) 他上週獲得升遷。
(B) 我十分鐘後要去開會。
(C) 我去年辭職。　　　　答案 (B)

15. 美國 M 英國 M

Didn't you have a doctor's appointment yesterday afternoon?
(A) Yeah, that's why I left work early.
(B) Here is your prescription.
(C) He is not available today.

你昨天下午不是要去看醫生嗎？
(A) 沒錯，所以我提早下班。
(B) 這是你的處方籤。
(C) 他今天沒空。　　　　答案 (A)

16. 英國 M 美國 W

How is our manager getting to the Seattle Convention?
(A) It was a great trip.
(B) Sure, I'd like to go there, too.
(C) I'm going to give him a ride.

我們的經理要如何去參加西雅圖大會？
(A) 那是一趟很棒的旅程。
(B) 當然，我也想去那裡。
(C) 我會載他去。　　　　答案 (C)

17. 澳洲 W 美國 M

You're attending the safety training on Thursday, aren't you?
(A) The desk for registration over there.
(B) The safety inspector is arriving in any minute.
(C) I'm leaving for the marketing conference.

你會參加星期四的安全培訓，不是嗎？
(A) 那邊的註冊櫃檯。
(B) 安全檢查員隨時會抵達。
(C) 我正要離開去參加行銷大會。　　　　答案 (C)

18. 美國 W 英國 M

Why has the storage closet been locked all day?
(A) Did you buy some more office supplies?
(B) It is close to our office.
(C) Because I misplaced the key.

為什麼儲藏櫃整天都鎖著？
(A) 你有多買一點辦公用品嗎？
(B) 它離我們的辦公室很近。
(C) 因為我把鑰匙搞丟了。　　　　答案 (C)

19. 美國 M 澳洲 W

The company is going to cover the damages for the shipment, isn't it?
(A) It was shipped out yesterday.
(B) I'm sure they will.
(C) The model has many advantages.

公司會賠償貨物的損害，不是嗎？
(A) 它昨天出貨。

(B) 我確定他們會。
(C) 那組模型有很多優點。　　　　　　答案 (B)

20. 美國 W　美國 M

Should we have the meeting this week or next week?
(A) We've met before, haven't we?
(B) It lasted for more than half an hour.
(C) Next Monday would be better.

我們該在這週還是下週開會？
(A) 我們之前有見過，對吧？
(B) 那持續了超過半小時。
(C) 下星期一比較適合。　　　　　　　答案 (C)

21. 英國 M　美國 W

When will the company outing be held?
(A) No, it hasn't been taken care of yet.
(B) I set it on the lawn yesterday.
(C) Management is still deciding.

員工旅遊會在什麼時候舉行？
(A) 不，還沒有處理好。
(B) 我昨天把它放在草坪上。
(C) 管理層還在決策中。　　　　　　　答案 (C)

22. 美國 M　澳洲 W

Who's helping you work on the quarterly sales report?
(A) It's already finished.
(B) Turn to the page 52 of the report.
(C) No, it comes out annually.

誰在協助你做季度銷售報告？
(A) 已經完成了。
(B) 翻到報告第 52 頁。
(C) 不，它每年出版一次。　　　　　　答案 (A)

23. 美國 W　美國 M

Doesn't the ticket office open at 7 P.M.?
(A) Aren't they closed on Mondays?
(B) Yes, the office is close to the bookstore.
(C) No, the performer will arrive at 6 P.M.

售票處不是晚上 7 點才開嗎？
(A) 他們不是星期一公休嗎？
(B) 沒錯，辦公室離書店很近。
(C) 不，那名表演者將會在晚上 6 點抵達。　答案 (A)

24. 澳洲 W　美國 M

Do you have the flight and accommodations details for our business trip?
(A) I flew to New York.
(B) Ms. Wilson is making arrangements for our travel.
(C) They had a paid vacation.

你有出差的航班和住宿詳情嗎？
(A) 我飛往紐約。
(B) 威爾遜女士正在安排我們的旅程。
(C) 他們有帶薪假。　　　　　　　　　答案 (B)

25. 澳洲 W　英國 M

Which one are we serving at the welcome reception, beef or chicken?
(A) The guests will have several options.
(B) The servers look busy.
(C) I didn't go to the party, either.

我們在歡迎會上提供的是牛肉還是雞肉？
(A) 客人將有多種選擇。
(B) 服務生看起來很忙。
(C) 我也沒有去參加派對。　　　　　　答案 (A)

26. 美國 M　英國 M

How many attendees are we expecting for the product demonstration?
(A) Right after 10.
(B) The number keeps changing.
(C) The upgraded version of the software.

我們預期有多少人參加產品展示會？
(A) 10 點剛過。
(B) 數字不斷變化。
(C) 軟體升級版本。　　　　　　　　　答案 (B)

27. 美國 W　澳洲 W

I'm wondering if you could e-mail me next quarter's sales projections.
(A) Yes, all items are on sale.
(B) I'd really appreciate it.
(C) Chris faxed it to you this morning.

我在想，你能不能把下一季的銷售預測用電子郵件寄給我。
(A) 是的，所有商品都在打折。
(B) 我不勝感激。
(C) 克里斯今天早上已經把它傳真給你了。　答案 (C)

28. 英國 M　美國 M

There isn't Internet access available on this shuttle bus, is there?
(A) This is one of the older buses our company has.
(B) About 30 minutes at rush hour.
(C) The tickets are available on the Internet.

這輛接駁車上沒有網路，對吧？
(A) 這輛車是我們公司所擁有的、較舊的巴士之一。
(B) 尖峰時段約 30 分鐘。
(C) 門票可在網路上購買。　　　　　　答案 (A)

29. 美國 W 澳洲 W

Why don't we publish this article in the May issue of our magazine?
(A) In the publisher conference.
(B) Yes, I think it's very timely.
(C) I don't subscribe to the magazine.

我們何不把這篇文章放在 5 月號雜誌裡呢？
(A) 在出版商會議上。
(B) 是的，我認為這時機非常合適。
(C) 我沒有訂閱那本雜誌。　　　　　答案 (B)

30. 美國 M 澳洲 W

Is the art gallery under renovation this month?
(A) I forgot to close the drawer.
(B) I don't work there anymore.
(C) Oh, I was there last month.

那間藝廊這個月在裝修嗎？
(A) 我忘了關抽屜。
(B) 我不在那裡工作了。
(C) 哦，我上個月去過那裡。　　　　答案 (B)

31. 美國 M 英國 W

This article looks at ways to improve energy efficiency.
(A) Can I read it when you are done?
(B) The magazine editor-in-chief.
(C) The new vehicle is fuel-efficient.

本文著眼於提高能源效率的方法。
(A) 你讀完後，我可以讀一下嗎？
(B) 雜誌總編輯。
(C) 新車很省油。　　　　　　　　答案 (A)

Part 3

問題 32-34，請參考以下對話內容。 美國 M 美國 W

M: Hello. You've reached the Perkins Art Gallery. How can I help you?
W: Good morning. (32)**I'm calling from Russell Publishing. (33)I saw a work of art in your digital collection last weekend, and I'd love to use it on the front cover of a book I'm working on. Can I do that?**
M: Of course. (34)**Could you let me know the image ID number of the work?** Each and every document here in our museum collection has one. If you do that, I can provide you with a digital image.

男：你好，這裡是帕金斯藝廊。需要什麼協助呢？
女：早安，我這裡是羅素出版社。上週末我看到你們數位收藏中的一件作品，想用它作為我正在製作的書籍封面。可以嗎？

男：當然可以。你可以給我那件作品的圖像識別號碼嗎？我們館藏的每一件作品都有一個編號。提供圖像識別號碼後，我就會給你那件數位圖像。

32. 女子在哪裡工作？
(A) 藝術品商店
(B) 藝廊
(C) 出版社
(D) 書店　　　　　　　　　　　答案 (C)

33. 女子為什麼打電話？
(A) 詢問照片使用相關事宜
(B) 了解新作品
(C) 詢問企業的營業時間
(D) 安排特殊旅遊　　　　　　　答案 (A)

34. 男子請女子提供什麼？
(A) 報名費
(B) 數位圖像
(C) 截止日期
(D) 識別碼　　　　　　　　　　答案 (D)

問題 35-37，請參考以下對話內容。 澳洲 W 美國 M

W: All right, (35)**the party to celebrate Mary's promotion is soon**, so we need to figure out what we need to buy for it. We definitely need a cake as well as some drinks, cups, and plates.
M: Don't worry about the cake. There's no need to buy one. (36)**Remember how Mary loved that chocolate cake I made at the party last spring? I can make another one.**
W: That sounds perfect, Dave. So let's just get the other things I mentioned. (37)**I'll visit the store tomorrow after work to purchase the cups and the plates.**

女：各位，慶祝瑪麗升職的派對馬上就要到了，我們得想想該買什麼。蛋糕是絕對不能少的，還要飲料、杯子跟盤子。
男：別擔心蛋糕，沒必要買。還記得去年春天的派對上，瑪麗有多喜歡我做的巧克力蛋糕嗎？我可以再做一次。
女：太好了，戴夫。那就買我說的其他東西吧。明天下班後，我會去店裡買杯子和盤子。

35. 談話者正在準備什麼活動？
(A) 慶祝派對
(B) 員工旅遊
(C) 募捐活動
(D) 紀念日慶祝活動　　　　　　答案 (A)

36. 男子表示願意做什麼？
    (A) 發送邀請
    (B) 裝飾房間
    (C) 烤蛋糕
    (D) 向瑪麗求助　　　　　　　　答案 (C)

37. 女子說要做什麼？
    (A) 申請修改後的預算案
    (B) 購買物品
    (C) 預訂房間
    (D) 拜訪蛋糕店　　　　　　　　答案 (B)

問題 **38-40**，請參考以下對話內容。 美國 W　英國 M

W: Hello, Kevin. Are you having a good time at this year's book tradeshow?

M: It's really great. (38)**I've discovered several new authors whose works I can sell at my bookstore.** I'm also pleased about the new venue this year. (39) **This convention center is much closer to my hotel.**

W: I know what you mean. (39)**I only had to walk for three minutes and didn't need to take a taxi like I did last year.** Oh, by the way, you told me that you purchased some tablet computers for the sales staff at your store to use. How well are they working out?

M: Quite well. (40)**My employees find them convenient, especially when it comes to checking on item availability.**

- -

女：嗨，凱文。你在今年的書展上玩得開心嗎？
男：真的很棒。我發現幾位新作家，他們的作品可以在我的書店裡販售。另外，我也很喜歡今年的新場館。這個會展中心離我的飯店近多了。
女：我懂你的意思。這邊走三分鐘就可以到，不用像去年那樣搭計程車。哦，對了，你說你為書店的銷售人員買了平板電腦。情況如何？
男：不錯。員工們覺得平板電腦很方便，尤其是確認庫存的時候。

38. 男子在自己的店裡賣什麼？
    (A) 電子產品
    (B) 書
    (C) 家具
    (D) 服裝　　　　　　　　　　　答案 (B)

39. 關於會展中心，談話者指出什麼事？
    (A) 會展中心在大眾運輸附近。
    (B) 貿易博覽會去年在那裡舉行。
    (C) 他們的飯店在會展中心附近。
    (D) 他們要搭計程車才能抵達。　　答案 (C)

40. 平板電腦在男子的店裡有什麼用途？
    (A) 註冊新會員
    (B) 進行付款
    (C) 收集顧客意見
    (D) 確認庫存　　　　　　　　　　答案 (D)

問題 **41-43**，請參考以下對話內容。 美國 M　澳洲 W

M: Samantha, (41)**I just learned that the vice president changed his schedule.** He's going to arrive tomorrow instead of on Friday.

W: In that case, we'd better complete our presentation file by this afternoon. (42)**We only have a couple of slides left and still need to rehearse it a couple of times, too.**

M: You're right, but I think we'll be ready by the time he arrives. Let's not stop working today.

W: Okay. You know, it's nearly lunch time. (43)**How about having some food delivered from the Marcos Deli?** That way, we won't need to waste time going out to a restaurant.

M: Sure, good idea. Let's do it.

- -

男：薩曼莎，我剛剛聽說副總改變行程，明天就會抵達，而不是星期五。
女：這樣的話，我們最好今天下午之前把報告檔案完成。我們還有幾頁投影片沒做，而且要彩排一下。
男：你說得對，但我覺得副總到之前，我們就能準備好了。今天就別休息，一直工作吧。
女：沒問題。不過午餐時間快到了，點馬科斯餐館的外送如何？這樣就不用浪費時間去餐廳了。
男：當然，好主意。就這樣吧。

41. 男子最近得知了什麼？
    (A) 管理層的行程變更。
    (B) 研討會剛剛取消。
    (C) 貨運今天會送達。
    (D) 會議室被預訂了。　　　　　　答案 (A)

42. 談話者需要做什麼？
    (A) 檢查素材
    (B) 安排培訓日程
    (C) 練習報告
    (D) 清理部分文件　　　　　　　　答案 (C)

43. 女子建議做什麼？
    (A) 點外送
    (B) 預訂餐廳
    (C) 為了明天的彩排早點抵達
    (D) 完成工作後吃午餐　　　　　　答案 (A)

問題 **44-46**，請參考以下三方對話內容。 英國 M　澳洲 W　美國 W

M: Hello, Alice. I'm Robert. It's great that you're joining us on the staff here at Watson Medical Center. I'm your supervisor, and (44) **I'll be teaching you how to handle office assistant duties.**

W1: Hi, Robert. It's a pleasure to meet you.

M: This is Karen. Karen, this is Alice, our newest office assistant.

W2: Hi, Alice. I'm glad to meet you. I guess we'll be working together.

M: Here's Alice's new employee binder. (45) **Could you help her fill out some of these orientation forms, please, Karen?**

W2: (45) **Sure. I've got some time now.**

M: Thanks. Once you are done, I'll show Alice how to use the patient tag software program.

W1: (46) **Actually, I used one at my previous job.**

男：你好，愛麗絲。我是羅伯特。很高興有你加入華生醫療中心，成為我們的一份子。我是你的主管，我會帶你掌握辦公室助理的工作。

女1：你好，羅伯特。很高興見到你。

男：這是凱倫。凱倫，這是新來的辦公室助理愛麗絲。

女2：你好，愛麗絲。很高興見到你。看來我們要一起工作囉。

男：這是愛麗絲的新進職員文件夾。你能協助她填寫這個入職訓練的表格嗎，凱倫？

女2：可以，我現在有空。

男：謝謝。你們完成後，我再向愛麗絲示範如何使用患者身分驗證軟體程式。

女1：其實，我在之前的工作中使用過了。

---

44. 愛麗絲的職業是什麼？
    (A) 研究員
    (B) 實驗室技術員
    (C) 辦公室助理
    (D) 辦公室主管　　　　　　　　　　答案 (C)

45. 愛麗絲接下來最有可能做什麼？
    (A) 參觀辦公室
    (B) 填寫書面資料
    (C) 面試工作
    (D) 跟執行長談話　　　　　　　　　答案 (B)

46. 關於軟體，愛麗絲暗指了什麼？
    (A) 她希望它被替換掉。
    (B) 它不能正常運作。
    (C) 它的費用很高。
    (D) 她知道它的使用方法。　　　　　答案 (D)

問題 **47-49**，請參考以下對話內容。 美國 M　美國 W

M: Pardon me, but where is the honey? (47) **I thought I knew where it was, but I can't seem to find it anywhere in this supermarket store.**

W: Ah, (48) **the building was recently remodeled, so we changed the locations of some merchandise.** You can find the honey in aisle number three. Do you need anything else?

M: Yes, please. (49) **Do you still sell Denton's frozen pizzas?**

W: (49) **Let me ask my manager. We no longer carry a few brands anymore.**

男：不好意思，這款蜂蜜在哪裡？我以為我知道它在哪裡，但我在這家超市裡似乎找不到它。

女：啊，最近大樓改建，所以我們改變了一些商品的位置。你可以在三號走道找到那款蜂蜜。還需要什麼嗎？

男：是的，麻煩了。你們還有賣丹頓的冷凍披薩嗎？

女：讓我問問店經理。我們已經不再經營某些品牌了。

---

47. 談話者的位置在哪裡？
    (A) 超市
    (B) 保健食品店
    (C) 餐廳
    (D) 倉庫　　　　　　　　　　　　　答案 (A)

48. 女子提及這家店的什麼資訊？
    (A) 那裡即將進行折扣。
    (B) 剛進行完翻修工程。
    (C) 開設了第二家賣場。
    (D) 顧客越來越少。　　　　　　　　答案 (B)

49. 女子說「我們已經不再經營某些品牌了」，是在暗示什麼？
    (A) 她不再待在那一區工作。
    (B) 她正在等待新配送的冷凍披薩。
    (C) 有些商品可能買不到。
    (D) 她認為男子應該買其他東西。　　答案 (C)

問題 **50-52**，請參考以下對話內容。 英國 M　美國 W

M: Hello, Janet. (50) **Stefan told me your design for the new multi-purpose tool is almost finished.**

W: That's right. I'm really pleased with it. The lightweight and compact tool has seven separate units that fit into one holdable hardwood handle.

M: Wonderful. How far along are we on the ad campaign for the multi-use tool?

W: I'm not sure yet. (51) **We're still in the process of deciding what to call it. We have come up with** some interesting ideas, but we have yet to agree on the best one.

M: (52)**Why don't you ask everyone to give some comments at the staff meeting tomorrow?** Maybe you'll get an idea or two of what name might appeal to most customers.

男：嗨，珍妮特。史蒂芬說，你的新款多功能工具設計快完成了。

女：沒錯，我非常開心。這個輕盈又小巧的工具有七個獨立部件，全都裝進一個手持的堅硬木柄上。

男：真厲害。還要多久才能進入廣告活動階段呢？

女：還不確定。我們還沒決定要幫它取什麼名字。我們提出了一些有趣的想法，但哪一款最好，我們還沒達成共識。

男：明天員工會議，你何不問問大家的意見？也許你會得到一兩個點子，了解什麼名字能吸引多數顧客。

---

50. 談話者在討論哪種產品？
(A) 食品
(B) 電器
(C) 工具
(D) 轎車　　　　　　　　　　　答案 (C)

51. 哪一方面還有待達成共識？
(A) 名稱
(B) 價格
(C) 上市日期
(D) 廣告活動　　　　　　　　　答案 (A)

52. 男子建議怎麼做？
(A) 實施顧客問卷調查
(B) 重新設計產品
(C) 與同事商議
(D) 在網路上投放廣告　　　　　答案 (C)

問題 **53-55**，請參考以下對話內容。 澳洲 W　美國 M

W: Ted, I just got off the phone with the manager of all the Dynamo Fitness Center locations in the city. (53) **He confirmed that our location will be closing ten days from now to undergo renovations that will last for two months.**

M: Okay, we'd better put some signs up to inform our members of what's going to happen. We can provide directions to other Dynamo Fitness Centers nearby.

W: Oh, one more thing. Mr. Sullivan informed me that (54) **any members who travel to alternate locations should receive half off their monthly fee.**

M: Sounds good. (55)**I'll send a mass e-mail to our members at once.**

女：泰德，我剛跟掌管本市所有活力健身中心分店的經理講完電話。他證實了我們分店十天後將暫停營業，進行為期兩個月的翻修工程。

男：好的。我們最好發布告示，讓會員知道接下來會發生什麼事。我們也可以提供前往附近其他分店的路線指引。

女：哦，還有一件事。蘇利文先生通知我，去其他分店的會員，月費可以打五折。

男：聽起來不錯。我馬上發團體信件給會員。

---

53. 十天後會發生什麼事？
(A) 新經理要上任了。
(B) 運動場館將進行翻修。
(C) 新的運動課程要開始了。
(D) 另一家分店會開門。　　　　答案 (B)

54. 將提供什麼給會員們？
(A) 折扣
(B) T 恤
(C) 新課程
(D) 商品禮券　　　　　　　　　答案 (A)

55. 男子說要做什麼？
(A) 面試應徵者
(B) 打電話給所有會員
(C) 更改日程
(D) 發送電子郵件　　　　　　　答案 (D)

問題 **56-58**，請參考以下三方對話內容。 美國 M　美國 W　澳洲 W

M: (56)**Susan, are you having any problems planning this year's company retreat? I know it's your first time working on this.**

W1: No worries. I've already got all the activities planned.

M: I'm glad to hear that. How about reserving the venue? Did you reserve the hotel rooms?

W1: Mary is handling that. She's right over there. Mary, have you booked the hotel reservations for our company retreat yet?

W2: No, I haven't. I haven't been told how many will participate in it. (57)**I need a final list of attendees.**

M: Okay, but we're running out of time. (58)**Just make sure the hotel rooms are available at that time. I recommend that you make a reservation as soon as possible even without that information.**

男：蘇珊，今年員工旅遊的策劃有什麼問題嗎？據我所知，這是你第一次準備這樣的活動。

女 1：不用擔心。我已經把所有活動都規劃好了。

男：很高興聽到你這麼說。場地預約進行得怎麼樣？你訂了飯店房間嗎？

女 1：那是瑪麗負責的。瑪麗就在那邊。瑪麗，你訂好員工旅遊的飯店了嗎？

女2：不，還沒。我還不知道會有多少人參加。我需要最終出席名單。

男：好吧，但是沒剩多少時間了。一定要確保到時候能訂到飯店房間。我建議就算沒有那個資訊，最好還是盡快預訂。

---

56. 談話者主要在討論什麼？
(A) 更改飯店房間
(B) 遷移辦公室
(C) 為客戶安排發表會
(D) 策劃員工旅遊　　　　　　答案 (D)

57. 瑪麗缺少什麼資訊？
(A) 活動報價
(B) 確定的場地
(C) 完整出席名單
(D) 潛在買家名單　　　　　　答案 (C)

58. 男子建議盡快做什麼？
(A) 預約活動場地
(B) 提前預訂機票
(C) 聯繫當地外燴服務
(D) 變更公司活動日程　　　　答案 (A)

問題 59-61，請參考以下對話內容。英國M 美國W

M: Hello, Ms. Sanders. I want to talk about the employee appreciation dinner with you. We're having it next month, but (59)**we still haven't selected the winner of the TV host of the year award.**

W: How about Peter? His morning show has been very popular with our viewers and gets great ratings.

M: (60)**He has won the award three times. And a lot of other hosts have also made a remarkable contribution to our program.**

W: You're right. (61)**Why don't we nominate three people and send the list to our employees? We can let them choose.**

M: (61)**That's a good idea.** It will be a first for us to have our staff members vote for the winner.

男：你好，桑德斯女士。我想跟你談談員工感謝晚宴。下個月就要舉行晚宴，但我們還沒選出今年的電視主持人獎得主。

女：比德怎麼樣？他的晨間秀一直很受觀眾歡迎，收視率也很好。

男：他已經拿了那個獎三次。而且其他主持人也對我們的節目做出了令人矚目的貢獻。

女：你說得對。提名三個人，然後把名單發給員工怎麼樣？我們可以讓他們選。

男：好主意。這是我們第一次讓員工投票選出獲獎者。

---

59. 談話者最有可能在哪裡工作？
(A) 電視臺
(B) 電影工作室
(C) 廣播電臺
(D) 餐廳　　　　　　　　　　答案 (A)

60. 男子為什麼說「他已經拿了那個獎三次」？
(A) 為了稱讚同事
(B) 為了修正
(C) 為了表示滿足
(D) 為了拒絕提議　　　　　　答案 (D)

61. 談話者同意做什麼？
(A) 徵詢員工的意見
(B) 延長最後期限
(C) 延期頒獎典禮
(D) 僱用新的電視主持人　　　答案 (A)

問題 62-64，請參考以下對話內容及草圖。澳洲W 美國M

W: Welcome to Delvin Interior. How may I help you?

M: Hello. (62)**I spoke on the phone with you about placing an order for some curtains for the travel agency I work at.**

W: Oh, hello, Mr. Carter. How did you like the samples I sent?

M: They were great.

W: Did you get the sketch of the design I e-mailed you?

M: I did. It looks nice, and I want to get some curtains made for the office. However, the windows in the office go from the floor to the ceiling, (63)**so I'd like them to hang down longer than what you have recommended so that they can reach all the way to the floor. I want them to be 280 centimeters long instead.**

W: No problem at all. But I think this will affect the cost slightly. (64)**Could you please hold on while I calculate the new price?**

女：歡迎光臨戴爾文室內裝修。請問需要什麼協助？

男：你好，我曾跟你通過電話，討論為我任職的旅行社訂購窗簾一事。

女：噢，你好，卡特先生。你滿意我寄的樣品嗎？

男：很滿意。

女：你有收到我用電子郵件寄出的設計草圖嗎？

男：收到了，看起來很棒。我想為辦公室製作窗簾，不過，辦公室的窗戶是落地窗，所以希望窗簾能比你推薦的再長一點，這樣才能及地。希望窗簾有 280 公分左右的長度。

女：完全沒問題。但我想這會稍微影響費用。在我計算新價格的時候，你能稍等一會兒嗎？

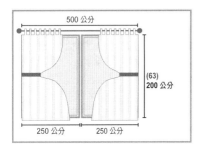

62. 男子在哪裡上班？
    (A) 室內設計公司
    (B) 書店
    (C) 旅行社
    (D) 建築公司　　　　　　答案 (C)

63. 請看圖表。哪一項數值將會變更？
    (A) 200 公分
    (B) 250 公分
    (C) 300 公分
    (D) 500 公分　　　　　　答案 (A)

64. 女子接下來最有可能做什麼？
    (A) 決定新價格
    (B) 追加訂購材料
    (C) 重新設計草圖
    (D) 打電話給其他供貨商　　答案 (A)

問題 65-67，請參考以下對話內容及圖表。 澳洲W 美國M

W: (65)**Here are last year's sales figures for our high-end laptops.** What do you think?

M: Hmm… I had expected sales for the third quarter to rise, (66)**but I'm shocked by how much they declined the following quarter.**

W: Well, we did have a few special sales during the third quarter, but we didn't do anything at the end of the year.

M: (67)**We'd better talk to Jacob Green, the new director of marketing. He should be able to arrange a promotional campaign or two for us.**

- -

女：這是我們去年高規格筆記型電腦的銷售數據。你怎麼想？

男：嗯……我有預期到第三季的銷售量會上升，但是下一季的銷售量下滑了這麼多，我真的很震驚。

女：嗯，第三季我們有幾次特別折扣，年底則是什麼都沒做。

男：我們最好還是跟新任行銷總監雅各‧格林談談。他可以為我們安排一兩場宣傳活動。

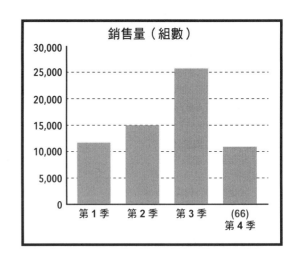

65. 談話者最有可能在哪裡工作？
    (A) 手機製造商
    (B) 廚房用品店
    (C) 電腦製造商
    (D) 玩具製造商　　　　　　答案 (C)

66. 請看圖表。男子對哪一項銷售數據感到驚訝？
    (A) 12,000
    (B) 15,000
    (C) 26,000
    (D) 11,000　　　　　　　　答案 (D)

67. 雅各‧格林是誰？
    (A) 公司經理
    (B) 行銷專家
    (C) 設計師
    (D) 會計師　　　　　　　　答案 (B)

問題 68-70，請參考以下對話內容及海報。 美國W 英國M

W: Dave, I can't wait to go to the music festival tomorrow.

M: I agree. There's such a big variety of musical acts that will be performing this year.

W: (68)**I am wondering if you need a ride to the festival.** I'm going to drive with some other colleagues in the sales department.

M: Actually, I have a dental appointment tomorrow morning, (69)**but I'll be sure to arrive there in time for the performance by my favorite act at 3:00.** Shall we meet near the blue stage?

W: No problem. (70)**Be sure to wear a jacket. I hear it's going to be a bit windy tomorrow.**

- -

女：戴夫，我等不及要參加明天的音樂節了。

男：我也是。今年要演出的表演者非常多元。

女：我在想，你要不要搭便車去慶典，我要和銷售部的男：幾位同事一起開車過去。

男：其實我明天早上要看牙醫。但是為了 3 點看我最喜歡的組合演出，我一定會準時抵達。在藍色舞臺附近見吧？

女：沒問題。記得要套一件夾克，聽說明天有點風。

麥迪森秋季音樂節
10 月 4 日

演出節目表

黃色舞臺		藍色舞臺	
中午 12 點	鄉村樂	上午 10 點	爵士樂
下午 4 點	搖滾樂	(69) 下午 3 點	流行樂
		下午 5 點	古典樂

68. 女子表示願意為男子做什麼？
(A) 為他買票
(B) 檢查他的報告
(C) 載他一程
(D) 為他保留位子　　　　　　答案 (C)

69. 請看圖表。男子最喜歡的音樂類型是什麼？
(A) 鄉村樂
(B) 流行樂
(C) 爵士樂
(D) 搖滾樂　　　　　　　　　答案 (B)

70. 女子提醒男子什麼事？
(A) 提前購票
(B) 穿夾克
(C) 帶很多水
(D) 準時抵達慶典　　　　　　答案 (B)

Part 4

問題 71-73，請參考以下介紹。 美國 W

Hello, everyone. **(71)I hope you've been having a great time at this year's engineering conference.** We're about to hear from the final speaker of the day, Brandon Morris. Anyone who has kept up on innovations in engineering would be familiar with his name since he's been recognized for a variety of innovative ideas. **(72)In fact, just one month ago,**

Mr. Morris won the prestigious Lorentz prize for designing a solar-powered portable water pump. Mr. Morris is going to tell us more about his latest work momentarily. **(73)But first I'd like to remind you all about the reception we'll be having as soon as his talk ends.**

大家好。希望各位在今年的工程技術大會度過了愉快的時光。今天最後一位演講者，布蘭登・莫里斯的演講即將開始。莫里斯先生以多樣的革新創意廣獲認可，凡是關注工程技術革新相關資訊的人，想必對他很熟悉。事實上，就在一個月前，莫里斯先生設計出以太陽能為動力的攜帶式抽水機，獲得著名的洛倫茲獎。莫里斯先生稍後會帶來更多新作品的消息。但首先要提醒大家，莫里斯先生的演講結束後，還有歡迎會在等著各位。

71. 大會的主題是什麼？
(A) 車輛製造
(B) 軟體開發
(C) 工程技術
(D) 圖書出版　　　　　　　　答案 (C)

72. 據說話者所說，布蘭登・莫里斯上個月做了什麼？
(A) 他安裝了太陽能板。
(B) 他獲獎了。
(C) 他參加了一場大會。
(D) 他發表了演說。　　　　　答案 (B)

73. 說話者提醒聽者什麼事？
(A) 產品展示會
(B) 歡迎會
(C) 演講
(D) 展覽　　　　　　　　　　答案 (B)

問題 74-76，請參考以下語音訊息。 英國 M

(74)Thank you for choosing Lincoln Electricity as your energy provider. We are well aware that **(75)the severe thunderstorms caused numerous power outages throughout the city during the night.** Work crews are busy attempting to restore power. We anticipate that all homes and businesses in the city will have full power no later than 10 a.m. this morning. **(76)If electricity has not been restored to your location by that time, please call us again** and press the number five to speak with one of our representatives.

感謝您選擇林肯電力公司作為供電商。我們深知，猛烈雷雨導致昨晚全市數度停電。工作組成員正忙著恢復電力。我們預計，本市所有家庭和事業單位最晚在今天上午 10 點前將恢復全面供電。屆時若您所在的地方還沒有恢復電力，請再次來電，並按 5 與專人通話。

74. 說話者最有可能在哪裡上班？
(A) 政府機關
(B) 地方氣象局
(C) 建築公司
(D) 電力公司　　　　　　　　　答案 (D)

75. 引發問題的原因是什麼？
(A) 曾有惡劣的天氣。
(B) 部分機器已經過時。
(C) 沒有足夠的工作人員。
(D) 電費上漲。　　　　　　　　答案 (A)

76. 如果問題持續下去，聽者應該做什麼？
(A) 造訪網站
(B) 晚點再打電話
(C) 親自造訪辦公室
(D) 取消電力服務　　　　　　　答案 (B)

問題 77-79，請參考以下介紹。 美國 M

(77)**Thank you for attending the opening celebration of our museum's Native American art exhibit**. It's wonderful to see so many people from the local area here today. This exhibit features all kinds of artwork made by Native Americans in this region. (78)**Now, before the tour begins, let's head to the auditorium to watch a short video about Native American art.** And please be aware that as a way of expressing gratitude for your support, (79)**we're offering a 30% discount for purchases made at our gift shop today only.**

感謝各位參加本美術館的美洲原住民藝術展開幕式。很高興今天能在這裡看到這麼多當地人。這個展覽主要展示此地美國原住民製作的各種藝術品。開始參觀之前，我們先去大禮堂觀看有關美國原住民藝術的短影片。也請留意，為了感謝各位的支持，今天一天在禮品店購買的商品，我們會提供七折優惠。

77. 美術館在慶祝什麼？
(A) 紀念日
(B) 管理層退休
(C) 新展覽
(D) 圖書館開館　　　　　　　　答案 (C)

78. 聽者首先將會做什麼？
(A) 自我介紹
(B) 進行參觀
(C) 收聽演講
(D) 觀看影片　　　　　　　　　答案 (D)

79. 聽者將會得到什麼？
(A) 免費入場
(B) 禮品店折扣
(C) 免費餐券
(D) 免費紀念品　　　　　　　　答案 (B)

問題 80-82，請參考以下電話留言。 澳洲 W

Hello. (81)**One of my colleagues that just got back from a vacation highly recommended your agency.** (80) (81)**So I'm calling because I'd love for you to assist me with my own trip for this winter.** I noticed on the Swiss Railways website that an unlimited travel pass is being offered in January for the equivalent of $400. (82)**I know it's the peak season for travel, which is why the fare is rather expensive. However, I heard that the scenery in Switzerland is stunning that time of the year.** So I thought I'd check with you before I reserve anything. Please call me back at 867-3339.

你好。我有一位剛剛度假回來的同事強烈推薦了貴社，本次來電，是希望你們能協助我今年的冬季之旅。我從瑞士鐵路網站上得知，1 月分會有價值相當於 400 美元的無限制旅行券。我知道 1 月分是旅遊旺季，所以費用有點貴。但聽說瑞士每年此時的風景都很美，所以我想在預約之前，向貴社確認一下。請撥打 867-3339 與我聯繫。

80. 說話者在計劃什麼？
(A) 商務會議
(B) 客戶拜訪
(C) 公司募款活動
(D) 假期　　　　　　　　　　　答案 (D)

81. 聽者最有可能是誰？
(A) 旅行社職員
(B) 列車車長
(C) 研討會籌辦者
(D) 飯店職員　　　　　　　　　答案 (A)

82. 說話者說「聽說瑞士每年此時的風景都很美」，意思是什麼？
(A) 她因旅行被取消而心情不好。
(B) 她認同聽者推薦的事物。
(C) 她鼓勵聽者與自己同行。
(D) 她認為花錢購買是值得的。　答案 (D)

問題 83-85，請參考以下電話留言。 美國 M

Hello. I'm calling from Sanderson Consulting. (83) **We'll be attending the Northeastern IT Trade Show next month**, and we need a display designed for us. I've gone over some of the designs you did for prior exhibitions on your website, and (84)**I must admit that they're quite unique. I'd love for you to work for us.** We didn't rent a big space, but I hope that your team can work with it and make something nice. Will you be available this Friday? (85)**If you are free, how about getting together to discuss what I'd like to have done?**

你好，我這裡是桑德森顧問公司。我們下個月要參加東北部的 IT 貿易博覽會，希望你能為我們設計一個展示空間。我在你的網站上，瀏覽了你為過往展覽設計的作品，不得不承認它們非常獨特。希望你能為我們工作。我們公司雖然沒有租下大空間，但希望你的團隊能善加利用，做出很棒的東西。這週五有空嗎？有時間的話，見面討論一下我的需求如何？

83. 說話者的公司下個月打算做什麼？
    (A) 更新公司網站
    (B) 推出新產品線
    (C) 額外招聘 IT 團隊職員
    (D) 參加貿易博覽會　　　　　　　答案 (D)

84. 說話者說「不得不承認它們非常獨特」，意思是什麼？
    (A) 他需要更詳細的說明。
    (B) 他才剛開始在顧問公司工作。
    (C) 他對某些設計印象深刻。
    (D) 他不願意聽從推薦。　　　　　答案 (C)

85. 說話者請求什麼？
    (A) 報價單
    (B) 會面
    (C) 客戶名單
    (D) 配送地址　　　　　　　　　　答案 (B)

問題 86-88，請參考以下會議摘錄。 澳洲 W

(86)**I wanted to have this meeting to discuss a new strategy for our department stores.** (87)**We're going to experiment with a strategy where the prices of items change all throughout the day.** We'd like to encourage customers to make more purchases at off-peak times. For example, young adult clothing sells quite well in the evenings. So if we lower the prices in the morning, we can sell more clothing items throughout the day. That should also encourage young adults to make other purchases. (88)**David Lowell, the vice president of Marketing, came up with this idea, and he's going to tell us exactly how we're going to implement the strategy in our departments.**

我召開這場會議，是想討論我們百貨公司的新策略。我們將實驗全天商品價格變動策略。我們要鼓勵顧客在離峰時段多買一些。比如，年輕人的服裝晚上賣很好，所以上午如果降價的話，一整天下來可以銷售更多服裝。這樣應該也會促使年輕人買其他東西。行銷副總大衛·勞威爾提出了這個想法，他會讓我們知道，如何在各部門實施這一項策略。

86. 說話者在哪種企業上班？
    (A) 百貨公司
    (B) 超市
    (C) 廣告公司
    (D) 行銷公司　　　　　　　　　　答案 (A)

87. 這家企業會開始做什麼？
    (A) 提供折扣給老顧客
    (B) 重新整理賣場的陳列
    (C) 全日調整價格
    (D) 更新供貨商合約　　　　　　　答案 (C)

88. 說話者說大衛·勞威爾將會做什麼？
    (A) 調到總公司
    (B) 邀請志願者
    (C) 僱用額外員工
    (D) 說明新策略　　　　　　　　　　答案 (D)

問題 89-91，請參考以下新聞報導。 美國 W

This is Helen Watson with Channel 3 News. In tonight's financial news, banking combines technology with Cisco Bank's new mobile banking app. (89)**With this new app, you can access the details of your account and complete transactions on your own electronic devices within minutes.** Some industry experts have doubted whether Cisco could be successful in the competitive banking technology field. (90)**However, there have already been 15,000 users since the application was released two days ago.** To promote the app, (91)**any users who complete two transactions within five days of downloading the app will automatically be entered into a raffle to win a new laptop.**

我是第 3 頻道新聞的海倫·華生。在今晚的財經新聞中，銀行業將科技與西思科銀行的行動銀行 APP 結合。有了這款新 APP，你可以取得自己帳戶的詳細資訊，幾分鐘就能在電子設備上完成交易。部分業內專家始終質疑西思科能否在競爭激烈的銀行技術領域取得成功，但該應用程式自 2 天前推出後，用戶已達 15,000 名。為了宣傳該 APP，下載 APP 並在 5 天內完成 2 筆交易的用戶，將自動參加筆記型電腦的抽獎活動。

89. 行動應用程式讓用戶得以做什麼？
(A) 下載銀行地圖
(B) 編輯照片和影片
(C) 線上進行銀行交易
(D) 提供建議　　　　　　　答案 (C)

90. 說話者說「用戶已達 15,000 名」，暗指了什麼？
(A) 另一間分行將開張。
(B) 服務很受歡迎。
(C) 系統因為用戶太多而超載。
(D) 專案需要更多員工。　　答案 (B)

91. 某些用戶可以參加什麼？
(A) 抽獎活動
(B) 歡迎會
(C) 訓練計劃
(D) 焦點團體討論　　　　　答案 (A)

問題 92-94，請參考以下語音訊息。 英國 M

You've reached the Burton Public Library. This month, our library building is closed for some remodeling. (92) **During the period of renovation, library patrons can visit our temporary location at 58 Creek Avenue. (93) Detailed directions can be found on our website.** Since the space in the temporary library facility is small, it does not have a multi-media room for patrons to use. However, this facility can provide laptop computers upon request. (94)**To borrow one, what you have to do is show your library card at the front desk.**

這裡是伯頓公立圖書館。這個月，我們的圖書館大樓因為裝修需要閉館。裝修工程期間，圖書館訪客可以前往位於克里克大道 58 號的臨時圖書館。詳細指引可以在我們的網站上瀏覽。臨時圖書館空間小，因此沒有可供訪客使用的多媒體室。但是，如果您提出要求，館內可以提供筆記型電腦。如有借用需求，只要在服務臺出示圖書館證即可。

92. 此訊息主要關於什麼事？
(A) 臨時場所
(B) 圖書館搬遷
(C) 新程序
(D) 讀書社團　　　　　　　答案 (A)

93. 據說話者所說，網站上能看到什麼？
(A) 可用服務列表

(B) 優惠代碼
(C) 會員申請書
(D) 方向指引　　　　　　　答案 (D)

94. 聽者要如何借用電腦？
(A) 寄送郵件
(B) 在到達之前打電話
(C) 填寫表格
(D) 出示圖書館證　　　　　答案 (D)

問題 95-97，請參考以下指引及地圖。 美國 M

(95)**Thank you all for participating in this year's three-mile race for charity fundraising.** We hope everyone enjoys themselves today. Now, let me review the event instructions with you today. First, all participants need to report to the registration booth by 9:30 A.M. (96)**Here at the registration booth, you can not only check in but also pick up a free T-shirt.** Go ahead and wear it during the race. While you run, you should keep to the designated course. (97)**Remember that once you make it to the end of the course, cross Maple Avenue to have your picture taken.** Several photographers we hired will be waiting for you there.

感謝大家參加今年的三英里慈善賽跑。希望今天大家都能度過美好的時光。現在，讓我說明一下今天的活動。首先，所有參賽者必須在早上 9 點 30 分以前至登記處報到。在登記處這裡，不僅可以辦理報到手續，還可以免費領取 T 恤。歡迎領取，並穿上那件 T 恤賽跑。跑步的時候，要遵照指定路線。不要忘記，一旦跑完賽道，就請穿越楓葉大道去拍照。我們聘請的幾位攝影師會在那裡等候大家。

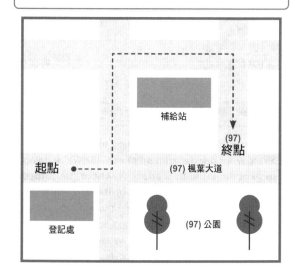

95. 聽者最有可能在參加什麼活動？
    (A) 運動賽事
    (B) 社區大掃除
    (C) 慈善拍賣
    (D) 城市遊行　　　　　　　　答案 (A)

96. 據說話者所說，聽者應該領取什麼？
    (A) 水瓶
    (B) T 恤
    (C) 鞋子
    (D) 名牌　　　　　　　　　　答案 (B)

97. 請看圖表。聽者可以在哪裡拍照？
    (A) 公園
    (B) 登記處
    (C) 起跑線
    (D) 補給站　　　　　　　　　答案 (A)

問題 98-100，請參考以下公告及目錄。 美國 W

Your attention, please. (98)**Before we get the lights dimmed down for today's three-hour flight to Houston, I have a couple of announcements to make.** First, for the sake of passengers' convenience, (99)**complimentary blankets are available for use during your flight.** If you are feeling cold and need a blanket, please let me or any of the other flight attendants know and (99)**we'll provide you with one.** We'll also be opening the duty-free shop in around an hour. Feel free to check out the catalog listing a great selection of items that you can purchase on the flight. (100)**Unfortunately, Item number 183 is not in stock at the moment**, but we have all other items in the catalog available for purchase today.

- -

請注意。今日往休士頓的飛行時間為三個小時，在把燈光調暗之前，有幾點要告知各位。首先，為了乘客方便，飛行期間可以取用免費毛毯。如果您覺得冷，需要毛毯，請告訴我或其他空服員，我們會拿一條給您。另外，大約一個小時後，免稅店將開始營業。歡迎查看商品目錄，裡面列出了您可以在機上購買的品項。遺憾的是，編號 183 的商品目前沒有庫存，但目錄中的其他品項皆已備妥，今天就可以購買。

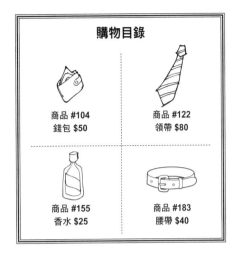

購物目錄

商品 #104
錢包 $50

商品 #122
領帶 $80

商品 #155
香水 $25

商品 #183
腰帶 $40

98. 此公告以誰為對象？
    (A) 飛機乘客
    (B) 大會與會者
    (C) 飯店客人
    (D) 購物中心職員　　　　　　答案 (A)

99. 說話者表示願意做什麼？
    (A) 接受飲料訂單
    (B) 提供毛毯
    (C) 將個人貴重物品上鎖
    (D) 免費供餐　　　　　　　　答案 (B)

100. 請看圖表。哪一項商品無法取得？
    (A) 錢包
    (B) 領帶
    (C) 香水
    (D) 腰帶　　　　　　　　　　答案 (D)

Part 5

101. 如對您的帳單、繳費方式、申請或領取財務補助有疑問，請立即與我們聯繫。　　　　答案 (D)

102. 下班前，請關掉天花板上的燈，打開舒心、柔和的夜燈。　　　　　　　　　　　　答案 (A)

103. 副總通常獨自出席行銷會議，卻決定帶華山先生參加在洛杉磯召開的會議。　　　　答案 (C)

104. 對於經營企業的能力，以種族為基礎來評價人選是不公平的。　　　　　　　　　　答案 (B)

105. 數據顯示，煤炭、天然氣和石油等化石燃料的使用量在過去 150 年間穩定增加。　　答案 (C)

106. 自從約書亞製藥公司將製造工廠遷至斯波坎，該市的住房需求在近幾年大幅增加。　答案 (B)

107. 我們藝廊裡的每幅畫，都有讓人留下深刻印象的歷史片段。　　　　　　　　　　　　答案 (C)

108. 遠程會議技術讓我們的職員不用離開辦公室，也能跟其他國家的客戶會面。　　　　答案 (C)

109. 貝拉公司現在每 3 年提供高年資職員最多 21 天的假期。　　　　　　　　　　　　答案 (C)

110. 附件是居民對購物中心建設計劃提案的最新問卷調查結果。　　　　　　　　　　　答案 (B)

111. 經過大約三個月的裝修，位於底特律的艾斯科技公司製造廠在昨天恢復運作。　　　答案 (C)

112. 很多公司現在面臨人力不足的問題。此外，擁有專業技術的職員也有所短缺。　　　答案 (C)

113. 通過樓層經理職位面試的應徵者，將在下週接到人事主任的聯繫。　　　　　　　　答案 (C)

114. 部分董事對新專案計劃存疑，但執行長讓他們相信該計劃的潛力。　　　　　　　　答案 (D)

115. 隨著新的會議中心和飯店建設，倫敦具備了成為歐洲出差者首選目的地的所有資格。　答案 (A)

116. 對地區型公司來說，企業品牌化遠比過去重要許多。因為如今，消費者辨識度和信賴度是事業繁榮的必備條件。　　　　　　　　　　　　　　　　　　　答案 (B)

117. 請注意。由於天氣惡劣，能見度低，所有航班都延誤了。　　　　　　　　　　　　答案 (C)

118. 知悉安全規範卻不遵守的建設工人們被通知解僱。　　　　　　　　　　　　　　　答案 (B)

119. 最新行動通訊技術的年會結束後，飯店餐廳將供應晚餐。　　　　　　　　　　　　答案 (A)

120. 我們的新車型自上一季問世以來，人氣高得驚人。　　　　　　　　　　　　　　　答案 (B)

121. 為確保客觀性和透明性，企業貸款申請人必須提交經獨立審計的多個財務文件。　　答案 (D)

122. 部分客戶對 GB 公司製造的新產品整體品質感到失望。　　　　　　　　　　　　　答案 (B)

123. 為了降低價格，我們公司簡化生產流程，減少包裝體積和重量。　　　　　　　　　答案 (D)

124. 本公司的保固不適用於消費者誤用產品所造成的缺陷或破損。　　　　　　　　　　答案 (D)

125. 查看股票研究網站時，他們一般會提供以過去收益和未來預期收益為基礎的收益率。　答案 (B)

126. 我們通常會為下一學年提供暫時課表，日後可能還會有變化。　　　　　　　　　　答案 (C)

127. 如果沒有至少一名的父母同行，未滿 15 歲的未成年人禁止進入電影院和遊樂園。　答案 (C)

128. 此次線上報告將探討對貴企業有效的多種行銷技巧與策略。　　　　　　　　　　　答案 (D)

129. 遺憾的是，國內有些偏遠地區無法使用我們的無線寬頻手機服務。　　　　　　　　答案 (D)

130. 考量本季我們蒙受較多損失，除了開始全面大幅度降低成本外，似乎沒有其他辦法可以擺脫這種糟糕的局面。　　　　　　　　　　　　　　　　　　　答案 (B)

Part 6

問題 131-134，請參考以下電子郵件。

寄件人：工廠廠長哈利·休斯頓
收件人：工廠員工
日　期：3 月 25 日
主　旨：外部評鑑

本次來信是為了通知各位，科米汽車公司的 3 名調查員將在 2 週後到訪我們工廠。他們的任務是監控正在進行的生產製程，並確認我們的汽車零件有按照他們的要求和標準製造。此外，他們還會對製程的清潔度進行評估。

他們的評鑑書將在 4 月 15 日至 4 月 17 日間公布。它將發送給我們，並發布於我們的官方網站。在他們到訪期間，遵循正規流程非常重要。如果你打算在 4 月 8 日至 4 月 10 日間休假，請事先通知主管，以利代理者接替你的職責。

哈利·休斯頓
工廠廠長
休斯頓精密機械

131. 　　　　　　　　　　　　　　　　　　答案 (B)

132. 　　　　　　　　　　　　　　　　　　答案 (A)

133. (A) 他們的到達日期還沒有確定。
　　(B) 儘管如此，我們的產品在同業中仍具很高的商業性。

(C) 申請書務必在下個月底之前提交。

(D) 它將發送給我們，並發布於我們的官方網站。

答案 (D)

134. 答案 (C)

問題 135-138，請參考以下廣告內容。

世紀家居室內設計
完美改造您的住宅！

想改造房子或擴建，卻不知道該怎麼做嗎？不用再四處打聽了。世紀家居室內設計最懂如何打造完美住宅。我們為希望將房子變成家的家庭，提供全方位的裝修解決方案。

從選擇新壁紙到建造後院平臺，我們的設計顧問幾乎可以達成您的所有要求。

無論室內設計、住宅管線或建築物結構變更等項目，我們聘請來自住宅設計所有領域的專家，確保負責您住家的職員，具備滿足您需求的資歷。

如需更多資訊，可至我們的網站 www.chid.com 或直接前往國王街 1123 號辦公室諮詢。

135. (A) 我們有對於您技術問題的解決方案。
(B) 您的裝修工程已經開始了。
(C) 不用再四處打聽了。
(D) 我們的目標是幫助大家找到這個地區最好的住房。

答案 (C)

136. 答案 (A)

137. 答案 (B)

138. 答案 (A)

問題 139-142，請參考以下信件內容。

銀河科技
列治文大道 5174 號
77506 德洲，休士頓

貝克先生，

感謝您諮詢我們的 X63 筆記型電腦系列。

很高興附上最新的型錄。請留意以紅色標示強調的物件，這些是我們和波浪印表機、極速顯示卡配套提供的特別產品。促銷活動僅為期一個月，所以不要錯過這次機會，敬請善用本次活動。

我們可以保證，X63 筆記型電腦系列是目前市場上最值得信賴的個人電腦。我們對本系列的信心，立基於 2 年

保固和 24 小時回答用戶疑問的線上支援系統。

期待獲得您進一步諮詢或寶貴的訂單。

誠摯感謝。

唐納·哈里森
銷售總監
銀河科技

139. 答案 (B)

140. 答案 (D)

141. 答案 (C)

142. (A) 期待獲得您進一步諮詢或寶貴的訂單。
(B) 他們還要不斷努力改善工作績效。
(C) 信用卡訂單處理及配送需要 3 個工作日。
(D) 公司以我們製造的高品質產品為傲。

答案 (A)

問題 143-146，請參考以下電子郵件。

戴維斯女士，

對於您 6 月 24 日至 29 日在貝拉度假村住宿期間遇到的問題，我們深感抱歉。希望讓您知道，您在客房裡發現的毛巾和未更換的寢具，並不代表本度假村長期享譽的高水準服務。本度假村的所有客房，通常在客人辦理入住手續前就會備妥乾淨的毛巾和寢具。對於本次疏失，我們深表歉意。

我們很樂意為您提供度假村的單日免費住宿券，包含在路易吉思千層義大利餐廳的用餐。下次預訂本度假村客房，只須印出電子郵件中的優惠券，在辦理入住手續時，向前臺工作人員出示即可。

再次對您體驗到的不當服務致歉。

誠摯致意。

詹姆士·威廉斯
總經理
貝拉度假村

143. 答案 (C)

144. 答案 (D)

145. 答案 (B)

146. (A) 和往常一樣，您會非常滿意我們的新產品。
(B) 如果您需要更多關於本次促銷活動的資訊，請查看我們的網站。
(C) 感謝您對本飯店及附設設施的大力稱讚。
(D) 再次對您體驗到的不當服務致歉。

答案 (D)

問題 **147-148**，請參考以下廣告內容。

BUYNSELL.COM

瑞秋・凱格爾 <rcagle@easymail.com>
1 小時前發布

產品：(147A)《草本療法的一切》賈奎琳・寇區著

本書 (147D) 狀況良好，(147B) 約 **6** 個月前以 **25** 美元的價格購入。

(147A) 對草本或其他藥用植物感興趣的人，可以用 **15** 美元的價格向我購買這本書。(148) 本書最晚在下週三前，於布魯克賽德地區領取。布魯克賽德社區中心是最理想的地點。我只收現金。如果想知道更詳細的內容，請發簡訊至 (647) 555-3921。

---

147. 關於這本書，沒有提到什麼事？
(A) 它是給想要將植物用於醫藥用途的人。
(B) 原本是 25 美元。
(C) 有作者簽名。
(D) 沒有受損。　　　　　　　　答案 (C)

148. 買家要做什麼？
(A) 造訪布魯克賽德社區中心
(B) 帶一張 15 美元的私人支票
(C) 留下電話號碼
(D) 在下週三之前拿書　　　　　答案 (D)

問題 **149-150**，請參考以下網頁內容。

---

http://www.carltonuniv.edu

首頁	訂閱	最新消息	聯絡我們

一年一度的卡爾頓大學慈善舞會
發布於 9 月 1 日

大家好。一年一度的卡爾頓大學慈善舞會即將來臨！今年的主題是「巴黎午夜」。10 月 16 日，花 50 美元於海灣街的達爾文大廳體驗在光之城度過一個夜晚的感覺。門票可在我們的網站購買 www. carltonuniv.edu/ charityball，截止日期為 10 月 11 日。線上購買的門票會發送到你的電子信箱。(149) 收益將全數捐贈給大自然保護組織。無法退款。

4 則留言	
凱文・斯尼德 10 月 12 日 晚上 7:11	我錯過買票的最後期限。(150) 有人要出售多的門票嗎？
蘿拉・詹金斯 10 月 12 日 晚上 8:05	我有！我的出差時間延長，無法參加活動，所以正好想找一個人來賣我的票。(150) 你要買我的票嗎？
凱文・斯尼德 10 月 12 日 晚上 8:18	是的，麻煩你了。(150) 謝謝！
(150) 蘿拉・ 詹金斯 10 月 12 日 晚上 8:19	(150) 我的榮幸。你可以打電話給我了解詳情。我的號碼是 (905) 555-2938。

---

149. 關於卡爾頓大學慈善舞會的敘述，何者正確？
(A) 限時退票。
(B) 在巴黎舉行。
(C) 門票將於 10 月 11 日開售。
(D) 它正在支持一個環保組織。　　答案 (D)

150. 晚上 8:19，蘿拉・詹金斯寫道「我的榮幸」，意思是什麼？
(A) 她很高興要去出差。
(B) 她很樂意幫助凱文・斯尼德。
(C) 她有興趣參加下一屆慈善舞會。
(D) 她喜歡打電話。　　　　　　　答案 (B)

問題 **151-152**，請參考以下行程表。

藍天旅行社
塔斯馬尼亞鄉村之旅
8 月 14 日上午 9:00 － 下午 6:30

* 請於早上出發時間前 30 分鐘抵達漢彌爾頓中心。

上午 9:00	巴士從漢彌爾頓中心出發 （請在抵達前享用早餐）
上午 10:00	抵達塔斯馬尼亞原住民村
上午 10:15	大鷹山健行 霍克瀑布觀景
上午 11:00	(152) 參觀塔斯馬尼亞原住民博物館的卡布・瓦希陶器特展
下午 12:30	在乾草堆自助餐廳享用午餐及自由活動時間 － 提供免費餐點。
下午 2:00	塔斯馬尼亞村現場參觀
下午 4:00	塔斯馬尼亞自由活動時間 (151) 鼓勵遊客參觀塔斯馬尼亞長屋，那裡有傳統糖果和各種紀念品可供購買。
下午 5:30	離開塔斯馬尼亞原住民村
下午 6:30	抵達漢彌爾頓中心

---

151. 遊客最有可能去哪裡購物？
(A) 漢彌爾頓中心
(B) 塔斯馬尼亞原住民博物館
(C) 乾草堆自助餐廳
(D) 塔斯馬尼亞長屋　　　　　　　答案 (D)

152. 卡布‧瓦希最有可能是誰？
　　(A) 導遊
　　(B) 策展人
　　(C) 藝術家
　　(D) 部落首領　　　　　　　　　　答案 (C)

問題 153-154，請參考以下電子郵件。

收件人：蓋爾‧萊瓦 <gleyva@enlightfinancials.com>
寄件人：史考特‧亞當斯
　　　　　<sadams@enlightfinancials.com>
日　期：11 月 2 日
主　旨：員工晚宴

親愛的萊瓦先生，

我就即將舉行一年一度的啟明金融員工晚宴的空間布置事宜聯繫了格雷葛里‧傑克森，他正在出差，讓我聯繫您。我需要貴團隊設立一個可容納 130 人左右的會議室，(154) 裡面需要 20 張圓桌，每張圓桌有 7 個座位。桌子要分散在會議室裡，以便每個座位都能看到舞臺。此外，請準備好一座講臺、兩個無線麥克風、一組投影機和投影幕。

以下是員工晚宴的時間表。
下午 3:30　　　　－ 大廳設置
下午 5:00　　　　－ 大門開啟
(153) 下午 5:30　－ 開幕致辭 － 拉羅謝爾‧史密斯／員
　　　　　　　　　工頒獎典禮
晚上 7:30　　　　－ 晚餐

史考特‧亞當斯
人力資源助理經理

153. 賓客應該在什麼時間到達啟明金融員工晚宴？
　　(A) 下午 5:00
　　(B) 下午 5:30
　　(C) 晚上 7:00
　　(D) 晚上 7:30　　　　　　　　　　答案 (B)

154. 亞當斯先生在電子郵件中提出什麼要求？
　　(A) 可使用的會議室列表
　　(B) 之前的晚餐賓客資訊
　　(C) 具體的家具布置
　　(D) 簡報設備清單　　　　　　　　答案 (C)

問題 155-157，請參考以下資訊。

薩默塞特湖景飯店
無線上網

(155) 請閱讀以下內容，以使用本飯店的無線網路。
1. (156C) 在前臺購買網卡。
2. (156A) 打開您裝置上的網路共享中心。從可用網路

列表中選擇名為「薩默塞特湖景飯店」的網路。
3. (156C) 輸入印在網卡上的密碼。
4. (156D) 閱讀並接受網路使用條款。
5. 點選「連接網路」。

請注意，您可以在商務中心的桌上型電腦免費使用網路。(157) 停車場和室外游泳池不提供無線網路。若需協助或諮詢，請致電前臺分機號碼 #555。

155. 此資訊的目的是什麼？
　　(A) 告知顧客取得服務所涵蓋的步驟
　　(B) 宣布推出新功能
　　(C) 解釋飯店政策的詳情
　　(D) 概述使用程序的優點　　　　　答案 (A)

156. 此資訊中，哪些內容沒有被提及為顧客應該做的事？
　　(A) 啟用他們電腦上的某項功能
　　(B) 輸入個人資訊
　　(C) 從接待處獲得密碼
　　(D) 同意遵守一些條件　　　　　　答案 (B)

157. 哪裡的無線網路連接受到限制？
　　(A) 飯店房間內
　　(B) 前臺周圍
　　(C) 商務中心
　　(D) 室外泳池周圍　　　　　　　　答案 (D)

問題 158-160，請參考以下電子郵件。

收件人：全體員工
寄件人：喬斯‧史考特 <jscott@beauchamparts.edu>
日　期：2 月 17 日
主　旨：地下停車場

致全體員工，

(158) 昨天，技術人員發現員工地下停車場存在滲漏問題。請注意，由於管道加固施工，地下停車場在二月分將無法使用。(160) 建議所有員工使用學校周圍的當地停車位。學校將報銷停車費。(160) 可用停車場列表將發布於 www.beauchampartsschool.com/staff。本次施工既不會直接影響我們即將舉行的春季音樂會，(159) 也不會為下週的新生迎新活動帶來問題。感謝您的配合。

喬斯‧史考特
博尚藝術學院秘書

158. 此電子郵件的目的是什麼？
　　(A) 解釋一個新程序
　　(B) 宣布興建新停車場
　　(C) 告知員工可能造成的不便
　　(D) 描述如何到達停車場　　　　　答案 (C)

159. 下週會發生什麼事？
(A) 音樂會將延期至下週。
(B) 將可使用地下停車場。
(C) 停車費將會增加。
(D) 將舉行教學活動。　　　答案 (D)

160. 員工被建議做什麼？
(A) 避免開車去學校
(B) 瀏覽網站
(C) 獲得汽車損壞賠償
(D) 參與建設　　　答案 (B)

問題 **161-163**，請參考以下公告內容。

玫瑰化妝品的顧客們，看過來！

(161) 應顧客的一再要求，玫瑰化妝品決定延長營業時間，以迎接更多賓客。請參考以下新的時間表：

地點	營業時間	
里奇蒙	週一至週五	早上 8:00 - 下午 6:00
	(162) 週日	**早上 9:30 - 下午 4:00**
薩弗克	週一至週五	早上 8:00 - 下午 6:00
	週六	早上 9:00 - 下午 5:00
朴次茅斯	週一至週五	早上 9:00 - 晚上 7:00
	週六	早上 9:00 - 下午 6:00

為了感謝顧客的支持，我們向所有在 5 月 5 日至 6 月 4 日期間光臨的消費者，提供精選商品折扣，(163) 並且**每筆消費都會贈送一份特別禮物**。如需折扣商品的完整列表，請查看我們的網站 www.rosecosmetics.com。玫瑰化妝品期待盡快與您見面！

---

161. 玫瑰化妝品為什麼要改變營業時間？
(A) 恢復區域競爭力
(B) 吸引其他地區的人
(C) 適應日益增加的顧客
(D) 處理顧客投訴　　　答案 (C)

162. 里奇蒙分店與其他分店有何不同？
(A) 每天開門時間較早。
(B) 週日營業。
(C) 目前正提供折扣。
(D) 近期將進行翻修。　　　答案 (B)

163. 顧客如何在玫瑰化妝品獲得免費商品？
(A) 查看網站
(B) 購買產品
(C) 與銷售業務交談
(D) 在指定時間前往特定商店　　　答案 (B)

問題 **164-167**，請參考以下信件內容。

---

7 月 8 日

馬蒂・羅馬諾
日出路 3718 號
89109 內華達州，拉斯維加斯

(164) 親愛的羅馬諾先生，

恭喜！您申請擔任常青兒童醫院志工的文件已被接收，並在日間托育計劃中獲得一個職位。不過，在開始之前，您必須提供一些針對安全性的附加文件。

(164) (165) 您需要提供過去 5 年的醫療紀錄（可以從您的個人醫生那裡取得），以及學校信函，證明您目前正在那裡上課。此志工機會僅適用於大學生，因此此文件非常重要。相關文件請直接郵寄至常青社會工作辦公室。(167) 地址已發布於我們的網站上。(165) 文件必須是列印出來的正本。請在 7 月 15 日前提交。

(166) 應您的要求，我附上了今年的志工計劃時間表。一旦我們審核完您的文件，我們將向您發送一條簡訊，其中包含一個網頁連結。請於網站上創建帳戶，以便您查看每日志工服務時間表。

如果您對以上有任何疑問，請隨時與我聯繫。

誠摯感謝。

茱蒂・克魯茲
常青兒童醫院志工計劃協調員
附件

---

164. 羅馬諾先生最有可能是誰？
(A) 大學生
(B) 醫院職員
(C) 招聘專員
(D) 志工團體代表　　　答案 (A)

165. 羅馬諾先生要在一週之內做什麼？
(A) 申請志工工作
(B) 發送電子郵件給克魯茲女士
(C) 參觀克魯茲女士在常青兒童醫院的辦公室
(D) 收到醫生的文件　　　答案 (D)

166. 什麼東西跟這封信一起寄來？
(A) 志工證書
(B) 出席證明書
(C) 網址
(D) 時間表　　　答案 (D)

167. 以下句子最適合放在文中 [1]、[2]、[3] 和 [4] 的哪一個位置？
「地址已發布於我們的網站上。」
(A) [1]
(B) [2]
(C) [3]

(D) [4]　　　　　　　　　　　　答案 (B)

問題 168-171，請參考以下線上討論訊息。

珍妮佛・摩絲　　　　　　　　　　　[晚上 9:03]
(170) (171) 在此提醒大家，明天 6 月 10 日，廣告部全體同仁將搬遷至新辦公地點。

珍妮佛・摩絲　　　　　　　　　　　[晚上 9:05]
請於今晚完成桌子清理的工作。如果你尚未在新辦公室被分配到辦公桌，請立即告訴我。

(169) 歐文・韋伯　　　　　　　　　[晚上 9:08]
我還沒有被分配到辦公桌。我記得和你說過這件事，但你後續就沒有再回覆我。

(168) 珍妮佛・摩絲　　　　　　　　[晚上 9:10]
哦，沒錯！很抱歉。我當時正在忙其他事情，完全忘了告訴你。你的辦公桌已經安排好了。我會親自跟你聯繫，並提供你的辦公桌號碼。

歐文・韋伯　　　　　　　　　　　[晚上 9:12]
謝謝。

(170) 賽門・哈洛姆　　　　　　　　[晚上 9:14]
(170) 終於有新辦公室了！那麼，明天是正常工作日，還是我們只是來搬東西？

珍妮佛・摩絲　　　　　　　　　　　[晚上 9:15]
(171) 明天就是一個搬遷日。我們的新辦公室將於上午 9:00 至下午 6:00 開放，務必確保在這期間內搬走所有物品。

提姆・貝爾文斯　　　　　　　　　[晚上 9:18]
我好像也沒有被分配到辦公桌。

珍妮佛・摩絲　　　　　　　　　　　[晚上 9:19]
提姆，你的辦公桌沒有像其他人那麼早分配，因為你幾天前才剛剛調到我們部門。不過，我有一張桌子可以給你。我也會親自跟你聯繫。

提姆・貝爾文斯　　　　　　　　　[晚上 9:21]
好的。謝謝。

---

168. 關於摩絲女士，文中提到什麼？
　　(A) 她沒有被分配到辦公桌。
　　(B) 她這一段時間很忙。
　　(C) 她在一家搬遷服務公司工作。
　　(D) 她是新的廣告經理。　　　　答案 (B)

169. 韋伯先生之前為何聯繫摩絲女士？
　　(A) 取得轉調其他部門的許可
　　(B) 提及他的升遷
　　(C) 要求分配工作位置
　　(D) 諮詢工作時間　　　　　　　答案 (C)

170. 晚上 9:14，哈洛姆先生寫道「終於有新辦公室了！」最有可能是什麼意思？
　　(A) 他在暗示明天不想工作。
　　(B) 他計劃最後一次參觀新辦公室。
　　(C) 他對新職位感到擔憂。
　　(D) 他對在新環境工作感到興奮。　答案 (D)

171. 員工被指示在 6 月 10 日上午 9:00 到下午 6:00 間做什麼？
　　(A) 在線上開設新帳號
　　(B) 搬移一些辦公家具
　　(C) 造訪新辦公室
　　(D) 聯繫摩絲女士　　　　　　　答案 (C)

問題 172-175，請參考以下文章內容。

納許維爾周邊──商業焦點

7 月 19 日

本週的商業焦點是貝兒洗衣店及其業主莫妮卡・貝兒女士。如果您不知道的話，(172) 貝兒洗衣店是一家位於傑克遜街的一站式商店，集自助洗衣店、咖啡廳和書店於一體。這種新型自助洗衣店，是當今納許維爾最成功的獨立企業之一。

(175) 起初，貝兒洗衣店並不像現在這麼成功。周圍有大型自助洗衣店環伺，讓它無法獲得足夠收入。然而，貝兒女士不願放棄自己的事業。經過幾個月的計劃，她將洗衣店的一部分改造成咖啡廳式的休閒空間。在這個等候區，顧客可以一邊喝咖啡、看書，一邊洗衣服和烘衣服。

貝兒洗衣店的顧客對其提供的便利和高品質服務，(173) 給予高度評價。該地區有許多住戶是韋爾奇學院的學生，他們需要洗衣服，也要購買課程書籍；他們知道，貝兒洗衣店是同時處理這兩項任務的完美場所。

(174) 許多當地大學請貝兒女士為計劃創業的學生提供祕訣和建議。作為一名年輕的企業家，她似乎很高興能夠開課，課程名稱為「化困難為轉機」。

---

172. 關於貝兒洗衣店，文中指出什麼？
　　(A) 它位於大學校園內。
　　(B) 它已被當地雜誌專訪過。
　　(C) 它透過網站銷售書籍。
　　(D) 這是一家運用獨特概念的企業。　答案 (D)

173. 第 3 段第 1 行中的「value」，含義最接近
　　(A) 評估
　　(B) 賞識
　　(C) 預估
　　(D) 支持　　　　　　　　　　　答案 (B)

174. 貝兒女士未來打算做什麼？
    (A) 教導大學生
    (B) 加入某個組織
    (C) 開設分店
    (D) 開展新業務　　　　　答案 (A)

175. 以下句子最適合放在文中 [1]、[2]、[3] 和 [4] 的哪一個位置？
    「周圍有大型自助洗衣店環伺，讓它無法獲得足夠收入。」
    (A) [1]
    (B) [2]
    (C) [3]
    (D) [4]　　　　　答案 (B)

問題 **176-180**，請參考以下公告及電子郵件。

巴哈音樂中心

(176) 巴哈音樂中心擴展到奧克維爾囉！我們將為老客戶開放免費參觀奧克維爾的全新中心。該中心配備了最新、改良後的系統和樂器。成為第一個在我們音樂中心體驗真正音樂的人吧！

(177) 日期：**7 月 8 日**
時間：上午 10:00 – 下午 5:00。
值得期待：參觀設施，試吃我們的咖啡廳產品，並與才華橫溢的指導老師會面。

(177) 在奧克維爾的巴哈音樂中心：
– 抒情咖啡廳有美味的新鮮烘焙食品及多種飲料可供選擇。
– 聖托馬斯禮堂，設有 150 席座位的室內表演廳。
(180) – 艾森納赫學程方案，針對 **11 歲以下**兒童的初級音樂課程。
(178) – 巴哈工作室——向專業歌手學習如何唱歌。巴哈音樂中心首次開設的聲樂培訓課程。

(176) (179) 奧克維爾的巴哈音樂中心將於 **7 月 11 日**首次對外開放。我們將為訪客提供免費的音樂書和巴哈音樂中心 T 恤。另外還有烘焙美食和飲料試吃等著您！

收件人：丹尼爾・魯伯特 <drupert@bachmusic.com>
寄件人：艾咪・雷耶斯 <areyes@fastmail.com>
日　期：(179) 7 月 12 日
主　旨：求職

親愛的魯伯特先生，

(179) 再次感謝您昨天抽出時間。我很高興看到該設施擁有所有最新的系統和設備。奧克維爾的巴哈音樂中心無疑展現出令人興奮的氛圍，這也是為什麼我很想成為貴音樂中心的指導老師之一。

我過去曾在幾所音樂學院擔任鋼琴老師。(180) 我主要

教授年輕學生，因為我喜歡和孩子們一起努力，見證他們成長為音樂家，透過學習鋼琴邁出音樂教育的第一步。看到孩子們對音樂產生熱情，是我主要的動機和靈感。

請發電子郵件給我或致電 (510) 555-3937，進一步討論有關貴音樂中心可能的職位資訊。謝謝您的考慮。

誠摯感謝。
艾咪・雷耶斯

---

176. 此公告最有可能是給誰？
    (A) 音樂指導老師的應徵者
    (B) 音樂學校的在學學生
    (C) 奧克維爾的訪客
    (D) 音樂比賽參賽者　　　　　答案 (B)

177. 7 月 8 日將免費向訪客提供什麼？
    (A) 一件 T 恤
    (B) 一本音樂書
    (C) 課程試聽優惠券一張
    (D) 食物和飲料　　　　　答案 (D)

178. 奧克維爾巴哈音樂中心獨家提供什麼？
    (A) 樂器租賃
    (B) 音樂廳
    (C) 聲樂訓練
    (D) 音樂課程折扣　　　　　答案 (C)

179. 魯伯特先生最有可能在什麼時候與雷耶斯女士交談？
    (A) 音樂中心盛大開幕期間
    (B) 音樂會中場休息期間
    (C) 在他的音樂課上
    (D) 參觀活動期間　　　　　答案 (A)

180. 雷耶斯女士最有可能想在音樂中心的什麼地方工作？
    (A) 聖托馬斯禮堂
    (B) 艾森納赫學程方案
    (C) 巴哈工作室
    (D) 抒情咖啡廳　　　　　答案 (B)

問題 **181-185**，請參考以下電子郵件。

收件人：詹姆士・科貝特 <jcorbett@ranianelec.com>
寄件人：伊麗莎白・雷維斯 <erevis@harrell.com>
日　期：11 月 17 日
主　旨：需要建議

親愛的科貝特先生，

很抱歉昨天我不得不這麼早就離開會議。正如我所提到的，我正在考慮申請拉尼安電子的工作，如果你能分享作為目前在該公司工作的人有什麼經驗和想法，我將不勝感激。

---

(182) 我目前在哈勒爾公司工作，跟同事合作或交流的機會並不多。(182) 頻繁出國出差也讓我筋疲力盡。

(185) 我看到一篇題為〈拉尼安工作環境〉的文章，是由你們的公關經理所寫，並發布在貴公司的網站上。如果這篇文章 (183) 確實反映了拉尼安的情況，我很樂意在那裡工作。(181) 你最近有辦法抽出時間，來討論我在貴公司的就業機會嗎？

謝謝。
伊麗莎白·雷維斯

收件人：伊麗莎白·雷維斯 <erevis@harrell.com>
寄件人：詹姆士·科貝特 <jcorbett@ranianelec.com>
日　期：11 月 18 日
主　旨：回覆：需要建議

親愛的雷維斯女士，

我很高興你有興趣在拉尼安電子工作。我想在我們見面詳細討論拉尼安和你的聘僱之前，先簡要回答你的問題。

(185) 你提到的那篇文章出自瑪莉·維特女士，確實描述了拉尼安的工作環境。我們有許多小組作業，要求所有成員互相分享自己的點子和想法。(184) 在每日會議中，任何人都可以提出新的策略或見解，無論他的職級或頭銜為何。我們很少出差，這對你來說應該是一個正向因素。我們更注重內部工作。

下週四下午我有空。那天一起共進午餐如何？期待盡快見到你。

謝謝。

詹姆士·科貝特

---

181. 第一封電子郵件的目的是什麼？
(A) 安排會面
(B) 推薦工作
(C) 接受工作機會
(D) 要求賠償　　　　　　　　答案 (A)

182. 關於哈勒爾公司，雷維斯女士提及什麼事？
(A) 不負擔員工的差旅費。
(B) 有空缺職位需要填補。
(C) 會在網站上發布文章。
(D) 在多個國家開展業務。　　答案 (D)

183. 第一封電子郵件中，第 3 段第 2 行的「true」，含義最接近
(A) 確定
(B) 自然
(C) 直接
(D) 準確　　　　　　　　　　答案 (D)

184. 關於科貝特先生，文中暗指什麼？
(A) 他經常在家工作。
(B) 他曾經是雷維斯女士的同事。
(C) 他認識雷維斯女士很久了。
(D) 他經常參加會議。　　　　答案 (D)

185. 瑪麗·維特是誰？
(A) 人事經理
(B) 公關經理
(C) 記者
(D) 技術員　　　　　　　　　答案 (B)

問題 186-190，請參考以下指引、電子郵件及收據。

歡迎蒞臨貝爾納多購物中心

為了確保所有顧客都能有愉快安全的體驗，務必嚴格遵守、落實貝爾納多購物中心的停車政策。請詳閱以下規則和說明：

- 所有停車位均遵循先到先得的原則，僅在指定位置停車。(190A) 威爾斯區是卡車、公車或貨車等大型車輛的停車空間，位於及時樂玩具店旁邊。所有其他類型的車輛，應停放在購物中心西側附近的佩德羅區。

- 所有顧客前半小時免費停車，過後將收取每小時 2 美元的費用。(188) 在貝爾納多購物中心消費超過 20 美元的顧客將免收停車費。(187) 離開時，必須在出口出示收據。雖然本購物中心與附近幾家餐廳共用停車位，但不接受餐廳收據。

- (186) 貝爾納多購物中心於營業時間提供停車位，自上午 10:00 至晚上 10:00，全年無休。

- 如有任何疑問、需求或投訴，請透過 customerservice@bernardomall.com 聯繫貝爾納多購物中心。

收件人：<customerservice@bernardomall.com>
寄件人：查爾斯·阿拉納 <carana@upmail.com>
日　期：3 月 20 日
主　旨：貝爾納多購物中心停車
附　件：(190A) 停車收據 (215117648)

敬啟者，

(188) (190B) 昨天，我和兒子造訪貝爾納多購物中心，並在旁邊的薯條及塔可餅餐廳吃了一頓飯。離開商場時，我被收取了 5.73 美元的停車費。我沒想到會這樣。因為我想我曾被告知，消費超過 20 美元的人將免繳停車費。(188) (189) 雖然我沒有在商場買任何東西，但我在餐廳花了遠超過 30 美元。(187) 當時我太忙了，無法向 5 號出口的工作人員解釋清楚，但希望我能得到這個失誤的退款。

謝謝。

查爾斯·阿拉納

貝爾納多購物中心停車場

(190A) 收據號碼：**215117648**

(190A) 停車位置	威爾斯區	車位編號	B07
入場日期／ 時間	(190C) **3 月 19 日** 下午 3:19	離場日期／ 時間	(190C) **3 月 19 日** 下午 6:41
需要發票嗎？	否	是否使用折扣？	否
應付金額	5.73 美金	停車時數	3 小時 22 分鐘
實付金額	5.73 美金	(190C) 支付方式	現金

感謝您，祝您行車安全！

186. 關於貝爾納多購物中心，文中暗指什麼？
　　(A) 最近修改了停車政策。
　　(B) 一週中的每一天都開放。
　　(C) 目前正在招募客服人員。
　　(D) 特定季節可能無法前往。　　　　答案 (B)

187. 關於阿拉納先生 3 月 19 日使用的停車場，文中暗指什麼？
　　(A) 整個上午都關閉。
　　(B) 最近剛裝修完。
　　(C) 這是一個地下設施。
　　(D) 它有很多個出入口。　　　　答案 (D)

188. 為什麼阿拉納先生將無法獲得退款？
　　(A) 他沒有正確停放車輛。
　　(B) 他沒有在貝爾納多購物中心花費規定的金額。
　　(C) 他沒有閱讀說明。
　　(D) 他沒有及時聯繫客服人員。　　　　答案 (B)

189. 電子郵件中，第 1 段第 4 行的「far」，含義最接近
　　(A) 真的
　　(B) 非常
　　(C) 超越
　　(D) 遙遠的　　　　答案 (B)

190. 關於阿拉納先生，以下敘述何者錯誤？
　　(A) 他駕駛一輛大型車輛前往貝爾納多購物中心。
　　(B) 他和兒子一起在薯條及塔可餅餐廳吃飯。
　　(C) 他於 3 月 19 日以現金支付停車費。
　　(D) 他不會再去貝爾納多購物中心。　　　　答案 (D)

問題 191-195，請參考以下廣告及網頁。

寧靜旅行社

寧靜旅行社自豪地推出特別的大峽谷一日遊。你可以在 6 人小團中，享受難忘而舒適的大峽谷南緣之旅。(195) 我們的專業導遊將用寬敞的廂型車，帶你前往大

峽谷和當地其他主要旅遊景點，並向你講述大峽谷的歷史以及每個地方的故事。(191) 請注意，只有寧靜旅行社的會員才能享有這個非常划算的價格。欲報名或了解有關大峽谷之旅的更多資訊，請至我們的網站 www.shermantours.com。

http://www.shermantours.com/tourinfo

寧靜旅行社

首頁	關於我們	旅遊資訊	旅程見證	預訂行程

(193) 特別的大峽谷一日遊

什麼時候：	上午 10:00 - 晚上 8:00 週日至週五（週六不開團）
什麼地方：	從弗拉格斯塔夫機場到大峽谷南緣（含接送服務）。(193) 在奧利瓦雷斯義大利餐廳享用午餐，(194) 在米切爾餐館或每逢週四在極盡法式餐廳享用晚餐。
多少錢：	每位成人 145 美元 16 歲以下兒童每位 80 美元
其他：	(192) 額外支付 **200 美元**，即可乘坐直升機遊覽大峽谷。飲食偏好務必提前告知。 點擊此處查看大峽谷和其他旅遊景點的照片。

http://www.shermantours.com/testimonials

寧靜旅行社

首頁	關於我們	旅遊資訊	旅程見證	預訂行程

「超棒的大峽谷之旅」

薩曼莎・瓦茲評論
10 月 10 日評論

這是寧靜旅行社提供的精彩又籌劃良好的旅程。我特別喜歡的是不會被催促，這使我能夠欣賞美麗的大峽谷景色和大自然。(195) 我們的導遊約書亞・歐尼爾知識淵博，所知甚多，而且很風趣。(194) 我也非常喜歡在極盡法式餐廳享用的美味晚餐。我會向所有想要在相對較短的時間內，在大峽谷獲得難忘體驗的人推薦此旅行套組。

191. 關於寧靜旅行社，以下敘述何者正確？
　　(A) 它為會員提供獨家優惠。
　　(B) 由六名員工組成。
　　(C) 每月發行一份電子報。
　　(D) 歷史悠久。　　　　答案 (A)

192. 關於乘坐直升機，文中提及什麼？
　　(A) 必須事先提出要求。
　　(B) 將贈送給回訪的客人。
　　(C) 需額外付費。
　　(D) 目前享有折扣價。　　　　答案 (C)

193. 大峽谷一日遊包含哪些項目？
    (A) 機票
    (B) 餐食
    (C) 紀念品
    (D) 拍照服務　　　　　　　　　　　答案 (B)

194. 瓦茲女士最有可能在什麼時候去大峽谷旅遊？
    (A) 星期四
    (B) 星期五
    (C) 星期六
    (D) 星期日　　　　　　　　　　　　答案 (A)

195. 關於歐尼爾先生，可以推斷出什麼？
    (A) 他是一名職業藝人。
    (B) 他為大峽谷之旅支付了 145 美元。
    (C) 他是寧靜旅行社的新員工。
    (D) 他載瓦茲女士前往大峽谷。　　　答案 (D)

問題 196-200，請參考以下網頁、公告及電子郵件。

---

http://www.booksworld.com/category

書的世界

首頁	最新消息	分類	訂購

各類別暢銷書：烹飪藝術

1.《廚房幕後》安東尼‧巴里
夢想開一家餐廳？借助巴里先生的見解和建議，(196) **學習如何在餐飲業賺大錢。**

2.《快樂餐桌》凱倫‧威爾森
餐桌上的食物，決定你和家人的健康幸福。關於選擇正確食材和使用正確烹飪方法的指南。

3. (198)《了解餐飲業》羅德尼‧桑福德
你必須了解這個行業，才能從中取得成功。了解如何避免餐飲業新手常犯的錯誤。如果你對擁有一家餐廳感興趣，這本就是你必讀的書。

4.《食物、語言和文化》羅德尼‧桑福德
是什麼決定了一個國家的食物、語言和文化？它們又如何影響國家及人民？你可以在桑福德先生的書中找到答案。本書已被翻譯成 10 多種語言。

布魯菲爾德公共圖書館
六月第四週的活動

(199) **6 月 20 日，星期一** —— (198) 暢銷作家兼餐廳老闆羅德尼‧桑福德蒞臨本圖書館，談論他新書中展示的餐廳經營法。活動結束後，桑福德先生將為參加者簽書。

6 月 22 日，星期三 —— (197) 為學齡前兒童、幼兒及其監護人舉辦的有趣互動音樂活動。有關不同季節和天氣的歌曲，將與各種樂器一起演奏。無須報名，即可參加這個令人激動的音樂課程。

收件人：<customerservice@bloomfieldpl.org>
寄件人：馬爾文‧查爾斯 <mcharles@opmail.com>
日　期：6 月 27 日
主　旨：布魯菲爾德公共圖書館

敬啟者，

(199) 我最近參加了布魯菲爾德公共圖書館主辦的活動。桑福德先生的知識和想法，讓我印象深刻。當我要執行自己的商業計劃時，他在討論過程中教我的內容，將會是很棒的資產。

(200) 此外，當《廚房幕後》一書可借閱時，我希望收到簡訊通知。我想借的時候，它已經被借走了。我的手機號碼是 (210) 555-3918。謝謝。

(199) 馬爾文‧查爾斯

---

196. 網頁中，第 1 段第 2 行的「good」，含義最接近
    (A) 愉快的
    (B) 可觀的
    (C) 慷慨的
    (D) 真實的　　　　　　　　　　　　答案 (B)

197. 關於布魯菲爾德公共圖書館，文中暗指了什麼？
    (A) 舉辦兒童活動。
    (B) 報名活動需要會員卡。
    (C) 目前正在招聘新員工。
    (D) 營業時間隨季節變化。　　　　　答案 (A)

198. 哪本書的作者最近在布魯菲爾德公共圖書館簽書？
    (A) 廚房幕後
    (B) 快樂餐桌
    (C) 了解餐飲業
    (D) 食物、語言和文化　　　　　　　答案 (C)

199. 關於查爾斯先生，以下敘述何者可能正確？
    (A) 他常常去布魯菲爾德公共圖書館。
    (B) 他在布魯菲爾德公共圖書館工作。
    (C) 他想買一本桑福德先生的書。
    (D) 他有興趣開一家餐廳。　　　　　答案 (D)

200. 查爾斯先生請求布魯菲爾德公共圖書館做什麼？
    (A) 告知他一本書的出版日期
    (B) 桑福德先生舉辦另一場活動時通知他
    (C) 某本書歸還至圖書館時讓他知道
    (D) 寄一本新書到他的地址　　　　　答案 (C)

Part 1

1. 美國 M
(A) He is leaving the window open.
(B) He is taking off his hat.
(C) He is wearing a coat.
(D) He is exiting an aircraft.

(A) 他讓窗戶開著。
(B) 他正在脫下帽子。
(C) 他穿著一件外套。
(D) 他正在下飛機。　　　　　　答案 (C)

2. 美國 W
(A) A hammer is placed in the tool box.
(B) New equipment is being installed in a work station.
(C) The man is leaning over his work.
(D) The man is measuring some building materials.

(A) 一把錘子放在工具箱裡。
(B) 新設備正被安裝到工作站裡。
(C) 男子正彎著腰工作。
(D) 男子正在測量一些建築材料。　答案 (C)

3. 英國 M
(A) One of the men is handing a pen to a presenter.
(B) Some folders have been left open on the table.
(C) A clock has been mounted on a wall.
(D) One of the women is reaching for a cup.

(A) 其中一名男子正將一支筆遞給講者。
(B) 一些資料夾攤開在桌子上。
(C) 時鐘設置在牆上。
(D) 其中一名女子正伸手拿杯子。　答案 (C)

4. 美國 M
(A) They are approaching a doorway.
(B) Some recycling bins have been left on the street.
(C) One of the men is parking a truck beside a store.
(D) Both of the men are hanging a sign on the wall.

(A) 他們正在接近門口。
(B) 有些回收箱被留在街上。
(C) 其中一名男子正在商店旁邊停放一輛卡車。
(D) 兩名男子在牆上掛了一個牌子。　答案 (A)

5. 澳洲 W
(A) Some branches of a tree are being trimmed.
(B) Some flowers are being planted in a parking lot.
(C) Some traffic cones have been put near a truck.
(D) A vehicle is being towed by a truck.

(A) 一棵樹的樹枝正被修剪。
(B) 一些花正被種在停車場。
(C) 一些三角錐放置在卡車附近。
(D) 一輛汽車被卡車拖走。　答案 (C)

6. 美國 W
(A) The audience is applauding the presenter.
(B) The audience is facing the front of the room.
(C) The presenter is walking toward a podium.
(D) The presenter is connecting a projector to a computer.

(A) 觀眾為講者鼓掌。
(B) 觀眾面向房間的前面。
(C) 講者正走向講臺。
(D) 講者正將投影機連接到電腦。　答案 (B)

Part 2

7. 美國 M 美國 W

Who's introducing the new marketing expert tomorrow?
(A) It will be on the market next week.
(B) The manager's going to.
(C) Nice talking to you, too.

明天誰來介紹新的行銷專家？
(A) 將於下週上市。
(B) 經理會做。
(C) 我也很高興跟你談話。　答案 (B)

8. 澳洲 W 美國 M

What ingredients are in this wedding cake?
(A) Not that I know of.
(B) Cookbooks will be on display today.
(C) Some blueberries and powdered nuts.

這個結婚蛋糕有什麼成分？
(A) 據我所知沒有。
(B) 今天將展示食譜。
(C) 一些藍莓和堅果粉。　答案 (C)

9. 美國 W 英國 M

Why did the management decide to hold the company picnic at the City Park?
(A) It was crowded.
(B) You should bring some paper plates and cups.
(C) They think it has lots of space.

為什麼管理層決定在城市公園舉辦公司野餐？
(A) 那裡很擁擠。
(B) 你應該帶一些紙盤和杯子。
(C) 他們認為那裡空間很大。　答案 (C)

10. 美國 M 澳洲 W

Could you water my potted plants while I'm away on business?
(A) Take a tour of the new plant.
(B) Sure. I'd be glad to.
(C) At the botanical garden.

我出差的時候，你能幫我的盆栽澆水嗎？
(A) 參觀新工廠。
(B) 當然。我非常樂意。
(C) 在植物園。　　　　　　　　　答案 (B)

11. 美國 W 澳洲 W

When did you last replace the water purifying filter?
(A) A few days ago.
(B) It should take about an hour to fix it.
(C) Because I was so thirsty.

你上次更換淨水過濾器是什麼時候？
(A) 幾天前。
(B) 修復它大約需要一個小時。
(C) 因為我太渴了。　　　　　　　答案 (A)

12. 美國 M 美國 W

Should we drive or take the bus to the conference?
(A) Half an hour if there's no traffic.
(B) I'd prefer to drive myself.
(C) On the conference table.

我們應該開車還是搭公車去參加大會？
(A) 不塞車的話半小時。
(B) 我比較喜歡自己開車。
(C) 在會議桌上。　　　　　　　　答案 (B)

13. 英國 M 美國 W

What is supposed to happen at his job interview?
(A) At the office on the second floor.
(B) He'll meet with the marketing director.
(C) It starts Tuesday morning at 9 o'clock.

他的工作面試中預計會發生什麼事？
(A) 在二樓的辦公室。
(B) 他將與行銷總監會面。
(C) 週二早上 9 點開始。　　　　　答案 (B)

14. 澳洲 W 美國 M

How long do you think it will take to fix the air purifier?
(A) No. I didn't repair it.
(B) It should be ready in about an hour.
(C) It will fit in the corner.

你認為修好空氣清淨機需要多長時間？
(A) 不，我沒有修理它。
(B) 大約一個小時內就可以準備好。
(C) 它將裝在在角落。　　　　　　答案 (B)

15. 美國 W 英國 M

Who's giving a speech first at the sales conference?
(A) Carrie is, I think.
(B) Not all of the attendees did.
(C) A very informative presentation.

誰會在銷售大會上第一個發表演說？
(A) 我認為是嘉麗。
(B) 並非所有與會者都這樣做。
(C) 資訊豐富的報告。　　　　　　答案 (A)

16. 英國 M 澳洲 M

Would you like to reschedule an appointment for next Monday?
(A) How about Tuesday at 2 P.M.?
(B) I scheduled a meeting.
(C) A new security policy.

你想重新安排下週一的預約嗎？
(A) 週二下午 2 點如何？
(B) 我安排了一場會議。
(C) 新的安全政策。　　　　　　　答案 (A)

17. 澳洲 W 美國 M

Why didn't Elaine attend the rock festival last night?
(A) I won't be able to be there until 7:00.
(B) I want to play some music.
(C) Because she had to work late.

為什麼伊萊恩昨晚沒有參加搖滾音樂節？
(A) 我 7:00 才能到那裡。
(B) 我想放一些音樂。
(C) 因為她必須工作到很晚。　　　答案 (C)

18. 美國 W 英國 M

Laura commutes an hour and a half to work every day.
(A) There was heavy traffic.
(B) That sure is a very long ride.
(C) Yes, my lunch break is in thirty minutes.

蘿拉每天花一個半小時通勤上班。
(A) 交通堵塞。
(B) 那真是一段很長的路程。
(C) 是的，30 分鐘後就是我的午休時間。　答案 (B)

19. 美國 M 美國 W

You're from Oxford, right?
(A) Wednesday afternoons will be fine.
(B) Yes, I lived there for 30 years or so.
(C) It was good to meet our overseas employees.

你來自牛津，對吧？
(A) 週三下午不錯。
(B) 是的，我在那裡住了 30 年左右。
(C) 很高興見到我們的海外職員。　　答案 (B)

20. 英國 M 澳洲 W

Does your company use any recycled materials in the factory?
(A) The recycling bin is over there.
(B) Please put on this safety gear.
(C) Not yet, but we are planning to.

貴公司在工廠是否使用回收材料？
(A) 回收箱在那邊。
(B) 請穿上此安全裝備。
(C) 還沒有，但我們正計劃這樣做。　　　答案 (C)

21. 美國 M 澳洲 W

Do you want to post the study results on the website or publish them in our magazine?
(A) The post office stays open until 4 o'clock.
(B) I think online would be much better.
(C) I subscribe to the magazine, too.

你想將研究結果發布在網站上，還是發表在我們的雜誌上？
(A) 郵局營業至下午 4 點。
(B) 我認為線上會好很多。
(C) 我也訂閱了這本雜誌。　　　答案 (B)

22. 英國 M 美國 W

The weather forecast said it is supposed to rain all day tomorrow.
(A) Joshua was supposed to handle that.
(B) Then we'd better cancel the outdoor event.
(C) Where did you buy that raincoat?

天氣預報說明天一整天都會下雨。
(A) 約書亞應該處理那個問題。
(B) 那我們最好取消戶外活動。
(C) 你在哪裡買那件雨衣？　　　答案 (B)

23. 美國 M 澳洲 W

Why can't I get this accounting program to work?
(A) He is a new accountant.
(B) I didn't watch that television program, either.
(C) You haven't installed the software update, have you?

為什麼我無法讓這個會計程式運作？
(A) 他是新會計師。
(B) 我也沒有看那個電視節目。
(C) 你還沒安裝軟體更新，對嗎？　　　答案 (C)

24. 美國 W 英國 M

You approved the remodeling of the employee breakroom, didn't you?
(A) Yes, construction will begin next Monday.
(B) His room has a nice mountain view.
(C) Let's take a coffee break.

你批准了員工休息室的改建，不是嗎？
(A) 是的，施工將於下週一開始。
(B) 他的房間可以看到美麗的山景。
(C) 讓我們喝杯咖啡，休息一下。　　　答案 (A)

25. 美國 W 美國 M

We need to formally announce when we are relocating.
(A) They require formal attire.
(B) Movers arrived late.
(C) Didn't Sue send an e-mail?

我們需要正式宣布何時搬遷。
(A) 他們要求正式服裝。
(B) 搬家工人遲到了。
(C) 蘇沒有發電子郵件嗎？　　　答案 (C)

26. 澳洲 W 英國 M

When will you be available to start working as a tour guide?
(A) Of course, I'm ready to work on it.
(B) He's been with us for 20 years.
(C) I still have three weeks left of school.

你什麼時候可以開始擔任導遊？
(A) 當然，我已經準備好去做這件事了。
(B) 他已經跟我們在一起 20 年了。
(C) 我還要上三個星期的課。　　　答案 (C)

27. 美國 W 英國 M

Will the farewell party for Jessy be held at the office or at a restaurant?
(A) Yes, it sure is more spacious.
(B) Our conference room is not large enough.
(C) Yes. We'll need more workers.

潔西的歡送派對會在辦公室還是餐廳舉行？
(A) 是的，它確實更寬敞。
(B) 我們的會議室不夠大。
(C) 是的，我們需要更多工人。　　　答案 (B)

28. 美國 M 澳洲 W

Where's the main entrance to the amusement park?
(A) He is the park ranger.
(B) You see a long line of people over there, don't you?
(C) There are many rides you can enjoy.

遊樂園的正門在哪裡？
(A) 他是園區管理員。
(B) 你有看到那邊排了很長的隊，不是嗎？
(C) 有很多遊樂設施可供你享受。　　　答案 (B)

29. 美國 W 英國 M

Will we discuss the expansion project at the manager meeting?
(A) Haven't you seen the agenda?
(B) Yes, it was well responded.
(C) Yes, that conference room will do.

我們會在經理會議上討論這個擴建計劃嗎？
(A) 你沒看到議程嗎？
(B) 是的，反應很好。
(C) 是的，那個會議室就可以了。 答案 (A)

30. 美國 W 美國 M

Haven't you ordered more of the rosemary shampoo yet?
(A) It's not that popular with shoppers.
(B) Actually, I'd like to rinse it.
(C) Put them back on the shelf.

你還沒有訂購更多迷迭香洗髮精嗎？
(A) 它不太受購物者青睞。
(B) 其實我想沖洗一下。
(C) 把它們放回架子上。 答案 (A)

31. 美國 W 英國 M

When can we reopen the factory we are expanding?
(A) Does the rent include utilities?
(B) The renovation project was delayed again.
(C) That tool belongs to Jenny.

我們正在擴建的工廠什麼時候可以重啟？
(A) 租金包括水電費嗎？
(B) 改造工程再次延期了。
(C) 那個工具屬於珍妮。 答案 (B)

Part 3

問題 32-34，請參考以下對話內容。 英國 M 美國 W

M: (32)**How is everything going with the development of the Dynasty sport utility vehicle?**
W: (33)**We're running a bit behind schedule with this vehicle. The engine is being overhauled. The one we had planned to use simply wasn't powerful enough.**
M: Good. When do you think we can start manufacturing it?
W: We'll need to let some potential customers test drive it first, but (34)**we are planning to begin production in two months.**

男：王朝休旅車的研發進展如何？
女：這款車型的進度有點落後。引擎正在改良中，我們原本計劃使用的那顆根本不夠有力。
男：好。你認為我們什麼時候可以開始生產？

女：我們得先讓一些潛在買家試駕，但我們計劃兩個月後才會開始生產。

32. 談話者正在討論什麼產品？
(A) 汽車
(B) 筆記型電腦
(C) 手機
(D) 電視機 答案 (A)

33. 是什麼導致延誤？
(A) 無法獲得材料
(B) 預算中沒有足夠資金
(C) 引擎問題
(D) 缺乏熟練的工人 答案 (C)

34. 兩個月後將發生什麼事？
(A) 開始生產。
(B) 設計獲得批准。
(C) 收集顧客調查結果。
(D) 工廠開始營業。 答案 (A)

問題 35-37，請參考以下對話內容。 澳洲 W 英國 M

W: Hello, Jeff. It's great to see you. Did you have a good vacation?
M: Yes, I did. Thanks for asking. You know, I noticed a sign on the front window when I came in. (35)**What's this about guaranteeing same-day delivery on all book purchases?**
W: (36)**I made the decision to do that while you were away. We have an arrangement with a local delivery service that will let us get books to customers within a couple of hours.**
M: (37)**That should help sales.** I imagine that our website will attract more customers if we keep ensuring that kind of reliability for swift delivery.

女：哈囉，傑夫。很高興見到你。假期過得愉快嗎？
男：是的，假期過得很愉快。謝謝你的詢問。那個，我進來的時候注意到前窗上有一個告示。保證所有書籍在購買當天送達，是怎麼回事？
女：你不在的時候，我決定這麼做。我們跟當地貨運服務達成協議，可以在幾個小時內將書籍送到顧客手中。
男：這應該有助於銷量。我想，如果持續確保快速交貨的可靠性，我們的網站將能吸引更多客人。

35. 談話者最有可能在哪裡工作？
(A) 雜貨店
(B) 電器行
(C) 書店
(D) 圖書館 答案 (C)

36. 女子決定做什麼？
   (A) 改善網頁
   (B) 保障服務
   (C) 向顧客收取會員費
   (D) 訂購更多產品　　　　　　　答案 (B)

37. 男子期望會發生什麼事？
   (A) 營業時間將延長。
   (B) 將提供免費貨運服務。
   (C) 將僱用更多員工。
   (D) 銷量將會提升。　　　　　　答案 (D)

39. 女子有什麼顧慮？
   (A) 材料
   (B) 期限
   (C) 價格
   (D) 地點　　　　　　　　　　　答案 (C)

40. 談話者同意下午做什麼？
   (A) 查看手冊
   (B) 簽訂租賃合約
   (C) 跟屋主會面
   (D) 參觀房產　　　　　　　　　答案 (D)

問題 **38-40**，請參考以下對話內容。 美國 M 美國 W

M: Hello, Ms. Buford. (38)**This is Samuel, the realtor with Kline Realty.** I've got some great news for you. There's a new home up for sale in the Golden Forest neighborhood. Are you interested?

W: I know that's a good neighborhood. Can you tell me about what the house is like?

M: Sure. It has four bedrooms and three bathrooms. It's selling for $250,000.

W: (39)**Well, the location and the house sound perfect, but it's a bit beyond my budget.** Would the owners consider negotiating a lower price?

M: They would. (40)**How about checking out the property first? Do you have time today at 1:00 P.M.?**

W: (40)**Yes, I do. If you tell me the address, I'll meet you there.**

男：你好，布福德女士。我是塞繆爾，克萊恩房地產公司的房地產經紀人。我有好消息要告訴你。金色森林附近有一棟新房待售，你有興趣嗎？

女：我知道那裡環境不錯。你能告訴我那是怎樣的房子嗎？

男：當然。它有四間臥室和三間浴室，售價為 250,000 美元。

女：嗯，地段和房子聽起來都很完美，但有點超出我的預算。屋主會考慮協商更低的價格嗎？

男：他們會的。不如先去看看房子怎麼樣？今天下午 1:00，你有空嗎？

女：沒問題，我有空。告訴我地址，我會在那裡跟你會合。

----

38. 男子在哪裡工作？
   (A) 園林綠化服務
   (B) 房地產仲介機構
   (C) 公共圖書館
   (D) 電信公司　　　　　　　　　答案 (B)

問題 **41-43**，請參考以下對話內容。 澳洲 W 英國 M

W: Well, that was a great party. (41)**It was wonderful to be all together and celebrate John's retirement.**

M: You can say that again. Now for the hard part, we have to clean up this mess.

W: (42)**I'm tired, so how about leaving that for tomorrow?**

M: (42)**All the recyclables get picked up tomorrow morning.**

W: I totally forgot about that. Okay, let's take care of it now.

M: Don't worry. We'll be finished in no time. (43)**I'll get the broom and dustpan, and you get some garbage bags from the back closet.**

女：嗯，那是一場很棒的派對。大家聚在一起慶祝約翰退休，感覺真棒。

男：你說得沒錯。現在最困難的部分，是我們必須把這團亂清理乾淨。

女：我累了，明天再說吧？

男：所有回收物都會在明天早上收走。

女：我完全忘記了。好吧，我們現在就處理。

男：別擔心。我們很快就會完成。我去拿掃把和畚箕，你從後面的櫃子裡拿一些垃圾袋。

----

41. 談話者正在談論什麼活動？
   (A) 退休派對
   (B) 培訓研討會
   (C) 新的清潔服務
   (D) 員工感謝派對　　　　　　　答案 (A)

42. 男子為什麼說「所有回收都會在明天早上收走」？
   (A) 提供警告
   (B) 提出請求
   (C) 表達驚訝
   (D) 婉拒建議　　　　　　　　　答案 (D)

43. 男子說他要做什麼？
    (A) 聯繫清潔服務機構
    (B) 早點回家
    (C) 撿起垃圾
    (D) 準備清潔用品　　　　　答案 (D)

問題 **44-46**，請參考以下對話內容。 美國 M 澳洲 W

M: Hello. (44)**You have reached the Everest Hotel.** How may I be of assistance?

W: Good morning. I need to reserve a room for this Thursday and Friday nights. Are there any rooms still available?

M: It's your lucky day. (45)**There's a trade show going on this weekend**, but we still have a couple of rooms available. Are you planning to attend the event?

W: Actually, I'll be hosting a booth there.

M: Just so you know, (46)**we will be providing shuttle buses to and from the convention center every thirty minutes. That should be convenient since you won't need to take a taxi or a bus.**

男：您好。這裡是聖母酒店。我可以如何提供協助呢？
女：早安。我要預訂本週四和週五晚上的房間。還有空房嗎？
男：您很幸運，這週末有貿易展，但我們還有幾個房間可用。您打算參加那場活動嗎？
女：事實上，我會在那裡設立一個展位。
男：讓您知道一下，我們每 30 分鐘就會提供往返會議中心的接駁巴士。這應該會方便很多，因為您不需要搭計程車或公車。

44. 男子在哪裡工作？
    (A) 火車站
    (B) 機場
    (C) 會議中心
    (D) 飯店　　　　　答案 (D)

45. 根據男子所說，本週將舉辦什麼活動？
    (A) 行銷研討會
    (B) 貿易展覽會
    (C) 音樂會
    (D) 新書發表會　　　　　答案 (B)

46. 男士建議做什麼？
    (A) 乘坐接駁巴士
    (B) 聘請當地導遊
    (C) 在餐館用餐
    (D) 搭計程車　　　　　答案 (A)

問題 **47-49**，請參考以下三方對話內容。 美國 M 美國 W 英國 M

M1: We appreciate your coming to this job interview, Anna. As you're aware, (47)**we need someone to handle our online advertisements as well as manage our social media accounts.**

W: Yes. I've been in charge of my company's social media campaigns for the past three years.

M2: We noticed that on your résumé. (48)**We checked out those online campaigns and were impressed. That's why you're the leading candidate for the job now.**

M1: (49)**Well, now that you're here at our resort, you can see its beautiful scenery and views for yourself.** Do you think you'd be able to incorporate images from here into our accounts?

W: Definitely. I can't believe how beautiful it is.

M1: We'll take you on a tour of the grounds soon so that you can see the natural beauty in person.

男1：安娜，我們非常感謝你參加本次工作面試。如你所知，我們需要有人來處理我們的線上廣告，並管理社群媒體帳號。
女：是的。過去三年，我一直負責公司的社群媒體宣傳活動。
男2：我們在你的履歷上注意到了這一點。我們查看了這些線上活動並留下深刻的印象。這就是為什麼你現在是這份職位的主要人選。
男1：那麼，現在你來到我們的度假村，可以親眼目睹這裡的美麗風景和景色。你覺得自己有辦法把這裡的畫面結合到我們的帳號裡嗎？
女：一定可以。我簡直不敢相信這裡有多美麗。
男1：我們很快就會帶你參觀環境，讓你親眼見證自然美景。

47. 這間公司希望女子做什麼？
    (A) 設計一個新的休閒區
    (B) 負責線上廣告
    (C) 創建一個新網頁
    (D) 管理客戶帳號　　　　　答案 (B)

48. 為什麼女子是最佳職位人選？
    (A) 她有在國外工作的經驗。
    (B) 她有很好的推薦資料。
    (C) 她的工作成果令人印象深刻。
    (D) 她的時程安排很有彈性。　　　　　答案 (C)

49. 男子們對他們的度假村有什麼評價？
    (A) 最近剛裝修過。
    (B) 這裡風景優美。
    (C) 很受客人歡迎。
    (D) 價格合理。　　　　　答案 (B)

W: Were you able to find everything you wanted?

M: I was. This grocery store just opened, right? It's my first time to see it.

W: We opened two days ago. We're still organizing everything. (50)**We'll be having a grand opening sale this weekend, and most items will be offered at a reduced price.** Please drop by.

M: I'm really pleased there's a supermarket so close to my home. (51)**Given that you have a good selection here, I think we'll be seeing each other a lot.**

W: If our sales so far are any criterion, it would seem that we can expect to see a lot of people here.

M: I'm happy to hear that. Anyway, I'd like to check out now. (52)**Do you take credit cards?**

W: (52)**I'm really sorry, but the card readers haven't been connected yet.**

女：找得到你想要的東西嗎？

男：沒問題。這家雜貨店剛開幕吧？這是我第一次看到它。

女：我們兩天前開幕，還在努力步上軌道。本週末我們將舉行盛大的開幕優惠活動，多數商品都將以折扣價出售。歡迎過來看看。

男：很高興有一家超市離我家這麼近。這裡的選擇很多，我想我們會經常見面的。

女：如果以我們迄今為止的銷售額為標準，我們似乎可以期待在這裡看到很多人。

男：很高興聽到這個消息。那麼，我想先結帳。你們接受信用卡嗎？

女：很抱歉，讀卡機還沒有連接。

---

50. 女子說週末會發生什麼事？
    (A) 部分商品會有折扣。
    (B) 新商品即將到貨。
    (C) 照明裝置將被安裝。
    (D) 商店營業時間將延長。 答案 (A)

51. 男子說「我想我們會經常見面的」，意思是什麼？
    (A) 他接受了商店的工作。
    (B) 他對新商店感到高興。
    (C) 他認識一位企業主很久了。
    (D) 他是購物俱樂部的會員。 答案 (B)

52. 女子為什麼道歉？
    (A) 她誤解了男子的要求。
    (B) 該商店目前不用招聘。
    (C) 付款方式無法使用。
    (D) 廣告中的商品缺貨。 答案 (C)

W: Hello. (53) (54)**I purchased this violin here two months ago, but yesterday I found a crack in it.** I wonder if I can get a refund.

M1: I'm not sure. Let me ask the manager. Oh, here he comes. Stuart, this customer has a question.

M2: Hello. I'm Stuart. What can I help you with?

W: Um, I bought this violin here two months ago, but it's already broken. Is it possible to return it for a refund?

M2: Sorry, but the store policy is that items must be returned within four weeks of purchase to get a refund. (55)**However, that particular item comes with a company warranty that's valid for one year.**

女：你好。我兩個月前在這裡買了這把小提琴，但昨天我發現它有裂縫。我想知道是否可以退款。

男1：我不確定。讓我問問經理。哦，他來了。斯圖爾特，這位顧客有疑問。

男2：你好。我是斯圖爾特。我可以怎麼協助你？

女：嗯，兩個月前我在這裡買了這把小提琴，但它已經壞了。可以退貨退款嗎？

男2：抱歉，商店政策規定，商品必須在購買後四個星期內退回，才能獲得退款。不過，這項特定產品附帶有效期一年的公司保固。

---

53. 談話者在談論什麼類型的產品？
    (A) 廚房用品
    (B) 樂器
    (C) 燈具
    (D) 智慧型手機配件 答案 (B)

54. 女子對該物品有什麼不滿？
    (A) 它缺少部分零件。
    (B) 它發出奇怪的聲音。
    (C) 它的電線有誤。
    (D) 它已損壞。 答案 (D)

55. 斯圖爾特建議做什麼？
    (A) 使用製造商的保固
    (B) 前往另一家維修店
    (C) 訂購一些替換零件
    (D) 當天晚點再回來 答案 (A)

W: Hello, Tim. Are you available now?

M: (56)**I'm just about to finish repairing this bicycle.** What's going on?

W: (57)**We finally received that shipment of electric motors.** I'm sure our customers will be pleased.

M: Great. There have been a lot of people asking if they could convert their bikes to electric ones. They're not hard to install, are they?

W: Not at all. You simply attach the motor. It's great for people who want to travel long distances on their bikes.

M: Wonderful. (58)**Could you please hang up a sign saying that the motors are currently in stock?** We need to inform our customers of their arrival as soon as possible.

女：你好，提姆。你現在有空嗎？

男：我馬上就要修完這輛自行車了。怎麼了？

女：我們終於收到那批電動馬達。相信我們的客戶會很高興。

男：太好了。很多人詢問是否可以將自行車改裝為電動自行車。它們並不難安裝，對嗎？

女：完全不會。你只需要接上電動馬達即可。對於想要騎自行車長途旅行的人來說，這非常有用。

男：太棒了。可以請你掛上告示，說明電動馬達目前有庫存嗎？我們要盡快通知客戶，它們已經到貨了。

---

56. 談話者在哪裡工作？
    (A) 回收廠
    (B) 技工學校
    (C) 製造工廠
    (D) 自行車店　　　　　　　　　　答案 (D)

57. 談話者在談論什麼？
    (A) 電動馬達
    (B) 一些安全裝備
    (C) 自行車架
    (D) 方向盤　　　　　　　　　　　答案 (A)

58. 男子要求女子做什麼？
    (A) 致電供應商
    (B) 張貼告示
    (C) 簽署文件
    (D) 發送電子郵件　　　　　　　　答案 (B)

問題 **59-61**，請參考以下對話內容。　英國M 澳洲W

M: Welcome back to my talk show on radio 103.4. (59) **My guest today is Susan Briggs, the owner of Briggs Furniture.** She'll be talking about how her industry has changed. Welcome, Susan.

W: Thanks for having me on the show.

M: I know that custom-made furniture isn't as popular as it once was. How has your store managed to remain profitable considering this changing trend?

W: (60)**Recently, we haven't gotten as many orders as we used to.** (61)**However, the orders we do get tend to be extensive.**

M: And is it profitable to fill those orders?

W: (61)**Many homeowners request custom-made furniture for every room in their home**, and those orders provide us with plenty of work, which helps us still stay competitive.

男：歡迎回到我在 103.4 電臺的脫口秀節目。今天，我的來賓是蘇珊·布里格斯，也就是布里格斯家行的老闆。她將談論她的產業發生了什麼變化。歡迎，蘇珊。

女：謝謝你邀請我參加節目。

男：我知道訂製家具不像以前那麼流行了。考慮到這種不斷變化的趨勢，你的商店如何設法保持盈利？

女：最近，我們的訂單沒有以前那麼多。然而，我們收到的訂單往往種類繁多。

男：完成這些訂單可以獲利嗎？

女：許多屋主要求為家裡的每個房間訂製家具，這些訂單提供了大量工作，有助於我們保持競爭力。

---

59. 女子在哪裡工作？
    (A) 廣播電臺
    (B) 家具行
    (C) 電腦商店
    (D) 百貨公司　　　　　　　　　　答案 (B)

60. 關於最近的訂單，文中提及什麼？
    (A) 它們數量較少。
    (B) 它們大多來自企業。
    (C) 它們總是透過網路下單。
    (D) 它們必須預先組裝好。　　　　答案 (A)

61. 據女子所說，她的企業如何保持競爭力？
    (A) 提供訂製家具折扣
    (B) 改善客戶服務
    (C) 加強網路行銷
    (D) 為個人戶提供許多品項　　　　答案 (D)

問題 **62-64**，請參考以下對話內容及報告。　英國M 美國W

M: Hello, Alice. (62)**I just inspected the office equipment here at the law firm.** But I need your advice about something before I turn in my report.

W: Sure. What's your question?

M: Almost everything is working properly, (63)**but there's one piece of equipment in the main conference room which hasn't worked in a while, and I don't know if I should repair it or throw it away.** What should I do?

W: Talk to Joseph. The main conference room is his responsibility. See what he wants to do.

M: (64)**He was in a meeting just a while ago, but I'll go there to see if it's over now.**

男：你好，愛麗絲。我剛剛檢查了律師事務所這裡的辦公設備。但在我提交報告之前，有些事需要你的建議。

女：沒問題。有什麼問題嗎？

男：一切幾乎全都正常運作，但主會議室裡有一個設備，已經有一段時間不能用了，我不知道該修理它還是丟掉。我應該怎麼做？

女：跟約瑟夫談談。主會議室是他負責的，看他想怎麼做。

男：他剛才在開會，我去看看現在結束了沒有。

檢查報告

項目	採取的行動
筆記型電腦	已升級作業系統
影印機	已更換碳粉
(63) 投影機	**破損－修復或移除**
印表機	已連接到新電腦

62. 談話者從事什麼類型的工作？
(A) 圖書館
(B) 電器行
(C) 大學
(D) 律師事務所　　　　　　　答案 (D)

63. 請看圖表。談話者在談論的是哪一件設備？
(A) 筆記型電腦
(B) 影印機
(C) 投影機
(D) 印表機　　　　　　　　　答案 (C)

64. 男子說他現在要做什麼？
(A) 訂購一些替換零件
(B) 與同事交談
(C) 清理會議室
(D) 購買一些新設備　　　　　答案 (B)

問題 65-67，請參考以下對話內容及行程表。 澳洲 W　美國 M

W: Sam, I thought you said you'd have to skip lunch with our clients.

M: (65)**My conference call with Fred got canceled, so I had time to make it to the restaurant.** I'm glad the clients aren't already here.

W: So am I. I'm pleased you're here. (66)**You worked on the design of the appliance a lot, so I hope you can help me describe it.**

M: Okay. However, (67)**I can't stay for too long because I have to be somewhere at 1:30.**

W: I understand. In that case, why don't you start by

talking about the new appliance when the clients arrive? Then, when you need to go, I'll take over and respond to all of their questions.

M: That sounds perfect to me.

女：山姆，我以為你說你必須取消跟我們的客戶共進午餐。

男：我和弗雷德的電話會議取消了，所以我來得及去餐廳。很高興客戶還沒有到。

女：我也是。很高興你在這裡。你對設備的設計投入很多，所以我希望你能幫我介紹它。

男：好的。不過，我不能停留太久，因為我必須在 1:30 到達某個地方。

女：了解。既然如此，何不在客戶到達時就先談談新設備呢？然後，你要離開的時候，我會接手並回答他們的所有提問。

男：這聽起來很完美。

山姆的行程表

待辦事項	時間
跟迪恩會面	上午 11:00
電話會議	上午 11:45
客戶午餐	下午 12:00
(67) 工廠參訪	下午 1:30
迎新演講	下午 4:00

65. 這場談話在哪裡進行？
(A) 迪恩的辦公室
(B) 餐廳
(C) 工廠
(D) 會議室　　　　　　　　　答案 (B)

66. 談話者將討論什麼？
(A) 產品價格
(B) 產品設計
(C) 產品銷售情況
(D) 產品廣告　　　　　　　　答案 (B)

67. 請看圖表。為什麼山姆需要提前離開？
(A) 他要和迪恩會面。
(B) 他有一個電話會議。
(C) 他要去參訪工廠。
(D) 他要發表迎新演講。　　　答案 (C)

問題 68-70，請參考以下對話內容及海報。 英國 M　澳洲 W

M: Hello. (68)**How are you enjoying the trade fair?**

W: It's interesting. I'm just checking out booths to see

what each company is offering.

M: I can tell you about an online management training program my company offers. It's helpful for those hoping to break into management.

W: It sounds good. I'll be applying for my boss's position when he retires next year.

M: This chart here shows the four phases of managing a project. Most people focus on the first and third phases and (69)**don't realize that a project can easily fail if they don't focus enough on the second phase.**

W: Interesting. Do you have any brochure about this program or whatever? I'm flying home tonight, (70)**but I can sign up for an online training program when I get back home.**

男：你好。你覺得這場貿易展覽會如何？

女：很有趣。我正在查看各攤位，看看每家公司提供什麼。

男：我可以告訴你我公司提供的線上管理培訓計劃。對於那些希望進入管理層的人很有幫助。

女：聽起來不錯。我的老闆明年退休之後，我將申請他的職位。

男：這張圖表顯示管理專案的四個階段。多數人只關注第一和第三階段，沒有意識到如果他們疏忽第二階段，整個專案就很容易失敗。

女：很有趣。你有關於這個計劃的小冊子或其他什麼嗎？我今晚要飛回家，但我到家之後可以報名參加線上培訓計劃。

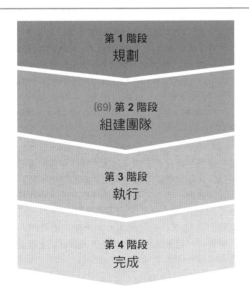

68. 這場談話在哪裡進行？
(A) 工作博覽會
(B) 經理會議
(C) 行銷公司
(D) 貿易展覽會　　　　　答案 (D)

69. 請看圖表。男子認為哪個階段對專案的成功很重要？
(A) 規劃
(B) 組建團隊
(C) 執行
(D) 完成　　　　　答案 (B)

70. 女子說她回家後會做什麼？
(A) 報名課程
(B) 申請職位
(C) 跟男子通話
(D) 提交履歷　　　　　答案 (A)

Part 4

問題 **71-73**，請參考以下會議摘錄。 美國 M

Hello, everybody. (71)**This is the last day of our special sale, and we expect lots of customers to come to purchase sporting goods.** (72)**Please be friendly and answer any questions customers have today.** I want you to make sure the shelves are fully stocked. (72)**But if a customer has trouble finding any item, help that person at once.** In addition, because it's the last day of the sale, we're giving away prizes today. (73)**All people need to do to win a prize is to make a purchase and then fill out a form you give them.**

大家好。這是特賣會的最後一天，我們預計會有很多顧客來購買體育用品。請保持親切有禮，並回答顧客今天提出的任何問題。我希望你們確保架上的貨品充足。但如果顧客找不到東西，請立即幫助他。另外，因為今天是促銷的最後一天，所以我們會贈送獎品。顧客若想贏得獎品，所要做的就是進行消費，然後填寫你們給他們的表格。

71. 說話者最有可能在哪裡工作？
(A) 體育用品店
(B) 五金行
(C) 百貨公司
(D) 珠寶店　　　　　答案 (A)

72. 據說話者所說，聽者應該關注什麼？
(A) 店內清潔
(B) 分發宣傳單
(C) 提供顧客服務
(D) 重新排列貨架　　　　　答案 (C)

73. 購物者要如何贏取獎品？
(A) 發送簡訊
(B) 提交收據
(C) 造訪網站
(D) 填寫表格　　　　　答案 (D)

Would you like a fun job during vacation? Then come to the career fair at Stanton Resort this Saturday. We're hiring part-time staff members for all kinds of positions, from lifeguards at our beach to servers at our restaurants. (74)**The Stanton Resort is recognized for one of the most popular hotels with tourists** (75)**as we attract visitors from all around the world.** We're also a great place to work. We have the highest hourly wages in the region, (76)**and we also offer other benefits, including flexible hours and paid days off.**

你想在假期期間找到一份有趣的工作嗎？那就來參加本週六在斯坦頓假村舉行的招聘會吧。我們正在招募各種職位的兼職員工，從海灘救生員到餐廳服務生。斯坦頓假村是公認最受遊客歡迎的飯店之一，因為我們吸引了來自世界各地的旅客。我們也是一個很棒的工作場所。我們有本地最高的時薪工資，還提供其他福利，包括彈性工時和帶薪假。

74. 什麼企業正在打廣告？
    (A) 遊樂園
    (B) 旅行社
    (C) 餐廳
    (D) 飯店　　　　　　　　　　　　答案 (D)

75. 據說話者所說，該企業受到哪種認可？
    (A) 舉辦游泳比賽
    (B) 採用環保材料
    (C) 吸引外國遊客
    (D) 向當地慈善機構捐款　　　　　答案 (C)

76. 員工有哪些工作福利？
    (A) 員工折扣
    (B) 全職工作的機會
    (C) 彈性的工作時間
    (D) 培訓機會　　　　　　　　　　答案 (C)

Hello, Dave. This is Carol at MTR, Inc. (77)**We just received a shipment of computer chips from you, but it's much less than we were expecting.** (78)**Please call me back at once. We have orders that we need to fill at the end of the month.** In addition, (79)**please be advised that I'll be out of the office most of the day.** If I don't answer, dial extension 78, please. Mark will be able to tell you how to get in touch with me.

你好，戴夫。我是港鐵公司的卡羅。我們剛剛收到你們

寄來的電腦晶片，但數量比我們預期的少很多。請立即回電給我，我們有訂單要在月底完成。此外，請留意，我整天大部分時間都不在辦公室。如果我沒有接聽電話，請撥打分機 78。馬克會告訴你如何與我聯繫。

77. 說話者為什麼打電話？
    (A) 申請取消
    (B) 追蹤訂單
    (C) 談論訂單
    (D) 詢問行車路線　　　　　　　　答案 (C)

78. 說話者說「我們有訂單要在月底完成」，是在暗示什麼？
    (A) 必須僱用更多工人。
    (B) 她的請求很緊急。
    (C) 她可以支付更高的價格。
    (D) 物品應透過特快專件發送。　　答案 (B)

79. 聽者被提醒什麼事？
    (A) 講者可能不在她的辦公室。
    (B) 工作時間可能會發生變化。
    (C) 無法預約。
    (D) 時間表已更改。　　　　　　　答案 (A)

(80)**I need to update you on the fundraiser we're holding for the local hospital next month.** (81)**It has just been confirmed that we can use the auditorium at city hall.** We're really pleased about that since it can hold 1,000 people. Now that we know the location is secured, (82)**we can start the next phase of the planning.** (82)**We need to put together a website for the fundraiser** to let people know why we're trying to raise money. I want the site to be up and running no later than next week.

我要向你們更新我們下個月為當地醫院舉辦的募款活動最新情況。剛剛確認可以使用市政府的禮堂。我們對此感到非常高興，因為它可以容納 1,000 人。現在我們知道地點已經確定，可以開始下一階段的規劃。我們需要為募款活動建立一個網站，讓大家知道我們為什麼要籌集資金。我希望該網站最晚在下週可以上線並投入運作。

80. 什麼類型的活動正在準備中？
    (A) 貿易展覽會
    (B) 當地節慶
    (C) 慈善拍賣
    (D) 募款活動　　　　　　　　　　答案 (D)

81. 說話者宣布什麼消息？
    (A) 廣告宣傳成功。
    (B) 海報已張貼。
    (C) 場地可以租用。
    (D) 晚餐預訂已確認。　　　　　答案 (C)

82. 據說話者所說，規劃過程的下一階段是什麼？
    (A) 投放廣告
    (B) 簽訂合約
    (C) 創建網頁
    (D) 獲取物資　　　　　　　　　答案 (C)

問題 83-85，請參考以下播客內容。 美國 M

It's time to get started with the local news podcast. I'm Tim Davis, the host of the show. (83)**Today, we'll be discussing how to expand your business.** It's important to know when you should open a new store or enlarge your present one. (84)**Today, our special guest is Tina Mellon. Tina started a small cosmetics manufacturer.** Two years later, she decided to hire more workers. At present, she employs more than 1,000 people. (85)**You can read an interview containing her thoughts on doing business by visiting her website. Go online to check it out.**

播放本地新聞播客的時候到了。我是節目主持人提姆·戴維斯。今天，我們將討論如何擴展你的事業。知道什麼時候應該開一家新店或擴大現有店面很重要。今天，我們的特邀嘉賓是蒂娜·梅隆。蒂娜創辦了一家小型化妝品製造商。兩年後，她決定僱用更多工人。目前，她擁有 1,000 多名員工。你可以瀏覽她的網站，閱讀她的採訪，裡面包含她對經商的想法。上網看看吧。

83. 這段播客的主題是什麼？
    (A) 了解市場趨勢
    (B) 拓展事業
    (C) 增加利潤
    (D) 幫助開展新事業　　　　　　答案 (B)

84. 蒂娜·梅隆擁有什麼類型的企業？
    (A) 服裝店
    (B) 餐廳
    (C) 金融服務公司
    (D) 化妝品製造商　　　　　　　答案 (D)

85. 說話者說可以在網站上找到什麼？
    (A) 訪談
    (B) 商業教程
    (C) 投資者名單
    (D) 工作機會　　　　　　　　　答案 (A)

問題 86-88，請參考以下旅遊資訊。 美國 W

Thanks for joining us on today's tour. (86)**I'd like to apologize for the late start**. The bus driver encountered some bad traffic on his way here. Fortunately, he took an alternate route, so he wasn't delayed too long. Our first stop will be the commercial district, where we'll stay for about an hour so you can shop. You'll see a variety of ceramic plates and bowls for sale there. (87)**But let me tell you something. Lots of the items for sale there are made in the artisan district. And that's our next stop.** In the afternoon, we'll have lunch at Rudolph Bistro where I think you'll have a good time (88)**because the Jackson Brothers, a popular local guitar duo, will be playing out on the patio there.**

感謝各位參加今日的旅程。我想為出發延遲向大家道歉。客運司機來這裡途中遇上交通堵塞。幸好他走了另一條路，所以沒有耽誤太久。我們的第一站是商業區，我們將在那裡停留大約一個小時，以便各位購物。您會看到那裡販售各種陶瓷盤子和碗。但讓我告訴大家一件事，那裡販售的許多物品，都是在工匠區製造的。那就是我們的下一站。下午，我們將在魯道夫小酒館吃午餐。我想各位會在那裡度過一段愉快的時光，因為當地高人氣吉他二人組傑克遜兄弟將在露臺上演奏。

86. 說話者為了什麼事情道歉？
    (A) 意外費用
    (B) 大排長龍
    (C) 延遲開始
    (D) 擁擠的客運　　　　　　　　答案 (C)

87. 說話者為什麼說「那就是我們的下一站」？
    (A) 建議稍後再購買物品
    (B) 投訴旅遊行程
    (C) 督促聽者加快速度
    (D) 回答聽者的問題　　　　　　答案 (A)

88. 說話者說聽者在魯道夫小酒館會享受到什麼？
    (A) 城市景觀
    (B) 藝術品
    (C) 音樂表演
    (D) 新鮮食品　　　　　　　　　答案 (C)

問題 89-91，請參考以下會議摘錄。 澳洲 W

Good morning. Our Human Resources meeting today will be about retaining employees. (89)**For the past several quarters, we've had problems with keeping staff members.** Lots of employees depart after working here a short time. (90)**Last month, I conducted a survey of every employee across the company.** I learned a lot from the results. Several people stated that they would like to have more support and training after being hired. (91)**To address this, we've decided to launch a mentoring program.** We are going to pair all new employees with experienced staff members to help them get settled into their position through informative guidance.

早安。我們今天的人力資源會議將討論如何留住員工。過去的幾季裡，我們在留住員工方面出現問題。很多員工在這裡工作一小段時間後就離開了。上個月，我對公司的每位職員進行了一項調查。我從結果中得知很多事情。不少人表示，到職後希望能得到更多支持和培訓。為了解決這個問題，我們決定啟動一個輔導計劃。我們將為所有新員工與經驗豐富的員工配對，透過扎實指導，幫助他們適應自己的職位。

89. 企業遇到什麼困難？
    (A) 僱用合格的員工
    (B) 推廣最新產品
    (C) 拓展國外市場
    (D) 留住員工　　　　　　　　　　答案 (D)

90. 說話者上個月做了什麼？
    (A) 她進行了一項調查。
    (B) 她面試了一些應徵者。
    (C) 她簽了一份新合約。
    (D) 她出差了。　　　　　　　　　答案 (A)

91. 說話者說公司將做什麼？
    (A) 啟動輔導計劃
    (B) 提供在職培訓
    (C) 製作更多廣告
    (D) 購買新房產　　　　　　　　　答案 (A)

問題 92-94，請參考以下新聞報導。 美國 M

Hello. This is News at Ten. (92)**Summerville has continuously made efforts to improve its bus operations in the city**, and we've been tracking its progress. The mayor just announced that the city is going to launch a mobile app, Bus-tracking Now to help passengers track where the buses are and look up real-time departures and arrivals. (93)**You may be wondering if it's worth downloading another mobile app. Well, we've been told that it has been successful in other cities.** If you download the app and use it, (94)**how about e-mailing your comments to newsatten@Summervillenews.org?** We'd love to know what you think.

大家好。這裡是十點新聞。薩默維爾不斷努力改善該市的公車營運，我們也持續追蹤其進展。市長剛剛宣布，將推出一款名為「即刻追蹤公車」的應用程式，幫助乘客追蹤公車位置，並查詢實時出發和到達情形。各位可能想知道，它是否值得讓你們下載另一個應用程式。嗯，我們收到消息，它在其他城市已經取得成功。如果你下載該應用程式並使用，何不將評論透過電子郵件發送至 newsatten@Summervillenews.org ？我們很想知道你的想法。

92. 薩默維爾打算做什麼？
    (A) 拓寬城市部分道路
    (B) 改善公車服務
    (C) 鼓勵居民使用大眾運輸
    (D) 吸引更多遊客　　　　　　　　答案 (B)

93. 說話者為什麼說「它在其他城市已經取得成功」？
    (A) 僱用更多公車司機
    (B) 提及新的培訓計劃
    (C) 開發另一個應用程式
    (D) 讚揚一項執行完善的工作　　　答案 (D)

94. 聽者被要求做什麼？
    (A) 透過電子郵件發送回饋
    (B) 開始乘坐公車
    (C) 參觀市長辦公室
    (D) 前往其他城市　　　　　　　　答案 (A)

問題 95-97，請參考以下電話留言及維修計劃表。 美國 W

Hello, Carl. This is Amy. (95)**I'm calling regarding the repairs you'd like to have done on your home.** We sent a crew to inspect your property two days ago, and they understand the work that you want done. (96)**Right now, I'm working on an estimate of the price you'll need to pay.** The price mostly depends upon the quality of the paint you want for the interior. (97)**Let me send you a few samples to choose from.** Once you do that, I can give you a final price quote. Please call me back if you have any questions. Thanks.

你好，卡爾。我是艾米。我打電話是為了你想對房屋進行的維修。兩天前，我們派了一組人員檢查你的房子，他們了解你想要完成的項目。現在，我正在估算你需要支付的價格。這主要取決於你想要的室內油漆品質。讓我寄一些樣品供你選擇。一旦你選好了，我就可以給你最終報價。如果你有任何疑問，請回電話給我。謝謝。

維修計劃表

步驟 1	檢查房子
(96) 步驟 2	進行成本估算
步驟 3	建立時間表
步驟 4	獲得許可證
步驟 5	開始執行

95. 說話者最有可能是誰？
   (A) 施工經理
   (B) 建築師
   (C) 五金行老闆
   (D) 室內裝潢師　　　　　　　　　答案 (A)

96. 請看圖表。說話者目前正在進行哪一個步驟？
   (A) 步驟 1
   (B) 步驟 2
   (C) 步驟 3
   (D) 步驟 4　　　　　　　　　　　答案 (B)

97. 說話者會向聽者寄送什麼？
   (A) 待簽合約
   (B) 修改後的藍圖
   (C) 一些材料樣本
   (D) 成本預估　　　　　　　　　　答案 (C)

問題 98-100，請參考以下電話留言及海報。　澳洲 W

Hello, Darlene. It's Lisa. I'm calling regarding the spring festival that's taking place in Fayetteville this weekend. **(98)Because of the approaching hurricane, the festival has been pushed back until next weekend.** That's good for me because I really wanted to attend it, but I'll be out of town this weekend. **(99)Anyway, that band we want to see is going to be performing on Saturday**, so how about going to see them together? If you want, **(100)I can pick the tickets up for you after work today.** Just let me know.

你好，達琳。我是麗莎。我打電話來，是關於本週末在費耶特維爾舉行的春祭慶典。由於颶風逼近，慶典延期至下週末。這對我是好消息，因為我真的很想參加，但這個週末我要出城。總之，我們想看的樂團將在週六演出，一起去看他們怎麼樣？如果你願意的話，我今天下班後可以幫你取票。請讓我知道。

費耶特維爾春季慶典

5 月 2 日星期六 – 5 月 3 日星期日
彩繪與繪畫
當地美食與表演者

◇◇◇◇◇◇◇◇◇◇◇◇◇◇◇◇◇◇◇◇◇◇◇◇◇

(99) 週六演出	週日演出
– (99) 馬歇爾彼得斯樂團	– 戴夫‧桑德斯喜劇劇目
– 費耶特維爾管弦樂團	– 紅木樂隊

98. 為什麼活動延期？
   (A) 部分費用尚未繳納。
   (B) 預期天氣惡劣。
   (C) 部分表演者缺席。
   (D) 需要進行修復工作。　　　　　答案 (B)

99. 請看圖表。說話者最有可能參加哪場演出？
   (A) 紅木樂隊
   (B) 費耶特維爾管弦樂團
   (C) 戴夫‧桑德斯喜劇劇目
   (D) 馬歇爾彼得斯樂團　　　　　　答案 (D)

100. 說話者表示願意做什麼？
   (A) 擔任節日志工
   (B) 籌辦活動
   (C) 買一些票
   (D) 開車去看表演　　　　　　　　答案 (C)

Part 5

101. 由於他樂觀開朗的性格，他後來在紐約當上了電臺主持人。　　　　　　　　　　　　　答案 (C)

102. 上週歐元和瑞士法郎對美元匯率都下跌了 3.1%。
　　　　　　　　　　　　　　　　答案 (A)

103. 我們公司決定聘用權先生為行銷負責人，因為他的行銷報告非常出色。　　　　　　　答案 (A)

104. 由於熱浪來襲，BK 建設要求延長新的橋樑建造計劃。
　　　　　　　　　　　　　　　　答案 (B)

105. 曼都電子的股價，在推出新的記憶卡後大約上漲了 25%。　　　　　　　　　　　　　答案 (D)

106. 隨著搜尋技術進步，要在網路上找到並購買 50-60 年代的老爵士樂專輯並不難。　　　答案 (B)

107. 詹金斯先生聘用的庭園造景師使用常綠灌木叢為花園創造額外的隱私，也為房子標記自然邊界。　答案 (C)

108. 一旦越南的新製造工廠建成,我們的生產力預計將增長約 30%。 答案 (A)

109. 新車型的外觀和內裝,為了吸引國內外買家而完全重新設計。 答案 (C)

110. 人們通常閱讀報紙和雜誌,以獲取關於各種社會現象的正確資訊。 答案 (A)

111. 應提醒求職者,面試時提供錯誤資訊可能會自動導致不合格。 答案 (B)

112. 新開發的電池充電器,幾乎可以與國內市場上所有類型的筆記型電腦相容。 答案 (C)

113. 帕克女士主張,新庫存系統的點子是她的,而非伊文斯先生的。 答案 (D)

114. 假如司機駕駛載運危險物品的車輛,應當遵守駕駛時間和休息時間的相關規定。 答案 (B)

115. 基於最近研究,部分科學家得出結論,北極冰帽消失得比 90 年代快了 7 倍。 答案 (A)

116. 有興趣參加科技研討會的人,請於下週三前跟麥高恩先生聯繫。 答案 (D)

117. 最近的問卷調查結果顯示,10 名青少年中有 3 名過度依賴手機。 答案 (B)

118. 這份市場分析報告裡,有霍普金斯先生在明天召開董事會議前要修改的一些錯誤。 答案 (D)

119. 詹姆斯・瓦特的最新專輯,是國內最暢銷的專輯,獲得很多知名音樂獎項。 答案 (D)

120. 請寫下您與全球電信相關的近期經驗,以便我們提升客戶服務水準。 答案 (D)

121. 演講嘉賓應站在聽眾面前,促進他們積極投入和參與。 答案 (D)

122. 人事部會精心規劃公司提供給新員工的許多活動。 答案 (B)

123. 建議所有人保留報稅表和收據副本,以備將來審計時使用。 答案 (A)

124. 儘管卡車和轎車銷售較少,但自動交易服務公司去年公布了破紀錄的利潤。 答案 (B)

125. 菁英電腦公司的製造工廠發現,自從生產線上的員工開始使用新機器後,生產力急劇增加。 答案 (A)

126. 公司部分交易檔案在轉入新數據儲存系統的過程中損壞。 答案 (C)

127. 新的辦公電腦講座共有 30 名員工參加。他們將學習電腦技術,包括文書處理及數據庫管理的進階知識。 答案 (B)

128. 雖然製造業工作在近幾十年減少,但由於生產力提升,製造業產量持續增加。 答案 (C)

129. 許多知名餐廳和飯店為了方便預約和信用卡支付,開設自己的官方網站。 答案 (D)

130. 包裝發貨的產品,如未拆下正品包裝盒,將予以退貨。 答案 (D)

Part 6

問題 131-134,請參考以下資訊。

課程公告

陽光山丘社區中心很高興宣布,從 4 月 10 日下週三開始,帕特里夏・埃爾南德斯女士將在社區中心教授基礎西班牙語。該課程於每週一上午 10:00 開始上課至 11:30,位置在 401 室。

您可以透過我們的網站 www.scc.org 報名,或親自前往任一服務檯。四個星期的學費為 80 美元。如果您在本週三之前報名,將自動獲得 20% 學費折扣。

陽光山丘社區中心從下個月開始提供綜合外語課程。所有 60 歲以上(含)的陽光山丘居民都可以免費參加我們的課程。更多資訊請見網站。

131. 答案 (C)

132. 答案 (C)

133. 答案 (C)

134. (A) 您需要大學學位才能滿足教學證照的要求。
(B) 我們的翻譯工作可能不需要其他經驗。
(C) 所有 60 歲以上(含)的陽光山丘居民都可以免費參加我們的課程。
(D) 社區中心將暫時關閉以進行大規模整修。
答案 (C)

問題 135-138，請參考以下文章內容。

首頁 > 本地新聞 >

山谷拓寬道路

作者：阿爾弗雷德‧布蘭特利，12 月 12 日上午 10:15

山谷市議會即將開始毗鄰山谷會議中心的倫巴第街道路擴建工程。此建設計劃包括拓寬倫巴第街的四線道，使其成為八線道道路。工作排定於 3 月 1 日左右開始，預計需要三個月左右完工。

為了確保施工安全進行，倫巴第街將禁止山谷會議中心和山谷美術館之間的車輛通行。山谷會議中心旁通往倫巴第街的天橋也將不對行人開放。

沿著倫巴第街通往山谷會議中心的人行道，不會受施工影響。不過，在此期間，途經倫巴第街的公車將改道瓦倫西亞巷。

135. 答案 (D)

136. (A) 我們關注道路交通擁塞和空氣汙染。
(B) 它將為本地工人創造許多新的就業機會，並帶動我們的經濟成長。
(C) 工作場所安全就是確保人們以正確的方式完成工作，使受傷的可能性為零或很小。
(D) 工作排定於 3 月 1 日左右開始，預計需要三個月左右完工。 答案 (D)

137. 答案 (D)

138. 答案 (B)

問題 139-142，請參考以下信件內容。

親愛的麥可‧韋斯特先生；

我們收到了您 6 月 1 日的來信。對於給您帶來的任何不便，我們深表歉意。

然而，據我們的運輸公司所稱，一百個箱子均在良好的冷凍狀態下交付。船上沒有人觀察到有任何箱子在抵達聖地亞哥之前有解凍狀況。因此，我們認為解凍過程是在貨物移至港口倉庫後開始的。

為了保持豬肉冷凍，冷凍室的溫度必須保持在攝氏負 15 度。我們認為，您的倉庫冷凍設施不足，箱子因此開始解凍。

雖然我們不打算向您提供全額退款，但很樂意為您提供下一筆交易的 30% 折扣。我們希望這種安排能夠彌補您所蒙受的部分損失。

我們期待將來再次為您服務。

誠摯感謝

妮娜‧李
產品品質控管經理
安德魯農場公司

139. 答案 (C)

140. 答案 (B)

141. 答案 (D)

142. (A) 我們對任何丟失、被盜或損壞的行李或個人物品不負任何責任。
(B) 冷凍食品可以除菌，並允許食物保存多年。
(C) 透過快速交貨和正確包裝，您可以將易腐爛的物品發送給您的客戶。
(D) 我們希望這種安排能夠彌補您所蒙受的部分損失。 答案 (D)

問題 143-146，請參考以下公告內容。

核桃溪飯店
特里蒙特街 1411 號
02120 麻州，波士頓
電話：(857) 770-7000~3
傳真：(857) 770-7004~5
www.walnutcreekhotel.com

很高興迎接您成為我們的貴賓，由衷感謝您選擇入住本飯店。核桃溪飯店設備齊全，時刻準備熱情接待您。因此，我們希望您像愛護自己的家一樣愛護它。

所有飯店客房最近都進行了極具品味的重新裝修和配備，將精緻織物及華麗大理石用最新技術結合，以確保飯店每一位顧客都能擁有最滿意的住宿體驗。

您可以在位於一樓的服務臺，獲取有關交通和各種便利服務的必要資訊。如果您需要更多資訊，請隨時撥打分機 101 與我們聯繫。

希望您在核桃溪飯店的留宿，成為波士頓之旅的美好回憶之一。再次感謝您選擇核桃溪飯店入住，並祝您度過愉快的時光。

143. (A) 我謹代表全體員工，由衷感謝您今年的慷慨禮物和支持。
(B) 預訂飯店房間時，客人可能會被要求預付押金。
(C) 無論一年中的什麼時候，這座小鎮的風景就在您家門口。
(D) 很高興迎接您成為我們的貴賓，由衷感謝您選擇入住本飯店。 答案 (D)

144. 答案 (B)

145. 答案 (B)

146. 答案 (A)

Part 7

問題 147-148，請參考以下廣告內容。

在寧靜水療中心放鬆身心

作為南加州首屈一指的水療中心，寧靜水療中心提供的服務，遠超出任何傳統水療。7 月 1 日當天，我們將在聖地牙哥開設另一家水療分館。

(147) 請留意，帶有星號 * 的服務，自 7 月 10 日起提供。

瑞典式按摩 *	治療按摩 *	(147D) 雷射護膚 *
(147A) 臉部護理	蜜蠟除毛	(147B) 石療
美甲	(147C) 換膚	香薰

(148) 請列印此頁面，並攜帶下方優惠券。

任何水療服務 15% 折扣	立即安排您的預約！ － 優惠有效期至 7 月 31 日。 － 每次到訪只能使用一張優惠券。

147. 7 月 9 日不提供哪些服務？
(A) 臉部護理
(B) 石療
(C) 換膚
(D) 雷射護膚　　　　　　　　　答案 (D)

148. 關於廣告中的優惠券，文中暗指什麼？
(A) 8 月分才可以使用。
(B) 僅在聖地牙哥分店提供折扣。
(C) 必須列印出來才能獲得折扣。
(D) 可與其他優惠同時使用。　　　答案 (C)

問題 149-150，請參考以下文字訊息。

大衛‧卡特　　　　　　　　　　　［下午 2:22］
下午好。感謝您聯繫桑德森汽車公司。請問需要什麼協助？

安娜貝絲‧墨菲　　　　　　　　　［下午 2:23］
你好。我去年買了一輛新的休旅車，(149) 我想知道它是否受到桑德森剛剛宣布的召回影響。

大衛‧卡特　　　　　　　　　　　［下午 2:24］
是的。過去三年生產的休旅車都包含在內。因此，請將您的車輛帶到最近的桑德森汽車經銷商，以維修安全

帶。

安娜貝絲‧墨菲　　　　　　　　　［下午 2:26］
我剛搬到一個新城市，不知道那在哪裡。

大衛‧卡特　　　　　　　　　　　［下午 2:27］
(150) 請至此處：www.sandersonautos.com/recall。點擊「尋找最近的經銷商」，您將找到要遵循的指示。

安娜貝絲‧墨菲　　　　　　　　　［下午 2:28］
(150) 這樣我能處理了。謝謝你的協助。

大衛‧卡特　　　　　　　　　　　［下午 2:29］
不客氣。祝您有個愉快的一天。

149. 墨菲女士為什麼聯繫卡特先生？
(A) 了解如何購買休旅車
(B) 詢問引擎問題
(C) 詢問公司召回事宜
(D) 要求提供部分退款　　　　　　答案 (C)

150. 下午 2:28，墨菲女士寫道：「這樣我能處理了」，最有可能是什麼意思？
(A) 她剛遵循卡特先生的指示。
(B) 她會自己解決這個問題。
(C) 她可以返回購買地點。
(D) 她明白她需要做什麼。　　　　答案 (D)

問題 151-153，請參考以下信件內容。

10 月 14 日

愛麗絲‧瓦茨
(151C) 帕特森地毯
朗文街 557 號
45662 俄亥俄州，樸茨茅斯

親愛的瓦茨女士，

(151) 很高興上週在肯塔基州列星頓舉行的家具博覽會上與您見面。(151B) 您花了不少時間，跟我談論貴公司生產的地毯。我很高興了解您的產品與競爭對手的產品有何不同。(152) 我與這裡的幾位員工分享了您給我的樣品，每個人都對它們的品質印象深刻。我的同事特別喜歡可供選擇的顏色。

(151C) 我們一直在為本室內設計公司尋找新的供應商。我們認為，貴公司絕對能夠滿足我們所有的需求。(153) 我想知道您是否有時間盡快面談，以便討論一筆大訂單。我還想談談可能的批發折扣。您什麼時候有空見面呢？

誠摯感謝

雷金納德‧威爾曼
樸茨茅斯室內設計

151. 關於威爾曼先生，文中沒有提到什麼？
(A) 他是一家公司的擁有者。
(B) 他親自與瓦茨女士交談。
(C) 他在一家賣地毯的地方工作。
(D) 他一週前去了肯塔基州。 答案 (A)

152. 關於樸茨茅斯室內設計公司，威爾曼先生暗指了什麼？
(A) 最近開業。
(B) 它有多名員工。
(C) 提供免費安裝。
(D) 即將展開折扣。 答案 (B)

153. 以下句子最適合放在文中 [1]、[2]、[3] 和 [4] 的哪一個位置？
「我還想談談可能的批發折扣。」
(A) [1]
(B) [2]
(C) [3]
(D) [4] 答案 (D)

問題 154-156，請參考以下資訊。

阿拉莫阿納的顧客看過來

感謝所有顧客光臨阿拉莫阿納。(155) (156A) 我們致力於透過我們的網站，為您提供最好的夏威夷風襯衫、帽子、配件和各種時尚單品。

(154) 今天，我們想宣布關於運輸政策的變化。(156B) 阿拉莫阿納之前為所有訂單提供免費運送服務，但由於燃料成本不斷上漲，我們不再提供這項服務。因此，我們必須對每筆 50 美元以下的訂單收取運費。(156C) 為了維持本地最低的產品價格，這是一項不可避免的決定。

我們請求您的諒解。阿拉莫阿納承諾將繼續成為最具競爭力的夏威夷時裝提供者。

154. 這項資訊的目的是什麼？
(A) 為線上業務打廣告
(B) 發布新產品價格表
(C) 確認最近的訂單
(D) 宣布服務變更 答案 (D)

155. 阿拉莫阿納最有可能是什麼類型的企業？
(A) 度假村
(B) 服裝店
(C) 旅行社
(D) 運輸服務 答案 (B)

156. 關於阿拉莫阿納，文中沒有暗指什麼事？
(A) 商品可以線上購買。
(B) 直到最近，它還提供免費運送服務。
(C) 產品價格低於競爭對手。
(D) 很快將舉行首次拍賣。 答案 (D)

問題 157-158，請參考以下公告內容。

致歐文居民的公告

(157) 由於第 4 屆德州春季遊行將於下午 3 點在弗里茨公園附近舉行，歐文市的一個區域將暫時關閉至 5 月 4 日晚上 8 點。

(158) 封路將影響：
－ 聖路易斯街介於漢普頓大道和凱斯路之間的路段

替代路線有：
－ 馬可尼街
－ 貝爾大道

如須了解更多訊息，請致電 214-885-0830 聯繫歐文市交通諮詢處。

157. 此公告的主要目的是什麼？
(A) 宣布體育比賽開幕
(B) 通知即將發生的交通中斷
(C) 通知預定的道路施工
(D) 提醒居民道路上可能存在的危險 答案 (B)

158. 活動期間，城市的哪些區域將關閉？
(A) 弗里茨公園
(B) 聖路易斯街
(C) 漢普頓大道
(D) 馬可尼街 答案 (B)

問題 159-161，請參考以下文章內容。

賈拉利奧的塔可餐廳在卡尼市中心開業
作者：克里斯提諾·盧森堡

卡尼，8 月 11 日——(159) 卡尼居民即日起將能夠在卡尼市中心享用美味的墨西哥美食。8 月 9 日，賈拉利奧的塔可餐廳盛大開幕，當地居民湧入餐廳。

(160) 店主亞伯拉罕·賈拉利奧和布倫娜·賈拉利奧是持有執照的廚師，他們在家鄉墨西哥城成功經營了三家餐廳。自從去年搬到美國後，他們就一直計劃在卡尼開一家餐廳。5 月 22 日，當一間閒置的鞋店出售時，他們毫不猶豫地買下了它，將其改造成一家餐廳。

賈拉利奧的塔可餐廳以合理的價格，提供帶有賈拉利奧現代創意的自製傳統墨西哥美食。賈拉利奧的塔可餐廳使用最新鮮的食材，提供美味而健康的食物。

賈拉利奧的塔可餐廳位於卡尼商業區最車水馬龍的街道上，即將成為眾多商務人士最喜歡的餐廳。(161)「我一直是墨西哥美食的忠實粉絲。開幕當天，我在前門免費試吃後，就情不自禁進餐廳吃飯。我對他們的餐點品質非常滿意。」顧客胡安·蘇亞雷斯說道。餐廳開幕前一天，我採訪了賈拉利奧先生，了解他的餐廳前景。他指出：「我很高興在卡斯坦丁街開設一家新餐廳。我計劃吸引大學生和商務人士。可能有人從未來過我們的店，但沒有人只來過一次。」

如需詳細資訊、菜色定價和訂位，請致電 201-331-9243。

159. 此文章的目的是什麼？
    (A) 發布閒置房產廣告
    (B) 提供有關傳統食品的資訊
    (C) 介紹該地區的新企業
    (D) 通知居民即將進行的施工   答案 (C)

160. 關於賈拉利奧先生和女士，文中暗指什麼事？
    (A) 他們在卡尼有親戚。
    (B) 他們以前擁有一家鞋店。
    (C) 他們使用從墨西哥進口的原料。
    (D) 他們還經營其他餐廳。   答案 (D)

161. 根據蘇亞雷斯先生所說，以下關於賈拉利奧的塔可餐廳的敘述何者正確？
    (A) 位置便利，靠近一所大學。
    (B) 它為來客提供了一些試吃品。
    (C) 客戶服務品質令人滿意。
    (D) 長期以來，這裡一直是蘇亞雷斯先生最喜歡的地方。   答案 (B)

問題 **162-164**，請參考以下評論內容。

藍色靈魂的神奇秋夜

(162) 昨晚，藍色靈魂為聚集在奧克拉荷馬城廣場的 500 人帶來了一場激動人心的表演。藍色靈魂由四位來自不同國家背景的音樂家組成，是美國最受歡迎的爵士樂團之一，並多次 (163) 獲文章報導。

藍色靈魂由世界著名鋼琴家大衛·雅卡爾於四年前創立。(164) 成立兩年後，雅卡爾先生的一位老朋友加入。曾在倫敦城市交響樂團演奏小號的泰勒·克萊頓作為樂團的新成員，豐富了他們的表演。在他加入後不久，藍色靈魂因其卓越的銅管樂聲和表演品質，而被奧克拉荷馬城授予年度最佳音樂家獎。

昨晚在奧克拉荷馬城廣場戶外舞台的現場表演，向觀眾展示了藍色靈魂演奏音樂的獨特光彩。除了他們最受歡迎的歌曲《形單影隻》外，他們還表演了即將於下個月發行的第三張專輯歌曲。他們的新專輯涵蓋不同風格的音樂，包括搖擺樂、巴薩諾瓦音樂和現代爵士樂。

藍色靈魂的表現一如既往地完美，但還是有一個小小的瑕疵。演奏會場地有點冷，如果主辦方在座位附近配備一些移動式暖器就更好了。

勞倫·塞古拉 發表

162. 正在評論什麼類型的活動？
    (A) 管弦樂音樂會
    (B) 爵士音樂會

    (C) 魔術表演
    (D) 舞蹈表演   答案 (B)

163. 第 1 段第 4 行中的「coverd」，含義最接近
    (A) 接受採訪
    (B) 以……為焦點
    (C) 付費買
    (D) 被封鎖   答案 (B)

164. 關於克萊頓先生，文中有哪些描述？
    (A) 他彈鋼琴。
    (B) 他兩年前加入藍色靈魂。
    (C) 他曾獲得倫敦城市交響樂團頒發的獎項。
    (D) 他最近成為藍色靈魂的隊長。   答案 (B)

問題 **165-167**，請參考以下信件內容。

米基·安德森
山路 31 號
12520 紐約，哈德遜河畔康沃爾郡

4 月 19 日
切爾西美髮沙龍
宇宙大道 98 號
12592 紐約，康沃爾郡

敬啟者，

(165) 我寫這封信，是為了申請新罕布夏州切爾西美髮沙龍分店廣告中的全職髮型師職位。雖然我已在這封信中附上了完整履歷，但我想簡要總結一下我的職業背景。

在獲得克拉克學院的髮型師認證後，我開始在布魯克萊恩的伯克希爾美髮店工作。在那工作的 6 年裡，我獲得專業認可，包括去年的全國最佳燙髮造型獎。(166) 在我的履歷裡，我也附上一些獲獎髮型的照片。

除了專業技能，我還是一個熱情、有藝術感和忠誠的人，(167) 準備為切爾西美髮沙龍的全國聲譽做出貢獻。我相信，我的美髮風格符合切爾西美髮沙龍的潮流品味。

謝謝您。期待有機會進行個人面試。

誠摯感謝

米基·安德森
附件

165. 安德森女士為什麼寫這封信？
    (A) 確認參加面試
    (B) 申請髮型設計比賽
    (C) 向潛在僱主介紹自己
    (D) 在美髮沙龍提供工作機會   答案 (C)

166. 信中包含什麼內容？
(A) 髮型師證照
(B) 獎項
(C) 範本圖像
(D) 來自他人的推薦信　　　　　答案 (C)

167. 關於切爾西美髮沙龍，這封信暗指了什麼？
(A) 全國知名。
(B) 已營業至少 6 年。
(C) 它的員工裡有許多獲獎的髮型設計師。
(D) 它在布魯克萊恩有一家分店。　　答案 (A)

問題 168-171，請參考以下線上討論訊息。

羅素·湯普森　　　　　　　　［上午 9:55］
嗨，史帝夫和馬克。默里住宅的工作進展如何？

史帝夫·吉爾摩　　　　　　　［上午 9:57］
我們快完成了。(168) 這項工作比預期花費的時間要長一些，因為默里先生要求我們在修剪樹籬後砍倒一棵樹。不用擔心。我把這件事記在他的帳單上了。

羅素·湯普森　　　　　　　　［上午 9:58］
聽起來不錯。我們剛剛收到新客戶的線上詢價。安娜·格蘭尼特要求對她的住所進行估價。她住在巴特勒大道 88 號。(169) (171) 你覺得有辦法在去斯坦頓廣場之前，先去那裡嗎？

馬克·斯圖爾特　　　　　　　［上午 10:00］
(171) 那裡只有幾個街區遠。

史帝夫·吉爾摩　　　　　　　［上午 10:01］
(169) 我們的下一場預約要等到下午 1:00，所以這裡結束後就會過去。她需要什麼？

羅素·湯普森　　　　　　　　［上午 10:02］
多謝你們。

羅素·湯普森　　　　　　　　［上午 10:02］
呃，她想要基本服務。但她說她的院子比多數人的院子還大。這就是為什麼我想讓你確認一下。

馬克·斯圖爾特　　　　　　　［上午 10:04］
我知道那個地方。它占地約三英畝。

(170) 羅素·湯普森　　　　　　　［上午 10:05］
我想這將是一項艱鉅的工作。(170) 根據你認為所需要的工作量，估一個價給她。

史帝夫·吉爾摩　　　　　　　［上午 10:06］
(170) 明白了。我們結束後會打電話跟你討論。

168. 傳訊息者最有可能在哪裡工作？
(A) 水池安裝公司
(B) 房地產仲介機構
(C) 建築公司
(D) 園林綠化公司　　　　　　　答案 (D)

169. 吉爾摩先生預計下午做什麼？
(A) 提供估價
(B) 返回辦公室
(C) 拜訪客戶
(D) 參加電話會議　　　　　　　答案 (C)

170. 與格蘭尼特女士會面後，吉爾摩先生會做什麼？
(A) 聯繫湯普森先生
(B) 提交帳單
(C) 採購物資
(D) 發送電子郵件　　　　　　　答案 (A)

171. 上午 10:00，斯圖爾特先生寫道「那裡只有幾個街區遠」，暗指了什麼？
(A) 他可以滿足湯普森先生的要求。
(B) 他沒有時間親自拜訪。
(C) 他不知道確切的位置。
(D) 他以前曾親自參觀過一棟房子。　答案 (A)

問題 172-175，請參考以下電子郵件。

收件人：披薩站全體員工
寄件人：傑森·博南扎
日　期：4 月 5 日
主　旨：新消息

各位，

(174) 感謝你們為了讓我們披薩店成為本市第一所做的一切努力。(172) 不幸的是，我們的成功導致模仿者出現，他們試圖搶走我們的生意。因此，我決定實施一些新策略來吸引更多顧客。讓我向你們詳細介紹一下。

首先，從明天，即 4 月 6 日起，我們將為店內顧客提供免費 Wi-Fi。密碼每天都會更改，因此服務生必須到桌邊通知用餐者。我們也會增加桌子附近的電源插座數量。這將使用餐者能夠為他們的電子裝置充電。(173) 我們將於 4 月 8 日關閉，以便電工在此進行這些變動。

接下來，我們最近進行的調查顯示，用餐者希望有更多披薩配料可供選擇。所以我將在 4 月 9 日變更菜單。我們將提供總共 25 種可能的披薩配料，而這會成為本市最多選擇的。

(175) 最後，我們向顧客推出披薩站會員卡。持有者可以獲得折扣和各種免費品項。請參閱我附在電子郵件中的文檔，以了解更多資訊。

致上問候。

傑森·博南扎
披薩站老闆

172. 披薩站為何要改變策略？
　　(A) 響應顧客要求
　　(B) 減少開支
　　(C) 增強自身競爭力
　　(D) 改進其廣告宣傳　　　　　　　　　　　　答案 (C)

173. 4 月 8 日會發生什麼？
　　(A) 商店不會營業。
　　(B) 菜單將會改變。
　　(C) 將安裝網路。
　　(D) 折扣將開跑。　　　　　　　　　　　　　答案 (A)

174. 關於披薩站，文中暗指了什麼？
　　(A) 目前有會員計劃。
　　(B) 為常客提供折扣。
　　(C) 很快就會添加更多桌子。
　　(D) 它是該市領先的披薩店之一。　　　　　　答案 (D)

175. 以下句子最適合放在文中 [1]、[2]、[3] 和 [4] 的哪一個
　　位置？
　　「持有者可以獲得折扣和各種免費品項。」
　　(A) [1]
　　(B) [2]
　　(C) [3]
　　(D) [4]　　　　　　　　　　　　　　　　　答案 (D)

問題 176-180，請參考以下網頁及電子郵件。

www.hudsoncollege.edu/notice

哈德遜大學

關於我們	公告	學術	社區

哈德遜大學兒童教育系列講座
兒童教育與發展系相當自豪地舉辦一系列關於幼兒教育
的講座。講座將於 6 月 14 日至 7 月 5 日每週五於該系
舉行。(176D) 哈德遜大學知名教授和來自國家組織的
專業人士，將深入介紹兒童發展的新想法和適當的教學
技巧。

研討會日程：

講座主題與講師	日期／時間	費用
幼兒語言發展 講師：米拉‧特朗德，哈德遜大學教授	6 月 14 日 (176A) 下午 2 點 - 4 點	60 美元
兒童課堂中的適當課程 講師：丹尼爾‧奎恩，哈德遜大學教授	(178) 6 月 21 日 (176A) 下午 3 點 - 5 點	70 美元
管理兒童和小學課堂 (179) 講師：大衛‧丹頓，國家早期兒童教育研究所兒童教育專家	(179) 6 月 28 日 (176A) 下午 2 點 - 4 點	90 美元
兒童的社會性發展：從出生到童年 講師：莉莉絲‧米爾斯，康沃爾醫院兒童精神疾患學家	7 月 5 日 (176A) 下午 1 點 - 3 點	80 美元

(176C)* 每場講座最多允許 100 人參加。

(177) 如欲報名參加其中一場講座，請點擊此處。(176B)
請注意，所有課程均遵循先到先得的原則，報名截止
日期為 6 月 1 日。如有任何疑問，請透過 cfelton@
hudsoncollege.edu 聯繫卡洛琳娜‧費爾頓。

(178) (180) 從事兒童教育和發展領域工作的參與者，將
獲得講座報名費 10 美元折扣。報名過程必須出示證明
文件。

收件人：卡洛琳娜‧費爾頓
　　　　 <cfelton@hudsoncollege.edu>
寄件人：(180) 奧莉維亞‧康
　　　　 <okang@hudsonelementary.com>
日　期：6 月 3 日
主　旨：詢問

(178) 我經常聽說哈德遜大學提供的主題講座非常有幫
助，所以我報名參加了 6 月 21 日舉行的講座。不過，
這封電子郵件其實是想詢問我是否可以更改課程預約。

(178) (180) 我是當地一所小學的老師。不幸的是，我的
同事由於一些家庭因素，突然請假三週。我不得不在 6
月 21 日星期五下午幫他代課。我仍然有興趣參加你們
的系列講座，(179) 想知道能否改成參加由大衛‧丹頓
主講的講座。我還想知道，如果可以更改，何時需要匯
出額外費用，(178) 以及我是否仍有資格享有折扣。

謝謝。希望能早日收到你的回覆。

奧莉維亞‧康

176. 網站上沒有提及以下哪項關於講座的內容？
　　(A) 它們被安排在下午。
　　(B) 報名截止日期為 6 月 1 日。
　　(C) 每次講座只有有限名額的參與者可以參加。
　　(D) 所有講師均為大學教授。　　　　　　　答案 (D)

177. 參加者如何報名參加系列講座？
　　(A) 發送電子郵件
　　(B) 進入網站
　　(C) 致電學校職員
　　(D) 前往活動場地　　　　　　　　　　　　答案 (B)

178. 康女士最初支付了多少錢？
　　(A) 60 美元
　　(B) 70 美元
　　(C) 80 美元
　　(D) 90 美元　　　　　　　　　　　　　　　答案 (A)

179. 康女士希望在哪一天參加講座？
(A) 6 月 14 日
(B) 6 月 21 日
(C) 6 月 28 日
(D) 7 月 5 日　　　　　　　　　答案 (C)

180. 關於康女士，文中暗指了什麼？
(A) 她將休三週病假。
(B) 她已經支付了額外費用。
(C) 她可能向哈德遜大學提交了所需文件。
(D) 她上一季參加了類似的系列講座。　　答案 (C)

問題 181-185，請參考以下廣告及信件。

第 7 屆年度 ISEE 全球心理學論壇
招募學生志工！

(181) ISEE 全球心理學論壇，是世界各地心理學家交流新想法的知名研討會。第 7 屆 ISEE 全球心理學論壇組委會目前正在招募學生志工，為即將於 7 月 5 日至 10 日在伊利諾州芝加哥米蘭飯店舉行的研討會提供各種支援服務。

志工的職責
• 活動助理 – 主要職責是 (182D) 在研討會期間和結束後布置和清潔場地。此外，活動助理還須協助影印、(182A) 向與會者分發講義或 (182C) 為講者準備飲水。這個角色可能涉及輕型家具的搬移。
• 視聽操作員助理 – 這項工作是檢查會議廳的視聽設備。如有必要，設置投影機和麥克風也將是視聽操作員助理的職責之一。

(184) 申請者條件
– 所在學校的正式信函，以表明你當前的學生身分
– (184) 下列語言中至少一種官方熟練程度證明：西班牙語、中文或德語
– 在會議中擔任志工的經驗
– 熟悉演講設備者優先

提交申請
(183) 請在 6 月 1 日前，將履歷影本、求職信和正式文件發送至 ISEE 全球心理學論壇組委會辦公室，如下所示：

克萊兒‧史丹利，人事經理
ISEE 全球心理學論壇組委會，60007 伊利諾州，
芝加哥，富蘭克林大道 30 號

---

5 月 10 日
克萊兒‧史丹利
ISEE 全球心理學論壇組委會
富蘭克林大道 30 號
60007 伊利諾州，芝加哥

伊凡‧哈菲爾德
羅斯貝爾特街 22 號
60608 伊利諾州，布里奇波特

親愛的史丹利女士，

我想申請 ISEE 全球心理學論壇的學生志工計劃。我是伊利諾大學的大三學生，對心理學領域非常感興趣。(185) 我過去參加過許多心理學研討會，包括 IWO 心理學和伊利諾大學研討會。

此外，我還參與許多不同的活動，包括在美國學生行銷協會工作。我在那裡與許多來自不同背景的人互動，非常努力完成所有交辦給我的任務。(184) 雖然除了英語之外，我不會說任何其他語言，但我相信，我可以為 ISEE 全球心理學論壇做出很多貢獻。

請參閱附檔所需文件。我希望能收到面試通知。提前感謝您撥冗考慮。

誠摯感謝

伊凡‧哈菲爾德
附件

181. 關於 ISEE 全球心理學論壇，文中暗指什麼？
(A) 已成功舉辦七屆。
(B) 由米蘭飯店贊助。
(C) 會有來自不同國家的與會者。
(D) 向志工提供證書。　　　　　　　答案 (C)

182. 何者不是活動助理的職責之一？
(A) 向與會者發放文件
(B) 會場照明
(C) 為講者做一些差事
(D) 會議結束後的清理工作　　　　　答案 (B)

183. 組委會什麼時候停止接受申請？
(A) 5 月 10 日
(B) 6 月 1 日
(C) 7 月 5 日
(D) 7 月 10 日　　　　　　　　　答案 (B)

184. 為什麼哈菲爾德先生可能無法成功擔任志工職位？
(A) 他不會說任何所需的語言。
(B) 他沒有提交大學文件。
(C) 他缺乏心理學領域的經驗。
(D) 他沒有心理學學位。　　　　　　答案 (A)

185. 關於哈菲爾德先生，文中暗指什麼？
(A) 他可能在會議期間的某一天缺席。
(B) 他畢業於伊利諾大學。
(C) 他擅長處理演講設備。
(D) 他以前參加過心理學研討會。　　答案 (D)

問題 **186-190**，請參考以下網頁、收據及電子郵件。

辦公棚竭誠為您服務！

| 關於我們 | 商品列表 | 政策 | 客戶回饋 |

運送方式

(186) 辦公棚對國內標準運輸（5-7 個工作日）收取 4.50 美元的固定費率，對國內快捷運輸（2-3 個工作日）則收取 6.50 美元的固定費率。我們目前的運送範圍涵蓋美國、英國和紐西蘭。詳細費率請參考以下：

地點	標準運輸	快捷運輸
美國	$11.00	$15.00
英國	$13.00	$17.00
紐西蘭	$6.00	$8.00

* 除非另有說明，所有價格均以澳幣為單位。

(187) 對於辦公棚的註冊會員，我們目前提供限時免費運送。此優惠僅適用於國內訂單。

訂單出貨後，您將收到一封電子郵件通知。之後，您可以使用我們的程式（www.officeshed.com/ordertracker）免費確認包裹遞送狀態。請注意，您可能無法追蹤某些訂單，例如國際運輸。

欲查看我們的退款和退貨政策，請點擊此處；要查看我們的會員政策，請點擊此處。

辦公棚
訂單確認和收據

訂單參考號：#4865436
下單日期：12 月 12 日

收件地址：
布魯克·賓德，4157 (187) 澳洲，維多利亞州格倫黑文謝爾頓路 43 號

產品資訊	數量	價格
4 層金屬桌面托盤（顏色：黑色）	1	$10.99
28 毫米迴紋針（100 個／包）	3	$6.75
(190) 優質白色信封（**25 個／包**）	1	$8.81
	小計：	$26.55
	稅額：	$2.65
	(187) 運費：	**$0.00**
	總計：	$29.20

付款方式：信用卡 (xxxx-xxxx-xxxx-0555) 付款金額：$29.20

(188) 若您需要有關訂購流程的協助，請在週一至週五上午 9:00 至下午 5:00 我們的工作時間內，致電 130-111 客戶服務中心。

收件人：<cs@officeshed.com>
寄件人：<brookebinder@goldcoastmail.com>
日　　期：12 月 17 日
主　　旨：請求

敬啟者，

(189) 我一直對辦公棚提供的服務非常滿意。然而，想像一下當我打開盒子卻 (190) 找不到訂購的信封時，我有多驚訝。我想有人在打包我的物品時，忘記把它們放進來。

(190) 我希望將缺漏商品的金額加到我的帳戶中，(189) 因為我會在不久的將來再次訂購。希望你們能盡快更正這個情況。

致上問候。

布魯克·賓德

---

186. 網頁中，第 1 段第 1 行中的「flat」，含義最接近
    (A) 不足
    (B) 固定
    (C) 減少
    (D) 垂直　　　　　　　　　　　　答案 (B)

187. 辦公棚可能位於哪裡？
    (A) 美國
    (B) 紐西蘭
    (C) 澳洲
    (D) 英國　　　　　　　　　　　　答案 (C)

188. 收據中提及哪些關於辦公棚的內容？
    (A) 賓德女士的訂單於 12 月 12 日出貨。
    (B) 銷售當地製造商生產的產品。
    (C) 分銷辦公家具。
    (D) 其客戶服務中心僅在工作日營業。　答案 (D)

189. 關於賓德女士，文中暗指什麼？
    (A) 她經常從辦公棚購買東西。
    (B) 她用現金支付訂單。
    (C) 她將收到一封來自辦公棚的電子郵件。
    (D) 她是一家小公司的老闆。　　　　答案 (A)

190. 賓德女士要求退還多少錢？
    (A) 2.65 澳幣
    (B) 6.75 澳幣
    (C) 8.81 澳幣
    (D) 10.99 澳幣　　　　　　　　　答案 (C)

問題 191-195，請參考以下公告、簡訊及電子郵件。

鴿子小窩檢查通知

所有房客請注意。(192) 大樓暖氣系統的年度檢查將於下週進行。(191) 這是為冬季做準備的過程，將有助於維持暖氣系統正常運作。和往常一樣，當地的四季維護公司將到訪並進行檢查。每戶檢查大約需要 20 分鐘。如果發現任何問題，我們將安排進一步檢查和維修。

詳細檢查時間安排如下：
－A 棟住戶：11 月 3 日中午 12:00 － 下午 6:00
－B 棟住戶：11 月 4 日中午 12:00 － 下午 6:00
－(193) **C 棟住戶：11 月 5 日上午 10:00 － 下午 4:00**

如果您因任何原因，無法在預定日期配合檢查，請立即透過 rvelasquez@dovecottage.com 聯繫物業經理羅莎・維拉斯奎茲，以利重新安排您的檢查時間。

請至四季維護網站，了解有關檢查的更多資訊。預先感謝您的合作。

致：安德魯・魯道夫
電話號碼：594-9584-1128

安德魯，我是大衛。(193) 我的公寓今天早上要進行檢查，所以想知道我們是否可以將會議重新安排到下午。檢查員到達之後，過程不會花太長的時間。我們下午 3:00 左右，在你的辦公室見面怎麼樣？讓我知道你是否方便。大衛。

收件人：羅莎・維拉斯奎茲
　　　　＜rvelasquez@dovecottage.com＞
寄件人：大衛・亞卡爾 ＜dyakal@smail.com＞
日　期：11 月 6 日
主　旨：詢問

我的公寓最近進行檢查，很高興得知我的暖氣系統沒有任何問題。然而，(194) 今天稍早，我注意到檢查人員打破了我陽臺上的窗戶。去年檢查人員來我家的時候也有同樣的問題。我認為他們使用的大型設備造成了損害。

(194) 我希望獲得更換窗戶的補償費用。(195) 我將購買一個新窗戶並自行安裝。我會將收據寄給你，以便順利得到賠償。請留意我這個週末要出差，兩週內不會回來，所以希望在出發前收到款項。

希望早日收到你的回覆。
謝謝。

大衛・亞卡爾

---

191. 鴿子小窩為何接受檢查？
　　(A) 讓大樓做好因應寒冷季節的準備
　　(B) 解決中央暖氣系統問題
　　(C) 遵守當地住宅建築法規
　　(D) 減少能源過度使用　　　　　　　　答案 (A)

192. 公告中對本次檢查的情況有什麼說明？
　　(A) 需要註冊。
　　(B) 定期進行。
　　(C) 由物業經理完成。
　　(D) 大約需要一天的時間。　　　　　　答案 (B)

193. 亞卡爾先生的檢查，最有可能發生在什麼時候？
　　(A) 11 月 3 日
　　(B) 11 月 4 日
　　(C) 11 月 5 日
　　(D) 11 月 6 日　　　　　　　　　　　答案 (C)

194. 亞卡爾先生為什麼寄送電子郵件？
　　(A) 重新安排檢查
　　(B) 要求解決問題
　　(C) 記下他要去哪裡旅行
　　(D) 查詢檢查費用　　　　　　　　　　答案 (B)

195. 關於亞卡爾先生，文中暗指什麼？
　　(A) 11 月 3 日他去出差。
　　(B) 他向鄰居推薦一家檢查公司。
　　(C) 他打算自行完成一些維修工作。
　　(D) 他之前曾聯繫過維拉斯奎茲女士。　答案 (C)

問題 196-200，請參考以下電子郵件、公告及評論。

收件人：(196A) 大衛・林德曼
　　　　＜dlinderman@kitavipi.com＞
寄件人：(196A) 山姆・班克爾
　　　　＜sbankole@kitavipi.com＞
日　期：7 月 9 日
主　旨：工作坊課程

親愛的林德曼先生，

本次來信是關於下個月在伊斯坦堡舉行的工作坊時程安排。我看了你今早上寄給我的時程表草稿，我認為必須提出修改。(196) (197) 在工作坊舉行的當天早上，我必須去安卡拉參加一位重要客戶的會議。客戶從布魯塞爾過來，只停留兩天，因此會議無法重新安排。(197) 我返回伊斯坦堡的航班將於上午 11:30 起飛。

(198) 我已經請求同部門的藤田小百合交換工作坊時間，她同意了。請在時程表印出並公布於全公司前做出調整，以免造成混亂。

謝謝你。

山姆・班克爾
編輯部助理編輯

基塔維出版公司

伊斯坦堡 · 安卡拉 · 伊茲密爾 · 布爾薩

第 15 屆年度員工培訓工作坊

(197) **8 月 14 日**，伊斯坦堡總部大樓

時間	工作坊名稱	主持人
上午 8:30 - 10:00	與客戶和同事交流	藤田小百合
上午 10:20 - 11:30	(200) 將想法發展成 偉大的故事	(200) 羅倫佐 · 蒙迪
上午 11:30 - 下午 1:00	午餐	
下午 1:00 - 2:30	設計吸引人的 書籍封面	凱瑟琳 · 孔法洛涅里
下午 2:50 - 4:00	自己的專欄自己編	泰勒 · 布徹
(198) 下午 **4:20 - 6:00**	時間管理 —— 讓它變得有意義	(196D)(198) **山姆 · 班克爾**

(199)* **每位參加者將受邀於午休期間參加午餐會。**

所有員工都必須完成本次工作坊的簡短評價。您可依個人意願決定是否匿名。您的回饋將幫助我們改進未來的課程。

整體品質如何⋯⋯

	極優	很棒	普通	不佳
講師	X			
簡報		X		
資料	X			

評論：(200) 我真的很喜歡蒙迪先生的發表。我從他身上學到很多。其他指導老師也都很好。布徹先生講話時，麥克風總是壞掉，所以很難聽清楚他講的話。

姓名：艾蜜莉 · 哈珀

196. 關於班克爾先生，文中沒有暗指什麼？
(A) 他最近聯繫了林德曼先生。
(B) 他要參加一個商務會議。
(C) 他下個月將造訪布魯塞爾。
(D) 他計劃主持一次工作坊。　　　　答案 (C)

197. 8 月 14 日上午 11:30，班克爾先生最有可能在哪裡？
(A) 布魯塞爾
(B) 伊斯坦堡
(C) 布爾薩
(D) 安卡拉　　　　答案 (D)

198. 藤田女士原定什麼時間主持工作坊？
(A) 上午 8:30
(B) 上午 10:20
(C) 下午 1:00
(D) 下午 4:20　　　　答案 (D)

199. 時程表中暗指什麼？
(A) 基塔維出版公司已營業 15 年。
(B) 蒙迪先生將主持一場關於文章編輯的工作坊。
(C) 班克爾先生將出席藤田女士的工作坊。
(D) 將為工作坊的參加者提供伙食。　　　　答案 (D)

200. 哈珀女士最喜歡哪一場工作坊？
(A) 與客戶和同事交流
(B) 將想法發展成偉大的故事
(C) 設計吸引人的書籍封面
(D) 自己的專欄自己編　　　　答案 (B)

Actual Test 03

Part 1

1. 美國 M
   (A) He is moving a rocking chair.
   (B) He's sweeping the yard.
   (C) He is reading a newspaper.
   (D) He is watering the garden.

   (A) 他正在移動一把搖椅。
   (B) 他正在掃院子。
   (C) 他正在看報紙。
   (D) 他正在為花園澆水。　　　　　答案 (C)

2. 美國 W
   (A) The woman is standing in the middle of an aisle.
   (B) The woman is trying on a blouse in the fitting room.
   (C) The woman is hanging up a blouse.
   (D) The woman is carrying a clothing rack.

   (A) 女子站在走道中間。
   (B) 女子正在試衣間試穿一件襯衫。
   (C) 女子正在掛一件襯衫。
   (D) 女子正拿著一個衣架。　　　　答案 (C)

3. 英國 M
   (A) A man is exiting a vehicle.
   (B) A woman is packing her backpack.
   (C) Some people are waiting to board a bus.
   (D) A man is rolling his suitcase down the aisle.

   (A) 一名男子正在下車。
   (B) 一名女子正在收拾背包。
   (C) 有些人正在等待上公車。
   (D) 一名男子正推著他的行李箱走下走道。　答案 (A)

4. 美國 M
   (A) One person is distributing some printouts.
   (B) One person is entering some data into a laptop.
   (C) Some people are listening to a presentation.
   (D) Some people are seated out on the patio.

   (A) 一個人正在分發一些列印文件。
   (B) 一個人正將數據輸入筆記型電腦。
   (C) 有些人正在聽報告。
   (D) 有些人坐在外面的露臺上。　　　答案 (C)

5. 澳洲 W
   (A) They are emptying their basket.
   (B) Shopping baskets are piled in rows.
   (C) Items are displayed on shelves.
   (D) Some shelves are being measured.

   (A) 他們正在清空籃子。
   (B) 購物籃成排堆放。
   (C) 物品陳列在貨架上。
   (D) 一些貨架正被測量。　　　　　答案 (C)

6. 英國 M
   (A) Pots are placed on the stove.
   (B) Some chairs are stacked near the entrance.
   (C) The refrigerator doors are closed.
   (D) Some tables have been pushed against a wall.

   (A) 鍋子被放在爐子上。
   (B) 一些椅子被堆放在入口附近。
   (C) 冰箱門關著。
   (D) 一些桌子被推到牆邊。　　　　答案 (C)

Part 2

7. 美國 M 美國 W
   How long will the bike race last?
   (A) It's a mountain bike.
   (B) It's a 200-meter race track.
   (C) It ends at around 5.

   那場自行車賽會持續多長時間？
   (A) 這是一輛登山自行車。
   (B) 這是一條 200 公尺的賽道。
   (C) 5 點左右結束。　　　　　　　答案 (C)

8. 英國 M 澳洲 W
   Where are you going for your vacation?
   (A) To a resort in Hawaii.
   (B) An informative presentation.
   (C) I'll reserve a ticket.

   你要去哪裡度假？
   (A) 去夏威夷的度假勝地。
   (B) 內容豐富的報告。
   (C) 我要訂票。　　　　　　　　　答案 (A)

9. 美國 M 英國 M
   Which manager is on duty after hours?
   (A) Yes, I have been.
   (B) It's an hourly rate.
   (C) I think Paul is.

   下班後是哪位經理值班？
   (A) 是的，我值班過了。
   (B) 這是每小時的費率。
   (C) 我認為是保羅。　　　　　　　答案 (C)

10. 美國 W 美國 M

Who do you think I should give this sales report to?
(A) To Ms. Kwon, please.
(B) The sales figures are up.
(C) What time do you report to work?

你認為我應該把這份銷售報告交給誰？
(A) 請給權女士。
(B) 銷售數字上升。
(C) 你幾點上班？　　　　　　　　　答案 (A)

11. 英國 M 美國 W

You should buy the sunglasses with the white frames.
(A) I bought a pair like that last year.
(B) Check the filing cabinet.
(C) A regular eye exam.

你應該買白色鏡框的太陽眼鏡。
(A) 我去年買了一副那樣的。
(B) 檢查文件櫃。
(C) 例行眼科檢查。　　　　　　　　答案 (A)

12. 美國 M 澳洲 W

Where should we place the new copier?
(A) You'd better ask Jeff.
(B) More than 10 copies might be needed.
(C) It is beyond our budget.

我們應該把新的影印機放在哪裡？
(A) 你最好問一下傑夫。
(B) 可能需要 10 份以上。
(C) 那超出我們的預算。　　　　　　答案 (A)

13. 英國 M 美國 W

Are you going to participate in the bike race for charity next week?
(A) More than 50 people.
(B) She has a yearly gym membership.
(C) My bike needs to be repaired.

你會參加下週的慈善自行車比賽嗎？
(A) 50 人以上。
(B) 她是健身房的年度會員。
(C) 我的自行車需要修理。　　　　　答案 (C)

14. 澳洲 W 英國 M

Which team had the best performance results last month?
(A) My train was delayed only 10 minutes.
(B) Some big yellow envelopes.
(C) The director is still reviewing the data.

哪支球隊上個月的表現最好？
(A) 我的火車只誤點 10 分鐘。
(B) 一些黃色的大信封。
(C) 領隊還在檢視數據。　　　　　　答案 (C)

15. 美國 M 澳洲 W

Why is it so cold in the conference room?
(A) Because the heater is not working.
(B) Can I have a room with a kitchenette?
(C) Just a brief weather update.

會議室怎麼這麼冷？
(A) 因為暖氣無法運作。
(B) 我可以要一間有小廚房的房間嗎？
(C) 只是簡短的天氣更新。　　　　　答案 (A)

16. 美國 W 美國 M

Have you seen the agenda for the board meeting?
(A) I haven't checked my e-mail.
(B) At a reduced rate.
(C) I saw that movie last week.

你看過董事會會議的議程嗎？
(A) 我還沒有確認我的電子郵件。
(B) 採折價後的費率。
(C) 我上週看了那部電影。　　　　　答案 (A)

17. 美國 W 英國 M

When is the new airport location opening?
(A) No, I didn't open it.
(B) In a week or so, I think.
(C) It is a full flight.

新機場何時開放？
(A) 不，我沒有打開它。
(B) 我想大約一週後吧。
(C) 飛機座無虛席。　　　　　　　　答案 (B)

18. 美國 W 英國 M

Do you like driving your car or the motorcycle to work?
(A) I thought he had left work early.
(B) I prefer my car.
(C) A car rental agency.

你喜歡開車還是騎摩托車上班？
(A) 我以為他提前下班了。
(B) 我更喜歡我的車。
(C) 汽車租賃機構。　　　　　　　　答案 (B)

19. 美國 M 澳洲 W

What's the monthly maintenance fee for my savings account?
(A) On a weekly basis.
(B) It's 4 dollars a month.
(C) At the accounting firm.

我的儲蓄帳戶每月管理費是多少？
(A) 每週一次。
(B) 每月 4 美元。
(C) 在會計師事務所。　　　　　　　答案 (B)

20. 英國 M 美國 W

None of the clients asked for me this morning, right?
(A) I was out of the office.
(B) It didn't last long.
(C) Sure, you can go ahead and use it.

今天早上沒有任何客戶找我，對嗎？
(A) 我不在辦公室。
(B) 它並沒有持續多久。
(C) 當然，你可以去使用它。　　　　　答案 (A)

21. 澳洲 W 美國 M

I just mailed out the survey to our regular customers.
(A) Refunds are possible at the customer service desk.
(B) Check with the director.
(C) I hope all of them complete it.

我剛剛將問卷寄給我們的常客。
(A) 可以在顧客服務臺辦理退款。
(B) 跟主任確認。
(C) 我希望他們都會完成它。　　　　　答案 (C)

22. 美國 W 美國 M

Jasmine hasn't submitted the reimbursement form yet.
(A) I don't agree with them.
(B) The manager is happy with our budget.
(C) She should do it today.

茉莉還沒有提交報銷單。
(A) 我不同意他們的觀點。
(B) 經理對我們的預算很滿意。
(C) 她今天應該交。　　　　　答案 (C)

23. 美國 W 英國 M

Why are you late for the morning staff meeting today?
(A) Did you see the traffic?
(B) No. He arrived last night.
(C) Neither am I.

今天早上的員工會議，你為什麼遲到了？
(A) 你有看到交通狀況嗎？
(B) 不，他昨晚到的。
(C) 我也不是。　　　　　答案 (A)

24. 美國 M 澳洲 W

How do you like your new job as a salesperson?
(A) Yes, I'd like to.
(B) My first day isn't until next Monday.
(C) Sure, I'll review the sales numbers.

你對銷售員的新工作感覺如何？
(A) 是的，我願意。
(B) 我第一天上班要到下週一。
(C) 當然，我會查看銷售數字。　　　　　答案 (B)

25. 澳洲 W 英國 M

Isn't this back door supposed to stay locked?
(A) I used to live in this neighborhood.
(B) Yes, but it broke this morning.
(C) Put it up on the door.

這個後門不是應該鎖著嗎？
(A) 我以前住在這附近。
(B) 是的，但是今天早上它壞了。
(C) 把它掛在門上。　　　　　答案 (B)

26. 澳洲 W 美國 M

Where did you purchase this smartphone?
(A) OK. That day works for me.
(B) Well, I got a great deal.
(C) Actually, it was a present.

你在哪裡購買這款智慧型手機？
(A) 沒問題，我那天可以。
(B) 嗯，我完成一筆好買賣。
(C) 其實，這是一份禮物。　　　　　答案 (C)

27. 英國 M 美國 W

You're not sold out of this smartphone model, are you?
(A) At an electronic store nearby.
(B) Call me on my cellphone.
(C) Yes, but can I order one for you?

你們還沒賣光這款智慧型手機，對吧？
(A) 在附近一家電子商場。
(B) 打電話到我的手機。
(C) 賣完了，但要我為你訂一支嗎？　　　　　答案 (C)

28. 美國 M 澳洲 W

Would you like any dessert this evening?
(A) A plastic tablecloth will do.
(B) Do you only serve vanilla ice cream?
(C) It was sold out yesterday afternoon.

今晚你想吃點甜點嗎？
(A) 一張塑膠桌布就可以了。
(B) 你們只提供香草冰淇淋嗎？
(C) 昨天下午就賣完了。　　　　　答案 (B)

29. 美國 W 英國 M

Are you comfortable leading the focus group by yourself or do you need some help?
(A) It's offered at a group rate.
(B) I've done it before.
(C) I came up with those ideas.

你比較想要自己主持焦點團體，還是需要協助？
(A) 以團體價格提供。
(B) 我以前這麼做過了。
(C) 我想出這些點子。 答案 (B)

30. 美國 M 美國 W

We should offer employees discounts to the local
fitness center.
(A) He is unemployed at the moment.
(B) I think that sounds great.
(C) Two hours every day.

我們應該為員工提供當地健身中心折扣。
(A) 他目前失業。
(B) 我覺得這聽起來很棒。
(C) 每天兩小時。 答案 (B)

31. 英國 M 美國 W

Who do I give my reimbursement form for travel
expenses to?
(A) It's an online process now.
(B) The job requires a lot of traveling.
(C) A two-hour flight to Michigan.

我應該將差旅費報銷表交給誰？
(A) 那現在是線上作業了。
(B) 這項工作需要頻繁出差。
(C) 飛往密西根州的兩小時航程。 答案 (A)

Part 3

問題 **32-34**，請參考以下對話內容。 英國 M 美國 W

M: Lisa, (32)**don't forget to take your carry-on
luggage from under the seat in front of you.**
W: Thanks for the reminder. (32)**This flight has been
pretty long.**
M: Well, at least we have landed five minutes ahead of
schedule. Once we get to the hotel, we can practice
the presentation we're giving at the expo tomorrow.
W: (33)**Did you remember to bring the pamphlets
we're going to hand out there?**
M: (33)**Yes, I did.** I've got them in my checked luggage.
I have a total of 500, which should be plenty.
W: Now that I think of it, (34)**I'm going to contact the
conference center** after we arrive. (34)**I want to
ask if we can check out the conference room**
that we'll be speaking in to see if it's good enough.

- -

男：麗莎，別忘了從前面的座位下方取出你的隨身行
李。
女：謝謝提醒。這次飛行時間真長。
男：嗯，至少我們比預定時間提早了五分鐘降落。到達
飯店後，我們就可以練習明天在博覽會上的報告。

女：你記得帶我們要在那裡發放的小冊子嗎？
男：是的，我記得。我把它們放在托運行李裡了。我總
共帶 500 本，應該綽綽有餘。
女：我想到，抵達之後我就去聯繫會議中心。我想問能
否參觀我們即將發表報告的會議室，看看那裡夠不
夠好。

32. 這場對話最有可能在哪裡進行？
(A) 飯店
(B) 辦公室
(C) 飛機上
(D) 會議中心 答案 (C)

33. 男子帶了什麼？
(A) 一些圖片
(B) 一些資料
(C) 飯店確認函
(D) 飯店路線指南 答案 (B)

34. 女子為什麼要打電話給會議中心？
(A) 預訂會議室
(B) 更改到達時間
(C) 請求看看會議室
(D) 獲取活動時間表 答案 (C)

問題 **35-37**，請參考以下對話內容。 美國 W 澳洲 W 美國 M

W1: (35)**Thank you for listening to Motor Chat on
Radio 99.8 FM.** I'm Tina.
W2: And I'm Diane, the cohost of the show.
W1: This evening, (36)**we're going to be talking with
a man who just launched a new car dealership.**
Hello, Tim.
M: Hello. It's a pleasure to be here.
W2: What made you decide to start your own car
dealership in the downtown area?
M: To be honest, my family has had a car business for
more than 30 years. After working there for quite a
long time, I realized I have personality traits suitable for
a car salesman and wanted to start my own business.
W2: That is so interesting. (37)**Do you think you could
give our listeners some advice on top things to
consider when buying a car?**
M: (37)**No problem.**

- -

女1：感謝收聽 99.8 FM 電臺的車市聊聊。我是蒂娜。
女2：我是黛安，節目的共同主持人。
女1：今晚，我們要採訪一位剛剛創設汽車經銷商的人。
哈囉，提姆。
男：大家好。很高興來到這裡。
女2：是什麼讓你決定在市中心開設自己的汽車經銷
商？

男：說實話，我家做汽車生意已經有 30 多年了。在那裡工作了很長一段時間後，我意識到自己有適合汽車銷售員的性格，也想自己創業。

女2：這太有趣了。你覺得你可以針對買車要考慮的優先事項，給我們的聽眾一些建議嗎？

男：沒問題。

35. 女子們最有可能在哪裡工作？
   (A) 廣播電臺
   (B) 電子商場
   (C) 汽車修理廠
   (D) 汽車經銷商　　　　　　　　　　　答案 (A)

36. 男子最近做了什麼？
   (A) 他讀了一本汽車雜誌。
   (B) 他找到一份新工作。
   (C) 他開了一家公司。
   (D) 他完成汽車維修課程。　　　　　　答案 (C)

37. 男子接下來會做什麼？
   (A) 出版一本書
   (B) 打進廣播電臺
   (C) 購買汽車
   (D) 提供一些建議　　　　　　　　　　答案 (D)

問題 38-40，請參考以下對話內容。 英國 M 美國 W

M: Have you heard that Jason's last day here is Friday?

W: Yes, I have. (38)**I can't believe he's taking a job at our main rival** after working here for 15 years.

M: It's hard to believe. (39)**By the way, have you made the arrangements for his going-away party yet?**

W: Yes, I have. The caterer will arrive with the food at 3:00. What are you buying for him?

M: (40)**I'm going to get together with a couple of other people in the office to buy him a set of golf clubs.** He'll love them.

W: That sounds good. Maybe I can contribute as well.

- -

男：你有聽說星期五是傑森在這裡的最後一天嗎？

女：是的，我有。不敢相信他在這裡工作 15 年之後，竟然接受了我們主要競爭對手的職位。

男：真難以置信。順便問一下，他的告別派對，你安排好了嗎？

女：是的，我安排好了。外燴商將於 3:00 把食物送達。你要買什麼給他？

男：我要和辦公室裡的其他幾個人一起，買給他一套高爾夫球桿。他會很喜歡的。

女：聽起來不錯。也許我也可以貢獻一點。

38. 談話者說了什麼關於傑森的事？
   (A) 他即將退休。
   (B) 他要調往國外。

(C) 他正接受升遷。
(D) 他要跳槽到另一家公司。　　　　　答案 (D)

39. 男子問了什麼事？
   (A) 派對的準備工作
   (B) 即將召開的會議
   (C) 出差
   (D) 客戶的緊急電話　　　　　　　　　答案 (A)

40. 根據男子所說，他打算做什麼？
   (A) 去高爾夫球場
   (B) 購買禮物
   (C) 尋找另一家外燴商
   (D) 捐一些錢　　　　　　　　　　　　答案 (B)

問題 41-43，請參考以下對話內容。 澳洲 W 英國 M

W: David, I spoke with the manager of the caterer who is going to provide food for our annual end-of-the-year party we are having this weekend. (41)**He told me the food we're planning to order for everyone will cost much less than we budgeted for.**

M: (41)**That's very surprising.** Fredo's is an expensive place.

W: That's the truth. (42)**So I was thinking that we could use the leftover money to buy some presents for our employees.** Would it be okay? I think that would impress a lot of people here.

M: I agree. Just be sure not to go over the budget. (43)**Oh, would you be sure to check the names on the invitation list?** I want to confirm that we haven't omitted any of the board members.

- -

女：大衛，我和外燴商經理談過了，他將為我們本週末舉行的年度年終聚會提供餐點。他告訴我，我們計劃為每個人訂購的餐點價格，將比我們的預算低得多。

男：非常令人驚訝。弗雷多可是一個很貴的地方。

女：真的。所以我就想，可以用剩下的錢買點禮物給員工。這樣行得通嗎？我想這會讓這裡的人留下深刻的印象。

男：我同意。請確保不要超出預算。哦，你可以檢查一下邀請名單上的人嗎？我想確認我們沒有漏掉任何董事會成員。

41. 男子對什麼感到驚訝？
   (A) 延長營業時間
   (B) 活動地點
   (C) 出席人數
   (D) 外燴服務價格　　　　　　　　　　答案 (D)

42. 女子想要得到做什麼的許可？
(A) 聘請外燴商
(B) 購買一些禮物
(C) 更換場地
(D) 邀請更多人 答案 (B)

43. 女子被要求接下來要做什麼？
(A) 取得價格估算
(B) 瀏覽賓客名單
(C) 發送邀請
(D) 與董事會成員交談 答案 (B)

問題 44-46，請參考以下對話內容。 美國M 美國W

M: (44)**Eastside Electronics. This is David speaking. What can I do for you?**
W: Hello. (44)**I am calling regarding the web cam I bought at your store on Sunset Street.** I do lots of videoconferencing with executives at my company's headquarters, (45)**but the audio keeps cutting in and out. To be honest, I'm pretty disappointed as I only purchased it two weeks ago.**
M: I'm terribly sorry, ma'am. How about if we walk you through a bit of troubleshooting now? First, have you tried unplugging the device and then plugging it back in?
W: Yes, but that didn't change anything.
M: Okay. How about the software? (46)**Did you get the most recent update?**
W: Hmm… Maybe not. (46)**Okay, let me take care of that, and then I'll call you back if there's still a problem.** Thanks.

男：東區電子您好，我是大衛。請問需要什麼協助？
女：你好。我打電話是想詢問我在你們日落街的商店購買的視訊鏡頭。我跟公司總部的高層進行大量視訊會議，但音訊一直斷斷續續。說實話，我很失望，因為我兩週前才買的。
男：非常抱歉，女士。我們來引導您排除一些故障如何？首先，您是否嘗試過拔下設備的插頭，再重新插入？
女：是的，但這並沒有改變任何事情。
男：好的。那軟體呢？您有進行最新更新了嗎？
女：嗯……好像沒有。好吧，我來處理，如果還有問題，我會再打電話給你。謝謝。

44. 男子最有可能是誰？
(A) 銷售員
(B) 人力資源員工
(C) 客戶服務專員
(D) 產品設計師 答案 (C)

45. 女子說「我兩週前才買的」，是在暗示什麼？
(A) 物品應該能發揮作用。
(B) 物品在運送過程中損壞。
(C) 訂單尚未交付。
(D) 她想購買另一個音訊設備。 答案 (A)

46. 女子接下來最有可能做什麼？
(A) 更新軟體
(B) 獲得商品退款
(C) 參閱使用者指南
(D) 為設備插電 答案 (A)

問題 47-49，請參考以下對話內容。 英國M 美國W

M: Lisa, (47)**do you have a moment to discuss your schedule here at the bakery?** (48)**Would you like to put in some more hours?**
W: That would be wonderful.
M: That's good. We could use another baker to work the morning shift on Saturday and Sunday. Lots of cakes and cookies are selling out by noon, so we need to make more. You'd begin your shift each day at 6 A.M. and finish at noon.
W: That's kind of early. (49)**How is the pay? Is the hourly rate the same as it is for my afternoon shifts on the weekday?**
M: No. You'll get paid seven dollars more for each hour.
W: Whoa. That's impressive. I'll work both shifts then.

男：麗莎，你有時間討論一下麵包店的班表嗎？你願意多上幾個小時嗎？
女：那太好了。
男：很好。我們可以讓另一名麵包師傅在週六和週日上早班。很多蛋糕和餅乾到中午就賣完了，所以我們要做更多。你每天早上 6 點開始上班到中午。
女：這有點早。那工資呢？時薪和我平日下午班的工資一樣嗎？
男：不。每小時會多付你 7 美元。
女：哇噢。太棒了。那我就輪兩個班。

47. 這場對話在哪裡進行？
(A) 超市
(B) 麵包店
(C) 餐廳
(D) 烹飪學校 答案 (B)

48. 男子為女子提供什麼機會？
(A) 續簽合約
(B) 轉移到另一個地點
(C) 經營一家麵包店
(D) 增加工時 答案 (D)

49. 女子詢問什麼資訊？
    (A) 工作時數
    (B) 公司福利
    (C) 時薪
    (D) 付款方式　　　　　　　答案 (C)

52. 根據愛麗絲所說，以下哪個資訊不正確？
    (A) 部分項目的成本
    (B) 建築物地址
    (C) 倉庫規模
    (D) 裝載點數量　　　　　　答案 (D)

問題 50-52，請參考以下三方對話內容。 澳洲 W ｜ 美國 M ｜ 美國 W

W1: Hello, Mr. Darvish. Thanks for agreeing to this meeting on short notice.

M: No problem. (50)**I'm eager to get started on the design of the new warehouse.**

W1: This is Alice Hastings, the warehouse manager. I've asked her to attend this meeting to discuss what needs to be done.

M: It's a pleasure to meet you, Alice. (51)**Did you look over my proposal?**

W2: (51)**Yes, each of us reviewed it this morning.** But I noticed there's a mistake in the specifications for the loading dock.

M: What mistake?

W2: (52)**We requested that there be enough room for ten trucks to load or unload simultaneously. But the specifications only noted that we'll be getting eight spots.** We're expanding, so we need those extra two slots.

女 1：您好，達維什先生。感謝您在臨時通知下參加這次會議。
男：小事。我等不及開始設計新倉庫了。
女 1：這位是倉庫經理愛麗絲·黑斯汀。我邀請她參加這次會議，討論要完成的事項。
男：很高興認識你，愛麗絲。你看過我的提案了嗎？
女 2：是的，今天早上我們都看了。但我注意到裝卸區的規格有誤。
男：什麼錯誤？
女 2：我們要求有足夠的空間，供十輛卡車同時裝卸。但規格僅指出我們將獲得八個位置。我們正在擴張，所以需要額外的兩個車位。

50. 這場對話的主題是什麼？
    (A) 搬遷
    (B) 高人氣產品
    (C) 聘用機會
    (D) 新設施　　　　　　　　答案 (D)

51. 女子們今天做了什麼？
    (A) 她們致力於一項新設計。
    (B) 她們親自參觀了倉庫。
    (C) 她們審查了企劃提案。
    (D) 她們面試了求職者。　　答案 (C)

問題 53-55，請參考以下對話內容。 澳洲 W ｜ 美國 M

W: Mr. Lewis, even though I just started here at the factory last month, I have an idea I'd like to discuss with you. (53)**It's regarding how we can make the production process of our kitchen tiles more efficient and cost effective.**

M: Okay. What's your idea on how to improve the process?

W: I noticed that we are manufacturing more tiles than we sell, and that's leaving us with plenty of leftover tiles. (54)**But we don't have enough of those tiles to put in a single kitchen, so we can't sell them.** Why don't we not make any tiles until we get an order?

M: You know, we tried doing that before. (55)**But our customers weren't pleased with how much longer it took them to receive their orders than promised.**

女：路易斯先生，雖然我上個月才開始在這間工廠工作，但我有一個想法想跟您討論。這是關於如何讓廚房瓷磚的生產過程更高效也更具成本效益。
男：好。你對改善流程有什麼想法？
女：我注意到，我們生產的瓷磚比銷售的多，導致留下大量剩餘的瓷磚。但我們又沒有足夠一個廚房使用的瓷磚量，所以賣不出去。那為什麼我們不在收到訂單之前，都不生產任何瓷磚？
男：你知道，我們以前嘗試過這樣做。但我們的客戶對於收到訂單的時間比預期還長而感到不滿。

53. 女子想討論什麼？
    (A) 完善安全規則
    (B) 僱用其他供應商
    (C) 改變生產流程
    (D) 提供有競爭力的價格　　答案 (C)

54. 女子提到什麼關於多餘瓷磚的問題？
    (A) 無法出售。
    (B) 沒有空間存放它們。
    (C) 其中一些在生產過程受到損壞。
    (D) 它們的尺寸不正確。　　答案 (A)

55. 男子為什麼說客戶不高興？
    (A) 近期價格上漲。
    (B) 網站出現一些問題。
    (C) 未按時收到訂單。
    (D) 部分產品品質差。　　　答案 (C)

問題 56-58，請參考以下對話內容。 美國W 英國M

W: Jason, do you know where we keep the paper cups in the employee lounge? (56)**Since we relocated to this new office last week, I can't seem to find anything.**

M: Look in the cupboard behind you. You know, it's good that we've moved a lot closer to our major clients, but this has been quite a change.

W: You can say that again. (57)**The old office was so close to my apartment that I used to walk to work.** But now I have to take the bus. It's not a big problem, but walking helped me stay in shape.

M: (58)**Are you aware that the company is offering free gym memberships to all employees? You can talk to Fred if you're interested.**

女：傑森，你知道我們把員工休息室的紙杯放在哪裡嗎？自從我們上週搬到新辦公室之後，我似乎什麼東西都找不到。

男：看看你身後的櫃子。你知道，我們離主要客戶更近了，這是件好事，但也是一個很大的變化。

女：你說得沒錯。舊辦公室離我的公寓很近，我之前常常走路上班。但現在我必須搭公車。這不是什麼大問題，但走路有助於我保持體態。

男：你知道公司向所有員工提供免費的健身房會員資格嗎？如果你有興趣，可以跟弗瑞德談談。

---

56. 公司最近做了什麼？
(A) 整理辦公用品
(B) 擴展到國外
(C) 為員工提供更多福利
(D) 搬遷至其他地點　　　　　　　答案 (D)

57. 女子說她以前會做什麼？
(A) 每天健身
(B) 步行上班
(C) 帶午餐去上班
(D) 工作到很晚　　　　　　　答案 (B)

58. 男子建議女子做什麼？
(A) 搬到另一個地方
(B) 調往其他部門
(C) 成為健身房會員
(D) 開車上班　　　　　　　答案 (C)

問題 59-61，請參考以下對話內容。 英國M 澳洲W

M: Jasmine, (59)**we need to talk about the van design for the Rubicon model. I think there's a flaw in the design.** The engine isn't powerful enough, and the van is too heavy for it to go very

fast. (60)**I'm worried because we're already running behind schedule.**

W: (60)**We have until August to finish the project.** Have you considered making the engine more powerful?

M: Of course, but doing that would cost more than we've budgeted.

W: Okay, (61)**let's have a meeting with Kevin to figure out what we can do.** He's gone today and tomorrow, but he'll be back in the office on Thursday.

男：茉莉，我們需要談談盧比孔型號的車款設計。我認為設計有缺陷。引擎不夠強，而且車身太重，跑不快。我有點擔心，因為我們已經進度落後了。

女：我們到八月分才要完成這個計劃。你有考慮過讓引擎變更強嗎？

男：當然，但是這樣做的成本會超出我們的預算。

女：了解。我們跟凱文開個會，看看能做什麼。他今天和明天都不在，但週四會回到辦公室。

---

59. 這場對話的主題是什麼？
(A) 產品設計
(B) 廣告變更
(C) 產品展演
(D) 新車上市日期　　　　　　　答案 (A)

60. 女子說「我們到八月分才要完成這個計劃」，是在暗示什麼？
(A) 他們沒有足夠的時間。
(B) 他們需要僱用更多工人。
(C) 他們必須工作得更快。
(D) 他們仍然可以按時完成任務。　　答案 (D)

61. 女子建議做什麼？
(A) 聘請顧問
(B) 與同事交談
(C) 增加預算
(D) 檢視一些計算　　　　　　　答案 (B)

問題 62-64，請參考以下對話內容及問卷。 美國W 英國M

W: (62)**Craig, have you done any work on the survey we're doing for our newest video game?** You know, the action one?

M: I've written something up. Could you look at it, please?

W: Sure. Let me look… I'd say you covered everything. (63)**How did you decide which questions to put in the survey?**

M: (63)**I took a look at the reviews of other video games on the Internet. (62)These questions were mentioned the most by game players in the** online reviews.

W: That was a good idea. Now, let me make one comment. (64) **I've noticed that most people don't respond to surveys if they have to write any kind of explanation.**

M: Ah, you're right. (64)**I'll remove that item from the survey.**

女：克雷格，你有為我們最新款電動遊戲的問卷做了什麼嗎？你知道，那款動作遊戲？

男：我寫了一些東西。可以請你看一下嗎？

女：當然。讓我看看……每一個面向你都涵蓋到了。你如何決定要在問卷中提出哪些問題？

男：我看了網路上其他電動遊戲的評論。這些問題是網路評論中，遊戲玩家最常提及的。

女：這是個好主意。現在我來提出一些建議。我注意到，如果問卷中必須寫出解釋，大多數人都不會回應。

男：啊，你說得對。我會從問卷中刪除那一項。

問卷調查

	滿意	不滿意
1. 性能	☐	☐
2. 故事	☐	☐
3. 畫面	☐	☐

(64) **4. 如果你有不滿意的地方，原因是什麼？**

_____

_____

_____

62. 這項調查是針對誰？
(A) 設計師
(B) 作家
(C) 遊戲玩家
(D) 電腦工程師　　　　　　　　答案 (C)

63. 男子如何選擇問卷中列出的項目？
(A) 他參考了一些網路評論。
(B) 他閱讀了線上雜誌的一些文章。
(C) 他跟同事開會。
(D) 他查看了產品手冊。　　　　　答案 (A)

64. 請看圖表。哪個項目將從問卷中刪除？
(A) 第 1 項
(B) 第 2 項
(C) 第 3 項
(D) 第 4 項　　　　　　　　　　答案 (D)

問題 65-67，請參考以下對話內容及長條圖。 美國 M 美國 W

M: Lisa, look at the numbers for the sales we made at the farmers' market last month. We sold a lot of strawberries.

W: (65)**I think the new organic fertilizers we purchased last year helped us harvest high quality strawberries**, so customers love them. But check out the graph. (66)**We only managed to sell 15 kilograms of this.**

M: (66)**We'd better lower the price the next time we sell them at the farmer's market.**

W: Good thinking. (67)**Oh, did you see that segment on the news last night? It was all about the farmers' market.** (67)**It should help attract more people this weekend.**

男：麗莎，看看我們上個月在農貿市場的銷售數字。我們賣了很多草莓。

女：我認為去年購買的新有機肥幫助我們收穫了高品質草莓，所以客人喜歡它們。但看看圖表，這一項我們只賣了 15 公斤。

男：下次去農貿市場販售的時候，最好把價格降低一點。

女：好主意。哦，你有看到昨晚的新聞片段嗎？全部都跟農貿市場有關。這應該有助於在這個週末吸引更多人。

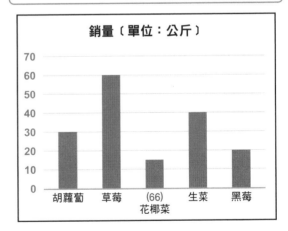

銷量（單位：公斤）

65. 談話者去年做了什麼？
(A) 他們買了一些肥料。
(B) 他們買了一輛新農用車輛。
(C) 他們獲得更多農田。
(D) 他們僱用更多農場工人。　　　答案 (A)

66. 請看圖表。哪項產品本週末將以更低的價格出售？
(A) 草莓
(B) 花椰菜
(C) 生菜
(D) 黑莓　　　　　　　　　　　答案 (B)

67. 為什麼女子認為會有更多客人去市場？
    (A) 新聞節目播出了報導。
    (B) 報紙刊登了一篇文章。
    (C) 稍後會有更多攤販蒞臨。
    (D) 所有價格都會打折。　　　答案 (A)

問題 **68-70**，請參考以下對話內容及地圖。 美國 W 英國 M

> W: Hello, Steve. It's Carla. (68)**I'm calling because Anderson Electric, one of our clients, wants to talk about the advertising campaign we're developing for them.**
>
> M: Right. We're supposed to make some changes to the print advertisement that's going to run in the paper soon, right?
>
> W: Correct. The team at Anderson wants to meet this Friday, so I said we'd be there at nine in the morning. (69)**The office is on the third floor of the building across from City Hall.**
>
> M: Okay. I know where it is. Oh, no… I just remembered I'm meeting Mr. Gruber from HHW at ten on Friday. I can't cancel on him.
>
> W: Don't worry. (70)**I'll reschedule the meeting for some time after lunch. Then, you can attend it.**
>
> ----
>
> 女：你好，史帝夫。我是卡拉。我打電話是因為我們的客戶之一安德森電器，想要談談我們正在為他們開發的廣告活動。
>
> 男：好的。我們應該對即將在報紙上刊登的印刷廣告做出一些改變，對吧？
>
> 女：沒錯。安德森團隊希望在本週五開會，所以我說我們會在早上九點抵達那裡。辦公室位於市政廳對面的大樓三樓。
>
> 男：好的。我知道那在哪裡。哦，不……我剛剛想起週五 10 點，我要和 HHW 的格魯伯先生見面。我無法取消這一場會面。
>
> 女：別擔心。我會把會議重新安排在午餐後。這樣你就可以參加了。

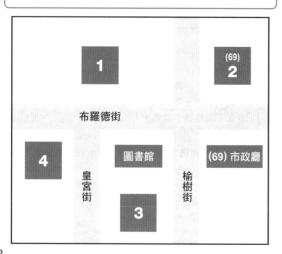

68. 談話者最有可能從事什麼行業？
    (A) 廣告公司
    (B) 會計師事務所
    (C) 電器製造商
    (D) 電力公司　　　答案 (A)

69. 請看圖表。談話者週五將造訪哪棟建築？
    (A) 1 號樓
    (B) 2 號樓
    (C) 3 號樓
    (D) 4 號樓　　　答案 (B)

70. 女子表示願意做什麼？
    (A) 跟她的主管交談
    (B) 更改會議時間
    (C) 重寫一些報告資料
    (D) 更改會面地點　　　答案 (B)

Part 4

問題 **71-73**，請參考以下廣告內容。 美國 M

> Attention, anyone who loves cooking. Do you cook dishes that require exact amounts of certain ingredients? (71)**Then the Devers 1500 is the kitchen scale you need for all your cooking needs.** It's the most reliable product on the market. (72)**You'll get precise measurements to the nearest gram** each and every time you weigh something. (73)**The Devers 1500 is so durable that we're ready and willing to immediately give you a special offer—a three-year extended warranty at no extra fee.** That means, if it breaks, you can return it and get a new one for free.
>
> ----
>
> 喜歡烹飪的朋友們注意了。您煮的菜餚，是否需要特定食材的準確份量？那麼德弗斯 1500 就是滿足您所有烹飪需求的廚房秤。它是市場上最可靠的產品。每次秤量某物時，您都會獲得精確至克數的準確測量值。德弗斯 1500 非常耐用，我們已準備好，願意立即為您提供特別優惠——三年延長保固——無需額外費用。這表示，如果它壞了，您可以退回，並免費獲得一個新的。

71. 正在促銷什麼產品？
    (A) 攪拌機
    (B) 咖啡機
    (C) 烤麵包機
    (D) 秤　　　答案 (D)

72. 說話者對產品的哪個部分讚譽有加？
    (A) 環境友善
    (B) 價格便宜
    (C) 便於攜帶
    (D) 數值準確　　　答案 (D)

73. 說話者提供什麼特別優惠？
    (A) 食譜折扣
    (B) 免費安裝
    (C) 延長保固期
    (D) 免費運送　　　　　　　　　答案 (C)

問題 74-76，請參考以下電話留言。 美國 W

Hello, Rick. This is Amy. Remember how Mr. Burgess asked us to come up with some ideas to save money? (74) (75)**He said we needed to present our cost-reduction proposal next Friday. (75)But he just told me he wants the proposal to be done this Thursday.** Apparently, he's meeting the CEO the following day, so he's counting completely on us to come up with some good ideas for saving money. I can start working on the slides, (76)**but to get the presentation done, we'll need additional financial data. You do know Peter from Finance, don't you? Let me know what you get from him.** I'll be in my office all day long. Thanks.

你好，瑞克。我是艾咪。還記得伯吉斯先生要求我們想出一些省錢的辦法嗎？他原本說我們要在下週五提出成本削減提案。但他剛剛告訴我，他希望提案在本週四完成。顯然他第二天就要見執行長，所以完全指望我們想出省錢的好主意。我可以開始製作投影片，但為了完成報告，我們需要額外的財務數據。你認識財務部的彼得，對嗎？讓我知道你從他那裡得到什麼。我會整天待在辦公室裡。謝謝。

74. 說話者將報告什麼內容？
    (A) 留住更多員工
    (B) 提供削減成本的想法
    (C) 提高辦公效率
    (D) 獲得更多成本預估　　　　　答案 (B)

75. 據說話者所說，發生了什麼變化？
    (A) 提案截止日期
    (B) 執行長到達的日期
    (C) 客戶來訪
    (D) 會面地點　　　　　　　　　答案 (A)

76. 說話者為什麼說「你認識財務部的彼得，對嗎」？
    (A) 表達對成本的擔憂
    (B) 確認會議日期
    (C) 建議人員變動
    (D) 要求聽者聯繫同事　　　　　答案 (D)

問題 77-79，請參考以下介紹。 英國 M

Hello. (77)**I'm very pleased to announce that the winner of the employee of the year award is Susan Darcey, the head of the R&D Department.** She not only manages a department with 120 people, (78)**but she also successfully developed a more fuel-efficient engine that's being used in most of our vehicles now.** Susan's contribution greatly helped our company, but she is also well known for her kindness. (79)**Susan is always willing to mentor employees. She helps them improve themselves whenever she can.** So, Susan, here's your award. Congratulations.

大家好。很高興宣布年度最佳員工獎的獲獎者，是研發部主管蘇珊·達西。她不僅管理著一個有 120 名員工的部門，還成功開發了一種更省油的引擎。目前我們的大多數車輛都在使用該引擎。蘇珊的貢獻，大大地幫助了公司，但她也以她的善良而聞名。蘇珊總是願意指導員工，盡可能幫助他們提升自我。所以，蘇珊，這是屬於你的獎。恭喜。

77. 正在介紹誰？
    (A) 執行長
    (B) 客戶
    (C) 公司主管
    (D) 政府官員　　　　　　　　　答案 (C)

78. 關於引擎，文中提到什麼？
    (A) 目前正被採用。
    (B) 它有時會故障。
    (C) 需要改善。
    (D) 正在開發中。　　　　　　　答案 (A)

79. 關於蘇珊·達西，文中暗指什麼？
    (A) 她剛剛升職。
    (B) 她經常出國旅行。
    (C) 她打算盡快退休。
    (D) 她喜歡幫助別人。　　　　　答案 (D)

問題 80-82，請參考以下電話留言。 澳洲 W

Hello. This message is for Mr. Griggs. (80)**I'm calling from Orlando Restorations about the sofa that you dropped off here. The fabric on the seating part of the sofa needs replacing.** I've checked with the furniture manufacturer to see if I could get some of the original fabric, (81)**but unfortunately they don't have any in stock.** The fabric for your sofa was a limited release design, so they didn't mass-produce it. However, I've found some other fabric that looks similar to it. I want to show it to you. (82)**How about dropping by the store when you have a chance?**

你好。這個訊息是給格里格斯先生的。我這裡是奧蘭多修復中心,來電詢問你送來這裡的沙發。座位部分的布料需要更換。我已經向家具製造商詢問是否可以獲得一些原本的布料,但不幸的是,他們沒有庫存。你的沙發布料是限量設計版,所以他們沒有大量生產。不過,我發現一些其他看起來與之相似的布料,想展示給你看。方便的話,可以來店裡看看嗎?

80. 說話者打電話的目的是什麼?
    (A) 家具廣告
    (B) 沙發運送
    (C) 她的特殊訂單狀態
    (D) 家具維修　　　　　　　　　答案 (D)

81. 說話者提到什麼問題?
    (A) 某些材料無法取得。
    (B) 物品無法修復。
    (C) 價格高於估計。
    (D) 未遵守最後期限。　　　　　答案 (A)

82. 聽者被要求做什麼?
    (A) 尋找其他供應商
    (B) 更改發布日期
    (C) 前往店面
    (D) 拿起他的裝備　　　　　　　答案 (C)

問題 83-85,請參考以下參觀資訊。 英國 M

Welcome to the Mandela Art Gallery. We'll start today's tour at the Impressionist Art Collection. (83)**This is among our most popular exhibits because it features paintings by a different famous artist every other month.** People enjoy seeing new artwork whenever they visit here. (84)**After the tour, please feel free to ask any questions. But you should know that I'm an intern here.** (85)**Oh, one final reminder – flash photography is prohibited inside the gallery without special permission as it might damage artwork.** Thank you very much.

歡迎來到曼德拉美術館。我們將從印象派藝術收藏開始今天的導覽。這是我們最受歡迎的展覽之一,因為它每隔一個月就會展出不同知名藝術家的畫作。人們每次來這裡都喜歡看到新的藝術品。參觀結束後,如有任何問題,請隨時提問。但各位應該知道我是這裡的實習生。哦,最後提醒一下——未經特別許可,館內禁止使用閃光燈攝影,因為這可能會損壞藝術品。非常感謝。

83. 據說話者所說,印象派藝術收藏為何受歡迎?
    (A) 免費入場。
    (B) 它出現在一部電視紀錄片中。
    (C) 這是博物館最大量的收藏品。
    (D) 經常更新。　　　　　　　　答案 (D)

84. 說話者說「我是這裡的實習生」,是在暗指什麼?
    (A) 他沒有因導覽而獲得報酬。
    (B) 他需要同事的幫助。
    (C) 他可能回答不出某些問題。
    (D) 他渴望給訪客留下深刻印象。　答案 (C)

85. 說話者提醒聽者什麼?
    (A) 美術館政策
    (B) 票價
    (C) 關門時間
    (D) 新展覽　　　　　　　　　　答案 (A)

問題 86-88,請參考以下廣播內容。 美國 W

WKEK is bringing you the news you need to know at 7 P.M. (86)**First, let's cover the main story. All the votes have been counted, and Peter Shaw is the new mayor.** Mr. Shaw is a leading member of the business community here in town. (87)**Before running for mayor, he was the CEO of Shaw Construction for twenty years.** He promised local residents to use his knowledge of the business world to improve the city's economy. (88)**We'd love to know what our listeners think about the election. How about calling in to the station during our 8 P.M. talk show to discuss your opinions?**

WKEK 將於晚上 7 點帶來您需要知道的新聞。首先,我們來報導一下頭條故事。選票已全數清點完畢,彼得‧尚恩成為新市長。尚恩先生是該鎮商界的重要成員。在競選市長之前,他曾任尚恩建設執行長長達二十年。他向當地居民承諾,會運用自身對商業世界的知識來改善該市經濟。我們很想知道聽眾對這次選舉的看法。在晚上 8 點的脫口秀打來,一起討論你的觀點如何?

86. 廣播主要關於什麼內容?
    (A) 經濟情況
    (B) 企業收購
    (C) 選舉結果
    (D) 已竣工的建設計劃　　　　　答案 (C)

87. 據說話者所說,彼得‧尚恩有什麼領域的經驗?
    (A) 教育
    (B) 商業
    (C) 娛樂
    (D) 旅行　　　　　　　　　　　答案 (B)

88. 聽眾被邀請做什麼？
(A) 點播音樂
(B) 註冊會員
(C) 分享他們的想法
(D) 參加抽獎 答案 (C)

問題 89-91，請參考以下語音訊息。 美國 M

Hello. This is the voice mailbox of Ronald Martinson at Robinson Consulting. (89)**At Robinson Consulting, we provide our clients with the investment advice they need to make their money grow.** (90)**I'm going to be out of the office this week at an investment management training program.** I'll be back in the office on next Monday with knowledge to better serve you. (91)**If you need some urgent financial advice, please get in touch with Rodney Chapman, assistant supervisor.** He can be reached at extension 9548.

您好。這是魯賓遜諮詢公司羅納德‧馬丁森的語音信箱。在魯賓遜諮詢公司，我們為客戶提供實現資金成長所需的投資建議。本週我不在辦公室，去參加一個投資管理培訓計劃。我將於下週一回到辦公室，帶著豐富知識提供更好的服務。如果您需要緊急財務建議，請與助理主管羅德尼‧查普曼聯繫。他的分機是 9548。

89. 此公司提供什麼服務？
(A) 財務諮詢
(B) 網路安全
(C) 網路行銷
(D) 物業管理 答案 (A)

90. 為什麼說話者本週沒有空？
(A) 他出國了。
(B) 他正在參加一場大會。
(C) 他正在參加員工會議。
(D) 他正在參加培訓課程。 答案 (D)

91. 如果聽者需要緊急建議，應該怎麼做？
(A) 發送電子郵件
(B) 造訪辦公室
(C) 致電另一名員工
(D) 用手機致電經理 答案 (C)

問題 92-94，請參考以下會議摘錄。 澳洲 W

(92)**And our monthly meeting here at the Davidson Health Clinic is now over.** Oh, I need to mention one more thing. A local hospital is offering a two-day healthcare workshop. Leslie Smith will be leading the program. She's well-known in the medical industry as a leading health expert. You don't want to miss out on this program. We'd love for everyone to attend it. (93)**You can register tomorrow. Please keep in mind that lots of people know about Leslie. (94)When we meet next month, be sure to have next year's budget requests with you.**

我們在戴維森健康診所舉行的月會現已結束。哦，我還需要提一件事。當地一家醫院正在舉辦為期兩天的醫療保健工作坊。萊絲莉‧史密斯將主持這項課程。她作為首屈一指的健康專家，在醫療業享有盛譽。你們不會想錯過這個課程。我們希望每個人都能參加。明天就可以報名了。請記住，很多人都知道萊絲莉。當我們下個月見面時，請務必備妥明年的預算需求。

92. 聽者在哪裡工作？
(A) 大學
(B) 醫療設備公司
(C) 醫療機構
(D) 製藥公司 答案 (C)

93. 說話者說「很多人都知道萊絲莉」，是在暗示什麼？
(A) 她計劃訂購更多辦公用品。
(B) 聽者務必趕快報名。
(C) 會議場地太小。
(D) 她需要立即聯繫萊絲莉。 答案 (B)

94. 說話者提醒聽者做什麼？
(A) 提出一些建議
(B) 聯繫一些客戶
(C) 提高效率
(D) 準備一些文件 答案 (D)

問題 95-97，請參考以下新聞報導及天氣預報。 美國 W

It's time for the local weather report. (95)**I'm pleased to say that the rain will end before the fall festival begins. We'll have some cloudy weather, but no rain.** In fact, it should be perfect fall weather. (96)**I'm looking forward to the festival because the Dingoes will be performing live. I love that band, so I'll definitely be at the performance.** (97)**And please remember that our radio station, KMSD, is giving away backstage passes.** Winners will also get the opportunity to meet the band after the concert ends. (97)**So visit our web page and enter.** You could be one of ten lucky winners.

又到了當地天氣預報時間。我很高興地宣布，雨天將在秋季慶典開始之前結束。我們將會有一些多雲的天氣，但不會下雨。事實上，這應該是完美的秋季天氣。我很期待這個慶典，因為野狗樂團將進行現場表演。我很喜

歡那個樂團，所以一定會去看演出。請記住，我們的廣播電臺 KMSD 正在贈送後臺通行證。獲獎者將有機會在音樂會結束後與樂團見面。因此，請前往並進入我們的網頁。你就可能成為十位幸運獲獎者之一。

天氣預報

星期一	星期二	(95) 星期三	星期四	星期五
雨天	雨天	(95) 多雲	晴天	雨天

95. 請看圖表。秋季慶典什麼時候舉行？
    (A) 星期一
    (B) 星期二
    (C) 星期三
    (D) 星期四　　　　　　　　　　　答案 (C)

96. 說話者說她對什麼感到興奮？
    (A) 藝術展覽
    (B) 音樂表演
    (C) 體育競賽
    (D) 音樂講座　　　　　　　　　　答案 (B)

97. 說話者建議聽者做什麼？
    (A) 帶上他們的朋友
    (B) 提前購票
    (C) 打進電臺
    (D) 參加競賽　　　　　　　　　　答案 (D)

問題 98-100，請參考以下會議摘錄及議程。 英國 M

Hello, everyone. (98)**Let me congratulate you on starting your first day of work here at Stephenson's.** I'm Stuart Preston, and I'm the head of the HR Department. (99)**Today, we'll let you know about what happens here at our camping equipment company.** We would like everybody to understand how the different departments and teams work together to manufacture high-quality equipment including tents and sleeping bags we sell around the world. We were supposed to start with Jude Crow in R&D, but he's in a meeting. (100)**So let's listen to the head of Sales instead.**

各位好。恭喜你們展開在斯蒂芬森工作的第一天。我是斯圖爾特·普雷斯頓，人力資源部的負責人。今天，我們將讓你們了解本露營設備公司的大小事。希望每個人都能了解不同部門和團隊如何共同努力，製造高品質的設備，包括在世界各地銷售的帳篷和睡袋。我們本來應該從研發部門的朱帝·克勞開始，但他正在開會。那我們先來聽聽業務主管的想法吧。

會議議程

13:45	介紹
14:00	朱帝·克勞 — 研發經理
14:15	伊麗莎白·迪恩 — 人力資源主管
14:30	(100) 安迪·湯普森 — 業務主管
14:45	威爾瑪·帕特森 — 執行長

98. 聽者最有可能是誰？
    (A) 潛在投資者
    (B) 國外客戶
    (C) 主管
    (D) 新員工　　　　　　　　　　　答案 (D)

99. 此公司生產什麼類型的產品？
    (A) 露營裝備
    (B) 車輛
    (C) 藥品
    (D) 體育用品　　　　　　　　　　答案 (A)

100. 請看圖表。接下來誰會發言？
    (A) 朱帝·克勞
    (B) 伊麗莎白·迪恩
    (C) 安迪·湯普森
    (D) 威爾瑪·帕特森　　　　　　　答案 (C)

Part 5

101. 詹姆士·華生，該國最受歡迎的歌手之一，已同意可可珠寶在即將推出的廣告宣傳中使用他的名字。
　　　　　　　　　　　　　　　　　答案 (B)

102. 貝拉通訊向當地居民提供網路和行動電話服務。
　　　　　　　　　　　　　　　　　答案 (C)

103. 多年來，該公司一直是教育大眾更有效設計廣告活動的領頭羊。　　　　　　　　　　答案 (D)

104. 人事部的某些辦公桌太重，布萊恩和哈利無法獨力搬動。　　　　　　　　　　　　　答案 (D)

105. 我們公司決定推進原定在中國合併兩家銀行的計劃。
　　　　　　　　　　　　　　　　　答案 (B)

106. 新的桌上型電腦配備了最新文字處理軟體和高解析度螢幕。　　　　　　　　　　　　答案 (C)

107. 經過兩週的音樂表演後，《貓的浪漫》現在將於本劇院上演至 11 月 14 日。　　　　答案 (A)

108. 許多公司一直熱切等待與歐洲國家簽訂新的自由貿易協定，希望提高歐洲的市場份額。　答案 (D)

109. 詹金斯先生昨天表示，出口的冷凍食品符合 20 個國家的食品安全法規。　　　答案 (A)

110. 數據顯示，近十年來，由火山活動引起的地震次數顯著增加。　　　答案 (B)

111. 乾淨又美觀的工作環境，足以對員工績效和情緒產生巨大影響。　　　答案 (A)

112. 該航班的部分乘客在抵達國際機場後生病並立即住院治療。　　　答案 (C)

113. 請注意，我們的數據必須安全地傳輸到中央數據庫，以供分析和回饋。　　　答案 (A)

114. 如果您無法遵守排定的醫療預約，請至少提前兩天通知我們。　　　答案 (C)

115. 請填寫表格，以了解你的辦公大樓是否可以免除消防演習和安全檢查的要求。　　　答案 (B)

116. 致電我們的客戶服務專員詢問問題時，最好準備一份問題清單。　　　答案 (B)

117. 第一國際的投資，是該國金融業最大的單一外國直接投資。　　　答案 (D)

118. 該報告以可查證的事實和證據為依據，以合乎邏輯與分析的方式進行。　　　答案 (B)

119. 麥克唐納先生兩個月前才獲聘，但他已經為公司制定了一些有效的銷售策略。　　　答案 (C)

120. 根據我們的辦公室政策，最後離開的人要負責關掉辦公室裡的所有燈並鎖上門。　　　答案 (D)

121. 許多上班族似乎在因工作和日常生活感到疲倦或壓力時，過度飲用能量飲料。　　　答案 (B)

122. 該雜誌非常成功，銷量比任何人預想都多，發行量卻在幾年內迅速下滑。　　　答案 (B)

123. 向亞洲商業網站下的訂單，通常都是來自越南倉庫的商品。　　　答案 (A)

124. 我們的員工將在今年年底獲得巨額獎金，前提是：公司淨利潤超出董事會預期。　　　答案 (A)

125. 星園運動致力於設計和生產每個人都想穿的各式跑鞋。　　　答案 (A)

126. 為了讓我們的品牌保持今天的人氣，需要在網路上以便利的形式提供高品質內容。　　　答案 (D)

127. 儘管風浪很大，天氣惡劣，飛機上的所有乘客仍全數成功獲救。　　　答案 (A)

128. 城市居民很少考慮栽種自己的花園，儘管建造一個小花園並不那麼困難。　　　答案 (D)

129. 偶爾，在國定假日之前，我們的多數員工獲准比平常早下班。　　　答案 (C)

130. 近年來，電子產品的消費增長如此之快，以至於如今它已成為環境問題最嚴重的產品類別之一。　　　答案 (B)

Part 6

問題 131-134，請參考以下資訊。

> **貝拉航空常見問題**
>
> 如果我沒有收到貝拉航空的航班確認電子郵件怎麼辦？
>
> 您的航班詳細資訊將發送至您提供的電子郵件。預訂後，貝拉航空通常最多需要三個小時，才能向乘客發送確認信。如果您在預訂後仍未收到確認信，請確保您已成功付款。如果您的信用卡上未顯示付款，則可能表示您的航班預訂未成功。
>
> 這種情況下，請致電 692-9815，以便我們查詢。撥打此號碼的費用，由貝拉航空公司負擔，因此我們的客戶可以免費撥打。

131. (A) 飛行期間任何時間均不得使用手機。
　　 (B) 如果交易資訊有誤，我們將更正您的帳戶。
　　 (C) 您的航班詳細資訊將發送至您提供的電子郵件。
　　 (D) 請保留您的訂單影本和確認號碼。　　　答案 (C)

132. 　　　答案 (B)

133. 　　　答案 (B)

134. 　　　答案 (D)

問題 135-138，請參考以下廣告內容。

> **幸運 7 超市**
> 「只有新鮮的！」
> 桑代爾弄 5801 號
> 93307 加州，貝克斯菲爾德
>
> 幸運 7 超市充滿各季最新鮮的水果和蔬菜！

我們的產品來自加州、亞利桑那州、佛羅里達州等地，超級新鮮！幸運 7 超市會向您的家人提供由附近農民種植的新鮮當地食材。

幸運 7 超市的產品，都是您喜歡的價格！我們提供精選午餐冷盤肉和奶酪，根據您的訂單新鮮切片！我們只提供最好的牛肉、A 級家禽肉、A 級新鮮豬肉、自製煙燻火腿和絞肉。您一定會喜歡我們的每日低價、特價商品和新品。

如果您在購物時需要協助，請詢問店員。他或她會很樂意帶您找到商品。

---

135. 答案 (C)

136. 答案 (A)

137. 答案 (A)

138. (A) 了解我們即將推出的特別促銷活動。
　　 (B) 顧客評價一直很正面。
　　 (C) 商業競爭可能非常激烈，尤其是在快速變化的市場中。
　　 (D) 您一定會喜歡我們的每日低價、特價商品和新品。
　　 答案 (D)

問題 139-142，請參考以下電子郵件。

收件人：夏洛特・帕克 <cp@hdmail.com>
寄件人：麗莎・普雷斯頓 <lpreston@nybc.com>
主　旨：您的申請
日　期：2 月 14 日

親愛的帕克女士，

感謝您申請行政助理職位。我們非常感謝您有興趣加入本公司。您申請的職位已不再開缺。然而，我們的人力資源團隊滿懷興趣地讀了您的履歷。您的專業經驗和教育背景令人印象深刻，這將使您成為本公司的優秀人才。

如果您不反對，我們會將您的履歷存檔，並在有合適職位時立即與您聯繫。

同時，祝您求職一切順利。

誠摯問候，

麗莎・普雷斯頓
人事主管
紐約商業諮詢

---

139. 答案 (C)

140. (A) 我們對您的求職面試結果感到擔憂。
　　 (B) 您申請的職位已不再開缺。
　　 (C) 您非常有資格擔任行政助理。
　　 (D) 我們的招聘人員必須審查多項申請，才能填補職位空缺。
　　 答案 (B)

141. 答案 (D)

142. 答案 (B)

問題 143-146，請參考以下信件內容。

米拉麥克斯家居裝修
桃樹街 265 號
30303 喬治亞州，亞特蘭大

6 月 20 日
經典色調公司
斯科特街 401 號
30303 喬治亞州，亞特蘭大

敬啟者，

昨天我們收到 40 罐一加侖的花白色房屋塗料，但它們並非我們從貴公司訂購的品項。因此，我們將把它們退回你們位於馬里蘭州洛克斯維爾的工廠。

請參閱我們 6 月 12 日的採購訂單 BK365020，其中我們要求購買 50 罐一品脫雪花房屋塗料，你們的產品型錄號碼為 SF-909。請盡快傳真至 1-800-521-6313，確認收到此信函並處理要求。

另外，請盡快完成該訂單，以便我們及時滿足客戶的需求。

誠摯問候，

歐若拉・雷恩
採購主管
米拉麥克斯家居裝修

---

143. (A) 我們很樂意為你提供你所要求的估價。
　　 (B) 不幸地，客戶對錯過最後期限表示失望。
　　 (C) 因此，我們將把它們退回你們位於馬里蘭州洛克斯維爾的工廠。
　　 (D) 你們的油漆產品最常用於保護物品或賦予其紋理。
　　 答案 (C)

144. 答案 (B)

145. 答案 (B)

146. 答案 (D)

問題 147-148，請參考以下表格內容。

東村公司

皮茨街 109 號

19028 特拉華州，多佛

訂購日期：6 月 5 日

訂單號：0194570

(147) 客戶姓名：安吉拉‧蘿絲

送貨地址：19010 特拉華州，海蘭阿克雷斯，慈善路
42 號

交貨日期和時間：6 月 9 日中午 12:00

(148D) 歸還日期和時間：6 月 10 日上午 10:00

品項	數量	價格
(147) 彩色接待餐具套組（租賃）	2	24 美元
花卉裝飾－白色和黃色（租賃）	5	20 美元
折疊宴會桌椅套組（租賃）	2	40 美元
派對帳篷（租賃）	2	50 美元
(148C) 運送及安裝		50 美元
總計		184 美元

* (148B) 我們為企業客戶提供 10% 折扣。

* 提取費包含在運費和安裝費中。

* (148D) 所有品項必須在上述歸還時間內備妥，以供提取。

147. 關於蘿絲女士，文中暗指什麼？
   (A) 她住在皮茨街。
   (B) 她是公司客戶。
   (C) 她正在準備一個活動。
   (D) 她將在早上使用送達的物品。　　　　答案 (C)

148. 關於東村公司，文中沒有暗指什麼？
   (A) 逾期歸還加收 10% 服務費。
   (B) 向某些客戶提供折扣。
   (C) 向客戶收取運費。
   (D) 將於 6 月 10 日提取租賃物品。　　　答案 (A)

問題 149-150，請參考以下文字訊息。

大衛‧羅伯茨　　　　　　　　　　[上午 9:11]
卡拉，(149) 我被指派的工作截止日是兩天後，但我還有很多要做。

卡拉‧瓊斯　　　　　　　　　　　[上午 9:12]
你需要幫忙嗎？

大衛‧羅伯茨　　　　　　　　　　[上午 9:13]
那就太完美了。(150) 今天早上可以見面嗎？

卡拉‧瓊斯　　　　　　　　　　　[上午 9:14]
(150) 午餐後怎麼樣？

大衛‧羅伯茨　　　　　　　　　　[上午 9:15]

沒問題。我會在 1:30 去你的辦公室。我會把我已經完成的工作帶去。如果你能給我一些如何繼續的想法，我將不勝感激。

卡拉‧瓊斯　　　　　　　　　　　[上午 9:16]
如果你需要一些額外的幫助，我也不介意待晚一點。我的客戶剛剛取消了我們的晚餐會議。

149. 羅伯茨先生的問題是什麼？
   (A) 他需要更多關於新專案的想法。
   (B) 他必須在今晚之前完成一個計劃。
   (C) 他的客戶剛剛取消了一場會議。
   (D) 他還沒有完成一些工作。　　　　　答案 (D)

150. 上午 9:14 時，瓊斯女士為何寫道「午餐後怎麼樣」？
   (A) 更改預訂
   (B) 拒絕提議
   (C) 道歉
   (D) 提議地點　　　　　　　　　　　　答案 (B)

問題 151-153，請參考以下公告內容。

第 2 屆布朗設計大賽

首屈一指的家居用品製造商布朗公司，很高興舉辦第 2 屆布朗設計大賽。今年的設計作品將是食品儲存容器，這是我們從未開發過的產品。

歡迎各種形式的參賽作品，包括使用不同藝術材料的草稿和草圖。請參閱 www.browninc.com，上面有布朗公司過往的產品設計。(151) 瓦特‧楚設計的攜帶式茶壺就是一個很好的例子，它是去年布朗設計大賽的獲獎設計，打破布朗公司以往的所有銷售紀錄。

今年的獲獎作品，將在下一個市場年度被選為布朗公司的官方產品並推出。此外，(152D) 一等獎獲獎者將獲得該公司的全職工作職位。(152B) 所有獲獎者將受邀參加 8 月 20 日在多佛總部舉行的頒獎典禮。此獎項將由布朗公司的設計主管頒發。

此外，獲獎者還將獲得共 6,000 美元的獎金。

(152A) 一等獎：3,000 美元

二等獎：2,000 美元

三等獎：1,000 美元

如果你有興趣參賽，請上我們的網站 www.browninc.com/application 下載詳細的交件指南，並將參賽作品透過電子郵件寄給我們。(153) 參賽作品於 7 月 1 日開始收件，截止日期為 7 月 31 日。

151. 關於布朗公司，文中暗指什麼？
   (A) 它只銷售食品容器。
   (B) 已營業兩年。
   (C) 攜帶式茶壺深受顧客歡迎。
   (D) 明年將舉行大賽頒獎禮。　　　　　答案 (C)

152. 一等獎獲獎者不會得到什麼？
    (A) 3,000 美元現金
    (B) 參加正式活動的邀請
    (C) 飛往多佛的機票
    (D) 布朗公司的全職職位　　　　答案 (C)

153. 關於報名，文中暗指什麼？
    (A) 需要支付手續費。
    (B) 截止日期為 7 月 31 日。
    (C) 由一組高層進行評審。
    (D) 必須透過郵寄方式交件。　　　答案 (B)

問題 **154-156**，請參考以下電子郵件。

> 收件人：約翰・貝克 <jbaker@easymail.com>
> 寄件人：安柏・李 <alee@hotelconcord.com>
> 日　期：9 月 20 日
> 主　旨：(155) 回覆：關於我上次造訪
>
> 親愛的貝克先生，
>
> 首先，感謝您最近蒞臨新奧爾良協和飯店。為您服務是我們的榮幸。
>
> (155) 我們已收到您的詢問。(154) 對於您上週在本飯店的不愉快住宿經驗，請接受我代表協和飯店誠摯致歉。我們的預訂系統發生不明錯誤，對於無法為您提供最初預訂的房間，我們深表歉意。
>
> (154) 為了彌補造成的不便，(156) 我們向您提供價值 200 美元的禮券，您可以在美國協和飯店的任何一分店使用。請透過我們的官方網站 www.hotelconcord.com 下載禮券。
>
> 謝謝您，希望能再次見到您。
>
> 誠摯感謝。
>
> 安柏・李
> 新奧爾良協和飯店經理

154. 此電子郵件的主要目的是什麼？
    (A) 感謝顧客光臨飯店
    (B) 為超額預訂給出藉口
    (C) 確認預訂
    (D) 彌補最近的錯誤　　　　　　答案 (D)

155. 關於貝克先生，文中暗示了什麼？
    (A) 他與家人一起造訪協和飯店。
    (B) 他最近寫了一封電子郵件給協和飯店。
    (C) 他住在新奧爾良。
    (D) 他為自己的房間支付了 200 美元。　答案 (B)

156. 根據此電子郵件，關於協和飯店，文中暗指了什麼？
    (A) 它將開設網站。
    (B) 房間目前已訂滿。

    (C) 它有多家分店。
    (D) 它向所有首次造訪者提供優惠券。　答案 (C)

問題 **157-158**，請參考以下優惠券。

> **山姆披薩**
>
> (157) 為慶祝山姆成立 5 週年，我們在整個 7 月，為顧客提供平日特別優惠。請攜帶下方優惠券，以優惠價格享用美味的披薩。
>
> **優惠券**
>
> ✂
>
> | | |
> |---|---|
> | 折價 3.00 美元
適用於任何特製披薩 | < 免費 >
2 份義大利辣香腸捲
或
2 種自選配料
* 須購買大披薩 * |
> | (158) 週三和週四
大優惠
起司大披薩
7.99 美元
2 件僅需 15.00 美元 | 買 1 送 1
任何大披薩 |
>
> － (158) 所有優惠券僅適用於「外帶」。
> － 每個訂單只能使用一張優惠券。

157. 關於山姆披薩，可以推斷出什麼？
    (A) 已營業五年。
    (B) 週末休息。
    (C) 顧客沒有配料可選。
    (D) 不提供外送服務。　　　　　答案 (A)

158. 如果顧客要花 15 美元購買兩個起司大披薩，應該怎麼做？
    (A) 現金支付
    (B) 7 月的星期四在餐廳用餐
    (C) 在特定日子使用優惠券
    (D) 再買一個原價披薩　　　　　答案 (C)

問題 **159-161**，請參考以下廣告內容。

> **樹屋解決方案**
>
> (159) 您是否受白蟻和臭蟲等家庭害蟲所擾？樹屋解決方案可以為您的家提供客製化三步除蟲解決方案，來解決您的昆蟲問題。
>
> 1. 檢測
> (161A) 我們的優質檢查員每年接受 10 小時培訓，(161B) 在與您協商後，首先會仔細檢查您的房屋。接著，我們將根據您的獨特情況，制定最佳處理方案，以提供最大程度的防護。

2.處理

檢測後，我們會透過 3 次滅蟲處理，有效、快速地消滅害蟲。(161D) 我們有兩種類型的處理方法，兩者都是無毒又環保的：液體和泡沫。液體適用於房屋的地基，泡沫則適用於外牆、管道等表面。

3.監控

(160) 我們的監控服務可確保防護的持續有效性。兩年內，我們將每季拜訪您的家一次，並根據需要進行額外處理。

---

159. 正在廣告的最有可能是什麼？
 (A) 房屋清潔服務
 (B) 害蟲清除服務
 (C) 環保室內設計
 (D) 園藝服務　　　　　　　　　　　答案 (B)

160. 樹屋解決方案的員工，多久上門一次進行監控？
 (A) 每年一次
 (B) 每年兩次
 (C) 每年三次
 (D) 每年四次　　　　　　　　　　　答案 (D)

161. 關於樹屋解決方案的員工，文中沒有暗指什麼？
 (A) 他們必須參加年度培訓。
 (B) 他們在發現原因之前，與客戶討論症狀。
 (C) 他們向續約客戶提供處理套組。
 (D) 他們使用對環境危害很小的處理方法。　　答案 (C)

問題 162-164，請參考以下電子郵件。

收件人：潔西卡・西斯內羅斯
　　　　<jcisneros@sevelia.com>
寄件人：馬克・德蒙特 <mdemont@sku.edu>
日　期：4 月 15 日
主　旨：昨天晚上

親愛的西斯內羅斯女士，

(163) 自從我在開幕之夜第一次造訪塞維利亞以來，就一直是它的忠實粉絲。我不敢相信，一家在地小餐館可以提供如此美味的泰國菜和優質服務。從那時起，我就經常去塞維利亞，(164) 每次我都很高興，直到昨晚為止。

(164) 昨晚，我和妻子去你們餐廳吃飯。我們點了兩道主餐，但只上了一道。儘管我們對這個錯誤感到非常沮喪，但我們沒有時間等待，所以決定分享同一道主餐後就離開。吃完飯後，我用信用卡付款，但沒有檢查帳單或收據。後來我查看收據時，發現你們收了我兩份主餐的費用，而不是一份。

(163) 這是我在你們餐廳用餐兩年以來收到最令人失望的服務。因為這次經歷，我不得不考慮以後是否再去你們餐廳。(162) 我請你立即關注此事。

謝謝你。
馬克・德蒙特

---

162. 此電子郵件的目的是什麼？
 (A) 推薦當地餐廳
 (B) 請求金錢補償
 (C) 投訴餐費上漲
 (D) 舉報一些不良服務　　　　　　　答案 (D)

163. 關於塞維利亞，文中暗指什麼？
 (A) 這是一家大型連鎖店。
 (B) 顧客不多。
 (C) 已營業約 2 年。
 (D) 最近僱用了一名新員工。　　　　答案 (C)

164. 以下句子最適合放在文中 [1]、[2]、[3] 和 [4] 的哪一個位置？
「昨晚，我和妻子去你們餐廳吃飯。」
 (A) [1]
 (B) [2]
 (C) [3]
 (D) [4]　　　　　　　　　　　　　答案 (B)

問題 165-167，請參考以下文章內容。

塵土飛揚的舊市政廳重生

6 月 17 日

位於維街的舊市政廳在過去 8 個月裡一直受到眾人的好奇與期待。終於，該建築將於 7 月 1 日晚間，以新名稱印第安納波利斯市藝術博物館向公眾展示。

建造這座城市地標——螺旋塔——的建築師伊恩・肯辛頓，承擔了博物館的設計責任。他與城市電力系統工程師多里安・韋伯斯特密切合作，讓整個空間變得環保。增加了兩個翼廊，將博物館與雕塑花園連接起來。偽裝成雕塑的風車和太陽能電池板，將產生足夠電力來運行整個博物館。

(165) 這次改造工程實際上是由建築師本人發起的。在向市議會提交提案後，他還為該計劃捐贈了大筆資金。「如果說是肯辛頓先生讓這個計劃成為可能，一點都不誇張。」(166) 印第安納波利斯市市長凱特琳・特里斯坦評論道。「他透過舉辦募款晚宴，募集了大部分裝修費用。我所做的只是批准他的提案。」

博物館開幕時，將舉辦著名攝影師艾米・尼金斯基的展覽。(167) 當晚她將代表市議會，向肯辛頓先生發表感謝致辭。

博物館將於週一至週五上午 9 點開放至晚上 7 點。有關城市博物館的更多資訊，請參閱網站 www.icma.org。

165. 肯辛頓先生對博物館有何貢獻？
    (A) 允許其私人財產用作建築工地
    (B) 規劃如何使用預算
    (C) 提出翻新市政廳大樓的想法
    (D) 籌辦開幕式 答案 (C)

166. 特里斯坦女士最有可能是誰？
    (A) 著名攝影師
    (B) 博物館館長
    (C) 市政府官員
    (D) 專業工程師 答案 (C)

167. 關於開幕式，文中提到什麼？
    (A) 隨後將舉行募款晚宴。
    (B) 將於星期一舉行。
    (C) 這是僅限受邀者參加的活動。
    (D) 將包含一場正式演講。 答案 (D)

問題 **168-171**，請參考以下線上討論訊息。

> 特蕾莎·哈珀 ［上午 10:48］
> (168) 不要忘記今天的腦力激盪會議。地點已改為 453 室，但仍定於 3:00 舉行。
>
> 凱特·馬丁 ［上午 10:50］
> 我沒辦法準時抵達。(169) 我在鄧肯公司的會議預計要到 2:30 才能結束。(171) 我為大家準備些茶點好嗎？
>
> 特蕾莎·哈珀 ［上午 10:51］
> (171) 為什麼不呢？噢，各位，請記得把我今天早上發給你們的資訊列印出來並隨身攜帶。
>
> 達里爾·沃爾特普 ［上午 10:52］
> 我正在查看我的收件匣，但沒有看到你的任何信。
>
> 埃里克·里德 ［上午 10:53］
> 我也沒有。
>
> 特蕾莎·哈珀 ［上午 10:55］
> 真的嗎？我一定是忘記寄出了。我現在就用電子郵件發給大家。
>
> 埃里克·里德 ［上午 10:56］
> 知道了。謝謝。
>
> 達里爾·沃爾特普 ［上午 10:57］
> (170) 我會在午餐時讀它，以便為會議做好充分準備。
>
> 特蕾莎·哈珀 ［上午 10:59］
> 感謝大家。我們真的需要簽下這份合約，(168) 所以希望你們對我們的提案發揮創意。截止日期為本週末。

168. 哈珀女士為什麼邀請兩位傳訊息的人參加會議？
    (A) 回顧調查結果
    (B) 考慮最近的提案
    (C) 審查合約條款
    (D) 提出一些新想法 答案 (D)

169. 馬丁女士開會為什麼會遲到？
    (A) 她還沒有做好準備。
    (B) 她需要完成一份工作提案。
    (C) 她必須參加一個商務會議。
    (D) 她將與她的主管會面。 答案 (C)

170. 沃爾特普先生表示自己會做什麼？
    (A) 閱讀一些資料
    (B) 為每個人列印一份文件
    (C) 設置會議室
    (D) 讓同事知道有一場會議 答案 (A)

171. 上午 10:51，哈珀女士為何寫道「為什麼不呢」？
    (A) 質疑馬丁女士的提議
    (B) 拒絕讓任何人會議遲到
    (C) 同意在會議上享用餐點和飲料
    (D) 批准更改會議時間的請求 答案 (C)

問題 **172-175**，請參考以下文章內容。

> ### 東京日報
>
> (172)「我仍然不敢相信這真的發生在我身上。」木本作太郎說。木本先生 16 歲時，隨父母從日本東京移居美國。「當我第一次來到紐約，我感到非常孤獨。一切都是全新的、令人困惑的，所以放學後我大部分時間都是一個人度過。緩解無聊的唯一方法，就是花時間在家做飯。」
>
> 20 歲那年，木本先生沒有上大學，而是開始在波士頓一家義大利餐廳查樂斯擔任廚房工作人員。憑藉出色的能力和努力，他在短短兩年內就晉升主廚。在那裡，他學會了管理廚房員工，並烹飪各種義大利菜餚。隨著廚師聲譽提升，木本先生開始考慮開設自己的餐廳。(173) 在那裡擔任主廚三年後，他便離開查樂斯，搬回家鄉，開了一家小餐廳，名為伊拉特謝義大利餐廳，專精於日義融合菜餚。(172) 該餐廳很快就引起當地人極大興趣，開業僅一年就成為該地最受歡迎的用餐場所之一。
>
> (175) 木本先生的餐廳規模不斷擴張。該店已進行翻修並擴大了兩次，但仍需要更多空間來滿足顧客的需求。(174) 事實上，第二家伊拉特謝義大利餐廳將於下週末在日本橫濱開業。「我很高興能再開一家餐廳。我很感謝我所擁有的機會。我將繼續盡己所能，為當地居民提供優質的日義美食。」木本先生說道。

172. 文章主要在討論什麼？
    (A) 個人成就
    (B) 本地企業成功的條件
    (C) 當地餐飲趨勢
    (D) 開餐廳的成功之道 答案 (A)

173. 木本先生在開設自己的餐廳之前，以什麼為生？
    (A) 餐廳廚房工作人員
    (B) 查樂斯餐廳老闆
    (C) 大學生
    (D) 當地企業經理　　　　　　　　　答案 (A)

174. 根據文章所述，木本先生很快就要做什麼？
    (A) 僱用更多員工
    (B) 搬遷原來的餐廳
    (C) 開設另一家餐廳
    (D) 投資其他商業領域　　　　　　　答案 (C)

175. 以下句子最適合放在文中 [1]、[2]、[3] 和 [4] 的哪一個位置？
    「木本先生的餐廳規模不斷擴張。」
    (A) [1]
    (B) [2]
    (C) [3]
    (D) [4]　　　　　　　　　　　　　答案 (C)

問題 176-180，請參考以下收據及調查內容。

(176) 神奇智能

(176) 沒有什麼是我們無法解決的，所以請相信我們！

(177) 分店地點：
■曼徹斯特　　　□倫敦　　　□布拉德福德

(178) 到訪及取件日期：7 月 6 日
工作完成日期：7 月 22 日　　　服務編號：CR7902

客戶資訊	服務資訊
姓名：史蒂夫‧傑克遜	物品：洗衣機
地址：曼徹斯特里奇大道 134 號	品牌：沙拉特
電話：161-555-2267	型號：S3

服務說明	價格
• (176) 洗衣機漏水：更換門封和水泵	65.00 歐元
• 親訪及取件服務	15.00 歐元
• 送貨及安裝費用	12.00 歐元
小結	92.00 歐元
稅額	9.20 歐元
總計	101.20 歐元

付款日期	7 月 22 日
付款方式	現金

(179) 我們特別重視服務效率。因此，對於所有修復並送返中的時間比預期還更長的服務，我們將退款30%。請在技術人員領取設備時向您提供的調查表中，註明服務過程的總時長。

神奇智能

感謝您選擇神奇智能！請您花一些時間完成以下調查，以便我們改進服務，下次為您提供更優質的服務。

顧客姓名	(178) 史蒂夫‧傑克遜
取件日期	(179) 7 月 22 日
服務編號	CR7902
技術人員	(178) 威廉‧路克

請說明對以下方面的滿意度是……

	極佳	很好	不錯	不好
即時性				V
品質	V			
費用			V	

技術員的表現……？

	極佳	很好	不錯	不好
專業度	V			
禮貌	V			
知識量	V			

請留下您可能有的任何意見：

我必須說，我對這次的服務感到非常失望。(180) 服務品質一如既往地不錯、令人滿意，但耗費的時間相當令人沮喪。我 7 月 2 日打電話給神奇智能時，(179) 我被告知維修將於 7 月 10 日完成。然而，我已經被迫去當地洗衣店兩個多星期了，而我的洗衣機昨天才送達。我想我將來勢必會重新考慮是否繼續回來使用你們的服務。

176. 神奇智能最有可能屬於哪種業務？
    (A) 當地洗衣店
    (B) 船運公司
    (C) 維修服務供應商
    (D) 電器行　　　　　　　　　　　答案 (C)

177. 關於神奇智能，文中暗指什麼？
    (A) 要求顧客自行領取電器。
    (B) 向所有顧客提供折扣。
    (C) 它有多家分店。
    (D) 提供免費運輸和處理。　　　　答案 (C)

178. 關於路克先生，以下敘述何者最有可能是正確的？
    (A) 他填寫了一份調查問卷。
    (B) 他擁有一臺沙拉特製造的洗衣機。
    (C) 他於 7 月 6 日拜訪了傑克遜先生。
    (D) 他是神奇智能的新員工。　　　答案 (C)

179. 將來可能會發生什麼？
    (A) 傑克遜先生將收到一定金額的退款。
    (B) 修好的洗衣機將會送達。
    (C) 神奇智能將再次派出技術人員拜訪傑克遜先生。
    (D) 折扣券將過期。　　　　　　　答案 (A)

180. 問卷調查中暗指了什麼？
    (A) 傑克遜先生對新洗衣機的品質感到不滿。
    (B) 神奇智能的費用是該地區最便宜的。
    (C) 傑克遜先生以前曾光顧神奇智能。
    (D) 神奇智能已在出版品中獲得專題報導。　　答案 (C)

問題 181-185，請參考以下電子郵件。

> 收件人：(181) 尼古拉斯・卡丁斯基
> 　　　　　<nkadinsky@relectronics.com>
> 寄件人：(181) 艾琳・傑克遜
> 　　　　　<ejackson@relectronics.com>
> 日　　期：10 月 10 日
> 主　　旨：10 月 23 日至 24 日時間表
>
> 親愛的卡丁斯基先生，
>
> 相信您已知悉，(181) 您即將於 10 月 23 日至 24 日前往東京出差，而我只是在此稍作提醒。
>
> 您的航班將於上午 7:15 從洛杉磯機場起飛，(183) 10 月 23 日中午 12 點 50 分抵達東京機場（當地時間）。(183) 東京分公司的代表拓也彰將在機場問候並迎接您。隨後抵達櫻花飯店，與分店經理本田翼共進午餐。
>
> (184) 您將在期貨大會上發表專題演講，於下午 4:00 在櫻花飯店大會議廳進行。隨後，您將出席邀請所有與會公司執行長和總裁的宴會。
>
> 第二天早上，(182) 您將參加東京分公司會議廳舉行的董事會會議，討論公司下一會計年度的發展方向。您的回程航班於下午 4:25 起飛，抵達後我會到機場接您。
>
> 誠摯問候。
>
> 艾琳・傑克遜
> 首席秘書
> 拉米電子

> 收件人：本田翼 <thonda@relectronics.com>
> 寄件人：艾琳・傑克遜 <ejackson@relectronics.com>
> 日　　期：10 月 23 日
> 主　　旨：午餐預約取消
>
> 親愛的本田女士，
>
> 很遺憾通知您，卡丁斯基先生的航班因機械故障而延誤，因此他今天無法與您共進午餐。(183) 我已安排了比原定晚 2 小時起飛的備用航班。請配合重新安排時間表，以便能夠及時從機場接到卡丁斯基先生。
>
> 卡丁斯基先生對未能親自與您會面表示歉意，並希望將來還有機會。儘管有所延遲，他仍會在會議上發表專題演講。(185) 其餘日程維持不變。
>
> 誠摯問候。
>
> 艾琳・傑克遜

> 首席秘書
> 拉米電子

181. 傑克遜女士為什麼寄電子郵件給卡丁斯基先生？
    (A) 提供有關活動的詳細資訊
    (B) 索取會議議程
    (C) 概述出差計劃
    (D) 提醒部門會議　　答案 (C)

182. 卡丁斯基先生最有可能是誰？
    (A) 企業高層管理者
    (B) 分店經理
    (C) 區域代表
    (D) 首席秘書　　答案 (A)

183. 拓也先生將在 10 月 23 日做什麼？
    (A) 下午 4:00 發表專題演講
    (B) 與本田女士共進午餐
    (C) 從櫻花飯店接卡丁斯基先生
    (D) 下午 2:50 之前到達機場　　答案 (D)

184. 關於期貨大會，文中暗指什麼？
    (A) 僅供拉米電子員工參加。
    (B) 隨後將舉行正式晚宴。
    (C) 它將在洛杉磯舉行。
    (D) 它是由傑克遜女士組織的。　　答案 (B)

185. 第二封電子郵件中，第 2 段第 3 行中的「rest」，含義最接近
    (A) 休息
    (B) 細節
    (C) 剩餘
    (D) 添加　　答案 (C)

問題 186-190，請參考以下資訊、網頁及電子郵件。

> ### 《自己做》雜誌
>
> 尼爾森出版社很高興宣布，我們的多樣雜誌又增加了新內容。(187) 過去十年，我們將關注點從女性興趣擴展到其他領域。今年的新增項目將於 5 月推出。
>
> 《自己做》是同類雜誌中的先驅。(186) 透過《自己做》，您可以選擇自己感興趣的主題，並將其編輯成個人化的月刊。(189) 尼爾森出版社提供十二種不同的類別供你選擇。訂閱費率根據您想要的類別數量而有所不同。

會員等級	類別數量	訂閱費率
白金會員	6	每年 200 美元
黃金會員	4	每年 170 美元
銀色會員	2	每年 145 美元

(190) 白金會員將額外獲得三個月分的雜誌，及一本免費暢銷小說。訂閱《自己做》時，請輸入您想要的小說圖書代碼。書籍和代碼列表，可以在尼爾森出版社的網站上找到。黃金會員將額外獲得一個月分的雜誌。

看看我們為已訂閱尼爾森出版社雜誌的人提供的獨家促銷活動。第一年訂閱《自己做》，將獲得 50% 折扣。此優惠將從 5 月持續至 8 月。

(188) 立即訂閱《自己做》，我們將在 30 天內把它交到您手中！

---

www.nielsenpublishing.com/subscribe/payment/
confirmation

尼爾森出版社
(187) **10007 紐約，錢伯斯街 120 號**

首頁	訂閱	贊助	聯絡我們

訂閱已確認。
感謝您訂閱《自己做》！

日期	(188) **6 月 19 日**
姓名	凱爾西・佩里
電話	917-659-7834
地址	12520 紐約，康沃爾哈德遜，山路 98 號

收到付款：200 美元
訂閱詳情：

商業經濟	**V**	科學自然		運動娛樂	**V**	時尚風格
親子教養		(189) 健康塑身	**V**	文學小說	**V**	音樂
V	生活風格	**V**	醫療		新聞政治		兒童相關

您的贈書代碼：＿＿＿＿＿＿＿＿＿＿＿＿＿＿＿

* 白金級會員如果將贈書代碼欄留空，將隨機選擇一本書籍。

收件人：<customerservice@nielsonpublishing.com>
寄件人：<kperry@personalmail.com>
日　期：6 月 20 日
主　旨：我的訂閱

敬啟者，

我剛剛發現我遺漏了訂閱時要一併發送的特殊代碼。(190) 我想要的代碼是 5954-93A。請確保將其添加到我的訂閱紀錄中。非常感謝。

期待盡快收到我的第一期雜誌。

誠摯感謝。

凱爾西・佩里

---

186. 關於《自己做》，文中提到什麼？
(A) 深受讀者歡迎。
(B) 每月出版一次。
(C) 將於 5 月在書店發售。
(D) 已出版十年。　　　　　　答案 (B)

187. 關於尼爾森出版社，文中暗指什麼？
(A) 專門提供女性雜誌。
(B) 在多個國家出版雜誌。
(C) 總部位於錢伯斯街。
(D) 出版許多暢銷小說。　　　答案 (C)

188. 佩里女士什麼時候會收到她的第一期《自己做》？
(A) 5 月
(B) 6 月
(C) 7 月
(D) 8 月　　　　　　　　　　答案 (C)

189. 佩里女士對哪個主題不感興趣？
(A) 文學小說
(B) 醫療
(C) 時尚風格
(D) 健康塑身　　　　　　　　答案 (D)

190. 佩里女士為了什麼寄電子郵件？
(A) 選擇一本免費小說
(B) 提出她想要的附贈雜誌名稱
(C) 讚揚雜誌的品質
(D) 要求延長她的訂閱期限　　答案 (A)

問題 191-195，請參考以下文章、電子郵件及新聞稿。

國際百利堡獎即將頒發
作者：弗蘭克・詹姆森

北阿靈頓（9 月 19 日）—— (191) **9 月 28 日**，國際百利堡獎頒獎典禮將一如過去 80 年，在百利堡中心舉行。此獎項旨在表彰在文學領域取得傑出成就的作家。(194) 獲獎者將得到 **8,000 美元**現金和一枚獎牌。今年，評選出了 4 位提名者：羅莎・佩里、賈斯汀・奧特、吉納維芙・斯威夫特和布魯斯・摩爾。

佩里女士和摩爾先生都是獲獎作家。佩里女士的提名作品《煙火》如同她的許多小說，屬於傳記類型。摩爾先生的《一路》講述了名叫盧克・韋斯特的年輕男孩的悲慘愛情故事。

賈斯汀・奧特的《永不言敗》獲得提名。奧特先生在上個月的巴黎圖書節接受我們採訪時表示，他的冒險主題作品，多少是基於自己年輕時在家鄉墨爾本的經歷。

(192) (195) 入選作品《歸屬》最值得注意的一點，在於它是吉納維芙・斯威夫特的第一部小說。「去年，我終於辭掉教師工作，專心寫作。(193) 當我在書店看到我的小說，我想我終於實現了夢想。」斯威夫特女士說道。

欲了解更多資訊和歷屆獲獎名單，請至國際百利堡獎網站 www.ipaliberqaward.org。

---

(194) 收件人：賈斯汀・奧特 <jotter@ccpmail.com>
寄件人：賽琳娜・傑特森 <sjetson@kearnyhs.edu>
日　期：9 月 30 日
主　旨：恭喜！

你好，賈斯汀。

(194) 恭喜你榮獲國際百利堡獎。當我在提名名單上看到你的小說時，就毫不懷疑你會得獎。

我注意到，書中的蘋果農場曾經是我父親所擁有的。我記得暑假期間，我們會一起幫父親的忙。幾年前我們搬到紐約後，我們就很難保持聯繫。讀你的書，讓我想起了我們在家鄉一起度過的時光。

再次恭喜！希望能早日收到你的消息。

誠摯問候。

賽琳娜

即時發布

報春花出版社剛剛與吉納維芙・斯威夫特簽訂了獨家寫作合約。斯威夫特女士將在未來 6 年內出版 5 本書。(195) 第一本書，書名暫定為《天鵝湖》，是斯威夫特幾個月前出版的《歸屬》續集。有關這項新交易的更多資訊，請參閱 www.primrosepublishing.com。

191. 關於國際百利堡獎，文中暗指什麼？
    (A) 它成立於大約 80 年前。
    (B) 只頒給了兩位小說作家。
    (C) 由當地企業贊助。
    (D) 接受作者私人報名。　　　　答案 (A)

192. 誰是前教育家？
    (A) 弗蘭克・詹姆森
    (B) 羅莎・佩里
    (C) 吉納維芙・斯威夫特
    (D) 盧克・韋斯特　　　　答案 (C)

193. 文章中，第 4 段第 3 行的「realized」，含義最接近
    (A) 擁有
    (B) 履行
    (C) 認可
    (D) 理解　　　　答案 (B)

194. 關於奧特先生，以下敘述何者正確？
    (A) 他被百利堡中心聘用。
    (B) 他獲得獎金。
    (C) 他過去因作品而得過其他獎項。
    (D) 他主修文學。　　　　答案 (B)

195. 關於斯威夫特女士，文中暗指什麼？
    (A) 她的第二部小說書名是《天鵝湖》。
    (B) 她無法出席頒獎典禮。
    (C) 她將與奧特先生合作一部新作品。
    (D) 她白天工作，晚上寫作。　　　　答案 (A)

問題 196-200，請參考以下備忘錄、電子郵件及意見表。

收件人：全體員工
寄件人：艾琳・林賽，人力資源總監
主　旨：員工培訓
日　期：9 月 21 日

我們將在本週末安裝新機器。我們正從合成公司購買電腦、從最佳康普購買印表機、(197) (198) 從泡德之家購買影印機，以及從廷代爾購買掃描機。我們更換了大量設備，(196) 因此必須盡快對所有員工進行如何正確使用所有設備的培訓。以下是 9 月 28 日星期一和 9 月 29 日星期二的培訓課程安排：

日期／時間	部門
9 月 28 日上午 9:00 - 中午 12:00	業務
9 月 28 日下午 1:00 - 下午 4:00	會計、人力資源
9 月 29 日上午 10:00 - 下午 1:00	研發
(199) 9 月 29 日下午 2:00 - 下午 5:00	行銷

請務必跟你的同事一起適時參加培訓課程。如果你無法參加指定的課程，請撥打分機 89 與我聯繫。我會盡力將你安排至另一場。

收件人：哈羅德・馬丁
　　　　<harold_martin@powderhouse.com>
寄件人：艾琳・林賽 <elindsey@watsontech.com>
日　期：9 月 23 日
主　旨：謝謝

馬丁先生，

(197) (198) 感謝你告知我泡德之家最近為長期客戶提供的促銷活動。根據這項資訊，我想購買 6 臺 XJ45，而不是只買 5 臺。希望你能滿足這個要求。我仍然希望在這週末將所有機器送達，並在公司安裝好。如果我的需求有任何問題，請讓我知道。

誠摯問候。

艾琳・林賽
沃森科技人力資源總監

(199) 培訓日期／時間：**9 月 29 日下午 2:00**

員工姓名：雷吉娜‧斯圖爾特

評論：

我認為培訓課程整體上非常有幫助。培訓師非常了解他
們要教我們使用的設備，也願意回答我們的所有問題。
(200) 不過，我希望廷爾代表可以向我們提供講義。
我不得不寫下她告訴我們的一切，我擔心會沒有記下所
有必要的資訊。

196. 此備忘錄的目的之一是什麼？
(A) 向員工索取工作時間表
(B) 確認即將搬遷的辦公室
(C) 為員工分配培訓時段
(D) 要求志工在週末工作　　　　　　　答案 (C)

197. 關於沃森科技，文中暗指什麼？
(A) 週末將把辦公室搬到新地點。
(B) 正為即將舉行的課程提供內部培訓師。
(C) 過去曾從泡德之家購買過設備。
(D) 需要新設備，因為它最近僱用了更多員工。
　　　　　　　　　　　　　　　　　答案 (C)

198. 林賽女士能夠以折扣價購買哪項設備？
(A) 電腦
(B) 印表機
(C) 影印機
(D) 掃描機　　　　　　　　　　　　　答案 (C)

199. 斯圖爾特女士最有可能在哪個部門工作？
(A) 業務
(B) 會計
(C) 研發
(D) 行銷　　　　　　　　　　　　　　答案 (D)

200. 斯圖爾特女士提到了什麼問題？
(A) 她提出的問題沒有得到答覆。
(B) 她的培訓沒有準時開始。
(C) 沒有向她提供書面說明。
(D) 她培訓時使用的某些設備無法正常運作。　答案 (C)

Actual Test 04
Part 1

1. 美國 M
(A) A woman is reaching for a test tube on the shelf.
(B) A woman is wearing a lab coat.
(C) A woman is stocking some cabinets.
(D) A woman is pulling on some gloves.

(A) 一名女子正伸手拿架子上的試管。
(B) 一名女子正穿著實驗服。
(C) 一名女子正在填裝櫥櫃。
(D) 一名女子正在戴上手套。　　　　答案 (B)

2. 美國 W
(A) The woman is lifting up some documents.
(B) The woman is leaning toward a display case.
(C) The woman is resting her arm on a cabinet.
(D) The woman is gazing out the window.

(A) 女子正拿起一些文件。
(B) 女子正俯身靠向展示櫃。
(C) 女子將手臂放在櫃子上。
(D) 女子正凝視著窗外。　　　　　　答案 (C)

3. 澳洲 W
(A) Both of the men are putting on their masks.
(B) One of the men is pulling his suitcase on the runway.
(C) Some people are stepping out of a vehicle.
(D) They are gathered around the tour group.

(A) 兩名男子正戴上口罩。
(B) 其中一名男子正在跑道上拉行李箱。
(C) 有些人正在走下車。
(D) 他們聚集在旅行團周圍。　　　　答案 (B)

4. 美國 M
(A) A piano is being worked on.
(B) A woman is singing to the piano.
(C) A man is seated at a piano.
(D) A piano is located near an entrance.

(A) 一架鋼琴正在修理中。
(B) 一名女子正對著鋼琴唱歌。
(C) 一名男子坐在鋼琴前。
(D) 一架鋼琴被擺在入口附近。　　　答案 (C)

5. 澳洲 W
(A) A man has stopped at a desk.
(B) A man is typing on a keyboard.
(C) A woman is drinking from her cup.
(D) A woman is arranging some office supplies.

(A) 男子停在辦公桌前。
(B) 男子正在用鍵盤打字。
(C) 女子正用她的杯子喝水。
(D) 女子正在整理一些辦公用品。　　　　答案 (A)

6. 英國 M

(A) A carpet is being installed in the conference room.
(B) A presentation slide is being projected on a screen.
(C) Refreshments are being served to the attendees.
(D) Some chairs have been arranged for a meeting.

(A) 會議室正在鋪設地毯。
(B) 簡報投影片正被投射到螢幕上。
(C) 茶點正提供給與會者。
(D) 已經為會議布置了一些椅子。　　　　答案 (D)

Part 2

7. 美國 M 澳洲 W

Do you know where the X-ray room is located?
(A) This morning, I think.
(B) Yes, she's a medical doctor.
(C) On the 3rd floor.

你知道 X 光室在哪裡嗎？
(A) 我想是今天早上吧。
(B) 是的，她是一名醫生。
(C) 在三樓。　　　　答案 (C)

8. 美國 W 英國 M

Will you be in the office this afternoon?
(A) Sure, here you are.
(B) The new copier in the office.
(C) No, I am supposed to meet a client.

今天下午你會在辦公室嗎？
(A) 當然好，給你。
(B) 辦公室裡的新影印機。
(C) 不，我要去見一位客戶。　　　　答案 (C)

9. 澳洲 W 美國 M

When will the new landscaping crew arrive?
(A) I like your new garden.
(B) Right after noon.
(C) I didn't do it until this morning.

新的造景人員什麼時候會到？
(A) 我喜歡你的新花園。
(B) 就在中午過後。
(C) 直到今天早上我才去做。　　　　答案 (B)

10. 美國 W 英國 M

How long have you worked for Mr. Sanchez?
(A) Work extra hours.
(B) 3 kilometers away from here.
(C) For about one and a half years.

你為桑契斯先生工作了多久？
(A) 加班。
(B) 距離這裡 3 公里。
(C) 大約一年半。　　　　答案 (C)

11. 美國 M 美國 W

How do you get to the laboratory from here?
(A) Aren't they included in the invoice?
(B) Just go upstairs and you'll see it on the right.
(C) I ordered more test tubes.

你從這裡怎麼去實驗室？
(A) 它們沒有含在發票裡嗎？
(B) 走上樓後，你就會看到它在右邊。
(C) 我訂購了更多試管。　　　　答案 (B)

12. 澳洲 W 英國 M

Who will take over now that Harry retires?
(A) In-Sook in human resources.
(B) Yes, I'll send a technician over right away.
(C) I'm tired of working overtime.

哈利退休後誰會接任？
(A) 人力資源部的仁淑。
(B) 是的，我會立刻派技術人員過去。
(C) 我厭倦了加班。　　　　答案 (A)

13. 美國 W 美國 M

The contract has to be sent out soon, doesn't it?
(A) Yes. I'll go ahead and mail it right away.
(B) You have the wrong contact information.
(C) You can get some at the post office downtown.

合約必須盡快送出，不是嗎？
(A) 是的，我會處理，馬上寄出。
(B) 你的聯絡資訊有誤。
(C) 你可以在市中心的郵局買一些。　　　　答案 (A)

14. 英國 M 美國 W

The chef's special soup doesn't have any meat in it, does it?
(A) I'd like a steak, too.
(B) Actually, it does.
(C) It looks like the restaurant is open.

主廚特調湯品裡面沒有肉，對吧？
(A) 我也想要一塊牛排。
(B) 事實上，裡面有。
(C) 看起來餐廳已經開門了。　　　　答案 (B)

15. 美國 M 英國 M

What time does the out-of-town client want to meet?
(A) No, they aren't in town.
(B) Anytime in the afternoon is fine.
(C) Probably from a local supplier.

外地客戶想要什麼時候見面？
(A) 不，他們不在城裡。
(B) 下午任何時間都行。
(C) 可能來自在地供應商。　　　　答案 (B)

16. 美國 W 澳洲 W

Make sure to reschedule your appointment for next week.
(A) I'm not sure if he did.
(B) I'll do it right away.
(C) An hour-long regular check-up.

務必重新安排你下週的預約。
(A) 我不確定他做了沒。
(B) 我馬上去做。
(C) 一個小時的定期檢查。　　　　答案 (B)

17. 美國 M 澳洲 W

Why is Joseph carrying a suitcase?
(A) Take it to the dry cleaners.
(B) His flight leaves at 7.
(C) We don't carry that suitcase brand.

約瑟夫為什麼帶著行李箱？
(A) 把它帶去乾洗店。
(B) 他的班機 7 點起飛。
(C) 我們不銷售那個品牌的行李箱。　答案 (B)

18. 美國 W 英國 M

Have you heard about the new movie directed by Tom Cameron?
(A) The movie theater is newly built.
(B) I heard it got great reviews.
(C) Aren't they moving today?

你有聽說湯姆・卡麥隆執導的新電影消息嗎？
(A) 這間電影院是新建的。
(B) 我聽說它獲得了很好的評價。
(C) 他們今天不搬家嗎？　　　　答案 (B)

19. 澳洲 W 美國 M

When can we see the safety training schedule?
(A) It was a great training session.
(B) Didn't you get the e-mail?
(C) We're expecting more than 100 people.

我們什麼時候會看到安全培訓的時間表？
(A) 這是一次很棒的培訓課程。
(B) 你沒有收到電子郵件嗎？
(C) 我們預計會超過 100 人。　　　答案 (B)

20. 英國 M 美國 W

Are you leading the workshop for new employees this afternoon or am I?
(A) He is unemployed at the moment.
(B) I work out every morning.
(C) Susan is going to take my place.

今天下午的新進員工工作坊是由你主持，還是我？
(A) 他目前沒有工作。
(B) 我每天早上都鍛鍊身體。
(C) 蘇珊會接替我的位置。　　　　答案 (C)

21. 美國 M 英國 M

Could you let Elaine know that a package has been delivered for her?
(A) She's at a doctor's appointment.
(B) I'd like to send this to her by express mail.
(C) We are out of packing materials.

你可以讓伊琳知道包裹已經送給她了嗎？
(A) 她正在看醫生。
(B) 我想用快遞把這個寄給她。
(C) 我們的包裝材料用完了。　　　答案 (A)

22. 美國 W 英國 M

Is Loraine here at the factory today?
(A) I saw her car in the parking area.
(B) Be sure to put on a safety helmet.
(C) Yours is down the hall.

洛蘭今天在工廠這邊嗎？
(A) 我在停車場看到她的車。
(B) 務必戴好安全帽。
(C) 你的在走廊那頭。　　　　　答案 (A)

23. 美國 M 澳洲 W

What location do you think would be good for a second store?
(A) There aren't any properties available nearby.
(B) You can buy it at a convenience store.
(C) Hang it on the wall above the table.

你認為什麼地點適合開第二家店？
(A) 這附近沒有任何可以取得的店面了。
(B) 你可以在便利商店購買。
(C) 把它掛在桌子上方的牆上。　　答案 (A)

24. 美國 W 美國 M

You watched the video about the workplace safety, didn't you?
(A) It was a requirement for all the factory workers.
(B) My watch needs to be fixed.
(C) A cabinet for safety goggles.

你看過關於工作場所安全的影片了，不是嗎？
(A) 這是對所有工廠工人的要求。
(B) 我的手錶需要修理。
(C) 放置安全護目鏡的櫃子。　　　答案 (A)

25. 美國 M　澳洲 W

Where do you think these summer blouses should be displayed?
(A) Yes, around five degrees Celsius below zero.
(B) Don't we have to move some items?
(C) I prefer winter sports.

你認為這些夏季襯衫應該在哪裡展示？
(A) 是的，大約攝氏零下五度。
(B) 我們不用移動某些品項嗎？
(C) 我比較喜歡冬季運動。　　　答案 (B)

26. 美國 W　英國 M

Why hasn't production on the commercial been finished?
(A) That sounds like a good idea.
(B) The deadline's been changed.
(C) Thirty seconds long.

為什麼那個廣告的製作還沒有完成？
(A) 這聽起來是個好主意。
(B) 截止日期已變更。
(C) 30 秒長。　　　答案 (B)

27. 美國 M　澳洲 W

Would you like me to show you where the human resources office is?
(A) Yes, I really enjoyed the talk show.
(B) All the positions have been filled.
(C) Nick gave me directions.

你需要我帶你看看人資辦公室在哪裡嗎？
(A) 是的，我真的很喜歡這個脫口秀。
(B) 所有職缺都已補齊。
(C) 尼克告訴我怎麼走了。　　　答案 (C)

28. 英國 M　美國 W

You want to buy a pair of glasses, don't you?
(A) Somebody broke the window.
(B) I'm having trouble with my car.
(C) I purchased some reasonable contact lenses.

你想買一副眼鏡，不是嗎？
(A) 有人打破窗戶。
(B) 我的車出了問題。
(C) 我買了一些價格合理的隱形眼鏡。　　　答案 (C)

29. 美國 W　美國 M

Who's the sales representative for Janson Medical Supplies?
(A) I think I have their business card.
(B) She got a promotion.
(C) A 20% discount on oxygen tanks.

傑森醫療用品的業務代表是誰？
(A) 我想我有他們的名片。
(B) 她獲得升遷了。
(C) 氧氣瓶有 20% 折扣。　　　答案 (A)

30. 美國 W　英國 M

Does Mr. Nelson have any experience in information technology?
(A) Yes, I am an experienced repairman.
(B) We need someone with a background in online marketing.
(C) It's a state-of-the-art technology.

尼爾森先生有任何資訊科技方面的經驗嗎？
(A) 是的，我是經驗豐富的維修人員。
(B) 我們需要具備線上行銷背景的人。
(C) 這是一項最先進的技術。　　　答案 (B)

31. 英國 M　澳洲 W

I'd like to promote Dan to marketing director.
(A) Do you have a promotional code for this item?
(B) No, it's already been on the market.
(C) He hasn't worked here long enough.

我想提拔丹擔任行銷總監。
(A) 你有這個品項的促銷代碼嗎？
(B) 不，它已經上市了。
(C) 他在這裡工作的時間還不夠長。　　　答案 (C)

Part 3

問題 **32-34**，請參考以下對話內容。　澳洲 W　美國 M

W: Greg, (32)**could I take a look at the budget for the yoga class I'm going to teach here at the community center this coming semester?**

M: Of course. I'll be able to pull it up on my computer in no time. Why do you want to see it?

W: (33)**I purchased some new yoga mats for some students yesterday,** but they cost a lot. I wonder if there's any money in the budget to get some other equipment I could use.

M: It doesn't look like there's much left. (34)**However, we could plan a community fundraiser for new supplies.**

W: That's a great idea. How about meeting tomorrow morning to discuss what to do?

女：格雷格，我可以看看下學期我在這個社區中心教瑜珈課的預算嗎？

男：當然。我很快就可以用電腦調出來。你為什麼想看？

女：我昨天買了一些新的瑜珈墊給學生，但它們花了很多錢。我想知道預算裡還有沒有錢可以買我用得上的其他裝備。

男：看來所剩無幾。不過，我們可以為新的用品規劃一次社區募款活動。

女：好主意。明早開會討論一下該怎麼做，如何？

32. 女子最有可能是誰？
   (A) 瑜珈教練
   (B) 烹飪老師
   (C) 實驗室技術員
   (D) 程式設計師　　　　　　　　　答案 (A)

33. 女子說她最近做了什麼？
   (A) 加入健身中心。
   (B) 轉換部門。
   (C) 購買一些用品。
   (D) 審視預算。　　　　　　　　　答案 (C)

34. 男子有什麼建議？
   (A) 重複使用某些物品
   (B) 添購額外的裝備
   (C) 與他們的上級會面
   (D) 舉辦募款活動　　　　　　　　答案 (D)

問題 35-37，請參考以下對話內容。 英國 M 美國 W

M: Good morning, Lucy. (35)**You are all prepared for the online marketing training session, aren't you?** I think I have all of the materials ready.

W: Yes, and the conference room is just about ready. (36)**The projector and the desks have been set up, but we need facility services to return. I requested 25 laptops.**

M: (36)**Oh, yeah? Okay, I'll give them a call.** In that case, why don't you go to the cafeteria? (37)**We are going to pick up the meal vouchers for the attendees before they arrive.**

男：早安，露西。你已經為線上行銷培訓課程做好準備了，對嗎？我想我已經準備好所有素材了。

女：是的，會議室快準備好了。投影機和桌子也都擺好了。但我們需要設備服務團隊回來，我要了 25 臺筆記型電腦。

男：哦，是嗎？好，我來打電話給他們。這樣的話，你何不先去員工餐廳呢？我們要在參加者到達之前領好餐券。

35. 談話者正在討論什麼活動？
   (A) 培訓計劃
   (B) 迎新會
   (C) 慈善午宴
   (D) 產品演示會　　　　　　　　　答案 (A)

36. 女子說「我要了 25 臺筆記型電腦」，是在暗示什麼？
   (A) 她計劃舉辦線上會議。
   (B) 請求沒有被妥善滿足。
   (C) 並非每個人都會參加活動。
   (D) 有些機器故障了。　　　　　　答案 (B)

37. 男子要求女子做什麼？
   (A) 付款
   (B) 領取一些餐券
   (C) 預訂活動場地
   (D) 打掃房間　　　　　　　　　　答案 (B)

問題 38-40，請參考以下對話內容。 澳洲 W 美國 M

W: Mr. Jacobs, I determined the nature of the problem. (38)**The leak is coming from your second-floor bathroom sink.**

M: Is that so?

W: Yes. I turned off the water there, so no more water is coming out. You're in luck because there doesn't appear to be any major water damage to the floor.

M: That's great. Thanks. (39)**Can you fix it now? I need to get this problem taken care of so that I can return to work.**

W: I don't know. (40)**Let me run out to my truck to see if I have the necessary parts.** I'll be back in a moment.

女：雅各布斯先生，我確定問題的源頭了。漏水來自二樓浴室的洗手臺。

男：是這樣嗎？

女：是的。我關掉那裡的水之後，就不再有水流出來了。你很幸運，因為地板看起來沒有受到水的嚴重損害。

男：那太好了。謝謝。你現在能修好它嗎？我需要解決這個問題，這樣才能回去上班。

女：我不確定。等我到我的卡車那裡，看看有沒有需要的零件。我等一下就回來。

38. 女子提到什麼問題？
   (A) 卡車的引擎無法發動。
   (B) 烤箱壞了。
   (C) 浴室窗戶卡住了。
   (D) 洗手臺漏水。　　　　　　　　答案 (D)

39. 男子問了什麼事？
    (A) 某些工具放在哪裡
    (B) 他需要付多少錢
    (C) 何時可以修好
    (D) 如何填寫表格　　　　　　　　答案 (C)

40. 女子說她接下來會做什麼？
    (A) 查看她的工具箱
    (B) 檢查房子的其他地方
    (C) 找一些零件
    (D) 打電話給她的主管　　　　　　答案 (C)

問題 41-43，請參考以下對話內容。 美國 M 美國 W

M: Mr. Reynolds is sending me to Paris next week.
   (41)**He wants me to make a presentation on our latest findings at a seminar there.**
W: That sounds fun. Have you visited Paris before?
M: No, I've never been there.
W: I went there on vacation once. Aside from the popular places, (42)**be sure to visit La Salle. It serves the best food in the city.**
M: Oh, yeah? Well, I do have one free evening. I wonder if I need to make a reservation. (43)**I'll do an online search during my next break.** Thanks.

男：雷諾茲先生下週要派我去巴黎。他希望我在那裡的研討會上，介紹我們的最新發現。
女：聽起來很有趣。你以前去過巴黎嗎？
男：不，我從來沒有去過那裡。
女：我度假時去過一次。除了熱門景點外，一定要光顧拉薩爾餐廳。它們有全城最好的餐點。
男：哦，是嗎？嗯，我確實有一個晚上有空閒時間。我好奇是否需要預約。我下次休息時會上網查看。謝謝。

----

41. 男子出差的目的是什麼？
    (A) 展現某些成果
    (B) 與新的供應商會面
    (C) 簽訂合約
    (D) 展示產品　　　　　　　　　　答案 (A)

42. 女子建議男子去哪裡？
    (A) 博物館
    (B) 劇院區
    (C) 餐廳
    (D) 紀念碑　　　　　　　　　　　答案 (C)

43. 男子說他在休息時間會做什麼？
    (A) 進行搜尋
    (B) 預訂機票
    (C) 找一些門票
    (D) 聯絡他的客戶　　　　　　　　答案 (A)

問題 44-46，請參考以下對話內容。 美國 W 英國 M

W: (44)**On this morning's show, we've got Eric Stark, the CEO of Wilson Media.** He's here to discuss his company's amazing rise to fame in the Internet news industry.
M: Thanks a lot for having me on.
W: Thank you for finding the time from your busy schedule to come to our show. (45)**I also know that you made a presentation at the New Haven Online News Convention last week.**
M: That's right. The convention was a lot of fun.
W: (46)**What do you think the key to your success is?**
M: (46)**Well, my employees are incredibly dedicated and reliable.**
W: I think that's a good point.

女：在今天早上的節目中，我們邀請到威爾遜媒體公司的執行長艾瑞克‧史塔克。他要來談談公司在網路新聞產業的驚人崛起。
男：非常感謝你邀請我來。
女：感謝你在百忙之中抽空參加我們的節目。我還知道，你上週在紐海芬線上新聞大會上做了報告。
男：沒錯。那場大會非常有趣。
女：你認為你成功的關鍵是什麼？
男：嗯，我的員工非常敬業又可靠。
女：我認為這是一個很好的觀點。

44. 女子最有可能是誰？
    (A) 報社記者
    (B) 公司老闆
    (C) 脫口秀主持人
    (D) 廣告公司主管　　　　　　　　答案 (C)

45. 根據女子所說，男子最近為什麼很忙？
    (A) 他參加了一場大會。
    (B) 他正在培訓一些新員工。
    (C) 他寫了一些新聞報導。
    (D) 他做了一些採訪。　　　　　　答案 (A)

46. 男子為什麼說：「我的員工非常敬業又可靠」？
    (A) 針對新工作推薦他的員工
    (B) 協助與客戶簽訂新合約
    (C) 處理客戶投訴
    (D) 認可其他人的貢獻　　　　　　答案 (D)

問題 47-49，請參考以下對話內容。 澳洲 W 英國 M

W: Hello, Stan. How about an update on the things you are currently working on?
M: No problem. (47)**I'm focusing on reading the**

results from customer satisfaction surveys about our travel magazine. Lots of readers have been complaining that we don't have many articles on foreign destinations.

W: (48)**Well, the cost of traveling overseas has significantly increased.** I'm afraid we can't afford to dispatch more writers abroad, which cost us a lot.

M: (49)**Why don't we reach out to writers and travel guides living in foreign countries?** I'm sure they would know about a lot of interesting stuff to do in their regions and (49)**willingly work for us on a part-time basis.**

女：哈囉，史坦。更新一下你最近在忙些什麼事情，怎麼樣？

男：沒問題。我正專注閱讀客戶對我們旅遊雜誌的滿意度調查結果。很多讀者抱怨我們沒有國外去處的文章。

女：嗯，出國旅遊的成本明顯增加了。恐怕我們無力負擔讓更多撰稿人到國外去，這會讓我們花很多錢。

男：我們何不聯繫住在國外的撰稿人和導遊呢？我相信他們知道當地有什麼有趣的事情可以做，也願意用兼差的形式跟我們合作。

47. 男子一直在做什麼？
    (A) 面試求職者
    (B) 撰寫關於國際旅遊的文章
    (C) 閱讀調查結果
    (D) 更新部分規則　　　　　　　　答案 (C)

48. 女子提到什麼問題？
    (A) 部分成本上升了。
    (B) 一家公司的分店即將關閉。
    (C) 某些設備故障。
    (D) 撰稿人不願意出國。　　　　　答案 (A)

49. 男子建議做什麼？
    (A) 把部分員工調往新分店
    (B) 允許電子支付
    (C) 製作雜誌的線上版本
    (D) 招募更多工作人員　　　　　　答案 (D)

問題 **50-52**，請參考以下對話內容。 澳洲 M 美國 W

W: (50)**Jason, I just reviewed the budget proposal. I like it. I think we can make a presentation to the board of directors this Friday.**

M: Oh, I was about to call you. (51)**I was given some updated numbers from the Accounting Department.** We have to revise the budget. There won't be major changes, but we need to start working on it now.

W: (52)**Well, I have a meeting with a client in ten minutes.** I don't have time to do it today.

M: I'll take care of it then. We can go over everything tomorrow morning.

W: Sounds great. Thanks.

女：傑森，我剛剛審視了預算提案。我喜歡。我想我們本週五可以向董事會做簡報。

男：哦，我正想打電話給你。會計部門給了我一些最新數字。我們必須修改預算。不會有重大變化，但我們需要現在就開始處理。

女：嗯，十分鐘後我要和客戶開會。我今天沒有時間做這件事。

男：那我來處理。明天早上我們可以把所有事情都討論一遍。

女：聽起來很棒。謝謝。

50. 談話者主要在討論什麼？
    (A) 空缺職位
    (B) 預算提案
    (C) 廣告活動
    (D) 出差　　　　　　　　　　　　答案 (B)

51. 男子說他收到什麼？
    (A) 工作機會
    (B) 餐券
    (C) 新資訊
    (D) 銷售數字　　　　　　　　　　答案 (C)

52. 女子接下來最有可能做什麼？
    (A) 與客戶會面
    (B) 進行一場簡報
    (C) 重新安排會議時間
    (D) 參加午餐會　　　　　　　　　答案 (A)

問題 **53-55**，請參考以下三方對話內容。 澳洲 W 美國 M 英國 M

W: (53)**Pardon me, but could either of you recommend a marble cutter? I have to cut and install a lot of marble soon, (54)but the cutting machine I have is heavy and bulky. I need something that's easy to use and carry to worksites by myself.**

M1: Of course. The 840T is the best item on the market. It's tough but lightweight and even on wheels.

M2: In addition, you can fold up its legs, so you can fit it in your van easily.

W: That sounds fantastic, but I'm not really interested in spending $1,300.

M1: It's not cheap, but it's a great investment if you stay in the business. I'm sure it is worth the price. (55) **Todd can demonstrate how to use it.**

M2: (55)**Sure. Let me show you how simple it is to use.**

女：不好意思，你們誰可以推薦一款大理石切割機？我很快就需要切割和鋪設大量大理石，但我的切割機又重又占空間。我需要易於使用，也方便自己帶到工作場所的機型。

男1：當然。840T 是市場上最好的產品。它堅固，重量又輕，甚至還有輪子。

男2：除此之外，你可以折疊它的腳架，這樣就可以輕鬆把它放進貨車中。

女：聽起來很棒，但我對於花費 1,300 美元不太感興趣。

男1：雖然不便宜，但如果你待在這行，這是一筆很好的投資。我確信它物有所值。陶德可以示範如何使用。

男2：沒問題。讓我來示範它有多容易使用。

---

53. 這場對話最有可能在哪裡進行？
    (A) 建築工地
    (B) 免稅店
    (C) 五金行
    (D) 租車公司　　　　　　　　　答案 (C)

54. 女子說她在尋找具備什麼的產品？
    (A) 延長保固期
    (B) 耐用的材料
    (C) 搬運便利性
    (D) 防水性　　　　　　　　　　答案 (C)

55. 陶德接下來可能會做什麼？
    (A) 展示使用者指南
    (B) 安排送貨
    (C) 給予示範
    (D) 提供折扣　　　　　　　　　答案 (C)

問題 56-58，請參考以下對話內容。 美國 W 美國 M

W: (56)**Thanks for coming to the Westside Hotel.** What can I do for you?

M: Hello. (57)**I'm the electrician you asked for. I heard there are some problems with the lighting in some of your guestrooms.**

W: Oh, thanks for coming. Please follow me to the second floor. (58)**We just underwent a few renovations on that floor last week**, and everything seems to be working fine, but the lights in some of the rooms have been flickering since we were done with the work. I am wondering if there might be a problem with the circuit.

女：感謝您蒞臨西區飯店。我能為您做什麼呢？

男：你好。我是你要找的電工。聽說你們某幾間客房的照明有問題。

女：哦，謝謝你過來。請跟我到二樓。上週我們剛對那層樓做了一些裝修，一切似乎都運作良好，但在我們完工之後，有些房間的燈光一直在閃。我想也許電路有問題。

---

56. 這場對話在哪裡進行？
    (A) 機場
    (B) 辦公大樓
    (C) 飯店
    (D) 超市　　　　　　　　　　　答案 (C)

57. 男子為何前往該企業？
    (A) 安裝照明燈具
    (B) 修理電燈
    (C) 重新裝潢房間
    (D) 粉刷牆壁　　　　　　　　　答案 (B)

58. 女子說上週發生了什麼事？
    (A) 購買一些設備。
    (B) 新房客入住。
    (C) 進行裝修。
    (D) 營業時間延長。　　　　　　答案 (C)

問題 59-61，請參考以下三方對話內容。 美國 M 美國 W 澳洲 W

M: Good morning. Thank you for visiting Star Bank.

W1: Hello. I'm Sarah Doyle. (59)**I have a car dealership here, and I'd love to take out a small business loan to fund some advertisements.**

M: That sounds great. (60)**But I'm not in charge of discussing business loans. Let me talk to one of our loan officers.** Excuse me, Justine. This is Ms. Doyle. She'd like to apply for a business loan.

W2: Wonderful. It's great to meet you, Ms. Doyle. Do you have an account with us?

W1: Yes, I have one.

W2: (61)**Good because that's a requirement for customers requesting loans. Only current account holders qualify for loans.**

男：早安。感謝您蒞臨星銀行。

女1：你好。我是莎拉・多伊爾。我在這裡經營一家汽車經銷商，我想申請一筆小額企業貸款來資助廣告費用。

男：聽起來很棒。但我不負責商議企業貸款。讓我和我們的信貸人員談談。打擾了，賈絲汀。這是多伊爾女士，她想申請企業貸款。

女2：太棒了。很高興認識您，多伊爾女士。您有我們的帳戶嗎？

女1：是的，我有一個。

女2：好的，因為這是對客戶申請貸款的要求。只有目前持有帳戶的人才符合貸款資格。

59. 莎拉‧多伊爾為什麼想要貸款？
(A) 添購一些設備
(B) 支付她的每月租金
(C) 投放一些廣告
(D) 僱用額外的工作人員　　　　　　答案 (C)

60. 男子為何尋求協助？
(A) 他不經手某項事務。
(B) 他正在協助另一位客戶。
(C) 他目前正在休息。
(D) 他搞不懂某個問題。　　　　　　答案 (A)

61. 文中提到什麼貸款要求？
(A) 推薦信
(B) 財產法律文件
(C) 財務紀錄
(D) 銀行帳戶　　　　　　　　　　　答案 (D)

問題 62-64，請參考以下對話內容及餐廳評比。 英國 M　美國 W

M: Hello, Emily. (62) (63)**I reviewed the presentation you'll be giving at tomorrow's meeting.** It was really good, but I e-mailed some suggestions on how to improve it.
W: Thanks, Ken. (63)**I'm a bit worried since this client has the potential to be big.**
M: I'm sure you'll do fine.
W: Oh, (64)**do you happen to know any good restaurants around here?** The client wants to have dinner after the meeting ends.
M: (64)**I know a really good one. It got four stars in a newspaper review last week**, and it's right around the corner from the bank. I'll e-mail you a link to the website.

男：哈囉，艾蜜莉。我審視了你在明天會議上要做的簡報。簡報真的很棒，不過我還是用電子郵件寄了一些改善建議。
女：謝謝你，肯。我有點擔心，因為這個客戶有潛力做大。
男：我相信你會做得很好。
女：哦，你知道這附近有什麼好吃的餐廳嗎？客戶想在會議結束後吃晚餐。
男：我知道有一間超棒。它在上週的報紙評比得到了四顆星，而且它就在銀行過去的轉角。我再把網站的連結寄給你。

餐廳評比	
蘇珊的角落	★★☆☆☆
西區咖啡廳	★★★☆☆
(64) 45 牛排	★★★★☆
湯普森之地	★★★★★

62. 男子為女子查看了什麼？
(A) 產品評比
(B) 會議時程
(C) 簡報
(D) 公司型錄　　　　　　　　　　　答案 (C)

63. 女子擔心什麼？
(A) 即將舉辦的培訓課程
(B) 她在研討會上的簡報
(C) 她的績效評估
(D) 與客戶的會面　　　　　　　　　答案 (D)

64. 請看圖表。男子推薦哪家餐廳？
(A) 蘇珊的角落
(B) 西區咖啡廳
(C) 45 牛排
(D) 湯普森之地　　　　　　　　　　答案 (C)

問題 65-67，請參考以下對話內容及配送選項。 美國 M　澳洲 W

M: Hello. (65)**I'm Steve from Harrison Manufacturing. We've gotten some new clients in Europe**, so we need a shipping provider that can deliver our products there.
W: We provide shipping by both ground and air for flat rates if you use the boxes we provide. How many packages do you intend to ship?
M: (66)**We'll likely ship around 70 boxes each week.**
W: Air is the faster method, but you can save money by using ground shipping. It's slower, though.
M: (66)**We guarantee speedy delivery, so we need to use airmail.**
W: Okay. (67)**Why don't you let me know your address**, and I can send you enough boxes for the first week?

男：你好。我是哈里森製造公司的史蒂夫。我們在歐洲獲得了一些新客戶，因此需要一家可以把產品運到那裡的貨運商。
女：如果您使用我們提供的箱子，我們可以提供單一費率的陸運和空運服務。您打算運送多少個包裹？
男：我們每週可能會運送約 70 箱。
女：空運是更快的方式，但你可以用陸運來省錢。不過，速度比較慢就是了。

男：我們保證快速交貨，所以需要採用空運。

女：好的。何不告訴我您的地址，以利我寄給您足夠第一週使用的箱子？

	陸運 （每件包裹的價格）	(66) 空運 （每件包裹的價格）
1-20 件包裹	$3.00	$6.00
21-50 件包裹	$2.50	$5.00
(66) **51-100 件包裹**	$2.00	(66)$4.00

65. 哈里森製造公司最近發生了什麼事？
(A) 它僱用了更多員工。
(B) 它獲得一些新客戶。
(C) 它在歐洲開了一間工廠。
(D) 它與供應商簽了一份合約。　　　　答案 (B)

66. 請看圖表。寄送一件包裹最有可能花費多少錢？
(A) 2.00 美元
(B) 2.50 美元
(C) 4.00 美元
(D) 5.00 美元　　　　　　　　　　　答案 (C)

67. 男子接下來最有可能做什麼？
(A) 寄送包裝箱
(B) 提供他的聯絡方式
(C) 簽訂合約
(D) 運送一些包裹　　　　　　　　　　答案 (B)

問題 68-70，請參考以下對話內容及會議議程。 美國 W 英國 M

W: (68)**Today, we need to discuss how to restore the Renaissance paintings in the B-wing.** I already handed out copies of the meeting agenda, (69)**but I'd like to skip ahead a bit and talk about who should lead the project.**

M: I'm in favor of letting Marcus do it. He'd be a great project leader since he has more than 10 years of experience in restoring paintings for many art galleries.

W: Hmm… He has never led a team before, has he? There is a huge difference between restoring individual paintings and taking care of multiple restorations while leading a massive team.

M: Well, I've worked on a few projects with him, and he's always been highly organized and efficient.

W: (70)**Sounds good to me. I'll give him a call and find out if he wants the assignment today.**

女：今天，我們需要討論如何修復 B 翼廊的文藝復興時期畫作。我已經發下會議議程的影本，但我想稍微往前跳一點，先談談誰應該領導這個專案。

男：我傾向讓馬庫斯來做，他會是出色的專案領導者，

因為他在修復許多美術館畫作方面，擁有超過 10 年的經驗。

女：嗯……他從未帶領過一個團隊，對嗎？修復單幅畫作與帶領龐大的團隊進行多項修復工作，其中存在很大的差異。

男：嗯，我和他一起做過幾個專案，他總是很有條理，效率很高。

女：聽起來不錯。我今天會打給他，看看他有沒有想要接下這份任務。

專案相關議題項目

1. 時程
2. (69) **專案管理**
3. 預算
4. 供應商

---

68. 談話者最有可能在哪裡工作？
(A) 圖書館
(B) 博物館
(C) 美術用品店
(D) 建築事務所　　　　　　　　　　答案 (B)

69. 請看圖表。談話者正在討論哪個議程事項？
(A) 第 1 項
(B) 第 2 項
(C) 第 3 項
(D) 第 4 項　　　　　　　　　　　　答案 (B)

70. 女子說她稍後要做什麼？
(A) 聯繫同事
(B) 審查提案
(C) 刊登廣告
(D) 召開會議　　　　　　　　　　　答案 (A)

Part 4

問題 71-73，請參考以下電話留言。 美國 M

Hello, Ms. Denton. This is David Stern from Travel Magazine. (71)**We received your application to work here as a writer.** (72)**Thanks for sending some of the articles you wrote in the past. I was quite impressed with them.** I would love for you to come in for an interview next week. (73)**Please call me back so that we can set up a day and time for you to come in.** My phone number is 596-2033. Thank you.

你好，丹頓女士。我是《旅遊》雜誌的大衛·史騰。我們收到了你想在這裡當撰稿人的應徵資料。感謝你寄來過去寫的一些文章，我對它們印象深刻。希望你下週能過來面試。請回我電話，以便安排你前來的日期和時間。我的電話號碼是 596-2033。謝謝。

71. 聽者最有可能是誰？
    (A) 總編輯
    (B) 撰稿人
    (C) 攝影師
    (D) 老師　　　　　　　　　　　答案 (B)

72. 據說話者所說，他對什麼印象深刻？
    (A) 預算提案
    (B) 職位描述
    (C) 一些照片
    (D) 一些作品樣本　　　　　　　答案 (D)

73. 說話者說他想做什麼？
    (A) 確認電子信箱
    (B) 安排面試
    (C) 提供估價
    (D) 安排發布日期　　　　　　　答案 (B)

問題 74-76，請參考以下廣告內容。 美國 W

The Jospin Institute can teach you everything you need to know about computers. (74) (75)**This Sunday from noon to three P.M., visit our building to learn more about us and computer courses we provide.** You can meet our instructors and sit in on some model classes. (75)**When you study at Jospin, you'll be taught by the best and get a computer programming certificate in as little as nine months.** (76)**Text 1234 on your cell phone in order to subscribe to our online version of the weekly newsletter.**

裘斯潘學院可以教授你需要的所有電腦知識。這週日中午到下午三點，蒞臨我們的大樓，了解更多關於我們的資訊，和我們提供的電腦課程。你可以與我們的講師會面，並旁聽一些試聽課程。當你在裘斯潘學習，將由最好的老師授課，最快能在九個月內獲得程式設計的證照。用手機發送簡訊 1234，就能訂閱我們的線上電子週報。

74. 週日會發生什麼事？
    (A) 產品展示會
    (B) 資訊說明會
    (C) 銷售會議
    (D) 工作面試　　　　　　　　　答案 (B)

75. 裘斯潘學院提供什麼？
    (A) 企業審計
    (B) 電腦課程
    (C) 線上市調
    (D) 安全諮詢　　　　　　　　　答案 (B)

76. 為什麼聽者要用簡訊傳送一組號碼？
    (A) 回覆調查
    (B) 接收電子報
    (C) 提出申請
    (D) 提出評論　　　　　　　　　答案 (B)

問題 77-79，請參考以下會議摘錄。 英國 M

(77)**The new phone system was installed in the conference room about a month ago.** This system is much better than the old one, but you may have noticed a problem regarding how it interacts with the two-way video. I've spoken with our IT expert, and he thinks the problem has been solved. (78)**But he wants us to let him know at once if any further problems arise.** Thanks to the new system, the conference room has become the most popular place for meetings, so we have to start reserving the room to avoid any conflicts. (79)**Call me whenever you want to use it since I'm handling the bookings now.**

大約一個月前，會議室安裝了新的電話系統。這套系統比舊系統好得多，但你們可能已經注意到，它與雙向影音的互動有問題。我已經跟我們的資訊科技專家談過，他認為問題已經解決了。但如果有其他問題出現，他希望我們立刻告訴他。受惠於這套新系統，會議室已成為最受歡迎的開會場所，因此我們必須開始進行預約，以免時間衝突。現在由我處理預約，所以你們想使用時，請打電話給我。

77. 說話者主要在談論什麼？
    (A) 部門預算
    (B) 會議演講
    (C) 新電話系統
    (D) 新會議室　　　　　　　　　答案 (C)

78. 據說話者所說，如果聽者還有其他問題，應該怎麼做？
    (A) 通知專家
    (B) 撰寫網路評論
    (C) 使用不同的設備
    (D) 重新啟動電腦　　　　　　　答案 (A)

79. 說話者為什麼要求聽者打電話給他？
    (A) 預約會議室
    (B) 申請新機器
    (C) 要求轉調
    (D) 訂購用品　　　　　　　　　答案 (A)

All of you are new members of the wait staff, so I want to speak with you before we get too busy at the dinner rush. (80)**First, you should know about this restaurant. I opened it twenty years ago**, and almost all the recipes I had were inherited from my mother and grandmother, and I wanted to share the delicious food recipes with people in the area. (81)**Even though many local restaurants have closed since then, our kitchen is always busy.** I'm pleased to welcome you here and I hope your first day goes well. (82)**In addition, please be sure to wear your name tags at all times.** That will enable both our diners and the other staff members to remember your names.

你們都是服務團隊的新成員，所以我想在我們因為晚餐尖峰時段而陷入忙碌之前，先和你們談談。首先，你們應該認識這家餐廳。我二十年前開業，幾乎所有食譜都是從我母親和祖母那裡繼承而來。我想與這個地方的人們分享美味的料理食譜。儘管在那之後，許多在地餐廳關門了，但我們的廚房總是很忙碌。很高興歡迎你們來到這裡，希望你們的第一天一切順利。此外，請務必隨時戴著名牌。這能讓我們的顧客和其他工作人員記住你的名字。

80. 說話者最有可能是誰？
   (A) 餐廳老闆
   (B) 政府稽查員
   (C) 廚房工作人員
   (D) 財務顧問　　　　　　　　　　答案 (A)

81. 說話者為什麼說「我們的廚房總是很忙碌」？
   (A) 告訴聽者等待時間可能會更長
   (B) 解釋出現變動的原因
   (C) 表明生意是成功的
   (D) 證明這份工作會很困難　　　　答案 (C)

82. 說話者要求聽者做什麼？
   (A) 確認他們的工作時間表
   (B) 加班
   (C) 一直戴著安全帽
   (D) 戴上名牌　　　　　　　　　　答案 (D)

Good afternoon, everybody. (83)**The R&D team just told me that work on our latest sneaker is almost complete.** They just need to implement a couple of changes suggested by the focus groups. The launch date has been moved up by two months. (84)**We therefore need to work on our marketing materials

as quickly as possible. We need both print and radio advertisements, and we'll be active on social media, too. This is our main priority. (85)**This week, I'll meet individually with each of you to talk about the specific role I want you to have on the project.**

大家午安。研發團隊剛剛告訴我，我們最新款的運動鞋已大致完成。他們只需要採納焦點團體建議的部分修改就好。發布日期已提前兩個月。因此，我們需要盡快製作行銷素材。我們需要平面廣告和廣播廣告，也會在社群媒體上積極活躍。這是我們的首要任務。本週，我將與你們每個人單獨會面，討論我希望你們在計劃中扮演的具體角色。

83. 說話者在談論什麼類型的產品？
   (A) 健身器材
   (B) 軟體程式
   (C) 護膚產品
   (D) 跑鞋　　　　　　　　　　　　答案 (D)

84. 聽者將開始處理什麼工作？
   (A) 與焦點團體合作
   (B) 創造行銷素材
   (C) 製作電視廣告
   (D) 培訓新員工　　　　　　　　　答案 (B)

85. 說話者說她這週會做什麼？
   (A) 與每位員工會面
   (B) 安排與員工的電話會議
   (C) 到國外出差
   (D) 參訪公司的工廠　　　　　　　答案 (A)

And now for our next story, (86)**let's talk about an announcement by Martin Motors, which today said that every car model the company makes in the future** will have both a gasoline engine and an electric battery engine. Apparently, (87)**this action toward manufacturing hybrid vehicles, which utilize both fuel sources, has been taken in an effort to make the firm more ecofriendly.** During the press conference, Martin Motors' president also showed some pictures of the new vehicles, (88)**proving that caring for the environment can be paired with nice-looking cars.** In case you haven't seen them yet, let me say that I've already ordered a new one.

緊接著是我們的下一個故事。讓我們來談談馬丁汽車公司的一項聲明。該公司今天表示，未來他們生產的每款車型，都將配備汽油引擎和電池動力引擎。顯然，採取邁向混合動力車的這一步，是為了使公司更加環保，也

可以有效利用兩種燃料來源。在記者會上，馬丁汽車總裁還展示了一些新車圖片，證明愛護環境可以與好看的汽車兩者兼顧。如果你還沒有見過它們，請容我說，我已經訂購了一輛新車。

86. 此新聞報導主要在談論什麼類型的企業？
    (A) 飛機製造商
    (B) 汽車租賃服務公司
    (C) 汽車製造
    (D) 攝影工作室　　　　　　　　　　答案 (C)

87. 據說話者所說，這間公司的行動目標是什麼？
    (A) 拓展海外市場
    (B) 協助保護環境
    (C) 降低生產成本
    (D) 減少原物料使用　　　　　　　　答案 (B)

88. 說話者說「我已經訂購了一輛新車」，是在暗示什麼？
    (A) 他認為這些汽車的需求很大。
    (B) 某些型號不會很快上市。
    (C) 這些汽車的價格不算太高。
    (D) 他喜歡新車型的外觀。　　　　　答案 (D)

問題 89-91，請參考以下會議摘錄。 [澳洲 W]

Good morning. (89)**This meeting was called due to the many recent complaints we've received about our items breaking while being shipped.** This is a major issue. After conducting an investigation, we determined that the damage to these items is caused by defective packaging. (90)**In an effort to fix that, our design team came up with three packaging options to protect the items better.** Since you're the employees who prepare the items to be shipped, we'd like your comments regarding which packaging works best. (91)**We've prepared samples of each package option.** Please come up here, take a good look, and let us know your thoughts on each type.

早安。召開這次會議，是因為我們最近收到很多商品在運輸途中破裂的投訴。這是一個重大問題。經過調查，我們確定這些商品損壞是包裝不良導致。為了解決這個問題，我們的設計團隊提出了三種包裝選項，以更好地保護商品。由於你們是準備、運送商品的員工，因此希望你們就哪種包裝最有用提出意見。我們已經為每個選項準備了樣品。請過來這裡，仔細看看，並讓我們知道你對每種款式的想法。

89. 說話者提到什麼問題？
    (A) 貨運商延遲寄送商品。
    (B) 建築物需要翻新。
    (C) 有些產品受到損壞。
    (D) 運送錯誤的品項。　　　　　　　答案 (C)

90. 公司打算做什麼？
    (A) 更改包裝
    (B) 僱用另一個運輸服務
    (C) 提供更多員工福利
    (D) 推出新的政策指引　　　　　　　答案 (A)

91. 已為員工準備了什麼東西？
    (A) 餐點和飲料
    (B) 包裝教程
    (C) 員工手冊
    (D) 一些包裝樣品　　　　　　　　　答案 (D)

問題 92-94，請參考以下發言。 [美國 M]

Thanks for coming to today's volunteer orientation session. I'm glad so many local residents are willing to help out with the art program for children again this summer. (92)**As you know, the community center offers a five-week program every summer** for children to participate in art classes and learn about all kinds of art forms. (93)**This year, we'll be adding activities like woodcarving and sculpture.** Unfortunately, we're running a bit short of money because of the cost of all the art supplies we need. (94)**So any financial help that we can get from local residents would be great. We hope you feel the same way.** I'll be placing a collection box at the registration desk. Any amount will be appreciated.

感謝參加今天的志工迎新活動。很高興今年夏天有這麼多在地居民，願意再次為兒童藝術課程提供協助。如各位所知，社區中心每年夏天都會提供為期五週的課程，讓孩子們參加藝術課，認識各種藝術形式。今年，我們將新增木雕和雕塑等活動。不幸的是，我們的資金有些短缺。原因在於，我們所需的各種美術用品成本。因此，若在地居民願意給予任何財務上的協助，那就太好了。希望各位也有同樣的感覺。我會把募款箱放在登記處櫃檯。任何金額都將不勝感激。

92. 說話者在哪裡工作？
    (A) 政府機關
    (B) 小學
    (C) 美術用品店
    (D) 社區中心　　　　　　　　　　　答案 (D)

93. 據說話者所說，今年夏天的課程有什麼不同？
    (A) 將納入額外的活動。
    (B) 將在不同地點舉辦。
    (C) 要花錢才能參加。
    (D) 將在夏季晚些時候才開始。　　　答案 (A)

94. 說話者為什麼說「希望各位也有同樣的感覺」？
    (A) 因更改日期向聽者致歉
    (B) 鼓勵聽者捐款
    (C) 感謝聽者的志工服務
    (D) 徵求聽者的回饋意見　　　答案 (B)

問題 95-97，請參考以下電話留言及型錄。 美國 W

Hello, Ms. Watson. This is Erin Harper calling. Last week, I visited your home decorating store, and you gave me a catalog of the items you sell. I'd love to buy some wallpaper to redo my living room walls. (95) **It's product R4854.** I remember that it was being discounted by 25% last week, (96)**but I wonder if the sale price still applies.** Would you mind calling me back at 954-3827 to let me know? (97)**I'm out of the house all day, so you need to contact me after 8:00 P.M.** Thanks.

你好，華森女士。我是艾琳·哈珀。上週，我參觀了你們的家居飾品店，你給了我一份販售品項型錄。我想買一些壁紙，來重新裝潢客廳的牆壁，也就是產品 R4854。我記得上週折扣是 25%，我想知道促銷價是否仍然適用。你方便回電 954-3827 讓我知道嗎？我一整天都不在家，所以請在晚上 8 點以後聯繫我。謝謝。

型錄	
象牙白 #R4852	淺藍色 #R4853
(95) 綠色 #R4854	米色 #R4855

95. 請看圖表。說話者對哪種顏色感興趣？
    (A) 象牙白
    (B) 淺藍色
    (C) 綠色
    (D) 米色　　　答案 (C)

96. 說話者想知道什麼？
    (A) 是否可以退費
    (B) 是否可取得特價
    (C) 某個品項是否缺貨
    (D) 是否可以免費送貨　　　答案 (B)

97. 說話者希望何時聯繫她？
    (A) 早上
    (B) 午餐時間
    (C) 晚上
    (D) 週末　　　答案 (C)

問題 98-100，請參考以下導覽及地圖。 美國 M

Welcome to Green Forest State Park. I'm Ranger Smith, and I'd like to give you some information before you set off. Take a look at this map. If you're an expert hiker, the south trail is the most challenging. It can get pretty steep as it goes up Mount Placid. (98)**However, the trail that goes around the pond is flat and is the easiest one.** Now, please remember that (99)**during this time of year, sudden rain showers can happen, so make sure you have a raincoat.** Okay, one last thing. (100) **I need you to look at these pictures of dangerous animals in the park.** Please familiarize yourself with them so that you can avoid them if necessary.

歡迎來到綠色森林州立公園，我是森林護管員史密斯。我想在你們出發前提供一些資訊。請看這張地圖。如果你是專業健行人士，南側步道最有挑戰性。當它向上通向普萊西德山時，會變得相當陡峭。然而，繞池塘一圈的小路很平坦，是最容易走的一條路。現在，請記住，每年的這個時候可能會突然下陣雨，所以一定要帶雨衣。好，還有最後一點。我需要你們看看這些公園裡的危險動物照片。請熟記牠們，以便在必要時閃避。

公園步道地圖
河川
普萊西德山
東側步道
南側步道
★
北側步道　　(98) 池塘
(98) 西側步道

98. 請看圖表。說話者說哪條路線最好走？
    (A) 北側步道
    (B) 南側步道
    (C) 東側步道
    (D) 西側步道　　　答案 (D)

99. 根據說話者所說，聽者應該隨身攜帶什麼？
    (A) 防曬乳
    (B) 雨具
    (C) 充足的水
    (D) 帳篷　　　答案 (B)

100. 聽者被要求接下來做什麼事？
(A) 完成針對健行者的調查
(B) 觀看一部短影片
(C) 看一些照片
(D) 獲得健行許可證　　　　　　答案 (C)

Part 5

101. 咖啡屋的常客對上週意外實施的大幅漲價感到驚訝。
　　　　　　答案 (C)

102. 這個氣象衛星計劃在十年前啟動，但經歷了數次延宕。
　　　　　　答案 (D)

103. 執行長發言的重點，聚焦在我們的詹金斯先生和他在
印度取得的成功。　　　　　　答案 (B)

104. 經濟不確定性是我們在這座城市做生意面臨的最大挑
戰之一。然而，只有相對較少的心力投入來解決這個
問題。　　　　　　答案 (B)

105. 我們這個城鎮，是由不同國籍、文化背景和宗教團體
所組成的多元社群。　　　　　　答案 (C)

106. 速達貨運服務總裁一直考慮兩年後要在多倫多再建一
座倉庫。　　　　　　答案 (B)

107. 大多數員工在錄用一年後都有資格享有休假和休假期
間的薪資。　　　　　　答案 (A)

108. 欲退費之顧客應在購買後三天內退回瑕疵商品，並帶
上當初的收據。　　　　　　答案 (B)

109. 由於我們收到大量申請，下週只會聯繫符合資格的申
請者。　　　　　　答案 (A)

110. 貝拉汽車公司僅在六年內就成為混合動力車產業的領
頭羊，真是令人驚嘆。　　　　　　答案 (B)

111. BK 藥品實驗室的所有研究人員在工作場所內都必須穿
戴安全裝備。　　　　　　答案 (B)

112. 政府最近宣布，外國公司來本國開展業務，將獲得優
惠的稅收減免。　　　　　　答案 (C)

113. 該環境計劃旨在提高對於海洋嚴重垃圾問題的意識。
　　　　　　答案 (C)

114. 必須偶爾關閉電腦數據伺服器來升級其作業系統。
　　　　　　答案 (B)

115. 某些經常工作到很晚的員工可能會認為，讓自己保持
活力的最佳方法就是來點能量飲料。　　答案 (A)

116. 不要推遲必要的修理或例行性保養，以使你的汽車盡
可能長時間保持最佳狀態。　　　　答案 (A)

117. 註冊成為 BK 有線電視會員，即可觀看數百個頻道，再
加上三個由你選擇、完全免費的體育頻道。　答案 (B)

118. 根據我們的人事紀錄，瓊斯先生是起司麵包廠裡最認
真工作的員工。　　　　　　答案 (C)

119. 醫療保健體系基本上是一個以服務為基礎的產業，充
其量與其他服務導向的產業沒什麼兩樣。　答案 (A)

120. 儘管目前原油價格大幅上漲，大多數人還是很少考慮
汽車共乘。　　　　　　答案 (C)

121. 帕克先生去年獲得了管理職位，但他婉拒了。因為他
正在找一份薪水更高的工作。　　　　答案 (C)

122. 國際旅遊協會將把「年度最佳旅行社獎」頒發給獲得
董事會最高票的旅行社。　　　　答案 (B)

123. 人力資源部將採取多項措施，激勵業務人員提高他們
在海外市場的競爭力。　　　　答案 (D)

124. 公司的員工餐廳在平日從上午 8 點開到晚上 8 點，因
此你可以安排相應的午餐和晚餐時間。　答案 (D)

125. 正如布朗先生所說，實際損益應準確反映在下一份會
計報告中。　　　　　　答案 (D)

126. 根據我們的政策，任何違反「禁用手機」規定的人都
可能被要求離開劇院。　　　　答案 (D)

127. 針對所有會導致我們公司財產和財務變動的商業交易，
負責追蹤的人是首席會計師布萊恩·沃克先生。
　　　　　　答案 (A)

128. 儘管多數顧客認為這款新產品易於使用，那些不太熟
悉的人仍應在使用前查閱使用說明。　答案 (A)

129. 羅德里茲女士將參加新職位的培訓課程，並負責統計
分析。　　　　　　答案 (B)

130. 檢測到問題之後，新的行動裝置已延後至少一週推出。
　　　　　　答案 (C)

問題 **131-134**，請參考以下信件內容。

親愛的席克勒女士；

關於我們的電子產業年度研討會，我們會邀請一位這個領域的專家來對談。今年，我們的重點是電子產業的未來，因此如果您願意根據商務經驗進行對談，我們將深感榮幸。

未來電子研討會將於 10 月 1 日上午 10 點至下午 3 點在洛杉磯大都會飯店舉行。我們已安排您在下午 1-2 點登臺。希望您能對談一個小時，包括問答時間在內。

我們很樂意為您支付車馬費，並提供小額講師費。

誠摯感謝。

西沃恩・凱利
副總裁
安德洛墨達電子公司

131. 答案 (A)

132. 答案 (C)

133. 答案 (B)

134. (A) 非常感謝您參加我們 10 月 1 日的演講。
    (B) 按照約定，你與我們的交易將以加幣付款。
    (C) 我們很高興舉辦一些與國際社會相關的研討會和演講。
    (D) 我們很樂意為您支付車馬費，並提供小額講師費。
    答案 (D)

問題 **135-138**，請參考以下電子郵件。

致全體員工，

我寫這封信是為了讓各位知道，我們最近修改了差旅費核銷政策。本政策適用於代表公司出差的員工，針對公司在哪些方面會補貼出差相關費用，界定了各項條件、規則和程序。

即日起，出差獲准之後，必須透過人力資源部預訂班機和旅館。這將有助於消除我們過去面臨的混亂。如果你有理由要自行預訂出差事宜，你必須在差旅費用報告中記下原因，並將所有收據提交給人力資源部。此外，員工每天最多可以有 100 美元用於雜費支出，包括餐飲和路上交通費用。

請注意，如果你預訂出差事宜時沒有遵守這些新政策，將不予補貼。

有任何問題或疑慮，請隨時與我聯繫。

誠摯感謝。

詹妮弗・格蘭特
會計經理

135. 答案 (D)

136. (A) 你將對我們這裡的服務品質感到滿意。
    (B) 我們應該在下週討論雜費的許可金額。
    (C) 這將有助於消除我們過去面臨的混亂。
    (D) 若要把握這個機會，你必須在 5 月 15 日之前回覆。
    答案 (C)

137. 答案 (A)

138. 答案 (D)

問題 **139-142**，請參考以下通知內容。

上城家具行
活動通知

非常感謝您購買我們的沙發套組。這將是讓全家人都可以舒服坐著的沙發。我們由衷感謝您的光顧，相信您會對新家具深感滿意。

我們始終致力於改善顧客服務。因此，如果您能花點時間，完成隨附的顧客滿意度調查，我們將不勝感激。您的回答將幫助我們確保未來能持續滿足顧客的需求。

此外，只要完成調查，就能參加特別的抽獎活動。得獎顧客將獲得價值 500 美元的禮券，可在店內使用。若要參加抽獎，請在 7 月 15 日前回傳您的調查問卷。8 月 1 日將會公布中獎名單。

139. 答案 (C)

140. (A) 有此職位經驗者為佳。
    (B) 我們始終致力於改善顧客服務。
    (C) 你們的所有投訴都會獲得公平處理。
    (D) 常用於抽屜櫃、餐桌等重物。
    答案 (B)

141. 答案 (A)

142. 答案 (D)

問題 **143-146**，請參考以下文章內容。

敘拉古紀事報
文化版

全新攝影展即將蒞臨小鎮

布蘭登・李

（11 月 1 日）從下週三開始，國立美術館將舉辦攝影師塞西爾・比頓女士的作品展。比頓女士的攝影作品曾榮獲多項國際獎項。這位新興藝術家以其描繪社會受壓迫者的黑白照片而聞名。她是已故知名攝影師彼得・傑克遜的唯一弟子，而傑克遜先生專注於捕捉原住民的生活。比頓女士依據從傑克遜先生身上所學，繼續為無家可歸者、乞丐、童工和其他被社會忽視的群體拍攝照片。「就像原住民在全球各地並未受到全然認可一樣，我們自己的城市裡也有人遭到忽視。」比頓女士說。「我想藉著攝影捕捉他們的生活，這樣我的觀眾就能看見身邊被遺忘的鄰居，並與他們重新建立連結。」這位攝影師希望透過她的作品為社會做出貢獻。她計劃將展覽的全部收益捐給慈善機構。本次展期為四個月。

143. 答案 (C)

144. 答案 (C)

145. 答案 (C)

146. (A) 展覽將以傑克遜先生拍攝的原住民照片為主。
(B) 幾家雜誌社很快就會聯繫她，以使用她的照片。
(C) 她計劃將展覽的全部收益捐給慈善機構。
(D) 這位攝影師提到拍攝無家可歸者的未來計劃。

答案 (C)

Part 7

問題 147-148，請參考以下電子郵件。

收件人：布蘭妮・薩德勒 <bsadler@runmail.com>
寄件人：<customerservice@mccarleyonline.org>
日　期：6 月 3 日
主　旨：需要重新啟用

(147) 親愛的薩德勒女士，

(147) 由於您嘗試登入時，密碼錯誤達到三次，我們已停用您的線上帳戶。若要重新啟用帳戶，請至 www.mccarleyonline.com/reactivation 重設密碼。

基於安全考量，您需要提供一些資訊，包括您的社會安全碼和住址。(148) 待您啟用帳戶後，您將重新取回借閱我們線下和線上資料的完整權限。希望您有興趣使用我們新推出的電子書檔案庫。請洽服務臺以獲得更多資訊。

客戶服務部門
(148) 麥卡利

147. 向薩德勒女士發送電子郵件，可能是出於什麼原因？
(A) 她無法在網路上買書。
(B) 她取消了與麥卡利的交易。

(C) 她需要更新她的帳戶。
(D) 她忘記密碼。　　　　　　　　　答案 (D)

148. 麥卡利最有可能是什麼？
(A) 銀行
(B) 網路書店
(C) 圖書館
(D) 保全公司　　　　　　　　　　　答案 (C)

問題 149-150，請參考以下傳單內容。

第 5 屆年度炙熱馬鈴薯市場
(149) 搖滾之夜

由當地日本餐廳伊拉特謝舉辦

(149) 快來享受一個充滿活力的夜晚吧！
(149) 表演嘉賓：綠番茄樂團

9 月 4 日星期五

下午 5:30 – (150C) 晚上 11:00

本森藝術劇院
68927 內布拉斯加州，伯特蘭，凱爾街 958 號
2 樓

門票：20 美元（8 月 30 日開始售票）
(150B) 收入全數捐給傑克遜維爾音樂學院。
(150A) 想了解更多資訊或預訂入場券，請至
www.hotpotatomarket.org。

行動要快！入場券預計很快就會售完。

* 伊拉特謝 10% 折扣優惠券將提供給所有參與者。

---

149. 正在為什麼類型的活動打廣告？
(A) 餐廳開幕週年紀念派對
(B) 劇院開幕
(C) 音樂表演
(D) 當地美食節　　　　　　　　　　答案 (C)

150. 關於這項活動，文中沒有提到什麼？
(A) 入場券可在網路上取得。
(B) 它會幫助某個教育機構。
(C) 晚上 11 點結束
(D) 9 月 4 日可以開始購票。　　　　答案 (D)

問題 151-152，請參考以下文字訊息。

喬治・麥唐納　　　　　　　　　［上午 11:19］
我聽說任命了一位新的行銷經理。

亞當・丹尼爾　　　　　　　　　［上午 11:20］
對，我也有聽說。韓先生終於退休了。我會想念他的。

喬治‧麥唐納　　　　　　　　　［上午 11:22］

(151) 你能相信韓先生在快速科技公司工作了將近 20 年嗎？(152) 他是一位很棒的領導者。

亞當‧丹尼爾　　　　　　　　　［上午 11:25］

我完全同意。

喬治‧麥唐納　　　　　　　　　［上午 11:26］

(151) 看到我們公司僅剩的少數創始成員又有一位離開，感覺很糟。

亞當‧丹尼爾　　　　　　　　　［上午 11:27］

你說得沒錯。但我相信希利女士會和韓先生做得一樣好。

151. 關於快速科技公司，文中暗指什麼？
　　(A) 營運時間不滿 20 年。
　　(B) 最近僱用了一名新員工。
　　(C) 不久就會發布徵才廣告。
　　(D) 正在擴編行銷部門。　　　　　答案 (A)

152. 上午 11:25，丹尼爾先生寫道「我完全同意」，是什麼意思？
　　(A) 指出麥唐納先生提供了不正確的資訊。
　　(B) 他也認為韓先生很棒。
　　(C) 他不再有親近的同事了。
　　(D) 他拒絕與希利女士一起工作。　　答案 (B)

問題 **153-154**，請參考以下表格內容。

優質裱框

學院大道 1086 號
45434 俄亥俄州，代頓

顧客資訊	
(154) 姓名：	維克多‧克拉克
電話：	(513) 555-2903

特別備註：
我想為一幅畫裱框。這幅畫是我祖父畫的，感情價值高不可計。(153) 如你所見，這幅畫已經放了很久，所以請特別小心照料。

畫框類型：米開朗基羅
顏色：　　　古典金色和銀色
(154) 取件日期：**7 月 10 日**

成本概要：
－服務費：　　　　　　　　　35.00 美元
－材料成本：米開朗基羅畫框（2 5/8 英寸）：
　　　　　　　　　　　　　　 95.00 美元
－會員折扣 (10%)：　　　　　 -9.50 美元
－預付金：　　　　　　　　　 -30.00 美元

(154) 取件時應付餘額：　**90.50 美元**

---

153. 關於這幅畫，可以推論出什麼？
　　(A) 由一位知名藝術家所畫。
　　(B) 原來的畫框壞了。
　　(C) 脆弱容易損壞。
　　(D) 價格昂貴。　　　　　　　　　答案 (C)

154. 7 月 10 日，克拉克先生需要付多少錢？
　　(A) 30 美元
　　(B) 35 美元
　　(C) 90.50 美元
　　(D) 95 美元　　　　　　　　　　答案 (C)

問題 **155-157**，請參考以下廣告內容。

爵士數字

(156B) 爵士數字是一支成立三年的爵士樂隊，成員演奏鋼琴、薩克斯風、單簧管、低音提琴和鼓。我們培養了許多著名音樂家，包括我們的創始成員之一亞倫‧米爾斯。(156C) (156D) 他最近加入了聲望卓著的埃塞爾管弦樂團，擔任單簧管首席。

你對爵士樂充滿熱情嗎？

(155) 那就別猶豫了，申請成為會員吧！(157) 作為一支自由爵士樂隊，我們隨時隨地為各種活動演奏，例如派對、婚禮和其他儀式。(155) 目前我們正在尋找新成員。你只需要在 11 月 3 日之前，錄製你的演奏和一份簡短的個人描述。一旦評估完你提交的內容，我們就會打給你進行試奏。若要提交試奏檔案或有任何疑問，請寄電子郵件至 jhenderson@boostmail.com 給傑佛瑞‧韓德森。

---

155. 此廣告的目的是什麼？
　　(A) 宣布退休
　　(B) 招募更多表演者
　　(C) 宣傳即將進行的演出
　　(D) 募款　　　　　　　　　　　　答案 (B)

156. 關於亞倫‧米爾斯，以下敘述何者不正確？
　　(A) 將對試奏進行評審。
　　(B) 大約三年前，他在爵士數字演奏。
　　(C) 他是一位著名的單簧管演奏家。
　　(D) 他目前是埃塞爾管弦樂團的成員。　答案 (A)

157. 關於爵士數字音樂家，文中暗指什麼？
　　(A) 他們用電子檔案記錄演奏。
　　(B) 他們是業餘愛好者。
　　(C) 他們會到不同地方旅行。
　　(D) 他們為韓德森先生工作。　　　答案 (C)

問題 **158-160**，請參考以下資訊。

巴尼山丘
巴尼的招牌穀物棒

(159) 巴尼山丘穀物棒採用加拿大農民巴尼・皮埃爾開發的傳統家常食譜所製成。50 年來，皮埃爾先生一直經營這家公司，但現在他的兒子羅密歐・皮埃爾先生已接棒經營。(158) 所有穀物棒都不含人工香料，裡面是滿滿的烘焙燕麥、腰果和杏仁，並浸泡在真正的楓糖漿中，創造出一種甜美、可口和健康的零食，方便你隨身攜帶到任何地方。我們的穀物棒富含全穀物的經典口感和營養成分，使其成為一種營養豐富的零食，能讓你充滿飽足感又不會感到罪惡。

- 高纖維和低糖
- 零反式脂肪，不添加麩質
- 簡便好吃
- 能量補充
- (158) 有機農場協會認證

(160) 請至我們的網站 www.barneyshill.com/naturebars 下載可列印的優惠券。購買一盒 12 入的巴尼山丘穀物棒時，向收銀員出示優惠券，即可再免費獲得一盒！

---

158. 此則資訊的目的是什麼？
(A) 描述一間企業的歷史
(B) 介紹傳統食物
(C) 宣傳用天然食材製成的產品
(D) 示範如何烹飪家常菜　　　　答案 (C)

159. 關於巴尼山丘，文中暗指什麼？
(A) 皮埃爾先生的簽名印在產品上。
(B) 其產品是在農場製造的。
(C) 這是一間家族企業。
(D) 它將與有機農場協會合併。　　答案 (C)

160. 網站上可以取得什麼？
(A) 訂購一盒穀物棒
(B) 下載申請表
(C) 索取免費試吃商品
(D) 領取買一送一優惠券　　　　答案 (D)

問題 **161-163**，請參考以下電子郵件。

收件人：蘇菲亞・艾略特 <selliot@neymail.com>
寄件人：奧斯卡・維倫 <oviren@valverdeshoes.com>
日　期：8 月 13 日星期一
主　旨：回覆：要求

親愛的艾略特女士，

(162) 感謝您於 8 月 9 日聯繫我們，告知您在 8 月 4 日用網路傳送的訊息尚未收到回覆。由於我們的網路伺服器發生技術問題，您提及在 8 月 2 日收到的鞋款尺碼

錯誤的訊息，延遲至今日處理。

(161) 如您所知，若提出的退貨要求是由巴爾韋德鞋業所引起的問題，將獲得免費處理。此外，對於造成您的不便，我們將提供 20 美元的折扣券以示歉意。請登入我們的網站，收取折扣券。

欲退回鞋子，請從網站下載退貨申請單，列印後填寫。在原包裝盒中，您會看到一張預付費用的貨運標籤。(163) 我們的辦公室地址印在上面，因此郵寄時請務必將其貼在您的貨運包裹上。請將鞋子、購買收據和填妥的退貨申請表一併放入包裹。

請確保您的退貨包裹在 8 月 20 日之前寄送給我們。

誠摯感謝。

奧斯卡・維倫
巴爾韋德鞋業客戶服務部門

---

161. 關於巴爾韋德鞋業，文中暗指什麼？
(A) 要求退貨通常會收費。
(B) 貨物中將附上折扣券。
(C) 目前遭遇技術問題。
(D) 為回頭客提供折扣券。　　　答案 (A)

162. 艾略特女士第一次向巴爾韋德鞋業回報訂單問題，是什麼時候？
(A) 8 月 2 日
(B) 8 月 4 日
(C) 8 月 9 日
(D) 8 月 13 日　　　　　　　　答案 (B)

163. 以下句子最適合放在文中 [1]、[2]、[3] 和 [4] 的哪一個位置？
「我們的辦公室地址印在上面，因此郵寄時請務必將其貼在您的貨運包裹上。」
(A) [1]
(B) [2]
(C) [3]
(D) [4]　　　　　　　　　　　答案 (C)

問題 **164-167**，請參考以下線上討論訊息。

艾曼達・梅斯特　　　　　　　　[晚上 7:37]
(165) 我剛剛買了搖滾襪子演唱會的門票！除了我還有誰要去嗎？

利亞姆・莫里斯　　　　　　　　[晚上 7:41]
我一直很想去聽他們的演唱會，(165) 他們的新專輯超棒。

佩德羅・路德　　　　　　　　　[晚上 7:42]
沒錯，可不是嗎？(165) 我試著在一些實體商店購買這張專輯，但它們很快就賣完了。

利亞姆・莫里斯　　　　　　　　[晚上 7:43]
門票多少錢？

(164) (166) (167) 艾曼達・梅斯特　　　[晚上 7:44]
我花了 90 美元買到一張一般門票。

(164) 佩德羅・路德　　　　　　　[晚上 7:44]
哇。我的票花了 120 美元。你是在哪個網站買的？

(164) (166) 艾曼達・梅斯特　　　　[晚上 7:47]
因為我是傳奇票券的會員，所以可以獲得折扣。

(166) (167) 利亞姆・莫里斯　　　　[晚上 7:48]
太誇張了！通常一場在托齊雅廳舉辦的演唱會，很容易
就會花超過 100 美元。如果我加入會員，也可以享有
折扣嗎？

艾曼達・梅斯特　　　　　　　　[晚上 7:49]
當然。那間公司還為第一次使用的人提供額外折扣。你
一定要看一下。

佩德羅・路德　　　　　　　　　[晚上 7:50]
我想，從現在開始我會在那個網站購買所有演唱會的門
票。

利亞姆・莫里斯　　　　　　　　[晚上 7:53]
謝謝你的消息，艾曼達！

艾曼達・梅斯特　　　　　　　　[晚上 7:54]
沒問題。到時候演唱會見！

164. 為什麼路德先生的票比梅斯特女士的票貴？
(A) 他的門票只限定給粉絲俱樂部會員。
(B) 他沒有用折扣價買票。
(C) 他買了前排座位的票。
(D) 他不小心付了超出應有金額的費用。　答案 (B)

165. 關於搖滾襪子，文中暗指什麼？
(A) 他們即將舉辦的演唱會門票已售罄。
(B) 他們最近首次亮相。
(C) 他們目前正在巡迴演出。
(D) 他們的新專輯大受歡迎。　　答案 (D)

166. 晚上 7 點 48 分，莫里斯先生寫道「太誇張了」，是什
麼意思？
(A) 他認為這個網站給了很棒的優惠。
(B) 他建議梅斯特女士在演唱會當天早點出門。
(C) 梅斯特女士為他買票之後，他立刻就會收到。
(D) 他很驚訝得知在網路上買票有多麼容易。　答案 (A)

167. 從線上討論訊息中，可以推斷出什麼事？
(A) 莫里斯先生將獲得門票退費。
(B) 搖滾襪子演唱會將大排長龍。
(C) 梅斯特女士會和莫里斯先生一起去聽路德先生的演
唱會。
(D) 即將登場的搖滾襪子演唱會將於托齊雅廳舉辦。
答案 (D)

問題 168-171，請參考以下信件內容。

12 月 18 日

(170) 莉莉・馬丁尼茲
副主編
德薩特出版社
老鷹路 551 號
92155 加州，聖地亞哥

親愛的馬丁尼茲女士，

(170) 我是科帕斯大學的新聞學教授。(169) 您在貴公司
網站的線上專欄中，說明了關於創造和運用數位出版品
的創新概念，讓我印象深刻。您在編輯和出版方面的知
識和專業，相當令人敬佩。

(168) (170) 為了向我的學生提供專業寫作領域的現況資
訊，我正在組織一個由特約嘉賓演講的學程。您是否有
興趣來我的其中一堂課與學生會面，並就您線上專欄的
同一主題進行授課？(170) 上學期，貴部門經理菲利普
先生曾為此為學生上課，他們全都獲益良多。

(171) 如果您有興趣，請透過 bsmith@cupouse.edu 聯
繫布蘭達・史密斯，以討論您來訪的日期和時間。我們
期待與您見面。

誠摯邀請。

約瑟夫・克利夫蘭
科帕斯大學新聞學教授

168. 這封信的目的是什麼？
(A) 針對即將來臨的活動提供資訊
(B) 表揚某位學生
(C) 請求網頁設計
(D) 邀請講師　　　　　　　　　答案 (D)

169. 克利夫蘭先生如何得知馬丁尼茲女士的概念？
(A) 他讀了她在網路上寫的文章。
(B) 他參加了她舉辦的研討會。
(C) 他在她的公司演講。
(D) 他為了做報告採訪了她。　　答案 (A)

170. 根據信件內容，誰之前曾到訪科帕斯大學？
(A) 一群網頁設計師
(B) 一名出版社員工
(C) 一名公司領導人
(D) 一系列研討會的籌辦者　　　答案 (B)

171. 馬丁尼茲女士為何需要聯繫史密斯女士？
(A) 預留研討會席位
(B) 提交一些文件
(C) 討論補償事宜
(D) 安排會面　　　　　　　　　答案 (D)

問題 **172-175**，請參考以下文章內容。

---

8 月 9 日－(172) (174) 月亮馬戲團在紐約首次演出，將帶來令人驚嘆的大自然故事《佐拉》。(173D) 經過兩年籌備，這場最新的精彩演出終於準備好登上舞臺。

(173D) (173A) 上週在費城舉行的記者會上，《佐拉》導演葛明格里·卡明斯基詳細描述了這場表演的誕生過程。這場表演靈感來自朱莉婭·西姆斯的流行小說《叢林故事》，裡頭包含叢林及其住民既雄偉又狂野的特徵。

卡明斯基先生在舞臺上著重於描繪《叢林故事》用文字傳達的自然色彩。他非常重視舞臺設計、服裝、道具的每一個細節，並盡可能讓一切看起來栩栩如生。(173C) (175) 他找來為《西雅圖天際線》編舞的編舞家艾瑞亞·費南迪茲一同合作，創造出讓觀眾彷彿置身於真正叢林中的舞蹈設計。創作《佐拉》的劇本時，導演還與得獎編劇路易·貝爾密切合作。(175) 這些努力都為一項傑作的誕生帶來貢獻，即是這場超乎想像的馬戲團表演。

(174)《佐拉》將於 9 月 3 日在洛倫茨劇院首演。未來的全國巡迴演出，則計劃前往波士頓和拉斯維加斯。別錯過這個機會，欣賞由月亮劇團帶來、有史以來最精彩的表演——《佐拉》。

---

172. 此文章的主要目的是什麼？
    (A) 替小說改編電影打廣告
    (B) 介紹首次亮相的導演
    (C) 分享一場表演的資訊
    (D) 描述以叢林動物為主題的活動　　　答案 (C)

173. 關於卡明斯基先生，文中沒有暗指什麼？
    (A) 他上週和一群記者談話。
    (B) 他為了準備表演而前往叢林。
    (C) 他與艾瑞亞·費南迪茲一起工作。
    (D) 他為《佐拉》花費了兩年心力。　　答案 (B)

174. 洛倫茨劇院在哪裡？
    (A) 紐約
    (B) 費城
    (C) 拉斯維加斯
    (D) 波士頓　　　　　　　　　　　　答案 (A)

175. 以下句子最適合放在文中 [1]、[2]、[3] 和 [4] 的哪一個位置？
    「創作《佐拉》的劇本時，導演還與得獎編劇路易·貝爾密切合作。」
    (A) [1]
    (B) [2]
    (C) [3]
    (D) [4]　　　　　　　　　　　　　答案 (C)

問題 **176-180**，請參考以下時間表及電子郵件。

---

(176) (179) **山谷健身中心**
～ 歡慶一週年 ～

(176)「我們只用了一年，
就成為這個地區最好的個人訓練服務提供者。」

(178) **12 月 12 - 16 日，201 個人訓練教室可用時間表**

(178) 星期一	(178) 星期一	星期二	星期三	星期四	星期五
(178) 早上 9 點－ 中午 12 點	(178) 丹尼爾·安德魯斯	羅伯特·史東	羅伯特·史東	亞歷山大·尼爾森	亞倫·葛瑞森
下午 1 點－ 下午 4 點	希薇亞·佩雷拉	亞倫·葛瑞森	羅伯特·史東	亞歷山大·尼爾森	希薇亞·佩雷拉
下午 4 點－ 下午 6 點	丹尼爾·安德魯斯	亞倫·葛瑞森	丹尼爾·安德魯斯	維多莉亞·柏克	維多莉亞·柏克

本週，由於艾許莉·史奈德女士正在從輕傷中復原，羅伯特·史東先生將代替她為客戶進行個人訓練。每週六，所有訓練教室都會保留供客戶進行補課。

收件人：琳達·克羅寧 <lcronin@cuzmail.com>
寄件人：卡爾·強森 <cjohnson@valleyfitness.com>
日　期：(178) (179) 12 月 10 日
主　旨：您的個人訓練

親愛的克羅寧女士，

(177) 我們很遺憾地通知您，由於沙加緬度遭逢意外的大雪，山谷健身中心將於本週一、二閉館。(178) 因此，您原定週一上午於 201 教室進行的個人訓練已被取消。請在方便時盡速聯繫本中心，以討論您方便至本中心訓練的日期。

(179) 我們的紀錄也顯示，您的年度會員資格將於 **12 月 20 日**到期。12 月 15 日之前續訂會員資格，即可獲得 15% 會員折扣和一份特別禮物。(180) 請上我們的網站，查看您可以從中挑選的 **20 多種禮物**。

卡爾·強森
山谷健身中心

---

176. 關於山谷健身中心，文中暗指什麼？
    (A) 這是一項快速成長的事業。
    (B) 每週六都會邀請化妝師前來。
    (C) 最近僱用了史東先生。
    (D) 計劃再開一間分店。　　　　　　答案 (A)

177. 此電子郵件的目的是什麼？
    (A) 警告惡劣天氣
    (B) 回覆一項要求
    (C) 確認一間公司倒閉
    (D) 宣布時程變更　　　　　　　　　答案 (D)

178. 克羅寧女士原本打算接受誰的個人訓練指導？
    (A) 亞歷山大‧尼爾森
    (B) 亞倫‧葛瑞森
    (C) 丹尼爾‧安德魯斯
    (D) 希薇亞‧佩雷拉　　　　　　　　　答案 (C)

179. 關於克羅寧女士，文中暗指什麼？
    (A) 她住在沙加緬度。
    (B) 她計劃在週六續約會員資格。
    (C) 她成為山谷健身中心的會員大約一年了。
    (D) 她是山谷健身中心的私人教練。　　答案 (C)

180. 克羅寧女士為什麼需要造訪該網站？
    (A) 重新安排會面
    (B) 查看一份清單
    (C) 續約會員資格
    (D) 取得折扣　　　　　　　　　　　　答案 (B)

問題 **181-185**，請參考以下廣告及電子郵件。

奧卡拉

(181) 奧卡拉是位於波茨維爾的會議中心，為波茨維爾和克靈頓的企業和居民提供場地。我們的場地專家不會停下腳步，直到您完全滿意為止。

特色活動場地

(183) 芭芭拉大廳	卡塔利娜花園
伯頓大廈的主廳是舉辦企業和私人活動的完美場所。設有點心吧。最多可容納 **200** 人。	這是座美麗的花園，適合舉辦婚禮和宴會等戶外活動。場地能否使用，將視天氣狀況而定。餐飲服務須額外收費。
(184) 迪斯基托大廳	專業人員室
此會議大廳配備投影機、**6** 人圓桌和舒適的椅子。適合舉辦約 **40** 人參加的簡報會議和研討會。	這是教室型空間，非常適合舉辦研討會、簡報會議和講座。有白板、麥克風、雷射筆、投影機和其他必要物品。可容納約 **50** 人。

(182) 本頁列出的所有場地均提供免費無線網路。想了解細節、場地價格以及更多奧卡拉相關資訊，請上我們的網站 www.auckara.com。如須預約，請寄信至 k.washington@auckara.com 給我們的場地經理凱瑟琳‧華盛頓。

收件人：凱瑟琳‧華盛頓 <k.washington@auckara.com>
寄件人：羅斯‧郭琳 <rguarin@voepublishing.com>
日　期：6 月 10 日
主　旨：活動場地

親愛的華盛頓女士，

我計劃在七月舉辦一場公共關係研討會。(183) 我在活動策劃部門工作的同事麥可‧格林米爾，4 月分在芭芭拉大廳舉辦宴會後，介紹了奧卡拉給我。他告訴我，這個地方設施齊全，價格也很合理。(184) 我正在尋找可容納 35 人左右的場地。由於研討會將包括討論環節，因此需要一個可以讓參與者分組的空間。

如果有符合我需求的場地，請回信附上您的建議。我想用電話與您討論更多細節和價格。(185) 此外，由於我的部門每半年就會舉辦一次研討會，我想知道是否可以獲得折扣。在此先感謝你的協助。

誠摯祝福。

羅斯‧郭琳

---

181. 關於奧卡拉，文中提到什麼？
    (A) 預訂場地時須繳納押金。
    (B) 可能根據天氣狀況而關閉。
    (C) 銷售商務會議的設備。
    (D) 有舉辦各種活動的場地。　　　　　答案 (D)

182. 根據廣告，所有特色活動場地都有什麼？
    (A) 茶點
    (B) 投影機
    (C) 桌椅
    (D) 網路　　　　　　　　　　　　　　答案 (D)

183. 關於格林米爾先生，文中提到什麼？
    (A) 他在奧卡拉工作。
    (B) 他會寄電子郵件給郭琳女士。
    (C) 他 4 月時造訪了伯頓大廈。
    (D) 他對公共關係了解很深。　　　　　答案 (C)

184. 華盛頓女士最有可能向郭琳女士推薦哪個場地？
    (A) 芭芭拉大廳
    (B) 迪斯基托大廳
    (C) 卡塔利娜花園
    (D) 專業人員室　　　　　　　　　　　答案 (B)

185. 郭琳女士在電子郵件中詢問什麼？
    (A) 她有沒有獲得折扣的資格
    (B) 餐飲服務的價格
    (C) 一系列研討會的日期
    (D) 場地大小　　　　　　　　　　　　答案 (A)

問題 **186-190**，請參考以下公告及網頁。

第三屆家常料理大賽

(190)《美食帝國雜誌》誠摯邀請業餘廚師參加第 3 屆家常料理大賽。我們正在蒐羅四類菜餚：

類別	評審
中式	唐納 · 劉，紅龍餐廳老闆，(186)《最好的食材，最好的菜餚》作者
法式	科琳 · 德西萊茲，大皇宮飯店主廚，(186)《生命中最重要的因素：食物》作者
(188) 義式	馬里奧 · 帕尼庫奇，電視節目《美食現場》美食評論家及 (186)《秘密食譜》作者
墨西哥式	艾麗西亞 · 羅德里格斯，屢獲殊榮的食品造型師及 (186)《如何拍攝最佳菜餚快照》作者

(187) 第一輪篩選將根據參賽者提交的照片和食譜來進行。請於 7 月 5 日之前在我們的網站上提交你的參賽作品。7 月 20 日將公布各類別的 15 名入圍者。入圍者將受邀於 7 月 30 日前往美食帝國會議中心，在評審委員面前展示烹飪技巧和菜理。每個類別的兩名優勝者將於 8 月 10 日公布。(189) 所有優勝者將在我們的 9 月號上刊登，並附上專業攝影師為他們拍攝的廚房和菜餚照片。(190) 第一名優勝者將獲得 2,500 美元獎金，第二名優勝者將能免費訂閱我們一整年的雜誌。

---

http://www.foodempire.com/contest_submission

家常料理大賽
線上申請表

姓名：(188) (189) 海倫 · 麥丹尼爾斯
電子信箱：hmcdaniels@riomail.com
電話號碼：843-555-5265
地址：29455 南卡羅萊納州，羅斯威爾，卡勒街 35 號

簡單描述你的料理：

> (188) 經典奶油義大利麵配上蘑菇、培根及自製奶酪披薩。搭配阿芙佳朵佐香草冰淇淋為甜點。

 (189) 如果我獲選為大賽優勝者，我同意《美食帝國》雜誌刊登我的料理和廚房照片。

請附上你的料理照片和食譜：

📄 Pasta_McDaniels.jpg	📄 Affogato_McDaniels.jpg
📄 Pizza_McDaniels.jpg	📄 Recipes_McDaniels.doc

---

http://www.foodempire.com/contest_winners

家常料理大賽
優勝者公告

終於到了公布第 3 屆家常料理大賽優勝者的時刻！

	第 1 名：	第 2 名：
中式	賈斯汀 · 哈諾伊斯	羅伯特 · 威爾遜
義式	金伯利 · 史密斯	海倫 · 麥丹尼爾斯
法式	布萊恩 · 洛佩茲	泰森 · 蘇利文
墨西哥式	(190) 第 1 名：米歇爾 · 梅森	第 2 名：約瑟夫 · 唐

恭喜所有優勝者！想看優勝者的菜餚照片和食譜，請點擊這裡。

186. 評審委員有什麼共同點？
(A) 他們都因烹飪而獲獎。
(B) 他們去了同一所烹飪學校。
(C) 他們各自三度擔任這個大賽的評審。
(D) 他們每人各寫了一本關於食物的書。　　答案 (D)

187. 第一輪選拔的交件截止日是什麼時候？
(A) 7 月 5 日
(B) 7 月 20 日
(C) 7 月 30 日
(D) 8 月 10 日　　答案 (A)

188. 誰最可能評審麥丹尼爾斯女士的參賽作品？
(A) 劉先生
(B) 德西萊茲女士
(C) 帕尼庫奇先生
(D) 羅德里格斯女士　　答案 (C)

189. 麥丹尼爾斯女士同意什麼事？
(A) 出現在電視節目中
(B) 讓美食帝國驗證她是不是業餘廚師
(C) 為比賽優勝者的廚房拍照
(D) 讓美食帝國的員工造訪她的廚房。　　答案 (D)

190. 關於梅森女士，文中暗指什麼？
(A) 她將獲得免費雜誌訂閱。
(B) 她將獲得獎金。
(C) 她在《美食帝國雜誌》工作。
(D) 她是一位專門做墨西哥菜的廚師。　　答案 (B)

問題 **191-195**，請參考以下電子郵件。

收件人：(191B) (193) 約瑟夫 · 金、安德魯 · 史密斯、安娜 · 格里森
寄件人：羅伯特 · 路納
日　期：5 月 8 日
主　旨：歡迎

大家好。

(191C) 歡迎來到鄧肯有限公司，我們致力於為兒童和成人提供最優質、最安全的迷你汽車、玩偶和拼圖。

(191B) (193) 鄧肯公司全體很高興與你們能和我們一起在業務部門工作。到職第一天，你們必須先到人力資源部，(192) 領取發放的員工證。人力資源部副理米歇爾·威廉斯也會帶你們參觀公司大樓。

(191A) (194) 5 月 17 日的新進人員培訓，各位也必須參加。(193) 部門經理會聯絡你們，說明培訓的地點和時間。再次歡迎加入鄧肯公司！

誠摯祝福。

羅伯特·路納

收件人：(193) 約瑟夫·金、安德魯·史密斯、安娜·格里森
寄件人：克里斯多夫·佩吉
日　期：5 月 14 日
主　旨：培訓課程

你好，

我希望你們已經漸漸適應鄧肯公司。(193) 這封電子郵件是關於你們即將接受的培訓課程。這些課程將於下午 1:30 在三樓會議室進行。(194) 培訓結束後隔天，將為所有新進人員舉辦簡單的歡迎會。請於下午 6 點前抵達波斯蒂奧餐廳。

誠摯祝福。

(193) 克里斯多夫·佩吉

收件人：克里斯多夫·佩吉
寄件人：蘿拉·摩根
日　期：5 月 21 日
主　旨：你的商務提案

親愛的佩吉先生，

(194) 感謝您選擇波斯蒂奧餐廳，作為貴公司近期迎新宴會的場地。希望大家能在我的店裡度過愉快的時光。(194) 正如我們在聚會上所討論的，波斯蒂奧餐廳很樂意在 6 月分，為貴公司於會議室舉辦的年度慶祝活動提供餐點。(195) 請再次來訪，以便我們討論合約的條款和細則。

謝謝您。

蘿拉·摩根

191. 關於鄧肯公司，文中沒有暗指什麼？
　　(A) 為員工提供培訓課程。
　　(B) 最近僱用了一批員工。
　　(C) 販售兒童玩具。
　　(D) 支付僱員的差旅費。　　　　　　答案 (D)

192. 第一封電子郵件中，第 1 段第 4 行的「issued」，含義最接近
　　(A) 印刷
　　(B) 收取
　　(C) 發放
　　(D) 公布　　　　　　　　　　　　答案 (C)

193. 佩吉先生最有可能是誰？
　　(A) 業務部經理
　　(B) 培訓課程指導員
　　(C) 企業主
　　(D) 人資主任　　　　　　　　　　答案 (A)

194. 摩根女士和佩吉先生可能是何時碰面的？
　　(A) 5 月 14 日
　　(B) 5 月 17 日
　　(C) 5 月 18 日
　　(D) 5 月 21 日　　　　　　　　　答案 (C)

195. 摩根女士要求佩吉先生做什麼？
　　(A) 提供餐飲服務
　　(B) 發送電子郵件
　　(C) 支付近期活動費用
　　(D) 去她的店裡　　　　　　　　　答案 (D)

問題 196-200，請參考以下廣告、訂單及電子郵件。

(196)Booktree.com 是一家網路書店，您可以在這裡用最合理的價格，找到新書和二手書。Booktree.com 已經營 20 多年，越來越受閱讀愛好者歡迎，去年被《今日趨勢》雜誌評為「年度最佳書店」。

(197) 我們推出一項特別的夏季促銷活動，會將您買書時支付金額的 20% 作為 Booktree 點數送還。這比您平時收到的 5% 還多了 15%。Booktree 點數是獎勵點數，您日後可用於購買更多書籍。(197) 本優惠僅適用於首次購買，有效期限至 8 月 30 日。

只需要 3 美元即可申請加急運送，讓訂單在 2 天內送達。本服務僅適用於國內顧客。

Booktree.com

始終以最好的價格提供最好的書

訂單編號：	FS094810	訂單日期：	8月28日
Booktree 帳號：	jbrown09	(198) 寄送日期：	9月2日
(197) 顧客姓名：	約瑟夫·布朗		
地址：	劍橋大道 425 號 85040 亞利桑那州，鳳凰城		

訂單明細

書名	作者	品項編號	價格
軟體設計的藝術	雷納德·卡斯楚	D148501	27.5 美元
程式設計的模式	(200) **法華克·莫斯利**	R720958	(200) **16.75 美元**
程式設計基礎知識	霍華德·傑克遜	R012290	31.10 美元
高效運算	露西·羅德里茲	C890271	28.80 美元
		小計	104.15 美元
		貨運和手續費	–
		稅額 (8%)	8.33 美元
		總計	112.48 美元

(197) 本次交易提供的 **Booktree** 點數：
22.50 點（促銷優惠 **-20%**）

- 退貨或退款必須在購買後 10 天內提出。上網提交申請或發送電子郵件至 returnrequest@booktree.com。欲了解詳細的退貨和退款政策，請前往我們的網站。

收件人：約瑟夫·布朗 <jbrown@bkmail.com>
寄件人：客戶服務 <customerservice@booktree.com>
日　期：9 月 5 日
主　旨：回覆：我最近的訂單

親愛的布朗先生，

(200) 我們聽說您今天早上收到了莫斯利博士所寫的《程式設計入門》一書。對於本次書籍寄送錯誤一事，我們深表歉意。我相信是在包裝您所訂購的書籍有所疏漏，因為本書的作者和價格與您實際訂購的書籍相同。我們會立即將正確的書籍加急運送到您的地址。請在您方便時，將收到的書籍寄至：73550 德州，休斯頓，伊爾福德大道 55 號。此外，為了對此過失表示歉意，我們會為您提供一張 10 美元折價券。請用您的帳號 (199) 登入我們的網站領取。

誠摯祝福。

Booktree.com 客戶服務

---

196. 關於 Booktree.com，文中暗指什麼？
　　(A) 它在網路販售二手書。
　　(B) 它榮獲多個獎項。
　　(C) 它只會寄送書籍給國內客戶。
　　(D) 它去年推出了一款雜誌。　　答案 (A)

197. 關於布朗先生，以下敘述何者最可能正確？
　　(A) 他製造電腦。
　　(B) 他訂閱《今日趨勢》雜誌。
　　(C) 他要求加急運送。
　　(D) 他第一次在 Booktree.com 上下訂單。　答案 (D)

198. 這筆訂單何時寄給布朗先生？
　　(A) 8 月 28 日
　　(B) 8 月 30 日
　　(C) 9 月 2 日
　　(D) 9 月 5 日　　答案 (C)

199. 電子郵件中，第 1 段第 7 行的「claim」，含義最接近
　　(A) 堅稱
　　(B) 抱怨
　　(C) 花費
　　(D) 拿取　　答案 (D)

200. 《程式設計入門》多少錢？
　　(A) 16.75 美元
　　(B) 27.50 美元
　　(C) 28.80 美元
　　(D) 31.10 美元　　答案 (A)

Actual Test 05
Part 1

1. 美國 M
   (A) They are sitting across from each other.
   (B) A man is pushing a chair under a table.
   (C) A woman is writing on a pad of paper.
   (D) They are removing a table from the room.

   (A) 他們面對面坐著。
   (B) 男子正把椅子推到桌子下。
   (C) 女子正在一疊紙上寫字。
   (D) 他們正把一張桌子移出房間。　　　　答案 (C)

2. 英國 M
   (A) The woman is applying some makeup.
   (B) The woman is removing an item from her purse.
   (C) The woman is packing her suitcase.
   (D) The woman is hanging a bag on her shoulder.

   (A) 女子正在化妝。
   (B) 女子正從她的包包裡拿出一樣東西。
   (C) 女子正在收拾行李。
   (D) 女子肩上掛著一個包包。　　　　答案 (B)

3. 美國 M
   (A) He is washing a cutting board in a sink.
   (B) He is stirring something in a bowl.
   (C) He is placing some containers in a cabinet.
   (D) He is preparing some food at a counter.

   (A) 他正在水槽洗砧板。
   (B) 他正在攪拌碗裡的東西。
   (C) 他正在把一些容器放入櫃子。
   (D) 他正在流理臺準備一些食物。　　　　答案 (D)

4. 美國 W
   (A) The woman is turning off a water faucet.
   (B) The woman is leaning against a windowsill.
   (C) Some potted plants have been arranged in a row.
   (D) Some tables are being moved into a room.

   (A) 女子正在關水龍頭。
   (B) 女子靠在窗檯上。
   (C) 一些盆栽被排成一列。
   (D) 一些桌子被搬進房間。　　　　答案 (C)

5. 澳洲 W
   (A) One of the women is rowing a boat.
   (B) Some people are boarding a boat.
   (C) Some people are standing on a dock.
   (D) One of the men is swimming across the river.

   (A) 其中一名女子正在划船。
   (B) 有些人正在登船。

   (C) 有些人站在碼頭上。
   (D) 其中一名男子正在游泳渡河。　　　　答案 (C)

6. 美國 W
   (A) Some trees are being planted near a river.
   (B) A cabin overlooks a fishing pier.
   (C) A bridge extends over a lake.
   (D) Some trees border a river.

   (A) 幾棵樹正被種植在河的附近。
   (B) 一間小屋俯瞰著一座釣魚碼頭。
   (C) 一座橋延伸到湖面上。
   (D) 河邊有幾棵樹。　　　　答案 (D)

Part 2

7. 美國 W 英國 M

   What are they constructing near the city park?
   (A) On the 20th floor.
   (B) A multi-complex shopping mall.
   (C) The parking space is limited.

   他們在城市公園附近建造什麼？
   (A) 在 20 樓。
   (B) 一座複合式購物中心。
   (C) 停車位有限。　　　　答案 (B)

8. 美國 M 澳洲 W

   We should consider Donald for the graphic designer position, shouldn't we?
   (A) Yes, we're reviewing his application now.
   (B) The repair should be done by 3.
   (C) Can I come in for an interview?

   我們應該考慮讓唐納擔任平面設計師，不是嗎？
   (A) 是的，我們正在審查他的申請。
   (B) 維修應該在 3 點前完成。
   (C) 我可以進來面試了嗎？　　　　答案 (A)

9. 美國 W 英國 M

   When will the next marketing report become available?
   (A) Not for another 2 weeks.
   (B) Yes, it was last month.
   (C) We are out of paper.

   下一份行銷報告何時可以拿到？
   (A) 至少要再過 2 週。
   (B) 是的，那是上個月的事情。
   (C) 我們沒有紙了。　　　　答案 (A)

10. 英國 M 澳洲 W

    Who's in charge of the expansion budget?
    (A) Neither did she.

(B) Forty thousand dollars.
(C) The project manager.

誰負責這次擴建的預算？
(A) 她也不是。
(B) 4 萬美元。
(C) 那位專案經理。 答案 (C)

11. 美國 W 美國 M

Doesn't this supermarket have a section for bread?
(A) The catering service.
(B) There's a new bakery across from the entrance.
(C) Are you applying for the position right now?

這家超市不是有麵包區嗎？
(A) 餐飲服務。
(B) 入口對面有一家新的烘焙坊。
(C) 你現在要申請這個職位嗎？ 答案 (B)

12. 英國 M 澳洲 W

Will the prototype for the 3D printer be ready in time for the trade fair?
(A) The decision is not fair.
(B) Yes, it'll be finished in 2 days or so.
(C) The flight was behind time.

這款 3D 列印機的原型趕得上博覽會嗎？
(A) 這個決定不公平。
(B) 是的，大約 2 天內就會完工。
(C) 航班延遲了。 答案 (B)

13. 美國 M 美國 W

Why didn't the shipment of computer keyboards arrive today?
(A) The truck broke down on the way.
(B) I like the computer game.
(C) The shipping department did yesterday.

為什麼電腦鍵盤今天沒有到貨？
(A) 卡車在半路拋錨了。
(B) 我喜歡這款電腦遊戲。
(C) 貨運部門昨天到了。 答案 (A)

14. 美國 W 英國 M

Our factory complex is locked on national holidays, isn't it?
(A) Go straight on Washington Boulevard.
(B) Just bring your company ID badge.
(C) To access the restricted area.

我們的綜合廠區在國定假日期間會鎖上，不是嗎？
(A) 沿著華盛頓大道直行。
(B) 只要帶著你的員工識別證即可。
(C) 進入管制區。 答案 (B)

15. 澳洲 W 美國 M

Do you want to purchase an inkjet printer or laser printer?
(A) I have the model number here.
(B) Yes, print it out, please.
(C) We are out of stock at the moment.

你想買噴墨印表機還是雷射印表機？
(A) 我這裡有型號。
(B) 是的，請列印出來。
(C) 我們目前缺貨。 答案 (A)

16. 英國 M 美國 W

Where can I sign up for the time management seminar?
(A) A new manager will be here soon.
(B) You can sign at the bottom.
(C) You can register on our website.

我在哪裡可以報名參加時間管理研討會？
(A) 新經理很快就會到了。
(B) 你可以在下方簽名。
(C) 你可以在我們網站上報名。 答案 (C)

17. 英國 M 澳洲 W

You know the supervisor at this assembly line, don't you?
(A) Yes, I've met her several times.
(B) It comes preassembled.
(C) No, several units in the line are not working.

你認識這條裝配線的主管，不是嗎？
(A) 是的，我見過她好幾次。
(B) 它是預先組裝好的。
(C) 不，線路上的多個元件無法使用。 答案 (A)

18. 美國 W 澳洲 W

Can I help you rearrange your office furniture?
(A) I bought a filing cabinet last Monday.
(B) The furniture store on Oak Street.
(C) I think I can manage on my own.

我可以幫你重新布置你的辦公室家具嗎？
(A) 我上週一買了一個文件櫃。
(B) 橡樹街的家具店。
(C) 我想我可以自己處理。 答案 (C)

19. 美國 M 澳洲 W

Can you tell me how to open a corporate account?
(A) A new accountant.
(B) There are additional office supplies in the cabinet.
(C) Here is the form you need to fill out.

你可以告訴我怎麼開立公司帳戶嗎？
(A) 一名新會計師。
(B) 櫃子裡還有額外的辦公用品。
(C) 這是你需要填寫的表格。　　　　答案 (C)

20. 美國 W　英國 M

Which client are we supposed to meet with this afternoon?
(A) We could possibly discuss the upcoming merger.
(B) From a local catering service.
(C) The Cattel Company representative.

今天下午我們要見哪位客戶？
(A) 我們可能會討論即將進行的併購案。
(B) 來自當地的外燴公司。
(C) 卡特爾公司的代表。　　　　答案 (C)

21. 澳洲 W　美國 M

How do you like this seafood restaurant?
(A) I'd like to do it.
(B) No, I haven't met the chef.
(C) I'd say it's my favorite place to eat.

你覺得這家海鮮餐廳怎麼樣？
(A) 我願意做這件事。
(B) 不，我還沒見過主廚。
(C) 我會說這是我最喜歡的用餐地點。　　　　答案 (C)

22. 英國 M　美國 W

Is there anybody who knows how to start a video conference?
(A) Tracy can do it.
(B) The registration fee for the conference.
(C) Yes, the video will be available.

誰知道要如何召開視訊會議？
(A) 崔西會。
(B) 會議的報名費。
(C) 是的，視訊可供使用。　　　　答案 (A)

23. 美國 M　澳洲 W

I don't think today is the best day for an outdoor baseball game, right?
(A) Yes, he is one of the baseball players.
(B) I agree. It is rather hot and humid.
(C) Mondays from 8 to 5.

我認為今天不是最適合戶外棒球比賽的日子，對吧？
(A) 是的，他是一名棒球選手。
(B) 我同意。天氣又熱又濕。
(C) 每週一 8 點到 5 點。　　　　答案 (B)

24. 美國 W　英國 M

It's raining so hard outside.
(A) With an umbrella and a raincoat.

(B) I can give you a ride to the store.
(C) Yes, that was really hard.

外面雨下得很大。
(A) 用雨傘和雨衣。
(B) 我可以載你去商店。
(C) 對，那真的很難。　　　　答案 (B)

25. 英國 M　澳洲 W

Which museum do you think I should take Mr. Ricardo to?
(A) I'm new to this town, actually.
(B) I'll take that one on the left.
(C) Thanks, but I've already submitted the report.

你認為我應該帶里嘉圖先生去哪間博物館？
(A) 其實，我才剛來這座小鎮。
(B) 我選左邊那個。
(C) 謝謝，但我已經提交報告了。　　　　答案 (A)

26. 美國 W　美國 M

Greg, will you be available to call our foreign clients back?
(A) Aron left them a message.
(B) Yes, he'll be back shortly.
(C) Haven't we met before?

格雷格，你有空回電給我們的外國客戶嗎？
(A) 亞倫留言給他們了。
(B) 是的，他很快就會回來。
(C) 我們以前沒見過面嗎？　　　　答案 (A)

27. 美國 M　美國 W

Are the new clients from overseas flying in today or tomorrow?
(A) Salma already picked them up from the airport.
(B) Two roundtrip tickets, please.
(C) I'll give them the contract.

海外新客戶是今天還明天搭機抵達？
(A) 薩爾瑪已經去機場接他們了。
(B) 兩張來回票，謝謝。
(C) 我會把合約給他們。　　　　答案 (A)

28. 英國 M　美國 M

When do you think you'll be able to work on this designing project?
(A) I can't agree with you more.
(B) Yes, they brought in a new designer.
(C) I haven't been trained yet.

你認為你什麼時候可以處理這個設計專案？
(A) 我非常同意你的觀點。
(B) 是的，他們引進了一位新設計師。
(C) 我目前還沒有受過培訓。　　　　答案 (C)

29. 美國 W 英國 M

This bill seems too high for the lunch we ordered, doesn't it?
(A) Okay, I'll add that dessert to the menu.
(B) No, that looks about right to me.
(C) I'll be right back with your bill.

以我們點的午餐來說，這個帳單似乎太貴了，不是嗎？
(A) 好的，我會把那道甜點加入菜單。
(B) 不，我覺得看起來差不多。
(C) 我會立刻帶著你的帳單回來。　　　　答案 (B)

30. 澳洲 W 英國 M

Why will the warehouse be closed for the next week?
(A) We don't have any in stock, either.
(B) No, that's a new factory.
(C) Didn't you receive the memo?

為什麼倉庫下週要關閉？
(A) 我們也沒有庫存了。
(B) 不，那是一座新工廠。
(C) 你沒有收到備忘錄嗎？　　　　答案 (C)

31. 美國 W 英國 M

The all-weather tires here in this section are really costly.
(A) A 10-minute taxi ride.
(B) They last a very long time.
(C) Stay tuned for the weather update.

這一區的全天候輪胎真的很貴。
(A) 搭計程車要 10 分鐘。
(B) 它們非常耐用。
(C) 請留意氣象最新動態。　　　　答案 (B)

Part 3

問題 32-34，請參考以下對話內容。 英國 M 美國 W

M: (32)**I'm pleasantly surprised by how well our clothing store is doing. Our customers seem satisfied with the blouses and sweaters we carry.**

W: That's right. (33)**And as soon as we install the new cash registers this weekend**, customers will have shorter waits at checkout.

M: For sure. Oh, one more thing. (34)**Since the holidays are approaching, several employees have asked about when you will have the overtime work schedule ready.**

W: (34)**I've been working on the schedule since this morning.** I think I should be done with it by tomorrow.

男：我們服裝店的經營狀況好得令人驚喜。顧客似乎對我們提供的襯衫和毛衣很滿意。

女：沒錯。一旦我們在這個週末安裝了新的收銀機，顧客結帳的等待時間還會縮短。

男：這點毋庸置疑。哦，還有一件事。由於假期快到了，幾位員工在詢問你何時會完成加班表。

女：我從今天早上就開始排班表了。我想明天之前應該會完成。

32. 說話者在哪裡工作？
(A) 零售商店
(B) 紡織品製造商
(C) 藥局
(D) 超市　　　　答案 (A)

33. 這個週末會發生什麼事？
(A) 將舉辦一場特賣會。
(B) 員工會加班。
(C) 將安裝新設備。
(D) 將舉辦一場培訓課程。　　　　答案 (C)

34. 女子說她一直在準備什麼？
(A) 班表
(B) 商店導覽圖
(C) 庫存清單
(D) 廣告　　　　答案 (A)

問題 35-37，請參考以下對話內容。 美國 M 澳洲 W

M: Hello. (35)**This is Jason in customer service at Harding International.** How can I help you?

W: Oh, it's about time. I've been on hold for more than 40 minutes. (36)**I'm so frustrated because I've never had to wait so long to talk to someone about a computer issue before.**

M: I'm very sorry about the wait, ma'am. We're experiencing much higher call volume than normal today, and we're trying to answer them as quickly as we can. Now, before we continue speaking, (37)**would you please let me know the eight-digit product code that's located on the back of your laptop?**

男：您好。我是哈汀國際公司客戶服務部的傑森。請問有什麼我可以效勞的地方嗎？

女：噢，總算接了。我已經等 40 幾分鐘了。我很不高興，因為我以前從來不需要等這麼久才能說明電腦的問題。

男：女士，很抱歉讓您久等。今天來電遠多於平日，我們正在努力盡快答覆。那麼，在我們繼續談話之前，能請您先告訴我，您筆記型電腦背面的八位數產品代碼嗎？

35. 男子最有可能是誰？
    (A) 客戶服務人員
    (B) 電機工程師
    (C) 銷售顧問
    (D) 行銷專家　　　　　　　　答案 (A)

36. 女子為何感到不滿？
    (A) 她沒有收據。
    (B) 她的電腦沒有修好。
    (C) 她無法獲得退款。
    (D) 她必須等待很久。　　　　答案 (D)

37. 女子被要求提供什麼？
    (A) 帳號
    (B) 產品編號
    (C) 優惠券代碼
    (D) 地址　　　　　　　　　　答案 (B)

問題 38-40，請參考以下三方對話內容。 美國 M 美國 W 英國 M

M1: Hello. (38)**I'd like to confirm that the bus bound for Lexington is leaving in thirty minutes.** I can't see a listing for it anywhere on the board.

W: (38) (39)**I regret to inform you that the bus has been delayed by two hours.** It's leaving at 10:30 now.

M1: Oh, no. That means we're going to miss our meeting with a customer in Lexington.

M2: (40)**We'd better give her a call and let her know.** Steve, would you mind doing that now?

M1: (40)**Not at all.** I'll see if she minds if we meet later in the evening.

- -

男 1：你好。我想確認開往萊辛頓的客運會在三十分鐘後出發。我在告示板上找不到這班車。

女：很遺憾通知您，這班車已延遲兩小時。10 點 30 分發車。

男 1：哦，不。這樣我們會錯過和萊辛頓客戶的會面。

男 2：我們最好打電話讓她知道。史蒂夫，你介意現在打通電話嗎？

男 1：一點也不。我看看她會不會介意我們晚上晚一點見面。

38. 女子最有可能是誰？
    (A) 公車司機
    (B) 鐵路工程師
    (C) 租車公司員工
    (D) 客運站員工　　　　　　　答案 (D)

39. 女子提到什麼問題？
    (A) 電話號碼不正確。
    (B) 會議取消。

(C) 客運誤點。
(D) 無法取得網路連線。　　　　答案 (C)

40. 史蒂夫接下來會做什麼？
    (A) 聯繫客戶
    (B) 取消會議
    (C) 支付票券費用
    (D) 要求票券退費　　　　　　　答案 (A)

問題 41-43，請參考以下對話內容。 澳洲 W 美國 M

W: Hi, John. (41)**Is there a bicycle rack somewhere on the office building property here?**

M: I'm not sure. Why do you ask?

W: (42)**I just had to take my car to the garage. The mechanic said he can't work on it for a week**, so I'm planning to ride my bike here until he's done.

M: Hmm… There might be a bicycle rack somewhere around here. (43)**But if there isn't, why don't you talk to Michelle? She lives in your neighborhood, so perhaps you could carpool to work together.**

W: I had no idea about that. I'll call her after lunch.

- -

女：嗨，約翰。辦公大樓這裡有腳踏車停放架嗎？

男：我不確定。你為什麼這麼問？

女：我剛把車開去修車廠。技師說他這一個禮拜無法著手修理，所以我打算騎腳踏車來這裡，直到他修好為止。

男：嗯……這附近可能有腳踏車停放架。但是如果沒有，你何不跟蜜雪兒談談呢？她住在你家附近，也許你們可以共乘上班。

女：我不知道這件事。午餐後我會打給她。

41. 女子詢問男子什麼事情？
    (A) 修車廠
    (B) 即將舉辦的研討會
    (C) 腳踏車停放處
    (D) 預約租車　　　　　　　　答案 (C)

42. 女子遇到什麼問題？
    (A) 她把車鑰匙搞丟了。
    (B) 她的車在店裡。
    (C) 她的電腦故障。
    (D) 她上班又遲到了。　　　　答案 (B)

43. 男子建議女子做什麼？
    (A) 休假一下
    (B) 搬到離公司更近的地方
    (C) 找一名同事談談
    (D) 列印一些文件　　　　　　答案 (C)

問題 **44-46**，請參考以下對話內容。 美國 W 英國 M

W: (44)**Congratulations on being transferred to the new office in London, David.** Here's a card that everyone in the office signed. We hope you enjoy working abroad.

M: Thanks. I'm going to miss working with everyone, (45)**but I'm looking forward to the chance to manage my own office.**

W: I know you'll do an outstanding job. We all wonder if you have some free time for dinner tonight. (46)**We'd like to take you out to celebrate before you leave for London.**

M: (46)**I heard about a new Indian restaurant downtown.**

W: Sounds great. Let's go there.

女：大衛，恭喜你被調到倫敦的新辦公室。這是辦公室裡大家簽名的卡片。我們希望你喜歡在國外工作。

男：謝謝。我會懷念跟大家共事的時光。但我也很期待有管理自己辦公室的機會。

女：我知道你會做得很出色。我們在想，你今晚是否有空吃晚餐。我們想在你出發去倫敦之前，帶你去慶祝一下。

男：我聽說市中心有一家新的印度餐廳。

女：聽起來很棒。我們就去那裡吧。

44. 女子因為什麼事情向男子祝賀？
    (A) 獲得升遷
    (B) 接受調任
    (C) 收到獎金
    (D) 獲得獎項　　　　　　　　　　答案 (B)

45. 男子期待什麼事情？
    (A) 搬回他的家鄉
    (B) 簽訂新合約
    (C) 擔任主管
    (D) 接待來自海外的員工　　　　　答案 (C)

46. 男子為什麼說「我聽說市中心有一家新的印度餐廳」？
    (A) 接受邀請
    (B) 指出市中心交通繁忙
    (C) 要求更改菜單
    (D) 表達對成本的疑慮　　　　　　答案 (A)

問題 **47-49**，請參考以下三方對話內容。 美國 W 英國 M 澳洲 W

W1: Hello, Mr. Ames. I'm Deanna Morris. I'm the head of HR here at Peterson Software. This is Alice Boyle, my coworker. (47)**We'll both be interviewing you now.**

M: It's a pleasure to meet both of you.

W2: Likewise. Thanks for coming in for an interview today. (48)**I see from your application that you want to work here as a software developer.** So why are you interested in applying to our company?

M: Well, I've done a lot of research on your company. It's not only a great place to work, (49)**but you also provide your employees with great opportunities for career development and growth.** I think Peterson Software has a good reputation for investing a lot in training and educating its workers.

W1: Yes, we do encourage our employees to get as much training as they can.

女1：艾姆斯先生，你好。我是迪安娜·莫里斯。我是彼得森軟體公司的人資部主管。這是我的同事，愛麗絲·博伊爾。現在我們要向你進行面試。

男：很高興認識你們。

女2：我們也是。謝謝你今天前來面試。我從你的應徵資料看出，你想在這裡擔任軟體開發工程師。你為什麼有興趣來我們公司應徵呢？

男：嗯，我對貴公司做了很多研究。它不僅是一個理想的上班場所，還為員工提供了職涯發展和成長的絕佳機會。我認為，彼得森軟體公司在員工教育訓練方面投入甚多，因而享有很好的名聲。

女1：是的，我們確實鼓勵員工盡可能接受培訓。

47. 談話者為什麼碰面？
    (A) 進行工作面試
    (B) 觀看產品展示
    (C) 執行實驗
    (D) 討論新的軟體專案　　　　　　答案 (A)

48. 男子的專業最有可能是什麼？
    (A) 化學工程師
    (B) 軟體開發人員
    (C) 汽車設計師
    (D) 業務代表　　　　　　　　　　答案 (B)

49. 男子說他喜歡公司的什麼地方？
    (A) 支付員工高薪。
    (B) 提供個人成長的機會。
    (C) 在海外多國設有辦公室。
    (D) 為員工提供健身房會員資格。　答案 (B)

問題 **50-52**，請參考以下對話內容。 美國 W 美國 M

W: (50)**Jackson Health Clinic.** This is Melissa. How can I help you?

M: Hello. I need to make an appointment to see a doctor. My name is Stanley Peters.

W: Are you a current patient here?

M: That's right. I want to get a flu shot.

W: (51)**Just so you know, it's no longer necessary to make an appointment with a doctor to get a flu shot.** You can visit us anytime during hours of operation. One of our nurses can administer the shot.

M: Wonderful. I'd like to visit tomorrow during my lunch break. Are you busy then?

W: Lots of people come then. If you don't want to wait, you'd be better off coming in early in the morning.

M: Okay. (52)**I'll be there first thing tomorrow morning.**

女：傑克遜健康診所，您好。我是梅麗莎。請問有什麼需要協助的地方？

男：你好。我要預約看醫生。我的名字是史丹利‧彼得斯。

女：您目前是這裡的病人嗎？

男：沒錯。我想接種流感疫苗。

女：知會您一聲，接種流感疫苗不再需要預約醫生了。您可以在營業時間內隨時過來。我們其中一名護理師會負責接種。

男：太棒了。我想明天午休時過去。你們到時候會很忙嗎？

女：那時候來的人很多。如果您不想等，最好一大早就來。

男：好的。我明天早上第一件事，就是過去那裡。

---

50. 女子最有可能在哪裡上班？
　　(A) 大學
　　(B) 醫療診所
　　(C) 購物中心
　　(D) 藥局　　　　　　　　　　　答案 (B)

51. 女子告訴男子什麼新政策？
　　(A) 他必須轉診。
　　(B) 他必須支付取消費用。
　　(C) 他必須提前登記。
　　(D) 他不需要預約。　　　　　　答案 (D)

52. 男子說他會做什麼？
　　(A) 填寫醫療表格
　　(B) 重新安排明天的預約
　　(C) 下班後到達
　　(D) 早上前往　　　　　　　　　答案 (D)

問題 53-55，請參考以下對話內容。 英國 M 美國 W

M: Hello, Sabrina.

W: Hello, Jason. What can I do for you?

M: (53)**Some sales representatives and I had a meeting about the office renovations starting next week. It looks like some of us have to move**

during that time of construction. (54)**I wonder if there's any room for us in the Marketing Department.**

W: Oh, (54)**we just got four new interns.**

M: I see… Well, I know you've got several tables set up in the area. Don't you think they take up a lot of room? I guess some desks could fit in that space.

W: That's a good point. (55)**I'll give a call to Facilities and have its team come to take them away.**

男：你好，薩布麗娜。

女：你好，傑森。我能為你做什麼？

男：我和一些業務代表開會，討論下週開始的辦公室整修事宜。看來我們其中一些人必須在施工期間搬離。我想知道行銷部有沒有空位可以給我們。

女：哦，我們才剛招聘四名新實習生。

男：我懂了……嗯，我知道你們在那個區域擺了幾張桌子。你不覺得它們占了很多空間嗎？我覺得那裡可以放一些辦公桌。

女：好主意。我會打給設備部，請他們團隊來把桌子搬走。

---

53. 說話者主要在談論什麼事？
　　(A) 變更時間的活動
　　(B) 擴建提案
　　(C) 施工計劃的影響
　　(D) 就業機會　　　　　　　　　答案 (C)

54. 女子說「我們才剛招聘四名新實習生」，意思是什麼？
　　(A) 空間不夠。
　　(B) 她需要額外的辦公設備。
　　(C) 他們需要新進員工訓練。
　　(D) 她的部門超出預算。　　　　答案 (A)

55. 女子表示會做什麼？
　　(A) 致電設備部門
　　(B) 查看預算報告
　　(C) 與顧客交談
　　(D) 處理顧客投訴　　　　　　　答案 (A)

問題 56-58，請參考以下對話內容。 美國 M 美國 W

M: Hello, Wendy. (56)**I'm hoping to put together a training session for the employees in this department all day next Monday.** How does that sound?

W: That's fine. Everyone seems to be having trouble with the new software we've been working with, so having an instructor to go over how to use it at a slower pace would be helpful. (57)**Since it's going to be so long, why don't we provide lunch for everyone?**

M: That's a good idea. That should make everybody happy.

W: I know we can get some money from the departmental budget to buy lunch, but I don't know how much is available.

M: (58)**I'll review the budget and let you know.**

男：你好，溫蒂。我希望下週一整天，為本部門的員工舉辦一次培訓課程。聽起來如何？

女：聽起來不錯。大家在使用目前的新軟體時，似乎都遇到了問題，因此請一位講師帶大家慢慢了解如何使用會很有幫助。既然課程要這麼久，我們何不為大家提供午餐呢？

男：這是個好主意。每個人應該都會很開心。

女：我知道我們可以從部門預算裡拿一些錢來買午餐，但我不知道能拿多少。

男：我查看一下預算再告訴你。

---

56. 男子想做什麼？
　　(A) 安裝新版本軟體
　　(B) 再多僱用一些員工
　　(C) 安排培訓課程
　　(D) 安排部門會議的時間　　　　答案 (C)

57. 女子建議做什麼？
　　(A) 查看網路評價
　　(B) 升級電腦
　　(C) 帶顧客去吃午餐
　　(D) 提供餐點　　　　答案 (D)

58. 男子接下來最有可能會做什麼？
　　(A) 尋找遺失的用品
　　(B) 聘請外燴廠商
　　(C) 查看預算
　　(D) 打電話　　　　答案 (C)

問題 **59-61**，請參考以下對話內容。 澳洲 W 美國 M

W: Hello, Mark. (59)**I just completed the installation of the XLS 500, our new electronic time recorder. As of now, information about all of the employees is entered, so the system is going to start tracking employee timesheets electronically.**

M: Employees just need to swipe their ID badges to clock in and out of work, right?

W: That's correct. (60)**And at the departmental meeting this afternoon, I can distribute their new badges.**

M: Okay. Do you think we need to extend the meeting to teach the employees how to use the new system?

W: Not at all. (61)**The XLS 500 is very straightforward**

---

and user-friendly. I can demonstrate it if you want, but it's a simple process.

女：你好，馬克。我剛剛完成 XLS 500 的安裝，這是我們新的電子時間記錄器。截至目前，所有員工的資訊都已經輸入，系統將開始以電子方式追蹤員工的考勤。

男：員工上下班打卡，只需要刷員工證就行了，對嗎？

女：正是如此。在今天下午的部門會議上，我會發下他們的新員工證。

男：好的。你認為，我們需要延長會議時間，來教員工如何使用新系統嗎？

女：完全不用。XLS 500 非常好上手又對使用者友善。如果你想要的話，我可以示範一下，但真的很簡單。

---

59. 說話者主要在討論什麼？
　　(A) 聘僱程序
　　(B) 耐用裝置
　　(C) 考勤記錄系統
　　(D) 數位門鎖　　　　答案 (C)

60. 今天下午將提供什麼給員工？
　　(A) 修改後的工作時程
　　(B) 新的安全碼
　　(C) 電子員工證
　　(D) 筆記型電腦　　　　答案 (C)

61. 關於 XLS 500，女子暗指了什麼？
　　(A) 員工使用方便。
　　(B) 在全公司安裝的成本高昂。
　　(C) 提供兩年保固。
　　(D) 安裝工作耗時。　　　　答案 (A)

問題 **62-64**，請參考以下對話內容及表格。 澳洲 W 英國 M

W: Hello, Steve. (62)**I'm just confirming that we have the necessary safety gear for the work we'll be doing on the four-story parking structure.**

M: That's the garage next to the river, right?

W: Yes, that's it. The project manager wants the workers on the site to wear color-coded safety helmets to keep track of the individual teams. (63)**But we don't have enough blue hard hats for the team that needs them.**

M: Hmm… (63)**Those construction workers won't be needed on the job site until one week from now.** Why don't we arrange to have some more blue hats delivered before then?

W: Yeah, that should be fine. (64)**I'll go ahead and place an order for them right now.**

女：你好，史蒂夫。我只是來確認，我們要在那座四層停車場施工時，會有必要的安全裝備。

男：那是河邊的車庫，對吧？

女：是的，正是它。專案經理希望現場的工人佩戴用顏色編碼的安全帽，以便追蹤各個組別。但我們沒有足夠的藍色安全帽給需要的小組。

男：嗯……一週後，工地才會需要那些建築工人。我們何不安排在這之前多送一些藍色安全帽過來？

女：好的，那應該沒問題。我現在就去下訂單。

各組安全帽顏色	
焊接工	黃色
(63) 水電工	藍色
砌磚工	橘色
屋頂修蓋工	白色

62. 說話者在談論什麼類型的建築？
(A) 體育場
(B) 工廠
(C) 停車場
(D) 購物中心　　　　　　　　答案 (C)

63. 請看圖表。哪個團隊的成員將在一週後上工？
(A) 焊接工
(B) 水電工
(C) 屋頂修蓋工
(D) 砌磚工　　　　　　　　答案 (B)

64. 女子接下來會做什麼？
(A) 上網刊登廣告
(B) 參訪專案現場
(C) 確認施工時程表
(D) 下訂單　　　　　　　　答案 (D)

問題 65-67，請參考以下對話內容及價目表。 美國M 美國W

M: Hello. Thank you for coming to Jackson's Ice Cream Shop.

W: Hello. (65)**I'm a teacher at Ridgewood Elementary School**, and I'd like to purchase some ice cream for our school party today.

M: Oh, my son is a student at your school. Today's your lucky day since we are having a sale on strawberry ice cream. I've got the price list right here.

W: My class is big, (66)**so I guess I'd better purchase a gallon of strawberry ice cream.** Oh, sorry. (67) **I left my purse in my car. I'll be back in just a moment.**

M: No problem.

男：你好。感謝蒞臨傑克森冰淇淋店。

女：你好。我是里吉伍小學的老師，我想為今天的學校派對購買一些冰淇淋。

男：哦，我兒子是你們學校的學生。今天是你的幸運日，因為我們有草莓冰淇淋促銷活動。這裡有價目表。

女：我的班級很大，所以我猜我最好買一加侖的草莓冰淇淋。哦，對不起。我把錢包留在車上了。我等一下就回來。

男：沒問題。

傑克森冰淇淋店 今日優惠價	
一球	$2.00
一品脫	$3.50
一誇脫	$5.00
(66) 一加侖	$9.00

65. 女子是誰？
(A) 餐廳老闆
(B) 送貨員
(C) 學校教師
(D) 公司經理　　　　　　　　答案 (C)

66. 請看圖表。女子要為她的點單支付多少錢？
(A) 2 美元
(B) 3.5 美元
(C) 5 美元
(D) 9 美元　　　　　　　　答案 (D)

67. 女子接下來會做什麼？
(A) 為冰淇淋付錢
(B) 試吃一點草莓冰淇淋
(C) 從她的車上拿回錢包
(D) 把她的車交給技師　　　　　　　　答案 (C)

問題 68-70，請參考以下對話內容及信用卡帳單。 英國M 澳洲W

M: Thank you for contacting Lexington Bank. What can I do for you?

W: Hello. I just received this month's credit card statement, (69)**and I see an incorrect charge on it dated February 11.**

M: (68)**Could you tell me the name as it appears on**

your credit card, please?

W: Sure. My name is Molly Carpenter.

M: Okay, Ms. Carpenter. It looks like you used your card at Jerry's Grill on February 11.

W: That's right. But the amount listed on the statement is different from the one on my receipt. I have the receipt I got from Jerry's Grill.

M: Okay. (70)**You'll need to fill out a form to dispute the charge.** I'll e-mail it to you at once.

男：感謝您聯繫萊辛頓銀行。請問需要什麼協助？

女：你好。我剛剛收到這個月的信用卡帳單，我發現上面日期 2 月 11 日的費用不正確。

男：請告訴我您信用卡上的姓名好嗎？

女：沒問題。我叫莫莉・卡彭特。

男：好的，卡彭特女士。您似乎於 2 月 11 日在傑瑞燒烤店使用了您的卡片。

女：沒錯。但對帳單上列出的金額和我收據上的金額不同。我有傑瑞燒烤店的收據。

男：了解。您需要填寫一份表格，來對這筆費用提出異議。我會立刻用電子郵件寄給您。

信用卡帳單

日期	明細	金額
2 月 5 日	希薇雅服飾	$73.45
2 月 9 日	公車總站	$15.00
(69) **2 月 11 日**	**傑瑞燒烤店**	**$42.00**
2 月 12 日	西岸雜貨店	$89.98

68. 女子被要求提供什麼資訊？
    (A) 她的名字
    (B) 她的電子信箱
    (C) 她的電話號碼
    (D) 她的住家地址　　　　　　　　答案 (A)

69. 請看圖表。女子說哪一筆金額有誤？
    (A) 73.45 美元
    (B) 15.00 美元
    (C) 42.00 美元
    (D) 89.98 美元　　　　　　　　答案 (C)

70. 男子告訴女子要做什麼事？
    (A) 親自前往辦公室
    (B) 提供她的帳號
    (C) 填寫文件
    (D) 和他的經理談話　　　　　　答案 (C)

Part 4

問題 **71-73**，請參考以下公告內容。 美國 W

(71)**I'm so happy to be here with everyone today for the opening of the Meridian Library's new multi-media center.** Thanks to the generous donations everyone provided, (72)**we were able to buy a subscription to a movie streaming service.** This service will allow us to get fast and easy access to a wide selection of films available online. Best of all, all library members can enjoy the service for free. (73) **There's further information about the streaming service on the library's web page.** Now, why don't we celebrate with some snacks and beverages?

很高興今天能和大家一起參加子午線圖書館新多媒體中心的開幕典禮。感謝大家慷慨捐助，讓我們得以付費訂閱電影串流服務。這項服務將使我們能夠快速、輕鬆連上多種網路影片。最棒的是，所有圖書館會員都可以免費享受這項服務。圖書館的網頁上還有更多關於串流服務的資訊。現在，我們何不用點心和飲料來慶祝一下呢？

71. 此公告在哪裡進行？
    (A) 電影院
    (B) 博物館
    (C) 電視臺
    (D) 圖書館　　　　　　　　答案 (D)

72. 說話者表示會提供哪一項新服務？
    (A) 線上客戶支援
    (B) 免費網路教學
    (C) 電子書下載服務
    (D) 電影串流服務　　　　　　答案 (D)

73. 聽者如何獲得更多資訊？
    (A) 閱讀手冊
    (B) 訂閱電子報
    (C) 諮詢圖書館員
    (D) 瀏覽某個網頁　　　　　　答案 (D)

問題 **74-76**，請參考以下工作坊摘錄。 美國 M

My name is Tim Chambers, and I'm your instructor at today's workshop. I know most of you here today are business owners, and you know plenty about your professions. (74)**However, knowing how to market your products properly can be the difference between succeeding and failing.** In the past, you'd have to hire a marketing agency to help with promoting your products, and that could cost thousands of dollars.

But today, (75)**I'm going to teach you some things you can do that will be much cheaper.** Now, before we get started, (76)**let's go around the room and introduce ourselves.** I want each of you to state your name and the business you run.

我叫提姆・錢伯斯，我是今天工作坊的講師。我知道在座多數人都是企業主，對自己的專業所知甚多。然而，學習如何妥善行銷你的產品，可能帶來成功和失敗的差別。過去，你們必須聘請行銷代理公司來幫忙推廣產品，這可能會花費數千美元。但是今天，我要教你們一些可以做的事情，而且會便宜得多。在我們開始之前，讓我們輪流自我介紹。我希望你們每個人都說出自己的名字和經營的事業。

74. 此工作坊的主題是什麼？
    (A) 聘僱新員工
    (B) 寫履歷
    (C) 行銷商品
    (D) 管理員工　　　　　　　　　　答案 (C)

75. 此工作坊能為聽者帶來什麼幫助？
    (A) 它能吸引更多顧客。
    (B) 它能讓他們留住客戶。
    (C) 它能讓他們省錢。
    (D) 它能改善績效。　　　　　　　答案 (C)

76. 說話者要求聽者做什麼？
    (A) 簽署表格
    (B) 觀看資訊豐富的影片
    (C) 安裝投影機
    (D) 自我介紹　　　　　　　　　　答案 (D)

問題 77-79，請參考以下會議摘錄。 澳洲 W

I'm pleased all of you could make it for a morning team meeting. (77)**We're going to open the restaurant soon, so I want to keep this meeting short.** As you're well aware, summer is rapidly approaching, (78)**so that means the tourists are flocking to this area. If any of you are interested in working additional hours, talk to me.** I'd also like to remind everyone about our rules regarding changing schedules. (79)**If you trade shifts with anyone, don't forget to update the online calendar so that I know who will be working that day.**

很高興你們所有人都能趕上晨間團隊會議。餐廳很快就要開始營業了，所以我想讓這次會議簡短一點。如各位所知，夏天即將來臨，這代表遊客會湧入這個地區。如果你們之中有人有興趣加班，請跟我說。我還想提醒大家，注意我們變更班表的相關規定。如果你和別人換

班，請別忘記更新線上行事曆，這樣我才知道當天誰會上班。

77. 聽者在哪裡工作？
    (A) 飯店
    (B) 超市
    (C) 餐廳
    (D) 百貨公司　　　　　　　　　　答案 (C)

78. 說話者提到「遊客會湧入這個地區」，是在暗指什麼？
    (A) 將僱用更多員工。
    (B) 會很難找到停車位。
    (C) 可能無法如期完工。
    (D) 生意將變得更忙碌。　　　　　答案 (D)

79. 說話者提醒聽者做什麼？
    (A) 拿他們的新制服
    (B) 準時上班
    (C) 更新行事曆
    (D) 配戴名牌　　　　　　　　　　答案 (C)

問題 80-82，請參考以下電話留言。 英國 M

Hello, Craig. (80)**I'm calling to get an update on the mobile phone application for the travel guide we just published.** Ms. Chapman informed me that she wants to include a few more cities on the app, and one of those is Hartford. (81)**I know you grew up there, so I'm sure you know the best places to see and where to shop and eat in the city, so you would be a great fit for this updated app project.** I'd like to add your suggestions to the guide. (82)**We need to schedule a meeting to discuss this new project**, so please give me a call back as soon as possible to let me know when you have time. Thank you.

你好，克雷格。我打電話給你，是為了更新我們剛發布的手機旅遊指南應用程式。查普曼女士通知我，她想在應用程式裡再納入幾個城市，哈特福就是其中之一。我知道你在那裡長大，我相信你知道城裡最好的景點，以及購物和吃飯的地方，所以非常適合這個應用程式更新專案。我想把你的建議加到指南裡面。我們需要安排一次會議來討論這個新專案，所以請盡快回電給我，讓我知道你什麼時候有空。謝謝。

80. 說話者為了什麼打電話？
    (A) 設備訂單
    (B) 行動應用程式
    (C) 職缺開放
    (D) 新手機上市　　　　　　　　　答案 (B)

81. 為什麼聽者適合新專案？
    (A) 他很了解某座城市。
    (B) 他具備良好的領導力。
    (C) 他是一名電腦程式設計師。
    (D) 他很有組織性。　　　　　　　答案 (A)

82. 說話者想做什麼？
    (A) 刊登廣告
    (B) 談論就業機會
    (C) 諮詢專家
    (D) 安排會議　　　　　　　　　　答案 (D)

問題 83-85，請參考以下發言內容。　美國 W

(83)**My newest book, Starting Your Career**, is for those looking for a job or wanting a career change. Job seekers spend long hours writing their résumés and completing job applications, but they seldom get a job interview call. (84)**My book explains some common mistakes people make in the job seeking process and also shows how to get the jobs and promotions you want. I've worked as a recruiting manager at a few large companies for more than two decades.** Following my presentation, I'll answer any questions you have and sign copies of my book. (85)**And be sure to visit my website, where you can sign up to get a free half-hour-long consultation from me regarding your career.**

我的新書《開啟你的職涯》，是寫給那些正在找工作或想要改變職涯的人。求職者花費大量時間寫履歷和申請工作，但他們很少接到通知面試的電話。我的書說明了人們在求職過程中常犯的錯誤，並示範如何爭取你想要的工作和升遷。我在幾家大公司擔任招募經理長達 20 多年了。簡報結束後，我會回答大家的問題，並開始簽書。請務必造訪我的網站。你只要註冊，我就會針對你的職涯提供半小時免費諮詢。

83. 說話者最近做了什麼？
    (A) 她創辦了一間公司。
    (B) 她要求面試。
    (C) 她寫了一本書。
    (D) 她進行了一場簡報。　　　　　答案 (C)

84. 說話者說「我在幾家大公司擔任招募經理長達 20 多年了」，是在暗示什麼？
    (A) 人們可以相信她的建議。
    (B) 她有一份很棒的工作。
    (C) 她撤回了履歷。
    (D) 她不跟小公司合作。　　　　　答案 (A)

85. 聽者查看網站可以得到什麼？
    (A) 課程教材折扣
    (B) 軟體試用版
    (C) 簽名書
    (D) 免費諮詢　　　　　　　　　　答案 (D)

問題 86-88，請參考以下廣播內容。　澳洲 W

Welcome back, everyone. I'm Meredith Warner, (86)**and we're halfway done with my show on Radio 103.4 here in Jacksonville.** You know, I often get asked how I chose this career, so I thought I'd share the answer with you. I've wanted to be a radio host since I was a kid. (87)**When I was nine, I was listening to the radio and heard an interview with a famous singer.** I realized that it would be wonderful to have conversations with famous people. (88)**Now, I'm going to play some music by that musician.** Try to guess who it is.

歡迎回來。我是梅瑞迪思‧華納。我們在傑克森維爾 103.4 電臺的節目已來到中場。你們知道，我經常被問到我是如何選擇這個職業的，所以我想跟大家分享答案。我從小就想當廣播主持人。九歲的時候，我聽著廣播，聽到一位知名歌手的訪談。我意識到如果能跟名人對談，那會有多棒。現在，我要播放那位音樂家的歌曲。試著猜猜他是誰吧。

86. 說話者是誰？
    (A) 歌手
    (B) 女演員
    (C) 廣播主持人
    (D) 體育記者　　　　　　　　　　答案 (C)

87. 說話者說，是什麼啟發她選擇了自己的職業？
    (A) 與一位知名歌手交談
    (B) 贏得獎項
    (C) 聽一場訪談
    (D) 環遊全國　　　　　　　　　　答案 (C)

88. 說話者接下來會做什麼？
    (A) 宣布消息
    (B) 採訪一些名人
    (C) 回答問題
    (D) 播放歌曲　　　　　　　　　　答案 (D)

問題 89-91，請參考以下會議摘錄。　英國 M

Thank you for coming to this meeting here at the community center. (89)**As you're all aware, our annual fundraiser will be held this Friday night.** We hope to raise enough money to pay for the renovations the center badly needs. Now, we've gotten plenty of volunteers from the community who are willing to help out, which I am really grateful for. (90)**The volunteers will be putting up decorations around the auditorium and arranging tables for the fundraiser.** Unfortunately, however, the caterer for the event just had to cancel our order since there was some water damage to the business last night. (91)**Does anyone know a caterer that can provide food for 250 people on short notice?**

感謝各位來社區中心參加這次會議。正如你們所知，我們的年度募款活動將於本週五晚上舉行。希望募集足夠的資金，來支付本中心急需的整修費用。現在，我們已經有很多來自社區的志工願意提供協助，我對此深表感激。志工將協助裝飾整個禮堂場地，並為募款活動擺放桌子。但不幸的是，活動的外燴廠商因為昨晚的水災，不得不取消我們的訂單。有人知道哪家外燴廠商，可以在短時間內為 250 人提供餐點嗎？

89. 什麼活動正在計劃中？
    (A) 慈善拍賣
    (B) 體育賽事
    (C) 募款活動
    (D) 音樂會　　　　　　　　　　答案 (C)

90. 據說話者所說，志工將為這次活動做什麼？
    (A) 為來賓提供食物
    (B) 在每張桌子擺放鮮花
    (C) 在入口處接待來賓
    (D) 布置禮堂　　　　　　　　　答案 (D)

91. 說話者向聽者提出什麼要求？
    (A) 簽訂合約
    (B) 對樂隊的建議
    (C) 信用卡號碼
    (D) 外燴廠商推薦　　　　　　　答案 (D)

問題 92-94，請參考以下發言內容。 澳洲 W

(92)**Thank you for attending the annual marketing conference and for coming to my presentation.** As a marketing consultant, I have one final tip. Before releasing new products, most businesses rely on outside product testers. (93)**In exchange for comments or any ideas to improve products, companies send products to these testers for free, which is costly. Your employees could turn out to be effective product testers.** It's because after all, they want their company to be successful. All you have to do is collect feedback from those who haven't worked on developing that particular product. That way, you

get a new point of view. (94)**Here is a brochure that should be helpful.** It has my contact information on it, so feel free to get in touch with me.

感謝各位參加年度行銷大會，並出席我的報告。身為一名行銷顧問，我最後還有一個建議。在發布新產品之前，多數企業都仰賴外部的產品測試員。為了換取評論或任何改良產品的想法，公司免費向這些測試人員發送產品，代價不斐。你的員工可能會是很有效的產品測試員。這是因為，畢竟他們希望自己的公司獲得成功。你要做的就是蒐集那些沒有參與開發該項產品的人員回饋。這樣一來，你就會得到新的觀點。這本小手冊應該會有所幫助。上面有我的聯絡方式，歡迎隨時與我聯繫。

92. 此發言在哪裡進行？
    (A) 一場大會上
    (B) 培訓課程中
    (C) 迎新活動裡
    (D) 就業博覽會　　　　　　　　答案 (A)

93. 說話者為什麼說「你的員工可能會是很有效的產品測試員」？
    (A) 建議銷售更多產品
    (B) 提議不同的方法
    (C) 表揚部分員工
    (D) 建議僱用更多員工　　　　　答案 (B)

94. 說話者給了聽者什麼？
    (A) 一張名片
    (B) 一個網址
    (C) 一本宣傳手冊
    (D) 一張圖片　　　　　　　　　答案 (C)

問題 95-97，請參考以下會議摘錄及圖表。 美國 W

(95)**Thanks for attending this afternoon's design team meeting.** We need to discuss the design for the limited-edition necktie we sell every year in celebration of the company's anniversary. Remember that this item will only be available for purchase for two months. (96)**Now, I need everyone to divide into small groups and come up with at least a couple of ideas for the style for the item.** In case it helps to know what the primary color will be, this chart shows last quarter's sales broken down by colors of the ties we sold. (97)**The decision has already been made to use the top-selling color for the new product.**

感謝各位參加今天下午的設計團隊會議。關於為了慶祝公司週年而販售的限量版領帶，我們需要討論一下這次的設計。請記住，這個品項只開放兩個月的販售時間。

現在，我需要每個人分成小組，並就這個品項的款式提出幾種想法。了解主色是什麼可能會有幫助，這個圖表將我們銷售的領帶根據顏色分類，顯示出上一季的銷售額。已經確定新產品要使用最暢銷的顏色。

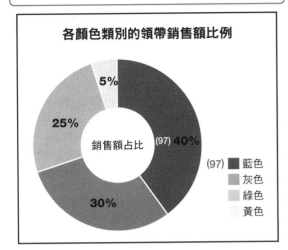

各顏色類別的領帶銷售額比例

銷售額占比
(97) 40%
5%
25%
30%

(97) ■ 藍色
　　 ■ 灰色
　　 ■ 綠色
　　 ■ 黃色

95. 聽者最有可能是誰？
(A) 行銷人員
(B) 設計師
(C) 業務人員
(D) 程式設計師　　　　　　　　答案 (B)

96. 團隊分成小組後，將討論新產品的什麼面向？
(A) 大小
(B) 顏色
(C) 款式
(D) 價格　　　　　　　　　　　答案 (C)

97. 請看圖表。新產品會是什麼顏色？
(A) 灰色
(B) 綠色
(C) 黃色
(D) 藍色　　　　　　　　　　　答案 (D)

問題 **98-100**，請參考以下發言內容及地圖。 美國 M

(98)**All right, this is one of the most important days of the year at our furniture store. It's our annual clearance sale.** This is a huge event, so we're going to be full of customers all day long. (99)**Make sure that every customer who enters the store knows we're giving away free drinks and snacks in the customer lounge.** There is one more thing: I'll need a few people to put up a few more signs promoting our new membership program. We've already got some in front of the furniture display areas and by the cash registers, but (100)**we need some more in front of the customer service desk.**

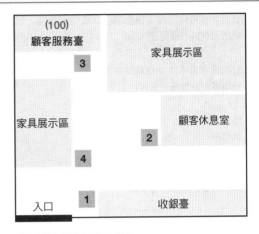

(100) 顧客服務臺　3
家具展示區
家具展示區
顧客休息室　2
4
入口　1　收銀臺

98. 說話者主要在討論什麼？
(A) 培訓課程
(B) 年度清倉拍賣
(C) 業務大會
(D) 顧客感謝日　　　　　　　　答案 (B)

99. 人們抵達時，聽者被建議要做什麼？
(A) 給他們購物車
(B) 幫他們找東西
(C) 發送促銷傳單
(D) 告訴他們茶點的事情　　　　答案 (D)

100. 請看圖表。新增的告示會出現在哪裡？
(A) 地點 1
(B) 地點 2
(C) 地點 3
(D) 地點 4　　　　　　　　　　答案 (C)

Part 5

101. 這家餐飲服務公司會為週年慶、企業宴會等特殊活動，提供各種義大利菜色和甜點。　　　答案 (A)

102. 消費者需要確認自己透過國外直送的產品是否被召回。
　　　　　　　　　　　　　　　　　答案 (A)

103. 如果你找書時遇到困難，請前往還書處，向我們的圖書管理員尋求協助。　　　　　答案 (C)

104. 如果有人干擾其他客人愉快的用餐時光，本餐廳保留拒絕為其提供服務的權利。 答案 (C)

105. 人事經理跟我說，董事會正在找人負責新的製造工廠。 答案 (B)

106. 由於缺乏新產品研發，可可運動公司無法維持其在體育用品市場的龍頭地位。 答案 (C)

107. 文章中有任何錯誤，都必須立刻通報編輯部，以便在報紙出刊前予以更正。 答案 (B)

108. 針對促進公平競爭以保障消費者的立法通過，幾位當地商界領袖發揮了重要作用。 答案 (D)

109. 該市將為參加 5 月 14 日至 19 日電影節的人提供多種免費飲料。 答案 (A)

110. 通過部門經理一職最終面試的應徵者，將在下週稍晚由人力資源經理進行聯繫。 答案 (D)

111. BK 電子昨天宣布新計劃，將擴大其位於阿拉巴馬州的半導體製造設施。 答案 (C)

112. 我們必須更努力提高顧客滿意度，讓公司更有競爭力。 答案 (A)

113. 在經濟成長趨緩之際，幾家投資公司看到了獲得財務回報的潛力，推出鎖定新興市場的金融商品。 答案 (B)

114. 請注意，此批貨物應在收到發票後 21 天內付款。 答案 (C)

115. 抵達機場後，每一位乘客都必須通過海關，歷時約 25 分鐘。 答案 (B)

116. 這場即將舉辦的論壇與會者，可以自行判斷便利性、舒適度，選擇入住貝拉飯店或格蘭德飯店。 答案 (C)

117. 為了確實證明開銷，在報銷費用時，必須附上收據或發票正本。 答案 (B)

118. 隨著原物料價格上漲，食品加工、鋼鐵和紡織產業的經濟前景相當黯淡。 答案 (C)

119. 史丹佛先生兩年前辭去執行長一職，放棄了對其父親公司的控制權。 答案 (D)

120. 價格可能會有所不同，具體取決於你的旅行日期、旅客人數、出發城市，以及你對航班、旅館和其他項目的選擇。 答案 (B)

121. 任何試圖改變幾條主要河流的行為，最終只會對環境和生態系統造成無以復加的破壞。 答案 (C)

122. 評估報告明確指出，我們的配送系統改良之後，在過去兩年節省了超過數百萬美元。 答案 (A)

123. 在消費性電子產業中，成功取決於及時將新產品引進市場的技術能力。 答案 (C)

124. 有鑑於當前經濟形勢，多數顧客無力購買我們昂貴的新產品。 答案 (B)

125. 王牌醫療開發了幾款低成本成像設備，其中兩款有望角逐今年的布蘭登技術獎。 答案 (D)

126. 如果捷紅航空開始將預約工作外包到海外，今年加州將創造約 1,000 個新工作。 答案 (D)

127. 我們每個人都必須負起個人責任，這不只是為了自己和家人，也是為了鄉鄰和社會。 答案 (B)

128. 一旦這個行政職位有人補上，公司的人事經理就會停止接受應徵。 答案 (B)

129. 新州長提議擴建四條主要高速公路，以因應增加的貨運量，並減少交通時間延誤。 答案 (D)

130. 如果你的報告需要協助或進一步支援，請不要猶豫，與我們聯繫。 答案 (C)

Part 6

問題 131-134，請參考以下文章內容。

舊金山日報

王牌超市進軍南美
彼得・史密斯

（舊金山 - 3 月 3 日）王牌超市的總部位於美國，是全球最大連鎖超市，現正計劃進軍南美市場。王牌超市總部昨天宣布，將在智利和巴西開設 5 家分店，首批兩家超市排定於 3 月 30 日在智利開業。其餘 3 家分店，將於下月底在巴西開幕。基本上，王牌超市採用獨特的經營策略，開設小型超市，並以親民價格提供自有品牌產品和在地農產品。王牌超市發言人班傑明・威爾森表示：「我們渴望在南美洲開設自己的超市，並向我們的顧客介紹價格實惠的優質產品。」

131.　　　　　　　　　　　　　　　　答案 (B)

132. (A) 其餘 3 家分店，將於下月底在巴西開幕。
　　　(B) 今年我們的超市約有五分之一會安裝節能照明。
　　　(C) 他們與整個南美洲的傳統雜貨連鎖店競爭。
　　　(D) 許多店面建在過度擁擠又土地稀缺的城市中。
　　　　　　　　　　　　　　　　答案 (A)

133.　　　　　　　　　　　　　　　　答案 (B)

134.　　　　　　　　　　　　　　　　答案 (D)

問題 135-138，請參考以下信件內容。

愛丁堡藝術與設計學院
勞瑞斯頓廣場 74 號
愛丁堡，EH3 9DF
eca@ed.ac.uk
+44 (0)131 651 5800

5 月 30 日
路易斯・伯頓先生
奇塔姆山路 184 號
英國，曼徹斯特
M4 1PW

親愛的伯頓先生，

感謝您詢問有關愛丁堡藝術與設計學院的夜間課程。我
聯絡您，是為了提供課程的詳細資訊，特別是您要求了
解的、每週二或週四開設的課程。

首先是我們的油畫入門課，教授基本技法，強調色彩的
重要性。其次，是我們的技術繪圖課，專為對工程和建
築感興趣的人所設計。

不幸的是，我們目前只有這些課程是開設於週中晚間。
不過，我們還提供各種線上課程，特別適合那些行程繁
忙的人。報名這些課程的人會收到一份清單，上面列出
必須提前購買的必需用品。關於上面列出的所有選項，
我們的網站上有更多詳細資訊。

誠摯祝福。

安娜貝爾・泰勒
學生服務經理
愛丁堡藝術與設計學院

135.　　　　　　　　　　　　　　　　答案 (D)

136.　　　　　　　　　　　　　　　　答案 (A)

137.　　　　　　　　　　　　　　　　答案 (B)

138. (A) 感謝您對本機構的就業機會感興趣。
　　　(B) 關於上面列出的所有選項，我們的網站上有更多詳
　　　　　細資訊。
　　　(C) 您的課程註冊申請，目前正在處理中。
　　　(D) 如果您想退出任何課程，請與我聯繫。　　答案 (B)

問題 139-142，請參考以下電子郵件。

收件人：斯嘉麗・威爾士 <sw@cocomail.com>
寄件人：埃莉諾・弗萊徹 <ef@sjfc.com>
主　旨：唱片店表演
日　期：4 月 21 日

親愛的威爾士女士，

很高興通知你，斯坦利・喬丹娛樂公司正在為我們珍貴
的粉絲俱樂部會員準備即將到來的表演。

喬丹先生將在音響工廠大廳進行 25 場演出，為粉絲們
提供絕佳機會，來體驗斯坦利・喬丹在小而溫馨的情境
下演出。之後，粉絲們可以在隨後進行的簽名環節上，
親眼見到他們最愛的流行歌手。現場有斯坦利・喬丹的
新專輯可供購買，粉絲也可以把專輯拿到簽名會上簽
名。

門票價格合理，可上網購買。唱片行音樂會將於 5 月
10 日至 15 日舉行，確切巡演日期將在未來幾天內公布
在 www.sjfc.com。別錯過這個機會，近距離接觸你最
愛的藝術家。

祝福順心。
埃莉諾・弗萊徹
斯坦利・喬丹粉絲俱樂部經理

139.　　　　　　　　　　　　　　　　答案 (D)

140.　　　　　　　　　　　　　　　　答案 (D)

141.　　　　　　　　　　　　　　　　答案 (B)

142. (A) 感謝你最近對斯坦利・喬丹先生的詢問。
　　　(B) 你將在 7 天內收到免費門票。
　　　(C) 別錯過這個機會，近距離接觸你最愛的藝術家。
　　　(D) 首場公演預計於本月底舉行。　　答案 (C)

問題 143-146，請參考以下資訊。

軟木塞本質上是一片軟木橡樹樹皮，也稱為栓皮櫟。軟
木樹自然生長在西地中海沿岸地區。全球其他地區已多
次嘗試培育該樹種。但到目前為止，結果並不振奮人
心。雖然有歷史證據表明，軟木在大約 2,000 年前就被
當成塞子，但隨著 17 世紀引入玻璃瓶，軟木塞的使用
變得更加廣泛。近年來，塑膠塞之類的各式替代品已被

引入作為酒瓶蓋。儘管如此，軟木塞仍然是優質葡萄酒的主要瓶塞。

143. 答案 (C)

144. (A) 全球其他地區已多次嘗試培育該樹種。
(B) 這表示某些樹木適應了地中海型氣候。
(C) 軟木塞機必須根據製造商的說明進行清潔和維護。
(D) 該地區出產一些世界上最知名的葡萄和葡萄酒。
答案 (A)

145. 答案 (C)

146. 答案 (D)

Part 7

問題 147-148，請參考以下資訊。

東西雅圖洗衣店
城裡最好、最乾淨的自助洗衣店！
24 小時營業

(147) **1.**將你的衣物放入其中一臺洗衣機。
2.把洗衣粉倒入洗衣機。洗衣粉可以在前門旁邊的自動販賣機購買。
3.設定洗衣機面板。一般而言，熱水適合白色衣服，冷水適合彩色衣服。
4.將洗衣機所需的正確金額投入投幣孔。在衣服尚未洗滌完成之前，請勿打開洗衣機。

(148) 如果你有任何問題，請致電 **(206) 408-3180**。

---

147. 這則資訊的目的是什麼？
(A) 告知人們如何購買洗衣機。
(B) 描述某個設施的使用程序。
(C) 告知如何申請設備維修服務。
(D) 為洗衣服務打廣告。 答案 (B)

148. 如果沒有熱水，顧客該怎麼辦？
(A) 到前檯去
(B) 將更多衣物放入洗衣機
(C) 打電話通知工作人員
(D) 投入更多硬幣 答案 (C)

問題 149-150，請參考以下文字訊息。

哈羅德・馬龍 ［上午 10:25］
艾達，你有收到迪肯飯店的斯託林斯先生回覆了嗎？
(149) 我們要求的預訂已經完成了嗎？

艾達・斯圖爾特 ［上午 10:27］
他大約 5 分鐘前剛打給我。(149) (150) 他說橙色房間已經在 9 號被預訂了，但如果我們願意，可以使用紅色房間。

哈羅德・馬龍 ［上午 10:28］
可以容納多少人？

艾達・斯圖爾特 ［上午 10:29］
空間最多可容納 250 人。(150) 它比橙色房間貴。

哈羅德・馬龍 ［上午 10:31］
(150) 如果有必要，我們隨時可以申請額外的資金。

艾達・斯圖爾特 ［上午 10:32］
好的。我馬上回電話給他。

---

149. 此文字訊息主要在討論什麼？
(A) 即將舉辦的活動準備事宜
(B) 租房價格
(C) 預訂飯店房間的需求
(D) 更改活動日期 答案 (A)

150. 上午 10:31，馬龍先生寫道「如果有必要，我們隨時可以申請額外的資金」，意思最有可能是什麼？
(A) 他必須提交一份預算報告。
(B) 他需要盡快和他的老闆談談。
(C) 他剛要求在預算中增加更多資金。
(D) 他願意預約紅色房間。 答案 (D)

問題 151-153，請參考以下廣告內容。

戲劇披薩
營業時間：10:00 A.M. – 11:00 P.M.
(153A) 每週營業 7 天

小	中	大	巨型
12.95 美元	14.95 美元	18.95 美元	20.95 美元

價格如有更改，恕不另行通知。
(153B) 訂單滿 20 美元，即可免費外送。

(151) 本月精選披薩（買一送一！）		
素食	(151) 番茄、蘑菇、紅洋蔥、青椒、香菜、橄欖	
豪華	義式辣香腸、(151) 番茄、蘑菇、紅洋蔥、紅椒、青椒、橄欖	
BBQ 烤雞	特製 BBQ 醬、雞肉、(151) 番茄、蘑菇、洋蔥、青椒	

想知道菜單上的完整品項，
(153C) 請上我們的網站 www.theatricalpizza.com。
(152) 添加配料

小	中	大	巨型
1.65 美元	2.25 美元	2.85 美元	3.55 美元

蘑菇、番茄、甜椒、切達起司、蝦、火腿、義式辣香腸、

雞肉、烘烤蒜片、洋蔥、橄欖等多種選擇！

我們為各式活動提供餐飲服務。

欲了解費用，請致電 555-329-0504。

151. 所有本月精選披薩都包含哪種食材？
(A) 香菜
(B) 番茄
(C) 雞肉
(D) 橄欖　　　　　　　　　　　答案 (B)

152. 廣告中提供了什麼資訊？
(A) 飲料價格
(B) 餐飲服務價格
(C) 配料選擇
(D) 商店地址　　　　　　　　　答案 (C)

153. 關於戲劇披薩，文中沒有暗指什麼？
(A) 週日營業。
(B) 為部分顧客免費外送。
(C) 它有一個網站。
(D) 最近開了一家新分店。　　　答案 (D)

問題 154-156，請參考以下資訊。

納撒尼爾 · 庫珀床鋪

(154) 感謝您向全市最好的家具供應商——納撒尼爾家具有限公司——購買納撒尼爾床鋪。(155) 這張床曾因其耐用度而獲獎。我們相信它會讓您完全滿意。開始組裝之前，請仔細閱讀以下說明。

組裝說明
步驟 1. 將床頭板安裝在所需位置。
步驟 2. (156) 將側邊床欄上的紅點對準床頭板上的點，將其安裝到床頭板上。對另一側床欄重複上述做法。
步驟 3. 將床尾板固定到床欄上。
步驟 4. 用螺絲把床頭板和床尾板鎖緊。
步驟 5. 放入床架，並用螺絲起子拴緊。
步驟 6. 將床墊放在床架上。

請到我們的網站查看以上步驟的照片。如果您對我們的產品有任何疑問，請致電 1-555-932-3333 或發送電子郵件至 staff@nathanielbed.com。

154. 此資訊是針對誰？
(A) 家具運輸公司員工
(B) 客戶服務人員
(C) 家具製造商
(D) 顧客　　　　　　　　　　　答案 (D)

155. 關於此產品，文中暗指什麼？
(A) 床欄可以當成扶手。
(B) 可以用附加組件來組裝床。

(C) 專為兒童設計。
(D) 此床因結構堅固而受到肯定。　　答案 (D)

156. 以下句子最適合放在文中 [1]、[2]、[3] 和 [4] 的哪一個位置？
「對另一側床欄重複上述做法。」
(A) [1]
(B) [2]
(C) [3]
(D) [4]　　　　　　　　　　　答案 (B)

問題 157-158，請參考以下收據。

(157) 關愛之手

富蘭克林大道 24 號
97160 俄勒岡州，海濱
(503) 762-0847

4 月 10 日上午 9:35

品項	數量	價格	金額
(157)《關於急救》袖珍書	1	2.80 美元	2.80 美元
(157) 繃帶（2 件）	1	2.00 美元	2.00 美元
(157) 消毒軟膏（25 毫克）	1	4.70 美元	4.70 美元
(157) 止痛藥（10 顆）	1	4.00 美元	4.00 美元
總品項	4		
小計			13.50 美元
(158) 常客折扣			-2.00 美元
支付金額			11.50 美元
信用卡			11.50 美元
*********5621			
找零			0.00 美元

感謝您！

157. 關愛之手最有可能是什麼類型的企業？
(A) 醫院
(B) 藥局
(C) 書店
(D) 美髮沙龍　　　　　　　　　答案 (B)

158. 關於這位顧客，文中暗指什麼？
(A) 他在診所工作。
(B) 他下午買了這些物品。
(C) 他以現金支付。
(D) 他經常在關愛之手購物。　　答案 (D)

問題 159-161，請參考以下電子郵件。

收件人：傑克 · 黑若德 <jherald@chelsea.com>
寄件人：莉蓮 · 馬爾維 <lmulvey@chelsea.com>
日　期：1 月 23 日

主　旨：查詢

(160) 親愛的黑若德先生，

1 月 2 日，行銷部門的影印機壞了。(159) (161) 因此，我在 1 月 8 日向 (160) 採購部門申請購買新的影印機。(159) 你告訴我會在一週內處理。但我提交申請已經兩週了，還沒有看到任何行動。

我們部門目前使用人力資源部的影印機。這導致 1 月 30 日的會議準備工作嚴重延誤。

我希望這個問題能盡快獲得解決。如果有什麼我能做的，請讓我知道。

感謝。

莉蓮·馬爾維

159. 問題是什麼？
(A) 某物品未被替換。
(B) 會議被延後。
(C) 沒有提供資金。
(D) 尚未聘請繼任者。　　　　　　答案 (A)

160. 黑若德先生在哪裡工作？
(A) 行銷部
(B) 人力資源部
(C) 採購部
(D) 維修部　　　　　　答案 (C)

161. 新影印機的提案是何時交出去的？
(A) 1 月 2 日
(B) 1 月 8 日
(C) 1 月 23 日
(D) 1 月 30 日　　　　　　答案 (B)

問題162-164，請參考以下電子郵件。

收件人：<jhbuskers@chmail.com>
寄件人：<tmyers@ggmail.com>
日　期：12 月 15 日
主　旨：恭喜！

致親愛的街頭藝人團員們，

祝賀你們最近在克魯斯劇場舉辦的音樂會大成功。(164) 我讀了《聖克勞斯市先驅報》後，了解到你們是第一個出道三年後就在那裡舉辦音樂會的音樂家。當我得知你們把部分收益捐給兒童醫院時，更是印象深刻。

(162) (163) 身為酒吧老闆和你們的大粉絲，我想邀請各位到我的酒吧表演。我們的客人多是 20 多歲的大學生，因此我認為你們很適合他們。我的酒吧「帆船」位於聖克勞斯市馴鹿區 46 號，每天從晚上 8 點營業至凌晨 4 點。你們的演出時間和酬勞都可以討論。如果你們有興趣，請回覆我。

謝謝。

(163) 泰莎·邁爾斯

162. 這封電子郵件的主要目的是什麼？
(A) 談論某個樂團的成就
(B) 提供一份酒吧工作
(C) 通知人們關於音樂會的詳情
(D) 確認一場表演的時程　　　　　　答案 (B)

163. 泰莎·邁爾斯是誰？
(A) 酒吧顧客
(B) 樂團成員
(C) 病患
(D) 樂迷　　　　　　答案 (D)

164. 關於街頭藝人，文中暗指什麼？
(A) 它成立於 4 年前。
(B) 它最近招募了新團員。
(C) 當地出版品對其進行專題報導。
(D) 在醫院舉辦了一場音樂會。　　　　　　答案 (C)

問題 165-167，請參考以下文章內容。

AMC 向前邁進

作者：薩曼莎·普羅布斯特，特約撰稿人

8 月 7 日－總部位於布魯塞爾的汽車製造商亞擴汽車公司（AMC）(167) 在北京的製造工廠終於完工，將於本週開始在中國生產汽車。

「這是 AMC 戰略的第一步，旨在領先汽車業界，並維持相對於中國其他競爭對手的 (165) 優勢。」AMC 執行長吉恩·伯格曼解釋道。「我們決定建造這座新工廠，是為了維持在中國市場穩定銷售汽車，並推廣未來的車型。」

自去年廣受好評的精實型車款「大白鯊」上市以來，AMC 在中國越來越受歡迎。「大眾對 AMC 汽車的需求迅速成長，(166C) 尤其是大白鯊系列。我認為本地客戶對大白鯊車型感興趣，因為它 (166A) 價格實惠、(166B) 省油、設計新穎。」上海當地汽車經銷商王周這麼說。

該公司計劃在 10 月推出「大白鯊 2」，正是大白鯊的升級版。這款新的大白鯊將配備內建導航系統、改良版的安全科技和更高燃油效率。(167) 新建工廠將聚焦生產該車型，以滿足重慶、天津等中國主要城市的需求。目前，AMC 正準備藉由電視廣告，在中國大力推廣此車款。廣告由高人氣比利時明星菲利普·吉列姆斯擔綱演出。大白鯊 2 一上市，廣告就會隨之播出。

165. 第 2 段第 1 行的「edge」，含義最接近
    (A) 刀片
    (B) 收入
    (C) 優勢
    (D) 趨勢　　　　　　　　　答案 (C)

166. 王先生的說法並未暗指大白鯊車款的什麼事？
    (A) 定價合理
    (B) 消耗相對少的燃料
    (C) 在中國買氣旺盛
    (D) 目前在中國製造　　　　答案 (D)

167. 大白鯊 2 主要在哪裡生產？
    (A) 布魯塞爾
    (B) 上海
    (C) 天津
    (D) 北京　　　　　　　　　答案 (D)

問題 168-171，請參考以下線上討論訊息。

羅斯瑪麗・沃特斯　　　　　　　　［下午 2:42］
你好，希薇亞。你的培訓計劃進行得如何？

希薇亞・史密斯　　　　　　　　　［下午 2:43］
(168) 這真的很有教育意義。我在這裡學到很多東西。這些資訊將對我下週正式開始工作時大有幫助。

羅斯瑪麗・沃特斯　　　　　　　　［下午 2:44］
很開心聽到這個消息。我相信你會適應得很好。

希薇亞・史密斯　　　　　　　　　［下午 2:45］
很高興你對我有信心。

特倫特・薩特　　　　　　　　　　［下午 2:47］
希薇亞，(169) 你下週一來上班時，上午 10 點請到我的辦公室。我有一個任務要交給你。

希薇亞・史密斯　　　　　　　　　［下午 2:48］
(169) 我很樂意，但我在 9 點到中午之間應該要與人力資源部的帕齊・羅斯會面。我們可以午餐後見嗎？

特倫特・薩特　　　　　　　　　　［下午 2:49］
我中午要離開辦公室，週五才會回來。(171) 我用電子郵件把任務寄給你如何？

希薇亞・史密斯　　　　　　　　　［下午 2:51］
(171) 這對我來說行得通。(170) 但我還沒有工作用的電子郵件帳號。

羅斯瑪麗・沃特斯　　　　　　　　［下午 2:53］
(170) 我現在就請資訊科技部門的人為你設置。我會在一個小時內，把你的用戶名稱和密碼傳給你。

希薇亞・史密斯　　　　　　　　　［下午 2:54］
謝謝。特倫特，一旦收到新的電子郵件，我會立即通知你。然後我們就可以上工了。

168. 史密斯女士最有可能是誰？
    (A) 經理
    (B) 試用期僱員
    (C) 顧客
    (D) 主管　　　　　　　　　答案 (B)

169. 史密斯女士遇到什麼問題？
    (A) 她無法在提議的時間見面。
    (B) 她經驗不足。
    (C) 她無法出差。
    (D) 她尚未填完一些表格。　答案 (A)

170. 沃特斯女士表示要為史密斯女士做什麼？
    (A) 準備一臺新電腦
    (B) 為她訂購一張新桌子
    (C) 開設網路帳號
    (D) 幫助她處理專案　　　　答案 (C)

171. 下午 2:51，史密斯女士為什麼寫道「這對我來說行得通」？
    (A) 抱怨新的任務
    (B) 主動提出加班
    (C) 表示她有多忙
    (D) 同意薩特先生的點子　　答案 (D)

問題 172-175，請參考以下文章內容。

在這裡感受非洲的靈魂！

布魯克萊恩，4 月 22 日 － (172) 非洲之聲來到布魯克萊恩了，這裡前幾年曾辦過許多音樂節。非洲靈魂音樂節是精彩的戶外非洲音樂節，(174) 將於 5 月 30 日至 31 日在布魯克萊恩廣場舉辦。預計會有數百名非洲音樂迷和當地居民前來參加。

由布魯克萊恩娛樂部門主辦的非洲靈魂音樂節具備多項知名特色。其一是音樂多樣性。現場將演奏多種非洲音樂，包括來自非洲東部、中部和南部的曲調。

許多著名的非洲音樂家都會飛來布魯克萊恩，在非洲靈魂音樂節上表演。(175) 第 4 屆非洲音樂大賽獲勝者巴巴・克勒將在第一天表演。第二天，因上電視而出名的斯卡風樂團黑磨坊將蒞臨現場。在各國頗受歡迎、持續累積國際知名度的幾位藝術家也將在音樂節上表演，包括艾倫・加莫拉、老爹所羅門和辛巴・奧蒙加。

(174) 活動第一天，晚上在入口處附近將提供免費非洲傳統餐點和飲料，供各位品嚐。

節慶期間，門票可以在布魯克萊恩廣場入口附近的售票處購買。(173) 5 月 20 日之前，也可以在 www.brooklinetickets.com 上以優惠價取得門票。

172. 這篇文章的主題是什麼？
    (A) 獻給居民的免費表演
    (B) 一趟非洲之旅
    (C) 非洲音樂史
    (D) 一場戶外活動　　　　　　　　　　　答案 (D)

173. 關於門票，文中提到什麼？
    (A) 會有限時折扣。
    (B) 不能現場購買。
    (C) 免費向當地居民提供。
    (D) 可致電娛樂部進行預訂。　　　　　　答案 (A)

174. 什麼時候會提供免費餐點？
    (A) 4 月 22 日
    (B) 5 月 20 日
    (C) 5 月 30 日
    (D) 5 月 31 日　　　　　　　　　　　　答案 (C)

175. 以下句子最適合放在文中 [1]、[2]、[3] 和 [4] 的哪一個
    位置？
    「第二天，因上電視而出名的斯卡風樂團黑磨坊將蒞
    臨現場。」
    (A) [1]
    (B) [2]
    (C) [3]
    (D) [4]　　　　　　　　　　　　　　　答案 (C)

問題 176-180，請參考以下傳單及網站。

呼叫提示
倫敦，西摩公園
10 月 1 日至 5 日

(176) (179A) 國際戲劇協會（ITS）再次回歸，舉辦第
5 屆「呼叫提示」！加入這個為期一週的年度慶典，現
場有來自主流和獨立製作公司的活力演出，其中也包括
(180) 克萊莫爾表演藝術學院（CCPA）！

(176) 主舞臺的表演包括：

第一天：詹姆斯‧加爾薩和羅克珊‧史旺森表演《與老
虎相伴的人》
第二天：安妮 - 索菲‧溫特表演一系列獨角戲；皇家劇
團演出《商人之城》
第三天：謝幕劇團演出《色彩噴泉》；伊萊恩‧艾迪娜
的單人表演
第四天：(179D) 今年 ITS 短劇比賽的獲獎劇本，包括
羅素‧陳的《黃雨傘》
第五天：由 JMS 製作、羅德演員協會演出的《龍的眼
淚》；(177) 羅德里克‧多爾蒂演出《孤獨的樹》

還有更多！有關每天的詳細演出節目表，請造訪我們的
網站 www.its.org/callthecue。

(180) 就讀 CCPA 的 (178) 學生可享受特別折扣。請在
結帳時輸入折扣代碼 CCASTD。輸入之後，請出示在

學證明。

（179B）國際戲劇協會
倫敦帕蒂森街 1 號
0844 555 0787

---

www.ticketbook.com/theatre/its-call-the-cue/payment
票券訂購

歡迎光臨，(180) 克里斯‧法夫！| 我的帳戶

首頁	音樂會	(176) 戲劇表演	展覽	運動賽事

快速搜尋	票券類型	單日入場券
	選擇日期	10 月 3 日
今日優惠	寄送方式	現場取貨
本週	優惠碼	(180) CCASTD
本月	入場券：	30 美元
	寄送費：	0 美元
我的頁面	(180) 折扣：	-5 美元
預訂	總計：	25 美元
書籤	付款方式	信用卡
我的點數		xxxx-xxxx-xxxx-0333

---

176. 「呼叫提示」最有可能是什麼類型的活動？
    (A) 美術展
    (B) 一連串動物表演
    (C) 一系列戲劇表演
    (D) 校慶　　　　　　　　　　　　　　　答案 (C)

177. 誰會演出《孤獨的樹》？
    (A) 史旺森女士
    (B) 加爾薩先生
    (C) 溫特女士
    (D) 多爾蒂先生　　　　　　　　　　　　答案 (D)

178. 傳單中，第 4 段第 1 行的「extended」，含義最接近
    (A) 延期
    (B) 創造
    (C) 提供
    (D) 擴展　　　　　　　　　　　　　　　答案 (C)

179. 關於國際戲劇協會，文中沒有暗指什麼？
    (A) 以前曾舉辦過慶典。
    (B) 總部位於倫敦。
    (C) 大約在 5 年前成立。
    (D) 會舉辦短劇比賽。　　　　　　　　　答案 (C)

180. 關於法夫先生，文中暗指什麼？
    (A) 他為別人買票。
    (B) 他是 ITS 的成員。
    (C) 他是藝術學院的學生。
    (D) 他將表演一齣短劇。　　　　　　　　答案 (C)

問題 181-185，請參考以下廣告及電子郵件。

瓦爾波洞穴之旅

歡迎來到瓦爾波洞穴，令人驚嘆的大自然傑作。這個千年洞穴位於菲律賓拉古納省的國家公園內，是該國最大的旅遊景點之一。選擇以下其中一個導覽行程，見證大自然令人嘆為觀止的壯闊！在每個導覽行程中，你將在 (185) 國家旅遊協會（NTA）認證的導遊協助下，了解當地歷史、地理和文化。

一般導覽
包含舒適地乘坐休旅車前往洞穴。成人每位 450 比索，兒童（4-11 歲）每位 300 比索，4 歲以下免費。

黃金時段導覽
在一天當中最多陽光照入洞穴的時間出發。成人每位 550 比索，兒童（4-11 歲）每位 380 比索，4 歲以下免費。

攝影導覽
親自拍攝美麗的瓦爾波洞穴照片。業餘或專業攝影師都適合。無論是設置相機或拍攝角度，都會有專家協助。(184) 你可以帶著三腳架。(184) 成人每位 650 比索，兒童（4-11 歲）每位 470 比索，4 歲以下免費。

(181) 365 天全年開放。(182) 如須預訂或了解更多資訊，請前往 www.valpoacave.com。若有任何疑問，請寄電子郵件至 customerservice@valpoa.com 或致電 632-555-9270。

收件人：瓦爾波洞穴之旅 <customerservice@valpoa.com>
寄件人：庫特・托卡 <ktoka@polemail.com>
日　期：7 月 5 日
主　旨：關於我上次的導覽行程

致相關人士，

(184) 上個月，我和太太造訪了瓦爾波洞穴。我們非常享受洞穴的美景。然而，現場太擁擠了，(184) 害我很難拍攝洞穴的照片，因為沒有足夠的空間來架設我的三腳架。(185) 我對我們的導遊大衛・尼森提到這個困擾，他也承認這有問題。他承諾將提供部分退款，(183) 並在一週內把一套瓦爾波洞穴的明信片寄到我家，作為補償。我收到了部分退費的 200 比索，這還算合理，因為我很喜歡這個洞穴之旅。(183) 但已經過了兩個多星期，我還沒有收到明信片。

如果你們還沒有寄出明信片，可以在包裹裡附上一本旅遊手冊嗎？我在你們的廣告上看到有折價券，而我最近還想再次參觀瓦爾波洞穴。

謝謝你。

庫特・托卡

---

181. 關於瓦爾波洞穴的導覽行程，文中暗指什麼？
(A) 要求遊客駕駛自己的休旅車。
(B) 每小時有一團出發。
(C) 全年無休。
(D) 不分年齡都收取相同費用。　　答案 (C)

182. 顧客如何預訂導覽行程？
(A) 告知導遊
(B) 寫電子郵件
(C) 瀏覽網站
(D) 撥打電話　　答案 (C)

183. 這封電子郵件的目的是什麼？
(A) 投訴導遊
(B) 告知某人某項物品沒有送達
(C) 索取完整導覽行程
(D) 詢問洞穴的位置　　答案 (B)

184. 托卡先生在 6 月旅遊時，最初付了多少錢？
(A) 200 比索
(B) 450 比索
(C) 470 比索
(D) 650 比索　　答案 (D)

185. 關於尼森先生，文中暗指什麼？
(A) 他會為托卡先生再帶另一團導覽。
(B) 他會寄明信片給托卡先生。
(C) 他獲得某個機構的認證。
(D) 他帶著自己的三腳架去瓦爾波洞穴。　　答案 (C)

問題 186-190，請參考以下時程表及電子郵件。

魯道夫玩具公司

(186) 魯道夫玩具很高興宣布，年度員工培訓課程將於下週舉行。這些課程是為了加強員工的效率和知識。請見以下課表：

專案規劃

淺田節子，行銷總監		
6 月 10 日星期二	上午 9:00 - 10:30	501 室

工程　　　　*(187) 工程部全體員工必須參加。

奧蘭多・伊布拉希莫維奇，首席工程總監		
6 月 10 日星期二	下午 1:00 - 3:00	502 室

溝通技巧

安娜・德沃爾金，會計副理		
6 月 12 日星期四	下午 1:00 - 2:30	401 室

(188) 安全規定及設備使用

金柏利・傑德，工廠經理		
(188) (190) 6 月 12 日星期四	(188) (190) 下午 3:00 - 6:00	603 室

(188) 6 月 12 日最後一堂課結束之後，將為參加者提供

晚餐。請在每堂課開始前 5 分鐘抵達入座。禁止攜帶食物或飲料。(189) 如有任何意見、建議和問題，請提交給人力資源部。

收件人：雷米・伊夫 <ryves@rudolftoys.com>
寄件人：淺田節子 <sasada@rudolftoys.com>
日　期：6 月 3 日
主　旨：培訓課程

(189) 親愛的伊夫先生，

(189) 本次來信是關於即將舉行的培訓課程。我本來應該負責其中一堂課，但我因為有個緊急商務行程，無法過去。幸好，我部門的副主任琳達・薩默斯在課程當天有空。她將代替我負責培訓課程。

請盡快更正關於課表的貼文，以免造成混亂。很抱歉造成不便。在我出差期間，可以用電子郵件或電話 (135)-555-6432 與我聯繫。

誠摯感謝。

淺田節子
行銷總監

收件人：雷米・伊夫 <ryves@rudolftoys.com>
寄件人：安娜・德沃爾金 <annad@rudolftoys.com>
日　期：6 月 13 日
主　旨：謝謝

(189) 伊夫先生，

(189) (190) 非常感謝你讓我與金柏利調換課程時間。很遺憾只提前一天通知你。我衷心感謝你協助做出更動。

此外，這是我第一次在這裡舉辦培訓課程。我全然享受這個過程，並希望將來還有這種機會。如果你以後需要我提供更多幫助，請隨時提出。

謝謝。

安娜・德沃爾金

---

186. 關於魯道夫玩具公司的時程表，文中暗指什麼？
　　(A) 要求培訓課程參加者提前報名。
　　(B) 目前正在招募新員工。
　　(C) 預計很快就會舉辦一場定期活動。
　　(D) 每年評估員工的表現。　　　　　　答案 (C)

187. 關於伊布拉希莫維奇先生舉辦的培訓課程，文中提到什麼？
　　(A) 需要特定人員參與。
　　(B) 將持續 3 個小時。
　　(C) 將為參加者提供茶點。
　　(D) 針對新工作人員。　　　　　　　答案 (A)

188. 哪堂課後會提供免費餐點？
　　(A) 專案規劃
　　(B) 工程
　　(C) 溝通技巧
　　(D) 安全規定及設備使用　　　　　　答案 (D)

189. 關於伊夫先生，可以推斷出什麼？
　　(A) 他將帶領一堂培訓課程。
　　(B) 他正計劃去出差。
　　(C) 他很快就會聯繫淺田女士。
　　(D) 他在人力資源部門工作。　　　　答案 (D)

190. 德沃爾金女士何時舉辦培訓課程？
　　(A) 星期二上午 9 點
　　(B) 星期二下午 1 點
　　(C) 星期四下午 1 點
　　(D) 星期四下午 3 點　　　　　　　答案 (D)

問題 191-195，請參考以下廣告、網頁及電子郵件。

緋紅之地
讓您的特別之日不同凡響

如果您要舉辦特殊活動，請選擇本市最受歡迎的場地——緋紅之地。我們連續五年，在活動管理領域被選為華盛頓特區的最佳服務提供者。

• 宴會大廳
這個選項包括由枝形吊燈照明的宴會廳，營造優雅的感受。它可以讓 200 位賓客舒適地分坐於十人桌，並設有可供發言的舞臺。

• 玫瑰花園
(191) 在陽光下的優雅涼亭裡舉辦您的活動。附餐點的長凳配置可容納 300 位賓客，宴會配置則可容納 150 位賓客。請注意，根據天氣情況，活動可能會移至空的宴會廳舉行。

• 禮拜堂
(192) 高高的拱門和大型彩繪玻璃窗，為您的特別之日提供神聖的空間。該房間僅供舉行儀式，不提供餐點。如有要求，賓客可以在其他大廳享用餐點。

• 攝影
(194) 當地攝影工作室「漢密爾頓」將捕捉這些日子的獨特時刻。除了 3 月至 5 月的旺季之外，此服務皆為免費提供。

---

www.scarlatium.com/testimonials

緋紅之地 讓您的特別之日不同凡響！

首頁	諮詢	預訂	客戶評價

完美

　　　　　　－ 娜塔莉・懷特撰文，發布於 6 月 13 日

(193) 在緋紅之地舉行婚禮，是我不會後悔的決定。這一天完美無瑕，感謝我的活動業務專員伊芙琳・喬治。伊芙琳在組織活動的每個細節上，帶來了無價的貢獻。當我早上接到電話，說我預訂的房間音響系統無法正常運作時，我壓力超大。聽說其他宴會廳都滿了之後，我變得更加著急。然後，伊芙琳安排在花園裡舉辦活動。(194) (195) 她還退還我為攝影支付的費用，以示歉意。緋紅之地提供的餐點也超乎預期。我已經沒什麼可以要求的了。

收件人：雅各布・湯馬斯 <jthomas@hamiltons.com>
寄件人：伊芙琳・喬治 <egeorge@scarlatium.com>
日　期：6 月 14 日
主　旨：回覆：付款

湯馬斯先生，

我剛剛讀了你寄的電子郵件。(195) 別擔心，你為懷特女士婚禮所提供的服務將獲得付款。即便我們退費給她，仍然打算付費給你。只要我們收到發票，款項將在 3 個工作天內存入你的帳戶。如果還有其他疑慮，請讓我知道。

誠摯問候。

伊芙琳・喬治
緋紅之地

---

191. 廣告中，第 1 段第 1 行的「occasions」，含義最接近
(A) 案例
(B) 活動
(C) 休息時間
(D) 日期　　　　　　　　　　答案 (B)

192. 關於緋紅之地，文中提到什麼？
(A) 成立於 5 年前。
(B) 只能舉辦婚禮。
(C) 有一個窗戶裝飾華麗的空間。
(D) 一次最多可容納 300 名賓客。　答案 (C)

193. 懷特女士為什麼在網頁上發布貼文？
(A) 要求退款
(B) 提出建議
(C) 提出投訴
(D) 讚揚服務　　　　　　　　　答案 (D)

194. 關於懷特女士，可以推斷出什麼？
(A) 她向緋紅之地要求退款。
(B) 她最初計劃在戶外舉行活動。
(C) 她在緋紅之地的旺季舉辦活動。
(D) 她使用了外部餐飲服務。　　答案 (C)

195. 湯馬斯先生最有可能是誰？
(A) 攝影師
(B) 緋紅之地員工
(C) 婚禮嘉賓
(D) 緋紅之地客戶　　　　　　　答案 (A)

問題 196-200，請參考以下廣告及電子郵件。

東方之星飯店

(196) 東方之星飯店位於曼谷市中心，已有 60 年歷史。飯店最近經過重新裝修。目前整間飯店均提供免費無線網絡。新裝修的客房特色如下：

標準房型	單人床、吹風機、空調
(197) 豪華房型	2 張單人床、吹風機、(197) 冰箱、空調
套房	2 張單人床、客廳、2 間有浴缸的浴室、吹風機、冰箱、頂級音響系統、高畫質電視、空調
(199) 商務套房	2 間臥室、客廳、2 間有浴缸的浴室、吹風機、2 臺冰箱、音響系統、2 臺高畫質電視、空調、(199) 免費早餐

東方之星飯店的餐廳「藍盤」提供由 (198D) 世界知名、(198B) 屢獲殊榮的主廚伊斯拉・塔料理的美食。(198C) 塔女士擁有 15 年烹飪經驗，菜色涵蓋泰國、韓國、日本和義大利傳統美食。

關於東方之星飯店的更多資訊，請造訪 www.orientalstarhotel.com。(200) 考慮到旺季遊客較多，建議您提前 2 個月預訂房間。

收件人：客戶服務
　　　　　<customerservice@orientalstarhotel.com>
寄件人：阿努拉格・霍維庫爾
　　　　　<ahorvejkul@pmtextiles.com>
日　期：11 月 20 日
主　旨：很棒的經歷

致相關人士，

我寫這封信，是為了感謝貴公司提供的美好體驗。上週，我的客戶塔漢・桑蒂薩庫來曼谷出差時，我安排他入住你們的飯店。桑蒂薩庫先生表示，他很滿意你們為他提供的整體服務。(199) 他特別喜歡每天早上享用的免費早餐。

此外，桑蒂薩庫先生和我都很喜歡藍盤的餐點。11 月 16 日，我們點了烤鮭魚，主廚親自為我們服務。與這位從前在電視上見過的人交談，是一次愉快的經驗。期待將來再次與貴飯店進行商務合作。

誠摯感謝。

阿努拉格・霍維庫爾

客戶經理
PM 紡織有限公司

收件人：<reservations@orientalstarhotel.com>
寄件人：<tahans@promenadecarpets.com>
日　期：12 月 1 日
主　旨：訂房

親愛的先生／女士，

我的名字是塔漢‧桑蒂薩庫，我想預訂你們飯店。我上個月入住過，而且非常享受那次經驗。我 12 月 6 日至 12 日會到曼谷。希望能有和上次入住時同樣的房型。

(200) 我知道我應該在幾個月前預約，但希望你們仍然能接受我的要求。如果有空房，請讓我知道。

誠摯問候。
塔漢‧桑蒂薩庫

---

196. 關於東方之星飯店，廣告暗指了什麼？
 (A) 它在特定期間沒有營業。
 (B) 它是曼谷最大的飯店。
 (C) 它位於幾個旅遊景點附近。
 (D) 它已經營業了幾十年。　　　　　答案 (D)

197. 豪華房型有什麼設備？
 (A) 高畫質電視
 (B) 冰箱
 (C) 客廳
 (D) 浴缸　　　　　　　　　　　　答案 (B)

198. 關於塔女士，文中沒有暗指什麼？
 (A) 她在東方之星飯店工作了 15 年。
 (B) 她曾因烹飪而獲獎。
 (C) 她會烹飪多種風格的料理。
 (D) 她為其他國家的人們所熟知。　　答案 (A)

199. 關於桑蒂薩庫先生，可以推斷出什麼？
 (A) 他是霍維庫爾先生的同事。
 (B) 他多次造訪曼谷。
 (C) 他住在商務套房。
 (D) 他最近讀了一本有關烹飪藝術的雜誌。　答案 (C)

200. 關於桑蒂薩庫先生，文中暗指什麼？
 (A) 他整個 12 月都會待在曼谷。
 (B) 他每天都會見到霍維庫爾先生。
 (C) 他想在下次旅行時住不同的房間。
 (D) 他計劃在旺季造訪曼谷。　　　　答案 (D)

---

1. 美國 M
 (A) A man is stacking some boxes on a shelf.
 (B) A man is lifting a box.
 (C) A man is carrying crates on a cart.
 (D) A man is packing supplies into a box.

 (A) 男子正把一些盒子堆到架子上。
 (B) 男子正舉起一個盒子。
 (C) 男子正用推車搬運箱子。
 (D) 男子正把物資裝進箱子。　　　答案 (C)

2. 澳洲 W
 (A) Some pillows are piled up on a sofa.
 (B) Some cartons are stacked on the floor.
 (C) A ladder is leaning against the fence.
 (D) Some plants are placed along the hallway.

 (A) 一些枕頭疊在沙發上。
 (B) 一些紙箱堆放在地板上。
 (C) 梯子靠在圍籬上。
 (D) 一些植物沿著走廊放置。　　　答案 (B)

3. 美國 M
 (A) They are constructing a brick walkway.
 (B) They are placing safety cones on a street.
 (C) They are kneeling to inspect a machine.
 (D) They are unloading bricks from a truck.

 (A) 他們正在建造一條磚砌人行道。
 (B) 他們正在街道上放置安全錐。
 (C) 他們跪著檢查機器。
 (D) 他們正從卡車上卸下磚塊。　　答案 (A)

4. 美國 W
 (A) Plastic bags are being distributed to people.
 (B) A broom has been propped up against a tree.
 (C) They are putting waste in the recycling bins.
 (D) They are cleaning up some debris.

 (A) 塑膠袋正被分發給人們。
 (B) 一支掃把靠在一棵樹上。
 (C) 他們正將廢棄物放入回收桶。
 (D) 他們正在清理一些殘骸碎片。　答案 (D)

5. 英國 M
 (A) The man is holding a cutting board.
 (B) The woman is putting some pans on the counter.
 (C) The man is placing some food onto a plate.
 (D) The woman is turning off a stove.

 (A) 男子正拿著一塊砧板。
 (B) 女子正把一些平底鍋放上流理臺。

(C) 男子正在將一些食物裝盤。
(D) 女子正關掉火爐。　　　　　　答案 (C)

6. 美國 W

(A) There is a deck overlooking a river.
(B) Some people are disembarking from a boat.
(C) A motorboat is passing under an arched bridge.
(D) One of the people is diving off a pier.

(A) 有一個俯瞰河流的甲板。
(B) 有些人正在下船。
(C) 汽艇正從拱橋下通過。
(D) 其中一人正從碼頭上跳水。　　答案 (A)

Part 2

7. 英國 M 美國 W

What kind of ice cream did you purchase?
(A) Yes, at the ice cream stand.
(B) I got the strawberry flavor.
(C) They seem to be reasonably priced.

你買了哪種冰淇淋？
(A) 是的，在冰淇淋攤。
(B) 我買了草莓口味。
(C) 它們的價格看起來很合理。　　答案 (B)

8. 澳洲 W 英國 M

When will the marketing expert arrive?
(A) The train will be here any minute.
(B) Right after noon.
(C) Sure, I will.

行銷專家什麼時候抵達？
(A) 火車隨時會到站。
(B) 中午過後。
(C) 當然，我會的。　　　　　　　答案 (B)

9. 美國 W 美國 M

Who is supposed to authorize this approval form?
(A) Yes, he is our new intern.
(B) The marketing director.
(C) By the end of the month.

應該由誰授權這份同意書？
(A) 是的，他是我們的新實習生。
(B) 行銷總監。
(C) 月底前。　　　　　　　　　　答案 (B)

10. 英國 M 美國 W

Please come here 15 minutes before your scheduled appointment.
(A) But I left work early yesterday.

(B) She is 10 minutes late.
(C) Okay. Is there parking for visitors nearby?

請在預約時間前 15 分鐘到達這裡。
(A) 但是我昨天提早下班了。
(B) 她遲到了 10 分鐘。
(C) 好的。附近有供訪客停車的地方嗎？　答案 (C)

11. 英國 M 美國 M

When will remodeling at the cafeteria be finished?
(A) This Friday at the latest, I think.
(B) Reserve a table for three.
(C) Try the first door on the left.

餐廳何時能完成裝潢？
(A) 我想，最晚這個星期五。
(B) 預訂三人的用餐座位。
(C) 試試看左邊第一扇門。　　　　答案 (A)

12. 美國 W 美國 M

How did your presentation for the board go?
(A) Actually it was a present from my mother.
(B) Is it okay if I join you?
(C) It really went well.

你在董事會的簡報進行得如何？
(A) 其實這是我媽送我的禮物。
(B) 我可以加入你們嗎？
(C) 進展得很順利。　　　　　　　答案 (C)

13. 澳洲 W 美國 M

How much of the budget is allocated to our computer lab?
(A) It was too expensive to buy.
(B) The software tracks your budget.
(C) Less than 5 percent.

我們的電腦實驗室分配到多少預算？
(A) 這買起來太貴了。
(B) 這款軟體會追蹤你的預算。
(C) 少於 5%。　　　　　　　　　答案 (C)

14. 美國 W 英國 M

Do you want to talk about the report after your conference call?
(A) The regional manager from Chicago.
(B) Yes, I report directly to Mr. Park.
(C) Actually, my call was postponed.

你想在電話會議後談談這份報告嗎？
(A) 來自芝加哥的區域經理。
(B) 是的，我直接向帕克先生報告工作。
(C) 事實上，我的通話被延後了。　答案 (C)

15. 英國 M 澳洲 W

Isn't the technician for routine maintenance coming later?
(A) Yes, after 3 in the afternoon.
(B) The renovation met our expectations.
(C) Downstairs and to the right.

負責例行維護的技師稍後不是會來嗎？
(A) 是的，下午 3 點之後。
(B) 這次整修符合我們的預期。
(C) 下樓右手邊。　　　　　　　　　答案 (A)

16. 美國 W 美國 M

Who's responsible for taking meeting minutes today?
(A) You should take the train.
(B) There's an extra table upstairs.
(C) I'll take care of it.

今天誰負責記錄會議摘要？
(A) 你應該坐火車。
(B) 樓上還有多一張桌子。
(C) 我會處理。　　　　　　　　　　答案 (C)

17. 英國 M 美國 W

Do you know why Sarah is out of the office this afternoon?
(A) The office space is rented out.
(B) She's picking up a client from the airport.
(C) You can take the stairs.

你知道為什麼莎拉今天下午不在辦公室嗎？
(A) 這個辦公空間已經租出去了。
(B) 她正在機場接一位客戶。
(C) 你可以走樓梯。　　　　　　　　答案 (B)

18. 澳洲 W 英國 M

Could you lend me your webcam for a video conference tomorrow?
(A) Arrange a conference call.
(B) Post it on the website.
(C) Sure, but I need it tomorrow afternoon at 5.

你可以借我視訊鏡頭來參加明天的視訊會議嗎？
(A) 安排電話會議。
(B) 把它張貼在網頁上。
(C) 當然可以，但我明天下午 5 點需要它。　答案 (C)

19. 美國 W 美國 M

What forms should I fill out on my first day of work?
(A) The ones in the welcome packet.
(B) Do it first thing in the morning.
(C) Sure, I'll fill it up.

第一天上班我應該填寫哪些表格？
(A) 員工迎新包裹裡的那些。

(B) 當成早上第一件事去處理。
(C) 當然，我會把它填滿。　　　　　答案 (A)

20. 英國 M 澳洲 W

Didn't the attendees have time to fill out their paperwork?
(A) No, I didn't attend, either.
(B) A 30 minute taxi-ride.
(C) Not yet, but that's next.

與會者沒有時間填寫文件嗎？
(A) 不，我也沒有參加。
(B) 搭計程車 30 分鐘。
(C) 還沒有，但那是接下來的事。　　答案 (C)

21. 美國 W 美國 M

I think this water faucet has a leak.
(A) Water the plants for me.
(B) Carl has a list of things to repair.
(C) The old microwave has been replaced.

我認為這個水龍頭會漏水。
(A) 替我為植物澆水。
(B) 卡爾有一份待修理物品的清單。
(C) 舊微波爐已被更換。　　　　　　答案 (B)

22. 英國 M 美國 W

We haven't already processed Ms. Wagner's order, have we?
(A) Place an order for more.
(B) I've gone over this book before.
(C) Yes, it was shipped out this morning.

我們還沒有處理華格納女士的訂單，對嗎？
(A) 訂購更多。
(B) 我以前看過這本書了。
(C) 已處理，今天早上出貨了。　　　答案 (C)

23. 澳洲 W 美國 M

Why don't we purchase the conference tables that Mr. Kwon recommended?
(A) A weeklong training session.
(B) We can't afford to get them.
(C) No, it's not in the conference room.

我們何不購買權先生推薦的會議桌呢？
(A) 為期一週的培訓課程。
(B) 我們買不起它們。
(C) 不，不在會議室。　　　　　　　答案 (B)

24. 美國 W 英國 M

Are you driving yourself or taking a taxi to the art museum?
(A) The buses do run on weekends, right?

(B) Just across the street.

(C) I get to work on foot.

你是自己開車還是搭計程車去美術館？
(A) 公車週末也有行駛，對吧？
(B) 就在對街。
(C) 我步行上班。   答案 (A)

25. 澳洲 W 美國 M

What street is the local community center on?
(A) They offer art classes at the center.
(B) Miranda's been there before.
(C) About a road repaving project.

當地社區中心位於哪條街上？
(A) 他們在中心提供藝術課程。
(B) 米蘭達以前去過那裡。
(C) 關於道路重鋪工程。   答案 (B)

26. 英國 M 美國 W

Was the 10 o'clock ferry to the island canceled?
(A) She went there by plane, too.
(B) That's what I heard.
(C) Yes, at the restaurant downstairs.

10 點去島上的渡輪取消了嗎？
(A) 她也搭飛機去那裡。
(B) 我是這麼聽說的。
(C) 是的，在樓下的餐廳。   答案 (B)

27. 美國 M 澳洲 W

Would you like me to give you a tour of the new motor parts factory today?
(A) Inspect assembly lines.
(B) I was there last Friday.
(C) A new automobile is launching today.

你今天想要我帶你參觀新的汽車零件工廠嗎？
(A) 檢查裝配線。
(B) 上週五我在那裡。
(C) 今天推出一款新車。   答案 (B)

28. 英國 M 澳洲 W

What's the fastest way to get to the modern art museum?
(A) Din might know.
(B) Just two more paintings.
(C) An hourly rate.

前往現代美術館最快的方式是什麼？
(A) 狄恩可能知道。
(B) 還有兩幅畫。
(C) 按小時收費。   答案 (A)

29. 美國 W 美國 M

Will the training for the new summer intern start on Monday or Tuesday?
(A) Can I come in for an interview?
(B) It wasn't a safety training session.
(C) The schedule hasn't been finalized.

新來的暑期實習生是週一還是週二開始培訓？
(A) 我可以進來面試嗎？
(B) 這不是安全培訓課程。
(C) 時間表尚未定案。   答案 (C)

30. 英國 M 美國 W

The copy machine in Marketing is out of order, isn't it?
(A) Yes, the manager's out of the office today.
(B) I used it 30 minutes ago.
(C) It's on the market now.

行銷部的影印機壞了，不是嗎？
(A) 是的，經理今天不在辦公室。
(B) 我 30 分鐘前使用過。
(C) 現在已經上市了。   答案 (B)

31. 澳洲 W 英國 M

Dr. Yoon has an appointment available this Friday after 3.
(A) Yes, I'm free at the moment.
(B) Chapter 7 starts on page 55.
(C) What about next Monday?

尹醫生本週五下午 3 點後可以接受預約。
(A) 是的，我現在有空。
(B) 第 7 章從第 55 頁開始。
(C) 下週一如何？   答案 (C)

Part 3

問題 32-34，請參考以下對話內容。 美國 M 美國 W

M: Carla, (32)**how did the trade show go yesterday?**

W: Very well. (32) (33)**I talked about the new sensor-laden smart watches we're producing, and people seemed really interested in it. We had an audience of more than 70 people, and everyone agreed that that's the future of our industry—designing high-tech devices that provide people with more immediate access to any information.**

M: Did you mention that (34)**we'll be conducting a product testing for our latest smart watches next Monday?**

W: I did. And several potential investors in the audience indicated that they'd be attending it.

男：卡拉，昨天的貿易展進行得如何？
女：非常好。我談到我們正在生產裝配感測器的新型智慧型手錶，大家似乎對此非常感興趣。我們的觀眾超過 70 人，每個人都同意這就是此產業的未來——設計高科技裝備，提供人們更直接獲取資訊的管道。
男：你有沒有提到，我們下週一將為最新的智慧型手錶進行產品測試？
女：有。聽眾裡的幾位潛在投資者表示會參加。

32. 女子昨天做了什麼？
    (A) 她進行了採訪。
    (B) 她發表了簡報。
    (C) 她招募了一名新員工。
    (D) 她更新了網頁。　　　　　　　　答案 (B)

33. 談話者在什麼產業工作？
    (A) 服裝
    (B) 電子產品
    (C) 工程
    (D) 餐飲服務　　　　　　　　　　　答案 (B)

34. 這間公司下週一會做什麼？
    (A) 與客戶開會
    (B) 更換部分設備
    (C) 協調收購案
    (D) 測試新產品　　　　　　　　　　答案 (D)

問題 35-37，請參考以下對話內容。 英國 M 澳洲 W

M: Elizabeth, (36)**I'm planning the event** that will be held in March. You know almost all the speakers. (35)**Would you mind introducing them to the audience before they talk?**
W: (35)**Not at all.** I would love to. Do you need any assistance with the planning? (36)**I know we're hoping to raise enough funds to finance some new projects, so it's vital for everything to go well.**
M: That's all right. I'm nearly finished. (37)**All I have to do is work on the invitations.** Thanks for offering, though.

男：伊麗莎白，我正在籌劃 3 月分舉行的活動。你幾乎認識所有講者。你介意在他們開講之前，向觀眾介紹一下他們嗎？
女：完全不介意。我很樂意這麼做。你在籌劃方面需要任何幫助嗎？我知道我們希望募集足夠資金，來資助一些新計劃，因此確保一切順利是至關重要的。
男：沒問題。我快完成了。我要做的只剩製作邀請函。不過還是謝謝你願意協助。

35. 男子請求女子在活動中做什麼事？
    (A) 介紹講者
    (B) 製作與會者名單
    (C) 準備場地
    (D) 銷售門票　　　　　　　　　　　答案 (A)

36. 正在籌備哪種類型的活動？
    (A) 慈善拍賣
    (B) 培訓課程
    (C) 募款活動
    (D) 產品展示　　　　　　　　　　　答案 (C)

37. 男子說他需要做什麼？
    (A) 製作邀請函
    (B) 聯繫客座講者
    (C) 聘請外燴廠商
    (D) 支付押金　　　　　　　　　　　答案 (A)

問題 38-40，請參考以下對話內容。 英國 M 美國 W

M: Hello, Lucy. (38)**You're leading the tours at the museum next week, right?**
W: That's right. I'll be here every day since Chester will be gone.
M: Okay. (39)**Then you should know we'll be getting a tour group from the local elementary school on Tuesday.** The kids are scheduled to take a special tour of the observatory.
W: Great. Do I need to do anything before they arrive?
M: Here's a list with the students' names on it. (40)**Make sure each of them has a visitor's badge when the group gets here.** They're scheduled to arrive at 10:00 A.M.

男：你好，露西。下週你會帶隊參觀博物館，對吧？
女：沒錯。因為切斯特要離開了，所以我每天都會在這裡。
男：好的。那麼你應該知道，週二我們要接待當地小學的導覽團。孩子們已排定要來一趟特別的天文臺之旅。
女：太棒了。在他們到達之前，我需要做些什麼嗎？
男：名單在這，上面有學生的名字。團體抵達的時候，要確保每個人都有訪客證。他們預計上午 10 點抵達。

38. 談話者在哪裡工作？
    (A) 主題樂園
    (B) 銀行
    (C) 動物園
    (D) 博物館　　　　　　　　　　　　答案 (D)

39. 根據男子所說，星期二會發生什麼事？
    (A) 有一個人會開始工作。
    (B) 一個團體會參訪一棟建築。
    (C) 將啟動一項新專案。
    (D) 一場展覽將開幕。　　　　　　　答案 (B)

40. 男子說女子應該做什麼？
    (A) 提供證件
    (B) 領取門票
    (C) 補充小手冊
    (D) 列印導覽行程表　　　　　　　答案 (A)

問題 41-43，請參考以下對話內容。 澳洲 W 美國 M

W: Eric, (41)**do you remember I said I'd research manufacturers for our new skateboard design?** Well, I think I found a good one.

M: Wonderful. Does the company have the ability to work with the lightweight materials we plan to use for the skateboards?

W: Yes, but the problem is that the company is in St. Louis.

M: Oh… You know that we have to make frequent site inspections to ensure quality. (42)**It would be pretty expensive to fly to St. Louis every two weeks.**

W: That's true. (43)**But why don't we outsource by hiring a quality control inspector who lives in St. Louis?** That would be much cheaper than having to travel there twice a month.

女：艾瑞克，你還記得我說過，會為我們的新滑板設計查一查製造商嗎？嗯，我想我找到一間不錯的。
男：太棒了。這間公司有能力處理我們計劃用於滑板的輕量材料嗎？
女：有的，但問題是，這間公司在聖路易斯。
男：噢……你知道的，我們必須經常執行現場檢查來確保品質。每兩週就飛往聖路易斯一次會相當昂貴。
女：確實如此。但我們何不聘請住在聖路易斯的品質檢驗人員，來外包這件事呢？這會比每個月去那裡兩次要便宜得多。

41. 談話者在談論什麼產品？
    (A) 跑鞋
    (B) 運動飲料
    (C) 滑板
    (D) 自行車　　　　　　　答案 (C)

42. 男子為了什麼而擔心？
    (A) 航班被取消。
    (B) 工廠位置太遠。
    (C) 工作負荷過重。
    (D) 專案沒有照進度走。　　　　　　　答案 (B)

43. 女子建議怎麼做？
    (A) 購買高燃油效率的車輛
    (B) 搬遷工廠
    (C) 變更生產時間表
    (D) 尋找當地檢查員　　　　　　　答案 (D)

問題 44-46，請參考以下對話內容。 英國 M 美國 W

M: Hello, Tina. Welcome to Dylan Manufacturing. I'm Paul Bernstein, (44)**and I'll be your trainer.** I understand you have quite a bit of career experience in our field.

W: That's right. I worked for an automobile manufacturer in Dayton for seven years. (45)**I took this job so that I can live closer to my parents.**

M: That's wonderful. I'm sure this training should go smoothly then. But before we begin, you have to learn about the safety procedures we follow.

W: Sure. I understand.

M: (46)**Here's the safety manual. Why don't you read it through now?** I'll return to go over everything with you in about twenty minutes.

男：你好，蒂娜。歡迎來到迪倫製造公司。我是保羅·伯恩斯坦，你未來的培訓員。我知道你在這個領域頗有工作經驗。
女：沒錯。我在代頓一家汽車製造商工作了 7 年。我接下這份工作，是為了能住得離父母近一些。
男：那太好了。我相信這次培訓應該會順利進行。但在開始之前，你必須了解我們所遵循的安全規定。
女：當然。我明白。
男：這是安全手冊。何不現在就讀一下呢？大約 20 分鐘後，我會回來和你一起全部看過一遍。

44. 男子是誰？
    (A) 招募人員
    (B) 培訓人員
    (C) 面試官
    (D) 汽車經銷商　　　　　　　答案 (B)

45. 女子為什麼接下一份新工作？
    (A) 為了更靠近家人
    (B) 為了獲得更高的薪水
    (C) 為了在本地大學修一門課
    (D) 為了獲得一些新技能　　　　　　　答案 (A)

46. 女子接下來最可能會做什麼？
    (A) 獲得實作經驗
    (B) 查看手冊
    (C) 填寫文件
    (D) 進行示範　　　　　　　答案 (B)

問題 **47-49**，請參考以下三方對話內容。 美國 M 澳洲 W 美國 W

M: Hello. I'm Kevin Lester. I reserved a room here for tonight.

W1: Good afternoon, Mr. Lester. Welcome to the Omni. This is your room keycard. (47)**Unfortunately, the elevator is out of service since it is being fixed right now.** But you can take the stairs over there. Emily can show you to your room.

W2: Follow me, sir. (48)**Do you have any luggage?**

M: (48)**Yes, I left them outside in my car. There are also a few boxes of books. Is that all right?**

W2: (48)**It's no problem at all.**

M: Great. (49)**I'm hoping to sell all those books at the international book fair tomorrow.**

男：你好。我是凱文‧萊斯特。我今晚在這裡預訂了一個房間。

女1：午安，萊斯特先生。歡迎來到奧姆尼。這是您的房卡。不巧的是，電梯目前正在維修，所以暫停使用。但您可以走那邊的樓梯。艾蜜莉會帶您前往房間。

女2：請往這裡，先生。您有行李嗎？

男：是的，我把它們留在外面的車裡了。還有幾箱書。這樣可以嗎？

女2：完全沒問題。

男：太好了。我希望明天在國際書展上，把那些書全部賣掉。

47. 電梯出了什麼問題？
(A) 因保養而停機。
(B) 正在清理。
(C) 空間不夠大。
(D) 正在維修中。 　　　　　　答案 (D)

48. 艾蜜莉表示願意做什麼？
(A) 拿一些行李
(B) 停車
(C) 開車送男子去機場
(D) 向男子提供折扣 　　　　　答案 (A)

49. 男子希望明天能做什麼？
(A) 租一輛車
(B) 賣掉一些書
(C) 在書店購物
(D) 預訂書展攤位 　　　　　　答案 (B)

問題 **50-52**，請參考以下對話內容。 美國 M 美國 W

M: Hello, Tina. (50)**I need to speak with you for a moment before you begin your next tour of the park.**

W: No problem. I won't start my next one until three o'clock.

M: Great. (51)**I've got some surveys of the park tour for our guests. Please distribute them to everyone.**

W: Sure. What's the survey asking about?

M: We're thinking of making some changes to the tours. But we want to find out what aspects of it people like and dislike so that we can retain the popular parts.

W: Sounds good. I wonder if we'd get more responses by e-mail. (52)**I have lots of e-mail addresses of people who went on tours before. I can e-mail them the survey.**

男：你好，蒂娜。在你開始下一趟公園導覽之前，我需要和你談談。

女：沒問題。我到3點才會開始下一輪。

男：太好了。我為顧客準備了一些關於公園導覽的問卷。請發給大家。

女：當然好。問卷會有什麼問題？

男：我們正在考慮對導覽做出一些改變。但我們想找出人們喜歡和不喜歡的地方，以便保留受歡迎的部分。

女：聽起來不錯。我想，用電子郵件會不會收到更多回覆。我有很多以前導覽參加者的電子郵件。我可以把問卷寄給他們。

50. 女子最有可能是誰？
(A) 政府檢查員
(B) 公車司機
(C) 導遊
(D) 旅行社代理 　　　　　　答案 (C)

51. 男子希望女子做什麼？
(A) 審查文件
(B) 參加公園導覽
(C) 發放問卷調查
(D) 寄一封電子郵件給他 　　　答案 (C)

52. 女子說她有什麼？
(A) 公園地圖
(B) 一些名牌
(C) 一些訪客通行證
(D) 一份電子郵件清單 　　　　答案 (D)

問題 **53-55**，請參考以下對話內容。 美國 W 英國 M

W: Sylvester Office Tower maintenance office. What can I do for you?

M: Hello. I'm calling from the Dustin Printing office on the fourth floor. (53)**The lights here in the office aren't working well.**

W: Maybe the light bulbs need to be replaced.

M: I did that, (53) (54)**but the lights go out a few seconds after I turn them on.**

W: Okay. (54)**Well, the maintenance team is working on some pipes this morning.**

M: (55)**Oh, unfortunately, I have to leave the office after twelve to inspect our warehouse.**

W: If you give us permission, we can access your office while you are gone.

女：西維斯特辦公大樓維護辦公室。有什麼我能效勞的嗎？

男：你好。我這裡是 4 樓的達斯汀印刷室。我們辦公室這裡的燈有些問題。

女：也許燈泡需要更換。

男：我換了，但才打開幾秒燈就熄滅了。

女：好的。嗯，維護小組今天早上正在處理一些管線。

男：哦，真不巧。我必須在 12 點後離開辦公室，去檢查我們的倉庫。

女：如果你給我們許可，我們可以在你外出時進去你的辦公室。

----

53. 此談話內容主要是關於什麼？
(A) 管線漏水
(B) 門鎖損壞
(C) 物品遺失
(D) 電路問題　　　　　　　　　　　答案 (D)

54. 女子說「維護小組今天早上正在處理一些管線」，意思是什麼？
(A) 男子需要打給別人。
(B) 某些維修作業會很昂貴。
(C) 某些工作無法立即完成。
(D) 團隊成員整天都很忙。　　　　　答案 (C)

55. 男子說他下午要做什麼？
(A) 造訪倉庫
(B) 會見客戶
(C) 參加員工旅遊
(D) 準備一些文件　　　　　　　　　答案 (A)

問題 56-58，請參考以下對話內容。 澳洲 W 英國 M

W: Hello, Steve. I remember that you asked for some suggestions on how we can encourage our employees to be healthy. (56)**I know some companies acquire gym memberships for their employees. How does that sound?**

M: I think it would be a wonderful way to get people healthy. But (57)**we have lots of employees here.**

W: (57)**I figured you would say that. So I did some research and learned that some local gyms offer corporate discounts.**

M: Really? That's fascinating. Would you please forward me the information you found regarding that? (58)**I'll put it on the agenda for tomorrow's staff meeting.**

女：你好，史蒂夫。我記得你曾詢問關於如何鼓勵員工保持健康的建議。我知道有些公司會為員工購買健身房會員資格。這聽起來如何？

男：我認為這是讓人保持健康的好方法。但我們這裡有很多員工。

女：我就猜你會這麼說。所以我做了一些研究，發現部分當地健身房會提供企業折扣。

男：真的嗎？這太棒了。你可以把你找到的相關資訊轉寄給我嗎？我會把它列入明天員工會議的議程。

----

56. 女子建議公司做什麼？
(A) 變更營業時間
(B) 提供健身房會員資格
(C) 提供更好的福利
(D) 開設內部保健中心　　　　　　　答案 (B)

57. 男子說「我們這裡有很多員工」，是在暗示什麼？
(A) 公司很快就會增加更多辦公室。
(B) 某項建議成本過高。
(C) 有些員工將被轉調。
(D) 許多員工必須居家上班。　　　　答案 (B)

58. 男子說他會做什麼？
(A) 延後員工會議
(B) 審查預算報告
(C) 自己研究一下
(D) 將某個主題加入議程　　　　　　答案 (D)

問題 59-61，請參考以下三方對話內容。 美國 M 澳洲 W 英國 M

M1: Thanks for coming to Jackson's. My name is Peter. What can I do for you?

W: Hello. I work for a law firm downtown, and we relocated to a larger office last week. (59)**I'd like to purchase some photo frames for our lobby.**

M1: If you would like a unique look, we suggest that your picture frames be engraved. Our custom engraving services are highly rated. (60)**We even won a Customer Satisfaction Award for our high-quality work this year.**

W: Sounds good.

M1: Our engraver is here behind us. Jason, this woman wants to have some photo frames engraved.

M2: I can definitely do that. Would you be interested in a few samples of my work that you can choose from?

W: That sounds great. Oh, what kind of price should I

expect for having the work done?

M2: (61)**As a first-time customer, you'll get 10% off the regular price and delivery is at no extra cost.**

男 1：感謝您光臨傑克森的店。我是彼得。我能為您做什麼嗎？

女：你好。我在市中心的律師事務所上班。上週我們搬到一間更大的辦公室，我想為我們的大廳購買一些相框。

男 1：如果您想要獨特的外觀，我們建議您選擇雕刻相框。我們的客製化雕刻服務大受好評。今年，我們還因為高品質的工作而獲得顧客滿意獎。

女：聽起來不錯。

男 1：雕刻師就在我們身後。傑森，這位女士想要雕刻一些相框。

男 2：我絕對可以處理。您有興趣看看我的幾款作品樣本，以便從中選擇嗎？

女：聽起來不錯。哦，這麼做大概需要多少錢呢？

男 2：對於首購顧客，您將獲得一般價格的 10% 折扣，而且不另外收取運費。

---

59. 女子想購買什麼？
(A) 明信片
(B) 相框
(C) 懸掛花卉
(D) 鑰匙圈　　　　　　　　　　答案 (B)

60. 彼得說了關於雕刻服務的什麼事？
(A) 需要額外的時間。
(B) 目前缺貨。
(C) 今年某雜誌對其做了專題報導。
(D) 這是一項獲獎的服務。　　　答案 (D)

61. 傑森說什麼是免費的？
(A) 雕刻服務
(B) 運送
(C) 維護保養
(D) 延長保固　　　　　　　　　答案 (B)

問題 62-64，請參考以下對話內容及行程表。 美國 W 美國 M

W: Hi, Jeff. (62)**I'm going over a few details for the biomedical conference I'm organizing.** I wonder if you can assist me with something.

M: Sure. What do you need?

W: Do you have some time available on Thursday? Kevin was supposed to be manning the information booth from 1:00 to 2:00, but he has to be away on business on that day. (63)**I need someone to substitute for him for that hour.**

M: Wait a second, let me check my calendar. Oh, sure. I can do it. (64)**I have something scheduled for**

1:00 on that day, but I can call Mr. Duncan and reschedule our meeting.

女：嗨，傑夫。我正在查看我所籌備的生技醫療大會細節。我想知道你能否幫我做些什麼。

男：當然可以。你需要什麼？

女：星期四你有空嗎？凱文原本應該在 1 點到 2 點之間在詢問處值班，但他那天必須出差。我需要有人替他值班這一小時。

男：稍等一下，讓我查看一下行事曆。哦，沒問題，我可以。那天我 1 點有事情，但我可以打給鄧肯先生，重新安排我們的會議。

傑夫的行程表
11 月 5 日星期四

上午 9:00 − 10:00	與都鐸製藥公司進行電話會議
上午 10:30 − 12:00	愛德華・萊特產品展示
(64) 下午 1:00 − 2:30	與斯圖爾特・鄧肯協商合約
下午 5:00 − 6:00	在哈珀會議中心進行簡報

62. 女子正在籌備什麼？
(A) 產品展示
(B) 大會
(C) 慈善拍賣
(D) 迎新活動　　　　　　　　　答案 (B)

63. 女子要求男子做什麼？
(A) 替補一位同事
(B) 統籌接待工作
(C) 出差
(D) 與客戶會面　　　　　　　　答案 (A)

64. 請看圖表。男子將重新安排哪項活動？
(A) 電話會議
(B) 產品展示
(C) 合約協商
(D) 簡報　　　　　　　　　　　答案 (C)

問題 65-67，請參考以下對話內容及圓餅圖。 英國 M 澳洲 W

M: Here is the sales report of my team for the store for last week.

W: Thank you. (65)**Oh, by the way, you know that the store manager is resigning next month, right?**

M: Yes, I heard about that.

W: I need someone who can take over her job. (66) **Your team has been pretty effective at selling refrigerators and air conditioners.** Would you be interested in the position?

M: Yes, I would. I think you ought to know that (67)**I**

actually had the third highest sales numbers last week, but I was also out of town for three days. I still believe I'm the best person for the job.

男：這是我們團隊上週在這間店的銷售報告。
女：謝謝。哦，順道一提，你知道這間店的經理下個月就要辭職了，對嗎？
男：是的，我有聽說。
女：我需要一個可以接替她工作的人。你的團隊在銷售冰箱和空調方面非常高效。你對這個職位有興趣嗎？
男：是的，我願意。我想應該讓你知道，我上週的銷售數字其實是第三高，但我當時出城了三天。我相信我還是這份工作的最佳人選。

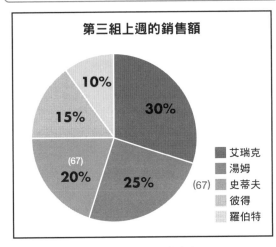

第三組上週的銷售額

65. 根據女子所說，下個月會發生什麼事？
 (A) 班表會調整。
 (B) 新員工將被調動。
 (C) 將會有促銷活動。
 (D) 某位員工停止上班。　　　　　　　答案 (D)

66. 談話者最有可能在哪裡工作？
 (A) 家電行
 (B) 服飾店
 (C) 露天市場
 (D) 工具製造商　　　　　　　　　　　答案 (A)

67. 請看圖表。男子叫什麼名字？
 (A) 艾瑞克
 (B) 湯姆
 (C) 史蒂夫
 (D) 彼得　　　　　　　　　　　　　　答案 (C)

問題 68-70，請參考以下對話內容及電腦螢幕畫面。
澳洲 W 美國 M

W: Hi, Walter. (68)**How do you like working at our marketing firm?**
M: I'm having a great time. In fact, I'm almost finished with my training program for new hires. However, I'm having some problems with the final assignment. I created a marketing plan, and I tried to e-mail it to my boss, Mr. Cameron. But I can't get it to go through. He's out of town on business and asked me to e-mail it to him.
W: The file is probably too big. You can't send files bigger than 30MBs.
M: (69)**Ah, the plan is around 40MBs.**
W: (70)**I think Mr. Cameron will return to the office tomorrow morning. Just wait until then and show the assignment to him.**

女：嗨，華特。你喜歡在我們這間行銷公司上班嗎？
男：我度過很棒的時光。事實上，我即將完成新進員工培訓計劃。但是，我在最後一項作業遇到了一些問題。我擬定了一份行銷計劃，並試著用電子郵件寄給我的老闆卡麥隆先生，卻寄不出去。他在外出差，要我用電子郵件寄給他。
女：檔案可能太大了。你無法寄送大於 30MB 的檔案。
男：啊，這份計劃約有 40MB。
女：我想卡麥隆先生明天早上會回來辦公室。等到那時再把作業給他就好了。

檔案名稱	大小
Kingswood.mov	15MB
Bernstein.mov	30MB
(69) **Perez.mov**	**40MB**
LIttlebrook.mov	25MB

68. 談話者在哪種產業工作？
 (A) 行銷
 (B) 廣告
 (C) 製造
 (D) 軟體　　　　　　　　　　　　　　答案 (A)

69. 請看圖表。男子試圖用電子郵件寄送哪個檔案？
 (A) Kingswood.mov
 (B) Bernstein.mov
 (C) Perez.mov
 (D) LIttlebrook.mov　　　　　　　　　答案 (C)

70. 女子建議男子做什麼？
 (A) 試著重新用電子郵件寄送檔案
 (B) 等待主管回來
 (C) 與資訊科技專家交談
 (D) 修理他的電腦　　　　　　　　　　答案 (B)

Part 4

問題 71-73，請參考以下電話留言。 美國M

Hello, Ms. Hamilton. (71)**This is Kyle, your new tenant.** I have a quick question about the policy here at the apartment regarding the recycling of paper, plastic bottles, and metal items. (72)**When should I take out my recycling bin? Does the city do pickups on Mondays or Friday mornings?** (73)**I hope you can call me back with the correct information when you have the opportunity.** Thanks.

你好，漢米爾頓女士。我是凱爾，你的新房客。對於這座公寓紙張、塑膠瓶和金屬物品的回收政策，我有一個小問題。什麼時候該把我的回收桶拿出來？這座城市是在週一還是週五早上清運呢？我希望你有機會時能回電給我，並提供正確資訊。謝謝。

71. 聽者最可能是誰？
    (A) 政府官員
    (B) 店主
    (C) 公寓經理
    (D) 送貨員　　　　　　　　　答案 (C)

72. 說話者想了解什麼資訊？
    (A) 公寓地址
    (B) 回收物品的場所
    (C) 清運日
    (D) 服務費金額　　　　　　　答案 (C)

73. 說話者請聽者做什麼？
    (A) 用電子郵件提供某些資訊
    (B) 回電話
    (C) 檢查房客政策
    (D) 致電維修部門　　　　　　答案 (B)

問題 74-76，請參考以下會議摘錄。 美國W

(74)**The final thing we need to discuss is office supplies.** At the last meeting, I gave everyone some request forms for office supplies. (74)**If you need any paper, pens, staplers, or other similar items, write down what you need.** (75)**Just be sure you provide the correct information on the form**, or the order won't be processed. Some forms were rejected last month because they had been filled out improperly or incomplete. (76)**Sharon, the office manager, has the catalog in her office** if you need to consult it when completing the form.

我們最後要討論的是辦公用品。上次開會時，我給了大

家一些辦公用品的申請表。如果需要任何紙、筆、釘書機或其他類似物品，請寫下你們的需求。請確保你們在表格上提供了正確的資訊，否則訂單將不會受理。上個月，某些表格因填寫不當或不完整而被退件。辦公室經理雪倫的辦公室裡有型錄，如果你們填寫表格時有需要，可以去參考看看。

74. 說話者在討論什麼事？
    (A) 改變規定
    (B) 訂購用品
    (C) 打掃辦公室
    (D) 尋找另一家供應商　　　　答案 (B)

75. 說話者要求聽者做什麼？
    (A) 提交他們的考勤單
    (B) 今晚加班到很晚
    (C) 準確填寫表格
    (D) 分享關於工作效率的想法　答案 (C)

76. 說話者說雪倫的辦公室裡有什麼？
    (A) 員工名錄
    (B) 產品型錄
    (C) 使用者手冊
    (D) 訪客證　　　　　　　　　答案 (B)

問題 77-79，請參考以下發言內容。 澳洲W

Hello, everybody. Before we close for the day, I have something to say. (77)**First, we haven't had any problems with the quality of our frozen pizzas or the packaging of them.** That's all thanks to your hard work. Next, I got some news from Justin Groceries, which is a big buyer. (78)**Due to the high demand for our pizzas, the supermarket has decided to increase its monthly order by fifty percent.** That means you'll be working a lot of overtime. (79)**Now, before we agree to the increase, I need to hear your thoughts.**

大家好。今天在結束之前，我有一些話要說。首先，我們冷凍披薩的品質或包裝沒有任何問題。這一切都歸功於各位的辛勤工作。其次，我從我們的大客戶賈斯汀雜貨舖那裡得到一些消息。由於顧客對我們披薩的需求很大，這間超市決定將每月訂貨量增加百分之五十。這表示你們必須大量加班。現在，在我們同意增加出貨量之前，我需要聽聽你們的想法。

77. 正在討論什麼產品？
    (A) 披薩
    (B) 麵包
    (C) 咖啡
    (D) 蛋糕　　　　　　　　　　答案 (A)

78. 賈斯汀雜貨舖最近做了什麼？
    (A) 取消一筆訂單。
    (B) 變更營業時間。
    (C) 推出新的披薩系列。
    (D) 增加訂貨量。　　　　　　　答案 (D)

79. 說話者說「我需要聽聽你們的想法」，意思是什麼？
    (A) 需要更多資金來滿足需求。
    (B) 會議每兩週召開一次。
    (C) 部分生產線運作不正常。
    (D) 需要一些資訊才能做決定。　　答案 (D)

問題 80-82，請參考以下公告內容。 美國 M

(80)**Attention, passengers on Grant Air Flight 29 bound for London.** We are still unable to find the problem with our electronic booking system, which means both passenger lists and boarding passes won't be available at the gate. (81)**However, please be aware that this kind of issue has happened before and we have a good team working on it now.** (82) **We'll keep you posted on our progress. We'll make another announcement in just a few minutes.** In the meantime, please be patient.

搭乘格蘭特航空 29 號班機飛往倫敦的旅客請注意。我們還無法找出電子訂票系統的問題，這表示登機門處仍無法提供旅客名單和登機證。不過，請知悉，這類問題以前發生過，而我們目前有良好的團隊正在處理。我們會持續向大家通報進度。我們將在幾分鐘內發布另一則公告。在此期間，請耐心等候。

80. 說話者在哪裡工作？
    (A) 餐廳
    (B) 醫院
    (C) 機場
    (D) 劇院　　　　　　　　　　　答案 (C)

81. 說話者說「我們目前有良好的團隊正在處理」，是在暗示什麼？
    (A) 替代零件很快就會到達。
    (B) 問題很快就會解決。
    (C) 所有員工都太忙了。
    (D) 並不需要更多培訓。　　　　　答案 (B)

82. 說話者說他接下來要做什麼？
    (A) 退款給大家
    (B) 變更登機門號碼
    (C) 回答任何人的問題
    (D) 盡快提供更新資訊　　　　　　答案 (D)

問題 83-85，請參考以下會議摘錄。 澳洲 W

Hello. We are meeting because I was just informed by the vice president that (83)**our most recent ad campaign for our running shoes has not been successful.** Basically, we tried to attract too many people. Our market research shows that our shoes appeal mostly to 20 to 40-year-old age group. They like the style and are also physically active. (84)**Our next campaign needs to specifically target this group.** (85)**We'll think about the details when we go over our new strategy at Friday's meeting.**

各位好。這次會議，是因為副總裁剛剛通知我，我們最近的跑鞋宣傳活動並不成功。基本上，我們試圖吸引太多人了。市場調查顯示，我們的鞋子主要吸引 20 到 40 歲這個年齡段。他們喜歡這種風格，也常常活動身體。下一次宣傳活動需要專門針對這個族群。在週五會議上討論新策略時，我們要來構思細節。

83. 聽者最可能是哪方面的專家？
    (A) 設計
    (B) 旅遊
    (C) 行銷
    (D) 電腦　　　　　　　　　　　答案 (C)

84. 說話者建議做什麼？
    (A) 聚焦在特定個體
    (B) 推出新的跑鞋系列
    (C) 提升某個品項的品質
    (D) 聘僱更多行銷顧問　　　　　　答案 (A)

85. 星期五會發生什麼事？
    (A) 將錄製一部廣告。
    (B) 將針對特定群體進行調查。
    (C) 將舉辦就業博覽會。
    (D) 將討論某項策略。　　　　　　答案 (D)

問題 86-88，請參考以下廣播內容。 美國 W

I hope you enjoyed listening to those songs on FM Radio 89.9. Right now, let's hear an important message from our sponsor. (86)**Couper Kitchen Supplies is looking for people to act as product testers.** (87) **You'll receive some of its new products in the mail such as hand blenders, toasters and even small cooking utensils.** What you have to do is use those products and simply report on how you liked using them. (88)**If you would like to be picked, post your recipe that you think is best on our website.** If you're selected, one of our customer service representatives will contact you.

希望你們享受在 FM 89.9 廣播電臺上收聽這些歌曲。現在,讓我們聽聽一則來自贊助商的重要訊息。庫柏廚房用品正在招募產品測試員。你們將收到一些寄送的新產品,例如手持式攪拌機、烤麵包機,甚至小型廚具。你們要做的就是使用這些產品,並簡單回報你們的心得。如果你想被選中,請在我們的網站上張貼你認為最棒的食譜。如果你被選中,我們的客戶服務人員將與你聯繫。

86. 根據廣播,贊助商正在尋找什麼?
    (A) 烹飪參賽者
    (B) 明星大廚
    (C) 產品測試員
    (D) 電視主持人   答案 (C)

87. 贊助商製造什麼類型的產品?
    (A) 電腦遊戲
    (B) 廚房用具
    (C) 園藝用品
    (D) 體育用品   答案 (B)

88. 有興趣參加的聽眾應該做什麼?
    (A) 前往店面
    (B) 寄出問卷
    (C) 寄送食譜
    (D) 撥打電話   答案 (C)

問題 89-91,請參考以下研討會摘錄。 英國 M

Good morning. Welcome to our management seminar. (89)**During the next two days, you'll learn about how to run and grow a small business.** We're going to start with a presentation by my colleague and our speaker, Eric Hooper today. (90)**He's going to talk about his own past experiences with starting a small bookstore. Today, he owns a chain of stores all across the country.** So I strongly encourage you to listen carefully to what he advises. He is also the co-author of an award-winning book on management. (91)**Everybody will get a complimentary autographed copy when we are all done with this presentation today.**

早安。歡迎參加我們的管理研討會。在接下來的兩天裡,你們將學習如何經營和發展小型企業。今天將由我同事兼講者艾瑞克‧胡伯的簡報開場。他會談談自己過去創立一家小書店的經歷。如今,他擁有遍布全國各地的連鎖店。因此我強烈建議各位仔細聆聽他的建議。他也是獲獎管理書籍的合著者。今天這場簡報結束後,每個人都會獲得一本免費的親筆簽名書。

89. 聽者最有可能是誰?
    (A) 大學生
    (B) 作家
    (C) 出版社社員
    (D) 企業主   答案 (D)

90. 說話者為什麼說「他擁有遍布全國各地的連鎖店」?
    (A) 強調講者的資歷
    (B) 感謝同事的貢獻
    (C) 鼓勵聽眾全力以赴
    (D) 提議議程主題   答案 (A)

91. 當天結束時,聽者會收到什麼?
    (A) 一本優惠券
    (B) 一張簽名海報
    (C) 一本簽名書
    (D) 免費訂閱資格   答案 (C)

問題 92-94,請參考以下會議摘錄。 美國 M

(92)**You should be aware that our winter clothing sale begins next week.** I need to tell you about a couple of things before the sale event. First, we're expecting plenty of customers since we advertised in many places. Our parking lot probably won't have enough room for all of the cars. (93)**I would therefore like you to park in the pay lot two blocks away.** You'll be reimbursed for the price of parking. Next, here's the list of the clothes on sale. (94)**Make sure to look it over by the end of the week so that you can answer any questions correctly that customers ask.**

你們應該知道,我們的冬季服裝特賣會將於下週開始。開始前,我需要告訴你們一些事情。首先,由於我們在很多地方都投放廣告,所以預期會有大量顧客。我們的停車場可能沒有足夠空間容納所有汽車。因此,我希望你們把車停在兩個街區外的收費停車場。停車費可以核銷。再來,這是打折的服飾清單。請確保在本週末之前看過一遍,以便你能夠正確回答顧客提出的任何問題。

92. 下週會發生什麼事?
    (A) 盛大開幕
    (B) 歡送會
    (C) 特賣會
    (D) 道路封閉   答案 (C)

93. 說話者希望聽者做什麼?
    (A) 準時上班
    (B) 在收費停車場停車
    (C) 使用大眾運輸工具
    (D) 查看店鋪資訊   答案 (B)

94. 說話者告訴聽者本週末之前要做什麼？
    (A) 張貼特賣海報
    (B) 完成培訓課程
    (C) 確認他們的工作時間
    (D) 閱讀一份文件　　　　　　　　答案 (D)

問題 **95-97**，請參考以下電話留言及天氣預報。　美國 W

Hi, Tim. This is Katherine, the symphony conductor. (95)**I'm calling about the concert we're supposed to perform tomorrow.** (96)**It looks like we'll be getting rain tomorrow. We need to reschedule it for the following day. It will be sunny then**, so there's no chance of rain. However, what do we do about the people who bought tickets but can't attend? I think we should refund their money. (97)**Please e-mail every ticket holder an announcement about the new date and also mention how to apply for a refund.** Thanks.

嗨，提姆。我是交響樂團的指揮凱瑟琳。我打電話來，是為了我們明天要演出的音樂會。看來明天會下雨。我們需要把時間改成隔天。那時會是晴天，不會下雨。不過，對於那些買了票卻無法參加的人，該怎麼辦呢？我認為我們應該退費。請寄電子郵件給每個持票人，公告新的日期，並說明如何申請退費。謝謝。

天氣預報

星期日	星期一	星期二	(96) 星期三	星期四
雨天	陰天	(96) 雨天	(96) 晴天	晴天

95. 說話者為了什麼活動而打電話？
    (A) 音樂會
    (B) 體育賽事
    (C) 面試
    (D) 大會　　　　　　　　答案 (A)

96. 請看圖表。活動將於何時舉行？
    (A) 星期一
    (B) 星期二
    (C) 星期三
    (D) 星期四　　　　　　　　答案 (C)

97. 聽者被要求做什麼？
    (A) 寄送通知
    (B) 張貼廣告
    (C) 銷售門票
    (D) 更改演唱會場地　　　　　　　　答案 (A)

問題 **98-100**，請參考以下會議摘錄及地圖。　英國 M

(98)**Right now, let's talk about some possible locations for our new restaurant.** We need a place large enough to accommodate indoor and outdoor dining. Check out this map. You can clearly see the large building available beside the theater. (99)**But I prefer the location across the street from the subway station.** It's more accessible by public transportation. (100)**Now, let's check out some photographs of the interior of that building.** I want to know what you think after viewing them.

現在，一起來談談我們新餐廳的可能地點。我們需要一個夠大的地方，來容納室內和室外用餐區。看看這張地圖。你可以清楚看到劇院旁可供選擇的大型建築。但我比較喜歡地鐵站對街的位置，搭乘大眾運輸工具更方便。我們來看看那棟大樓內部的照片。我想知道你們看完之後有什麼感想。

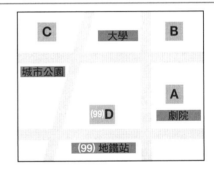

98. 說話者談論的是哪種類型的事業？
    (A) 零售店
    (B) 餐廳
    (C) 五金行
    (D) 劇院　　　　　　　　答案 (B)

99. 請看圖表。說話者推薦哪個地點？
    (A) 地點 A
    (B) 地點 B
    (C) 地點 C
    (D) 地點 D　　　　　　　　答案 (D)

100. 說話者說他接下來要做什麼？
    (A) 展示一些照片
    (B) 發放宣傳手冊
    (C) 談論財務狀況
    (D) 回答問題　　　　　　　　答案 (A)

Part 5

101. 社會學家能幫助我們意識到解決社會問題時面臨的阻礙。　　　　　　　　答案 (B)

102. 音樂劇表演期間，除了基本的燈光之外，還有雷射投影機和煙霧機，以達到最大視覺效果。　答案 (D)

103. 哈里森先生追求擁有一家企業的夢想，學習了從商業保險到企業會計的各種事情。　答案 (B)

104. 可可精品是歐洲最受歡迎的服裝品牌之一，創造了女性時尚界的最新潮流。　答案 (B)

105. 市議會最近立法要求所有跨國公司每年更新營業證照。　答案 (B)

106. 各國通往該市的入口受到嚴格控制，以在早期預防有害病毒散播。　答案 (C)

107. 有些報紙說，我們的新任執行長是一位很少改變管理風格和經營策略的領導者。　答案 (B)

108. 動用了多種方法，來向潛在受眾傳達訊息並增加門票銷量。　答案 (C)

109. 重要的是提前分發會議議程，讓與會者有時間針對規劃作必要的思考。　答案 (A)

110. 達美證券概述其經營改善計劃：透過整併雪梨投資公司與自身銀行業務，尋求更強的綜效。　答案 (C)

111. 由於柯林斯先生豐富的實務經驗，人事經理認為他在業務團隊將是備受歡迎的新成員。　答案 (D)

112. 由於商業區辦公空間租金上漲，越來越多公司希望搬到城市外圍。　答案 (B)

113. 在德文郡街安裝新交通號誌以減少交通擁塞的做法，只取得些許成功。　答案 (D)

114. 多虧精心的策劃和持續不斷的電視廣告，貝拉與安德魯斯公司最終成為全球玩具市場領導者。　答案 (C)

115. 社群媒體可說是一種新型網路媒體，其特徵包含參與、開放和連結。　答案 (D)

116. 銷售經驗有限的應徵者一旦獲得錄用，將被要求參加培訓課程。　答案 (A)

117. 航班乘客在入境該國之前，必須經過幾道嚴格的海關程序。　答案 (D)

118. 最近一項關於港口使用情況的調查中，許多旅客表示，在海關的漫長等待時間令人筋疲力盡。　答案 (A)

119. 顧客受邀參觀溫徹斯特家具製造廠，看看他們辦公家具的製造過程。　答案 (D)

120. 我們的員工績效評估，對於了解每位員工的能力、相對優勢、對公司的價值至關重要。　答案 (C)

121. 有些廣告商喜歡發放冰箱磁鐵，而非鋼筆、毛巾或鑰匙圈之類的宣傳品。　答案 (A)

122. 儘管最近發生了暴風雪，我們這個地區目前仍在經歷溫暖乾燥的冬季。　答案 (B)

123. 有鑑於最近油價上漲，公司會把購買新重型設備的合約延後到 11 月底甚至 12 月中旬。　答案 (D)

124. 我們的會員每在全國任何一家加盟店購物，都可以累積紅利點數。　答案 (D)

125. 根據醫學專家的說法，任何人外出都應該戴口罩，以保護自己免受病毒感染。　答案 (A)

126. 如果大眾運輸免費，就可以節省金錢、拯救樹木，因為不再需要列印車票。　答案 (B)

127. 全年都會舉辦公共節慶和活動，但大多數通常在夏季和秋季舉行。　答案 (A)

128. 麥高恩先生將帶來一場新手機的簡報，之後則會有 10 分鐘的問答時間。　答案 (C)

129. 根據我們公司的政策，最後下班的人要負責開啟安全警報系統。　答案 (C)

130. 近年來，電子產品的消費成長如此之多，以至於成為導致當今環境問題最嚴重的產品類別之一。　答案 (B)

Part 6

問題 **131-134**，請參考以下新聞稿。

---

585 號高速公路新收費

7 月 17 日－奧克蘭 > 肯伍德市長批准城市外圍的 585 號州際公路，竣工後徵收新的通行費。

市長的新收費標準，在高速公路竣工後立即生效。收費站將建在高速公路 1 英里標記處。亦會裝設電子收費系統，讓駕駛享有無需停車繳費的便利。

市長針對新高速公路及其徵收通行費的擔憂做出回應。市長表示，他知道收費不會受到歡迎，但最終將有助於減少車流量，同時讓該市無需增稅就有能力負擔新的地方道路費用。

---

131. 答案 (B)

132. 答案 (A)

133. 答案 (B)

134. (A) 從 8 月到 11 月，道路通行費可以用現金支付。
(B) 他加入觀光部門，負責宣傳旅遊景點，並提升遊客參訪意願。
(C) 市長針對新高速公路及其徵收通行費的擔憂做出回應。
(D) 高度發達的公路系統，將吸引遊客前來我們城市進行休閒娛樂。　　　　答案 (C)

問題 135-138，請參考以下資訊。

您剛剛購買的能量電池，設計成可以使用超過 4 年，或行駛約 40,000 英里。儘管如此，當電池最終達到使用年限時，請您務必妥善處理，勿直接把它丟進垃圾桶。目前，多數市政府建議使用者不要隨意把廢電池連同垃圾一起丟棄。

多數專家表示，如果廢電池放在裝有金屬物品的盒子或袋子中，可能會引發火災和爆炸。因此，本公司為客戶提供了一種快速簡便的處理方法。您所要做的，就是將耗盡的電池送回所在地區的任一回收中心。只要把它們交給我們，我們的回收專家將以適當的方式處理，無需額外收費。

135. 答案 (B)

136. 答案 (B)

137. 答案 (B)

138. (A) 請勿將新舊電池或不同類型、品牌的電池混用。
(B) 留在您車庫中的電池，可能會成為幾種安全問題的導火線。
(C) 您所要做的，就是將耗盡的電池送回所在地區的任一回收中心。
(D) 新的小型電池被用於手機和電動工具。　　答案 (C)

問題 139-142，請參考以下廣告內容。

快速購物的 VIP 會員資格

厭倦了等待您的包裹送達？迫切需要來點購物療法？討厭每次都為快捷到貨付費？立即加入 VIP 會員，免除這些問題。我們的 VIP 會員享有免費當日到貨服務，每年次數不限。不僅如此，他們每季還會收到一張 30 美元的電子禮券，可以在店內和網路使用。我們也為 VIP 會員提供購物特別優惠。只要年費 18 美元，今天就能成

為我們的 VIP 會員。好好把握這個黃金機會！您絕對不會後悔！

139. 答案 (C)

140. 答案 (A)

141. 答案 (B)

142. (A) 我們也為 VIP 會員提供購物特別優惠。
(B) 消費超過 100 美元，即可享有免費當日到貨服務。
(C) 感謝你們辛勤工作與奉獻，締造了今年的最佳銷售紀錄。
(D) 我們很意外您沒有收到商品，並對此延誤表示歉意。　　　　答案 (A)

問題 143-146，請參考以下備忘錄。

親愛的大家，

我想讓你們知道，哈利‧麥克貝恩先生將於 6 月 30 日離開我們公司，開展自己的事業。自 5 年前加入我們以來，麥克貝恩先生在提高公司競爭力方面扮演了關鍵角色。因此，我們的銷售額大幅增加，成為一家利潤更高的公司。

在麥克貝恩先生的領導下，我們重組了規劃流程，引入嚴格的品質標準，並制定全公司的競爭戰略。改變的過程並不總是平順，但由此而生的正面成果有目共睹。例如，我們估計上一季的營收和銷量都首度超越了所有競爭對手。這項成就應歸功於麥克貝恩先生。

請與我一同祝福麥克貝恩先生一帆風順，並在他未來的事業中繼續獲致成功。

誠摯祝福。

莎莉‧墨菲
人事經理

143. 答案 (B)

144. (A) 我們對客戶的全力奉獻，幫助我們實現擴張。
(B) 他將繼續擔任執行長一職，並參與重大決策。
(C) 我們的服務和產品價格差異很大，常常會造成混亂。
(D) 因此，我們的銷售額大幅增加，成為一家利潤更高的公司。　　　　答案 (D)

145. 答案 (C)

146. 答案 (B)

Part 7

問題 **147-148**，請參考以下廣告內容。

家
甜蜜的
家

《休斯頓日報》提供

正在為你的家人尋覓新食譜嗎？

(147) 在當地最受歡迎的餐廳貓咪熟食店支持下，《休士頓日報》將於下週開始為在地居民提供烹飪課程。課程將在貓咪熟食店舉行，餐廳老闆鳥羽實負責授課。

提供的課程包括：
創作你自己的壽司 － 週一下午 2 點
日本麵食 － 週一下午 3 點

(148) 你可以上網到這裡報名：**www.thehoustondaily. com**。想了解費用等詳細資訊，請致電 917-803-7552 聯繫凡妮莎‧康納利。

147. 此廣告在宣傳什麼？
(A) 一間餐廳
(B) 地方性刊物
(C) 烹飪課
(D) 住宅維修服務　　　　　　　　　　答案 (C)

148. 有興趣的讀者應該做什麼？
(A) 造訪某個網站
(B) 致電餐廳老闆
(C) 拜訪康納利女士
(D) 購買一本雜誌　　　　　　　　　　答案 (A)

問題 **149-150**，請參考以下文字訊息。

達斯汀‧彼得森　　　　　　　　　［下午 6:35］
(150) 南希，你還在辦公室嗎？我正在去機場的路上，但我剛剛才發現，我沒有帶到埃德森檔案的影本。

南希‧惠特克　　　　　　　　　　［下午 6:36］
(150) 你運氣很好。它在哪裡？

達斯汀‧彼得森　　　　　　　　　［下午 6:37］
(149) 它在我辦公室，桌子最上層的抽屜裡。你可以從安迪‧弗勞爾斯那裡拿到鑰匙。

南希‧惠特克　　　　　　　　　　［下午 6:45］
(149) 好，我拿到文件了。我該怎麼做？

達斯汀‧彼得森　　　　　　　　　［下午 6:46］
請掃描所有頁面，並用電子郵件寄給我。

南希‧惠特克　　　　　　　　　　［下午 6:48］
這是一份大文件。可能需要半個小時。

149. 關於惠特克女士，文中暗指什麼？
(A) 她與彼得森先生共用一間辦公室。
(B) 她走進彼得森先生的辦公室。
(C) 她通常在辦公室待到很晚。
(D) 她找不到弗勞爾斯先生。　　　　答案 (B)

150. 下午 6:36，惠特克女士寫道「你運氣很好」，最有可能是什麼意思？
(A) 她正在處理埃德森檔案。
(B) 她找到了彼得森先生需要的文件。
(C) 她有時間去機場。
(D) 她還沒離開辦公室。　　　　　　答案 (D)

問題 **151-153**，請參考以下備忘錄。

快樂電子公司

收件人：全體員工
寄件人：瑪麗‧戴維斯
日　　期：4 月 1 日星期一
主　　旨：新服務政策

相信大家都看過 ST 電子 3 月 27 日公布的新客戶服務政策報導。我們最大的競爭對手之一 ST 電子，宣布將推出現場維修服務。

(151) 為了維持業界領先地位，我們會 (152C) (153) 將所有產品目前的 1 年保固再延長 2 年。我們也會為前來中心的客戶，提供免費的軟體升級服務。新政策將於 4 月 5 日星期二生效。

此外，每間店 (152B) 都將舉辦 2 小時的培訓課程，以提升服務品質和顧客滿意度。所有銷售人員都必須接受培訓。各店的詳細培訓時程，將在下次 (152A) 月會結束時公布。會議將於 4 月 8 日在 302A 會議室舉行。

瑪麗‧戴維斯
行銷經理

151. 此電子郵件的目的是什麼？
(A) 提供某間公司的歷史
(B) 尋求顧客回饋
(C) 索取會議議程
(D) 通知員工某些變化　　　　　　　答案 (D)

152. 關於快樂電子公司，文中沒有暗指什麼？
(A) 它定期召開會議。
(B) 它擁有不只一家店面。
(C) 它不久後將提供 3 年保固。
(D) 它將開始提供現場維修服務。　　答案 (D)

153. 以下句子最適合放在文中 [1]、[2]、[3] 和 [4] 的哪一個位置？
「新政策將於 4 月 5 日星期二生效。」

(A) [1]
(B) [2]
(C) [3]
(D) [4]　　　　　　　　　　　　　　答案 (B)

問題 154-156，請參考以下傳單內容。

來夏洛特欣賞演出吧！

(154) 夏洛特市議會將帶來一系列精彩表演！
請蒞臨本市，享受眾多旅遊景點。

• 如遇下雨，演出可能會取消。•

5 月 4 日 / 賽奇 **夏洛特冒險世界 /** **晚上 7 點** 挪威年度音樂家賽奇，將帶來他第二張專輯中的歌曲。他被譽為世界上最熱情的歌手之一，並被《謬思》雜誌評選為年度音樂家。	**5 月 18 日 / 科威特劇團** (156) 夏洛特戲劇廳 / 晚上 7 點 (156) 科威特劇團將使用科威特樂器魯巴巴和坦巴拉，來表演科威特傳統舞蹈。
5 月 11 日 / **詹姆斯·麥克萊恩** **夏洛特主題樂園 /** **晚上 8 點** 麥克萊恩將使用蘇格蘭傳統樂器風笛，為各位演奏他自己創作的美妙歌曲。	(155) **5 月 25 日 / 斑馬** **夏洛特萊特工廠 /** **晚上 7 點** 蒲隆地的斑馬樂團將使用獨特的樂器和節奏，演奏傳統非洲音樂。

---

154. 為什麼會舉辦這些活動？
(A) 宣傳旅遊套裝行程
(B) 紀念新完工的主題樂園
(C) 促進夏洛特觀光旅遊
(D) 鼓勵市民演奏不同類型的音樂　　　答案 (C)

155. 根據傳單，斑馬樂團什麼時候表演？
(A) 5 月 4 日
(B) 5 月 11 日
(C) 5 月 18 日
(D) 5 月 25 日　　　　　　　　　　答案 (D)

156. 舞蹈表演將在哪裡登場？
(A) 夏洛特冒險世界
(B) 夏洛特主題樂園
(C) 夏洛特市議會
(D) 夏洛特戲劇廳　　　　　　　　　答案 (D)

問題 157-158，請參考以下表格內容。

彼得園藝

親愛的顧客，
(157) 感謝您使用我們的服務。邀請您填寫下表，以便借重您的寶貴意見，讓我們的服務更好。

姓名：　　(158) 史考特·杭特

電話號碼：214-860-2209

地址：　　德州，歐文，貝爾柏區 80 號

(157) 1. 您從彼得園藝獲得了哪種服務？
□ 修剪植物　　□ 除草　　□ 清潔　　☑ 整體解決方案

2. 您對價格的滿意度為何？
□ 非常滿意　　□ 滿意　　☑ 不滿意　　□ 非常不滿意

3. 您對服務所需時間的滿意度為何？
☑ 非常滿意　　□ 滿意　　□ 不滿意　　□ 非常不滿意

4. 您對成果的滿意度為何嗎？
□ 非常滿意　　☑ 滿意　　□ 不滿意　　□ 非常不滿意

5. 額外評論：
感謝彼得園藝的整體解決方案，成功改造了我的花園。我喜歡快速的改造過程和成果。然而，相較於競爭對手，這項服務的費用似乎過高。(158) 我建議增加折扣給像我一樣的常客。

---

157. 這份表格為什麼會寄給杭特先生？
(A) 蒐集員工意見
(B) 取得已完成工作的回饋
(C) 針對即將推出的服務，詢問客戶一些問題
(D) 確認來自客戶的服務訂單　　　　　答案 (B)

158. 根據表格，文中暗指了杭特先生的什麼事？
(A) 他向同事推薦了彼得園藝。
(B) 他認為服務的價格合理。
(C) 他的服務獲得了折扣。
(D) 他之前接受過彼得園藝的服務。　　答案 (D)

問題 159-161，請參考以下網頁資訊。

---

www.wholenewworlds.com/register

歡迎來到全新世界

(159) 你是否曾經想學一種新語言，卻沒有時間或機會？那麼，全新世界正好適合你。全新世界是實力雄厚又受人尊敬的教育供應者，提供以下服務：

• 與來自 50 多個國家的母語人士進行一對一配對
• 由認證講師教授的影音課程
• 採用便利自學工具——單字和片語教學閃卡
• 3 天免費試用期
• 分班考試

---

(160) 成為全新世界數千名會員的一份子，今天就開始提升你的語言專業！

向我們介紹你自己吧！	
姓名：	亞伯特・斯塔爾
電子郵件：	astahl@quickmail.com
你來自哪個國家：	德國 ▼
你使用的語言：	德文 ▼
你想學的語言：	中文 ▼

(161) 這是你第一次使用全新世界嗎？
□ 是　　(161) ☑ 否

註冊類型	可用服務
□ 3 天體驗課程（免費）	分班測驗、自學工具和影音課程
□ 1 個月（30 美元） ☑ 3 個月（80 美元） □ 6 個月（150 美元）	全新世界提供的服務包括： 分班測驗、一對一配對系統、自學工具、影音課程、技能評量測驗……還有很多

159. 此資訊的目的是什麼？
(A) 招募新的語言教師
(B) 為線上出版品提供折扣
(C) 為翻譯服務打廣告
(D) 宣傳教育計劃　　　　　　　　答案 (D)

160. 關於全新世界，文中提到什麼？
(A) 所有服務均免費提供。
(B) 它是最近成立的。
(C) 它有很多使用者。
(D) 總部位於德國。　　　　　　　答案 (C)

161. 關於斯塔爾先生，文中暗指什麼？
(A) 他計劃報名 3 天體驗課程。
(B) 他說中文。
(C) 他以前曾瀏覽過這個網頁。
(D) 他最近參加了分班測驗。　　　答案 (C)

問題162-164，請參考以下備忘錄。

備忘錄

收件人：神祕瀑布飯店的全體員工
寄件人：達蒙・薩爾瓦托
日　期：2 月 2 日
主　旨：(162) 提名結果

親愛的全體員工，

(162) 很高興宣布，埃琳娜・吉爾伯特獲選為本月最佳員工。飯店老闆羅伯特・胡德將在 (163) 6 月、每半年舉行一次的神祕瀑布之夜上，頒發區額以茲表揚。此外，她還將獲得兩天帶薪休假和 300 美元現金作為獎勵。

自從吉爾伯特女士 3 年前開始在神祕瀑布飯店擔任客房服務員以來，一直是相當出色的員工，表現出持之以恆的努力和奉獻精神。她出色的服務，多次得到顧客認可。

(162) 我希望全體員工祝賀她所取得的傑出成就。(164) 自從商業夥伴兼老友的諾曼・胡德和凱文・科斯特納最初創立飯店以來，我們一直延續對於展現奉獻精神和熱情員工的獎勵傳統，而我相信，你們之中的任何人，都有可能是下一屆最佳員工獎得主。

謝謝你們。

達蒙・薩爾瓦托
總經理
神祕瀑布飯店

162. 此備忘錄的主題是什麼？
(A) 一位獲獎者
(B) 即將到來的節慶
(C) 顧客滿意度調查結果
(D) 員工績效評估　　　　　　　　答案 (A)

163. 6 月最有可能發生什麼事？
(A) 薩爾瓦托先生將得到獎賞。
(B) 將開始提交提名。
(C) 飯店員工將獲得升遷。
(D) 吉爾伯特女士將參加一項活動。　答案 (D)

164. 科斯特納先生是誰？
(A) 飯店老闆
(B) 吉爾伯特女士的朋友
(C) 企業的共同創辦人
(D) 客房服務員　　　　　　　　　答案 (C)

問題 165-167，請參考以下銷售合約。

汽車銷售合約
J&G 汽車有限公司

合約編號：121590

本銷售協議由 (167D) **J&G 汽車有限公司（賣方）**與麥可・貝爾（買方）簽訂。

A. (165) **賣方應於 2 月 28 日**將下列車輛轉讓給買方。
(167A) 製造商：詹森公司　　　類型：皮卡車
型號：J3000i　　　　　　顏色：寶藍色
里程：76,291

B. (165) 買方同意以 **19,500 美元（含稅）**的價格向賣方購買該車輛。

C. (165) 買方將於當天支付部分金額，即 **14,500 美元**，並在收到車輛後支付剩餘款項。

D. 賣方已向買方出示車輛的所有檢查紀錄，而 (167B)

買方同意購買該車輛，且不附保固。

2 月 20 日於 (166) **J&G 汽車有限公司瓊斯維爾市分公司**簽署。

(167D) 約翰‧凱爾斯	2 月 20 日
(167D) 賣方（銷售人員）	日期
麥可‧貝爾	2 月 20 日
買方	日期
凱爾‧威爾森	2 月 20 日
證人	日期

165. 貝爾先生最有可能在 2 月 28 日做什麼？
(A) 出售車輛給 J&G 汽車有限公司
(B) 支付 5,000 美元尾款
(C) 購買 1 年的有限保固
(D) 將檢查紀錄影本寄給凱爾斯先生　　　答案 (B)

166. 根據合約，可以推斷出關於 J&G 汽車的什麼事？
(A) 擁有多個據點。
(B) 總部位於瓊斯維爾。
(C) 擁有眾多銷售人員。
(D) 將一輛寶藍色轎車賣給貝爾先生。　　答案 (A)

167. 合約中沒有暗指什麼？
(A) 該汽車是詹森公司製造的。
(B) 貝爾先生不會得到任何保固。
(C) 凱爾‧威爾森是該車的前車主。
(D) 約翰‧凱爾斯在 J&G 汽車有限公司工作。答案 (C)

問題 168-171，請參考以下線上討論訊息。

格倫‧卡特	［下午 2:29］

安珀咖啡館的珍妮特‧魯道夫寄了一封電子郵件給我。她想將每週的訂貨量增加一倍。我們處理得來嗎？

馬庫斯‧斯泰森	［下午 2:30］

沒有理由做不到。這個量不是那麼大，我們可以處理。你覺得怎麼樣，格雷格？

格雷格‧沃特金斯	［下午 2:31］

我能想見的唯一問題是運送。目前她每週一都會收到 6 盒，如果增加到 12 盒，(168) 她的貨物量可能過大，無法跟其他東西一起裝進我的卡車。

馬庫斯‧斯泰森	［下午 2:33］

啊，我沒想到這一點。

格倫‧卡特	［下午 2:34］

我可以重新安排送貨時間嗎？畢竟，她的店就在幾個街區之外。(169) 當天早一點把東西送給她，怎麼樣？

艾米‧瓊斯	［下午 2:35］

(169) 我來送吧。我每天早上都會開車經過她的店，這樣當我去哈羅德炸魚薯條店時，就可以把她買的所有東西交給她。我可以在早上 8 點 30 分前到那裡。

格倫‧卡特	［下午 2:37］

聽起來很棒。(170) 我會打電話告知珍妮特。還有什麼我需要知道的問題嗎？

馬庫斯‧斯泰森	［下午 2:38］

(171) 這個週末工作人員會短缺。布萊德‧霍華德辭職了，我們還沒找到人來替補。

艾米‧瓊斯	［下午 2:40］

(171) 我這週末沒有安排事情。

格倫‧卡特	［下午 2:41］

謝謝你，艾米。那我們週六見。

168. 關於沃特金斯先生，文中暗指什麼？
(A) 他駕駛送貨卡車。
(B) 他在咖啡廳工作。
(C) 他當面見過魯道夫女士。
(D) 他工作到深夜。　　　　　　　　　　答案 (A)

169. 瓊斯女士願意做什麼？
(A) 與魯道夫女士交談
(B) 尋找潛在的新員工
(C) 將物品送去一家店
(D) 每天早點開始工作　　　　　　　　　答案 (C)

170. 卡特先生接下來最有可能會做什麼？
(A) 打電話
(B) 重新安排時程
(C) 與霍華德先生交談
(D) 拜訪客戶　　　　　　　　　　　　　答案 (A)

171. 下午 2:40，瓊斯女士寫道「我這週末沒有安排事情」，是在暗示什麼？
(A) 她需要賺更多錢。
(B) 她這週工作時間不多。
(C) 她預期會獲得加班費。
(D) 她願意接替霍華德先生的班。　　　　答案 (D)

問題 172-175，請參考以下文章內容。

帕薩迪納，4 月 19 日－今天，總部位於洛杉磯的 (172) **國際乳製品通路暨供應商輝煌乳業**宣布，過去 10 年擔任執行長的傑克森‧霍夫施塔特將於 4 月 30 日退休。該公司現任副總裁佩內洛普‧加西亞將接替他的位置。

霍夫施塔特先生畢生職涯都在輝煌乳業度過，自公司 35 年前成立以來，便一直忠於公司。「很高興看到我投入全部熱情的公司，成長為業內第一。」霍夫施塔特回顧過去時說道。

霍夫施塔特先生的繼任者在公司也有同樣長久的歷練。25 年前，加西亞女士從波士頓大學獲得商管學位後不久，就加入該公司位於紐約的子公司──CBS 牛奶公司。在加入輝煌乳業之前，她曾在 CBS 牛奶公司擔任

11 年的行銷總監。

「加西亞女士是董事會無庸置疑的首選。(173) 當我在 CBS 牛奶公司擔任助理行銷經理、與加西亞女士共事時，我就知道她會被選中。她是我所見過最高效、最敬業的領導者，」現任 CBS 牛奶公司常務董事 (173) 肖恩·庫柏這麼說。

(175) 輝煌乳業在總部籌劃了一場活動，將歡送前任執行長，並歡迎新上任者。它將於 4 月 30 日舉行。此活動也將慶祝霍夫施塔特先生的新書《每個人都從底層開始》上市。「我在各方面都很感謝這個產業的許多人。(174) 現在，是時候透過書籍分享我的經驗和知識來幫助他人了。」霍夫施塔特先生說。

172. 關於輝煌乳業，文中暗指什麼？
(A) 產品出口海外。
(B) 它是 CBS 牛奶公司的競爭對手。
(C) 它在帕薩迪納有一座大型乳牛牧場。
(D) 目前正在招募新員工。　　　答案 (A)

173. 庫柏先生是誰？
(A) 輝煌乳業公司的新任執行長
(B) CBS 牛奶公司的前助理行銷經理
(C) 輝煌乳業公司的現任副總裁
(D) 《每個人都從底層開始》的作者　　答案 (B)

174. 霍夫施塔特先生打算做什麼？
(A) 開展新事業
(B) 學習企業管理
(C) 培訓加西亞女士
(D) 透過書寫分享他的專業　　　答案 (D)

175. 以下句子最適合放在文中 [1]、[2]、[3] 和 [4] 的哪一個位置？
「將於 4 月 30 日舉行。」
(A) [1]
(B) [2]
(C) [3]
(D) [4]　　　　　　　　答案 (D)

問題 176-180，請參考以下電子郵件。

收件人：錢德勒·德利恩 <cdeleon@stranton.com>
寄件人：艾弗瑞·比林斯 <abillings@stranton.com>
日　期：9 月 15 日
(176) 主　旨：系統存取錯誤

親愛的德利恩先生，

如你所知，我們部門目前正在準備與泰國分部和當地曼谷迪姆家居生活公司的聯合視訊會議。潔西卡·迪姆將出席會議，討論兩家公司未來可能的合作。(177) 本次會議將成為我們公司拓展亞洲市場的關鍵基石。

(179) 然而，在準備 9 月 19 日進行的會議時，我們遇到一個問題。(176)(178) 副總監伊芙琳·福斯特回報她目前無法存取公司內部網路。她指出，一週前登入系統時沒有出現任何問題。

她是這個潛在商業關係的關鍵成員，因此我們務必要讓 (176) 福斯特女士可以上網取得所有素材。請盡快解決此問題。在此先感謝你的協助。

誠摯祝福。

艾弗瑞·比林斯
行銷總監，斯特拉頓廚房用品

收件人：艾弗瑞·比林斯 <abillings@stranton.com>
寄件人：錢德勒·德利恩 <cdeleon@stranton.com>
日　期：9 月 16 日
主　題：回覆：系統存取錯誤

親愛的比林斯女士，

我已對你的詢問進行了調查，並找到問題的成因。由於我們每間分公司都有獨立的公司伺服器存取點，存取代碼並不通用。因此，(178) 你的副總監在從曼谷分部轉調之前收到的代碼只在曼谷分部有效。你需要取得一個新的代碼，才能在總部使用。

(179) 考慮到時間限制，我已發布了臨時存取代碼，並將透過另一封電子郵件寄給你。請注意，該代碼將在會議結束後的第二天到期。(180) 要獲得永久代碼，當事人必須上網提出申請。依照《員工手冊》中的規定，填寫 http://intranet.stranton.com/form/100254 上的表格，並上傳清單所列的資料。

我從 9 月 22 日開始出差，所以無法與你聯繫。如果我不在的期間，你有任何其他問題，請聯絡我的助理丹·哈德利。

誠摯祝福。

錢德勒·德利恩
技術支援經理，斯特拉頓廚房用品

176. 第一封電子郵件的主要目的是什麼？
(A) 要求出席會議
(B) 請求技術援助
(C) 告知關於商業計劃的資訊
(D) 讚揚某位員工的努力　　　答案 (B)

177. 關於斯特拉頓廚房用品，文中暗指什麼？
(A) 它遭遇財務困難。
(B) 它最近招募了新員工。
(C) 它想擴大業務。
(D) 它計劃不久後採用新系統。　　答案 (C)

178. 誰最近加入了比林斯女士的部門？
(A) 德利恩先生
(B) 迪姆女士
(C) 福斯特女士
(D) 哈德利先生　　　　　　　　答案 (C)

179. 臨時存取代碼什麼時候過期？
(A) 9 月 16 日
(B) 9 月 19 日
(C) 9 月 20 日
(D) 9 月 22 日　　　　　　　　答案 (C)

180. 福斯特女士接下來最有可能做什麼？
(A) 向她的經理提交報告
(B) 閱讀說明手冊
(C) 申請新的授權代碼
(D) 安排會議　　　　　　　　答案 (C)

問題 181-185，請參考以下公告及評論。

第 4 屆海沙音樂節
7 月 13 日至 14 日，(184A) 索爾茲伯里海灘

(181) 造訪索爾茲伯里，這個多位世界著名音樂家的故鄉，來參加第 4 屆年度海沙音樂節，享受夏季的日夜。這個橫跨週末的節慶在索爾茲伯里海灘舉行，將為遊客提供美味佳餚、興奮之情和難忘回憶！以下是你可以參加的活動清單：

沙雕展
沿著索爾茲伯里海灘的美妙海岸漫步，觀看令人印象深刻的沙雕展示。今年展覽的主題是「海底」。

沙灘排球賽（僅限 7 月 14 日）
(182) 參加混合沙灘排球比賽。你可以在 7 月 8 日前，快速簡便地上網報名。

夏夜音樂會
享受日落時迴盪的音樂聲。索爾茲伯里海灘沿岸將搭建一個舞臺。(184D)(185) 如果下雨，音樂會將在當地的酒吧舉行。

煙火表演
每天晚上 9 點觀賞令人驚嘆的美麗煙火秀。

- 如果對第 4 屆海沙音樂節有任何疑問，請致電 555-0095 與我們聯絡。
- (183) 媒體必須獲得官方許可，才能報導這個節慶。請於 7 月 10 日前透過 jseiz@salisbury.com 聯絡傑克・賽茲，預先進行登記。

索爾茲伯里時報

(183) 海琳娜・馬利奧薩撰文

索爾茲伯里，7 月 15 日－上週末，超過一萬人參加了在索爾茲伯里海灘舉行的第 4 屆年度海沙音樂節，享受激動人心的活動。

(184B) (184C) 我和兒子們最喜歡今年的沙雕展。去年我們一起參加這個節慶時，沙雕展中只有大約 10 件雕塑。今年的巨型海洋生物村，無疑呈現出壯觀的景象。來自全國各地的十位世界級沙雕藝術家創作了 30 件藝術作品。

第一天的爵士音樂會非常成功。海邊的大舞臺在圍觀的大批觀眾之中顯得相當渺小。(184D) 與爵士音樂會不同，第二天的流行音樂會則是令人失望。(185) 流行音樂會在當地酒吧舉行，但受限於酒吧的空間，許多人根本進不去。此外，酒吧的音響設備太舊，觀眾聽不清楚音樂。明年音樂節的籌辦者可能必須為音樂會找到另一個室內場地。

毫無疑問，節慶亮點是每天活動結束後的煙火表演。該地區的頂級煙火公司設計了今年的煙火秀，所有遊客都受邀免費觀看這場壯觀的演出。

181. 這份公告提到索爾茲伯里的什麼事？
(A) 它以每週的煙火秀而聞名。
(B) 僅在夏季對外開放。
(C) 遊客太多造成擁擠。
(D) 它造就了幾位著名音樂家。　　答案 (D)

182. 報名沙灘排球比賽，必須在什麼時候前完成？
(A) 7 月 8 日
(B) 7 月 10 日
(C) 7 月 14 日
(D) 7 月 15 日　　　　　　　　答案 (A)

183. 馬利奧薩女士在節慶前可能做了什麼？
(A) 註冊成為會員
(B) 聯絡賽茲先生
(C) 支付入場費
(D) 致電籌辦者　　　　　　　　答案 (B)

184. 關於今年的節慶，文中沒有暗指什麼？
(A) 它在靠近水的地方舉行。
(B) 它首度舉辦沙雕展。
(C) 它對兒童開放。
(D) 第二天下雨了。　　　　　　答案 (B)

185. 評論中，馬利奧薩女士暗指本屆節慶的什麼事？
(A) 節慶欠缺給兒童的活動。
(B) 煙火表演需要更多安全防護員。
(C) 音樂會的替代場地不足。
(D) 沒有足夠的地方供遊客用餐。　答案 (C)

不可議小屋

澳洲，北域，艾莉絲泉

+61 230777199

(186) 正在尋找獨特的度假場地嗎？請到不可議小屋，在澳洲大陸的中心地帶享受令人驚嘆的體驗。接觸古老的土地，挖掘埋藏在沙裡的故事。

- 烏魯魯之旅，與來自澳洲原住民部落的導遊同行
- (189) 參加當地部落阿南古人的節慶
- 探索澳洲中部的日出駱駝之旅
- 在美麗的沙漠星空下用餐

(187C) 作為該地區最大的旅館，(187B) 我們可以滿足您的所有需求，包括免費機場接駁車、洗衣服務和清潔服務。(187D) 為了慶祝十週年，所有客人均可享用免費自助早餐。

欲了解更多資訊，請上 www.incrediblelodge.com。
(188) 一月底前造訪我們的禮品店，可享 **10%** 折扣。

不可議小屋

顧客回饋意見

為了向客人提供更好的服務，請完成這份簡短的調查。

姓名：基蘭・阿奇諾　　電子郵件：kachino@mail.com
(190) 住宿日期：**1 月 20 日 - 25 日**

請註明您的滿意度（1= 最高 / 4= 最低）

	1	2	3	4
工作人員的禮貌	○	●	○	○
工作人員的回應	●	○	○	○
設施清潔度	○	●	○	○
房間品質	○	●	○	○

最難忘的體驗：烏魯魯之旅。(189) 參觀烏魯魯時，我由巴卡納帶隊。她是很棒的說故事者。她向我講述她部落的傳統夢境故事，為我的經歷增添了深度。(189) 很高興那天晚上在她的部落節慶上再次見到她，她在那裡告訴了我更多故事。

您遇到的問題：(190) 入住第二天，空調就停止運轉。不過，回報後 30 分鐘內，問題就解決了。服務水準讓我留下了深刻的印象。

收件人：維修部全體員工
寄件人：傑森・惠洛克
主　旨：房間問題
(190) 日　期：1 月 30 日

(190) **3 樓 34 號房**的空調上週發生第二次故障。經調查，我發現這臺是我們 10 多年前買的。因此，我訂購

了一臺新的，預計兩天後到達。收到後請立即安裝。在新設備正常運作之前，該房間將保持空房狀態。

186. 這份廣告的對象是誰？
(A) 歷史學家
(B) 企業主
(C) 遊客
(D) 傳統藝術家　　　　　　答案 (C)

187. 關於不可議小屋，文中沒有暗指什麼？
(A) 只接受網路預訂。
(B) 免費為客人洗衣服。
(C) 可以容納比附近所有旅館更多的客人。
(D) 10 年前開業。　　　　答案 (A)

188. 根據廣告，將限時提供什麼？
(A) 房間升級
(B) 免費租用駱駝
(C) 免費晚餐
(D) 禮品店折扣　　　　　　答案 (D)

189. 關於巴卡納，文中暗指什麼？
(A) 她是一位著名作家。
(B) 她來自阿南古部落。
(C) 她最近受聘於不可議小屋。
(D) 她對最近的旅行感到滿意。　答案 (B)

190. 關於阿奇諾先生，文中暗指什麼？
(A) 他覺得不可議小屋太貴了。
(B) 他對這趟旅行有些不滿。
(C) 他住在不可議小屋的三樓。
(D) 他計劃今年稍晚再次造訪烏魯魯。　答案 (C)

問題 **191-195**，請參考以下信件及優惠券。

7 月 25 日

巴貝多燒烤
普拉特大道 97A 號
多倫多 M4C5B5

親愛的店長，

(191) 這封信是為了詢問我上次光顧貴餐廳時的結帳流程。(192) 7 月 20 日下午 6:30，我和太太在參加音樂會之前去了你們的餐廳吃晚餐。我太太點了義大利香草羊排，我點了五花肉捲。每道料理的定價是 60 美元。然而，(195) 實際送來的餐點卻是主廚特餐，也就是洋蔥排骨。

(193) 當我向你反應時，你問我要等待正確的餐點，還是想吃已經送上的料理。你還說，既然是你們的錯誤，你會以我原來點餐的價格 (195) 計算我這道 90 美元的菜。因為時間緊迫，我當時就吃了排骨。

我們走的時候太匆忙，沒有仔細檢查帳單。但當我收到每個月的信用卡帳單時，(191) 我發現那一頓飯花了我 150 美元。因此，我要求退款 30 美元。

近兩年來，我們始終是貴餐廳的顧客，而這件事相當令人失望。我希望類似的事情不會再發生。

誠摯祝福。

布魯斯·麥基

---

7 月 31 日

布魯斯·麥基
維多利亞街 555 號
多倫多，M3M5G9

親愛的麥基先生，

請接受我對這項錯誤的誠摯歉意。(193) 我和馬克·哈林頓談及您的來訪，他證實為您意外上了錯誤的餐點，也承諾以折扣價提供給您。因此，30 美元已退還至您的信用卡。

(194) 很抱歉這件事發生在像您和您太太這樣的貴賓身上。請收下這份優惠券，以在下次光顧時使用。如果還有什麼我可以為您效勞的地方，請讓我知道。

誠摯致意。

洛林·布拉科
巴貝多燒烤店老闆

優惠券

巴貝多燒烤店

(195) 本優惠券可免費享用一份廚師特餐。
點餐時請向服務生出示本優惠券。
每位顧客限用一張優惠券。

有效期限：**12 月 31 日**

---

191. 第一封信是為了什麼而寫？
　　(A) 描述愉快的經歷
　　(B) 回報付款錯誤
　　(C) 預約用餐
　　(D) 詢問菜單　　　　　　　　答案 (B)

192. 關於麥基先生，文中暗指什麼？
　　(A) 他在音樂會遲到了。
　　(B) 7 月 20 日，他與配偶一起吃晚餐。
　　(C) 他喜歡嘗試新的菜單品項。
　　(D) 他再也不會去那家餐廳了。　　答案 (B)

193. 關於哈林頓先生，文中暗指什麼？
　　(A) 7 月 31 日，他在巴貝多燒烤店上班。

　　(B) 他的信用卡被錯誤扣款。
　　(C) 他是巴貝多燒烤店的管理者。
　　(D) 他通常會向顧客推薦羊排。　　答案 (C)

194. 關於巴貝多燒烤店，可以推論出什麼？
　　(A) 晚上 7:30 停止營業。
　　(B) 提供禮券給所有顧客。
　　(C) 開業約兩年。
　　(D) 老闆很重視他的顧客。　　答案 (D)

195. 這份優惠券值多少錢？
　　(A) 30 美元
　　(B) 60 美元
　　(C) 90 美元
　　(D) 150 美元　　　　　　　　答案 (C)

問題 **196-200**，請參考以下文章、備忘錄及電子郵件。

維多利亞（10 月 10 日）一蓬勃樹木組織（FTO）將於 10 月 13 日星期五上午 8 點半至下午 6 點，在吉爾摩公園舉辦「一個地球慶典」募款活動。(196) FTO 是一個非營利組織，致力於提醒人們環境和自然的重要性。本次慶典旨在向維多利亞人宣導環境的重要。

(197) (199) 慶典將邀請威洛·勞倫斯等嘉賓發表演說。「很高興這項活動終於在我的家鄉舉行。(196) 這是一件偉大的事情，肯定有助於提高該地區的環保意識。」勞倫斯女士說。

(197)「我希望維多利亞州的每個人，都能像之前在其他城市舉辦的節慶一樣享受這個慶典。屆時將會有食品攤販、當地居民的簡短表演和音樂會。」FTO 發言人德克斯特·沃里斯表示，(198)「今年慶典的特別之處，在於首次在戶外舉行。」

歡迎大家來參加這個慶典，並感謝所有捐款。(200) 捐贈 3,000 美元或以上的公司，將在本組織網站首頁和宣傳手冊獲得廣告空間。如須了解更多資訊，請致電 852-555-0958，聯繫規劃總監德克蘭·傑克曼，或發送電子郵件至 djackman@ftomail.com。

收件人：德克蘭·傑克曼、費莉西亞·史都華、羅德尼·韋斯特
寄件人：傑森·格林，執行長
日　期：10 月 11 日
主　旨：些微調整

關於維多利亞的慶典，需要做一些調整。請注意以下員工的新角色：

亞倫·漢普頓：　　　　娛樂專員
帕崔夏·埃爾敏：　　　餐飲專員
(199) 羅德尼·韋斯特：　公共演講主持人
南希·馬許：　　　　　公共關係顧問

如有任何疑問，請立即與我聯繫。讓我們把今年的慶典，打造成史上最棒的一次。

收件人：德克蘭・傑克曼 <djackman@ftomail.com>
寄件人：阿諾德・澤維爾 <axavier@lesfeuilles.com>
日　期：10 月 17 日
主　旨：謝謝！

親愛的傑克曼先生，

(200)感謝您在網站和宣傳手冊上張貼我們餐廳的標誌。很高興慶典進展順利。整場活動看起來都進行得很順暢。多虧了這份廣告，我們餐廳最近的顧客和銷售額都有所增加。

很高興能夠參加這次活動，希望將來也能繼續這麼做。請隨時通知我未來可能出現的任何機會。

感謝。

阿諾德・澤維爾
店長
法尤餐廳

---

196. 文章中，第 2 段第 4 行「cause」，含義最接近
   (A) 推廣
   (B) 目標
   (C) 資金
   (D) 結果　　　　　　　　　　答案 (B)

197. 關於勞倫斯女士，文中暗指什麼？
   (A) 她將帶領一支志工團隊。
   (B) 她創立了 FTO。
   (C) 她來自維多利亞。
   (D) 她享譽全球。　　　　　　答案 (C)

198. 根據沃里斯先生所說，以下關於「一個地球慶典」的敘述何者正確？
   (A) 預計將迎來史上最多的參加人數。
   (B) 它已在維多利亞舉行過幾次。
   (C) 只有維多利亞的居民可以參加。
   (D) 去年是在室內舉行的。　　答案 (D)

199. 誰最有可能跟勞倫斯女士共事過？
   (A) 漢普頓先生
   (B) 埃爾敏女士
   (C) 韋斯特先生
   (D) 馬許女士　　　　　　　　答案 (C)

200. 關於澤維爾先生，可以推論出什麼？
   (A) 他為慶典捐款超過 3,000 美元。
   (B) 他在慶典期間販售餐廳的餐點。
   (C) 他幾年前創立了法尤餐廳。
   (D) 他最近重新設計了餐廳的標誌。　答案 (A)

Answer Sheet

Actual Test 01

LISTENING (Part I ~ IV)

NO.	ANSWER				NO.	ANSWER				NO.	ANSWER				NO.	ANSWER			
	A	B	C	D		A	B	C	D		A	B	C	D		A	B	C	D
1	a	b	c	d	21	a	b	c		41	a	b	c	d	61	a	b	c	d
2	a	b	c	d	22	a	b	c		42	a	b	c	d	62	a	b	c	d
3	a	b	c	d	23	a	b	c		43	a	b	c	d	63	a	b	c	d
4	a	b	c	d	24	a	b	c		44	a	b	c	d	64	a	b	c	d
5	a	b	c	d	25	a	b	c		45	a	b	c	d	65	a	b	c	d
6	a	b	c		26	a	b	c	d	46	a	b	c	d	66	a	b	c	d
7	a	b	c		27	a	b	c		47	a	b	c	d	67	a	b	c	d
8	a	b	c		28	a	b	c		48	a	b	c	d	68	a	b	c	d
9	a	b	c		29	a	b	c		49	a	b	c	d	69	a	b	c	d
10	a	b	c		30	a	b	c		50	a	b	c	d	70	a	b	c	d
11	a	b	c		31	a	b	c		51	a	b	c	d	71	a	b	c	d
12	a	b	c		32	a	b	c		52	a	b	c	d	72	a	b	c	d
13	a	b	c		33	a	b	c		53	a	b	c	d	73	a	b	c	d
14	a	b	c		34	a	b	c		54	a	b	c	d	74	a	b	c	d
15	a	b	c		35	a	b	c		55	a	b	c	d	75	a	b	c	d
16	a	b	c		36	a	b	c		56	a	b	c	d	76	a	b	c	d
17	a	b	c		37	a	b	c		57	a	b	c	d	77	a	b	c	d
18	a	b	c		38	a	b	c		58	a	b	c	d	78	a	b	c	d
19	a	b	c		39	a	b	c		59	a	b	c	d	79	a	b	c	d
20	a	b	c		40	a	b	c		60	a	b	c	d	80	a	b	c	d

NO.	ANSWER			
	A	B	C	D
81	a	b	c	d
82	a	b	c	d
83	a	b	c	d
84	a	b	c	d
85	a	b	c	d
86	a	b	c	d
87	a	b	c	d
88	a	b	c	d
89	a	b	c	d
90	a	b	c	d
91	a	b	c	d
92	a	b	c	d
93	a	b	c	d
94	a	b	c	d
95	a	b	c	d
96	a	b	c	d
97	a	b	c	d
98	a	b	c	d
99	a	b	c	d
100	a	b	c	d

READING (Part V ~ VII)

NO.	ANSWER				NO.	ANSWER				NO.	ANSWER				NO.	ANSWER			
	A	B	C	D		A	B	C	D		A	B	C	D		A	B	C	D
101	a	b	c	d	121	a	b	c	d	141	a	b	c	d	161	a	b	c	d
102	a	b	c	d	122	a	b	c	d	142	a	b	c	d	162	a	b	c	d
103	a	b	c	d	123	a	b	c	d	143	a	b	c	d	163	a	b	c	d
104	a	b	c	d	124	a	b	c	d	144	a	b	c	d	164	a	b	c	d
105	a	b	c	d	125	a	b	c	d	145	a	b	c	d	165	a	b	c	d
106	a	b	c	d	126	a	b	c	d	146	a	b	c	d	166	a	b	c	d
107	a	b	c	d	127	a	b	c	d	147	a	b	c	d	167	a	b	c	d
108	a	b	c	d	128	a	b	c	d	148	a	b	c	d	168	a	b	c	d
109	a	b	c	d	129	a	b	c	d	149	a	b	c	d	169	a	b	c	d
110	a	b	c	d	130	a	b	c	d	150	a	b	c	d	170	a	b	c	d
111	a	b	c	d	131	a	b	c	d	151	a	b	c	d	171	a	b	c	d
112	a	b	c	d	132	a	b	c	d	152	a	b	c	d	172	a	b	c	d
113	a	b	c	d	133	a	b	c	d	153	a	b	c	d	173	a	b	c	d
114	a	b	c	d	134	a	b	c	d	154	a	b	c	d	174	a	b	c	d
115	a	b	c	d	135	a	b	c	d	155	a	b	c	d	175	a	b	c	d
116	a	b	c	d	136	a	b	c	d	156	a	b	c	d	176	a	b	c	d
117	a	b	c	d	137	a	b	c	d	157	a	b	c	d	177	a	b	c	d
118	a	b	c	d	138	a	b	c	d	158	a	b	c	d	178	a	b	c	d
119	a	b	c	d	139	a	b	c	d	159	a	b	c	d	179	a	b	c	d
120	a	b	c	d	140	a	b	c	d	160	a	b	c	d	180	a	b	c	d

NO.	ANSWER			
	A	B	C	D
181	a	b	c	d
182	a	b	c	d
183	a	b	c	d
184	a	b	c	d
185	a	b	c	d
186	a	b	c	d
187	a	b	c	d
188	a	b	c	d
189	a	b	c	d
190	a	b	c	d
191	a	b	c	d
192	a	b	c	d
193	a	b	c	d
194	a	b	c	d
195	a	b	c	d
196	a	b	c	d
197	a	b	c	d
198	a	b	c	d
199	a	b	c	d
200	a	b	c	d

Actual Test 02

LISTENING (Part I ~ IV)

NO.	ANSWER	NO.	ANSWER	NO.	ANSWER	NO.	ANSWER
1	ⓐ ⓑ ⓒ ⓓ	21	ⓐ ⓑ ⓒ ⓓ	41	ⓐ ⓑ ⓒ ⓓ	61	ⓐ ⓑ ⓒ ⓓ
2	ⓐ ⓑ ⓒ ⓓ	22	ⓐ ⓑ ⓒ ⓓ	42	ⓐ ⓑ ⓒ ⓓ	62	ⓐ ⓑ ⓒ ⓓ
3	ⓐ ⓑ ⓒ ⓓ	23	ⓐ ⓑ ⓒ ⓓ	43	ⓐ ⓑ ⓒ ⓓ	63	ⓐ ⓑ ⓒ ⓓ
4	ⓐ ⓑ ⓒ ⓓ	24	ⓐ ⓑ ⓒ ⓓ	44	ⓐ ⓑ ⓒ ⓓ	64	ⓐ ⓑ ⓒ ⓓ
5	ⓐ ⓑ ⓒ ⓓ	25	ⓐ ⓑ ⓒ ⓓ	45	ⓐ ⓑ ⓒ ⓓ	65	ⓐ ⓑ ⓒ ⓓ
6	ⓐ ⓑ ⓒ ⓓ	26	ⓐ ⓑ ⓒ ⓓ	46	ⓐ ⓑ ⓒ ⓓ	66	ⓐ ⓑ ⓒ ⓓ
7	ⓐ ⓑ ⓒ	27	ⓐ ⓑ ⓒ	47	ⓐ ⓑ ⓒ ⓓ	67	ⓐ ⓑ ⓒ ⓓ
8	ⓐ ⓑ ⓒ	28	ⓐ ⓑ ⓒ	48	ⓐ ⓑ ⓒ ⓓ	68	ⓐ ⓑ ⓒ ⓓ
9	ⓐ ⓑ ⓒ	29	ⓐ ⓑ ⓒ	49	ⓐ ⓑ ⓒ ⓓ	69	ⓐ ⓑ ⓒ ⓓ
10	ⓐ ⓑ ⓒ	30	ⓐ ⓑ ⓒ ⓓ	50	ⓐ ⓑ ⓒ ⓓ	70	ⓐ ⓑ ⓒ ⓓ
11	ⓐ ⓑ ⓒ	31	ⓐ ⓑ ⓒ ⓓ	51	ⓐ ⓑ ⓒ ⓓ	71	ⓐ ⓑ ⓒ ⓓ
12	ⓐ ⓑ ⓒ	32	ⓐ ⓑ ⓒ ⓓ	52	ⓐ ⓑ ⓒ ⓓ	72	ⓐ ⓑ ⓒ ⓓ
13	ⓐ ⓑ ⓒ	33	ⓐ ⓑ ⓒ ⓓ	53	ⓐ ⓑ ⓒ ⓓ	73	ⓐ ⓑ ⓒ ⓓ
14	ⓐ ⓑ ⓒ	34	ⓐ ⓑ ⓒ ⓓ	54	ⓐ ⓑ ⓒ ⓓ	74	ⓐ ⓑ ⓒ ⓓ
15	ⓐ ⓑ ⓒ	35	ⓐ ⓑ ⓒ ⓓ	55	ⓐ ⓑ ⓒ ⓓ	75	ⓐ ⓑ ⓒ ⓓ
16	ⓐ ⓑ ⓒ	36	ⓐ ⓑ ⓒ ⓓ	56	ⓐ ⓑ ⓒ ⓓ	76	ⓐ ⓑ ⓒ ⓓ
17	ⓐ ⓑ ⓒ	37	ⓐ ⓑ ⓒ ⓓ	57	ⓐ ⓑ ⓒ ⓓ	77	ⓐ ⓑ ⓒ ⓓ
18	ⓐ ⓑ ⓒ	38	ⓐ ⓑ ⓒ ⓓ	58	ⓐ ⓑ ⓒ ⓓ	78	ⓐ ⓑ ⓒ ⓓ
19	ⓐ ⓑ ⓒ	39	ⓐ ⓑ ⓒ ⓓ	59	ⓐ ⓑ ⓒ ⓓ	79	ⓐ ⓑ ⓒ ⓓ
20	ⓐ ⓑ ⓒ	40	ⓐ ⓑ ⓒ ⓓ	60	ⓐ ⓑ ⓒ ⓓ	80	ⓐ ⓑ ⓒ ⓓ
						81	ⓐ ⓑ ⓒ ⓓ
						82	ⓐ ⓑ ⓒ ⓓ
						83	ⓐ ⓑ ⓒ ⓓ
						84	ⓐ ⓑ ⓒ ⓓ
						85	ⓐ ⓑ ⓒ ⓓ
						86	ⓐ ⓑ ⓒ ⓓ
						87	ⓐ ⓑ ⓒ ⓓ
						88	ⓐ ⓑ ⓒ ⓓ
						89	ⓐ ⓑ ⓒ ⓓ
						90	ⓐ ⓑ ⓒ ⓓ
						91	ⓐ ⓑ ⓒ ⓓ
						92	ⓐ ⓑ ⓒ ⓓ
						93	ⓐ ⓑ ⓒ ⓓ
						94	ⓐ ⓑ ⓒ ⓓ
						95	ⓐ ⓑ ⓒ ⓓ
						96	ⓐ ⓑ ⓒ ⓓ
						97	ⓐ ⓑ ⓒ ⓓ
						98	ⓐ ⓑ ⓒ ⓓ
						99	ⓐ ⓑ ⓒ ⓓ
						100	ⓐ ⓑ ⓒ ⓓ

READING (Part V ~ VII)

NO.	ANSWER	NO.	ANSWER	NO.	ANSWER	NO.	ANSWER	NO.	ANSWER
101	ⓐ ⓑ ⓒ ⓓ	121	ⓐ ⓑ ⓒ ⓓ	141	ⓐ ⓑ ⓒ ⓓ	161	ⓐ ⓑ ⓒ ⓓ	181	ⓐ ⓑ ⓒ ⓓ
102	ⓐ ⓑ ⓒ ⓓ	122	ⓐ ⓑ ⓒ ⓓ	142	ⓐ ⓑ ⓒ ⓓ	162	ⓐ ⓑ ⓒ ⓓ	182	ⓐ ⓑ ⓒ ⓓ
103	ⓐ ⓑ ⓒ ⓓ	123	ⓐ ⓑ ⓒ ⓓ	143	ⓐ ⓑ ⓒ ⓓ	163	ⓐ ⓑ ⓒ ⓓ	183	ⓐ ⓑ ⓒ ⓓ
104	ⓐ ⓑ ⓒ ⓓ	124	ⓐ ⓑ ⓒ ⓓ	144	ⓐ ⓑ ⓒ ⓓ	164	ⓐ ⓑ ⓒ ⓓ	184	ⓐ ⓑ ⓒ ⓓ
105	ⓐ ⓑ ⓒ ⓓ	125	ⓐ ⓑ ⓒ ⓓ	145	ⓐ ⓑ ⓒ ⓓ	165	ⓐ ⓑ ⓒ ⓓ	185	ⓐ ⓑ ⓒ ⓓ
106	ⓐ ⓑ ⓒ ⓓ	126	ⓐ ⓑ ⓒ ⓓ	146	ⓐ ⓑ ⓒ ⓓ	166	ⓐ ⓑ ⓒ ⓓ	186	ⓐ ⓑ ⓒ ⓓ
107	ⓐ ⓑ ⓒ ⓓ	127	ⓐ ⓑ ⓒ ⓓ	147	ⓐ ⓑ ⓒ ⓓ	167	ⓐ ⓑ ⓒ ⓓ	187	ⓐ ⓑ ⓒ ⓓ
108	ⓐ ⓑ ⓒ ⓓ	128	ⓐ ⓑ ⓒ ⓓ	148	ⓐ ⓑ ⓒ ⓓ	168	ⓐ ⓑ ⓒ ⓓ	188	ⓐ ⓑ ⓒ ⓓ
109	ⓐ ⓑ ⓒ ⓓ	129	ⓐ ⓑ ⓒ ⓓ	149	ⓐ ⓑ ⓒ ⓓ	169	ⓐ ⓑ ⓒ ⓓ	189	ⓐ ⓑ ⓒ ⓓ
110	ⓐ ⓑ ⓒ ⓓ	130	ⓐ ⓑ ⓒ ⓓ	150	ⓐ ⓑ ⓒ ⓓ	170	ⓐ ⓑ ⓒ ⓓ	190	ⓐ ⓑ ⓒ ⓓ
111	ⓐ ⓑ ⓒ ⓓ	131	ⓐ ⓑ ⓒ ⓓ	151	ⓐ ⓑ ⓒ ⓓ	171	ⓐ ⓑ ⓒ ⓓ	191	ⓐ ⓑ ⓒ ⓓ
112	ⓐ ⓑ ⓒ ⓓ	132	ⓐ ⓑ ⓒ ⓓ	152	ⓐ ⓑ ⓒ ⓓ	172	ⓐ ⓑ ⓒ ⓓ	192	ⓐ ⓑ ⓒ ⓓ
113	ⓐ ⓑ ⓒ ⓓ	133	ⓐ ⓑ ⓒ ⓓ	153	ⓐ ⓑ ⓒ ⓓ	173	ⓐ ⓑ ⓒ ⓓ	193	ⓐ ⓑ ⓒ ⓓ
114	ⓐ ⓑ ⓒ ⓓ	134	ⓐ ⓑ ⓒ ⓓ	154	ⓐ ⓑ ⓒ ⓓ	174	ⓐ ⓑ ⓒ ⓓ	194	ⓐ ⓑ ⓒ ⓓ
115	ⓐ ⓑ ⓒ ⓓ	135	ⓐ ⓑ ⓒ ⓓ	155	ⓐ ⓑ ⓒ ⓓ	175	ⓐ ⓑ ⓒ ⓓ	195	ⓐ ⓑ ⓒ ⓓ
116	ⓐ ⓑ ⓒ ⓓ	136	ⓐ ⓑ ⓒ ⓓ	156	ⓐ ⓑ ⓒ ⓓ	176	ⓐ ⓑ ⓒ ⓓ	196	ⓐ ⓑ ⓒ ⓓ
117	ⓐ ⓑ ⓒ ⓓ	137	ⓐ ⓑ ⓒ ⓓ	157	ⓐ ⓑ ⓒ ⓓ	177	ⓐ ⓑ ⓒ ⓓ	197	ⓐ ⓑ ⓒ ⓓ
118	ⓐ ⓑ ⓒ ⓓ	138	ⓐ ⓑ ⓒ ⓓ	158	ⓐ ⓑ ⓒ ⓓ	178	ⓐ ⓑ ⓒ ⓓ	198	ⓐ ⓑ ⓒ ⓓ
119	ⓐ ⓑ ⓒ ⓓ	139	ⓐ ⓑ ⓒ ⓓ	159	ⓐ ⓑ ⓒ ⓓ	179	ⓐ ⓑ ⓒ ⓓ	199	ⓐ ⓑ ⓒ ⓓ
120	ⓐ ⓑ ⓒ ⓓ	140	ⓐ ⓑ ⓒ ⓓ	160	ⓐ ⓑ ⓒ ⓓ	180	ⓐ ⓑ ⓒ ⓓ	200	ⓐ ⓑ ⓒ ⓓ

Actual Test 03

LISTENING (Part I ~ IV)

NO.	ANSWER	NO.	ANSWER	NO.	ANSWER	NO.	ANSWER	NO.	ANSWER
	A B C D		A B C D		A B C D		A B C D		A B C D
1	ⓐ ⓑ ⓒ	21	ⓐ ⓑ ⓒ ⓓ	41	ⓐ ⓑ ⓒ ⓓ	61	ⓐ ⓑ ⓒ ⓓ	81	ⓐ ⓑ ⓒ ⓓ
2	ⓐ ⓑ ⓒ	22	ⓐ ⓑ ⓒ ⓓ	42	ⓐ ⓑ ⓒ ⓓ	62	ⓐ ⓑ ⓒ ⓓ	82	ⓐ ⓑ ⓒ ⓓ
3	ⓐ ⓑ ⓒ	23	ⓐ ⓑ ⓒ ⓓ	43	ⓐ ⓑ ⓒ ⓓ	63	ⓐ ⓑ ⓒ ⓓ	83	ⓐ ⓑ ⓒ ⓓ
4	ⓐ ⓑ ⓒ	24	ⓐ ⓑ ⓒ ⓓ	44	ⓐ ⓑ ⓒ ⓓ	64	ⓐ ⓑ ⓒ ⓓ	84	ⓐ ⓑ ⓒ ⓓ
5	ⓐ ⓑ ⓒ	25	ⓐ ⓑ ⓒ ⓓ	45	ⓐ ⓑ ⓒ ⓓ	65	ⓐ ⓑ ⓒ ⓓ	85	ⓐ ⓑ ⓒ ⓓ
6	ⓐ ⓑ ⓒ	26	ⓐ ⓑ ⓒ ⓓ	46	ⓐ ⓑ ⓒ ⓓ	66	ⓐ ⓑ ⓒ ⓓ	86	ⓐ ⓑ ⓒ ⓓ
7	ⓐ ⓑ ⓒ	27	ⓐ ⓑ ⓒ ⓓ	47	ⓐ ⓑ ⓒ ⓓ	67	ⓐ ⓑ ⓒ ⓓ	87	ⓐ ⓑ ⓒ ⓓ
8	ⓐ ⓑ ⓒ	28	ⓐ ⓑ ⓒ ⓓ	48	ⓐ ⓑ ⓒ ⓓ	68	ⓐ ⓑ ⓒ ⓓ	88	ⓐ ⓑ ⓒ ⓓ
9	ⓐ ⓑ ⓒ	29	ⓐ ⓑ ⓒ ⓓ	49	ⓐ ⓑ ⓒ ⓓ	69	ⓐ ⓑ ⓒ ⓓ	89	ⓐ ⓑ ⓒ ⓓ
10	ⓐ ⓑ ⓒ	30	ⓐ ⓑ ⓒ ⓓ	50	ⓐ ⓑ ⓒ ⓓ	70	ⓐ ⓑ ⓒ ⓓ	90	ⓐ ⓑ ⓒ ⓓ
11	ⓐ ⓑ ⓒ	31	ⓐ ⓑ ⓒ ⓓ	51	ⓐ ⓑ ⓒ ⓓ	71	ⓐ ⓑ ⓒ ⓓ	91	ⓐ ⓑ ⓒ ⓓ
12	ⓐ ⓑ ⓒ	32	ⓐ ⓑ ⓒ ⓓ	52	ⓐ ⓑ ⓒ ⓓ	72	ⓐ ⓑ ⓒ ⓓ	92	ⓐ ⓑ ⓒ ⓓ
13	ⓐ ⓑ ⓒ	33	ⓐ ⓑ ⓒ ⓓ	53	ⓐ ⓑ ⓒ ⓓ	73	ⓐ ⓑ ⓒ ⓓ	93	ⓐ ⓑ ⓒ ⓓ
14	ⓐ ⓑ ⓒ	34	ⓐ ⓑ ⓒ ⓓ	54	ⓐ ⓑ ⓒ ⓓ	74	ⓐ ⓑ ⓒ ⓓ	94	ⓐ ⓑ ⓒ ⓓ
15	ⓐ ⓑ ⓒ	35	ⓐ ⓑ ⓒ ⓓ	55	ⓐ ⓑ ⓒ ⓓ	75	ⓐ ⓑ ⓒ ⓓ	95	ⓐ ⓑ ⓒ ⓓ
16	ⓐ ⓑ ⓒ	36	ⓐ ⓑ ⓒ ⓓ	56	ⓐ ⓑ ⓒ ⓓ	76	ⓐ ⓑ ⓒ ⓓ	96	ⓐ ⓑ ⓒ ⓓ
17	ⓐ ⓑ ⓒ	37	ⓐ ⓑ ⓒ ⓓ	57	ⓐ ⓑ ⓒ ⓓ	77	ⓐ ⓑ ⓒ ⓓ	97	ⓐ ⓑ ⓒ ⓓ
18	ⓐ ⓑ ⓒ	38	ⓐ ⓑ ⓒ ⓓ	58	ⓐ ⓑ ⓒ ⓓ	78	ⓐ ⓑ ⓒ ⓓ	98	ⓐ ⓑ ⓒ ⓓ
19	ⓐ ⓑ ⓒ	39	ⓐ ⓑ ⓒ ⓓ	59	ⓐ ⓑ ⓒ ⓓ	79	ⓐ ⓑ ⓒ ⓓ	99	ⓐ ⓑ ⓒ ⓓ
20	ⓐ ⓑ ⓒ	40	ⓐ ⓑ ⓒ	60	ⓐ ⓑ ⓒ ⓓ	80	ⓐ ⓑ ⓒ ⓓ	100	ⓐ ⓑ ⓒ ⓓ

READING (Part V ~ VII)

NO.	ANSWER	NO.	ANSWER	NO.	ANSWER	NO.	ANSWER	NO.	ANSWER
	A B C D		A B C D		A B C D		A B C D		A B C D
101	ⓐ ⓑ ⓒ ⓓ	121	ⓐ ⓑ ⓒ ⓓ	141	ⓐ ⓑ ⓒ ⓓ	161	ⓐ ⓑ ⓒ ⓓ	181	ⓐ ⓑ ⓒ ⓓ
102	ⓐ ⓑ ⓒ ⓓ	122	ⓐ ⓑ ⓒ ⓓ	142	ⓐ ⓑ ⓒ ⓓ	162	ⓐ ⓑ ⓒ ⓓ	182	ⓐ ⓑ ⓒ ⓓ
103	ⓐ ⓑ ⓒ ⓓ	123	ⓐ ⓑ ⓒ ⓓ	143	ⓐ ⓑ ⓒ ⓓ	163	ⓐ ⓑ ⓒ ⓓ	183	ⓐ ⓑ ⓒ ⓓ
104	ⓐ ⓑ ⓒ ⓓ	124	ⓐ ⓑ ⓒ ⓓ	144	ⓐ ⓑ ⓒ ⓓ	164	ⓐ ⓑ ⓒ ⓓ	184	ⓐ ⓑ ⓒ ⓓ
105	ⓐ ⓑ ⓒ ⓓ	125	ⓐ ⓑ ⓒ ⓓ	145	ⓐ ⓑ ⓒ ⓓ	165	ⓐ ⓑ ⓒ ⓓ	185	ⓐ ⓑ ⓒ ⓓ
106	ⓐ ⓑ ⓒ ⓓ	126	ⓐ ⓑ ⓒ ⓓ	146	ⓐ ⓑ ⓒ ⓓ	166	ⓐ ⓑ ⓒ ⓓ	186	ⓐ ⓑ ⓒ ⓓ
107	ⓐ ⓑ ⓒ ⓓ	127	ⓐ ⓑ ⓒ ⓓ	147	ⓐ ⓑ ⓒ ⓓ	167	ⓐ ⓑ ⓒ ⓓ	187	ⓐ ⓑ ⓒ ⓓ
108	ⓐ ⓑ ⓒ ⓓ	128	ⓐ ⓑ ⓒ ⓓ	148	ⓐ ⓑ ⓒ ⓓ	168	ⓐ ⓑ ⓒ ⓓ	188	ⓐ ⓑ ⓒ ⓓ
109	ⓐ ⓑ ⓒ ⓓ	129	ⓐ ⓑ ⓒ ⓓ	149	ⓐ ⓑ ⓒ ⓓ	169	ⓐ ⓑ ⓒ ⓓ	189	ⓐ ⓑ ⓒ ⓓ
110	ⓐ ⓑ ⓒ ⓓ	130	ⓐ ⓑ ⓒ ⓓ	150	ⓐ ⓑ ⓒ ⓓ	170	ⓐ ⓑ ⓒ ⓓ	190	ⓐ ⓑ ⓒ ⓓ
111	ⓐ ⓑ ⓒ ⓓ	131	ⓐ ⓑ ⓒ ⓓ	151	ⓐ ⓑ ⓒ ⓓ	171	ⓐ ⓑ ⓒ ⓓ	191	ⓐ ⓑ ⓒ ⓓ
112	ⓐ ⓑ ⓒ ⓓ	132	ⓐ ⓑ ⓒ ⓓ	152	ⓐ ⓑ ⓒ ⓓ	172	ⓐ ⓑ ⓒ ⓓ	192	ⓐ ⓑ ⓒ ⓓ
113	ⓐ ⓑ ⓒ ⓓ	133	ⓐ ⓑ ⓒ ⓓ	153	ⓐ ⓑ ⓒ ⓓ	173	ⓐ ⓑ ⓒ ⓓ	193	ⓐ ⓑ ⓒ ⓓ
114	ⓐ ⓑ ⓒ ⓓ	134	ⓐ ⓑ ⓒ ⓓ	154	ⓐ ⓑ ⓒ ⓓ	174	ⓐ ⓑ ⓒ ⓓ	194	ⓐ ⓑ ⓒ ⓓ
115	ⓐ ⓑ ⓒ ⓓ	135	ⓐ ⓑ ⓒ ⓓ	155	ⓐ ⓑ ⓒ ⓓ	175	ⓐ ⓑ ⓒ ⓓ	195	ⓐ ⓑ ⓒ ⓓ
116	ⓐ ⓑ ⓒ ⓓ	136	ⓐ ⓑ ⓒ ⓓ	156	ⓐ ⓑ ⓒ ⓓ	176	ⓐ ⓑ ⓒ ⓓ	196	ⓐ ⓑ ⓒ ⓓ
117	ⓐ ⓑ ⓒ ⓓ	137	ⓐ ⓑ ⓒ ⓓ	157	ⓐ ⓑ ⓒ ⓓ	177	ⓐ ⓑ ⓒ ⓓ	197	ⓐ ⓑ ⓒ ⓓ
118	ⓐ ⓑ ⓒ ⓓ	138	ⓐ ⓑ ⓒ ⓓ	158	ⓐ ⓑ ⓒ ⓓ	178	ⓐ ⓑ ⓒ ⓓ	198	ⓐ ⓑ ⓒ ⓓ
119	ⓐ ⓑ ⓒ ⓓ	139	ⓐ ⓑ ⓒ ⓓ	159	ⓐ ⓑ ⓒ ⓓ	179	ⓐ ⓑ ⓒ ⓓ	199	ⓐ ⓑ ⓒ ⓓ
120	ⓐ ⓑ ⓒ ⓓ	140	ⓐ ⓑ ⓒ ⓓ	160	ⓐ ⓑ ⓒ ⓓ	180	ⓐ ⓑ ⓒ ⓓ	200	ⓐ ⓑ ⓒ ⓓ

Answer Sheet

Actual Test 04

LISTENING (Part I ~ IV)

NO.	ANSWER	NO.	ANSWER	NO.	ANSWER	NO.	ANSWER
	A B C D		A B C D		A B C D		A B C D
1	ⓐ ⓑ ⓒ	21	ⓐ ⓑ ⓒ ⓓ	41	ⓐ ⓑ ⓒ ⓓ	61	ⓐ ⓑ ⓒ ⓓ
2	ⓐ ⓑ ⓒ	22	ⓐ ⓑ ⓒ ⓓ	42	ⓐ ⓑ ⓒ ⓓ	62	ⓐ ⓑ ⓒ ⓓ
3	ⓐ ⓑ ⓒ	23	ⓐ ⓑ ⓒ ⓓ	43	ⓐ ⓑ ⓒ ⓓ	63	ⓐ ⓑ ⓒ ⓓ
4	ⓐ ⓑ ⓒ ⓓ	24	ⓐ ⓑ ⓒ ⓓ	44	ⓐ ⓑ ⓒ ⓓ	64	ⓐ ⓑ ⓒ ⓓ
5	ⓐ ⓑ ⓒ ⓓ	25	ⓐ ⓑ ⓒ ⓓ	45	ⓐ ⓑ ⓒ ⓓ	65	ⓐ ⓑ ⓒ ⓓ
6	ⓐ ⓑ ⓒ ⓓ	26	ⓐ ⓑ ⓒ ⓓ	46	ⓐ ⓑ ⓒ ⓓ	66	ⓐ ⓑ ⓒ ⓓ
7	ⓐ ⓑ ⓒ ⓓ	27	ⓐ ⓑ ⓒ	47	ⓐ ⓑ ⓒ ⓓ	67	ⓐ ⓑ ⓒ ⓓ
8	ⓐ ⓑ ⓒ ⓓ	28	ⓐ ⓑ ⓒ	48	ⓐ ⓑ ⓒ ⓓ	68	ⓐ ⓑ ⓒ ⓓ
9	ⓐ ⓑ ⓒ ⓓ	29	ⓐ ⓑ ⓒ	49	ⓐ ⓑ ⓒ ⓓ	69	ⓐ ⓑ ⓒ ⓓ
10	ⓐ ⓑ ⓒ ⓓ	30	ⓐ ⓑ ⓒ	50	ⓐ ⓑ ⓒ ⓓ	70	ⓐ ⓑ ⓒ ⓓ
11	ⓐ ⓑ ⓒ ⓓ	31	ⓐ ⓑ ⓒ	51	ⓐ ⓑ ⓒ ⓓ	71	ⓐ ⓑ ⓒ ⓓ
12	ⓐ ⓑ ⓒ ⓓ	32	ⓐ ⓑ ⓒ	52	ⓐ ⓑ ⓒ ⓓ	72	ⓐ ⓑ ⓒ ⓓ
13	ⓐ ⓑ ⓒ ⓓ	33	ⓐ ⓑ ⓒ	53	ⓐ ⓑ ⓒ ⓓ	73	ⓐ ⓑ ⓒ ⓓ
14	ⓐ ⓑ ⓒ ⓓ	34	ⓐ ⓑ ⓒ	54	ⓐ ⓑ ⓒ ⓓ	74	ⓐ ⓑ ⓒ ⓓ
15	ⓐ ⓑ ⓒ ⓓ	35	ⓐ ⓑ ⓒ	55	ⓐ ⓑ ⓒ ⓓ	75	ⓐ ⓑ ⓒ ⓓ
16	ⓐ ⓑ ⓒ ⓓ	36	ⓐ ⓑ ⓒ	56	ⓐ ⓑ ⓒ ⓓ	76	ⓐ ⓑ ⓒ ⓓ
17	ⓐ ⓑ ⓒ ⓓ	37	ⓐ ⓑ ⓒ	57	ⓐ ⓑ ⓒ ⓓ	77	ⓐ ⓑ ⓒ ⓓ
18	ⓐ ⓑ ⓒ ⓓ	38	ⓐ ⓑ ⓒ	58	ⓐ ⓑ ⓒ ⓓ	78	ⓐ ⓑ ⓒ ⓓ
19	ⓐ ⓑ ⓒ ⓓ	39	ⓐ ⓑ ⓒ	59	ⓐ ⓑ ⓒ ⓓ	79	ⓐ ⓑ ⓒ ⓓ
20	ⓐ ⓑ ⓒ ⓓ	40	ⓐ ⓑ ⓒ	60	ⓐ ⓑ ⓒ ⓓ	80	ⓐ ⓑ ⓒ ⓓ

READING (Part V ~ VII)

NO.	ANSWER	NO.	ANSWER	NO.	ANSWER	NO.	ANSWER	NO.	ANSWER
	A B C D		A B C D		A B C D		A B C D		A B C D
101	ⓐ ⓑ ⓒ ⓓ	121	ⓐ ⓑ ⓒ ⓓ	141	ⓐ ⓑ ⓒ ⓓ	161	ⓐ ⓑ ⓒ ⓓ	181	ⓐ ⓑ ⓒ ⓓ
102	ⓐ ⓑ ⓒ ⓓ	122	ⓐ ⓑ ⓒ ⓓ	142	ⓐ ⓑ ⓒ ⓓ	162	ⓐ ⓑ ⓒ ⓓ	182	ⓐ ⓑ ⓒ ⓓ
103	ⓐ ⓑ ⓒ ⓓ	123	ⓐ ⓑ ⓒ ⓓ	143	ⓐ ⓑ ⓒ ⓓ	163	ⓐ ⓑ ⓒ ⓓ	183	ⓐ ⓑ ⓒ ⓓ
104	ⓐ ⓑ ⓒ ⓓ	124	ⓐ ⓑ ⓒ ⓓ	144	ⓐ ⓑ ⓒ ⓓ	164	ⓐ ⓑ ⓒ ⓓ	184	ⓐ ⓑ ⓒ ⓓ
105	ⓐ ⓑ ⓒ ⓓ	125	ⓐ ⓑ ⓒ ⓓ	145	ⓐ ⓑ ⓒ ⓓ	165	ⓐ ⓑ ⓒ ⓓ	185	ⓐ ⓑ ⓒ ⓓ
106	ⓐ ⓑ ⓒ ⓓ	126	ⓐ ⓑ ⓒ ⓓ	146	ⓐ ⓑ ⓒ ⓓ	166	ⓐ ⓑ ⓒ ⓓ	186	ⓐ ⓑ ⓒ ⓓ
107	ⓐ ⓑ ⓒ ⓓ	127	ⓐ ⓑ ⓒ ⓓ	147	ⓐ ⓑ ⓒ ⓓ	167	ⓐ ⓑ ⓒ ⓓ	187	ⓐ ⓑ ⓒ ⓓ
108	ⓐ ⓑ ⓒ ⓓ	128	ⓐ ⓑ ⓒ ⓓ	148	ⓐ ⓑ ⓒ ⓓ	168	ⓐ ⓑ ⓒ ⓓ	188	ⓐ ⓑ ⓒ ⓓ
109	ⓐ ⓑ ⓒ ⓓ	129	ⓐ ⓑ ⓒ ⓓ	149	ⓐ ⓑ ⓒ ⓓ	169	ⓐ ⓑ ⓒ ⓓ	189	ⓐ ⓑ ⓒ ⓓ
110	ⓐ ⓑ ⓒ ⓓ	130	ⓐ ⓑ ⓒ ⓓ	150	ⓐ ⓑ ⓒ ⓓ	170	ⓐ ⓑ ⓒ ⓓ	190	ⓐ ⓑ ⓒ ⓓ
111	ⓐ ⓑ ⓒ ⓓ	131	ⓐ ⓑ ⓒ ⓓ	151	ⓐ ⓑ ⓒ ⓓ	171	ⓐ ⓑ ⓒ ⓓ	191	ⓐ ⓑ ⓒ ⓓ
112	ⓐ ⓑ ⓒ ⓓ	132	ⓐ ⓑ ⓒ ⓓ	152	ⓐ ⓑ ⓒ ⓓ	172	ⓐ ⓑ ⓒ ⓓ	192	ⓐ ⓑ ⓒ ⓓ
113	ⓐ ⓑ ⓒ ⓓ	133	ⓐ ⓑ ⓒ ⓓ	153	ⓐ ⓑ ⓒ ⓓ	173	ⓐ ⓑ ⓒ ⓓ	193	ⓐ ⓑ ⓒ ⓓ
114	ⓐ ⓑ ⓒ ⓓ	134	ⓐ ⓑ ⓒ ⓓ	154	ⓐ ⓑ ⓒ ⓓ	174	ⓐ ⓑ ⓒ ⓓ	194	ⓐ ⓑ ⓒ ⓓ
115	ⓐ ⓑ ⓒ ⓓ	135	ⓐ ⓑ ⓒ ⓓ	155	ⓐ ⓑ ⓒ ⓓ	175	ⓐ ⓑ ⓒ ⓓ	195	ⓐ ⓑ ⓒ ⓓ
116	ⓐ ⓑ ⓒ ⓓ	136	ⓐ ⓑ ⓒ ⓓ	156	ⓐ ⓑ ⓒ ⓓ	176	ⓐ ⓑ ⓒ ⓓ	196	ⓐ ⓑ ⓒ ⓓ
117	ⓐ ⓑ ⓒ ⓓ	137	ⓐ ⓑ ⓒ ⓓ	157	ⓐ ⓑ ⓒ ⓓ	177	ⓐ ⓑ ⓒ ⓓ	197	ⓐ ⓑ ⓒ ⓓ
118	ⓐ ⓑ ⓒ ⓓ	138	ⓐ ⓑ ⓒ ⓓ	158	ⓐ ⓑ ⓒ ⓓ	178	ⓐ ⓑ ⓒ ⓓ	198	ⓐ ⓑ ⓒ ⓓ
119	ⓐ ⓑ ⓒ ⓓ	139	ⓐ ⓑ ⓒ ⓓ	159	ⓐ ⓑ ⓒ ⓓ	179	ⓐ ⓑ ⓒ ⓓ	199	ⓐ ⓑ ⓒ ⓓ
120	ⓐ ⓑ ⓒ ⓓ	140	ⓐ ⓑ ⓒ ⓓ	160	ⓐ ⓑ ⓒ ⓓ	180	ⓐ ⓑ ⓒ ⓓ	200	ⓐ ⓑ ⓒ ⓓ

Answer Sheet

Actual Test 05

LISTENING (Part I ~ IV)

NO.	ANSWER
1	a b c d
2	a b c d
3	a b c d
4	a b c d
5	a b c d
6	a b c d
7	a b c
8	a b c
9	a b c
10	a b c
11	a b c
12	a b c
13	a b c
14	a b c
15	a b c
16	a b c
17	a b c
18	a b c
19	a b c
20	a b c

NO.	ANSWER
21	a b c
22	a b c
23	a b c
24	a b c
25	a b c
26	a b c
27	a b c
28	a b c
29	a b c
30	a b c
31	a b c
32	a b c
33	a b c
34	a b c
35	a b c
36	a b c
37	a b c
38	a b c
39	a b c
40	a b c

NO.	ANSWER
41	a b c d
42	a b c d
43	a b c d
44	a b c d
45	a b c d
46	a b c d
47	a b c d
48	a b c d
49	a b c d
50	a b c d
51	a b c d
52	a b c d
53	a b c d
54	a b c d
55	a b c d
56	a b c d
57	a b c d
58	a b c d
59	a b c d
60	a b c d

NO.	ANSWER
61	a b c d
62	a b c d
63	a b c d
64	a b c d
65	a b c d
66	a b c d
67	a b c d
68	a b c d
69	a b c d
70	a b c d
71	a b c d
72	a b c d
73	a b c d
74	a b c d
75	a b c d
76	a b c d
77	a b c d
78	a b c d
79	a b c d
80	a b c d

NO.	ANSWER
81	a b c d
82	a b c d
83	a b c d
84	a b c d
85	a b c d
86	a b c d
87	a b c d
88	a b c d
89	a b c d
90	a b c d
91	a b c d
92	a b c d
93	a b c d
94	a b c d
95	a b c d
96	a b c d
97	a b c d
98	a b c d
99	a b c d
100	a b c d

READING (Part V ~ VII)

NO.	ANSWER
101	a b c d
102	a b c d
103	a b c d
104	a b c d
105	a b c d
106	a b c d
107	a b c d
108	a b c d
109	a b c d
110	a b c d
111	a b c d
112	a b c d
113	a b c d
114	a b c d
115	a b c d
116	a b c d
117	a b c d
118	a b c d
119	a b c d
120	a b c d

NO.	ANSWER
121	a b c d
122	a b c d
123	a b c d
124	a b c d
125	a b c d
126	a b c d
127	a b c d
128	a b c d
129	a b c d
130	a b c d
131	a b c d
132	a b c d
133	a b c d
134	a b c d
135	a b c d
136	a b c d
137	a b c d
138	a b c d
139	a b c d
140	a b c d

NO.	ANSWER
141	a b c d
142	a b c d
143	a b c d
144	a b c d
145	a b c d
146	a b c d
147	a b c d
148	a b c d
149	a b c d
150	a b c d
151	a b c d
152	a b c d
153	a b c d
154	a b c d
155	a b c d
156	a b c d
157	a b c d
158	a b c d
159	a b c d
160	a b c d

NO.	ANSWER
161	a b c d
162	a b c d
163	a b c d
164	a b c d
165	a b c d
166	a b c d
167	a b c d
168	a b c d
169	a b c d
170	a b c d
171	a b c d
172	a b c d
173	a b c d
174	a b c d
175	a b c d
176	a b c d
177	a b c d
178	a b c d
179	a b c d
180	a b c d

NO.	ANSWER
181	a b c d
182	a b c d
183	a b c d
184	a b c d
185	a b c d
186	a b c d
187	a b c d
188	a b c d
189	a b c d
190	a b c d
191	a b c d
192	a b c d
193	a b c d
194	a b c d
195	a b c d
196	a b c d
197	a b c d
198	a b c d
199	a b c d
200	a b c d

Actual Test 06

LISTENING (Part I ~ IV)

NO.	ANSWER				NO.	ANSWER				NO.	ANSWER				NO.	ANSWER			
	A	B	C	D		A	B	C	D		A	B	C	D		A	B	C	D
1	a	b	c	d	21	a	b	c	d	41	a	b	c	d	81	a	b	c	d
2	a	b	c	d	22	a	b	c	d	42	a	b	c	d	82	a	b	c	d
3	a	b	c	d	23	a	b	c	d	43	a	b	c	d	83	a	b	c	d
4	a	b	c	d	24	a	b	c	d	44	a	b	c	d	84	a	b	c	d
5	a	b	c	d	25	a	b	c	d	45	a	b	c	d	85	a	b	c	d
6	a	b	c	d	26	a	b	c	d	46	a	b	c	d	86	a	b	c	d
7	a	b	c	d	27	a	b	c	d	47	a	b	c	d	87	a	b	c	d
8	a	b	c	d	28	a	b	c	d	48	a	b	c	d	88	a	b	c	d
9	a	b	c	d	29	a	b	c	d	49	a	b	c	d	89	a	b	c	d
10	a	b	c	d	30	a	b	c	d	50	a	b	c	d	90	a	b	c	d
11	a	b	c	d	31	a	b	c	d	51	a	b	c	d	91	a	b	c	d
12	a	b	c	d	32	a	b	c	d	52	a	b	c	d	92	a	b	c	d
13	a	b	c	d	33	a	b	c	d	53	a	b	c	d	93	a	b	c	d
14	a	b	c	d	34	a	b	c	d	54	a	b	c	d	94	a	b	c	d
15	a	b	c	d	35	a	b	c	d	55	a	b	c	d	95	a	b	c	d
16	a	b	c	d	36	a	b	c	d	56	a	b	c	d	96	a	b	c	d
17	a	b	c	d	37	a	b	c	d	57	a	b	c	d	97	a	b	c	d
18	a	b	c	d	38	a	b	c	d	58	a	b	c	d	98	a	b	c	d
19	a	b	c	d	39	a	b	c	d	59	a	b	c	d	99	a	b	c	d
20	a	b	c	d	40	a	b	c	d	60	a	b	c	d	100	a	b	c	d

READING (Part V ~ VII)

NO.	ANSWER				NO.	ANSWER				NO.	ANSWER				NO.	ANSWER			
	A	B	C	D		A	B	C	D		A	B	C	D		A	B	C	D
101	a	b	c	d	121	a	b	c	d	141	a	b	c	d	181	a	b	c	d
102	a	b	c	d	122	a	b	c	d	142	a	b	c	d	182	a	b	c	d
103	a	b	c	d	123	a	b	c	d	143	a	b	c	d	183	a	b	c	d
104	a	b	c	d	124	a	b	c	d	144	a	b	c	d	184	a	b	c	d
105	a	b	c	d	125	a	b	c	d	145	a	b	c	d	185	a	b	c	d
106	a	b	c	d	126	a	b	c	d	146	a	b	c	d	186	a	b	c	d
107	a	b	c	d	127	a	b	c	d	147	a	b	c	d	187	a	b	c	d
108	a	b	c	d	128	a	b	c	d	148	a	b	c	d	188	a	b	c	d
109	a	b	c	d	129	a	b	c	d	149	a	b	c	d	189	a	b	c	d
110	a	b	c	d	130	a	b	c	d	150	a	b	c	d	190	a	b	c	d
111	a	b	c	d	131	a	b	c	d	151	a	b	c	d	191	a	b	c	d
112	a	b	c	d	132	a	b	c	d	152	a	b	c	d	192	a	b	c	d
113	a	b	c	d	133	a	b	c	d	153	a	b	c	d	193	a	b	c	d
114	a	b	c	d	134	a	b	c	d	154	a	b	c	d	194	a	b	c	d
115	a	b	c	d	135	a	b	c	d	155	a	b	c	d	195	a	b	c	d
116	a	b	c	d	136	a	b	c	d	156	a	b	c	d	196	a	b	c	d
117	a	b	c	d	137	a	b	c	d	157	a	b	c	d	197	a	b	c	d
118	a	b	c	d	138	a	b	c	d	158	a	b	c	d	198	a	b	c	d
119	a	b	c	d	139	a	b	c	d	159	a	b	c	d	199	a	b	c	d
120	a	b	c	d	140	a	b	c	d	160	a	b	c	d	200	a	b	c	d

以正確答題數量為基準，可以概略換算實際考試的得分。
請留意，這是推測值，而不是完全正確的計算方法。

Listening Comprehension		Reading Comprehension	
正確答題數量	換算分數	正確答題數量	換算分數
96-100	470-495	96-100	470-495
91-95	440-470	91-95	450-470
86-90	410-440	86-90	420-450
81-85	370-410	81-85	380-420
76-80	340-370	76-80	350-380
71-75	310-340	71-75	330-350
66-70	280-310	66-70	300-330
61-65	250-280	61-65	270-300
56-60	230-250	56-60	240-270
51-55	200-230	51-55	210-240
46-50	170-200	46-50	190-210
41-45	150-170	41-45	170-190
36-40	120-150	36-40	140-170
31-35	90-120	31-35	110-140
26-30	70-90	26-30	90-110
21-25	40-70	21-25	70-90
16-20	30-40	16-20	50-70
11-15	10-30	11-15	30-50
6-10	5-10	6-10	10-30
1-5	5	1-5	0
0	5	0	0

核心 900 單字表

聽力訓練筆記

訓練筆記音檔

Actual Test 1

訓練筆記音檔

Actual Test 2

訓練筆記音檔

Actual Test 3

訓練筆記音檔

Actual Test 4

訓練筆記音檔

Actual Test 5

訓練筆記音檔

Actual Test 6

不方便掃 QR Code？輸入網址也可以！

Actual Test 01

https://www.suncolor.com.tw/2023Toeic/index.aspx?id=1

Actual Test 02

https://www.suncolor.com.tw/2023Toeic/index.aspx?id=2

Actual Test 03

https://www.suncolor.com.tw/2023Toeic/index.aspx?id=3

Actual Test 04

https://www.suncolor.com.tw/2023Toeic/index.aspx?id=4

Actual Test 05

https://www.suncolor.com.tw/2023Toeic/index.aspx?id=5

Actual Test 06

https://www.suncolor.com.tw/2023Toeic/index.aspx?id=6

解析

https://www.suncolor.com.tw/2023Toeic/index2.aspx?id=2

單字表

https://www.suncolor.com.tw/2023Toeic/index2.aspx?id=1

聽力訓練筆記

https://www.suncolor.com.tw/2023Toeic/index2.aspx?id=3

訓練筆記音檔 Actual Test 01

https://www.suncolor.com.tw/2023Toeic/index.aspx?id=a1

訓練筆記音檔 Actual Test 02

https://www.suncolor.com.tw/2023Toeic/index.aspx?id=a2

訓練筆記音檔 Actual Test 03

https://www.suncolor.com.tw/2023Toeic/index.aspx?id=a3

訓練筆記音檔 Actual Test 04

https://www.suncolor.com.tw/2023Toeic/index.aspx?id=a4

訓練筆記音檔 Actual Test 05

https://www.suncolor.com.tw/2023Toeic/index.aspx?id=a5

訓練筆記音檔 Actual Test 06

https://www.suncolor.com.tw/2023Toeic/index.aspx?id=a6